KISMET

A Creation Inc. Series Novel

BJ CUNNINGHAM
& MISTY CLARK

KISMET - A Creation Inc Novel

© 2016 by BJ Cunningham & Misty Clark

Published: 16th June 2017

Cover Art: Morgan-Cunningham Publishing/Creation Inc.

Publisher: Morgan-Cunningham Publishing/ Creation Inc.

Thank You...

I'd like to thank M. Shadows for how he looks in a pair of jeans and those damn dimples. Thank you Mr. Brock O'Hurn, may you never cut your hair or lose your smile. You two are responsible for countless hours of distraction, and without you, this novel would have been finished months ago...

But seriously, I'll keep this short. My love and deepest appreciation go out to Decatur, Tom, Sandy, the LMP counter crew, Flipper and Annie, Humo, Smokey, Toni Palmeri Brass, Sir Mistretta, Mikhaïella, Lishy, every single one of our awesome readers, and most of all, my amazing coauthor, Misty Clark.

Lots of love and shit,
~BJ

I would like to thank my family and friends for all their love and support while writing this book. Also, a huge thank you to everyone who took the time to read and review our first book. I hope you enjoy Kismet as much as we did, writing it. Lastly, I want to thank BJ for sticking with me and believing in what we started. We have a lot more stories to tell and I know it's not always easy, but the best things in life rarely are.

Much love to all.
~Misty

To all of those out there who refuse to stop believing that your dreams will come true, this book is for you.

Other Titles:

Creation Inc. Series
(BJ Cunningham & Misty Clark)

BLACK ON BLACK: THE MATING
KISMET

Coming Soon:
BLACK ON BLACK - A novelette
ALPHA PRIDE

The Bjorn Clan Series
(BJ Cunningham)

CURSED
FLESH & BLOOD

Chapter 1

"Where did you get it?" Brock grabbed the redhead with the stupid skull tattoo on his face, by the back of the neck and slammed his head down on the bar. "Don't make me ask again," his growl was low, calm, deadly and left no doubt that one wrong twitch or word and he was going to open the kid like a Hefty bag. Leaning closer, Brock's lip curled up in disgust. The kid stunk of Fox. Sneaky, thieving, opportunistic, good for nothing, fucking Fox.

Koen's dark brow arched and he turned his brown eyes to the Djinn beside him.

Balden sighed, put down his fork and began peeling the black calfskin gloves off his hands.

"I'll get the pin cushion?" Koen shook the hair from his eyes and grinned when big, blonde and silent nodded and smirked at the comment about the pierced kid that should have been wearing an 'I'm with Stupid' T-shirt.

"Watch for the butterfly knife in his back pocket," Balden warned, pushing his chair back like he was gonna hit the head and not like the shit was about to hit the fan. The Djinn dropped his gloves on the table and nodded to the bear behind the bar holding a towel and drying a glass. Or he had been until his hands froze. Now Bart's eyes were locked on the least violent of the Navarro brothers wiping the bar with someone's face.

Koen followed suit and crossed the room to stand behind the brunette with so many facial piercings that an MRI might prove fatal. When the kid tried to jump on Brock, Koen looped an arm around the kid's throat, yanking the shifter back against his chest. Koen's fingers dipped into the punk's pocket, snagged the knife and dropped it to the floor before wrenching the kid's arm up, behind his back. "How's about we let the grownups hash this shit out, Junior?" He winced at the voices that tunneled through the earpiece and into his skull as everyone else got with the program and prepared for crowd control and the potential mop up.

Bart tossed the towel into the sink and pressed the button under the bar that jammed cell signal. *Thank you, Ryker, you antisocial, brilliant mother fucker.* The last thing they needed was someone dialing 911 and having human cops getting in their way. 'We have a situation in the bar,' he said calmly through mindlink.

Multiple voices hit back in a chorus, all asking the same question. 'Who?'

'Brock.' An assortment of curses bounced inside Bart's head, making him smile. His older brother, even if it was by mere minutes, didn't lose his shit often, but when he did, they were left washing the blood splatter off the ceiling and walls for days.

"The fuck?" The fox with the face tat snarled just before he was forced to eat the heavily lacquered pine of the bar top. "Get what, Man? I don't know what the fuck you're talking about. Get off me!" He tried to push himself up, but Brock's grip tightened.

"The jacket, Douche Bag. And where is the female it belongs to?" The more the kid struggled, the tighter Brock squeezed. He had to fight to control himself when he felt the bones starting to give.

2

"I found it!" The kid froze. This big son of a bitch was going to snap his neck. "I don't know nothing about no chick!"

The kid Koen had contained, laughed. "You're wearing a girl's jacket."

Koen and Balden exchanged glances. That's what had set the bear off? Fuck, this was going to get messy. No one ever talked about it, but only an idiot didn't see that Brock had it bad for the Valkyrie. Well, her mate didn't seem to, but Dane could be damn oblivious when it came to anything but his drums and, more recently, Kara. Both the lion and the Valkyrie had been missing for close to a week.

"Shut up, Kyle," the kid growled out before his voice turned pleading. "Honest, Mister. I just found it."

"Let the POS go," Bart tugged at his brother's arm. "She would have wiped the floor with these panty wastes." He kept his voice low, but the room had gone silent, so his voice carried, and a murmuring of agreement from the peanut gallery filled the quiet.

Balden walked through the crowd, laying his hand on humans and shifters that didn't need to remember this shit before they were escorted to the door and sent on their way to enjoy the high that the Djinn's touch caused.

Brock felt his brother's hand and the stronger tug that followed, but he wasn't letting go. Not until he knew what happened to Kara. She never went anywhere without that black leather jacket with the ODIN'S RAVENS patches, flying proudly on the back. "Where?"

"Where what?" The kid started to cry. He was scared shitless and broke down.

"Jase, just give him the jacket. It ain't worth dying for." The pierced friend piped up.

"He can have it!"

"Where. Did. You. Find. It." Brock ground out between clenched teeth and shrugged off Bart's hand. His lip curled up in disgust as a snot bubble came out of the kid's nose and burst on the bar while the punk made a gurgling sound.

3

"The park! We found it in the park," Kyle said, struggling in Koen's hold. "C'mon, Dude. He's turning blue!"

"Which park?" Brock ground Jase's face into the wood a little harder and glared at the friend.

"The one in the French Market. Crescent, I think. On Peters Street!"

"There. Now you know. Let the little shit go," Bart grunted and tried to pull his brother off the Fox.

"Seriously, Brock," Koen spoke up, exchanging worried looks with the staff and crew gathered around them and getting closer to jumping on the bear to defuse the situation before he killed the canine. "He's graying out, and we don't need a bunch of Ghuardians poking around our shit or Reese kicking our asses for letting it happen."

"Fine." Brock leaned down and whispered into the kid's ear. "If I find out that you lied or did anything, and I mean ANYTHING, to her, I'm coming for you and your entire clan. Feel me, Kid?" The subtle nod was the only reason that Brock released him with a shove. Pushing his hands through his long, blonde hair, Brock tried to feel Kara's presence in the park.

The collective exhale of held breaths filled the room when Brock stepped back, and Bart slapped a relieved hand on his brother's shoulder.

The kid sagged, holding his throat and eyed the bear wearily. "She was already dead," he coughed, his voice barely more than a ragged hiss as he gulped air, but it cut through the silence like a gunshot.

"Fuck," Bart groaned and grabbed Brock around the chest, planting his feet and holding on tight. He flashed Jared an appreciative glance when the panther put himself between the bear and what was about to be a bloodstain if he didn't shut his fucking yap.

Brock's head swung back to pin the kid with a glare, his blue eyes glowed as his bear clawed its way to the surface, painted his vision in a blood red hue and demanded to be set free to shred the prick. "What did you say?" He didn't

4

feel the arms or the hands that gripped him or see Jared who he shoved out of the way when he lunged forward and fisted the kid's hair, yanking his head back to see his face.

"Already. Dead." The kid panted, his eyes showing a ring of white around the amber iris and rolling from Brock to his friend. "Kyle. Tell. Him."

"Fuck me running," Koen sighed and shook his head. Why the fuck didn't the kid keep that to himself?

Rage pulsed from Brock, forcing the bodies of those standing around him to sway to its beat.

Koen shook the pin cushion who chose now to fall silent. "Tell him kid, or this might be the last thing you see."

"Yeah... Umm..." Kyle stammered and tried to shrink away from Brock's barely contained bear. "We found a dead chick. The jacket, well it was cool, and she didn't need it, so we took it. She wasn't breathing or anything. We hid her in some bushes off the path. We just found her! I swear!"

Words just kept spewing from the kid as he broke into begging them not to kill him and other stuff that Brock wasn't tracking. A roar ripped free of his aching chest. The rafters shook, filling the air with a fine mist of dust. The little fucker had to be lying. Had to be. Brock ignored the fact that he hadn't seen Dane for days either. Kara could not be dead. What the kid said was a bold-faced lie. "Show me. NOW!" He shook the Fox.

"Okay. Sure." He ghosted himself and the bear that still had a handful of his hair to the bench where they'd found the woman and pointed with a shaky hand. "She was there."

Brock swallowed hard, trying to hold onto the rage because it was the only thing keeping him upright. "Where is she now?" He growled, his eyes already searching and praying that she'd pop out at any moment with her usual, beautiful smile.

"Those bushes." Jase turned and looked over his shoulder at a thicket of swamp doghobble.

Brock stomped towards the bushes, dragging the kid by the hair that was still wrapped around his fingers. He saw a boot, and his legs crumbled, dropping him to his knees. He released his hold on the kid, parting the branches carefully until his worst fears became truth. He could barely breathe as what he was seeing sucked the air from his lungs, and his throat closed. Sounds echoed in the distance, and everything grayed out, except for the Valkyrie's glassy and unfocused blue eyes. His bear roared inside his head, but Brock couldn't make a sound.

Gently, he pulled her free of the branches and picked the dead leaves from her hair before rolling her up and cradling her in his arms. His heart shattered for a woman that barely even knew that he existed and now she never would. Brock lowered his head to rest his forehead against hers, hating how cold her skin was. His world shrunk down to just the two of them as he whispered the things that he'd never said, but should have. Tears streaked down his face, but he didn't feel them.

Brock's pulse tripped over itself, and a tiny glimmer of hope flickered in his chest when the wind fluttered her long blonde hair. The movement created the brief illusion of life, only to be dashed when her neck allowed her head to fall back, limp and boneless when he stood. Kara was gone, and Brock felt lost.

Holding her to his chest, Brock ghosted to the clinic forgetting about the fox or the mess he'd left at The Pit. So many things that he wished he'd done or told her echoed inside his head but now, he'd never have the chance.

Chapter 2

Ty ghosted to his chambers in the Shadowlands to peruse his newest acquisitions. He needed fresh souls to replace those that were fading or had dwindled down to nothing but the hollow husks that blew through the realm like tumbleweeds in an old western. It took power, a lot of it, to ensure that the entrance to Niflheim remained closed. The Pit, as his minions called it, was an apt description. Beyond the layers of gates were the things that not even Ty wanted to be unleashed.

Mudd paced and muttered to himself, drawing Ty's attention and causing his brow to arch. The drogher demon never came out in the open, preferring the shadows where it could slink away and hide rather than risk Ty's displeasure and punishments. The corner of Ty's mouth curled up as he considered what the cost of invading his inner sanctum would be. The screams and the pain would be delicious. "Why are you here, Mudd?"

The emaciated creature jumped, lifting its bulging gray eyes to see his master. His feet took him two steps away before he remembered the last time he had fled and the loss of some of his favorite parts that were the result. "I have news, Master. Don't blame Mudd. He didn't do nothing." His body shook, and the need to flee grew stronger.

Sinking onto his throne, Ty rested his hands on the bony ends of the chair's arms and waited. "And?"

Mudd swallowed and dropped his eyes to his gnarled toes. He didn't want to tell him. The master did not like bad news. "Two new souls came, and one went," his voice shook and was barely louder than a whisper.

"What?" Ty growled. "How can one just leave? That's not how this place works. No one leaves." Ty leaned forward on his throne, his reddish-brown hair tickled his ears as it fell to cover his eyes until he lifted his head and stared at the drogher demon. He didn't bother to hide his disdain for the creature. Drogher were like rats with no real power and not the sharpest knives in the kitchen, but they went unnoticed, and that could be useful.

"Yes, Master. There was two that came in. A female and a male. The female didn't stay long. We tried to stop her, but whatever she was, it was not a shifter. Her soul smelled different," Mudd rambled on, looking up at Ty and shrinking away from the Master's glare.

Ty was so much older than anyone knew. He was, some said, eviler than Satan himself. He stood at six foot seven and looked like something out a fashion magazine. "Different? How?" Ty asked the demon.

"Yes, Master. She smelled like..." Mudd cringed when he met Ty's eyes and forgot what he had been about to say.

"Well?" Ty was growing impatient.

The demon knew that if he told the truth, it would send his master into a rage but if he lied his suffering would be worse. "She smelled of Asgard," Mudd whispered and waited for pain or death to follow.

Asgard. That meant one thing. Ty's blood began to boil. He had to see this for himself. "Show me."

Whimpering, Mudd stumbled forward and dropped to his knees at Ty's feet. His bare chalky colored skin hit the black marble with a fleshy splat. Bracing his palms on the smooth cold floor, Mudd bowed his head, praying that what happened to Stayn, didn't happen to him. A choked sob

8

squeezed his chest as he remembered poor Stayn, sniffing out cheese and coming home with rat traps decorating his loose skin, some in places that made Mudd cover himself reflexively. That wasn't the worst part. Stayn forgot who he was, everything was gone and replaced with the belief that he was a rodent and had died trying to cram himself into a mouse hole in some human's garage. Mudd didn't want to die like that.

Ty grimaced and laid his hand on the bald head of the sniffling drogher, disgusted by the thing. It was weak and didn't deserve to call itself a demon. Tightening his fingers on the pathetic wretch's head, Ty smiled at the whimper of pain it made and closed his eyes. His palm grew hot, searing through the skin and bone to tease the memories from Mudd's cranium. Pulling his hand away, Ty leaned back in his seat and pushed the thing away from him with his boot.

Mudd cradled his head in his hands, and his body rolled into a tight ball. Blood seeped through his fingers, but he didn't notice as his mind raced to remember everything he could. The image of Scabbs, his mate, filled his head and those of their children. He couldn't remember their names! He calmed himself, he couldn't remember them before, that was Scabb's job. Relief flooded Mudd when he realized that he still remembered where his most prized possessions of colorful pieces of yarn were hidden, and he wasn't craving cheese. Slowly, eyeing Ty cautiously, Mudd sat up and waited to be dismissed.

Ty turned his hand and watched the scenes play in his palm. A lion shifter and a woman had crashed into the sand, holding one another before they were ripped apart and flung to opposite corners of The Shadowlands. Comfort was not to be had here. The lion had roared for her, ready to fight anything that neared him as his form slowly dissolved to a vague, wispy version that was no threat. Already the power was being siphoned from the lion's soul.

Ty smiled as everything went as planned. Waving his free hand over the hologram, the lion disappeared, and the woman took his place. His brow arched and his jaw ticked as her form wavered, but did not change. A bright gold light surrounded her, forcing Ty to squint to continue to watch as she manifested her weapon and stabbed it through the barrier. She sliced her palm and slapped it over the hole she'd created, leaving a scar on the surface. She fought a beam of silver as it curled around her, but it yanked her through and then out of his realm.

Growling, Ty closed his hand into a fist and snuffed out the images. He could have used her. Not only could she have powered his gates for centuries before she dried up, but she was also the key to his revenge. His eyes rolled to Mudd who flinched back, expecting to be hit. Perhaps the demon wasn't as stupid as Ty had thought. He tilted his head thoughtfully, his mind turning to the Princess and the lion holding one another. Like lovers would. "Mudd."

"Yes, Master." Mudd's gray eyes bulged wider and were close to popping out of his skull.

"Would you like to live?"

"Yes, Master," he repeated nodding his head enthusiastically.

Ty smirked and turned the ring on his finger. "Take me to this lion." Sure, Ty could find it on his own, but this was faster, and he needed to know the value of the feline before he was drained beyond the point of being useful.

Chapter 3

One minute Kara was washing the blood off her face and the next she was landing on her bruised ass in Odin's throne room. Cursing, she didn't try to get up. Until she had time to heal there wasn't a damned thing that was worth moving for. Tilting her head back, she locked her azure eyes on her father, watching as the Ravens on his wide shoulders fluttered their wings and then hopped closer to whisper into his ears. Her gaze moved over the lines etched into his ancient face, caressing the hollowed socket of his missing eye and, across his broad, sculpted nose and lips that only appeared from the depths of his beard when he talked. Everywhere but his one good eye that she knew saw more than she wanted it to. The man she had loved as her father for centuries, and now she felt... nothing.

"I didn't know you were there, Kara." Odin's deep voice rolled like thunder through the room, echoing back and bouncing off the walls. "You know I wouldn't have left you there, child." His voice cracked, and Kara lowered her eyes to the stone floor, following a vein of quartz through the polished rock.

Kara shrugged her shoulders, ignoring the broken rib impaling her left lung, making her want to cough up the blood she could feel slowly filling it. She kept her face blank and shut the instinct down. If you were stupid enough to show pain affected you during training, then you were taught the difference between discomfort and suffering. She'd learned that lesson the first time and didn't plan to have it repeated.

Pulling her eyes to the jagged cut down her right arm and the shards of bone that poked through her scarred skin, she jabbed at the bone with her fingertips, pushing it back inside the skin and yanking her wrist, hard, to set it as straight as she could. Blood pooled in the hole, she dipped her finger in the thick, murky maroon fluid, lifting her hand and tilting her head as it ran down her finger to fill the webbed hollow before spilling over the back of her hand.

"What do you want to do, Kara?"

She could hear Odin shift on his throne. It was not like her father to fidget. Her gaze was pulled over the floor and back to the God, who now leaned forward, elbows on knees and hands clasped beneath his chin. It was the concern that twisted his features that made her growl low in her throat. Too little too late. They could all fuck off. Every, last one of them. Gods, other beings, and humans. She didn't care about any of them. She'd gone numb to them all.

"Do you know what happened, Little One?"

The sneer surfaced to curl her lip up in disgust before Kara quickly erased all emotion from her face again. "Yes. The Buffalo has jokes." How could she not know? She lived the humiliation of being taken out by a fucking ungulate of all things, and she heard about it every mother fucking day she was in Valhalla. The constant jabs and taunts made her blood boil even now. "Is the lion alive?"

Odin tapped his knuckles against his lips while his gaze measured her and found something he didn't like.

Before all of this, that wrinkle to his brow would have her sitting straighter, smoothing her clothes and flashing a killer smile to please him. That Kara was, at this very moment, considering finger painting curse words on the floor in her own blood. Yeah, that probably wasn't taking her father to his happy place, and she didn't fucking care.

"Do you want to go back, Kara?"

12

"Doesn't matter." His not answering was answer enough. She flexed the fingers of her broken arm, her eyes rolling back in her head at the sharp pain and for the first time, she smiled as though greeted by an old friend. "The mark is gone for good?" She lifted her head to show that her eyes had lost the hazel starburst around the pupil to her father, who again nodded. "Good. Send me where the hell ever you want to, Dad. None of it matters anymore."

"You know that's not true, Kara."

"And you know that wanting it to be that way, doesn't make it so, Fadir. Burn it all to the fucking ground. I'm not shedding a tear." She ghosted out choosing her destination before it could be selected for her.

Kara felt like she was being sucked down a drain. She twisted and turned, but the harder she fought for control, the faster she plummeted toward the city streets below. A roof grew from a speck in the distance until it blocked everything else from sight. She growled and braced for impact. This was going to hurt.

She gasped when she fell through the steel as if it wasn't there. Kara didn't have time to think about it as the scenes of people in hospital beds flashed by, floor after floor. *What. The. Fuck?* A loud zipping noise threatened to shatter her eardrums, and she stopped with a jolt. She couldn't breathe. Something was covering her. No. She was sinking into it. It coated her and weighed her down. She struggled to pull free in a panic.

"Fuck!" She cursed when her head smashed into something, hard enough for her to see stars and sound like a gong being struck. Kara fell back, smacking her elbow when she tried to reach for her head. "Son of a," she growled and blinked her eyes to be sure that they were open. No matter how many times she did, all Kara saw was black. Carefully she slid her hand over the thing covering her face. Her brow arched as she felt skin tighten and her jaw tense. There was nothing there. Just her. She groaned as the injuries she'd had before the fall seemed to settle into the meat suit that

13

was her. She'd been a shade? *A fucking shade? How was that possible?*

Curling her broken arm to her chest, Kara grimaced at the scratchy material that covered her. Her teeth began to chatter, and something fluttered when she moved and tickled the sole of her foot. Her mind churned, trying to do the math. Reaching out slowly, she ran her palm over the smooth cold surface above her. It bent and flowed down, surrounding her in a metal box. A coffin? Weren't they usually all cushiony and lined with silk? Had she been buried?

Twisting and almost getting her shoulders stuck, she managed to roll onto her stomach. Hissing as her broken arm was pinned beneath her, Kara stretched her good arm out until it hit another dead end. When she pushed against it, the thing she was on rolled further back with a rusty squeal. *Claustrophobia. That's what they called it when you felt like the walls were closing in on you, right?* She was rocking that, and it made it hard to think.

Closing her eyes, Kara concentrated, tapping her barely-there reserves and channeling the last of her energy into a bolt that blasted through the metal. She winced at the loud clanging noise of something hitting the floor when it fell. Kara squinted against the bright light that flooded the box. "Ugh," she groaned and stretched her arm out to hook her fingers over the lip to pull her toward the opening. Another scream of metal against metal was at odds with how smoothly the thing she was on rolled. Inching forward, she ignored the throbbing of her body and peered down at a green commercial tile floor that had been waxed within an inch of its life. *A morgue. She was in a fucking morgue?*

Growling again, Kara continued inch worming to the edge until she spilled out, rolled herself into a ball and landed in a fleshy splat to lay sprawled on the floor, blinking up at the rows and rows of refrigerator doors. Was Dane in one of those? Kara rubbed at the ache in her bare chest and rolled herself up to read the label on the closest one.

14

Hugging her arm to her chest, she managed to get her feet under her on the third try and walked the wall of stored bodies, not finding the name she was looking for. That was good. Maybe.

Sighing she pushed the hair back from her face and grabbed a long white lab coat from a hook and shrugged it on, holding it closed with her good hand. She needed to get home so she could find out what happened to Dane. Kara tried to ghost, but she was too weak. It was going to be a long walk.

Kara's legs were already shaking by the time she finally found her way out of the hospital and stepped into the darkness. Her head was pounding, and she took a second to be grateful that she wouldn't have to squint against the bright Louisiana sun. Forcing her eyes to focus, she read the street signs, trying to get her bearings. Home was ten blocks north, but The Pit was only two blocks east. She wasn't ready to deal with people yet, but she didn't think she'd make it back to her apartment.

Sighing, she pulled the white coat tighter around her and ignored the rough asphalt under her bare feet. Looking down, concentrating on putting one foot in front of the other, she heard a horn blare and staggered back. The black VW bug sped by, and the kid in the driver's seat flipped her the bird, yelling something that Kara couldn't hear.

Looking up, her eyes swept the intersection wondering when she'd gotten here. She sagged against a streetlight, taking a moment to calculate just how to cross the busy street and then get down the sidewalk to the bar. She was exhausted and not sure that she could make it as her legs trembled violently, the muscles spasmed and threatened to dump her on her ass. Sighing, she pushed away from the cold iron pole when the walk light, lit up and shuffled across the crosswalk. The Pit's sign grew larger as she got closer and continued past the lined-up humans waiting to get it, not stopping until she bumped into Brandon at his usual post at the door.

15

"Kara?" His eyes all but bugged out of his head.

She nodded and sighed her relief when his arm circled her waist, and she could lean on him.

"Okay." The Coyote licked his lips and looked around for someone to take over for him. They were going to shit when he got her inside. Brock was going to... His eyes closed when he remembered the stricken look on the bear's face when he'd come back with her body. They'd all seen her. Seen Asher take her pulse shaking his head no, and gaped as those damned machines gave a pretty clear visual with the red flat line. Kara had been D-E-A-D, dead.

Brandon glanced at her face and shook his head, not believing his eyes. "Blade. Do me a solid?" He called inside to the Panther leaning against the wall beside the door and surveying tonight's crowd for troublemakers.

"Whatcha need, kid?" Blade looked over his shoulder, and his eyes flared when he saw who was with Brandon. One side of his mouth quirked up. He may have been gone for a while, but he'd fought beside the Valkyrie more than once, and she was hard to forget. "We thought you were dead, Doll. Dane out there with you?" He stepped outside and eyed the crowd, expecting the lion to appear, until he saw the flatness of her eyes and the shake of her head. "If you're here, he won't be long, I'm sure." Blade stomped down the disappointment, not letting it show on his face. Their numbers were too few as it was, losing one of their own hurt.

"Cover here, or get her inside. She's about to drop."

"I'll take over here. Don't need to be part of what's gonna happen inside. Might slip and catch a feeling or some shit." Blade chuckled and reached for the ID of the next person in line and shined the flashlight that Brandon tossed him. 'Heads up. Got one hell of a surprise coming through the door. Someone might wanna get ready to catch Grizz or get his big ass into a chair.' He mindlinked the shifters and other beings inside. "Good to have you back, Doll." He grinned and waved the next three people inside.

16

"Thanks," Kara croaked and cleared her throat. Her mouth was so damned dry, and she wasn't tracking much. Higher thought had been reduced to tree pretty, fire bad. More than anything else she wanted to see Dane and sit the hell down.

Brandon rolled his eyes at the nickname that Blade insisted on using for Brock. Holding Kara tighter, he stepped inside. Heads turned to stare at them with mouths hanging open. He could feel the silent shock of his brethren, even over the buzz of the human's chatter and the loud music.

Kara searched the crowd for Dane, even though she knew that he wasn't here from Blade's words. Still, she hoped and tried to sense him. She sighed and held the white coat closed with her injured arm and waited, not sure that her presence would be welcomed and expected to be tossed out on her ass. One of their own was dead, and it was probably her fault. "Can I just go to my room, please?" She glanced up at Brandon, not liking the feel of so many eyes on her.

Brock was bussing tables and trying to keep his mind off shit. If he stayed busy, he was good, but when it got quiet, it was hell. Thank fuck that they were shorthanded, and everyone was covering everything as it came up. He felt the wave of shock and awe flow through the room and growled at Blade's pet name. Picking up the gray rubber tub, he turned to see what had his crew at a standstill. "Shit isn't gonna get done on its own!" He barked before he froze and his eyes locked on a ghost. Time stopped, and he wasn't sure that he was breathing.

Something crashed, breaking the spell. Brock glanced down at the shards of white plates, cups and the clear pieces of glass, mixed with the metal of the flatware. His eyes bounced back to the ghost and his legs almost folded under him. He wanted to rub his eyes but was afraid that that would erase the mirage and he wanted her to be real. He needed her to be real. Pushing the long blond hair back from his face, he stared and tried to speak, but all he got

17

was a croak. His pulse was pounding, and he felt like he had an elephant on his chest.

"Cher?" Brock's voice had no strength as he ordered his legs to work and crossed the bar to her. He didn't see the bodies that he pushed through. He couldn't see anything but the Valkyrie. Reaching out a hesitant hand, he cupped her chin, tilting her head back. He needed to touch her, to prove that she was real because she couldn't be. "How," he whispered in awe as his eyes caressed every detail of her beautiful face. "I told them that you'd be back."

Kara's brows shrugged together as she looked up at one of the very few that she had to tilt her head back to see his face. "Yeah. It's me. Long story." A brief, sad smile flickered over her face, and she closed her eyes at the warmth of his hand.

His nose twitched at the scent of blood. "You're hurt. We should get you to the clinic." Brock couldn't stop the wide grin that took over his face or stop himself when he pulled her into his arms and hugged her tightly. He barely felt the shake of her head, but her hiss of pain had his full attention. He loosened his grip on the female to arch a questioning brow.

"No doctors. They put me in a box. A cold, dark box," Kara growled, knowing that she wasn't making sense and pushed against his chest to free her broken arm from where it was being squashed. "I just need a place to rest and heal. I'll be fine." A laugh echoed in her head. Kara and fine weren't even in the same hemisphere.

"Anything you want, Cher." Brock hugged her again, more gently this time before releasing her and grabbing her again when her legs began to give out. Quickly, he reached to pull and hold the lab coat she was wearing shut but not before the image of her bare skin and one perfect breast were branded into his memory. He ignored the tightening of his jeans and hoped that she didn't notice as he gave Brandon a nod. "I've got her."

18

Brandon held up his hands and stepped back, shooting Brock a knowing smirk. "I'll just get back to my post then."

"Thank you." Kara didn't know who she was thanking. The Coyote for bringing her in. The bear for trying to save her modesty and help. To everyone else for not throwing her out. It could have been any or none of them. She let the bear lead her through the people and through the saloon style doors of the kitchen and winced when she heard Brax cursing in French.

Brock felt her fingers tighten their hold on his shirt and shot his brother a glare. "Don't start. Not. Now." He ghosted one of his t-shirts and a pair of sweats on Kara before he scooped her up in his arms and carried her through the door and up the stairs. He stopped outside the room Kara had shared with Dane and realized that he didn't have a key. He doubted that she did either, considering that she'd been all but naked when she came through the door. "You can stay in my room, Cher. I promise you'll be safe."

Kara nodded. She didn't care where she went, she just needed to sit down and maybe pass out. She held onto his shoulder when he stopped again and adjusted her so that he could get his own key out of his pocket and swing open the door. She numbly watched the kitchen become a small dining room and living room combo and then she was in a large bedroom and being lowered onto the biggest bed she'd ever seen.

He rethought where he'd put her, but not until it was too late. "Is here okay?" Brock pushed his hair back and stood, stuffing his hands into his pockets. His mind was going apeshit and seeing her in his bed wasn't helping. How many times had he dreamed it, but never like this? He reached down to pull a blanket over her, wishing that he'd thought to clean up before work. "Excuse the mess, Cher. I wasn't expecting company." He grinned, wanting to touch her again to confirm that she was really here.

Kara nodded. "Thank you. Where will you sleep? I mean..." She rubbed her face, realizing how that sounded.

19

"It's your bed. You should use it. I'm fine on a pallet of blankets in the corner. It's big enough to share, but I'd feel like shit if I had a nightmare and zapped you after you've been so kind to me."

Brock felt his face flush a bit. "No, we wouldn't want that, Cher. I'll take the couch." He held his hand up when she opened her mouth to argue. "I insist. Can I get you anything?"

She shook her head no and relaxed back onto the pillows with a sigh. She wanted to ask about Dane but already knew the answer. She swallowed hard and rubbed at her eyes. She would have been better off with Brax throwing shit at her and cussing her out than this kinder and gentler Navarro brother. His being kind to her made her want to cry, and she didn't understand why.

Brock ghosted a bottle of water into his hand and loosened the cap before setting it on the small table beside the bed, grinning when she reached for it and took a long drink. "How long have you been..." He wasn't sure how to phrase it. He didn't want to say, dead. "Back?"

"Not long. Woke up in a morgue and came here." She arched her brow and took another drink when she noticed the tag sticking out from under the blanket. "I think I'm still wearing the toe tag."

He bent and tugged the blanket up higher and chuckled. "I don't believe that you'll be needing this. Mind if I take it off?"

Kara shook her head no, but still jumped at the feel of his fingers on her foot. "Don't lose my souvenir, Bear," she teased with a growl, smiling softly when he gave her an unsure look. "No one gets my humor." She sighed and finally put down the water. Her stomach felt like it was going to burst and if she didn't stop she was going to be sick.

Brock chuckled and dropped the tag on the bedside table. "Sorry, Cher. I'm kind of expecting you to bolt me or turn me inside out or something." He rubbed the back of his neck. It was the truth.

20

"Why?" She covered a yawn and eyed him curiously. "Why would I want to do that? I mean, you're giving me your bed. I count that as a favor that I owe you for, not something to be punished. Besides," she yawned again. "Punishing is not my job."

"I am glad to hear that, Cher. I won't lie, I was worried. I don't have a lot of experience with gods and goddesses. I might slip and offend you." He grinned. "But now that I know that doling out hurt to clumsy bears with verbal diarrhea falls to someone else, I'll rest easy."

Kara smiled, and sank further down on the bed, hissing when her arm snagged the blanket. "Good. You're safe with me. I'm sorry. I can barely keep my eyes open, but I mean it when I say I owe you and I always pay my debts."

Brock shook his head no, his heart stammering when her smile shone brightly in her eyes. For the first time, he saw the life in her and knew that she wasn't a cruel hallucination. "Then rest, Cher. If you need anything, just call me." He wrote his number on the pad of paper from the drawer.

"I don't have my phone." She snorted. "I don't even have underpants."

He chuckled again, finding her amusing. "We'll talk to Asher about getting your things, but until then, use this." He pulled out his earpiece and set it on the table beside the water. "Just press the button and say that you need me, Cher. I'll come."

"I will." Her eyes moved from the headset to the bear. She had to blink to keep them open. "Thank you, Brock, for everything." Kara lost the battle to keep her eyes open.

"You are welcome, Kara." He smiled, surprised that she knew his name. He watched her for a few minutes before he forced himself to turn away. Thinking that sunrise would be arriving too soon and that he didn't want it to wake her, he unhooked the bands that held the heavy blackout drapes open.

"Bear?" Kara's voice was little more than a sigh.

21

"Yes, Cher." He glanced back over his shoulder to meet her sapphire eyes.

"Leave them open, please?" She smiled, and her eyes drifted shut again. "I need the sun. It helps me recharge."

"Then I'll leave them open." One side of his mouth curled up when he heard her soft snore. Fixing the drapes, Brock returned to the bed, squatted down and brushed the blonde hair from her face. He'd never had her, but he'd lost her anyway. If that wasn't a life lesson about taking advantage of every minute alive, he didn't know what was. For the first time since she'd gone MIA, his chest didn't ache, and that was indeed a gift. That she was back was an even greater gift. One he didn't intend to squander. Not this time.

Chapter 4

"It's your turn to open the bar." Sirus's voice boomed from the hall.

"No, it's not. It's yours, damn it," Drew growled.

Brock groaned and rolled his too large for the too small furniture, grizzly bear body off the couch before shifting into his human form. He rotated his neck on his shoulders until it snapped and popped, relieving the dull ache that sleeping on that damned thing gave him. He moaned and tried to make his eyes stay open. Who needed an alarm when he had Frick and Frack having the same argument, every morning, like clockwork?

Stretching and scratching his bare chest, Brock pulled open the door and leveled the twins with a glare. "Will you please, for the love of God, keep it down? Kara is sleeping," Brock growled in a loud whisper.

"She's been passed out for days…" Drew's voice died and was followed by a groan as he slapped his hand over his eyes. "Dude, you're naked."

Drew's twin mimicked the eye covering. "It's too early to see your junk, Man. Way too fuckin early. Put some clothes on. Like, seriously, I'm scarred. For life."

"Is there a good time to see his junk?" Drew shuddered and made a face behind his hand.

Sirus shook his head no. "Where's the eye bleach?"

Brock rolled his eyes at their dramatics.

"Maybe she isn't gonna wake up Dude. Then there ain't no point in us tiptoeing around and being quiet." Drew dropped his hand but kept his eyes above Brock's neck. "I don't get why she's our problem anyway."

Brock's growl rumbled in his chest, his hands balling into fists as he considered just how badly AP needed the canine pain in the asses. Oh. Wait. They didn't need them.

All heads turned at the loud crack of someone taking a bite out of an apple. Blade strolled down the hall, arched a brow at Brock's nakedness and slapped Drew on the back of the head. The Wolf pitched forward and almost fell over.

"Hey!" Drew cursed under his breath when he saw who had smacked him.

"Show some respect, Pup. She's put her ass on the line and bled with us more than once. More than you have." He nodded to Brock and continued walking down the hall. "And if you wake up the Cubs, Hayley is gonna wear your balls as earrings. Just saying." Blade smirked over his shoulder.

"And it's my turn to open this morning." Brock slammed the door and winced at how loud it was. Ghosting on some sweats, he stepped into his bedroom and eyed the mound of blankets and one long, shapely leg sticking out and hanging over the edge of the bed. Brock couldn't help the grin that crept over his face. He'd imagined her in his bed before, but it was nothing like this.

Shaking his head, he quietly opened the dresser drawers until he found everything that he needed. He draped the shirt over the high-backed leather chair that had belonged to Papa and took the boxers and jeans into the bathroom. After showering, he made sure that the clean towel and clothes that he'd borrowed from his sister's room, were piled neatly on the vanity. He hoped that Kara woke up soon. Sighing heavily, he zipped and buttoned his jeans, grabbing the towel he'd draped over the doorknob. Towel drying his hair, he opened the door and stepped back into his bedroom.

Kara woke to the sound of water running. Talk about your weird ass dreams. Nightmare was a better description. Groaning, she nestled under the blankets, her brow quirking when she realized that she didn't recognize the scent surrounding her. "What the hell?" She mumbled and stopped talking to herself when she heard a door open. She rolled and sat up, the blanket falling to pool around her waist. Her sword appeared in her hand, ready to cut through anything that so much as said fucking boo.

"What the," she repeated, seeing the large bare-chested male rubbing a towel against his head in the doorway. Holy hell, he filled the entire thing, ducking his head slightly when he moved through the opening, and his broad shoulders left mere inches between them and the frame.

Brock froze in mid-step when he heard her voice. Lowering the towel and lifting his head, he stared at her. It wasn't the broadsword in her hand that had his attention, or the look in her eyes that told him he was about to be in trouble. Sure, that shit registered, but it was in the darkest recesses of his mind. It was the blanket falling away, sliding down over painfully perfect breasts to pool around her slender, but toned waist. "Whoa," not so much a word, more of an exhale. Brock's bear growled. Finally, her voice broke the spell, and he could lift his eyes to hers. The corner of his mouth curled up at her mussed hair and sleepy eyes. He couldn't help it, she was just too cute, not that he'd ever dare utter those words out loud to the Valkyrie.

His face warmed when he realized that he was staring. Holding his hands up, he slowly reached to hook the shirt he'd left on the back of the chair with his finger and tossed it to her. "You're not wearing any clothes, Cher," he murmured and shook the wet hair back from his face, feeling water drip down his back. "How's about we put down the sword and pick up the shirt because I don't wanna lose bits of me because you make it hard to look you in the eye."

25

Kara's eyes narrowed. She knew him, she was almost positive. She reached for the Avenged Sevenfold t-shirt, never taking her eyes off the male that smelled like bear. "Brock? Right?" She tried to remember how she got here and other than the nightmare, she couldn't remember shit. That probably meant one thing. "Did I drink too much mead again and did we... Umm.... You know?" She lowered the sword to the bed and pulled on the shirt before pulling the blanket up and looking to see that she was completely naked.

Had they what? His brows shrugged together until she looked under the blanket and blushed a little. Brock laughed. She shot him an unamused look, and that made him laugh harder.

She arched a brow. "It's not THAT funny!"

Brock sat on the foot of the bed and wiped at his eyes. "It truly is, Cher."

"Why am I naked?" Kara arched a brow, not finding this funny at all. "And, where am I?"

Shaking his head, he turned to look at her. "That I can't say, Cher. You had clothes on when I put you in there. You're in the rooms over The Pit. Three doors down from yours and Dane's. You didn't have your key. Remember?"

"Oh." She did the math, and it added up to the nightmare being reality. She sighed and felt her chest constrict painfully. "So, all of that, actually happened?" Kara looked down at the blanket and reminded herself that she didn't cry because she felt like she should, and if she did, she might never stop. "Then I should probably stop imposing on your kindness." She pushed back the blanket and pulled the t-shirt down further to cover more of her. She swung her legs over the side and blinked at her bare feet on the floor. She didn't know where to go or what to do.

Brock's laughter died when her mixed emotions spilled into the air to churn around him. "I'm sorry, Kara." He wanted to hug her but was afraid the goddess would bolt him or something worse. "And you're not imposing. I promise. What do you say, we don't deal with any of it right now? Take a shower. Get dressed. I have some clothes in the bathroom, they're not yours, but they should fit. After that, when you're ready, come downstairs and get something into your stomach. You haven't eaten for days." He held up his hand when she opened her mouth to argue. "Humor a bear, please? I'll feel better if I know you've eaten and everything else will still be there, waiting, after. It always is." He tilted his head and watched her.

"Yeah. Okay," Kara agreed, her voice rough as she fought to control the shit storm that felt like it was turning her inside out.

"Good." He reached out and patted her hand, surprised when she turned hers and squeezed his. He jumped and growled when someone banged on the door.

"Go away!" Kara yelled and gave him a weak smile. "Thank you." She snorted and shook her head. She wasn't used to anyone trying to help her. It was usually the other way around. "You're okay, Brock." She gave his hand another squeeze, not wanting to give up the strange way it grounded her, but she had to. "You know they aren't going to stop until you go down." She'd experienced their persistence while living with Dane. "I'll see you down there."

"Promise, Cher?" He eyed her skeptically.

"You have my vow, Bjorn, and that's not something that my kind take lightly." She ghosted away her sword and stood up. "Bathroom is through there?" She pointed at the gaping door and walked toward it when he nodded. She smiled at him sadly before closing the door, keeping her mask firmly in place until she managed to step under the spray of the hot water.

Brock watched the door close and sighed. She was hurting. Not 'boo hoo, you hurt my pride.' No. She was a black hole of pain. Fuck, it even made his chest ache. He considered waiting for her, not sure that he trusted her to come and get something to eat. The banging on the door

27

was louder this time. "Keep your pants on. I'll be there in a minute!" He yelled and got up to find another shirt.

He looked at the pile of clothes on the floor and picked the cleanest one. Brock pulled it on and headed out of his room. The twins were still standing there. He ignored them and headed down to open the bar. Brock flipped on the lights and went to turn on the open sign. Taking the keys from his pocket, he unlocked the door. "Goddamn, this was so hard." He growled, looking at the twins. "I think I broke a fucking nail."

Brock shook his head, going to the back to unlock the door for the day's deliveries. He hoped she'd come down. He also hoped she wouldn't think he was some creepy stalker and that once all her marbles were rolling together, she wouldn't decide to off him and give his hide to her father for a new rug or blanket. His stomach twisted for a moment.

After a minor mental breakdown in the shower, Kara stepped out and picked up the clothes that Brock had left for her. It was very sweet of the Bjorn, and she appreciated the hell out of it but had no idea why he bothered. She was all but a dead man walking at the moment, and it wasn't likely to get better anytime soon. Not until she knew if Dane was dead or alive and not until she made the Ghuardian pay for this in blood.

She wiped the fog off the mirror and blinked at her eyes, missing the hazel sunburst that used to be there. "Please be okay, Babes. I'm not gonna make it if you're not." Kara's voice died, and she blinked back the tears that wanted to start up again. Sighing, she shook out the jeans, and after a brief search for underpants that weren't there, she pulled them up her long legs. They were a little tight for her liking, but she was going to eat, not fight, so she could live with it. She ignored the cute pink blouse and dropped the A7X t-shirt back over her head. It was more her style, and she liked how it smelled.

28

Her stomach growled, reminding Kara of her promise. She sighed and looked around for shoes, but other than a few pairs of size two hundred and three boots, there was nothing. Shrugging, she made the bed and found those clothes that Brock said that she'd gone to bed in. She folded them and left them on the dresser, not sure where he put the dirty laundry. Looking around again, she couldn't put this off any longer. It was time to face the real world. Kara opened the door and walked through the hall, stopping briefly to press her palm against the door to the room that she shared with Dane, and then down the stairs, through the kitchen, and into the bar. She kept her head down, hoping that Brax wouldn't notice her. Fate was kind this one time.

Brock heard the kitchen door open and close. He did his best not to run right to her. The last thing Kara needed was someone that she didn't know, playing helicopter. He went to check if it was her, and sure enough, it was. He was happy that she'd come down and didn't bolt. "So, what can I get you, Cher?" He asked, standing there for a moment before remembering that she might need a menu. He got one and put it in front of her.

She hadn't picked a seat yet, but he wasn't gonna push her into one. "I haven't made coffee yet, but we've got juice and all that if you want that too." He was rambling on, and he knew it. He closed his mouth and went to start the coffee.

Looking around, Kara felt completely exposed. Rubbing her bare arm, she stepped closer to the bar and slid onto the stool closest to the menu he'd put out for her and curled her bare toes around the brass pipe that ran around the perimeter of the bar seating. Not sure what to do, she flipped open the bifold and read through the options. Her stomach felt like it was eating itself and everything looked good, but the stuffed French toast made her drool.

She watched him make the coffee and wondered if it would be considered weird to have a beer with a coffee

29

chaser. She grinned at the image in her head. "Water will be perfect until the coffee's ready." Kara closed the menu and pushed it away, observing the room in the mirror behind the bottles of booze. "I can get it if you've got your hands full. I think I remember where everything is." She smiled and snapped the corner of the menu against the bar top absently.

"Water it is." Brock was about to get a glass when she said she could get it herself. Maybe letting her do things on her own would help. "Ok cool, that would be great. I need to get a few kegs from the back," he said pointing to the sticky notes above the cash register. "My honey do list is long." He took down the bright pink notes and lifted the bar divider up. "Did you figure out what you want? If not, I'll just bring you what I'm having," he said giving her a small smile.

She nodded and slid off her stool, grimacing when she stepped in something gritty. Wiping the bottom of her foot off on the leg of her pants, she eyed the sticky notes. "I feel your pain, mine come in the form of scrolls from my Mother." She made a face and continued behind the bar to scoop a bottle of water from the chest cooler and looked around for a glass. "I'm feeling the French toast. The stuffed kind, but anything is fine." She pulled a pint glass from the shelf and poured the water into it, watching him over the rim as she took a long drink and tried not to moan at how good it tasted. If she hadn't eaten in days, she also hadn't drunk anything, but until the water wet her tongue, she didn't realize how badly she needed it.

"Coming right up." Brock noticed the lack of footwear, so he ghosted a pair of slippers onto her feet. They were black rabbit skin they were a pair of his he kept in case someone pranked his footwear. Nothing like literally stepping in shit. He made a face thinking about it. "Scrolls sound harsher than my pink sticky note, hell." He left her to her water and placed the order.

She smiled her thanks and wiggled her toes in the soft, warm fur. "Hell is Hell, right? I've tried to explain email to

30

her, but she tells me this interweb thingy, as she calls it, won't last. Scrolls are forever." Kara called after him and rolled her eyes.

Brock headed to the back to start on his list of shit to do. If the Twins would just pull their weight, he could have been... *Been what, you stupid ass? She's mated to Dane, and she thinks you're just some nice shmuck.*

She watched him walk away and leaned her hip against the bar. Why was he so damned nice to her? He didn't have to and they'd never even really talked before she died. Well, there was that time... Kara shook her head, sighing and trying not to think about it. Instead, she found the broom and went to the bar to sweep around the stools. Having something to do made her feel better and kept her out of her head.

A thought hit him, *Kara's jacket.* Brock had taken it from the kid that found it. He went to the office and pulled open the closet. He'd cleaned it for her. Brock pulled it off the hanger and headed back to the bar with the jacket in hand. His to-do list could wait.

Kara glanced up, her hands flexing and becoming fists when she spotted movement in the hall. Too many years of fighting for the right to breathe made her pulse pound faster as her muscle memory prepared for a fight. When Brock emerged from the dimly lit corridor with her jacket in his hand, she couldn't help her smile. It was like seeing an old friend. "Where did you find that?"

Brock held the black leather out to her. He didn't want to tell her that some punk kid took it off her dead body. "In the hall, upstairs." He looked at the broom in her hands and tried not to arch a brow. "If you're sweeping, the booths need it too."

Kara leaned the broom against the bar and took the jacket, sliding her arms inside and shrugging it on. She wrapped her arms around herself and arched a brow at the strange scent coming from it. "Booths. I can do that."

He was only joking, and this time he couldn't hide his surprise. "Your food should be ready soon." He watched her take the jacket, and then he laughed, hoping to lighten the mood. "Interweb. Well, scrolls have been around longer than most things, nowadays. A classic never dies, plus the way I see it if it's not broken, don't fix it." He chuckled again. "Interweb."

Kara eyed him, not sure what that look was about and picked up the broom again. Her nose wrinkled at the unmistakable odor of fox. There was more to the story. In a closet? Her ass. She should let it go. He'd been nothing but nice to her, she thought to herself as she worked her way down the row of booths and swept the dirt back to her first pile. "Mother would be pleased that you agree with her. Course she might decide to keep you too." Kara snorted and returned to her sweeping. She caught the scent of fresh death and canine again and wrinkled her nose. "Thanks for trying to spare my feelings, but you can't get the smell of fox out of leather. I do appreciate that you tried." She looked around. "Dustpan?"

Brock sighed and took the dustpan to her. "I don't know the whole story. I know a punk kid found it and I took it from him. I cleaned it as best I could. I'm sorry." He heard her order being called, so he left her to get it, trying to block out the image of her dead eyes from his mind.

She eyed him and knelt to sweep the pile of dirt into it. Taking it behind the bar, she dumped it in the trash and put it back where she'd seen him get it from. She tapped his shoulder, pulling back when a weird peacefulness flooded through her but left as soon as the contact was broken. "I'm sorry. Thank you for getting it back. I'm just a little raw when it comes to people not telling me what's really going on, right now. I didn't mean to take it out on you." She leaned the broom in the crevice between the ice machine and the sink. "I'm not used to people doing nice things for me. I guess there's a learning curve." She smiled softly and picked up her glass of water, draining and then refilling it.

32

He nodded and set her food down. "It's okay, Cher. I know it's a mess right now. But I'm not good at talking to people. So, I'm sorry if I seem slow to you." He went to get his food and took a seat not too far from her. He ghosted in the silverware that he had forgotten to grab for them.

Her brows shrugged together with confusion. "Who said anything about slow? You're doing just fine. I don't want to hit you with an 'it's not you, it's me,' line. But it's true." She moaned as the scent of cinnamon raisin French toast surrounded her and made her knees weak. She wiped at her mouth just in case she'd begun to drool. Kara felt like one of those cartoon characters floating on air as she zeroed in on the plate of delicious. She slid the plate closer to him, with only a stool separating them and grinned when the flatware appeared. "I think talking to you is pretty easy, and I like it." She grinned at him and cut into the pile of egg dipped bread and lifted it under her nose, groaning softly as she sniffed it. "I'm skittish. That's all on me, Babes."

Brock picked up his fork and knife and nodded. "Well, I'm glad I don't scare you too much," he said cutting into his omelet. He forked food into his mouth chewing it slowly. He noticed some people staring at them as they ate. Like a weird sideshow attraction. "So how is your breakfast?" He asked pushing her French toast back onto the plate. It was trying to make a break for it.

She laughed, and it felt weird. "Nope, not scared. I was a little startled earlier this morning, but I've got it under control now, and no blood was shed." Kara finally stopped torturing herself and slid the fork into her mouth, chewing slowly to savor it and moaned. "Foodgasm. No joke." She closed her eyes happily before standing on the brass bar and reaching over the bar to get the bottle of honey, squeezed some onto her plate and then held it out to him.

Brock smiled. "Yes, I'm still alive, so I call it a win." He took the honey and put it on his toast and bacon. Making sure it didn't touch the omelet, he put the small plastic bear down. "I don't know why it comes in this damn thing." He pointed at the bear. "It's racist."

She eyed him and then covered her mouth as she busted out laughing. "Poor Bjorn, being stereotyped by humans." She snickered and drank some of her water. It felt wrong to laugh and to enjoy herself and his company, but that didn't change the fact that both were happening. "Oh, crap." She groaned and looked down at her plate. "I just realized that I have no cash, ID or anything, on me. Can I work this off?" She pointed at her plate with her fork.

"Humans are the devil." He said with a laugh. "Don't worry about the food, Cher. Your tab is always open. So, it's cool. If you wait it out till Christmas, it all goes away anyway, but don't tell anyone I said that. It's a trade secret." He eyed the plastic bear. "They could at least give him claws and make him better. He's so puny and fragile."

"Your secret is safe with me." Kara leaned over to bump him with her shoulder. "And thank you. I'll get this all sorted out as quickly as I can, as soon as I know if Dane..." Her voice died off, and she sighed, pushing the food around on her plate before she forced herself to take another bite and chew slowly. Who was she fooling? She knew the lion was dead, but knowing that he hadn't ended up in his own version of hell mattered. "You're right. The bear could be more intimidating. It really should be the Cheerios bee, that would make more sense.

"You'd think that, but no. Damn humans. And thank you, Cher, for keeping my secret." He felt bad not knowing more about Dane for her. He'd vanished when she had. Who knew? Maybe the lion was laying low somewhere, and mourning the loss of his mate. God knew that would have left a gaping hole in Brocks' chest.

"I owe you one." she grinned at him. "You looked like you saw a ghost when I walked in." She teased him, finding it easier to joke about it than drown in the ache she was inside. "I'm not sure why you decided to take pity on me, but I'm glad you did."

"Well, mostly it's for my own safety. You know, there's always that one person that could kill off everyone if they wanted to? While others run from them, I run towards them. Self-preservation, plus I hope if things were different someone would show me some kindness," Brock said with a shrug.

She snickered and shook her head. She wanted to tell him that she wasn't dangerous unless provoked, but with the random thoughts of watching everything burn, bathing in a certain Ghuardian's blood and random fun facts of violence racing through her skull, that wasn't exactly correct. And now her eyes were watering again. "I hope they would too, Babes, because if I hear they don't? I'm going to take that personally. You've got a Valkyrie watching your back." She groaned and covered her face with her hand. "That wasn't supposed to sound creepy as shit."

He laughed and nodded. "It wasn't, and I'm glad. It may come in handy someday. Do you have a card or a secret word I say to make you appear?" He joked. He finished his food and pushed his plate away.

Kara shook her head. "Cards. I knew I forgot something!" She grinned. "All you gotta do is call my name, and I'm there. I never forget when I owe someone. It doesn't happen often." She looked down at her empty plate, barely remembering cleaning it. "So how does it work when a mating is broken?" She glanced up at him. "Sorry. I'm foggy on how all this works and what I'm supposed to do next or how I'm expected to act." She rubbed at the ache in her chest and drank some of her water. "I don't mean to make you my Yoda, but if the big green ears fit..." she trailed off and smiled softly.

He chuckled. "I'll remember that." He thought for a moment about the broken mating thing. "Well if you're here, that means he could be. Alive, I mean. I don't know where he is. I haven't gone to look for him. So, don't give up hope. If he can, he'll come back to find you. Hell, he needs clean underwear at some point, right?" He joked.

"True. Hope D has his key, cuz I'd kill for my own underpants right now." She grinned and tried not to think about it. "I'm just afraid..." She swallowed hard and cleared her throat. "If this was my fault, he could blame me. Hate me even, and I can't blame him. All that I know is that I can't feel him and it's killing me. Maybe I should start drinking now, and after a while, it won't hurt anymore." She was only half joking. "I'm sorry to be unloading on you like this, but I don't really have anyone to talk to." Yeah, she was that pathetic.

"Well, if you give me a few minutes, I can find the extra key to the room so you can get in. Maybe you'll find some clues there. And it's totally okay, Cher. I'm here to listen. Just think of me as a venting valve. Besides, not too many pretty women talk to me. It's mostly at me. It gets on my nerves."

"Thanks, but I'm kind of afraid to go in there. I mean, what if he's dead on the floor? I know our lives were tied together when we were alive, but that shit should have been broken when we died. Right? Isn't it 'until death do we part,' or some shit?"

Brock nodded, knowing what she meant. The fear of the unknown could be a mother fucker. "If you want me to go with you. I can, then if it's got bad juju or some shit I'll be there with you," he said, standing to take their plates away and came back a few moments later with the key to Dane's room.

Kara chewed at her lip and nodded, brushing the hair back from her face nervously. She stared at her hands, folded together on the bar when he disappeared and looked up when he returned. If Dane was in there, dead, she was going to snap like a cheap plastic toy and leave a trail of death and rubble. The Ghuardian would be first, then she was shutting down Asgard, and if she survived that, this planet was doomed. Her jaw ticked as her fury pushed the fear out of its way. "I'd like that, but if we do find a body, duck, because shit is gonna get bad, fast." She sighed and lowered her head again. "I don't want you to get hurt in the blowout, and I don't think I'll be able to control it." She was honest. Kara was hanging by a tattered thread.

Brock nodded and let her lead the way to the room. He unlocked the door and stepped back. He wanted to say something profound, but nothing came. Part of him wanted to choke Dane for not going to find her. But he didn't know Danes side. Not yet. There was still time to put a knot in his tail.

She watched the door swing open, and she knew that she was supposed to step through, but she couldn't convince her feet to move. Kara wrapped her arms around her middle and noticed that she didn't smell death. Her brow arched. She was relieved, but the disappointment she felt was a surprise. Glancing up at the bear, she finally broke through whatever held her rooted to the floor and walked inside, looking around at Dane's things, her things and the stuff that belonged to them both. Slowly she wandered through the small group of rooms. They were empty. She dropped her head and blinked back the tears and somehow felt even more empty and lost. "Maybe I shouldn't have told Dad to fuck off until I had more info," She snorted to herself.

Brock stepped through the doorway and stopped, letting her roam the rooms. He didn't want to be in her way. A thought came to him about tracking Dane. "Can Odin's ravens track? I mean isn't that one of their charms and horrors for other people?" He hoped that he didn't sound utterly stupid. He could smell the tears she was holding back.

"Probably," her voice was a hoarse whisper. She opened a drawer and grabbed a handful of underwear, shoving them into her pocket and then circled the bed to find her boots. She needed to get the stuff that she'd had on her when she died. For all she knew, the lion had been blowing up her phone, and she didn't even know. She scrubbed her face with her hand as the scents and memories mocked her.

37

She glanced up at Brock. He was going above and beyond anything that she could have asked. Kara didn't know why, and she wasn't capable of putting a lot of thought to it, not when he stood there looking concerned and smelling of sincerity. The bear was a rare breed, indeed. "I guess I need to swallow my pride and go grovel to dear old Dad," she growled and curled up her lip.

Brock wanted to hug her and tell her it would all work out, but this was real life, not some romance novel where she'd stare into his eyes, and his muscles and long hair would be enough to make her forget or heal the pain she was in. No, real life was hard, bloody, and painful. She was Valkyrie. He knew what she was and hell, death didn't stop her. It might have slowed her down a tick. The clock didn't mean shit to her or her kind.

Her kind, the words boomed in his head. His clan was responsible for the portal. And in his family, he was seen but not heard. He always got lost in the shuffle of the deck of life. Brock knew what it was like to love someone and then shit changed on a dime. He decided long ago that being stone silent was best for him. But Kara needed answers. She deserved the truth even if it ended the world. It was the price you paid for playing with forces that should be left alone. And what's a little death and bloodshed in her world? A blip on the radar.

"Why was I so damned stupid? I knew better than to think I could have this." Kara hadn't meant to say it aloud, and the sound of her voice made her jump a little. She lowered her head and wiped at her eyes. She was feeling sorry for herself, and that was a waste of time. She needed to remember what she was. "Anyway," she blew out her breath and squared her shoulders. "He isn't here, so ..." Her voice trailed off, and she tried to smile. "Yeah, I don't think I need to be here. It doesn't feel right."

Kara looked up when she heard footsteps in the hall and sighed her disappointment when Blade strolled by. She shook her head and fought through the need to feel

38

grounded and connected to the world around her. Instead of dropping her head against the poor bear's chest like she wanted to, just for a moment while she regrouped, she reached out and touched his arm. "Thank you. I'm not sure I could have come in here alone." He could have no idea how much it meant to her, and she couldn't explain it without shedding a tear or sounding batshit insane, so she kept it to herself.

Brock watched Blade go by. The Panther had his blinders on. He would find out later what was going on with him. When Kara touched his arm, he smiled a bit. "I get it. It would be super weird being around here without Dane. But you are welcome here anytime. I shouldn't tell you, but if your father can't help with answers, I might know a hail Mary pass, kind of way."

"I appreciate that, and honestly, this place is like home now, as weird as that sounds." Her laugh was shaky. Did she dare hope that he had an in for getting information? "What are you thinking? I left stuff in a bad place with Dad and he never really cared for Dane, so another option would save me from saying a lot of BS that I don't mean to convince him to help." She noticed the curiosity in Brock's clear blue eyes.

"When I died, I didn't go down fighting. So, I was sent to a place where they train the foot soldiers for the final battle. It was days here, but a decade or more there. Every day, I got up and had to face, fight and kill the people that I love. Dane was one of them, probably why it's so hard for me to believe he's alive. I saw him die every mother fucking day and I was the one who killed him."

Kara shook her head, pulling herself out of the nightmare looping inside her skull. "Anyway, Dad finally got me out, but I wasn't exactly understanding about any of it. So, yeah, that's it in a nutshell."

Brock took in her words in and didn't show any emotion on how it made him feel. "That is harsh, Cher. My thought is taking you through the portal to The Mountain, itself. I can find someone to go with you as a guide."

As Brock spoke, his father's voice screamed in his head. *'Never let anyone cross over, that's not one of us. You hear me son? Doing it could send you to your death. We don't hold anything powerful enough to save you from that or to make the Ghuardians overlook something like that.'*

Kara stared at him, trying not to let her mouth drop open. "You'd do that, for me?" She knew the cost too well. She'd spent eons hiding Odin's secret from her mother and knew what the price was for breaking the rule. Banishment. That was worse than death for a portal keeper. And knowing that, did her in. A tear rolled down her cheek. "I can't ask you to make that kind of sacrifice. Not for me. But knowing that you would?" She shook her head as her throat closed off painfully making talking near impossible. "You are truly one of a kind, Brock Navarro." She rolled up on her tiptoes and pressed her lips to his bearded jaw. "

Brock didn't move when her lips touched him. "Yes, I would do that, for you. And I'm not tied to anyone, so if I lost my life, it wouldn't be that hard for anyone. I'd gladly give it to help someone in need. As I said, Hail Mary, and all of that. You let me know what you decide, Cher. I don't know about one of a kind. Looking around here you'll find a few that are just like me." He laughed hard at his own personal joke about his family.

"It would matter to me." Kara smiled. "I think this world just might be a little better for having you in it." She was still reeling from his suggestion and nodded her head, knowing that she couldn't play so loosely with the bear's life. She got his joke about the quints and shook her head no. "They may look like you, but they've got nothing on you."

Kara stepped back and shoved her hands into her jacket pockets, looking around the room one last time. She knew that if Dane didn't come back, she would never set foot in this place again. "Would it be too much to ask for you to be my friend?" She grimaced at how lame and pathetic that sounded. "I mean, wow that sounded sad. What I meant is that you're easy to talk to and right now, I don't really have anyone else who wants to listen and there is something about you that makes me feel like I'm really here, not just a ghost floating through." She rubbed the back of her neck and checked out the toes of the slippers she was still wearing. "Yeah, forget I said all that. Girl moment or some shit."

"Well, thank you for your kind words. And friends? I'm good with that. I don't have many myself. I'll leave you to do whatever you need to." He took the key off the key ring and gave it to her. "You keep this and try not to lose it." He joked and patted her shoulder. "When, or if, you go to speak with your father, my advice is to let him do most of the talking and then just speak. Let him get it all out before you give him the truth of your visit." He turned to leave.

"If all else fails, Hail Mary time," Brock said over his shoulder as he started down the hall wondering if he should go find Blade and make the Panther talk. But he really wasn't in the mood to have the cat give him an attitude and fight with him to spill it. Panthers and their tight-lipped, better than thou attitude, pissed Brock off. Maybe it was a feline thing, thinking their shit don't stink. He chuckled thinking about the fact the place was owned and run by cats. When the patients take over the asylum, came to mind.

Kara smiled and tucked the key into her pocket. She nodded when Brock turned to go and watched his back disappear down the hall. Looking around again she ghosted to the roof, to sit, think and recharge as she soaked up the sun.

Chapter 5

Bree sighed as her taxi stopped in front of The Pit. Groaning and stretching her legs, she paid the cabbie, got out and collected her bags. Sliding her backpack over her shoulder, she looked up at the two tall buildings that were so close together that they may as well have been one. To those who lived inside, they were. Closing her eyes, she breathed in the air, savoring the scents of Brax's cooking that leaked through the walls and the faint tinge of swamp battling the salty air of the Delta. "There's no place like home," she sighed.

Pulling the rolling suitcase behind her, she stepped through the family entrance in the side alley and pushed the handle back into the case, to make it easier to carry up the stairs. Photos of the Navarro clan, dating back to the invention of photography, dotted the walls and made Bree smile. This gentle reminder was far easier to swallow than the new age BS that they'd tried to shove down her throat at the training retreat ordered by Salvation. As she began climbing the stairs, she felt something pass through her. Bree stopped, shivered and searched the air around her. Nothing was in the stairwell. "You're letting the old people get to you."

Salvation's words came to her, *'You are your clan's medium. It's your job to protect and direct the lost souls.'* It was all a bunch of hoodoo voodoo. Too much peyote bull crap, if you asked her, not that anyone did. They just told her to be seen, not heard and be the golden child of the Navarro clan.

As she continued up the narrow flight of worn steps, Bree felt it again. A whisper of something just out of reach that made her skin goose bump. She shook her head, knowing that whatever it was, it would be seen when it was ready. She set the suitcase on the floor at the top of the stairwell and rolled it beside her as she continued toward her room. Bree eyed the door where the Valkyrie was rumored to live. Bree had never met the female. She didn't have to, to know about her. It was so odd that she was mated to Dane. Bree's head tilted as she passed the door and heard strange noises coming from inside.

After soaking up the sun, Kara's powers were still a joke, other than ghosting her sword this morning, which was a classic fear response, she couldn't even drop a fly. It was annoying as hell, and so were these jeans. They chafed in a spot she'd rather never feel that sensation. She hadn't wanted to come here again. It felt too empty and everywhere were things that brought memories crashing back to mock her, but she needed jeans that fit and shoes. "I'll make it quick and then walk to my place." She growled to herself, not looking forward to the long walk in the heat.

Kara pawed through the two drawers that belonged to her and found her own jeans, underwear and thank fuck, one of her bras. She held it up and considered kissing the soft lace. She hadn't seen one, let alone worn one in what felt like forever. It wasn't part of the armor issued while she was in the lower levels of Valhalla. Talk about chafing. Kara made a face and tossed the clothes on the bed before trying to shimmy her way out of the too-tight jeans.

She growled her frustration, glad that Dane wasn't here to watch and narrate this disaster. She could just hear him now, *"The Valkyrie had the upper hand folks, but Levi Strauss has turned the tables, trapped her knees and she's*

43

going down! Will she stay down, or is she tough enough to get back in the fight?"

Kara landed on her ass on the floor with a thump and a curse. There was no dignity being trapped in her body with no powers.

Bree poked her head into the room. She watched the Valkyrie fall over. Without a thought, she rushed to help her up. "Oh geez, are you ok?" She asked reaching down to take hold of an arm to help Kara up.

Kara yelped like a startled school girl when she heard a voice. Her laugh was a little shaky as she felt her face flush with embarrassment. "Yeah, I just hurt my pride and my rep." She shook her head as the female helped her up and leaned over to catch herself on the bed. The jeans still had a strangle hold on her knees. When she finally found her balance, she looked at who had come to her aid.

Bree's long dirty blond hair fell in her eyes blocking her view of the Valkyrie. A cold chill went through her. She tipped her head back, so her hair fell away. She blinked and thought she saw Dane for a moment. His mouth moved like he was trying to tell her something.

She looked familiar, but it wasn't until the she-bear shook the hair back from her face that Kara could see eyes almost identical to Brock's looking back at her. "Thanks." Kara plopped down on the bed, reaching out to steady the female when she blinked like she had a migraine and her face went blank. "But are you okay?"

Dane's outline vanished making Bree wonder if she was just overly tired. It was his room so, yeah, she was cracking up. "Oh yes. I'm fine. I just had a moment there." She smiled at the female. "I don't think we've officially met. I'm Bree Navarro." She looked at the jeans around the woman's ankles. "Skinny jeans are the devil. I'd rather wear a trash bag as a dress then wear those. It's like a corset for your lower half, plus they give you camel toe." Once the words came out of her mouth, she closed it biting her lip.

"I'm sorry that was a bit much. I apologize." Bree looked away.

'Ladies of this clan do not have a trash mouth. Manners, Bree! How many times must you be told?' Her mother's voice filled Bree's head.

"I couldn't agree more." Kara smiled and used her feet in the crotch to push the tight denim down her calves and finally over her bare feet. "I think I want to burn them." She blinked at the pile at her feet and kicked them away. "I've seen you around, I think. I'm Kara." She stopped talking and tilted her head to the side. "Camel toe...." She made a face, shook out the ones from the drawer and slid them on, breathing a sigh of relief. "Do I remember you being away for a while, or is my brain still mush?"

Bree nodded. "Yes, I just returned today as it happens." She wasn't sure how much the female knew of her kind, so she kept it short. "Where is Dane? I have a gift for him," she said opening her backpack and pulling out a carving made of black onyx that was in a shape of a lion. She knew it was silly, but he had joked with her that he wanted a gift and not a key chain that said, my friend went to where ever and all I got was this crappy keychain. Bree held out the small knickknack.

Kara pushed the hair back from her face and eyed the beautiful carving, but didn't reach for it. "Umm," she stalled for time until she could figure out what to say. "While you were gone, he and I kind of died and I haven't been able to find him yet." She swallowed hard and let her eyes fall to inspect the floor. "My powers are still shit. Who knew being dead, took so much out of you?"

Bree quickly pulled the small lion back. "I'm so sorry. I had no idea." She felt the chill again. Looking past Kara, she saw Dane. "But if you're here..." Her voice trailed off.

Dane's outline moved around the room and went right through Kara. Bree backed up a little. She had never had spirits come at her before. In her dreams, she was haunted

45

by them. They asked her to help find rest or speak to their family that still lived. But nothing like this.

'When you return home, things will be different for you, Little One. You have unlocked your inner magic.' One of the elders had told her.

Dane kept coming at her. Bree skittered back, slamming into the dresser and knocking things off it. "P..please," she stammered, her voice shaky.

Kara shivered as a cold breeze raced up her spine. "Don't worry about it, I'm getting used to it. Dane being MIA, not so much, though." She sighed, her brows shrugging together when she felt the bear's panic and watched a ring of white circle the blue iris as the girl backed up and slammed into the furniture. Odds and ends rolled to hit the floor like machine gun fire. Kara slid her hand between the mattresses to grab the dagger she always kept there and jumped up to block the female from... She slowly scanned the room. From nothing. What the fuck? "What is it? What's wrong?"

"Dane!" Bree squeezed out. She let Kara shield her, though it didn't stop Dane from coming at her. The lion's spirit reached out, taking hold of Bree's arm. She screamed in pain as her flesh started to turn freezing hot. "No! You will not take me," Bree yelled at Dane's outline.

Brax heard his sister's scream and ghosted into the room. He saw Kara and Bree, but nothing else. Brax couldn't see anything, but he felt something. He used his magic to shield the females.

Kara didn't see anything. She wanted to, but Dane wasn't there. She pushed everything else out of her mind and let her senses see what her eyes couldn't. She had just begun to pick up on something moving when a shield surrounded her, and Brax was in the room with them. Her nose twitched as the scent of the room changed. For a split second, she would have sworn that she smelled Dane and then it was gone. Kara gasped when she saw Bree's arm and the red fingerprints that wrapped around it laced with frost crystals that were quickly melting and dripping to the floor. "Are you okay?" She put her arm around the bear's shoulders hoping to comfort her or at least be there to catch her if Bree went down.

Dane had vanished when the bear's shield hit him. *Do not freak out,* Bree told herself. "Yes, I think so. Thank you," she said leaning on Kara.

"What happened?" Brax demanded of his sister and looked around the room.

"Dane, his spirit..." Bree couldn't explain it, but when it touched her, she felt his pain. He was lost and suffering. His pleading voice echoed in her head. *'Help me, please help me.'*

Kara closed her eyes against the tears that flooded them. Spirit meant not alive. She'd known but hearing it was like putting a grenade in her chest and pulling the pin. She opened her mouth to say something but her mind was a jumble, and nothing came out.

Brax moved to check on his sister. "Jesus, we need to get you looked at." He arched a brow at Kara. "You going to be okay?" He asked her, dismissing the Goddess.

Bree shook her head. "No Bubba I'm okay. I don't need to be babied."

Brax growled. "Not up for debate."

"But Bubba!" She protested. Brax stared her down. "Okay," she said looking at Kara. "I'm sorry."

"Nothing to be sorry for. Now I know. Listen to your brother. That looks like it hurts. He wouldn't have wanted to hurt you." Kara felt like she had a pound of sand in her throat and talking through it wasn't easy. She was barely holding her shit together. It was probably a good thing that her powers had shit out because if they hadn't, NOLA would see a lightning storm of apocalyptic proportions. Kara forced a reassuring smile that she didn't feel, and knew that she had to get the hell out of here before she broke completely. "It's okay. Really."

47

Bree apologized once again before Brax took her out of the room. Bree knew something was horribly wrong. Dane wasn't a violent person. She needed to find out what was going on. Now that her brother had seen her get hurt, she'd have him all over her. "Poor Dane," she whispered softly.

After they had gone, Kara dropped onto the bed and lowered her face into her hands as she leaned her elbows on her knees. "I can't do this," she whispered to the empty air and refused to cry. She knew that Dane was gone now, but he should have moved on. Why hadn't he?

Growling at herself, she pulled on her boots, fished her spare set of keys from the bed stand and left. She couldn't stay here, not now that she knew. She rubbed her chest as she made her way through the halls, down the stairs and outside. She didn't have any idea where she was going. It didn't matter. Everything that mattered was gone.

Chapter 6

Dane came awake. His body felt like it was on fire and yet freezing at the same time. He couldn't remember what happened. He snarled in pain and tried to get up. When he did, he floated away. "What in the hell?" He said looking down at his body.

Before he could do anything or say anything else, a portal opened, and he was sucked in. Everything went black, and his eyes couldn't seem to adjust to wherever he was.

"Kara!" His mind raced. Where was she? He screamed her name. Nothing... He let whatever was happening, take him. Dane moved like a leaf in the wind. Still screaming her name, he didn't stop until something hard hit him.

"You can scream all you like. The Kara thing isn't going to come," a voice said.

Dane growled. "Who are you? Show yourself!"

The voice laughed. "Show myself? Oh, for a body of my own, I'd kill. You animals are really stupid, ain't you?"

Dane snarled. "Show yourself, coward!!" The blackness faded for a moment. A flicker of something bright green appeared, and then Dane saw it the most horrifying thing he'd ever seen in his life. All that he could think of as he stared was, this is death. All around him, death. They looked like zombies that time had forgotten. Dane tried to turn, but his body was nothing more than a wisp of air. Did he look like them? "What is this place?"

"It is where the damned go to suffer. We are not living, and we're not dead. We just here."

He watched more color flickers appear each different from the next. Then a flash of silvery gold went by him. Dane knew that light. *KARA!* His mind screamed. She was gone before he could do anything. "KARA!" He screamed, and everything went black again.

"You are dead, and she got a reprieve. She is not one of us. Lucky her."

Dane felt her rage. He needed to get out of here. He needed to find her. He closed his eyes and focused on her and their home. Instead, he saw Bree in his mind, and he reached out to her. He knew that she could see him. "Help me!" He screamed over and over. He had to make her understand. He willed himself closer and took ahold of her.

For just a moment, he felt Kara, but it was short-lived. Something blasted him away, He bounced off it and back into the darkness. "NO!!!" He roared. Even though he was a wisp, that blast still hurt like hell. His 'body' hummed in pain as he roared out in rage.

"Are you finished with your tantrum?" The voice asked him.

"I don't belong here." He said trying to look down at his body to see if the damage matched how he felt.

"Sure, we are all innocent. That's why we are trapped." The voice turned condescending.

"Who are you?"

"Honestly? I've been here so long, I forget my name," it said.

"Is there truly no way out? I mean Kara got out." Dane said hoping the voice was just fucking with him.

"I told you she is not one of us. Her blood is different as is her power. Here in the Shadowlands, once you are here, you stay here. No one gives a damn about us. Not like they used to. The old ways have been lost. The elders no longer help us find our way home whether it be home at rest within the mountain or cast out into his pit."

His pit? Dane was confused. "His pit?" He asked.

"Yes, his pit. Did your clan not teach you the story of the mountain and the Ghuardians?" The voice asked.

"No, not really. It's all Boogie Man stories."

The voice laughed coldly and then things were silent a while.

"Hello?" Dane asked.

"Hush. He comes," the voice whispered.

Dane felt something evil approaching. No, it was scarier than evil. He tried to see what the voice was talking about, but he couldn't see anything. The darkness seemed to get darker as the footsteps drew closer.

Ty walked through the Shadowlands, trying to zero in on the smell left by the escapee. He hoped he wasn't too late to find it. "Dear sister, I will be coming to see you very soon," he said into the darkness that really didn't bother him. He could see everything perfectly. This was his realm.

As he walked along, Ty felt a ping of leftover power. He stopped and looked down at the wisp that was Dane's body. Ty's eyes glittered with rage. "You?" He reached down into the darkness for Dane.

Dane heard the footsteps stop then he heard the thing's voice. It was chilling as he felt someone take hold of him. Then he saw its face. Dane was expecting to see Satan himself. Instead, he saw a male that was a straight up, pretty boy. He laughed a bit. They feared this GQ looking motherfucker?

"Speak. Tell me who you are," the male said, shaking him hard. Ty gave form to the souls here, if only for his pleasure, while he tortured them.

Dane growled at him. "Fuck you!" His eyes glowered at the male.

"I just might, for the fun of it. You smell a bit like Asgard. It's faint, but it's there, on you. Why?" Ty asked, his voice as even as he could make it.

"I have no idea what you're talking about. Who the hell are you?" Dane asked.

51

Ty's face twisted into a grin. "Who am I?" Who am I?" He laughed hard and picked Dane up from the ground. "I am the thing the darkness fears and makes the devil cry. And you are about to piss me off."

Dane didn't waver in fear, not at first. Not until he looked into the male's eyes. He saw something straight out of a Clive Barker movie. His face paled, and Ty grinned wider.

"Now tell me who you are."

Dane swallowed before he answered. "My name is Dane Lyons."

"Tell me, Dane, why do you smell of Odin's realm? You're a shifter, and I can tell that nothing else about you is special. You don't have any powers the Viking King would want."

Dane's mind raced to Kara, but he said nothing.

"Speak, or I'll make you talk," Ty said, shaking him again.

"I have no idea." Dane lied.

Ty snarled at him. "Fine. We'll do this the hard way." Ty placed his free hand on Dane's head. "Don't say I didn't ask nicely." Ty let his magic see Dane's life up to the point of his death. At first, there was nothing special, then he saw it. A Valkyrie. Not just any Valkyrie, the daughter of Odin himself. He smiled and removed his hand, but not before seeing that Salvation was the one that killed the shifter and the princess. The Ghuardian had balls of steel to bring the wrath of the Norse pantheon down on himself. Ty snorted. Or the bastard was just fucking stupid. He dropped Dane to the ground letting him return to a wispy form.

Dane growled. "What did you do?"

Ty said nothing and walked away.

"WHAT DID YOU DO!!" Dane roared at him.

"Me? Nothing. You though? You did a lot. You may have just given me the keys to ending the world." Ty smirked over his shoulder at the shifter.

Dane tried to attack him but went right through him.

52

"This is my realm. Nothing and no one can hurt me here. So, you can try all you like, but I'd get comfortable. You'll be here for a long time. Sooner or later someone will come for you. The princess has gone soft, and so has her daddy. One of them will come looking for you, and I'll be sure to be here to slaughter them." Ty's voice was so cheerful that you'd think he was talking about getting a puppy for Christmas.

Chapter 7

"Well I don't know how a body got up and walked out of your god damn morgue either, but I still need to get the personal effects for her family!" Asher growled into the phone, missing the days when you could slam a receiver into the cradle, like you meant it and feel some satisfaction. "Just email me the paperwork, and I'll get it back to you." He rolled his eyes at the yammering coming through the phone and burrowing into his ear. "Fine, I'll hand deliver the stupid fucking thing. Happy?" He couldn't help wondering just how much shit he'd be in if he killed the humans, or whoever fucked up, and sent the Valkyrie's body to a human morgue.

Brax pushed the heavy doors of the clinic open and waited for a protesting Bree to go inside.

"Honestly Bubba, I'm okay." Bree lied and sighed when her brother snorted and raised his arm to point down the hall.

"Work on the fibbing, Little Sister." Brax shook his head and smirked when she gave up and went in the direction that he wanted her to.

Asher looked up when he heard voices in the hall. "I got patients. Just send it. Email. Fax. Fucking carrier pidgin. I don't care. Just do it." He pulled the cordless phone away from his ear to jab the end button hard. It just wasn't the same. Groaning, he considered banging his head against the desk.

He rolled his chair back and stepped into the hall to see what the newest emergency was and found two of the Navarro bears. Bree was holding her arm against her chest. "When did you get back, Little Bit?" Asher smiled and walked toward them to hug her gently. "Your brothers have been unbearable to live with, without you here."

Bree tried to smile at him. Brax yanked her arm away from her and held it out so Asher could see. "Today. You can tranq them, right?" She sighed and rolled her eyes, feeling embarrassed. "I'm fine. I don't need to be here."

Asher chuckled and gently palmed her arm to see it better. "I like how you think. What happened?" He tugged her gently, making her follow him into an empty exam room, motioning to the table while he pulled on gloves. "Maybe you don't, but humor the Doc and let me check it out anyway. I gotta earn my keep, or they'll toss me out on my ass." He grinned and held his hand out for her arm again. "Does it hurt?"

Bree followed him to the exam table and hopped up onto it. "I was attacked by a spirit. And it feels like I guess freezer burn would."

Brax stood in the doorway, watching them. Though Bree was the same age as the rest of the Quints, she didn't look it. The elders had kept her on the mountain longer, so she aged slower than her brothers. To the humans, she looked like a senior in high school or freshmen in college. They all babied her. Brax knew she hated it, but instinct dictated that they protect her and there was no fighting that.

Asher feathered his fingers over the welts, watching her face for a grimace. "That's what it looks like, too." There was too much happening lately, and all of it was straight out of the twilight zone. "Anyone, I know?" He teased and let go of her arm to turn and rummage through a cabinet for some burn ointment.

"Dane," she whispered, afraid that if she said his name too loud, he would come for her again.

55

"Well, fuck." Asher shook his head. That was a pity, but the news that Dane was pushing up daisies wasn't a surprise. "I've been expecting his furry ass to walk through that door. I guess I can stop waiting." They had to stop losing people. He followed her eyes as they ping-ponged around the room and shivered slightly.

"I think it's safe to say he won't unless he can find a way back," she murmured, not wanting Brax to hear her. "Am I gonna be okay?"

"You're going to be fine." Asher smiled and returned with a small tube of ointment, opened it, squeezed a dab onto his finger and smoothed it over the raised red skin. "Just keep it from drying out, and this should help with the pain." He looked up at her. "How does that feel?"

She winced at first and then relaxed. "A lot better. I should have waited to come home. Maybe I'm not ready to be here."

"Why would you think that? There's no place like home, and if you waited for everything to be normal, you'd never come back." He patted her shoulder affectionately. "And this place would suck without your smile, Little Bit."

"Thank you, Asher." She tried to smile but she felt like something bad was coming or going to happen. "Well, they already kept me there long enough to make me look like I'm thirteen. And I don't think my training worked, cuz." She held up her arm. "Cuz, yeah, this crap. When he touched me, the things I felt," she shook her head and looked down at the floor. "There's something wrong."

"I'm betting he's pissed. What did they teach you for dealing with that? Can you play shrink for them or something?" Asher could feel how scared she was, even though she was trying to hide it from her brother.

"I'm supposed to guide them to their resting place and protect their souls. But Dane didn't feel like he was lost. He felt trapped. The first day on the job and I get hurt. I hate being a girl."

"Did you try talking to him, maybe he didn't know he had your attention?" Asher screwed the cap on the tube and put it in her hand. "Not that I have a clue what I'm talking about." He chuckled and scratched his jaw.

She laughed. There was something about Asher that always put her at ease and made her feel like she wasn't some stupid kid. "I couldn't. Brax came in, and then he vanished. I think Brax's shield bounced him back to where he was. Poor Kara, I think I made things worse for her. I mess up everything."

"Kara has had a tough week, but she'll bounce back." Asher snorted "Or she'll kill us all. Who knows? All you can do is the best you can with what you know. Maybe if you try to reach out to him, he'll be more mellow. Dane wasn't a violent guy, I don't think he'd be happy to know that he hurt you."

Bree thought about it, but how could she do that with Brax there? Once he told the others, she'd never be left alone, not even to use the bathroom. Beyer and Bart had no problems standing in there with her. "I hope so, and as for Dane, I'll think of something."

"You know where to find me if you need help. Or you could ask Kara and do what you've got to while she beats the snot out of them. Let me know first though so I can have the popcorn ready." He winked and looked at Brax innocently. "What?"

Brax growled. "The Viking doesn't scare me."

Bree laughed. "You're stupid if that's true." *God, her brother was thick headed.*

"Lots of popcorn." Asher laughed. "Seriously though, I can be there when you do whatever you need to do. If anything happens or goes wrong, we'll deal with it ASAP."

"Thank you so much. I can use the support." Bree smiled and hopped off the table to hug him. "How much do I owe you?" She looked around and realized that she'd left her bag and her wallet in Kara's room.

"Buy me dinner the next time we're both at the bar, we can catch up, and we're square. Sound okay?" He hugged her back. He might be a different species, but he still thought of her as his little sister. Gods knew she needed someone around that didn't treat her like she was too fragile to live.

"Deal, and a game of darts. I'll let you win this time," Bree teased him before looking at Brax. "All done warden, take me back to my cell."

Brax was not amused and grunted, "We do have cells. It might not be a bad idea."

"Lighten up, Bubba. It'll be okay." She said, squeezing Asher's hand before leaving.

Asher laughed. "Let me win, my feathered ass. I'm gonna beat you so bad your grandcubs are gonna feel it, Little Bit." He watched them leave and shook his head. Her brothers needed to lighten up. She'd been chosen for a path that they couldn't walk for her and smothering her wasn't going to change that fact.

Brax escorted Bree to her room. She tried closing the door, but he shook his head and pushed his way inside. She growled at him and went to her bed to pass out. She really needed to upgrade to a suite of rooms, like the others had. Slamming a door would feel darn good right now.

Brax took out his phone and texted the family about what had happened. Eyeing her as she flopped on the bed and ignored him, he let his amusement show before he sunk into the big pink chair in her room. Leaning back, he got comfortable and kept watch over her, whether she liked it or not.

Chapter 8

Kara killed the rumbling motor of the classic Harley-Davidson pan head and slid her hand over the glossy sheen of the black on black gas tank. She remembered when it had been a heap of parts and frame that she'd rescued from the junkyard, and the months she'd spent rebuilding it with her own hands. It was her baby. At least it was still here. Sighing, she swung her leg over the airbrushed rear fender and began walking through the thick matted plants of the spongy swamp ground. She made her way to the small waterfall that she'd found last year.

Stripping off her clothes, she sunk into the tepid, sun-warmed water. A cool breeze played with her hair. It was silent here. Quiet and serene. Utterly empty, almost as empty as she was. She dropped her chin to rest on the knees curled to her chest, looking at nothing but the sun's reflection on the water and hoping for clarity. Maybe she just needed to face that she was not meant for the realm of man.

Kara sighed and turned her face to study the arm that she pulled from the water, watching as the water ran and then slowed to single drops pooling together to stagger from her skin. She used her magic to show her real skin. The one that showed every scar earned and to her kind were a badge of honor, but she felt none. Hell, she didn't feel much of anything anymore but emptiness and fetid, festering rage. Her eyes crawled over her bare skin from shoulder to wrist, searching for one unmarred bit of flesh. There was no peace to be found, just like there was no solace in the lion's appearance.

Inside she'd gone pitch black, thoughts and phantom emotions drifted and echoed. A hollow husk, that's all she was now, and she was so damned tired of it all. Tired of trying to be normal. Tired of going through the motions when in the end, it changed nothing. Tired of watching this world change, yet always be the same. Tired of watching everything she built crumble. Tired of seeing, breathing, and existing. Just tired. When was enough, enough? She couldn't even cry anymore, she'd run dry. Nothing could make this right or bring back that small flame of hope that she'd guarded and fought for with the entirety of her soul. It had been snuffed out when she had. When she was brought back, it remained just a charred, cold wick.

Reaching below the water's surface, Kara scooped up a handful of the coarse sand from the bottom and savored the gritty texture as she rubbed it between her fingers and thumb. Grinding it against her calf, feeling it chafe off her skin she shivered at the sensation. Feeling anything had become so foreign to her since she'd come back, that even pain was welcome. For the love of the Gods anything but the bottomless pit of empty.

She heard the faint call of one of her charges humming at the base of her neck and spreading at a snail's pace to slither inside her ear. Sighing, Kara stood to let the water sheet from her skin, her feet sinking into the coarse sand before finding the way to the mossy bank. She didn't want to go. There was too much for her to face, too much that would suck away any hidden shred of humanity that lingered and just another opportunity to sink further into her hell. Her fingers ran over the countless puckered scars that covered her abdomen as her azure gaze swept over the endless field of tall swaying plants. It moved like the ocean, she thought randomly as she pulled on the clothes that she'd left on the bank

It was time to cut ties and take care of business and then... Maybe stasis would be nice, because neither this world or any other, had anything to offer her anymore.

Closing her eyes and lifting her face to the warmth of the sun, Kara found the one calling and appeared at his side as he gasped his last breath on a slab of cracked asphalt in a pool of his own blood. She ached to feel the pity that had always hit her or the prickle of tears at that final heave of the chest. Instead, she felt nothing because she was nothing now.

Chapter 9

Brock slipped away from The Pit. He needed to clear his head and think. That was impossible at the bar. Someone always needed him to do something, like he didn't have a life of his own. He sighed. He didn't. He wanted that to change, but how? His mind was crammed full of so much stuff that he couldn't think clearly. It was no surprise that Kara was front and center.

She was back, but she wasn't herself. Something about her was different. It wasn't just the, she used to be dead part. Her typical easy grin was slow, and she didn't walk with the same confidence that she had before. He didn't even think it was the mess with Dane. Brock didn't doubt that was part of it, but it didn't explain the shift in her aura. It was darker now, the colors muted and dull. He'd never known her to be vulnerable, but now she felt fragile, and it made him want to hold her and keep her safe. Brock shook his head and sighed. Something soul deep was wrong with her.

Brock ghosted to the shed he'd converted into his makeshift woodworking shop. Glancing around, hoping that no one saw him come here, he unlocked the door and stepped inside. As he closed the door, the comforting scents of the shop filled his nose, and some of the tension drained out through a deep breath. The smell of freshly milled wood and varnish was thick. He breathed it in as he flipped on the lights, and made his way to the workbench that held his tools and the plans for his projects.

His hands ran over the trunk he was building for the foot of Bree's bed. Brock had hoped to have it finished before she came back, but as with everything else, he'd been helping others instead of having time for what he wanted to do. He was growing tired of it and running away from home was becoming a better idea by the day. He knew that he couldn't, but it was a nice fantasy.

Pulling his hair back and securing it with a rubber band, his eyes went to the photo pinned to the wall above the work bench. It was old, yellowed and the last one taken of his family when it was still whole. Brock sat down on the stool in front of the bench, still staring at the photograph. "What am I supposed to do? I know she's not my mate, but I want to help her. I'd do anything to see her happy," he said to the photo that held the smiles of his parents.

He sighed and dropped his eyes, knowing what Papa would say, and he felt compelled to plead his case. "I know my job is to always put the family first, but the last time I did that," Brock's voice trailed off. The last time, the person he loved was killed. Not just her. His parents were taken, too. All because of that damn portal and the rules.

Brock growled as tears stung his eyes. Kara's face filled his mind, and he hated the lost and haunted look in her azure eyes. He'd heard what had happened with Bree and if his baby sister was saying that Dane was a spirit, then the lion was dead. He wasn't coming back. Was it wrong that Brock wanted to help her? Maybe suggesting that he take her to The Mountain had been too far, but now she knew Dane was gone and she could... What? Move on with him? He closed his eyes and growled. Why the hell not? Brock would treat her better than Dane ever had, and he could make her happy. He knew it. All he needed was the chance. For now, he'd be the friend she'd asked for, but he'd be damned if he'd sit back and watch her, self-destruct. It was

63

coming, he felt it as surely as he felt the grain in the wood under his hands.

"Not this time. I can't let her suffer like I have. She's lost enough. Dane has lost enough. There is too much loss and not enough happiness. I know you'd want me to protect the family, but putting others first was always something you told me to do," he said lifting his eyes to the photo before dropping his head into his hands. He missed his parents so much. Though he was the oldest only by minutes, he seemed to be the one that got lost in the mix. He didn't want Kara to get lost too. If the chance came for Brock to make things right for her, he would take it. Still blinking back the tears, he made up his mind, then and there.

A sense of peace settled over him with the decision, and he smiled softly. Who knew? Maybe he'd even get the chance to be part of her life if she was serious about being friends. He picked up the sanding block and ran it over the surface of the chest, wearing down anything rough that might put a splinter in Bree's hands. For the first time since Kara had died, he felt like his old self as he hummed and lost himself in his work.

His phone beeped in his back pocket. Sighing, Brock fished it out and looked down at the screen. It was a reminder about one of the delivery trucks scheduled for today. He'd forgotten and knew better than to believe that someone else would handle it. Brock growled and ran his hand over the wood one last time before he turned off the lights, locked the door and, after a longing glance, headed back to The Pit. How could he have a life of his own when he couldn't even find forty minutes for himself?

Chapter 10

Kara's hand brushed the cold stone labradorite countertop when she tossed her keys on it. Her brow quirked at the layer of dust that coated her fingers and a soft smile played on her lips when the sunlight from the window caught a vein of the blue that sliced through the stone, glowing and mocking her with its beautiful perfection. Kara sighed and wiped her hand on her jeans. She'd been gone too long, preferring to spend her time with Dane, than in her small apartment, alone. That was over now.

Finger combing the hair back from her face, she walked through the space, seeing nothing as she followed the hardwoods to the balcony where the floor beneath her feet turned to blue slate. Kara leaned her palms against the wrought iron rail and turned her face up, closing her eyes as the sun warmed her skin, but did nothing to change the cold knot in her chest.

She didn't want to do this. Swallowing her pride had never been in her skill set. If it were anyone other than Dane... She groaned and let her head roll forward, to hang limply. For Dane, she would sell her soul to the devil, himself. One corner of her mouth curled up. That was a solid plan B.

"Dad?" Kara whispered, letting his face fill her head and waiting a moment, before looking up into the sky again.

"I need your help," the words almost stuck in her throat. She felt Odin's presence behind her. She didn't have to turn to know that he was there, but she did because groveling was done better face to face.

"You called, Little One?" Odin was alone, with no ravens hopping across his broad shoulders and his face showed his pain. He stepped closer and brushed the hair away from her face tenderly, wishing that he could siphon the unbearable ache that was crushing his daughter.

Kara flinched away from his touch and dropped her eyes from his. The love she saw there hurt and caused her stomach to twist. "I get it now, Fadir."

"What is that?" Odin dropped his hand with a sigh.

"What you said about love being both Valhalla and Helheim." Kara leaned her ass against the rail and wrapped her arms around herself, hoping that they would hold her together when she was so close to blowing apart.

"Aye."

"I made a promise that day, and I've kept my end of the deal. Haven't I?" She glanced up at his one blue eye.

"Aye. You have." His brow wrinkled as he tried to figure out what she was asking.

"Until now. I failed, and I lost one. He's a shade, Dad. A shade that I can't see. We both know what that means."

Odin swallowed a groan. "That he was not meant for you to reap." He already knew who the shade was. It was etched in the pain on her face and pulsed with her heartbeat. "The lion?"

"Dane." Kara nodded, ignoring the tear that trailed down her cheek. "I need to talk to Gaia. I need her help to save him."

His jaw fell open. "That's impossible. Freya will never allow it."

Kara snorted. "I didn't plan to ask Mother, and it's not impossible. Not with the right distraction."

"What are you hatching in that head of yours, Kara?" Odin chuckled at the flicker of life he saw beginning to return to his daughter's eyes.

"Fenrir. Take and leave me in his cell. Tell Hel that I'm calling in that favor she owes me. You stay somewhere safe. Give me ten minutes and meet me at Gaia's door."

"You'd risk Ragnarok to save your lion?" Odin arched a skeptical brow and stared at his daughter.

"That's the plan. Either it works, or there is nothing left to save." Kara shrugged.

Odin laughed. Leave it to his child to taunt the end of days to save a single soul. "You're right. You do understand the duality of love." He held out his hand to her. "Shall we go and shake up the entire pantheon, Little One?"

"Yes." Kara slid her hand into his and closed her eyes as his power bled into her palm and surrounded her, reminding her of being trapped in a box of packing peanuts. When she no longer felt like she was falling, she opened her eyes and smiled at the huge blocks of black obsidian that built the walls, reflecting and refracting the torchlight. She slid her hand over the roughly cut oak of the door to her left. Her eyes caressed the dwarven made hinges and the marks of their hammers in the mystical metal.

The door was thick, it was strong, and it was beautiful in its simplicity. In utility, it held back the giant wolf god, destined to kill her father and bring about the end of the world. Her fingers curled around the runes that covered the round pull as her hand on the lock spelled out the combination that would open the door.

"Ten minutes, Kara." Odin pressed his lips to her forehead and then he was gone.

The lock released and the door opened slowly. Kara waited for a moment for her eyes to adjust to the dim light before stepping inside. A wolf, the size of a minivan, lay in the corner, his muzzle resting on his paws as he watched her. His fur was matted from lack of care during his last shed, and the cell stunk. Kara shook her head as sadness

67

filled her. Keeping him like this wasn't right. If he tore her apart for allowing it, the kill would be just.

"Hey, Pup. Remember me?" She held up her hands to show that she wasn't armed and slowly edged her way closer and held out her palm. She remembered all too well, those jaws severing Tyr's hand when they had decided to bind the wolf. At the time, she'd cheered at Fenrir's show of defiance. None of that had set well with her when she was a young girl, and that hadn't changed.

Fenrir lifted his head, the beautiful hues of brown, auburn and black giving his coat a golden jet appearance that begged to be touched. His brows worked as he watched her approach and stretched his head forward, ignoring her hand and sniffing at her chest. Kara held her breath as he tilted his head, not releasing it until his tail thumped against the pallet and he licked her face.

"That's my Baby Boy." She grinned and scratched the sides of his head, stretching her arms to be able to scratch his ears as she nuzzled him. "I've missed you, Big Guy."

Fenrir whined and rubbed against her feverishly. If she'd been a human his affection would have crushed her, but she was Valkyrie and Father had bled just enough of his power into her on the trip to have her almost back to normal. Dropping to her knees, she moved closer and leaned against his massive body to pick out the mats in his fur and run her fingers through the hair to reach and massage the skin beneath. Fenrir groaned his appreciation and rolled onto his back offering his belly.

"I need your help," she cooed to the wolf, obliging him with a belly rub. "I know it's not fair of me to ask, but I am." She pulled back to see his intelligent brown eyes, wondering if he even understood the old language anymore. Kara made a habit of visiting him regularly, not able to stand the idea of him in total isolation. Imprisoning him made no sense. How was cutting him off from the world supposed to grow any feelings of not wanting to end it?

68

Fenrir rolled over and dropped his head on her bent knees. 'How can I help? I'm trapped here.' His lip curled up to expose fangs the size of her leg and his breath left him in a huff.

"Well, it begins with you getting to stretch your legs and make every god in Asgard lose their shit." She grinned and stroked between his eyes.

The wolf chuckled. 'But what is the catch?'

Kara sighed. "The catch is that they will put you back here when they finally find you and they'll probably make me do it."

'Then why bother?' Fenrir dropped his head again and closed his eyes.

"Remember the male I told you about? The lion? He died and is trapped somewhere that I can't get to. I need a distraction so that I can talk to someone who may be able to help him be free. We both know what it's like to wear chains, Big Guy. It's not fair of me to ask, but you can be free of yours for a little while."

'Does this world where man and animals live in one body, surviving among the humans truly exist, or is it just a fairy tale you tell me to keep hope alive, Kara?' He cracked one eye.

"It is real, and I have not given up on finding a way to show it to you, Pup." She leaned her forehead against his. "I will see you free, somehow. I gave you my vow."

'I know, Puny Girl,' he teased, lifted his head and stood to tower over her. 'Just know that I have no plans of going down easy, for anyone. Not even you.'

Kara laughed and kissed his cold, wet nose. "I wouldn't have it any other way, Big Guy." One by one she released the tethers that held him prisoner, until he was free. Looking up at him, she threw herself into his chest and hugged him fiercely. "Thank you."

The wolf held her close by lowering his snout against her back. 'I like knowing that you owe me.' He chuckled and pushed her away. 'Now get out of my way, Girl. I have terror to strike into the hearts of Gods.'

She laughed and stepped back, out of the path to the gaping door. "Have fun with it, Babes," she whispered as he slunk through the opening.

He looked back at her once he was out and chuffed before stretching and then he was gone. Moments later the shouts and screams began. It was time. Kara ghosted to the foyer close to where Gaia was rumored to be held and waited for her father to appear.

Odin felt like he was walking on air. There was a battle brewing, blood was sure to be spilled, and he was in mortal danger with that damn wolf roaming free again. It made him feel alive. His single azure eye sparkled as he ghosted to where he felt Kara waiting. He'd never doubted that she could talk the wolf into helping her. His daughter had a way with beasts. He chuckled to himself. If her becoming the mate to a lion didn't prove it, nothing did. He was not as pleased with the way she was a slave to her emotions when it came to them, but she would find her path. He hoped.

"You know where we're going?" She looked up at him when he appeared.

"Three doors down on the left." He led the way, thinking of the thousands of times that he'd come to stand outside the door and imagine the beautiful female inside, but never daring to try to enter. The cost was too high if Freya found out.

Kara fell into step beside him, grinning when she heard something break in the distance. Fenrir was doing his part. "You should really let me take him with me one of these days, to see the world and be part of it." She shook her head at her father's snort. He stopped, and his face was a little pale as he looked at the door in front of him. They were here. Kara lifted her arm and knocked.

"Hel, is that you? It's a little early for our tea, isn't it?" A melodic female voice came closer to the door before it was pulled open. Her hand went to her throat, and her eyes widened when she saw Odin standing there. "Oh, my God! What happened to your beautiful eye?" Gaia reached up to cup his face in her hands, her eyes searching his remaining one for answers. "What have they done to you?"

Kara's brows popped as she watched the woman touch her father with love and reverence and he was melting to her touch like warm butter. Freya's sentence was cruel. She lifted her hand and gently pushed Odin inside the room. Gaia backed up, not releasing him from her hold. Yeah, this could be harder than she'd planned. "I don't mean to interrupt," Kara closed the door behind her and turned to find them locked in an embrace. "Okay. Third wheel here and trust me when I say, I'd rather be somewhere else."

Gaia's head turned to pin her with a cold glare. "Then go."

Odin's chest stuttered as he took the woman's hand in his and draped his arm around her waist protectively. "Gaia, meet my daughter, Kara. She has been helping us take care of the kids below."

Gaia arched a brow, first at Odin and then at Kara.

"Okay. You don't know me. I get it. You want me to go so you can be alone with Dad. I'm totally on board with that. Help me, and I'm happy to be on my way. Hell, I'll even take my time getting Fenrir back under control so you can have some alone time. But I NEED your help."

"It's one of the children, My Love. He's trapped in the Shadowlands. That's your realm, not mine."

"Why does she care?"

"He's my mate. Long story. We both died. He's stuck and I can't, no I won't leave him there to suffer, but I can't get in. Can you help?" Odin's words sunk in and Kara leveled him with a glare. "Wait. You fucking knew where he was and you kept it from me? Honestly, Fadir?" Kara was livid and done with this bull shit. The only thing keeping her here was that she couldn't help Dane on her own. Just one more thing to chap her ass.

Odin closed his eye, realizing too late, his mistake. Having the reason his heart beat in his arms had made him a fool. "Kara, I."

"Don't give me the same line of bullshit that you fed me about not knowing where I was, or Dane. I was going to tell you, wears a little thin when all you do is lie to me. No more Dad. No more."

"There is a way," Gaia stepped between them, amused at seeing someone dress down her Viking with no care for their safety. "But it won't be easy or safe." She was getting pummeled with the whirlwind of emotions flying around the Valkyrie. Love. Hate. Betrayal. Vengeance. Gaia had no doubt that the girl would do it. She was beyond caring if she lived or died, but her father wasn't.

"Nothing ever is. What do I have to do?"

Gaia crossed the room and opened a small chest, looking through the vials until she found the one she wanted. Straightening her gown, she turned and eyed the girl, measuring her. "That is true, Child, but are you willing to enter the shadow plane, knowing that you may never return and that if you do, you will lose the one you seek anyway?"

Kara nodded and silenced her father's protests with a glare. "I don't care what happens to me. Dane doesn't deserve this, he's a damn good male, and he is needed. Loved. I'm dispensable. There are hundreds of my sisters to take my place if I fall."

Gaia smiled and took her hand, leading her to a chaise lounge and motioning for her to sit as the goddess took the chair across from her. She placed the vial in her hand, on the table between them. "Some call it a potion. Others call it poison. Either way, it will get you into the Shadowlands. Getting out is a different story."

Kara reached for the vial and held it up to the light. "How so?"

"You will be freed when the toxin leaves your system, but you will need a seer to guide your friend. Before he can

72

pass the barrier, he will be asked to give up something that he cherishes deeply. You must convince him to let it go, or he'll never be free."

"Thank you." Kara closed her fist around the delicate vial.

"You thank me now, but after this is done, you may not feel the same." Gaia offered her a small smile.

"If Dane is free, then that's all that matters." Kara stood and glared at her father before bowing her head in a show of respect to Gaia. "I'll leave you now. I have no intention of stuffing Fenrir back in his cell until after this is done. That should buy you some time with him." She nodded in Odin's direction. Yeah, she was mad as hell at him, but she couldn't deny him what she had lost, no matter how badly she wished that she could be so cold.

Gaia's mouth fell open in surprise and tears shone in her eyes. "Thank you, Child." She carefully embraced Kara, expecting to be struck for trying such a stupid and familiar thing.

Kara allowed the hug and gave the goddess a gentle squeeze, whispering, "He still loves you. Never once did that falter. Not when it comes to you." She stepped back and ghosted to her apartment in NOLA. Now all she had to do was figure out how to convince the Navarro brothers to let Bree help her.

Chapter 11

Bree shifted her weight on the bed as she sunk deeper into sleep. Her mind kept drifting to Dane and what she saw and felt. She knew her brother would never let her go through the portal to find the lion. And from everything that she was taught and believed, he was in the Shadowlands. It was forbidden for the living to go there. The elders spoke of things that would take your soul in seconds, grab your spirit and then come back wearing your skin as a costume.

She didn't realize it, but her magic was taking her there, forbidden or not. The elders called it shadow walking. Only mediums of the clans could do this, but it took years to perfect it. Young shifters were warned not to do it alone, because you could be killed, even in shadow form. Nothing was ever totally safe.

Bree wandered into the darkness. *Where am I?* She couldn't see, but she could hear and feel things. Her medium magic gave off a light in the darkness.

She caught the attention of a creature the elders called a Skitter. It fed off the spirit and souls of anything they could get a hold of. It had been centuries since they had been so close to something this pure and alive. They crept down from their hiding places.

Bree stopped in her tracks. She heard a skittering noise off in the distance. No, it was above her. As she slowed, the louder the skittering became.

No one stopped Kara when she began up the back stairs to the living quarters above the bar that had expanded to the warehouse next door. The only way in from The Pit was a short, covered land bridge on the third floor that only the residents or the invited could see. Crossing it, she wound her way through the long maze of halls until she stood outside Bree's living quarters.

Raising her arm, Kara rapped her knuckles against the door, ghosting a tray of burgers, wings, and fries into her free hand. She hoped that if she got one of the more reasonable Navarro brothers, the food might distract them enough to let her talk to Bree privately. She was just about to knock again when she heard footsteps approaching the door.

Kara smiled when it swung open and tired, red eyes looked her up and down. "Hi," she grinned and pushed the tray of food into the bear's hands, using it to push him back and step into the room. "I thought you might be hungry and need a break." She looked around trying to spot Bree, frowning at the strange energy she felt coming from the bed. The she-bear was up to something. Kara kept the smile on her face and acted like there was nothing out of the norm as the vial in her pocket began to warm. "I'm happy to take a watch or two. I know ya'll have a lot to do. Me, I got nothing but time." She shrugged, hoping he wouldn't notice that she was laying it on a little too thick.

Brax hadn't realized he was hungry until Kara appeared with food. Part of him was leery of letting her stay here alone with Bree, but he needed to eat and hit the head. "Okay, I'll be back in an hour." Brax said taking the tray of food. "If anything happens to her, Viking or not, you'll be sorry," he warned leaving the two alone as he headed to his room down the hall, to use the bathroom and eat.

"You're welcome," Kara called after him, poking her head into the corridor in time to catch the single digit salute. "Back at you, Buddy," she grumbled under her breath, closed the door, locked it and pulled over a chair to jam

75

under the doorknob. If the girl said no, she'd move it, but if she was down for helping, Kara didn't want to waste a second. "Bree?" She moved through the room, finding her on her bed asleep.

Kara's head tilted to the side. The strange pulse of energy was growing stronger, and Bree's heart was pounding fast. "Bree!" She shook the girl and got nothing but a slight shock. What the fuck? Dropping onto the bed, she closed her eyes and concentrated on the bear's emotions. Flashes of darkness. The sound of knitting needles sliding against each other and clicking boomed around them. Kara was late, but hopefully not too late.

Laying back on the bed, Kara fished the vial from her pocket and pulled the cork with a pop. She turned her head away and grimaced at the foul stench, somewhere between month old dirty gym socks and epic BO. Pinching her nose, she dumped it down her throat, trying to miss her tongue and failing. It tasted worse than it smelled. Scraping her tongue with her teeth and making a face, Kara took the bear's hand, ignoring the cramps that were twisting her gut and growing until she felt like she was being turned inside out. Her eyelids were suddenly too heavy to keep open, and she was falling, drifting on an unseen gust of wind and then floating, surrounded by darkness, so thick that even the lightning produced by rubbing her fingers together couldn't pierce it.

Bree backpedaled, trying to get away from the noise. As she moved backward, something sticky touched her hair. She threw her arms up, but that only made her hair tangle in whatever was behind her and the noise grew so loud that she felt like it was inside her head.

The skitters had her surrounded. Their webbing started to wrap around her. The magic she held, made them salivate.

Bree began to panic and struggled to get free. She screamed. As her mouth opened, one of the skitters tried to crawl into her mouth.

76

Dane was still reeling from Ty's visit. He was trying to rack his brain on what to do when he heard a noise clicking and growing louder. "The fuck?" He saw a dim light glowing in the distance. His mind went to Kara. She got her power from the sun, and he knew that lightning was one of her powers. He started for the light, ignoring the noise that grew louder until it was all he could hear. The scream of a female cut through it. Bree!

"No!" He moved faster, and once he got to her, the light was peeking out between something that looked like a webbing of some sort. Her screaming had stopped, but the sounds she was making weren't good. Dane reached out, trying to help her and felt something land on him.

"What the..." He didn't get a chance to finish his sentence when he felt his body being overtaken by something, a lot of somethings crawled over and on him. Their legs scraped against his form. It hurt like hell, feeling like hundreds of small metal cuts. He felt his energy dim, as though he were being sucked dry, like a juice box.

Concentrating on Bree, Kara felt herself dragged sideways before she hit the ground with a thud. She pushed off the sand that embedded itself in any exposed flesh, burrowing deeper like ravenous slivers of glass. She looked at herself. Okay, so skin wasn't exactly a good description. She was more like a gelatinous water balloon person or some shit. Her head snapped toward the scream.

Kara tried to run toward it, but it felt like she was moving through thick mud. Growling, she stopped. This body was useless. She willed herself toward the almost deafening knitting needles sound and grinned when she started moving faster. Until she ran into something, knocking her on her ass. Hundreds of sharp points poked and ran over her. She pushed them off, fighting through them to get closer to the dimming glow that she sensed was Bree. Raising her arm, she rubbed her fingers together. Lightning forked into the sky. Her eyes flared wide when she saw the surging ground, and some of the things above them

77

caught fire and began to rain down. "What the fuck?" Something tackled her from behind forcing her face into the seething mass of legs.

Bree gagged as the thing crawled into her mouth. Unable to pull it free, she felt her life draining away. She heard someone coming for her. They stopped behind her, and she heard someone else. Light flashed through the darkness, and the fire made the creatures run for their lives. As they ran, the webbing slipped away. She yanked the thing out of her mouth once her hands were free.

"Oh gross!" Bree looked down at the squirming thing in her hand. Eight metallic legs flailed, and its body looked like a melted clown face in a wax museum. Its eyes were slits that ran vertically. The skitter blinked at her and screamed before shooting more webbing from the tiny hairs on its legs. "Ewww." Bree shook her arm and threw it into the ones already burning. The fire flared bright and then died, leaving her in thick darkness. She could hear breathing. "Who's there?"

"I'm here," Dane answered, but who was the fire starter?

When the wave of stampeding pointy legs finally subsided, Kara lifted her face from the dirt and spit out some grit that had found its way inside her mouth. Hearing one of the things to her right, her hand snaked out and grabbed it, tearing its legs from the head, she tossed the bozo after napalm thing away from her. It was dark again. "It's me," Kara groaned, blinked and rolled until she was sitting on her ass, facing the glow of Bree. "I came to help." She snorted and started to laugh. Epic fail there, but it was funny. "Dane? Babes, is that you?" She turned her head, pissed that she couldn't sense him. Who the fuck was blocking him from her and how soon could she kill them?

Dane heard Kara's voice. "Kara!" He yelled, but he couldn't see her clearly.

Bree swayed but remained standing. She felt weak and nearly dead, but that wasn't the biggest problem. Kara was.

78

She didn't understand how the Valkyrie had come to the Shadowlands. "You can't be here. You must go. The living can never be here!" Bree warned as Dane drew closer.

Kara crawled closer to the voices. "Hate to break it to you Pooh, but you're not exactly pushing up daisy's, either."

"Dane, are you okay?" Bree rolled her eyes at Kara and watching Dane's strange form float closer.

"Take me out of here," he begged. If he had a heart, it would be pounding louder than a snare drum.

"I don't know how."

"You have to! Kara came for me. Tell her to get me out of here." Dane pleaded, not willing to give up.

"Now you've done it," the voice that had been haunting Dane, whispered.

"What?" Dane tried to see whatever it was.

"He's coming back. You have set in motion, the end."

Dane had no time to tell Bree anything because Ty appeared and hurled Dane into the darkness.

Kara reached for Dane when whatever was cloaking him from her lifted, growling as he slipped through her fingers and sped away.

Ty let light fill the darkness so they could see him. "Thank you, Little Bear. You've done me a huge favor." Ty grinned coldly and summoned the souls of the darkest creatures in the Shadowland. "I want the Princess. Kill the shifter female," he commanded.

Walls shot up through the sand around them. Pieces peeled off like old wallpaper falling began toward them like something out of Night of the Living Dead. Things that were once nothing more than wisps of air were given solid form and mutated into bodies of horrifying creatures.

One grabbed Bree by her throat, lifting her off her feet. She was still so weak that all she could do was choke and struggle.

"Son of a Bitch!" Kara cursed and blinked against the sudden brightness. One side of her mouth curled up, and she held her hands out for her weapons to appear.

79

"Figures," she growled when nothing happened. She grabbed the legs that she'd ripped off the clown spider thing and stabbed them into the throat of the beast that had Bree, wrapping her arm around its neck and pulling until its head came off.

The GQ looking fuck's words sunk in. At first, Kara thought he must have meant Bree when he said Princess, but the words that followed told her no. "Princess? I got your fucking Princess right here." She stood between Bree and the oncoming hordes of nightmares, with bloody spider legs in one hand and her fingers wrapped in the hair of the head of the monster that had dared touch the bear. "Just wake up, Bree. You need to get out of here, or your brothers are going to have my ass."

Ty laughed at them as Kara took her battle stance. "Princess, you will not leave here again. You could always do the honorable thing and trade your life for the shifters." Ty smiled coldly, lifting his gaze to the female behind the Valkyrie. His creatures lumbered closer, circling them and waiting for Ty to give them the order to feast on the soft living flesh. "Just say the word, and they go free."

Bree choked out a no, still holding her throat. "You can't do that. She's not one of us! She can't stay here. Don't do it, Kara! It's bologna." Bree remembered something the elders said about shadow walking, there was a word you spoke to automatically wake up. What was it? Crap, it wasn't coming to her! She closed her eyes and willed herself awake, chanting every random word she could think of.

Bree bolted upright in her bed, choking and gasping. She bumped something beside her and turned her head. Kara's body told her that it hadn't been a nightmare. Bree's eyes grew wide as she panicked.

Kara returned the cold smile when she felt Bree leave. One down, now she just needed to get Dane out. "Why would you want little ole me?" She eyed the talking douche bag. He looked familiar, but she couldn't place from where. "And what's the catch? What happens if I stay here?" She

80

remembered Gaia's words and let the grin play at her lips. This fucker didn't know as much as he thought he did. She looked at the beings that circled her and yawned to show her boredom.

Ty didn't bat an eyelash when the she-bear disappeared. It didn't matter. The one that the Princess really cared for was still here and trapped. "I'm not telling you jack shit, but I know that you just being here has set in motion something that I've been waiting for since your species came to be." He curled his lip in disgust. "It's a shame, you won't be around to see your family go the way of the dinosaur."

Bree felt something and looked down at Kara's hand in hers. She gripped it tightly. "Kara wake up!" Nothing happened. "KARA!" She yelled and still, nothing. Bree's panic grew. She felt Kara's body tense. Something was going on. She slapped the Valkyrie across the face as hard as she could. "Wake the hell up!" She felt Kara stir. "Oh, thank goodness," Bree sighed, hoping it worked.

Kara laughed. He really thought that she cared if most of Asgard died bloody? Hell, she'd been ready to burn it all to the ground just yesterday. "It really is, I could have used the laugh." Kara chewed at the inside of her cheek, hearing Bree's calls in the distance but she ignored them. "Me for the Lion. That's still the deal on the table? How do I know that you won't just drop him as soon as he's out of here?" She didn't care if she lived or died, and there weren't many that would even miss her if she was gone, but she couldn't do it if Dane wasn't safe.

Ty shrugged and lied, "I don't care either way. I only want one person. You're my ticket to them, Princess." Ty crossed his arms over his chest. "You don't know. It's a take it or leave it, type of thing."

"Why the hell not? I was looking at stasis after this, and your option sounds more entertaining." She tossed him the head and dropped the spider legs. "Let Dane go free, and as long as I'm here, I'll take his place."

Bree let go of Kara's hand and put both her hands over the female's heart. Using her powers of healing, she sent a jolt into Kara's chest and made her body jump. "Wake up!" She screamed doing it again. This time it worked, and Kara's eyes flew open.

Ty was just about to tell the Princess it was a deal when she vanished. "No!" He roared in rage.

Dane lay in a heap in the darkness. He had been so close. Maybe he was doomed to stay in this hell.

Kara sat up, gasping at the pain in her chest and pushed at whatever was touching her, knocking Bree to the floor. "No! What did you do? I had a way out!" She was on her feet and stomping around the bed. "Send me back. Now!"

Bree landed on the floor and looked up to see her brother staring at her and cussed under her breath.

Brock had to come to check on Bree but hadn't expected to find her on the floor or Kara looming over her and demanding to be sent back. "What's going on here?" Brock knelt to help his sister up. Her body felt cold. "What happened?" He asked Bree. Brock saw the wild and angry fire burning in Kara's eyes and pushed Bree behind him while he waited for someone to tell him what was going on.

"I almost had him out. So fucking close!" Kara wrapped her arms around herself and began pacing. She was so pissed that she couldn't stop shaking. What if she didn't get another chance? What if Dane was stuck there, in that hell, forever? Her chest ached, and she couldn't breathe.

"Had who out? Someone tell me what the hell is going on? What did you two do?" Brock demanded in a growl. He wanted to grab Kara by the shoulders and shake her until she started making sense, but he knew better. She was spiraling, and in that condition, she may not care who she hurt.

Kara sighed and closed her eyes. "Don't be mad at her. It was all me. I almost had Dane out, but now I've lost my chance." She turned away from them, not sure that she could hold back the tears of frustration and heartbreak that were choking her.

Brock was speechless.

Bree smoothed her hair and leaned out, to look around her brother. "I think it's time we spoke to Salvation about this."

Brock's brow quirked.

Kara's jaw clenched at the Ghuardian's name. "Good luck with that." She laughed coldly and headed for the door, but Brock was in the way. "If you don't mind?" She nodded to the door. Kara felt like she was about to blow apart and she needed to get away from them before it happened. Lightning was already flashing outside the windows, much longer and it wouldn't just be outside.

He moved, keeping Bree behind him so Kara could leave. He didn't know what to say. Brock felt like he was missing a big piece of the puzzle. After she'd gone, he saw the empty vile on the bed. He picked it up and glared at his sister. "You are going to be the death of us all."

Kara walked through the halls, not paying attention to where she was until she looked up and found herself in front of the portal. She touched the cold brick that was solid under her hand. Sinking down in the dead ended corner, she hugged her legs to her chest and dropped her head to her knees.

Brock listened to Bree explain what happened. Brax came back to watch over their sister and Brock went to look for Kara. He found her huddled in front of the portal. "Cher? I meant what I said about helping you. You just tell me what I can do." His heart broke for her. His family teased him about how much he loved her. He denied it, but deep-down Brock knew that he'd been in love with her since the moment he first saw her. Something about her called to him.

Kara didn't move, when she opened her mouth to speak a broken sob choked out her voice. She felt like she had a bus parked on her chest and she couldn't breathe. She shook her head. "Make it stop," she whispered, her voice barely more than a raspy sigh. She'd never dealt with failure well, but knowing that Dane was stuck and he was suffering, probably more after what they'd done, was strangling the tiny bit of good that was still left in her soul. What was the point of being alive, if you were dead inside?

"Okay, Cher," he said, leaning down and scooping her up into his arms. "It's time to stop fucking around," Brock growled and lowered her to rest on the table that sat near the portal. He shifted his right hand from human to bear and clawed his left, making it bleed. Lifting his bloodied palm, he spoke softly so she couldn't hear him and placed it on the wall where the portal hid. Brock growled as the gateway bit into his hand before it opened and light spilled through.

He didn't give Kara a chance to get up on her own. Instead, he scooped her up and held her against his chest. His eyes closed as he allowed himself to savor it, for just a moment. The situation was fucked, but having her in his arms felt right. That was good because this stupid fucking thing might be the last thing he ever did. Common sense told him not to do it, but one glance at the agony on the Valkyrie's face made him step through, then into the mountain and march straight to Salvation.

Kara gasped her disbelief when he picked her up. No one did that, ever. For one, she was too big, and for another, she was apt to kill someone for trying. When he did it the second time, it was less of a shock. She discovered that she liked it and allowed herself to relax even though she had no idea what he was doing or where he was taking her. Hell, if he was taking her to throw her over a cliff, she didn't care. She needed his warmth, his scent and to be held together when she was falling apart. No one else dared to try, but he did, and it was helping.

Brock knew that he'd just signed his death certificate, but if this fixed her pain, so be it. He had no one to live for. He walked over the miles of plains and desert holding Kara tightly. The scenery didn't change until he stopped at a large mud hut. "And here we are."

Kara lifted her head from Brock's shoulder when he stopped and spoke. Her eyes crawled over the house, her brows shrugging together in confusion as she turned her face to look at him. "Where are we?" She knew that they were on the other side of the portal, but other than that, she was clueless.

"We're standing in front of Salvation's home. I know it doesn't look like much, but trust me, it's his place. Bree told me everything. And it's time to get shit straight. I'm sorry if I've upset you by doing this. I know that you're hurting, and that is hard enough to take, but I can't allow your pain to put my sister in danger. I can't stand by and let two people I care for, be hurt." Brock set her on the ground gently.

She looked up at him, closing her gaping jaw and hugged him tightly. "Thank you." She blinked back the tears that always seemed ready to spill over and embarrass her by showing her weakness lately. When he'd said that he wouldn't let anyone hurt those he cared about, she liked him a little more for knowing that he included Dane in that list, because he had to mean the lion. She was on no one's list. Not anymore.

"Do me a favor?" She tilted her head back to be able to see Brock's eyes. "Don't let me kill him until Dane is out?" She let a small smile curl up one side of her mouth. "Only half joking, just so you know." Kara stuffed her hands into her back pockets to stop herself from bolting the place and burning it to the ground as she walked over the sparse scraggly grass toward what looked like the front door.

Brock followed behind her. "You're welcome, and you're not going in alone. No one will be dying today," he said as they got to the front door of the old mud hut. The door was a quilt of animal hides. Brock looked at it and wondered if they were supposed to scare off visitors. He reached for it and pulled it back so Kara could go in. "Salvation, we have to talk to you," Brock called into the hut.

85

Kara ducked inside and was surprised. The interior did not match the outside. The ceilings were high, it was light and airy and had every modern amenity that one could hope for. She was also shocked to see Salvation in a pair of plaid pajama bottoms, no shirt and checking waffles in the press thing. Kara arched a brow and honestly didn't know what to say. This was not how she imagined the son of a bitch who'd killed her. She wasn't the only one that looked surprised. Salvation looked like he saw a ghost before his face reddened and his glare fell on the bear behind her.

"I made him bring me, so put the dirty look away. After what you did, you have no right to play holier than thou with anyone. If you try it with him, I swear to fucking God, that I will slaughter you, fill your body with stuffing and serve you for Thanksgiving dinner. Don't even think of trying me." Kara felt Brock wrap his hands around her wrists and hold them loosely. She hadn't realized that she'd pulled her hands from her pockets and had been about to bolt the Ghuardian.

Salvation was making breakfast when Kara and Brock appeared. He was shocked that she was alive. He arched his brow at her word and plated his waffles. "We have rules and laws. The bear knows this," he said, getting the syrup from the high-end refrigerator. "I didn't kill you. I killed Dane, but I guess the myth that Viking magic is stronger than mine, was just that, a myth." He sat down and looked at them, waiting. "What is it that you want?" He cut the waffles with his fork.

Kara almost took the bait and showed him the myth. If Brock hadn't had her hands, she would have. "It wasn't your magic, Little Brother, it was that mated bullshit that took me out. When you think you've got the juice, bring it, and we can crown a winner once and for all, but until then, we both have jobs to do. Why did you dump Dane in the Shadowlands to be tortured while whoever the fuck wit that is in charge there, gets to try to use him to get into Asgard? Unless you are TRYING to bring the end of days?"

Sal forked waffles into his mouth. "Is that so? I didn't know that Dane was in the Shadowlands, but if he went there, there was a reason. You know I didn't take him out just for the fuck of it, right? He was batshit. He needed to be put down. I had no idea that he would end up there."

Kara wanted to call bullshit at the top of her lungs. Her hands balled into fists. Him sitting there, being calm and reasonable chafed her last nerve raw. "Whatever helps you sleep at night. The simple fact is that he's there. I've seen it with my own two eyes, and if I got in once, you know me, I'm stubborn, and I'll get there again. He will be freed, and I don't care if the price is this little ball of water and stone burning to ash. Meaning to or not, you succeeded in one thing. I'm dead and other than that lion, I don't give a shit about anything or anyone. Not even myself."

She felt Brock's thumb stroking her wrist, attempting to calm her down. Kara took a deep, shuddering breath and allowed his touch to help her find and center herself. "Please," she almost choked on the word. "Help me get him out. I know you can."

Salvation had no idea the lion would go there, but he knew his sister well enough to know that she would not just let it go. "Give me your hand," he said as calm as he could. Part of him wanted to slap her into next week for thinking he did what he did, just to fuck with her. His job was a lot harder than hers. Playing Daddy's girl and scary Viking bitch must be so taxing.

Kara eyed him for a moment and then held out her hand. She didn't even remember why they didn't get along, sure his 'accidentally' killing her hadn't helped, but it hadn't been the start of it. She wanted to trust him, wanted to have one member of her fucked up family that she could, but experience had shown her reality.

She slid her other hand free of Brock's and turned it to slide her palm against the bear's and thread her fingers with his. Looking back over her shoulder, she let her gaze slide over his poker face before meeting his eyes. Brock, she

87

trusted, although she didn't know why. 'I claim you as one of mine,' she mindlinked him, smiling when his eyes flared. 'Don't worry, Big Guy. It just means that I'll take anything done to you, personal and I will do anything in my power to see you safe." She turned back to Salvation and softened her face and her tone. "Thank you."

Salvation arched a brow at what was going on between the bear and his sister. Locking his fingers with hers, he closed his eyes and let the events of that night be known to her, as well as his feelings for her. He hadn't meant to hurt her, or even Dane, but the thing that had taken over the lion, infected him and embedded itself so deep that Salvation could do nothing to save him.

She watched the images as they flowed through her mind, seeing what had happened from her brother's point of view, the lack of malice and the pain that it caused him. Kara swallowed hard, trying not to crumble under the weight of it all. When the images stopped, she felt his regret. Their kind were always hurting others without meaning to, but it couldn't be helped. She knew that, deep down.

He dropped her hand when he was done. The pain she was in, stabbed deep to his core. Salvation didn't open his eyes for a moment. He spoke as he did, "To get him back from the Shadowlands, we need his body. I have to go alone. I can't take the chance if something happening to you." He looked at her. "I'm sorry, Kara. I was only doing my job," he said, letting his eyes fall to his plate.

Kara took and squeezed his hand. "You should have come to me, maybe I could have helped." She closed her eyes and let out her breath in a slow exhale. "I know we've had issues, but I would never turn you away if you needed me. Never. Just ignore the past few days." She laughed shakily. "Thank you, Salvation. I've been looking for his body, but he's blocked from me. I can't find it, him, or any parts of him, without help."

88

"You're welcome. Coming to you might have made me look weak, but I see now, that I should have. Wait, you can't find his body?" Sal's brows shot up. "Was it not sent to Asher?" If not, it could be any place. He snorted. The animal in him was growing upset.

"I have no idea. I woke up in a human morgue and in all honesty, I haven't even thought to ask Asher." Kara sighed and shook the hair back from her face. "Until Bree saw him as a shade, I was still hoping that he was alive." She looked over her shoulder at Brock. "Do you know?"

Brock shook his head. "I thought he was with you until we learned you were dead. We should see if Ozzy can find him. What about what I asked you before, about Odin's ravens?"

Salvation racked his brain. "I can do a summoning spell to bring his body here, but to get his soul back from the Shadowlands, that is another matter," Sal said.

"Is there anything I can do to help? You don't have to ask, I'm offering." She looked at Brock and blushed a little. "Dad is um... occupied with Sal's Mom, at the moment. Well, until I put Fenrir back in his cell. Gotta love prophecies for keeping people right where you left them." She shook her head. "I know that the mating is broken between Dane and I, but we did bond, can that be used somehow? Use my blood, my soul? I don't know. Nothing is too much to ask, not if it might work."

Salvation thought for a moment and then shook his head no. "Let's go outside. I'll call his body home to The Mountain."

Brock wondered if there was a reason that Kara couldn't sense Dane. Unless she wasn't Dane's true mate, she should be able to, even after death. He wanted to tell her that, but she'd already been through too much.

Stepping outside, Kara braced herself. She'd seen so many bodies over the years. She wondered if seeing Dane's would be different. She chewed on her lip and for the first time saw the land that surrounded them and the herds and

89

packs of animals living together peacefully. "It's truly beautiful here."

She sighed and looked at her brother, she'd seen the shadow that had crossed his eyes and the way he dropped them. "Don't worry Sal, I've thought the same thing myself, not being meant to be. I'm prepared to let him go if I have to, I just can't stand him being stuck where he is and being hurt." She wiped a tear that escaped to roll down her cheek. She was prepared, but that didn't make it hurt less.

Salvation gave her a small smile before walking away from them. He waved his hands out in front of himself, and then he spun in a circle, kicking up dirt.

As Sal turned, Brock realized he was creating a vortex. In a language that Brock didn't understand, Salvation chanted, spinning until he was nothing more than a black void. For a moment, the air around them rippled as a wave of energy blasted from him, knocking Brock and Kara on their asses. Seconds later, Dane's body appeared off to the left of them in a patch of soft grass.

Brock stared at the body. Dane looked a little dirty, but like he was asleep. Finally, Salvation stopped spinning the air around him and took a moment to calm before he looked at them. His real form flickered, and Brock blinked. So, the old stories were true, Salvation was the mythical Tatanka.

Kara watched curiously, right up until she landed on her backside with the bear almost falling on her. Her breath froze in her chest when Dane appeared on the grass. She didn't need to move closer to know that it was just the shell of his body. Her brows popped when Sal shifted to his buffalo form and blinked back to human. She wondered what Brock's bear looked like. *Where the hell had that come from?* She shook her head and turned her eyes back to her brother, ready to let him siphon her power if he needed it.

Salvation felt a bit dizzy. "That was the easy part," he said, smoothing his long hair. "I'm going to the Shadowlands to get his soul. I want you two to stand watch over him. If anyone comes, call for me." Sal ghosted out.

Brock sat close to Dane's body. He wondered how long it would take for Salvation to come back. "He's really what they say he is?" Brock asked looking up at Kara.

She sat beside him and reached out to stroke Dane's hair. It was so strange to see his eyes closed like this in human form. When he slept, he'd always shifted to lion. She glanced up at Brock when he spoke. "The great white bison? Yeah." The bear looked a little shaken. "You okay? You've heard a lot today that I'm not sure you knew before." She patted his knee hoping that it would have the same grounding effect that his touch had on her.

Brock blinked. "I'll be okay. It's a lot to take in."

Salvation appeared in the Shadowlands and called out for Dane. He felt someone move closer but knew that it wasn't the lion even before the spark of light flared to show Ty's Cheshire Cat smile.

"Oh. Look. It's the great white cow. Come to get the Princess's pussy cat? Sorry, but he's not here anymore. I fed his soul to the skitters," Ty taunted with a grin.

Sal grabbed Ty by the throat. "I am in no mood for this shit. Give me the lion's soul, or I'll tell everyone your one weakness. I will sing it from the mountain, take out ads in the god damn papers, and spam the hell out of every fucker on this planet and every other. Anything that I can think of. Want to call my bluff?"

Ty growled and made Dane appear.

Sal dropped him and eyed the broken mess that was left of the lion.

"I warn you, he will not be himself. The things he saw here have driven him mad as a hatter, but with slightly better fashion sense. Why does she want him back so bad? She is not his mate. Not his true one." Ty rubbed his throat and glared at Dane with disgust and veiled interest.

"What?" Sal played dumb. Let this stupid son of a bitch think that he knew he was aware of something that Sal wasn't. Let him flap his gums because Ty was the type that just couldn't help himself.

91

"You heard me. She's not his true mate. Take the mangy rug and get out. If you ever come here like this again? I'll kill you, and I'm not bluffing. I'd love nothing more than a big buffalo steak, extra rare. Oh, and Sal? I'll be by to collect for the soul you're taking." Ty winked and ghosted out.

Sal looked at Dane, who looked like he was in shock. "Let's go cat. I hope you appreciate the shit that has hit the fan for you."

Dane cowered. He didn't know what to do. He'd seen so many horrible things since he'd come here. And now he had the head Ghuardian in charge, glaring at him. He backed away, shaking his head.

Sighing, Salvation squatted and held his hand out. "You don't want to stay here. Kara sent me to bring you home. I'm not going to be the one to tell her I couldn't do it. Are you?" He tilted his head. Madness shone brightly in the lion's hazel eyes. "You let me help you once, let me do it now."

Dane eyed the Ghuardian, not sure that he trusted him until he heard Kara's name. Hope bloomed in his chest, and he crept forward allowing Salvation to touch him.

Salvation absorbed the lion and ghosted back to Dane's body. He knelt on the grass beside it, trying not to look at Kara's hopeful face. He opened his mouth and placed it over Dane's, pinching the lion's nose closed. Exhaling a long breath, Salvation let Dane's soul find its way back into his body.

Kara watched as Sal leaned over Dane and her heart skipped when he twitched. When he started screeching, she jumped back. She leaned down to try to calm him, but all she saw in his eyes was madness. Gaia's words rang in her head. "*He must give up something that he cherishes deeply. You must convince him to let it go, or he'll never be free.*" The meaning became clear. It wasn't asking him to give something up, but her, because he wouldn't remember any of it.

92

"Dane." She leaned over him, filling his field of vision. His head tilted as he looked at her with vague recognition and the screaming became a series of insane rants and words strung together that made no sense. "I can make it stop. Nod, if you want me to take it away."

His head bobbed rapidly as the babbling continued.

"Okay, Babes." Her breath hitched, and she ignored the tears that rolled unchecked down her face. Leaning down, she pressed her lips to his forehead and whispered, "I love you," as she siphoned the memories, tracing them back to any that the madness had infected. Kara ignored the heat that burned her palm as a bright orb formed to hold what she was taking. Memories were like souls. They could never be destroyed, but they could be contained.

When Kara pulled away, Dane was silent and blinking at the blue sky above. When she looked into his hazel eyes, she saw his typical humor return and knew that he was himself again. The price? Every memory of her, and their time together. For him, they had never met. She cradled the delicate orb between her palms, hiding it from view and keeping it safe as it burned her skin.

Brock wanted to reach out to her and pull her into his arms after she made Dane stop screaming, but he didn't. His brow arched at the thing in her hands that she held like a baby bird. *What the hell was that and where had it come from?*

Dane looked around confused and not sure where he was until he saw Salvation. "I swear I didn't do anything. At least this time. Don't kill me!" He rambled, and his eyes grew wide.

Salvation gave him a smile. "Okay Kid, this time I'll let it slide. Brock, would you see that he gets home safe?"

Brock nodded at Sal's request, waiting for the but, that didn't come. He wasn't stupid enough to think that his transgression would be forgotten.

"Sister, if you need anything else, let me know. I have some place I need to be." Without another word, Salvation ghosted out.

Kara turned away from them for a few moments, smiling softly as Dane defended himself. He was going to be alright, and she could live with that. A strange thought hit her when Salvation spoke, he was gone before she could say it aloud, so she mindlinked him, 'Thank you. I'm not sure if you have ever had the chance to see your mother and our father face to face. Meet me at The Pit tomorrow, and we can change that, Brother Mine.'

Wiping her face on the tail of her shirt, Kara tried to smile for the two males behind her. "Mind if I tag along? I don't know my way out of here."

Dane looked at her curiously. "Oh, good, I'm not the only one who is lost as hell," Dane said, following Brock as he led the way over the prairie and then back through the portal to The Pit.

Brock closed the portal behind them, ghosted them upstairs and wondered what his punishment for this would be.

They stood in silence a long ass moment before Dane rubbed the back of his neck. "Awkward as this is, and the blast that it was, I think I'm going to my room." He felt out of sorts, like he was having that dream that he was naked in church again.

Kara smiled softly. "It was nice meeting you, Dane." She smiled weakly and tried to remember how to breathe. She would not break down in front of him. She would not. He had the right to go on and live a happy life, and she would fight for it with her dying breath.

Chapter 12

Dane left Brock and the cute blonde to go to his room. His body felt stiff and weird as he opened the door and stepped inside. It smelled different. His nostrils flared as his lion tried to sort out and identify the scents that lingered here. Dane checked his pockets. They were empty. His wallet, his phone, and even his keys were all missing. His clothes smelled like... Well, they stunk of death.

"Must have been some party," he snickered and began pulling off his clothes. He needed a shower to hold the headache that he felt buzzing behind his eyes from gaining ground. He passed the bed, his head tilting with confusion at the quilt he didn't remember owning, that covered it. Shaking his head, he pulled open the dresser drawer that he kept his towels and boxers in. They weren't there.

A pile of soft and lacey bras and panties filled the space, with the occasional rolled up pair of socks as he pushed his hands through them. He snagged a pair of underwear, or what was pretending to be underwear, holding it up in front of his face to eye it skeptically. There wasn't a lot to them, and they weren't hiding a thing from what he could tell. Arching a brow, he turned them and finally dropped them back inside the drawer with the others. Sure, they were nice, and he'd be cool with seeing them on, and then taking them off an attractive female, but that didn't shed any light on why they were here.

Shaking his head, he pushed the drawer shut and yanked open the one beneath it, almost afraid of what he'd find there. If it was full of sex toys, then he'd be ninety-nine percent sure that Brian or Ripper were fucking with him again. A sigh of relief escaped his lungs when he found his shirts and socks but not where he usually kept them. "What the hell?"

Closing his dresser, Dane stepped back. The room smelled of bears and someone else. It was a scent that seemed familiar to him. If he didn't know better, he'd think that it was that chick that was with Brock, but that made no sense because Dane had no clue who she was. Not that he'd mind finding out. She was kinda hot.

Pulling open the other dresser, he continued the search for his boxers and a towel. Finally finding them, he closed the drawer too hard and knocked something off the top of the dresser. A small lion nick knack that he didn't remember owning stared up at him from the floor. As he picked it up, he looked it over and set it back on top of the dresser.

He looked around his room, the things that were wrong were bugging him. It was the same and yet different. Maybe it was all in his head, and the band was playing with him after he had some bad moonshine or something. That had to be it. Dane shook off the feeling that something was missing.

He showered and got dressed, ignoring the girly things in the shower and medicine cabinet. It was the band. It had to be. They'd upped their game and paid attention to detail this time. Hell, they'd even left him a slightly used toothbrush in the holder beside his. Dane laid on his bed, plotting his revenge but he didn't get far. Once his head hit the pillow, he was out cold.

Chapter 13

"I think I need to drink. A lot." Kara glanced up at Brock. "You're a bartender, I bet you could help a girl out with that."

"Of course, Cher." Brock nodded to Dane and watched the lion walk away before he started downstairs for the bar. He didn't say anything as they walked. He wanted to tell her it was going to be okay, but he wasn't psychic and losing someone you loved was always hard as hell.

Kara waited for Dane to veer off in the hall that would take him to his room, and as soon as she heard his door close, she stopped, leaned against the wall and sunk down into a squat. She struggled for air and tried to figure out how she could hurt this bad without being wounded. *I have to let it go. Let him go. How do I do that?* She remembered her original idea. Booze. Lots of Booze. "Sorry," she whispered, trying to stand and shake off the embarrassment that she felt. "Mini meltdown. Won't happen again."

Brock waited for her to catch up. Something weird was happening. Dane didn't seem to have a clue who Kara was, and he didn't understand why. His brow arched again when she slid the small glowing ball into her jacket pocket. "I saw nothing. Now let's get you that drink, Cher."

"Thank you." She stretched up and kissed his bearded jaw. "Seriously. For everything." She forced a smile and fell into step with him. "Now, onto drinking my face off and making bad decisions!" She tried to grin and bumped him playfully.

"After you," he said bumping her back. Brock followed her to the bar and then went behind it. "What do you wanna have first?" He asked leaning on the bar.

She sat on a stool and leaned forward on her elbows. "What's the strongest thing you have back there? I'll take three." Kara pulled the replacement debit card that she'd gotten from the bank, out of her pocket and tossed it on the bar top.

Brock nodded, selected a bottle and poured the shots.

Kara sniffed the first, making a face, before tossing them back, one after the other and then tapped the bar for a refill. She savored the warm burn of whatever she was drinking as it made her way to her stomach. She eyed him as he repeated the pours. "How do you feel about dancing?"

"I feel like I shouldn't do it."

She laughed, surprised that she still could. "I'll talk you into it." Kara nodded and took another drink. "Do you mean in public, or at all?"

"Public mostly. What I do in my boxers in my room is my own business." Brock nodded seriously.

"So, if I want you to dance with me, it's in your room with you stripped down to your skivvies?" Kara arched a brow and leaned over the bar to check him out. "Okay, if that's how you want to play it, Bjorn." She teased.

He nodded. "Yes, Cher. It is."

"Your call, bring the bottle." She shrugged, calling his bluff.

"I agreed to nothing, Cher. I think you're just trying to hog my bed again."

"I did not hog it!" She pretended to be offended before she laughed. "You offered it to me. HUGE difference. It was big enough for two." She pushed the hair back from her face and watched the people in the mirror behind the bar. "God's honest? I need to feel something else right now, and I was being selfish." She took a long haul of her drink. "This is good. What is it?"

"It's a secret. And I offered part of the bed. Not all of it and the covers and my pillows. It was traumatizing for me." He teased.

"But they were just so soft and warm," she grinned over her glass. "I would have shared if you'd said anything."

He nodded at her, mockingly. "Oh sure. Right, okay. And I'm a bunny."

"That would explain the size two hundred and three boots in your room." She nodded with a smirk. "I'm a good sharer-er!" She wrinkled her brow and looked at her glass, feeling the warm buzz of the alcohol warming her slowly. "Damn good secret you have here."

Brock smirked. "I know, right? And my boots are small and dainty, just like me. I'll have you know." He poured her another shot. "And I wouldn't talk, you and your clodhoppers. Those are some big and stinky feet you've got there, Cher."

Kara looked down at her boots and then back at him. She could burst into tears, it would be easy right now. The very idea struck her as funny, making her laugh hard. "My feet are perfect, and they smell fine." She twitched her lips back and forth, no idea if that last part was true or not. She'd never actually sniffed them. "Dainty? You? Not the words I'd use to describe you, bear."

"Sure, if you call swamp gas and old tacos, smelling fine." he said sticking his tongue out at her.

"Hey!" She toed off one of her boots and pulled her socked foot up to show him. "It does not stink! Sniff it bear. Sniff the foot!" She laughed at the strange looks she was getting, not giving a shit.

"No. Put that thing away. You're gonna kill the customers," he said, pretending to gag and covering his face with his shirt.

Laughing, she lowered it, but only because it was hard to balance on the bar stool like that. "Fine. You win for now.

You will worship them later." She teased and tossed him an evil grin, sliding her empty glass to him. "Tell me something about you, Brock."

"I hate stinky feet," he said, refilling the glass.

She sighed and pushed her lower lip out into a pout. "And?"

"I have a birthmark on my ass that looks like Africa," he joked, leaning on the bar.

She perked up. "Really?"

You'll never know, Cher," he teased.

"Is that a challenge? Cuz never is a really, really looooong time." She laughed and wiggled her brows as she lifted her glass.

Brock barked out a laugh. "You're wasted."

"Possible," she nodded her agreement. Kara frowned when she realized that the only place she had to go to sleep was halfway across town. She should care more about that, but she was pleasantly numb, at the moment. Kara covered his hand with hers and looked at Brock thoughtfully. "All joking aside, why is it that when I touch you, I feel real?" Her brows shrugged together with confusion. "That's the wrong word, but I know what I mean."

Brock didn't know what to say. "Maybe it's the hair. Chicks dig the hair."

Kara shook her head no and took a drink. "I don't think so. Your hair is nice and all, but no." She shrugged. "Whatever it is, I like it."

He smiled. "Well, thank you. And bad news. The bottle of secret is empty, but you timed it just right, though, because by the time on my magical, not even real watch, it's bed time." Brock dropped the bottle in the trash. "You can have my room. I'll go crash on the office couch."

"So, you can accuse me of hogging the bed again? I think not!" Kara gasped dramatically and finished her drink. "I can walk back to my place, and you can be comfortable." She slid off the stool but wasn't ready for the entire room to turn quickly to the left. She sank back down. "Yeah. I'll do that in a minute."

He came around the bar and helped her off the stool. "Come on, Cher. It's not the time to argue," he chuckled, taking her up to his room. "You can sleep on the bed, and I'll sleep on the floor. I have an air mattress." Brock opened his door and let her wobble inside.

Kara stepped inside, holding onto the door frame for balance, before walking carefully to the kitchen countertop and holding on to that. "Your bed is huge. You're huge. You take the bed and give me the air mattress. And help me get there cuz I feel like I'm on the deck of a ship and seas are getting rough." She grinned at him.

"Okay, Cher," he said going to get the air mattress ready for her. He came back a few moments later, and she was wobbling from the living room to the bathroom. "Cher," he said watching her carefully. "The mattress is made up for you." He ghosted her into a large t-shirt and sweats.

She looked down at herself when her clothes changed and blinked at them for a second. "Right, bed. Good idea." She tried to go to him but veered right, so she closed her right eye and tried to correct direction, reaching out to him. "I think my rudder is broken," she whispered loudly.

Brock laughed and helped her to the air mattress. Shaking his head and chuckling, he watched her flop down with a bounce. This was the Kara he remembered. Brock placed a trash can and a bottle of water on the floor next to her, hoping that this was a sign that she could come back from the darkness that had surrounded her since her return. Too bad she was probably going to spend half of the night recycling the top shelf booze into the waste basket, but it was progress. He scratched his bearded jaw as he watched her. A rogue thought made him smile. Dane was back, but she was here, in his room. It probably meant nothing, but just for tonight, he could savor it and allow himself to dream.

101

Kara eyed the trash and the water, blinking at them. "Vikings don't vomit, we can hold our liquor." She reached out to push it away, but then the room pivoted left and she thought better of it when her stomach rolled. Laying back, she pulled the blanket over herself and watched him get settled and turn out the lights. Everything was quiet and left her alone with nothing but the crap in her head. She sighed and stared at the ceiling. Kara closed her eyes, but the room began to spin. She groaned.

Brock adjusted his pillows and yawned, suddenly exhausted. He rolled onto his side, shoving his bent arm under the pillow so that he could see her better, smirking when one of her legs crept out from under the blanket and her knee bent to brace her foot against the floor. *Keep telling yourself that, Cher,* he thought with a silent chuckle. *But even Vikings get the room spins, and the puking usually isn't far behind.*

"Brock?" Kara turned her head to see his silhouette on the bed, grinning when she saw the reflection of the dim light on his eyes that told her that he wasn't asleep yet.

He yawned out a yes.

"Can I come up there? I'll be good. I promise." Kara waited, expecting him to tell her to shut up and go to sleep. Not that she didn't want to, but she felt exposed down here alone. There was nothing to press her back against to convince her mind that nothing could creep up on her.

"Okay, Cher." Brock stared at her for a second and inappropriate images flashed through his head, before he hitched his body further into the center of the bed to make room for her. "No puking in my bed, though."

"Deal." Smiling triumphantly, Kara pushed off the blanket and crawled into the bed beside him. Her body curled against his and she groaned happily as the tension drained away. "Thank you."

Brock's brow arched at the feel of her against him. His bear chuffed. He let his arm slide over her side and his hand rested on the small of her back. "You're welcome, Cher." He

102

waited for her to protest or move away from him, but she didn't. She must be drunk and his conscience wouldn't allow him to try anything else. He yawned one last time and shifted into form, drifting off to sleep with a smile on his lips.

Kara curled her fingers in his fur and closed her eyes. The switch in her brain that had been on alert flipped to off when his arm curled around her. She was safe and could relax. Sighing again, she snuggled into his fur and let his scent soothe her as she fell asleep.

Chapter 14

Salvation tied his hair back and dropped the long black tail of hair down the center of his back. He rotated his tense shoulders and eyed the pieces of the torn apart skitter that still twitched on his pillow. Ty's way of saying that it was time for them to have a chat. A nice bottle of wine would have been better appreciated, but the pompous prick didn't work that way. Blowing out a deep breath and turning the monstrosity to ash, Sal ghosted to Ty's throne room.

Demons surrounded the Ghuardian, shoving an assortment of pointed weapons at him, but Sal brushed them away with an annoyed wave of his hand and tried to see through the inky darkness. He hated these games. "Okay, I'm here. Let's get this over with."

Torches flared to life, bathing the cavernous room in a cold light. Salvation's eyes swept over the room. It reminded him of a giant mouth with numerous throats fading into darkness as their fetid odors offended his sensitive sense of smell. Ty sat at its center in a gaudy throne rumored to be built from the bones of those Ty had found no further use for, dipped in copper and fused to create the piece of furniture. No one knew what the leather pouches that hung randomly were about. *Game of Thrones, eat your heart out,* he thought, wondering how long it would be until his own skull became part of the macabre art piece.

Ty wore a confident grin. His hands were folded together in front of his chest and his elbows rested lightly on the arms of the throne. The loss of the Princess and the lion had been eating at him all day and his servants wore the evidence of his irritation. But it was a loss that could be regained. His head tilted as Salvation appeared and the Greeters scattered at Salvation's will. Nice trick, but it changed nothing.

"What's your hurry? You don't even know what I want yet. I know that you think you did the right thing, but the truth is that you royally fucked up. You have thrown things out of balance. Not just for us, but for that Viking bitch and her, now ex, mate."

Salvation wanted to slap the smirk off Ty's pretty boy face. "Look, I didn't come here for you to bore me to death. Tell me what you want. You know that I cannot reap a soul without cause. It is not allowed." Salvation growled.

Ty's expression was bored. He, better than most, knew the rules and he knew how to bend them. His brow arched and he chuckled at the ridiculousness of the Ghuardian's words. "No? But you did. It's the reason you're here in the first place." Sal's growl made him laugh harder. "Lie to yourself, if it gets you off, but don't try to play me." He lowered his chin to rest on the point of his steepled finger tips. "I have decided who will replace the loss of those you took. And I don't have to tell the walking rule book, that you can't bring them until it's their time. Do I?" Ty's amusement sparkled in his hazel eyes, but his voice was cold.

Trying to control himself, Salvation locked his jaw tightly and shook his head no. He wanted to blast Ty into the next century. Maybe he should. He was just as sick of the god damn rules as Ty was, but he, unlike that prick, was bound by them. "Yes, I know the rules," he growled. "Wait. Them? More than one?"

Ty nodded, tapping his fingers against his chin as the Ghuardian finally caught up. The ungulate wasn't very bright, and that's what made their relationship useful. It was

105

what had set in motion a way for Ty to have his revenge and the stupid cow didn't even know it.

"Why? You couldn't have kept my sister if you wanted to."

Ty's brow quirked. Sister? Interesting. His eyes gleaming, he nodded and grinned again. "But I could have. I still can. She offered herself for the lion. But, being the sweet son of a bitch that I am, I'll let that go." *For now, he thought to himself.* "Consider it an act of good will to strengthen our relationship. Instead, I want Jared Morgan's parents and firstborn son." He watched Salvation's face, still grinning, enjoying the way the color drained leaving the Ghuardian pasty white. "The Morgan's have become too big for their britches, and they need to be taken down a peg or seven. When the time comes, they will die. You will not step in. You will not help Jared save them. And you will not warn them. Are we clear? Now leave me."

Salvation couldn't believe what he'd just heard. He wanted the elders of The Morgan clan and their grandson? The price was too high for one lion. Sal shook his head as the repercussions chilled him to the bone. "That's three, Shit for Brains. I owe you one."

"Is it? I count three owed to me." Ty leaned back and placed his booted ankle on his knee and ticked off the names as he extended fingers. "The lion. The Princess. The Shadow Walker. Three. Or you can just bring back the Princess and hand her over, and we'll call it square." Ty groaned and licked his lips. "The sounds that I could make that one utter." He shifted in his seat and adjusted his crotch, eyeing Salvation. This was so much more fun now that he knew that Sal was the Princess's brother. "Your sister might be worth sparing the Morgan Clan. What do you say?"

"Fuck you." Salvation ghosted back to his hut in The Mountain. Sal had done his job, done what he was supposed to. Kara had gotten pulled into the avalanche when it began to snowball and she was still there. One soul for three. He scrubbed his face. If Gaia would just deal with Ty once and for all, shit would be so much easier. Sal went to his bed and fell face down on his pile of furs. "Why fucking me?" He groaned into them, closed his eyes and tried to relax, even though he knew that wasn't possible as he waited for the other shoe to fall.

"And yet, you're still going to do it." Ty grinned at the empty space where Sal had been. He'd offered the Ghuardian an easy way out and only a fool wouldn't jump on it. To wipe out the better part of the Morgan Clan would upset Sal's precious Gaia, but one Princess? It was an easy choice. Scratching the stubble on his jaw, Ty chuckled and ghosted to inventory the souls gathered in the Shadowlands. The young shifters had become lazy and no longer cared for their dead, leaving their souls to be trapped and used by him, here. Soon, with just a few more, less if he got the Princess, he would be ready. They all would pay.

Chapter 15

Kara bobbed and floated in that realm of not quite awake but not quite asleep. She tried to drift back down but something poked into her back pulling her closer to waking. She wiggled, not wanting to leave the soft furs or the warmth that allowed her body to feel liquid and relaxed in a way that she could barely remember. The wiggle didn't work. She tried again. It was still there.

Not opening her eyes, she reached a clumsy hand behind her to move whatever it was. Her brows worked as she tried to figure out what her fingers had curled around and why it was in her cocoon of comfortable. *Oh!* Her eyes flew open and her face flushed when her groggy mind finally coughed up where she was, and she realized what was in her palm.

Shifting in his sleep, Brock's giant bear form made the bed creak. Lost in dreams of Kara, he wasn't sure what it was about her that made it impossible for him to forget her. She was perfection in every way. From the tips of her toes to the top of her head. Something about her made the bear in him stir and stay that way. He shifted his weight on the bed again and felt something touch him in a place no one ever did, or at least hadn't in a long, long time. A soft growl of pleasure rolled up his throat as his hips rocked into it.

Kara's brow arched at the growl. It wasn't exactly menacing. In fact, it was... nice. She shivered at the goosebumps that broke across her skin and snuggled into the furs only to realize that it wasn't a blanket at all, but the bear's body. Her face grew warmer. She never blushed, but she'd guess that she was crimson right about now. She should leave the poor bear alone and get back to the nightmare that waited for her out in the real world. She didn't want to.

Brock opened his eyes and realized what was going on. If a bear could turn red, he was sure that he was. 'Oh! I'm sorry,' he mindlinked her. He felt like hiding in a hole, and he hoped she didn't gut him. She had been through so much, and the last thing she needed was to be sexually molested in her sleep by a strange male. *Although,* he mused, *I'm not really the one doing the molesting.*

He's sorry? Kara groaned and buried her face in his fur. And then she realized that she still hadn't let go of him. "Ummm..." She searched for the right words to say and shook her head, finally uncurling her fingers and trying to stealthily pull her hand back. "I think I'm the one who owes you the apology, Big Guy." She blushed even darker and looked at him over her shoulder, flashing him an impish grin.

He shifted to human form and chuckled. "No, it's my fault." The look on her face made him laugh harder. Brock swept her hair out of his face. It felt like silk against his skin. That didn't help his problem. Brock tried to move back and lost his balance. He hit the floor with a thump. Laying there, looking up at the ceiling, a thought made him laugh. *In form, he was a lot smoother. As a human, he was a klutz. You'd think a big ass bear would do more damage, but no.* "Well, that was smooth as hell," he said with a laugh.

She watched in awe as his bear face was replaced with his human one. She never got used to that. Her lips curled up when his laugh filled the room. It was deep, natural and soothing. And then he disappeared with a thump. Kara sat up and eyed the acres of bed that she had apparently pushed him across while they slept, to leave him teetering on the edge. Fuck. She WAS a bed hog.

109

Crawling to the edge, she flopped down and dropped her chin onto her folded hands, eyeing him with a grin. "I don't know. Didn't I promise to behave, or something like that? Not sure and early morning grope counts as being good." She snickered and dropped her face to the bed with the sight of him naked and hard branded into her memory forever.

He laughed again. "That is very true, Cher. It could be worse, you could have snapped it off. So, I thank you for not making my part detachable." Brock sat up and ghosted shorts on himself. "Does that mean I get a free grope later?" He asked, teasing her. His eyes focused on her hair, cascading over his bed. It was as beautiful as it was soft.

Kara laughed, lifted her head to see him and laughed harder. So many things popped into her head and balanced on the tip of her tongue, and not a single one was even slightly appropriate. "Yeah, I think it does." She shook her head. "Not sure I'm strong enough to be snapping... Never mind." She blushed and dropped her face again, still laughing. Finally, she got herself under control. "So, you gonna stay down there, or are you coming back to bed? We can negotiate the grope." She grinned, wiggled back to make room and patted the bed with her hand. "You can't be comfortable down there."

She wanted him to join her, in HIS bed? His mouth watered and his heart hammered. It was a dream come true. Trying to play it cool, he didn't listen to his bear who screamed, *Get up there now. Touch her. Roll her under you and make her ours!* Instead, he pulled a shoe out from under him. "What do you mean? I love having your boots lodged in my back." He took his time getting up and crawling onto the bed and laying on his stomach next to her. Flipping his hair out of his face, he laughed again. "That was super manly." He tried to regain his self-control, but she made him feel like he was a youngster, looking at boobs for the first time.

"But you made it look hella cute." She grinned and reached out to brush back the hair that clung to his beard. "I feel like I owe you dinner or something, for the show." She eyed him, wondering why she felt so relaxed around him. "I want to apologize and tell you I'm sorry, but," Kara trailed off and made a 'whatcha gonna do' gesture with her hands. "I'm kinda not."

"Cute huh?" Brock grinned. "Dinner. Do you cook?" He asked, staring at her, savoring the whisper of her touch. He still couldn't wrap his head around her being in his bed and in no hurry to leave it. "No need to apologize, Cher. We're both adults, right? Or I pretend to be."

Kara nodded and grinned. "Hella cute." She laughed at the look he gave her. "That we are." She dropped her head and blew at the hair that fell over her eyes as she tried not to think about the BS that waited for her outside this room. It was hard not to mourn what she'd had, but she didn't have that right when she'd erased it from ever having happened. All a figment of her imagination, that ached. "I have cooked." She made a face. "I'm told that potatoes exploding aren't normal, but I beg to differ. It happens. No matter how many times the kind humans with the firetrucks say that it doesn't."

Brock blinked at her before roaring with laughter. "What do you mean, explode? Cher, they are not supposed to go boom." He shook his head, still laughing.

She eyed him and made a face, before laughing herself. "I put it in the oven. Turned it on and BLAM! Potato shrapnel everywhere!"

"What kind of oven do you have, Cher?" He quirked his brow, wondering how someone could do that. "What did you set the oven on? Kill?"

"The kind with a handle and knobs? What do you mean what kind of oven?" She blinked at him, confused. "Okay, so maybe the answer should have been, I shouldn't cook. I didn't even know there was a kill setting. That would have been useful!" She leaned her head to the side and looked at

111

him. "I'm better with a sword than an apron." She rolled closer and bumped him playfully.

Brock bumped back, again ignoring the demands of his bear. "Well, cooking can be learned, like killing." He smiled. "So, tell me some things about yourself. What kind of food do you like?" He wanted to know more about her. Now that he finally had the opportunity, he had no plans on wasting it.

"Anything that I don't cook." She grinned. "Not a fan of charcoal. I'm not sure. I like almost everything. How about you?" She flopped onto her back to look up at him, her gaze falling to his lips. All she would have to do was raise her head to taste them. *Stop it! He's just being kind, and you have a mate!* Well, she did have, but not now. Kara sighed and refused to think about it. "Has anyone ever told you that you smell amazing?" She covered her face with her hand. "Sorry, I think it, and it pops out of my mouth. It's a curse."

Brock was about to tell her his favorite food when she made her comment. He paused for a moment, tilting his head and feeling her eyes on his lips. *Those are kiss me eyes,* his bear screamed. *Do it! She wants it. KISS HER!* Instead of doing what he wanted to, Brock licked his own and tried to take the high road. "Well, thank you. You do too. I'm not a picky eater, myself. What about hobbies? What little free time I have, I like to play guitar and do a little woodworking."

"Thank you." Kara smiled, unable to deny that the compliment pleased her. "Like carving and building things? I admire that, I've always wished that I was better at doing something creative with my hands." She thought about it for a few moments. "I'm not sure I remember, the last few years," she wrinkled her brow as she remembered that time passed differently here. "I guess it was only days, have been all about training and trying not to die." She sighed. "I have a hot spring that I love. It's beautiful, peaceful and quiet." She smiled softly and closed her eyes. "Here, I like movies, awful,

112

B horror flicks. I mean the REALLY bad ones. And I like to play pool. I don't understand why there is no Mrs. Brock." Groaning, she slid her hand to cover her eyes again. "Or maybe there is, and I should be apologizing to a pissed off female for copping a feel of her mate?" Kara chuckled and peeked at him through her fingers.

Brock felt a pang of pain for her. She was a warrior. It's not like she was going to tell him that she liked shopping and collecting glass unicorns. "No. There is no Mrs. Anything. There was once, but she was taken from me. Wait. B movies? Seriously? You?" He snorted and shook his head because he didn't expect that.

Kara watched his face for a moment, hating the way her chest ached and her throat closed off. "I'm sorry. I wouldn't wish that on anyone." She brushed her hand over his and bit back the stupid things that wanted to flow out of her. She pushed it away and nodded in answer to his question. "Evil Dead 2, Slumber Party Massacre 2 and Trick or Treat are my top three. Don't judge." She gave him a warning look that crumbled into a grin.

"Pool is a good game if you're not trying to hustle money out of people. Not that I would ever do that." He grinned and winked at her.

"We should play sometime."

He smiled at her touch and the way his body warmed. "I don't think I've seen any of those. I'd love to play you. Are you a betting woman, Cher?" Brock teased, mustering his courage to turn his hand and thread his fingers with hers. He had to swallow the pleased growl his bear pushed up his throat when their palms touched.

Kara laughed, liking the way he smiled when she touched him. "We have to fix that. You haven't lived until you've experienced the driller killer and his guitar." She arched a brow, rubbing her thumb against his and wiggled closer. She liked how his touch felt. "As a matter of fact, I am. What are you thinking Bjorn? Name your stakes." She accepted the unspoken challenge and dared him to call her bluff.

"Well, let's play for dinner. If I win, you let me teach you how to cook something. And if you win, then you can take me to dinner."

Her lips twitched back and forth as she considered his terms. "I am so gonna kick your furry ass." She grinned and tugged on his beard gently. "I'm in."

He pretended to bite her hand playfully. "We'll see about that, Cher," he chuckled, getting off the bed and pulling her up with him. "Please don't cry when you lose."

"Vikings rape and pillage. We don't lose." She laughed at how that sounded and crawled to the edge of the bed on her knees, not wanting to let go. "Usually I kill anyone unlucky enough to see me cry, but I like you and might miss you if you weren't around."

Brock laughed hard. "Okay Motor Mouth, let's do this." He ghosted more clothes on himself. "I thought it was rape, pillage, and burn?"

Kara shrugged and ghosted on a pair of jeans and a tank top, Folding and handing the sweats and his shirt back to him. She stretched and stepped off the bed. Gods it felt good to have her powers working right again. "The burn part is optional. You know, for the diehards." She pushed him towards the door, "I'm gonna make you beg, Big Guy." She laughed at the look he gave her.

He laughed and slipped on his shoes. *If only she would.* "Sure, you are, Cher. You keep thinking that." Brock opened the door and stepped aside so she could go out first. He ghosted his wallet, phone, and keys into his back pocket.

"Knowing that, you mean?" She teased and looked down the hall before stepping out. She ghosted her jacket into her hand and draped it over her shoulder. Stretching up, she whispered into his ear, "Oh, and I play dirty." She grinned and snagged one of his belt loops with her finger, pulling him down the hall.

Brock closed the door as she pulled on him. *This is going to be interesting,* he thought as they strolled down to the pool room. It was empty and that was all right with him. He pulled his keys out and unlocked the first table. "You rack them, and I'll go get us a couple of beers." He left her to get things started. As he made his way to the bar, he noticed that no one had opened for the day yet. *Good*, he thought. *Having the place to ourselves will be nice.* And having time to spend alone with Kara would be heaven. She was more than just the beautiful face that he'd fallen for. She made him laugh, and very few could do that, these days. He got two beers and headed back.

Kara dropped the balls into the triangle rack, rearranged them into a stripe and solid pattern with the eight-ball nestled in the middle. Rolling the wooden triangle up the table and pinching the balls tight to the frame, she removed it and tucked it back into its space. Pulling the white ball from the hole, she placed it on the green felt and took her time, rolling cue sticks on an empty table until she found two that were straight. She looked up and grinned when he came back. "I don't want you blaming faulty equipment when you lose." Kara snickered and took the beer he held out. "Those two are pretty straight. You can pick and break."

Brock chuckled, put his beer on the nearby table and picked a cue stick. "Okay, Cher." He chalked his cue and moved into position. He pulled the stick back and let it connect with the cue ball. It hit the colored balls and scattering them in a clean break and sinking two. He stood up and grinned at her. "I guess that makes me solids, Cher."

Kara took the remaining stick and braced the butt of it on the toe of her boot while she watched him break. She arched a brow as the two solids slammed into the pockets with a light puff of blue chalk dust. "I look better in stripes." She grinned, shrugged and leaned her ass against the closest table to reach for her beer. She knew the swagger of a male that was in his comfort zone, and the bear had it in spades.

115

"Don't choke Babes," she smirked over the rim before taking a sip.

He took his next shot and sank another ball. "I'll try hard not to." Brock chuckled and looked for his next move, but her balls blocked him. Arching an amused brow, he tapped the cue ball into one of her balls lightly, leaving it close enough to kiss it. "Your turn," he said, smirking at her.

"Really? You leave me like that?" Kara laughed as she put down her drink and chalked her stick as she circled the table looking for her shot. He wasn't going to take it easy on her, and she liked him just a little more for it. "Game on, Bjorn." She grinned and set down the cube of blue chalk to line up what she could see.

The ball he'd left the cue parked beside would be one hell of a cut, but... Kara leaned over the table, braced her bent fingers on the green felt and held up her thumb, creating a cradle for the stick to slide through. She lifted her eyes and winked at him.

"Nine ball. Back here," She bumped the table near the side pocket in front of her hips with the butt of the stick. "One bank." She sunk the next two shots and scratched on a straight shot when she was looking at him instead of concentrating on the English that would have prevented the cue ball from following in the twelve.

Brock gave her an impressed nod, took a long pull of his beer and then set it on the table, before taking his stick in his hands again. Watching her bend over the table and remembering how he'd woken up made him twitchy. He looked at the table and took aim. He hit the cue too hard, and it flew off the table, bouncing off another and then onto the floor. " I meant to do that," he said laughing.

Kara leaned down and caught it on the second bounce. "Uh huh," she teased and tossed the white ball, catching it before lowering it to the table behind the dot on the green felt, and rolled it left with the tip of the stick as she considered her options. She leaned over the table again when a thought hit her. Kara looked back over her shoulder

116

and narrowed her eyes. "You wouldn't be letting me win? Would you?" She turned back to the table and dropped the ten. She stood up to study the table. "That would get you punished."

He laughed and arched a brow. From the teasing tone of her voice, he wasn't sure that he wouldn't enjoy a little punishment that she was threatening to dish out. "I wouldn't dare, Cher."

Kara grinned and couldn't see a shot that the eight wasn't blocking. "Thirteen, two banks, or some shit." She shook her head and laughed doubtfully, tapping the cue ball with the stick's tip and wincing as the eight ball began rolling down the table. "Didn't think so."

After that, all of his mojo left him. Brock blamed her for the direction his thoughts went in. He growled as Kara mopped the table with him. "Well that was sad as hell," he sighed, shaking his head. He drained his beer and made a face.

Kara reached up and wiped a little foam from the corner of his stash. "But you get a free dinner on me and don't have to suffer through anything that I tried to cook. Trust me, that's a win," she grinned and leaned in beside him, closing her eyes at his scent.

He shrugged. "The world may never know." He lowered the stick to the table.

"If you're a glutton for punishment, we can give it a go."

Brock laughed. "Next time. You don't seem to be up to battling the oven, Cher. And I don't wanna die by potato."

Kara eyed him wearily. "True. Not a good way to go." She braced her hands on the table behind her and lifted herself up to sit on it, swinging her feet as she studied him the same way she had the pool table earlier. She didn't understand how he seemed able to see her in a way that others couldn't. She was putting up a damned good front, but she knew that she cringed at each sound in the bar, knowing that Dane could appear at any moment and then she couldn't pretend that reality didn't exist and that it wasn't eating her alive inside. "So, when and where, Big guy?"

"Winners call," he said putting the pool table glass back on and locking it up.

She shrugged and looked at the clock, sighing as he put things back to right in the room. She'd been enjoying her time with him and didn't want it to end. "I have to lock up Fenrir. If I live through that, tonight? The steakhouse on Bourbon?" Impulsively, she hooked one of his legs with her boots when he stepped closer. She suddenly felt self-conscious and had no clue why.

He moved closer to her as she hooked him. "Okay, it's a date, Cher." Brock leaned in and kissed her cheek, surprised when she turned to meet his lips with hers and felt the tip of her tongue trace the seam. He heard Brax call for him and growled. "Well, I think that's my queue to get some work done." He didn't want to go, afraid that if he did, whatever magic was at work would fade.

She bit her lower lip and smiled, tucking the hair that hung into his face behind his ear, before he pulled away. Kara was relieved and confused by the fluttering of her stomach. "Okay, and Brock? Thanks. For everything." She lowered herself to the floor and after looking around, ghosted on her armor. "I should be done by seven. See you then?"

"You bet, Cher. Kick some ass." Brock growled, seriously considering killing Brax. He forced himself to walk away, even though both his bear and the man wanted another taste of her, especially if it could be the last. He didn't like the idea of her putting herself into another situation that could kill her. He'd just gotten her back. *No*, he corrected himself. *You haven't gotten shit. It's a dinner and just a kiss. She probably turned her head by mistake*. When he glanced back to get another eyeful of her in the armor that was hot as fucking hell, he saw that she'd already ghosted out. "At least she knows I'm alive," he sighed and listened to Brax bitch.

Chapter 16

Kara ground her molars trying to keep the scream bottled in her throat where it belonged. Jumping on the back of the giant wolf, destined to end the world, was not one of Kara's smarter moves, but was hella effective until he rolled over, crushing her under his weight. The pain was bad, but it was the nasty sound of crunching bones that made her want to hurl. Rank saliva dripped from the snarling jaws mere inches from her face. Damn the bastard needed a breath mint. Drool hit her cheek, running back into her hair making her grimace and turn her head.

Voices from the others finally catching up, echoed and bounced around the cavern. About fucking time yet Kara dreaded their arrival in her current sitch. Bumbling idiots storming in could turn the not so good that was going down, to deadly and she had no plans to be wolf chow today. She had a dinner date to make, damn it. Curling her fingers around the charmed dwarven rope, she watched the wolf in her peripheral vision as she inched her arm closer to her body, trying to figure out the safest way to slip it over Fenrir's massive head as the sound of boots splashed and pounded toward her. She was out of time.

Her hand shot forward, looping the lasso under his bottom jaw and moving quickly to try sliding it over his muzzle. Fire exploded in her forearm as teeth penetrated the leather armor sinking into flesh and closing in a vice tight grip that shattered bone. Kara's eyes rolled back in her head and she fought against the darkness that closed in around her. As long as he had her arm, he wasn't likely to take her head off. *Way to find the bright side of things Kara,* she silently chided. Surging her shoulders off the stone floor, she flicked the rope over one ear and then the other.

Then the shaking began. Her body flopped around like a rag doll. Kara tried to bolt him, but in her condition, it was only a pathetic static charge and just pissed the wolf off. She was going to die. Again. Kara knew it and was strangely calm. This time she was going down fighting. She caught a glimpse of legs appearing from the tunnel and then lost them as she was savagely shaken and everything went dark leaving only the echoes of voices. Then silence.

Her eyes opened. She was sprawled on the cold stone floor. Her clothes, or what was left of them, sponged up the puddled water leaving Kara's chin quivering from the cold as every inch of her body screamed. Blinking she tried to figure out where she was. The chipped and uneven ceiling above gave no clues other than a cave, maybe? A soft rustling turned her head. Hel, the goddess of Helheim, knelt beside her. Of all the gods to come to her aid, it had to be one who could not heal. Shit luck that.

"Thank you, child." The beautiful woman cupped Kara's face in her cold palms, making her teeth chatter. How ironic that the half-rotted goddess was the only one who would think to thank her. Her fucking family sucked. "What can I do?"

Kara gave a tight smile and tried to roll up, but it was a no go. Her body was too broken and weak. "Send me back?" Her voice was little more than a soft growl. "And tell Dad that time is up."

Hel nodded her understanding, brushed her hand down over Kara's face to close her eyes and pressed her lips to Kara's forehead.

Then Kara was falling. That scream she'd locked inside, broke free as she landed in the bed, jostling her and reminding her that being immortal sucked ass. Silent tears rolled back into her hair. She tried not to move, not to breathe or do anything that would send another jolt of agony shooting through her. She envied mortals who could simply die before shit got this bad. They had no idea how lucky they were.

Clenching her teeth, she looked for a clock and finally found one on the dresser in the corner. Kara used the last of her energy to open the blinds wide and let in the sunlight. If she closed her eyes now, she should be able to move by tonight. A smile curled her lips. Dinner with that sweet-smelling bear with velvety soft lips. That was something worth living for.

Chapter 17

Kane's hand covered the stitch in his side that was making it hard to breathe and made his legs keep pumping. His boots pounded out a steady rhythm down the empty street. Whoever it was that claimed that New Orleans never slept was full of shit. When he was searching for a crowd, he couldn't find a living soul. Fucking humans, undependable twat waffles. He cut down an alley between two brick buildings that had seen better days, back before Katrina had made NOLA her bitch. The roofs leaned together like conspiring thieves plotting their next job while the wind blew over abandoned glass bottles, mimicking the sound of voices. The growl came again. It was behind him, and it was getting closer.

His body pivoted right, but his foot slid left in the grease leaking from a busted corner of a restaurant dumpster. Kane pinwheeled his arms, fighting for balance. It was a battle he was destined to lose. Gravity demanded her due, and he pitched forward before the split that was sure to turn him soprano was avoided. He wrapped his arms around his head just before he skidded over the rough asphalt, grunting at the cheese grater over mozzarella feel of skin chafed off his arms, chest, and knees. The coppery scent of his blood filled the alley. Fuck. He might as well have a flashing neon arrow pointing to his location.

Panting heavily, he scurried into the crevice between the dumpster and the crumbling brick wall, praying that the stink of tonight's tossed out special would mask his scent. He held up his arms to inspect the damage and shook his head. Kane didn't know how many layers of skin he had between the outside world and his exposed muscle, but he'd lay money that he'd scraped through most of them. He ground his molars to dust and wiped the blood dripping from his raw elbows on the bent knees of his jeans. They were ruined too, and that pissed him off. Kane liked these jeans. He'd finally broken them in so that they didn't ride up and try to divide and conquer his boys or pinch anything. Now, they were just another casualty.

Kane listened for the ones who chased him. Insects buzzed, and a paper cup chattered over the broken tar. Maybe he'd lost it. Sighing, he let his head roll forward on his chest and hang loosely. There were so few of his kind left. Why would anyone be hunting them to extinction? Kane snorted. Stupid question. Someone wanted one of the Ghuardians, one of the first Buffalo and wiping out the Seven was the quickest way to pass go and collect their two hundred dollars.

He inched closer to the edge of the dumpster and peered down the alley. Maybe the coast was clear. A door flew open. Kane jumped back, catching his shoulder on the ragged metal and losing more skin. He cursed silently and palmed the fresh oozing wound. Humans stepped outside, laughing and talking in thick Cajun accents that might as well have been a different language for all the sense it made to him. He pulled back into the shadows, listening to them as they threw the heavy bags of rubbish into the dumpster. Pieces of chicken and the rinds of fruit rained down on him. The bag must have ripped. Kane made a face and bit his lips against the second round of curses that demanded out.

Oh, fucking great. Now they're going to take a smoke break. Kane leaned back into the shadows and pulled his hand away from the cut on his shoulder. There was too much blood. He hadn't fed in weeks, and he didn't have the reserves to be spilling this much. His ears began to buzz and his vision dim. He needed food. Now. He gathered his legs under him and lunged just as the humans disappeared inside and the door closed behind them. He growled and searched for a knob, anything that would let him inside. There was nothing. No knob. No handle. Just a deadbolt lock, flush with the door.

He wouldn't go back. He couldn't. Not to the Shadowlands. Not to the darkness, the Skitters and the Unmentionables. Kane shuddered and staggered down the alley, his shoulder scraping against the brick. He heard the bass of loud music ahead. If he could get inside, he could find a meal. Just enough to take the edge off and give him enough of a boost to heal. He hadn't taken an unwilling meal in over half a century. Not since he had happened across that shifter female in the desert, hanging like a Scooby Snack and begging to be tasted and licked. His eyes rolled back in his head at the memory of the honey and spice that had coated his tongue. She had been a delicacy that should be savored over the centuries on special occasions.

A growl rolled through the alley. It echoed and built until it surrounded him. Kane's heart pounded in his chest. Adrenaline flooded his veins and made his feet move faster. Holding his hand against the wall to keep his balance, he stumbled and ran toward the music, looking over his shoulder every few steps. If death was creeping up on him, he sure as shit wanted to see it coming so he could gouge out its fucking eyes.

His eyes snapped forward when the wall he'd been using to stay upright disappeared. A bright green light burned his eyes, forcing him to blink and squint. Kane looked up that the sign that hung over his head. He scoffed as he read, *The Dungeon*, and in smaller print, *the Quarter's most unique late night spot*. Kane laughed as he staggered down the long red lit hallway. How fitting that he'd escaped the Shadowlands to die in The Dungeon. Ironic shit right there.

Chapter 18

Kara's eyes flew open, and her chest heaved. Cold sweat beaded and trickled down her face and into her hair. It was all a lie. She knew when she'd taken Dane's memories that they would unlock and she'd have to live them, but she hadn't been ready for this. She owed her brother an apology, and that didn't make her happy either. And this Kane son of a bitch, she was going to kill him slow.

She closed her eyes and covered them with her arm, grimacing as the movement pulled and sent a jolt of pain through her ribs and shoulder. Again, the images played out in her mind's eye. Dane, a few of The Violent Offenders and a handful of the new AP recruits sitting at a table in the back making bets on who could bag the new chick talking to the Navarro bear at the bar. Kara's jaw tightened. She'd been the girl, but that wasn't the worst part.

Kane was already boarded up inside Dane, twisting his thoughts and actions to serve the demon spawn before Kara had even arrived in NOLA. It was Kane's blood that had fired up when he saw her, not Dane's. Hell, the damn thing had purred at the idea of bedding her and finding a way to tap into her power, and he knew that Dane was the perfect tool to get the job done. Tall, rugged and good looking, with an easy humor that glowed in his hazel eyes. He was a smooth talker too, always seeming to know just what the ladies needed to hear to flip the switch of their better judgment to off and follow him anywhere. Kara hadn't been immune. Before she knew it, she was kegs deep in the mead and following Dane up to his room for some 'talking' that she knew wasn't going to happen, when the bar closed. It had seemed like a brilliant plan.

It was all fun and games until the starbursts of color had formed around the irises of their eyes. Kara snorted. She'd been such a fucking idiot. He played the 'don't let this poor loveable lion be limp for eternity' card like a pro, and she'd eaten it up, letting him play her conscience like a finely tuned violin. Meanwhile, Kane had been doing emotional backflips of joy inside his host, and when it came time to decide if they should tie their life forces together, it was his words of undying love and not being able to live without her that had done her in.

BEEP. BEEP. BEEP. The shrill sound of her alarm clock cut through the silence but barely registered inside her head as the rest played out. What had been some of the happiest times of her life were a set of cold and calculated moves, designed to gain access to her power and then Asgard itself. Her lips curled up at Kane's pissed off and disappointment when Dane dropping dead had dumped the demon back into its shit pit of a life with less power than he'd had before.

Banging on the wall drew her out of her thoughts, and finally, she reached over and slapped the alarm clock until it was silent again. Thank fuck Odin hadn't liked Dane, and she'd never taken him home. Kara scrubbed her face with her hands, playing what if until she saw stars. It was her own fault. She wasn't human. She wasn't shifter. She couldn't have what they had, and she shouldn't want it. She needed to take a step back and either remember her place in this world or choose to stay the hell out of it other than to reap the souls that she was assigned. Love wasn't for her kind, and she knew it. Nothing that surrounds itself with the darkness of death can live in the light. Forgetting that, was all on her.

127

Rolling her head, Kara looked at the clock. She was supposed to meet Brock soon. She scoffed. What was the point? He was alive and having her as a friend was just a cement block around his neck, destined to pull him under to drown. It was selfish on her part. Sighing, she clamped her teeth together and swung her legs over the edge of the bed. Shuffling as quickly as her sore and bruised muscles would allow she arched a brow at the kegs and kegs of mead that filled her kitchen. Dad and Gaia must have had one hell of a visit to merit this kind of gift giving.

Something fluttered on one of the stacked mini barrels. Her curiosity piqued, Kara moved closer and picked it up. A beautiful scrawling script spelled out her name on the lavender paper. Unfolding it carefully a small smile played at the corners of her mouth as she read.

Kara. Thank you for your thoughtfulness. Trust yourself to know the difference between what you think you want and what you need. When it's right, they are one and the same. Don't give up. I won't. Until I see you again. -G

If Gaia could hold onto hope, maybe she could too. Kara refolded the note and slid it into the drawer that held the takeout menus. Yeah, she could give it a try. Wasn't that the argument she'd tried to make for Fenrir? How can he be expected to care about the world that he has no place in? She could find a small niche, maybe. She wouldn't go in blind, but there was no reason that she couldn't enjoy being alive, just a little. Shaking her head at the mountain of mead, she headed for the shower to get ready to meet Brock for dinner.

Chapter 19

Reese crouched on the rooftop with one hand on the concrete ledge between her feet for balance. Something powerful had been stalking their streets and tearing into demons and the occasional shifters. Although popular culture dictated that all demons were evil, vile creatures, the reality is that they were just what came before man and shifters alike. Most were older than both, and it wasn't a surprise when they walked among them. The question was, was the demon in the alley below friend or foe?

She'd arrived too late to see what had left him bloody and bruised, but she was here now. Reese tilted her head to the side as she watched him jump out from behind the dumpster and stagger away. To humans, he would appear to be just another drunk that had been rolled for his wallet, but Reese knew better.

His hunger was so intense that it made her mouth water with anticipation and she could sense him becoming feral. That was too dangerous of a combination for her to ignore. Adjusting her position as the dark-haired demon turned down the side street, she arched a brow. Why was he laughing? She ghosted to the shadows when he disappeared.

Following the scent of his blood and the booming music, Reese stepped inside. Macabre instruments of torture hung on the walls, bathed in a pulsing red light. Her body was tense, not knowing what to expect. The red light was screwing with her vision, the fade and flash of it made her feel like the floor was shifting under her feet. Her fingertips scraped the stone of the wall as she continued deeper. It was like being swallowed, and her instincts screamed that this was a bad idea.

Turning the corner, she looked left, down another long hall that seemed to spill into the club. To the right was a small alcove filled with a cage made of thick oak slats and bolts designed to look like they were straight from a forge. The door was slowly swinging shut. She stepped closer and eyed the male huddled in a heap inside.

His breath was an uneven series of ragged pants that seemed to be slowing and the periods of apnea growing. She inched forward, her hand creeping to the knife on her hip. Although as loud as it was in here, she doubted anyone would notice a single gunshot.

He watched the boots stop and then cautiously come toward him. As places to hide went, this one sucked, but it was as good as any to die in. Kane's nose twitched. That scent. He knew that smell. Even after all of these years, he'd never forgotten it. His mouth watered as he forced his head up to see if he was dreaming. He blinked and grimaced when his head thudded against the stone. Yeah, just when he needed to help the hallucinations, a concussion. Letting the wall brace him up, his eyes moved down her form to the arm that disappeared inside her jacket.

"Do it." His voice was hoarse and had a full metric ton of gravel in it, but it carried. He coughed, not bothering to cover his mouth even as he felt the blood mist on his lips. "Do us both a favor and finish it clean."

Reese's eyes narrowed as she swiped her booted foot to the side to swing the door that separated them open, wincing at the screech of old hinges. "What happened? Why did someone do this to you?" She knelt beside him, ready to bury the blade in his neck if he so much as twitched wrong.

130

Kane tried to laugh, but it came out as a cough, "Because I ate their sister," he lied, watching her for a reaction.

She knew he was lying, but what the hell? If he wanted to play games? His funeral. Not hers. "Why?" Reese tilted her head. He was familiar. Not his face, but something about him and she didn't like missing pieces of the puzzle. "Have we met before?"

Kane shook his head no. *'Remember that time you were hanging, and someone snacked on you? Yeah, that was me. How the hell you been?'* seemed more likely to buy him a toe tag then break the ice. "I was starving, and I snapped." Like he was about to now. His mind was already calculating the distance between them and if he had the strength to grab and hold her arm while he tore into her throat.

"You still are. So, let's drop the bullshit, shall we?" Reese let go of the knife and shrugged out of her jacket, holding her arm out to him. "Take it."

It was his turn to be suspicious. "Why?" He groaned as she held her wrist under his nose. "No." He pushed it away.

"Why the fuck not? You need it." She growled.

"It's a choice," he growled back, pulling back his lips to show the tips of his fangs.

"It's a stupid fucking decision." Reese reached under her jacket and pulled out the blade, watching the demon close his eyes and wait for death to come. Shaking her head, she gripped the pommel tight and swung, striking the male in the knockout button near his temple.

Leaning back, she pushed the button on her earpiece. "Send the bus for pick up." She slid the dagger back into its sheath and shrugged her jacket back on. They weren't taking chances of this one waking up in mid ghost. He was too valuable if they could use him and too dangerous if they couldn't.

131

Chapter 20

After showering and getting dressed, Brock tried to shake off the annoyance that his family caused. Sure, his patience was shorter than usual because he believed that Kara was going to come to her senses and blow him off. That did not change the fact that his brothers were idiotic asses, all three of them. It was a relief to leave for the steakhouse and wait to find out that Kara wasn't going to show and he couldn't help the spring in his step because of the possibility that she just might.

On the walk, he let his mind wander to this morning. He couldn't help feeling like he'd stumbled and missed a chance at a real kiss, but that was stupid. If she were going to drop one on someone, it wouldn't be him. *And why not?* His bear demanded with a growl. *We wash, and she likes how we smell.*

Brock silenced the bear's voice in his head and noticed a lady selling flowers from a small cart. Smiling, he looked through the bouquets until he found a small bunch that reminded him of Kara's eyes and paid for them. The woman wrapped the stems in brown paper that protected the delicate petals but allowed them to show. Brock thanked her and crossed the street to the restaurant. He looked around and either he was there before she was, or he was going to be stood up. Wanting to hold onto the dream for as long as possible, he refused to look at his watch to check the time.

Kara was late. She shoved her new phone back into her pocket when she realized that she didn't have Brock's number. *Sure, hog his bed, but don't get his digits. Smooth!* She rolled her eyes and ducked behind a dumpster to ghost to the restaurant, stopping to check her reflection in the window before stepping around the corner. She didn't look like she'd been dead just days ago, so that was a win.

She saw the people parting to walk around Brock. He wasn't easy to miss, standing six foot eight and looking all male model like. She grinned, doubting that he'd see it that way. Kara picked up her pace to a jog. "Sorry, I'm late. I hope you haven't been waiting long." She stopped in front of him and hit him with her best smile, hoping he wouldn't be mad, before stretching up to kiss his cheek. "I would have texted, but I don't have your number."

"No, I just got here myself." Brock smiled his relief that she was here and held the flowers out to her, suddenly feeling nervous and wondering if he should have kissed her. "You look lovely." He pushed his hair back, out of his face.

Her brows popped at the flowers. "Thank you. You're looking good too, Babes." She leaned her nose over the bouquet and inhaled, closing her eyes. "This is sweet. I've never gotten flowers unless it was an apology." She thought about it and scrunched up her face. "Maybe at my funeral. Did I have a funeral?" She grinned and looked up at him. She couldn't figure out why he was so sweet to her. She smelled the flowers again before glancing up. "Sorry. I ramble. I hope you're hungry."

Brock laughed and felt himself relax. "I was thinking a nice salad. I need to watch my girlish figure." He opened the door for her and let her go in first.

She stepped inside, making sure to be obvious about checking him out. "Well, then I'm about to look like a pig." She laughed and stopped at the podium. "Two," Kara told the beautiful brunette with her hair twisted and piled neatly on top of her head. When the woman looked up, she froze, staring up at Brock. Kara hid her laugh, "I don't think you need to worry, Big Guy."

Brock quirked his brow. "Why? And I didn't know we were having an eating contest. I'd have worn my eating britches." He joked, following them to the table. He pulled the chair out for Kara and waited for her to sit.

Kara looked at the seat and arched a brow before she sat down and set the flowers on the table carefully. It would be a shame to bruise or break them. She waited for Brock to take his seat across from her before she answered. "No contest. I like to eat." She leaned her elbows on the table and dropped her chin onto her folded hands. "And as for having to watch your figure, from what I saw this morning, you can eat what you want. You're in excellent shape." She grinned when the menus were placed on the table. "How was your day?"

He blushed, pleased by her kind words and picked up his menu. "Well, I like a woman who can eat. Not many enjoy food as much as us Bears," he said opening his menu. He didn't look up when he answered her. "Oh, you know, it was just another day. It seemed to drag on and on." He couldn't decide what he wanted. "Everything on this thing looks good."

She grinned at his blush and watched him for a moment before scanning the options. He was right, everything did look good, and the smells of the meals around them wasn't helping her decide. Her body was still knitting itself back together, and while she didn't need food to help it along, the process always made her ravenous. "Would it be wrong to order everything and just work our way through it?" Kara sipped her water and grinned hopefully.

Brock thought about it for a moment. "Sounds good to me. And their dessert menu, too." He made a face at the water in front of him. It had a lemon wedge in it. "Why do they always pollute the water with those damn things?

Mmm water, with seeds." He flipped over the menu to look at the back for the drink options.

"Keep being all agreeable, and I'm going to decide that I want to keep you," Kara teased and twisted her lemon, laughing when a seed sank to the bottom. "You might have a point about the seeds. Are you a wine drinker?" She looked over the list, that might as well have been written in Egyptian hieroglyphs for all the sense it made to her.

Brock grinned at her threat. "See? Some places charge an arm and a leg for water with seeds. I haven't tried many wines. If you see anything you want, let me know?" He read the wine list. It all looked the same to him.

Kara shook her head no. "It all reminds me of what I think dirty feet would taste like." She shuddered and made a face. "I could go for a beer, though." She closed the menu, laid it on the table and watched him browse the list. "Can I ask you something?"

"Sure," he said still looking at the drink list. They had a lot of different beers. "What kind do you want? They've got some white girl beer, I see." Brock laughed when he realized what he'd said. "God, I've been around Blade too long."

"White girl beer?" Kara looked down at the list, confused. "I don't know what that is. I'll take a Guinness." She narrowed her eyes, trying to figure him out. "Okay, not that I don't appreciate it and enjoy your company, but why have you been so nice to me? I mean, until a few days ago, you never even spoke to me other than to ask what I wanted to eat or drink."

Brock looked up at her surprised. Kara was a straight shooter, and that wasn't something that he was used to with females. "The pumpkin spice beer." He tried to think of something witty or funny to say, but that wasn't him. "Do you want my honest answer, Cher?"

Kara made a face. "Who would put pumpkin anything, in beer? Fricken humans." She shook her head, and sure enough, she found the pumpkin spice beer on the menu.

"That's just nasty. And yes, I'd appreciate honest." That was no joke after the shit she'd just learned about Dane.

"I like pumpkin pie, but to answer your question?" Brock watched her face, wondering if she would leave or throw her seed water in his face when he answered. "Well, I've had a crush on you for a while and after what happened? I saw this as my second chance. I figured it was time to nut up or shut up," he answered honestly and waited for her to laugh her ass off at him.

"Pie is not beer. Beer should be beer flavored like coffee should taste like coffee damn it." Kara rambled as she let what he'd said sink in. A surprised smile played at the corners of her mouth. "Really? Me? Why didn't you tell me?" She felt his anxiety and reached out to cover his hand with hers. "I'm surprised, but..." She searched for the right word. "Flattered sounds like a kiss-off, so insert a word here that isn't." She grinned.

Brock relaxed at her hand on his. "I know I'm not popular and all that. Not like Dane. Women love him. I don't really let any get that close to me. Not after what happened to..." His voice trailed off. Just then, their server came and asked what they would like. *Saved by the bell*, he thought to himself. He let Kara go first. He wasn't one of those males that ordered for them both. Not that he'd been on many dates. Not since his Maggie. He'd decided if the gods wanted him to have someone, it would happen one way or another. There was no sense trying to troll for one. He also thought that his clan might go the old fashion route, and pick one for him. He was shocked they still did that in this day and age, but it happened sometimes. Something about bloodlines and such. He didn't really listen.

Kara cursed the waitress's bad timing. "I'll take page two. Just bring extra plates, please." She smiled and tried not to laugh at the look of shock on her face, the name tag said Becky. "And a Guinness." She held out the menu and waited for Brock.

136

"I think we're gonna share that. I'll have a house draft." Brock handed the menu to Becky. "Also, can you bring us the dessert menu? The good one. Not the little sleeve thing on this."

"Of course! I'll be right back." Becky winked at Brock and left with the menus.

"You were saying? What happened?" Kara watched him and could tell that he wasn't comfortable. "How about we make a deal. We can do that Silence of the Lambs thing. Not the lotion on the skin part. That would be weird. But the quid pro quo. And we take each other's secrets to the grave." She tilted her head, allowing herself to really see him after stripping away what she'd thought she knew. "And being popular doesn't impress me. That you bothered to inconvenience yourself to help me, that does. A lot. You didn't have to, and most wouldn't have."

Brock nodded and smiled. "Okay. I'd like that. And the lotion in the basket thing kinda always made me laugh. Humans taste better without all that extra wax stuff on them," he joked. "I was with someone for a long time, and the mating thing happened. Or I thought it had. Her clan wasn't happy about it. She went to her father to try to talk some sense into him. In the end, she was killed for it. They told me that it wasn't true and that they didn't do it. In my heart, I know differently. Plus, Ozzy had one of his team investigate the fact that she went MIA. If she just went back to the mountain that would have been one thing, but she vanished entirely. So, yeah," He dropped his eyes, looking down at the tablecloth.

"I'm sorry. They would have been damn lucky to have added you to their clan." Kara shook her head and took hold of his hand. She frowned, surprised that she didn't like knowing that someone had hurt him. "I can go wrath of the goddess on them, if you'd like. Just point me in the right direction."

Brock smiled softly at her comment. "No, it's okay. They will pay for what they did. I believe in karma and that

137

the elders will handle it in their own way. Plus, she was the only pretty daughter they had. The rest are uggos."

Kara laughed and squeezed his hand. "If karma moves too slow, just give me the nod. Fair is fair, what do you want to know? Open book here." She grinned and picked up the beer that Becky placed on the table. "Thanks."

"Thank you," Brock said taking his draft and sipping it. "Not bad," he said thinking about her question. "How did you come to be here? I don't see the appeal of NOLA for you. Nothing left to rape and pillage. The hurricane got most of it." He sipped his draft again, enjoying being able to watch her as much as he wanted to without having to hide it.

"I came here for work. I was assigned this cranky old bastard that shouldn't have been here, but when he died something else snatched him up, screwed him over and he was just a shade lost and wandering. Mom wanted him, so I gave him the option of Valhalla or being with her. He'd earned the right to pick his own fate, or at least that's how I saw it. He chose the great hall, which was the better choice. Mom took my wings for a while, as punishment, and I kind of fell in love with the place." Kara shrugged. "There isn't a lot more beautiful than the swamps at daybreak, and the culture is strange enough, that it's easy to blend in." Kara watched his face. "Not what you expected to hear?"

Brock loved the way she spoke about her people and smiled. "No, not what I thought, but I'm glad you stayed. So, tell me about the great hall, and what it's like to be able to control birds." He paused a moment. "Wings? Like for real, you can fly, wings?"

She nodded and winked. "Maybe I'll show them to you sometime. I'm glad I stayed too." Kara smiled softly, noticing that she was completely relaxed with him and that was strange but pleasant. "The great hall." She smiled, remembering growing up there and getting under foot. "It's huge. High ceilings. Massive hearths that always have some stew bubbling over the flames, no matter the time of year

138

and making the place smell like heaven. Rows and rows of wooden tables, all filled with retired warriors, telling tales of battles and conquests. And the mead never stops flowing." She sighed happily. "It is heaven. The only birds that we have to deal with are Dad's Ravens, and they stay on his shoulders, except when he forces them onto their perch."

He smiled at her tales. He was about to ask another question when Becky and another server appeared with the food and three stands for the rest that was still coming. "Wow, look at the size of these things." Brock was shocked at the portion sizes.

Kara blinked and laughed. "My eyes may have been bigger than my appetite. Glad I have back up." She grinned and unwrapped her flatware, shaking out the napkin and dropping it into her lap as they slid plate after plate onto the table.

"Yes, it seems so." Brock followed suit with his own napkin and silverware. "I think we may need a to-go wheel barrel." He smiled and waited for all the food to get there. "So where do you want to start? Ladies first and all."

Kara just shook her head and stared. It was overwhelming. Shrugging, she reached for the lasagna closest to her and scooped a little onto one of the additional plates they'd brought. "I'm going with this. It's closest." She shrugged and laughed. "How about you?"

He reached for a plate of eggplant something or other. He wasn't sure. "Does eggplant taste like egg?" He asked, never actually having tried it before. Brock put some on a plate and put the rest back. He worked some into his mouth and made a face.

"More like a sponge, I think. I don't know, I only tried it once and yep." She laughed. "That was the look I had." She took a bite of the lasagna and moaned happily, scooping some more onto her fork and holding it out to him with her other hand under it to catch anything that dripped. "But this is incredible. So, when you said this was your second chance..." Kara trailed off, not knowing where she was going with it. "I guess I'm not sure if you are thinking a fling or what you're going for?" She tilted her head curiously, smiling as he took the bite. "Good. Right?"

Brock swallowed the food she offered and nodded. "Yes, very." His face twisted into a frown and he shook his head. He poked at his eggplant. It was gross. He set it off to the side and took a plate of shrimp linguine. "A second chance to know you. That's all I want. Nothing in the way of disrespect, Kara," he said forking some of the food into his mouth. This time he growled a bit, it tasted so good.

"That I can do." Kara grinned and blushed at his growl, remembering the last time that she'd heard it. Reaching over to the next plate, she scooped a little shrimp scampi onto her plate and bounced happily when she tried it. "And just so you know, I'm enjoying the hell out of getting to know you, too." She grinned and pulled a roll from the covered basket and searched for the butter, finally finding it at the very end of the table. "Dad's honeyed mead would be perfect with this." She bit her lip, thinking about it.

"Mead? I tried it once. It was gross," he said making a face. Brock watched her for a moment as she ate. "You have butter on your chin, Cher." He gestured to his jaw, trying to show her where she had it. "I'm glad I haven't bored you to tears yet."

She wiped at her chin with the napkin. "You haven't tried Dad's private stock." She grinned and shook her head. "Far from bored. Intrigued is more like it. Did I get it?"

"Yes. And why is that?" He quirked his brow. "I'm sure Odin's is perfect. What I drank smelled like pig piss and old socks. I drank it on a dare." He ate more pasta and then spotted steak. "Oh, that looks fantastic. What is it?" He pointed at the large plate in the middle with steak swimming in something.

Kara eyed the platter. "I think that is the filet mignon, not sure what it's in." She thought for a moment before she answered. "I'm trying to figure out what it is about you that puts me at ease. It's hard to explain. I feel grounded and real

140

when I'm with you. Safe. Alive." She took another bite and chewed. "In all honesty, the only times that I've really been able to sleep since I've been back, have been with you. Yet, at the same time, every now and then when you give me a look, my stomach kinda flops, but in a good way." She blushed and sipped her beer. "I don't think I'm making sense or maybe I'm just too honest. I've had enough lies to last me a lifetime, and I'm not wasting time with them."

He eyed the plate of meat. "I feel the same, Kara. I feel comfortable and not like a big doof," Brock said and went for the plate of steak. He smelled it. "Bacon," he groaned. "Good gods! It's steak wrapped in bacon." He sounded almost turned on. He laughed at himself.

What?" Her eyes zeroed in on what had to be a foodgasm in the making. "We have got to try that!" If her mouth watered anymore, she was going to be drooling. "You do?" She smiled, more pleased than she probably should have been. "I'm glad. Have you talked to Dane yet?" She winced, not sure that she should talk about him or not.

Brock took some and passed her the plate. "No, I haven't. His truck was gone when I took out the bar trash this afternoon. I think he might need some time to do whatever he needs to do." He looked at the new meat thing in front of him, trying not to let it bother him that she was asking about her mate, ex-mate, or whatever he was. Brock wasn't sure. He cut it into pieces and then forked them into his mouth. He moaned. "Oh gods," he said forking more into his mouth. Juice dripped into his beard.

She followed his example and leaned back in her chair, closing her eyes and groaning happily. "This is giving sex a run for its money." She covered her mouth and laughed when she realized that she'd said it out loud. "I hope he's okay. Take it easy on him when he comes back. His memory is swiss cheese right now, and he's not going to remember some stuff. Like me. The divorce papers are going to confuse the hell out of him." She sighed and took another bite.

141

"Is that what you did? I was going to ask, but I didn't want to open wounds that I shouldn't."

Swallowing hard, Kara nodded. "The papers are why I was late. You saw how he was. The only thing I could do was take the memories that caused it. Unfortunately, his past with me was tangled up with them, so..." She trailed off and chewed as she stared at her plate.

"So, you took those too," Brock filled in for her, wincing at the gaping hole that would leave in his chest. He wasn't sure that he could have made that sacrifice if he were in her place. "Damn, Cher. I'm sorry."

She nodded again and sipped her beer, hoping to melt the lump in her throat.

"You're right about this being better than sex." Brock nodded in agreement and ate some more, trying to change the subject when he wanted to pull her into his arms. "I'm sure he's okay. I think he may just need some time to think and process everything." He looked at the rest of the food. "Do you believe that we'll make it?"

"Through this?" She looked at the food. "I hear that's one of the perks of being an adult. You don't have to finish your dinner before you can have dessert." She took another bite and chased it with a swallow of her beer. "I hope you're right." While it may be true that she'd never known the real Dane, she did want him to be okay. She had no ill will against him, just the demon spawn that had worn him like a cheap suit. The rest she had to figure out how to let go. "Tell me more about you, Brock. How did your family end up with portal duty?"

"True but I forgot that." He looked at the menu Becky had left with the last tray of food. "My mother's clan were the Keepers. When the last male member of her clan died, my parents took ownership of it. They weren't happy about it. My mother had other things in mind for us," he said tapping the dessert menu. "They have turtle cheesecake. What the hell is that?" He asked looking up at her.

142

She tried to see what he was reading, but the mounds of food were in the way. Kara moved her chair closer to him and leaned in to see what he was talking about. God, his scent. It was like coming home after too long away. What the fuck? She glanced up at him and then back at the menu. "Either it arrives in the half shell or is it like the chocolate candy with nuts and caramel? Apple crisp! We gotta get that."

"I hope not in the half shell. Apple crisp with ice cream. Is it bad I want to eat just for the pleasure of it?" Brock chuckled and pushed the menu to her so she could read it better. "So, tell me something about you that no one knows."

Kara grinned and didn't change her position when the menu came closer. She liked being near him. "Oh yes, ice cream," she groaned not sure how much more she could eat, but she was willing to give that a shot. "That nobody knows?" She thought about it. "That's tough, but there is this one thing." She eyed him and tried not to blush. "I kind of horde those carved animal sculptures that the Native Americans make. No joke. I have a storage unit full of them. No idea why I like them so much. Your turn." She bumped his shoulder with hers.

"Is that so?" Brock grinned, looking at her. "I make those just for shits and giggles. Well sometimes, for weddings, I get asked to do it. But now I know that if my stuff poofs, gremlins did not take it," he teased her. He liked her being close and not shying away from him.

Kara laughed and joked. "Yep, if they disappear, I'm probably the culprit." It was weird that being with him felt so natural. "And if you want something more personal and slightly embarrassing?" She chewed her lip, not sure that she should admit it or not, especially to him. "Your growl. Like you did this morning when you were waking up?" She blushed. "It makes me melt and fills my head with impure thoughts." She reached across the table for her beer. "Probably should have kept that to myself."

143

Brock smiled wide and said nothing. Becky reappeared and asked if they needed anything. "I think we'll try everything on the dessert menu. Box up the other food for us, except for the eggplant. Burn that. It's gross."

Becky apologized for him not liking it.

"I just don't think it's for us," Brock reassured her, reaching for his draft.

"And another of these please," Kara held up her Guinness. She watched as a small team of servers came to take away everything to doggy bag it. She glanced up at him when he didn't say anything and blushed a little darker. *Yep. She should have kept that under wraps.* "Throw me a lifeline and tell me something about you that no one knows, before I die of humiliation, please."

He thought for a moment. "I don't like the smell of coins," he said making a face after the table was clear. "Do you think that they think we're nuts?"

"Probably, but I don't care what they think. Coins?" Kara looked at him for a minute and then grinned. "So, if I want to hide something, I just need to cover it in change. Note made," she teased.

"Yes. Because the smell lingers. It's gross." He playfully pulled her hair.

Laughing, she reached up and tugged his beard in retaliation, pulling back a little when the urge to nip his jaw surprised her. *Yeah, that was a good way to scare the poor bear half to death.*

He growled at her and took the beer that Becky came back with. Brock held it up over Kara's head and teased, "How bad do you want this, Cher?" The servers returned with the desserts and eyed them like they were loons.

Kara closed her eyes at that growl. "Really, really bad." She opened her eyes and realized that he was talking about the beer. *Yep, that was smooth.* She smiled her thanks to the wait staff and reached blindly for her beer, making a face at Brock when he pulled it out of her reach.

He teased her a bit more before setting it down. "Well, thank you for not blasting me." He smiled and looked at the table. "Look at the diabetes on this table."

"I'm not going to blast the guy that comes to my rescue when I show up naked and wearing a toe tag." She snickered. "Yeah, never thought that would come up in dinner conversations, but bring on the sugar coma." Kara grinned, handing him a fresh bundle of silverware and dipping her finger into some whipped cream from one of the desserts to smear on the end of his nose.

He went cross-eyed looking at the smear. Then he licked it off with his tongue. "Not bad," he said looking at her. "Well, I'll keep that in mind if I upset you some time. So where to start?" He smelled honey cakes with fresh fruit. He beelined for the plate of that.

Kara laughed at his reaction and the fact that his bear was in control when it came to the honey. "With the comfort food," she groaned happily, spooning some of the apple crisp and ice cream into her mouth and leaning back in her chair, closing her eyes and moaning. "Now that is what I'm talking about."

Brock inhaled the cakes and realized he didn't leave any for her. "I'm sorry." He licked his lips savoring the honey on them.

Watching him lick his lips was a fine line between heaven and torture. The thoughts it put in her head and the way her stomach fluttered... Kara licked her lips, biting the lower one and looked down at what was on her plate. "No worries. I know better than to get between a bear and his honey," she teased.

Brock chuckled. "How is the apple crisp?" He asked looking for the turtle thing he saw on the menu. "None of this is turtle shaped."

"Delicious." She scooped up some of the apples and the crumble topping with her spoon, being sure to get a healthy dose of the soft vanilla ice cream and held it up for him. "I think they make their own ice cream. And you're

145

right, I think that might be it over there." She looked past the assortment of pie slices.

He ate the dessert from her spoon and moaned a bit, both at the taste and because sharing food was almost foreplay for a bear. He wondered if she knew. *Probably not*, he told himself, dismissing the idea. "That's wonderful." He followed her eyes to the turtle dessert. "Have you had it before? Another eggplant is not cool."

"I've had the candy, but not the cheesecake." She laughed and crooked her finger, waiting for him to lean in so she could wipe a drop of the ice cream from the hair over his lip.

He leaned in for it and his bear chuffed. "You don't like cheesecake, Cher?" He asked taking hold of the one that he assumed was turtle.

Kara shrugged and licked the ice cream off her thumb without thinking about it. "Honestly? The crust on the bottom is my favorite part, as long as it doesn't get soggy."

"Bones of your enemies, huh? Fe fi fo fum!" He said picking up his fork again getting ready to taste it.

"Something like that," Kara laughed. God if felt good to laugh again. Looking at him, she wondered what if could have been like if she hadn't followed Dane upstairs that night and had stayed at the bar talking to this sweet bear. She sighed and leaned back, sipping her beer and glancing around the room, biting her tongue against just laying it all out there. "Is it any good?"

He forked some into his mouth and shrugged. "Not bad. And the rest goes something about making bread. I don't think that applies to you, though, since a poor potato in your hands is C-4!"

Her jaw hung open, and she stared at him over her bottle. "You got jokes, bear?" Kara laughed.

Brock grinned and put some in her mouth as she laughed. "Try it. You'll like it." He said taking some of the pie closest to him.

146

Her brow arched at him stuffing some of the desert into her mouth. He was right, it was delicious. "Not the first time I've heard that line." Kara snorted.

He laughed. "I'm sure, Cher. What next? Between us, I have a pants issues right now." He leaned back and showed her his food belly.

"I'm stuffed too." Kara grinned and patted her stomach. "I don't know. We can call it a night, go find a way to work off what we ate or just sit around pantless for a while," she teased.

"Well, I'm all for pantless. You may have to roll me out of here." Brock waved Becky over and asked for the check. "Box all this up, too."

Kara wiggled her brows at him and grinned. "That was easier than I expected. My place or yours, Big Guy?"

He whistled at the check amount. "Yours," Brock said fishing his wallet out. "Let me know when no one is looking, please."

She gave him a confused look but played look out anyway. "Okay. Wait for it.... hold on... now... no, wait." Kara eyed the room. "Clear."

He ghosted all the to-go boxes away. "Okay, are you ready?"

She nodded and groaned as she stood up. "Yes. God, I'm too full." She reached across the table to pick up the flowers. There was no way that he could know that irises were her favorite, but that's what he'd brought her. She leaned over them to inhale the delicate sweet fragrance and smiled at him. "Do you know where we're going or should I drive?" She teased and took his hand.

Brock paid the bill and left a big tip. "Flying blind again." He laughed, following her outside after he got the door for her.

"Thank you." She looked up at the night sky and smiled back at him. "I like you being at my mercy." Tugging his hand, Kara led him around the corner, looking for a secluded spot to ghost them back to her apartment. "Ignore the mess. I haven't been here that much lately, and Dad has been leaving gifts." She eyed the stacked casks of mead that took up most of the area where her table was hidden and buried under it.

He looked around. "I have to say I'm a little letdown. I don't see any human skulls or anything like that. Tell the truth, you keep them in the back, right?"

Kara made a face at him and bit his shoulder, teasing, "I could show you, but I'd have to kill you."

Brock laughed. "I'm too full to die," he groaned "Really, it's a nice place,"

"Thanks. Make yourself comfortable, and I'll take advantage of this stockpile. Any chance ya'll could use some of this at The Pit? I'd like my table back." She grinned. "Pick a movie, and we can just chill and enjoy being fat." She grinned and stretched up to kiss his cheek.

"Okay. Maybe I could build you some shelves or something." He offered, realizing that his hand was resting on her hip. Brock pulled it away before he pulled her closer and fixed that mistake he'd made this morning in the billiards room, and went to look for a movie. Her collection was interesting.

"You'd do that for me?" Kara grinned over her shoulder and pulled down two glasses, filling them with the mead Dad had been kind enough to stick in the fridge for her. Picking them up, she carried them into the living room and sat down on the sofa, putting his on the coffee table, watching as he perused the options. "I warned you. Bad B horror flicks are my guilty pleasure."

"Course, Cher. You seem to need it." He laughed and picked out some cheerleader one. "I guess we can try this one. And why B movies?" He asked, handing her the DVD. " I don't see any Norse documentaries or any seasons of Vikings," he teased.

Kara stuck her tongue out at him and slid the movie into the blue ray player. "I don't know, really. I like things that are less polished and not pretending to be what they're

148

not." She looked at Brock over her shoulder and rolled her eyes at the mention of Vikings. "I saw it in person, and when they get things wrong," she made a face and dropped down beside him. "It's sad to see how they choose to interpret our history. Are you a fan?" She teased and leaned back on the cushions, toeing off her boots and tucking her feet under her, turning so she could see him better.

"No, I haven't watched it yet. I assumed since you liked bad movies you'd like bad television too." He got comfortable. "So, you don't think what's his name is hot?"

Kara arched a brow and tried to decide if she should be offended or not. "I don't know who you mean."

Brock laughed and picked up the mead from the table. "Sure, you don't, Cher." He sipped it and groaned. "Wow."

She blinked at him, having no idea what or who he was talking about, but shrugged it off. "You like, or you hate?" She wiggled closer to him and pressed play, tossing the remote onto the table. She really had no interest in the movie, but spending time with the bear, that was a different story. The timing was bad, but she was curious about the things he made her feel and he was good company.

"It's good," he said smiling at her. "Tell me about this movie. What's so special about it?" Brock looked at the liquid in the glass. "The mead I tried was a different color. Humans, I tell ya."

"Dad will be pleased that you like it." Kara looked at the television and shrugged. "Well, there is the driller killer. The drill is part of his guitar. An original idea. Other than that? Not much. Reminds me of simpler times, I think." She pulled a throw pillow onto her lap, feeling a little self-conscious about her weirdness. "Oh, and epically bad singing and dancing." She grinned and sipped from her glass.

His brow quirked as he imagined the scene she was talking about. "Interesting. A lot of boobs in this one? I ask because of cheerleaders and all." Brock joked and hoped that she didn't punch him for the comment. "What kind of television shows do you like, Cher?"

149

Kara laughed. "Yes, there are. So, there is a perk for you," she teased. "I don't watch a lot of TV. I mean The Walking Dead and Ink Master. Other than that?" She shrugged. "What about you? It's not fair that you know all of my embarrassing habits and I know none of yours."

Brock took another drink and thought for a moment. "Well, I like those shows also. I DVR a lot of stuff, and binge watch shows like Ice Road Truckers and Man vs. Wild. Manly stuff, you know." Brock pushed the hair out of his face. "Okay, I'll tell you something that you won't believe. Try not to laugh too hard when I say this. I loved watching Here Comes Honey Boo Boo. When it was on and that one show, with Hillbillies. Hollywood Hillbillies, or something like that."

She blinked at him, her lip twitching as she tried not to laugh. "Honey. Booboo." Kara lost her battle to control her laugh and dropped her head to his shoulder. "You're right, Babes. That one is hard to believe, but I feel we're on slightly more equal ground now."

Brock nodded and drank some more. "See? Don't let the hair fool you. I'm a closet dork. And anything remotely redneck or inbred? I dig it. I just do it secretly. Not very classy, I know, but we all have our secret shames." He said looking at the tv screen. "So, do they get killed when their doing that pyramid thing? That would be pretty good!"

"Sadly, no. It would be good, though." She glanced up at him. "I like your dorky side, just saying, Big Guy. And sadly, after the last few days, you probably know more about me than anyone else." She snorted and leaned back. That was sad as hell when she said it out loud.

"Really?" He was shocked. "I figured you being with Dane, he'd know all of that? Sadly, I can say the same thing. Look at us, sharing and growing together, like real people." Brock laughed thinking the mead was starting to kick in. He felt warm and a little floaty.

"Yeah, well, not everything is what is seems, I guess." Kara finger combed her hair back and grinned at him. "We are real people, either that or the beginning of a bad joke... A bear shifter and a Viking walk into a bar...."

He chuckled. "That's gotta be a tall damn bar for us to walk into."

Kara laughed. "I want more. What other secrets are you hiding in there?" She patted his chest with her palm.

"I don't know, Cher. That's a large can of worms to open. It's your turn, I think." Brock drained his glass.

She twitched her lips back and forth thinking. "Refill?" She stalled with a grin, getting up and snagging her glass from the coffee table. "Something no one knows? I've been thinking about stasis a lot lately." She shrugged, playing it off like it was nothing.

"Oh?" He held out the glass to her, suddenly feeling too sober. "Why stasis? The theory of it or what? Because I have some thoughts."

Kara took the glass and went to the kitchen to refill them both before returning. Shrugging, she sat beside him again and held out his glass. "Ninety-nine percent of the time, I feel like I'm drowning and... Yeah. I don't know. The big bad Viking is having trouble coping, I guess." She shrugged and tried to smile. "What are your thoughts?"

Brock remembered seeing her dead body in the park and the feeling it gave him. Now that he knew her, it would be worse. "Cher, you've been through a lot, and the fact you're not in a corner crying or off on a killing spree, is a miracle. I personally think I would have ended the world, just for the fuck of it." He took the glass in one hand and placed his free hand on her leg gently.

"A lot of the time, I'm a breath away from doing either of those, or both," Kara admitted. "The only time that I'm not is when I'm with you. The rest?" She shook her head. "I don't have a place that I fit here anymore or a purpose. I feel useless and lost."

He thought for a moment, trying to find the words to make her feel better. "Well, maybe you're just here to learn about yourself and to have some place to just be Kara, not

151

Viking Warrior Princess. I mean, would Odin let you stay here if you weren't needed for one reason or another?" Brock wasn't sure if that came out right, but he hoped it did.

"Yeah, Maybe. Or maybe I've learned the lesson I needed to, and he's waiting for me to catch up. I don't know who I am anymore." Kara let her head fall back on the cushions and stared at the ceiling, hating the tightness of her chest and the lump in her throat. "Sorry, I'll zip it."

"You shouldn't define yourself, by the person you're with. You are still you. You just need time to process everything."

"Well, that's easy. I'm not with anyone. Hell, Dane's been dead for a decade, even if it was only days here. Him breathing again doesn't change that. It's not just Dane. I did a lot of shitty things that still haunt me, while I was dead."

Brock downed his mead and burped loudly. "Well damn, I'm sorry. See? I'm as classy as they come, Cher." He hoped it would make her laugh and change the mood that had started to creep in like little black rain clouds.

Kara arched a brow at the burp and grinned. "How fucked up is it that I'm a little turned on by that?" She teased.

He roared with laughter. "Really Cher?!" Brock looked at her a moment trying to keep a straight face. It didn't work, though. He lost it laughing.

She grinned and blushed. "Hey! I know it ain't right. I was just saying..." She covered her face with her hand and laughed.

"Well, that proves it. And I gotta say, I like that. Oddness is an attractive quality. I mean, I've been making a list in my head of things, but the being turned on by burps just made it to the number one slot."

"You have a list? You've gotta share that with me." She handed him her glass seeing that his was empty.

He took the glass and smiled. "Sorry Cher, that's classified. Just know that they are all good things when it comes to you." Brock looked at the glass. "You trying to get

152

me drunk? Between you and I, I'm starting to feel it. Or maybe not feel. My face is a tad numb."

Kara shrugged and grinned. "Maybe, a little. For purely selfish reasons." She reached up and stroked his cheek. "You feel fine to me," she teased. "I will break you, Bjorn. I have ways of making you talk."

"I don't know, I'm stubborn. It'll take more than some liquor to make me break." He leaned into her hand, not able to help himself. "Selfish reasons, huh?"

She leaned closer and rubbed her nose against his softly, groaning at the heat of his skin and that damn scent. "Purely selfish and I am prepared to use more than liquor, to make you talk."

Brock smirked a bit. "Is that so? Do your worst. I'm sure it won't have any effect on me." He had thought about her being this close many times. In his dreams, this is the part where reality came crashing in on him. So, in his mind, Brock was holding his breath. Part of him thought maybe he should go and not take advantage of her in this state. It wasn't very gentlemanly, but this was one of those once in a lifetime moments, or it sure as hell felt like one.

"Really?" Kara opened her eyes to look into his and sucked in her breath. Him being this close made her heart pound and her stomach flutter. She moved so that she was closer and leaning against him. Cupping his face between her palms she brushed her lips over his, tracing his lower lip with the tip of her tongue and sucking it into her mouth to nip it lightly.

A soft growl came from his chest as her tongue touched his lip. Brock didn't move a muscle. He was dreaming this. That was what was happening. The moment he moved, the alarm would go off or his family would be banging on his door.

Kara shivered as he growled, goose bumps breaking over her skin. But he sat there, ramrod stiff and not moving a muscle. Hell, she wasn't sure he was even breathing. She pulled back and looked at him. "Do you want me to stop?"

153

Brock shook his head no. He didn't realize that he was holding his breath until then. He let the air out of his lungs slowly. "Please don't."

Grinning, Kara swung her leg over his to straddle his hips with her knees. "Thank fuck. I've wanted to do that since this morning." She pushed his hair back from his face with her hands and kissed him again, her lips curling up when she felt his breath. He was breathing, and that was good. "Kiss me, Brock," she whispered against his lips, not sure if he was scared to death or not into this.

He reached up and cupped her face gently. Brock stared at her for a long moment, trying to memorize her face and the way everything felt at this moment. He kissed her softly at first, then deepened it. If he was dreaming, he might as well enjoy it before the alarm went off. He let his hands leave her face and slide through her silken hair.

Kara's heart hiccupped when he finally touched her and pulled back to look at her. The reverent expression on his face shattered something in her, and for the first time since she'd come back she didn't feel cold, and a wave of warmth washed over her. Moaning when he kissed her, she felt it with her entire body. Never in her life had she felt something so deeply, and it was just a kiss. Who was he and what magic did he possess, that he could do this to her? Kara didn't care, as long as he didn't stop. The whimper that rolled over her tongue when his lips demanded more surprised her and made her blush and tangle her hands in his hair to keep him with her. Somewhere in the back of her mind she almost expected him to disappear, like smoke through her fingers.

Brock kissed her with all the passion and love for her that he held. He let his hands drift slowly down her back. His heart raced, and he could feel his blood start to boil.

The world fell away. She knew nothing put the feel of his mouth on hers, his scent, his touch and the burning ache that was growing and blocking out everything else. Kara pressed against him harder. She couldn't seem to get close enough. Her pulse hammered and she forgot how to breathe. Was this what drowning felt like? Her hands released his hair and slid down to cup his neck, scraping her nails lightly over the back of it.

A growl vibrated in his chest as she scraped his neck and his bear gave his vote of approval for what was happening. Brock laid back on the couch. Her weight on him felt good. He pushed her hair back so he could see her face.

That growl did her in, making her temperature spike and her skin goose bump and tingle. Kara let him pull her down with him, loving the way he felt beneath her. Solid, warm and a little dangerous. She pinned her lower lip with her teeth when he looked at her like he was searching for something. "What are you thinking?" Her voice was barely a whisper as she met his gaze, turning her head to brush her lips against his hand when her hair fell free, and he swept it back again.

Brock blinked at her for a moment, he wasn't thinking, honestly. "I'm waiting for my alarm to go off," he whispered staring up at her.

Kara arched a brow and grinned, shaking her head and dipping to nip at his jaw and nuzzle his neck. "Like a warning alarm or a wake-up call?" She teased and tugged his earlobe with her teeth. "No one's coming, and you're not asleep."

"Are you sure, Cher?" He whispered. Brock wasn't too sure that he wasn't still in his bed, dreaming this.

Lifting her head, she stroked his face and nodded, noticing how her hair pooled and mixed with his. There was something in his sapphire eyes that squeezed her heart and vacuumed the air from her lungs. Kara opened her mouth to speak, but all she could do was nod.

Brock kissed her again and held her tight to him. He had a lot of females that drooled over him, but he never let himself take it to this point, He hadn't been with a female in years, and Kara made his groin ache with lust. Losing himself in the sensation, he cupped her ass. Her scent was all he could think of, and he didn't care if it was wrong.

155

Damn, he was good. The way his tongue swirled and fought with hers set her nerve endings on fire. She moaned against his lips when his hands covered her ass, holding her against him more firmly and reminding her how hard he was. Holy hell that was a turn on and she remembered what it felt like to be alive.

Kara clung to him just as tightly, afraid that if she let go, he would disappear and be just another dream meant to torture her. "Don't let go." The words were out before she knew that she'd said them. "Please," but the please came from the darkest corners of her soul, and she knew that this bear had power. Not just that his magic could level a city block, but he could save her in a way that no one else could.

"I won't, Cher," Brock whispered, rubbing her back. "Thank you," he whispered a bit lower.

Kara sighed her relief and pressed her lips to his neck, closing her eyes and feeling his pulse under them. Strong and steady, like him when she was feeling anything but. She lifted her head to see his face. "For what?"

"Taking a chance on me and letting me get to know you," he murmured. "I know it's a big thing for you to let people in and close. Then again that's people in general, but still, I know what it means for you."

Kara smiled softly and was a little choked up. Not just that he understood that about her, but that he said it out loud, wanting her to know. She lifted her head to brush her lips over his softly. "Thank you for making it easy, Brock." She prayed silently that he wouldn't regret it.

"No need to thank me, Cher." He kissed her softly and squeezed her tighter.

She grinned. "Your wrong. It's important that you know that you're not disposable. Not to me." Kara closed her eyes as his arms tightened and she felt solid and grounded. "You are one of a kind."

Brock didn't know what to say. He just enjoyed being there with her and for her to say something like that, meant the world to him. He wished that he'd taken the time before, to get to know her and hadn't let fear cloud it all.

Kara smiled and played with the thin chain around his neck. She sighed and nuzzled him, growling softly as she inhaled his scent and felt her body relax completely and melt to mold to his, reminding her that he was all male and he made her ache in the sweetest way. "I don't want to mess this up, whatever it is. But I'm not going to lie. I want you, but I don't want you to feel like you have to do anything that you don't want to. Ever. I know I'm a complicated mess. I couldn't bear it if I screw up what I have with you or if I hurt you."

He didn't know what to say. "I want you too. I have for a long time. But I mean, not just for tonight. I don't think what we've started here can be screwed up. I'd be honored if you were mine. I know I am now just becoming your friend, Kara." Brock stroked her back, not wanting to do anything stupid like the falling off the bed incident.

"No. Not just for a night. The more time I spend with you, the more necessary you are, and I don't mean the physical stuff." She crossed her arms on his chest and pushed up to look into his face, dragging herself up his body a little, and groaning at how good he felt against her. "But, if we can't screw it up, then what's stopping us?" She rubbed the bridge of her nose along his bearded jaw and dropped soft kisses along his neck.

"Nothing," Brock whispered and groaned as she kissed his neck. "I am yours, Kara. I have been since the moment I set eyes on you. I want nothing more than for you to claim me." He moved under her. His long legs were hanging over the couch, and he tried to toe off his boots, but they were stuck, and he could feel the back of his legs going to sleep. He growled his frustration.

Closing her eyes as his words made them water, Kara lowered her lips to his again, raising her head when she felt him start to fidget. A grin curled her lips at his growl. The sofa was not built for someone his size, and he was too sweet to complain. Kara kissed him again and pushed herself up until her feet were on the floor, mourning the loss of his body's heat against hers. "Maybe we should move somewhere more comfortable?"

"If you want, Cher." He said moving his legs into a normal sitting position. They were tingling with a pins and needles sensation, but Brock stood up anyway. "After you," he said holding his hand out to her.

"I do." Biting her lip, Kara took his hand and led him to her bedroom, hoping that she hadn't left anything embarrassing out. She glanced back when he walked very slowly. "Second thoughts?"

Brock shook his head no. "Just be gentle with me. I'm fragile," he joked, watching her as she bit her lip. He couldn't believe how sexy and cute it was.

She laughed and rolled up on the tips of her toes to kiss him. "I thought I warned you earlier that I would break you?" Kara placed her hand on his chest and looked up at him, putting her heels back on the floor. "Do you know what it means when my kind claim someone?"

He honestly didn't. "No, but I've heard stories about slavery and sacrifice."

Kara arched a brow and growled. "That god damn TV show." She shook her head. "It's nothing so demeaning, and I'm the only one that feels the sacrifice. When I say the words, I give you a little piece of me. If you are ever in danger, no matter where you are, I can find you. Well, even if you're not at risk. In a way, I am enslaved to you, by choice. I've never done it before, and only you can choose to break it."

Brock blinked for a moment. "Well, I'll leave that up to you. I can tell, you love that show a lot," he teased and smirked.

She stuck her tongue out at him. "Smart ass, bear." She shook her head and reached up to cup his face. "It's important to know that you're not stuck. If you release me, there are no hard feelings, but I will watch over you and any

158

children you sire and on and on, as long as I'm able." Kara eyed him, trying to read what was going on in his head. "But enough of the doom and gloom." Her hands caressed his face and slid down his neck to his chest. Pinning her lower lip between her teeth, she blushed and reached down to pull her shirt over her head and tossed it into the chair in the corner of her bedroom.

He was about to thank her when she started peeling off clothes. His heart skipped a beat, and his jeans suddenly felt too tight. Brock removed his shirt and threw in the same direction that she threw hers. He thought about toeing off his boots again, but he remembered that he'd double knotted them. They would not be slipping off anytime soon. He wanted to be smooth, but all he could think was that he was going to fall off something again and make another super manly noise. He'd already done that in his own room, no less. The horrors that could happen here, in hers? He ghosted his boots off and wrapped his arms around her waist.

Kara groaned her appreciation of him shirtless and again when her bare skin touched his, her skin buzzing as though tiny static charges were going off everywhere they touched. She let her hands stroke his sides, grinning when the skin and muscles beneath twitched and jumped. "Don't laugh, but I'm nervous." She tilted her head back to look at him timidly and stretched up to suck on his lower lip. God, she felt tiny next to him, not something that she was used to, but damn, she liked it. Nothing was sexier than a male you thought could take you in a fair fight, not for her kind.

The growl started in his chest. Brock normally didn't let females put him in this position. His blood boiled and his jeans were crushing him. He kissed her softly, though his bear wanted to be rough with her. She made the animal he was, come alive in a way he wasn't used to.

Kara closed her eyes and shuddered as his growl vibrated through her chest and caused bolts of current to race up her spine. "I love when you do that," she whispered against his lips. It was too damn hot in here and it was his fault. So were her growing wetter by the second panties and the way her core clenched and ached with need and anticipation.

"Do you?" He growled again and chuckled when her knees shook and she nodded. Grinning, he drank her in with his eyes. He could smell her arousal and the animal in him had to have her. Leaning down to pull her against him and claim her mouth, Brock ghosted away the rest of their clothes before he ripped them off her. He couldn't stand anything keeping them apart. He needed to feel the softness of her skin against his. Driven by his bear, but fighting for control, he walked her backward to her large bed covered in furs and skins. For a moment, he wondered if there were any bear skins on there, but only for a moment. Picking her up, he laid her on the bed carefully. As her hair fanned out behind her, he fought the urge to bury his face in it. Crawling onto the bed, his fingers danced over her skin, wanting to touch every part of her.

Being carried was out of her comfort zone. Picked up and thrown down, sure, but this was done with care, as if he was afraid of hurting her. Her heart constricted in her chest, and she kept her eyes on his face when he joined her on the bed. Biting her lower lip to stifle the soft moan that rolled up her throat, Kara reached out and cupped his face, rubbing his lip with her thumb as her other hand explored his bare skin, surprised at how soft it was. She lifted her knee to run her toes down his leg. Growling softly, she captured his lips, nipping and sucking on them and his tongue. "I love how you taste," she whispered, tasting him again.

Brock smiled and kissed her, sucking her tongue into his mouth gently. He got comfortable, lowering his weight over her, and propping himself up on his elbows. He kissed her jaw then her neck, nipping her collar bone.

She grinned and tangled one hand in his hair and let the other explore the hard planes of his back. She jumped at

160

the nip and moaned softly as his lips burned a trail over her skin, erasing her nervousness and awakening needs that had been ignored for too long. Arching her back, rhythmically she stroked his hot and hard cock between them with her belly as her nails dug into his back, pulling him closer.

He growled against her collarbone. Brock slid his hand between her thighs and gently teased her core with his fingertips. She was slick and ready for him, making his mouth water and his bear growl. He looked down her body as he touched her and then back to her face with reverence, expecting her to tell him to stop.

Kara gasped and tightened her leg's grip on his, opening to him and covering the hand at her core with hers. Her eyes fluttered shut and her body arched into his touch. After such a long time of feeling nothing but pain and exhaustion, every tender brush of his fingers against her skin felt magnified. Her skin burned and threatened to devour her, heat growing and swirling through her until every nerve ending begged for him. And the look in his eyes? That shattered any doubt that this was right. "Please, don't stop."

His eyes narrowed, not sure that he'd heard her right, but the yes, burned in her azure eyes with passion and lust. It was for him and him alone, Brock Navarro. His chest felt like it was going to burst with the love he felt for her and the anxiety drained from him. His smile grew, knowing that she wanted him. "I won't, Kara. Not until you tell me to." Gently, he slipped a finger into her wet core, growling at the heat and the wetness that closed around him tightly.

She reared up and kissed him hard and nipped his lip. "Gods, what you and your growl do to me." She moaned against his lips and released his hand to curl her fingers around his length, squeezing and sliding her thumb around the tip, licking her lips when she felt him jerk and thicken in her palm. His skin was soft over the hardness beneath, and she bit her lip as she felt his heartbeat throbbing in her palm.

Brock growled again when he felt her hand on his cock. Gliding over his skin. Squeezing. The light scrape of her nails over his tip that wept. Chills raced down his spine. Muscles tightened. His sack stuttered. Brock's entire body, down to the last hair, burned to make her his. He added another finger, loving the way she felt around them. "Is that so, Cher?" He whispered, feeling himself harden to the point that it hurt, but he wasn't about to just force himself on her.

Kara shuddered. The mix of his growl and his fingers unraveled her control. "Oh, god yes," she hissed, rocking against him and stroking his cock in time with his fingers sliding inside her. Her hand squeezed tighter around his hot and hard cock, needing to feel Brock push deep inside her and claim her wet, aching core. Feral, Kara lost herself in the heat consuming her, knowing only Brock and the need to have him, threatened to break her beyond repair. A desperate whimper tore free of her throat. "Don't be shy." She nipped his jaw and captured his mouth possessively. Tearing her lips from his before she lost her mind, Kara met Brock's unsure eyes. "I want this," she panted, tightening her fingers as they slid over his rock hard shaft. "I want you, Brock."

His bear roared in answer to her words. Her voice thick with lust and the heaving of her chest brought a smile to Brock's lips and erased his doubt that she wanted him. Meeting her eyes, Brock licked his lips, nodded and pulled his fingers from her slowly, growling at the moistness that glimmered on his fingers. He moved his hand to cover hers, groaning at the bite of her nails against his shaft. "Guide me in, Cher," he whispered into her ear. He didn't want to do anything to ruin the moment. The closer his tip got to her core, the more he felt himself jerk in her hand. He'd never felt this way before. It was truly a dream come true. Brock wasn't sure why the gods had granted him this chance, but he was forever grateful, even if it was all he got.

She was having trouble keeping still, her core throbbed, slick and begging for him. She shivered as his breath tickled her ear and her chest swelled at his words that told her that he would not take what was not given. Kara raised her head to see between them, her breath caught in her throat as his fingers wrapped around hers and he slid her hand over him in another long stroke, moaning against her neck. He was beautiful and seeing the head of his cock spear through and retreat in their hands was erotic as fuck. Muscles flowed and flexed under her hand on his back as he pulled his hips back, giving her a new appreciation for the brute strength of this male as he lowered himself for her to position him to enter her. Kara's body jumped, and she whimpered a curse when the hot tip brushed over her clit and she almost lost it. Biting her lip, she rolled her hips, her breath stuttering as she slid him through her folds to cover his tip in her juices. Shaking with anticipation, Kara held the blunt head against her and lifted herself, moaning his name when she felt him nudge her open.

Brock lifted his head to see that she was ready and rocked his hips into her slowly. A growl vibrated in his chest as he sunk into her inch my inch. Her heat burned, gripping him snugly. He closed his eyes and stopped for a moment to just savor how she felt and let her body adjust to having him inside. Brock started with a slow pace, going deep with each thrust. He felt himself dancing dangerously on the edge. She felt better than he'd dreamed she would. "Kara," He moaned her name putting his face on her neck.

Kara gave a husky moan, watching him fill her slowly. Her walls stretching to accommodate his size stung, just enough to heighten the pleasure and almost send her tumbling over the edge on the first thrust. She whimpered his name stroking his back and ass as she curled her hips against his, meeting each surge. "God, you're perfect," she whispered, pulling his lips to hers and kissing him passionately, feeling herself begin to shatter and her core tighten and pulse around him. "Brock," she panted.

163

He rocked his lips faster, feeling that she was close to breaking. He growled again as he felt himself right there with her, but he wanted to feel her break first. To hear the sounds she would make and know that he was the cause. His bear growled its approval.

Her head jacked back. Kara was so close that it hurt and then he sunk into her again. She whimpered and felt her tightly coiled body explode. She was spiraling. Clinging to him. Only aware of him. His scent and his warmth wrapped around her as her body pulsed and vibrated from the pleasure that continued to build with each wave. "Fuck, Brock!" She screamed and bit his shoulder to stop herself from screaming it again. Nothing had prepared her for this, this never ending, crashing orgasm that would not let her go.

Brock held on as Kara bucked under him. He thrust deep and felt his cock kick. "God!" Her core pulsed around him, tightening, sucking him deeper and milking him as she came. He growled his own pleasure and fought against her dragging him over the edge with her. His body was on fire. His skin goose bumped at her touch and her bite. He growled softly.

Forcing herself to stop biting before she broke his skin, Kara feathered her fingertips over his sides and tried to remember how to breathe as his cock slid snugly against the walls of her core so deep that it made her tremble. God, nothing was supposed to feel like this. Every cell was vibrating and drowning in the incredible sensation of him moving inside her. Cupping his face in her hands, Kara pulled his mouth to hers to stop herself from saying something that she shouldn't, something that she couldn't take back and would ruin everything. She arched into him, meeting his rhythm effortlessly, as though they had always been like this. She wanted to feel him break, to see his face. Kara closed her eyes and growled at the thought as her body pulsed, milking him and pulling him in deeper.

164

As they kissed, he growled again at the feeling of her tightening around him. He wasn't sure if he should stop or keep going. He slowly thrust into her pulling almost all the way out and rocking back in again. "Gods," he mumbled against her lips. His mind was swimming with pleasure. He was drunk with it.

"Yes," She gasped, as another wave of bliss swept through her, tightening her hands in his hair. The skin between her shoulder blades tingled and burned. Her brows popped in surprise when she realized what was about to happen and she didn't think she could control it. Curling one leg around his hips she reared and threw her weight to roll him onto his back and trap him between her thighs.

"I'm sorry," she whispered, capturing his lips and mimicking the long stroke, almost pulling free, before sinking over him again. "Please don't freak out, I don't know how to stop it." Kara barely got the words out before she cried out and her wings sprouted from her back, spreading wide and then curling around them.

At first, Brock thought that she'd changed her mind or that he'd done something wrong. He braced himself to be bolted or run through. His pulse pounded and it took him a moment to realize that she was apologizing. For what? His brain stopped working when she demanded his lips and moved on him. Fuck, she felt so good.

His brow arched when he felt something brush his arms and thighs. Cracking one eye, he growled at the white wings that shielded them from the world, leaving only him and her. It was sexy as hell and one more thing that made her like no other. Growling, he kept the same pace, his hands on her hips pushing her down to cover him completely. "It's okay, Cher. They're perfect, like you."

A smile played at Kara's lips as she watched his face, seeing only acceptance and passion. She froze this moment in her mind to save forever. It was perfect and allowed her to give herself over to him completely, even though her wings had never appeared against her will, and she didn't know what it meant. His hands and the way he moved, demanded her full attention and pulled her out of her head. She lifted her chest, pushing against his with her hands to sink back and take all of him. She moaned his name, loving how it felt on her lips.

Brock grinned when he felt her relax and come back to him. She was breathtaking. An angel blessing him with the ride he'd never dare dream of, not like this. Once would never be enough for him after this. The fantasy had been strong, but this was addicting, and now he wanted nothing more than to please her and leave her too tired to kick him out of her bed. If he was lucky, this wouldn't be the last time.

Kara didn't miss the shadow that misted across Brock's perfectly chiseled features. She leaned down to kiss him and whispered into his ear. "Don't hold back. You can't do anything wrong. I want you, Brock. All of you or nothing."

Brock grunted as her words stirred the bear in him. He thrust into her with a primal need he'd never felt before. Even if he had wanted to, he couldn't stop. His body wasn't listening, high on the pleasure that he hadn't imagined possible. His heart hammered as fear and adrenaline pulsed through him. His body shook, and he had to fight his bear for control as he teetered on the verge of shifting and coming at the same time. He didn't want to hurt her or to have his bear take over and ruin everything. Her wings were still folded around them, trapping the energy that radiated from her and the smell of their lovemaking. It made it hard for him to focus and stay in control.

Whimpering his name when he let himself go, even if not completely, Kara's body felt like it was blowing apart. Lacing her fingers with his, she braced her wings for leverage and lost herself in everything he made her feel. Her breath froze in her lungs, and her core squeezed him tightly, strangling the curse she barked into a mangled yelp.

166

He felt his form waiver from human to bear and back when he finally fell over the edge again. A roar of her name filled the room, and his body shook from the force of it.

A smile broke over her face, and her chest swelled. Kara couldn't believe that he'd dropped his guard like that and she was surprised that he'd done it with her. His roar made the framed art on the walls rattle, and the force of his release rocked her, shattering her and pushing her over the edge to join him. "God. Brock." She panted, squeezing his hands and leaning down to lick a bead of sweat that was about to run over his collar bone.

He panted hard and felt sweat running down his chest. "Cher," he whispered.

Grinning, Kara lowered herself to nip his lower lip and then sucked away the sting. "Holy. Hell."

"Are you satisfied?" Brock asked softly.

She nodded and tried to catch her breath. "That was…" She shook her head, not having the words. "You?" She looked at her wings and blushed. "That never happened before. I'm sorry."

"Yes, very. Don't apologize." Brock nuzzled her and ghosted himself beside her, not wanting to hurt her wings.

Kara stretched out on her stomach and pushed herself up to brush her lips over his. "Please, tell me that you can stay?"

He nodded, still trying to collect himself. "My body will not allow me to move, even if you threatened my life, Cher," he said, wishing he wasn't so sweaty.

Kara grinned and snuggled against him. "You're safe and good." She touched his face, a bit in awe of him. "I like having you here." Mischief flashed in her eyes as a smirk clung to her lips. "I think I saw your bear, for just a second."

He blushed and cleared his throat. "That has never happened to me before. I'm sorry if it weirded you out."

She shook her head no. "Never be sorry. If I have you, I want the real you, not a cheap imitation." She grinned and kissed him, sighing her relief when her wings retracted back

167

inside her shoulder blades. "I guess we both had a first or two."

Brock nodded. "Well, I am yours. And I hope we share many more firsts," he said holding her to him.

Kara nodded and laced her fingers with his, pulling his hand closer to brush her lips over his knuckles. "We will, if you'll have me." She glanced up at him feeling like a dorky teenager.

"Yes, Kara." He squeezed her hand. A yawn started to slip from his lips. He closed his mouth to cut it off.

"You're tired." She stroked his jaw and smiled softly. "Sleep, Babes. I'll be here when you wake up."

"I'm sorry, Cher. Long day and great company." He kissed her head and closed his eyes. It did not take long before he was fast asleep.

She felt his skin sprout fur and continued stroking and curling her fingers in it, breathing in his scent. She laid awake for a while, thinking about what he was offering her. A chance for a life that wasn't empty and meaningless and another chance to have her heart ripped out of her chest and run over by a bus while she watched. Gaia's note and her words drifted across Kara's barely conscious mind. *Don't give up.*

Brock growled in his sleep, and Kara felt the shiver bone deep. That was all the answer that she needed. Sighing and snuggling into his body a little more, Kara allowed herself to drift off.

Chapter 21

Bree couldn't shake the feeling that something wasn't right. She hadn't seen Dane in days, and that made her restless. He hadn't come to pick up his paycheck or gone to the regular weekend poker game that the guys played. She worried that she was somehow responsible for him feeling the need to avoid everyone.

Slipping on her jacket, Bree decided to put an end to this, or at least tell him to stop being an ass. Maybe she'd get lucky and find him out in the employee parking lot, working on his bike or something. It was an idiotic idea, but she had to try.

Glancing around to double check that none of her brothers were following her, she snuck into the alley where the dumpsters were. Unless there was trash to take out, no one ever came out this way. She sighed and looked around, thinking she heard one of her brothers as the door closed behind her. Bree waited, but none of them appeared. Maybe it was an alley cat or a giant rat. She shivered and her skin crawled. She hated rats.

Bree skirted the dented green dumpster, staying as far away from it as the narrow walkway allowed, hoping to hear Dane's usual singing, humming or tapping. Eying the door and dumpster over her shoulder, she turned the corner into the parking lot. Crap. Nothing but employee vehicles. Dane's spot was taken by one of the bus boys. She couldn't remember the human's name, But Dane was going to kick the guy's ass if he kept that up.

Gore waited. The energy signature of the one Ty wanted was inside the stucco and brick building. Not the princess, but the one that would deliver her. Sighing, he looked at his watch, again and flicked away a speck of dried blood from its previous owner. Only five minutes had passed since the last time he'd checked. Sighing, he shook his head. It would be so much easier to just go inside and take the female, but his orders were clear. Wait and grab but do not kill it or break it too much.

His head tilted to the side as a new scent cut through the stench of rotting garbage, and he heard a door click. Stretching his wings, he flexed them before the harder flap that lifted him into the air. Gore remained hidden from sight, the only sign of his presence was the subtle wind from his wings. It made the trash bags in the dumpster shift and rattle.

Gore watched the female go down the alley. A cold smile curled at his lips exposing fangs. It was the one that had helped the lion and the Princess. Gore snorted at the pet name. Ty had made him pay dearly for the loss of the Viking bitch, even though he'd played no part in her escape. He followed his mark down the alley and into a parking lot.

It was the female bear's fault that he'd been forced to suffer and he wanted nothing more than to take every lash out of her hide. He could snap her neck right now and leave her there for her family to find. His smile grew wider. It was tempting, but not worth what Ty would do to him this time. He watched her curiously as she seemed to search for something.

Bree's mind wandered. She wondered if she could use her training to seek Dane out, using his aura and scent. She'd been taught the mechanics of how everything worked, but she was still learning how to harness the power and use it in the real world. Bree crossed her arms over her chest and stared at Dane's parking space.

The hair on the back of her neck bristled. She could feel the weight of eyes boring into her. Bree turned in a circle and saw nothing, but the feeling grew stronger. "Who's there?" She called out and snorted at her stupidity. *Like a serial killer is going to answer, 'Hey, over here! Can I interest you in some fava beans and a nice Chianti?'* Bree tried to push the feeling out of her head and focus on Dane's scent.

Closing her eyes, she opened herself and listened to the spirits around her. 'Can you help me find the soul I seek?'

'Run little one,' a spirit answered.

Bree's eyes snapped open. 'Run. Why?' She asked silently.

'There is something evil near.'

There's always evil near, she thought. Bree dismissed the warning and kept walking through the parking lot.

'It follows,' the spirit warned.

Bree stopped and called out again. She waited, but no one answered. Her nostrils flared, annoyed that someone was playing games or the spirits were messing with her for fun. They did that sometimes, she'd been warned. Pushing her hands out and weaving them to stir the still air, Bree cast a spell that was supposed to force death and evil to show itself. Nothing happened. She growled. A bright red flash made her jump and gasp. The spirits were right. "Whoever you are, do not come any closer," she warned and tried to sound bad ass.

Gore stalked the one Ty wanted, planning to watch and wait for the bear to lead him to the Viking. The first time she asked who was there, he said nothing. He held true to form with the second, but something had spooked her. He sniffed his shoulder but smelled nothing that would have given him away. His head tilted when she threw her hands out and moved them like she was playing an invisible game of cat's cradle.

171

A wave of something came from them that sent a charge through him, crawling inside his pores and burning painfully. He growled. Was the little bitch trying to infect him with the psychic version of the clap or some shit? He dropped the camouflage that bent the light around him and let himself be seen. "Hello, Bear. For a little thing, you have some pretty powerful tricks. Maybe they'll come in handy when I'm draining you dry." He rushed her and grabbed her by the neck. She let out a strangled growl. He laughed. "But I doubt it."

Bree spun around when she heard someone talking to her. Her eyes bugged when she saw the demon appear in front of her. She raised her hands to blast him with her magic. He was too quick for her. She struggled to break free as he lifted her feet off the cracked pavement. Bree clawed at the hand around her throat. The air in her lungs burned. The tendons stretched. Bones quivered, on the verge of shattering under the pressure of his grip. Darkness surrounded her as the voices of the dead filled her head.

Gore was about to choke her to death when Ty's voice echoed in his head, demanding that Gore not kill her. "What? Why not?"

'Because I fucking said so. Bring her to me,' Ty ordered.

Gore snarled and argued. "She'd be of better use elsewhere. Her power could be useful."

Ty growled 'Fine do whatever you want with her but do not kill her. She's going to bring the princess to me.'

Gore smiled. "I don't think this will kill her." He ghosted the smooth metal cylinder into his free hand and eyed the beveled needle as he licked the tip of a fang with his tongue. Honestly? He wasn't sure if it would or not. It was a prototype, and they hadn't begun testing on shifters yet. No time like the present. He jammed the tip of the needle into her shoulder, laughing when he felt the metal grow cold as the CO_2 exploded and shot the new serum into the bear. He raised her to watch her face, hoping that there would be some visible sign that she'd been infected, but was disappointed and dropped the empty dart to clatter on the tar.

Bree's fight or fight reflex struggled to the surface as she panicked. She screamed out to her brothers through mindlink as the demon seemed to be talking to himself. 'Help me!' She managed to get out, hoping that Bart, Brock, Brax, and Beyer would hear her. She silently screamed again when the demon stabbed something into her shoulder. She still couldn't breathe, and the darkness was getting thicker until the world went dark.

Brax's head snapped up as he heard Bree's voice faintly. He was on his way through the portal to bring another set of new shifters from the mountain to the human realm. As he was making his way through, he mindlinked Bart, knowing that his brother was the only free one in the building. 'Bart, did you hear that? Sounded like Bree. Can you please go check on her? I have Clan duties, and I don't know where anyone is.'

Bart was already jogging up the stairs and vaulting over a stray cub that darted out through one of the doors. 'Yeah. On it.' He linked Brax back, pitying the poor shifters whose first experience with the outside world would be his brother. They may change their minds. Bart shook his head and didn't bother to knock on Bree's door. In their family, a call for help canceled out polite.

"Bree!" He called to the empty room. "Where the fuck are you, Cub?" He growled and looked everywhere, even under the bed. How many god damn times had they told her to check in before she left The Pit? She could be anywhere. 'Bree Leigh Navarro, you answer me, NOW!' he growled over mindlink, pushing his hands through his hair, not sure what to do.

'Your pain in the ass sister is MIA. Not in her room, gonna check outside.' Bart mindlinked Brock and Beyer before ghosting back to the kitchen and stepping out through the door.

173

He followed his sister's scent to the parking lot, to Dane's spot. His brow arched and he growled. It was empty. If that mother fucking lion had harmed so much as a hair on her precious head, Bart would wear the fucker as a coat. He stepped back when Beyer appeared in front of him too close for comfort and felt something roll under his foot.

"Where is she?" Beyer's head whipped from side to side trying to locate Bree. "Don't give me that look. Reese is standing guard until we get back."

Bart growled again, not even slightly pleased with his brother's explanation as to why he had left his post. "Brax is gonna have your ass." Feeling the thing under his boot again, Bart moved his foot and looked down. "What the..." his voice trailed off as he bent to pick up what looked like one of those tranquilizer darts that Asher used when a shifter lost his shit. He sniffed it and curled his lip. It smelled like a mix of garbage and shit, but it also carried his sister's scent. "I'm going to fucking kill that lion," he growled, glaring at the empty parking space.

Beyer took the dart and repeated the sniff and learn, his eyes going wide. "You don't think Dane has anything to do with this?" He watched the Alpha Pride crew spill into the back lot and begin combing the area while giving the brothers plenty of space.

"Yeah, I really fucking do," Bart growled. That lion had been off for a long God damn time, and he was the only one who saw it. His head turned at the sound of shitkickers pounding the pavement, and Rycker took off. Not his problem if it didn't have to do with Bree, and Reese would know better than to send her people out here and not tell them if they knew something. They worked together, but something like that would end the cooperation but fucking quick.

"You're wrong, Bro." Beyer shook his head and slid the dart into his shirt pocket.

"He'd better hope so," Bart growled and continued searching for signs of Bree being here but found none. "He'd better fucking hope so."

Chapter 22

Stepping behind the bar, Reese poured three cups of coffee, nodded and returned the good mornings that were tossed her way, before placing the steaming mugs with a tiny pitcher of cream and some sugar packets on a tray. She stretched, waiting to see if anyone was going to bitch about this morning's assignments or if for once, people could do what the fuck they were told. She saw Bree duck out the kitchen door, through the big cut out order window to the kitchen. It was good that the kid was back, maybe her brothers would lighten up a little now.

Reese balanced the tray and headed for the basement and the cells. Feeling the fourth step shift, she cursed at the loud creak that cut through the silence. She'd asked the Navarros to fix it repeatedly, but they insisted that it was an early warning that someone was nearing the portal. Their place, their rules and she wasn't going to nitpick something so stupid and chance fucking up their mutually beneficial relationship. The simple fact was that the Navarro clan was the glue that held her merry band of misfits together. They were what made them family.

Finally reaching the bottom, she gave Beyer a smile and held out the tray while he took one of the mugs and doctored it to the way he liked it. "We still expecting newbies today?"

Beyer scratched at the stubble on his jaw and nodded before lifting the coffee for a sip and growling his appreciation. "Brax is on it now. How long is the cell gonna be occupado?" He nodded toward the row of cells and the demon inside.

Reese followed his eyes. The demon was sitting on the cot attached to the wall with one arm on his bent knee and the other foot dangling over the edge with his eyes closed. She doubted that he was sleeping. "That's up to him. Has he given you any trouble?"

"Other than me almost puking when he sucked down the blood bags like a Capri Sun?" He shuddered and made a face. "He's been quiet." His hand tightened on his mug causing the porcelain to make a cracking sound.

"Something wrong?" Reese lowered the tray to an empty chair and reached for her weapons.

"Bree's in trouble." He pushed the hair back from his face and looked like he was about to come out of his skin. He needed to go, but duty kept him planted here, especially if the Lioness was considering letting the demon out, this close to the portal.

Reese tossed the dagger up and caught the blade as she flipped the safety to on and spun it so that the pommel and the butt were facing the bear. "I've got this. Take them. Go. I saw her leave through the kitchen."

"Thanks." Beyer was on his feet, towering over her and palming the weapons. "Don't let him out until one of us is here?"

Reese nodded. "Roger that. Now go." She was talking to empty air before she finished. She pushed the button on her earpiece and spoke to the crew upstairs in the bar. "Navarro sitch in the back. Assist, but don't interfere." Once a satisfactory number of acknowledgments came back, she turned her attention to the occupied cell. "Hi, I'm Reese." She picked up the tray and walked across the stone floor to the bars. "I'm sorry about the accommodations, but you didn't exactly come willingly. Coffee?"

177

Kane listened to them talk, getting a little satisfaction from knowing that he'd made the bear sick. He waited until her voice was closer and she seemed to be talking to him before he cracked one eye. She was seriously going to play Little Miss Hostess after locking his ass up in here? Kane fought the urge to scoff and then he noticed the bandage on her bicep and the memory of taking a chunk out of her, hit him.

"Not exactly the Ritz," he mumbled pulling his other knee up and leaning forward a bit. "But not exactly a torture chamber, either." He eyed the tray in her hands and arched a brow. "Did you poison it?"

Reese laughed and shook her head no before lowering it to the floor and stepping back. "No need. You're under control now." She turned away and crossed the room to get a chair, returning to spin it around, so the back was facing the cell. Dropping onto the seat, she straddled the padded back and reached for one of the cups, keeping her eyes on him. She sipped. "See? And if you're hungry, I can have food, or more blood sent down." She crossed her arms on the back of the chair, holding the mug with the tips of her fingers on the rim, watching him for signs of aggression.

You make it sound like I'm not a prisoner." This time he snorted and slowly lowered his feet to the floor. The coffee did sound good, and the smells of food from upstairs were reminding him that not only had he not fed for too long, but he hadn't eaten anything for longer. Even if he didn't need it to survive, he enjoyed the taste of food. He got up, moving slowly, not wanting to give her a reason to off him and sat on the floor near the tray. Taking care, he reached through the bars, making sure not to touch them. He'd made that mistake last night, and the muscles in his arms were still spasming from the shock.

"You don't have to be." She watched him get settled and sniff the coffee before he lifted it to his lips to test it. A smile curled up one side of her mouth when he reached through again to get the cream. "I didn't catch your name last night..."

He arched a doubtful brow and savored the hot, nutty liquid on his tongue. "Kane. Okay, if I don't HAVE to be a prisoner, how do we make that happen?" He picked up one of the packets of sugar, ripped it open and poured half of it into the cup, stirring it with his finger and looking up at her when he sucked the wetness from it. "The way I see it, it's easy. Open the door. Problem solved."

She shook her head no again. "First, we talk, then we'll see what happens. Do you need a doctor for your wounds?" Reese's jaw tensed as the reports of Bree not being found hit her ear through the headset. That was not an acceptable outcome. And when Rycker said some shit about thinking he saw Heather lurking, her blood boiled. The bitch was supposed to be dead, but more and more sightings were being reported. 'Keep an eye on her, but don't get spotted,' she linked the snow leopard and closed her eyes to rub them when he answered in the affirmative.

Kane laughed. "No. Trouble in paradise, Kitten?" He smirked when he noticed her jaw ticking. The glare she gave him was priceless, and he couldn't help chuckle. "So, talk. Tell me what I can do to get out of here."

Even her father didn't call her Kitten, for fuck sake. She sipped her coffee and eyed him. Did she dare to do what she was considering? There had been one other demon in their ranks before Caleb, and it had ended in a blood bath. Her father wasn't going to let her forget that little page in their history and the ones that were alive to remember it, probably wouldn't be happy either. "I have a proposition for you, Kane."

He smirked at her, his brows popping in surprise. "Not all of us eat every living thing that wanders too close." The indecision that altered her scent intrigued him. "Hit me with it, Kitten. Please tell me that we're getting naked for it." He wiggled his brows and raised his cup with a grin.

Reese rolled her eyes. "No, no getting naked." She shook her head. This was probably a terrible idea. "We're fighting a war, and we need bigger numbers. Demons are getting wiped out by the dozen, and we don't know why. I'm asking you to help us put an end to it."

"Pity," He shook his head with a sigh, trying to look sad. "Partial nudity then?" He grinned and shrugged. "I'd settle for topless."

"What the hell is wrong with you? No!"

"That is a long list, Kitten." He drank his coffee, finishing it. "If I agree, you'll let me out?" *And never be seen again*, but he kept that part to himself.

"Yes, when the current sitch is handled and after Ana inserts the transmitter." She smiled sweetly waiting for him to balk.

"Will she be naked? This Ana?" Kane returned her grin, knowing that he was needling her and hitting his mark.

"No," Reese growled. "Will you pull your head out of the gutter, for fuck sake?"

He shook his head no and pretended to think about it. "I'll get back to you, Kitten. You know, when the whatever is taken care of. Thanks for the coffee, though." He smiled and returned to the cot and his previous position. "Until you're ready to open the door, we got nothing to talk about." He closed his eyes and leaned against the pillows that were a far better quality than one would expect in a cell. When she opened her mouth, Kane shushed her. "No talky. Nap time."

Reese blinked at him and growled again, not missing the way her frustration made him smirk. Shaking her head, she shrugged and moved her chair back to where Beyer had it and sat down again to keep watch until one of the Navarros came back.

Chapter 23

Brock woke slowly. At first, he wasn't sure where he was and looking around with his eyes still blurry from sleep, wasn't clearing anything up. His jaw popped when he yawned as he tried to remember the night before, but all he was getting was a beautiful dream. His brows popped when her scent hit him. Brock chuffed as it caressed the inner lining of his nose and made all tension disappear. It had been a dream. Hadn't it? He wasn't so sure now, and the more he looked around at the weapons and art on the walls, the more certain he was that he was in her bed. His lips curled up, and he wondered if she thought he may just be a bit nuts.

Why are you so nice to me? Her voice drifted through Brock's head. He wished that could put it into words that she'd understand. He'd been hooked from the moment he set eyes on her. He remembered it like it was yesterday. The thundering roar of that black seventy-nine Harley Panhead that warned that something was coming and he had damn well better pay attention. It had vibrated inside his chest, and his head had raised from sweeping up the discarded cigarette butts that littered the walk, in front of The Pit. It wasn't the sound of it that made him stop what he was doing and stare. It was the aura that surrounded her when she parked and slid off it. Brock had never seen anything sexier in his life. If Cupid was real, that was the moment that he shot Brock in the ass with a love arrow.

Her air of *just try me, motherfucker,* did something to him. His bear had stirred under his skin, begging to answer her, even though Brock was positive that it would be a suicide mission. Still, he couldn't tear his eyes away. She was beautiful and everything that he could ask for in a woman. Tall. Strong. God, that mane of blond hair that hung over her eyes, the color of the sky when it threatened to rain. The slight curve of her full pink lips when she met his eyes and his mind lost the ability to string together a greeting. Her scent was heaven. It was a mix of leather, sunlight, the ocean, and a hint of iron. He assumed that the metallic smell was the blood of her enemies.

Brock chuckled to himself thinking about that day. Had it really been a year? All it took for him to work up the nerve to finally get off his ass and know her was her dying. His bear form sighed and closed its eyes with regret. He'd wasted so much time on doubting that she'd want anything to do with the likes of an average bear. She was a fucking goddess. He was beneath her. Brock's insecurity had opened the door wide, for Dane to swoop in and snatch her up. Brock sighed again. He'd been a fool. If only...

Kara stirred when she felt her pillow's breathing change. Stretching, she snuggled into the furs wrapped around her bare skin and tickling her nose. She mumbled something about the best smell on earth, the sound of her voice pulling her from a blessedly dreamless sleep. Opening her eyes, she pulled her head back to smile up at him. Was she supposed to be disturbed by the giant grizzly bear that opened its sapphire eyes and blinked at her? If so, whoever made that stupid rule was going to be disappointed. "Morning." She rubbed her face with her hand and stretched up to kiss the end of his nose.

'Morning,' he answered through mindlink. He hadn't realized she was using him for a pillow until she moved. As she kissed his nose, he wrinkled it, breathing out a sigh of relief when she didn't scream, and her scent gave no signs of being scared or upset. He let his eyes roam over her face and the mussed hair that fell over one of her eyes, making her blow at it and fail to make it move. She was... Beautiful, taking his breath away and at the same time cute as hell.

'Did I snore? I'm not sure if I do, or not. My brothers say I do, but I think they are just messing with me.' He knew he was babbling and made himself shut up. *She's cool with this. Don't fuck it up,* he told himself, afraid that she would come to her senses and kick him out. One brow arched. *She could kill him with a thought, and he was worried that she'd tell him to go to hell? How fucked up was he?*

Brock flexed his front paws, taking care not to scratch her flawless, sun-kissed skin with his claws. He winced. They had fallen asleep, but the moment he moved it, pins and needles to shoot through them and up his arms. He wanted to stretch more, but he was afraid he'd do something super smooth, like fall off the bed or knock her onto the floor. Instead, he ignored the pain.

Kara laughed and shook her head no, "But I think that I drooled on you a little." She made a face and wiped at the damp fur of his chest. Seeing the flicker of discomfort in his eyes, she reluctantly eased off him. "Yeah, that's not even a little sexy." She blushed and wiped her mouth with the back of her hand.

Sliding down beside him, she tried to give his large bear frame plenty of room. The last time they'd woken up together, she'd made him fall off the bed and groped him. The time before that, she'd waved a sword in his face. Kara wanted one morning where she didn't give the bear a heart attack since they seemed to be making a habit of their sleeping arrangement. Before she realized it was happening, her hand crept over the space between them to his fur, curling it around her fingers and stroking the skin beneath.

'You did? I thought one of my brothers had played the paw in a bowl of warm water prank again. What a relief,' he joked, closing his eyes at the feel of her fingers brushing

183

through his hair and against his skin. He could feel her confusion and chuckled. "They think they're funny." Needing to see her, he opened his eyes and stared, his eyes drifting down over her nakedness and then back to her face. Three days in a row, he'd woken beside her, and he was afraid that there wouldn't be a fourth. Her smile brightened her eyes and melted the nervousness churning in his stomach.

"I'm glad you stayed." She grinned and bit her lower lip.

Stretching, a long bass groan punched past his lips as his body cracked and popped. 'I'm glad I stayed too, Cher.'

Brock shifted his weight to see her better. His paws were still half asleep. For a moment, he thought that even his tail was. *How in the hell did my ass literally go to sleep?* Once his legs started to wake up and feeling returned, he realized that his foot had slipped between the bed frame and the mattress, cutting off the circulation to that part of his body. He yanked his foot free with a growl. *So far so good. I haven't thrown her off the bed or done anything to make me wish I was dead, yet.*

Kara winced at the sounds his body made. Her own had that used and abused ache that stamped a permanent smile on her face, the way only good sex could. *Scratch that. Great sex*, she corrected. "Trust me, I'd say something if you did," she teased. "You okay?" She sat up, pulled the pillows behind her and wiggled until she was comfortable. "Let me help." She held out her hand and eyed the paw closest to her, smiling when he settled it softly against her upturned palm. Sandwiching it between her much smaller hands, she rubbed the fur and rough pad, pressing on the pressure points that released the tension she found. "Has anyone ever told you that you're cute, in a dangerous bear that could rip my head off and use it for a bowling ball, kinda way?" She smiled when he flexed his claws and gripped her hand gently.

184

Brock laughed, through mindlink. 'Can't say as they have. I'm okay for the most part. I guess I pulled a princess and the pea kind of thing and I'm not sure that I moved at all after I passed out.' Her rubbing his paw felt great, even better when it cracked in her hands. Watching her, Brock groaned his appreciation. It may be a small gesture, but it was the nicest thing anyone had done for him in a long time. 'Now, if the other three would do that, I'd be in heaven.' He watched her tiny hands massaging his paw. *What was he saying? He was already there.* "If I ever do wet the bed, it's time for me to be a rug.' He was serious. He knew that no female wanted to put up with that, period. Bear piss was not something you can just wash out. No amount of Febreze or Clorox could kill it.

"Yes, because finding Depends in your size?" Kara shook her head and teased, "That would be a challenge." She dropped his paw and repeated the give me gesture, waiting until he placed another in her hand and got to work, smoothing away the ache with her fingers and thumbs. Shaking her head, she chuckled at a random thought. "Another first with you. No one has ever spent the night here with me." It had never struck her until now how much she had changed her life to accommodate Dane and how little he had tried to be part of hers. Wow, talk about blowing one's mind. "If we're gonna get up, I can make coffee without needing to call the fire department," she offered with a grin.

'Depends. Ha ha!' He nudged her a bit. 'Coffee would be good. Wait. I'm the first to sleep here?'

Kara made a face and nodded. "I'm really starting to wonder if D had Emma put a whammy on me like she did on Jared." She tried to laugh it off and changed the subject. "Coffee flavored coffee or something else?"

'That was super uncool. She was a freaking wacko! I feel sorry for Jared and Brian both.' He shifted into human form and ghosted on sweats. "Denis Leary just popped into

185

my head, Cher. Got any waffle flavored coffee?" He laughed hard.

Kara nodded, her breath caught in her throat when he shifted exposing acres of kissable flesh before the clothing appeared. A pity that. In bear or human form, he was a pleasure to see. She slid off the bed and reached down to grab his shirt he'd worn the night before from the floor. She sighed her delight at his scent washing over her as she pulled it over her head and freed her hair. "I belonged to a coffee of the month thing once. I believe there is still some maple stuff left. Maybe some of the chocolate raspberry?" She shook her head as he laughed. His humor was contagious. It made her feel lighter, and she couldn't help her smile. "No waffle, though. Just the Eggos in the freezer."

He swung his legs over the edge of the bed and stood up, making sure that he could feel his legs before he attempted to follow her. "Damn, I had my heart set on Eggo flavored java. I'm okay with whatever you make." He pushed his hands through his long hair trying to get it out of his face. Some days he thought about shaving his head and his beard, but as a bear, his hair or fur in any form came back quickly. It was pointless.

She bumped into the kitchen island while watching him over her shoulder. "Smooth, Kara," she muttered to herself and pulled down a couple of mugs before opening the drawer that held the K-cups. Dropping one into the machine, she pushed a cup under it, closed the top and pressed brew. "Sumatran Reserve, it is. Help yourself to anything you want or need, Babes." She leaned into the fridge to pull out the new carton of half and half.

Brock smiled when she bumped into the island, liking that she was distracted by him for a change. "That thing came out of nowhere. I saw it. Wait, isn't that the fish-scented coffee?" He paused a moment thinking about a bag he'd tried once. Making a face, he took a seat in the kitchen and watched her long, lean legs as his shirt crept up them. His mouth watered and his palms itched to pull her into his lap and pull them around him as he... Brock cleared his throat and adjusted his weight on the seat as his cock hardened and kicked. "On second thought, I'm good with the coffee."

"I know, right?" She grinned and closed the cupboard door. "Fish? I don't think so, I also have French roast if you'd prefer?" She lifted the mug and sniffed it before holding it out to him. "I don't smell any weirdness. Do you?"

He smelled it and shook his head no, wondering what she would do if he acted on the thoughts cycling through his head. *That's right. We're talking about coffee,* he reminded himself. *Don't perv out on her.* "All good, must have been that brand." He looked around her kitchen. It looked super clean. "So, did the potato grenade happen here?"

Kara nodded and glared at the oven before making herself a cup of coffee. "Yes. Right in there. I was finding bits of potato shrapnel for weeks. Sugar?"

Brock held back a laugh. "Yes, please. You should stick to the ones that are already dead!"

She got the sugar container and set it beside him. "Well, they need to label them better or something. I'd settle for a non-exploding sign at the store." She circled the island pressing her lips to his shoulder before she slid onto the ladder-backed stool beside him. "I keep waiting for this to feel awkward or weird, but...." She gave him a slightly confused look. "It really doesn't." She grinned and sipped her coffee, cursing when she burned her tongue.

He took the sugar and poured it into his cup until it looked about right, ghosted himself a spoon and stirred it. "Try the boxed potatoes. Those may not kill anyone," he teased, picking up his cup and testing the coffee. It wasn't bad. He set the cup down. "No, it doesn't. That, in and of itself, should be weird, but it's not."

She stuck her tongue out at him for suggesting instant potatoes. "Exactly! I blame you," she teased and blew over the surface of her mug and arched a brow at him nodding. "But I'm glad. Think we can keep it up?"

He nodded and held the large cup between his hands and nodded gravely. "I'll take the blame when shit goes sideways, Cher." Leaning an elbow on the countertop, he swiveled his seat to see her better. "In all seriousness, I have no idea, but I'm game to try if you are, Cher."

"Good to know. Thank you." She leaned over and kissed his cheek. "I think I could get used to this, Brock Navarro." She grinned and sipped her coffee, this time not burning her tongue. "At least until you get sick of me," she teased.

"I don't know, Cher. Have you met my family? I don't think that will happen. You smell nicer than most of them do." He winked at her.

She laughed and rubbed his thigh, "Yeah. I'm willing to give it a shot." Her head tilted at a weird noise coming from the bedroom. *What the hell?* It took her a moment to realize that it was her phone and that she hadn't had time to set the sounds to her usual tones yet. Arching a brow, she ghosted it into her hand and slid her thumb over the screen. "Well, crap," she sighed and glanced up at him.

"Speaking of your family, Bart wants to know, and I quote, 'Where the good for nothing fucking lion is.'" She handed him the phone so he could see for himself. "The reprieve couldn't last forever, I guess. So, before it all goes to hell, I'm gonna ask, do we want to do this again? The, you and me, thing. Or have you been horrified enough for one lifetime?" Kara watched his face, fully expecting him to find an excuse to make this a one-time thing.

He looked at her phone and wondered what the hell was going on. "Are you kidding? I would love to do this again. I wonder what's got Bart's balls in a bunch?"

Kara grinned. "The question is, should we go find out, or hide here and build pillow forts to play in?" She turned on her stool and rubbed his calf with her toes. She couldn't help it. It was like she was compelled to touch him and although she didn't understand it, she didn't want to fight it. She needed just one single thing that felt right, and he was it until he changed his mind.

"We should find out, just to be safe. If it's idiotic, we can ignore him." Brock finished his coffee.

Nodding, Kara picked up her phone and typed [Haven't seen D. What's up? I can try to track him down if needed.] Her lip curled up a little as she hit send. She hadn't even set down the phone before Bart hit her back and her jaw dropped when she read the text. She looked up at Brock and winced a little, ghosting on her clothes. "He says Bree is missing, Babes. That she linked for help and they can't find her. If you want my help, I'm in. But if you prefer me to stay the hell out of it, I'll go with that."

Brock said nothing at first, letting it sink in. "Well, shit." His mind started racing. *Dane wouldn't hurt her. Would he? No. Dane knew better*, or Brock thought he did.

Kara watched him process everything and waited for a reaction. She held her breath, not knowing him well enough to know what to expect. She finished her coffee and mulled over the shit Bart thought Dane was capable of. Closing her eyes, Kara shook her head. Maybe before, when Kane was in there, but not now, not unless the demon had crawled back inside. She didn't want to think about that possibility.

"I would appreciate any help you can give us." He stood up and sighed. "I hope she's just off working on her training."

She nodded and slid off her stool, dropping her mug in the dishwasher. "It's going to be okay." Kara hugged him for a moment.

His arms slid around her waist. It felt as though he'd done it a thousand times. "Thank you, Cher." He kissed the top of his head and smiled before letting go to put his cup in the dishwasher beside hers and closing the door. "I guess we should go. I mean if you want to come with me. It's up to you." He ghosted himself fully dressed. He didn't want to assume anything, no matter what she said. Brock had an optimistic pessimist outlook for what they'd started. He

189

hoped for the best but expected it to go to shit at any second.

Kara glanced up at him as she scooped her cards and her phone from the counter and stuffed them into her pockets, but held her keys out to him. "You can drive this time." She linked a finger with his and shot him a grin. "Yeah, I'd like to help, if I can. Even if that is just to be the barrier that gets between Dane and Bart if it comes down to it."

"You want me to drive your baby?" Brock's brow arched with disbelief, and a surprised grin ghosted over his lips. "Yes, we may need a wall between them."

She nodded and laughed as she leaned against him. "Yes. Yes, I do."

He took the keys and headed outside. A few minutes later they were speeding down the road headed for The Pit.

Chapter 24

Bart paced, but it was doing nothing to calm him down. The more he moved, the more pissed off he became. *What the fuck did Kara mean? She didn't know where Dane was? Bullshit. She was his mate, for fuck sake.* He growled and kicked at a chair that was in his way, drawing weary looks from a table nearby. He didn't care. *His sister was missing, and there would be hell to pay if anything happened to her. And where the hell was Brock?*

"Calm down. You're making the natives restless." Beyer dropped a hand on his shoulder only to let it fall with a sigh when Bart hit him with a glare that could burn through titanium. "Seriously, man, if your head explodes, you ain't gonna be much help to anyone. True?"

Bart growled again and flipped his brother off.

Brock drove Kara's bike to the employee lot and kicked down the kickstand with his heel. "I see why you love this thing," he yelled over the thundering engine, killing the beast and handing the keys back to her once she slid off the bike. The hair on the back of his neck bristled. Things felt off. His eyes swept the lot or anything out of the norm but showed nothing. Still, the things he was smelling didn't add up.

Kara grinned and finger combed her hair, taking the keys and shoving them into her pocket. "Gotta love a classic." Her brow arched as he froze like he was doing .

191

complicated geometry in his head. She shivered. The air had a weird charge causing her arms to pebble with goosebumps. "You feel it too?" It wasn't so much a question as letting him know that her Spidey sense was tingling.

Beyer cursed when the sound of Kara's bike moved along the building, and the engine cut off. This wasn't going to be pretty, especially if she didn't have Dane with her. Hell, odds were, it was gonna get messy even if she did. "Try to play nice. She can bolt your ass, remember?" He said to Bart's back as the bear stomped through the bar.

Bart shoved through the saloon style swinging doors and then through the kitchen staff and outside. "Did you bring him?" He growled, his head rocked back on his shoulders when he saw that Brock was with her.

Brock's head snapped up when he heard Bart's voice. "The lion isn't here. He wasn't here last night either," Brock said, looking at his brother. The look on his face read a mix of shock and rage. "Did you check his room and the basement?" Brock hoped that Kara didn't just take his brother out at the knees.

Kara turned to face the pissed off bear and tried to remind herself that Bart was like a Momma bear trying to find its cub. She counted to ten and pushed the hair back from her face. "I turned in the spare key, it should be in the office." She stepped closer to Brock and crossed her arms over her chest. "Do you have a reason to think Dane lost his mind and decided to take her or are we just throwing out theories that could get someone killed, for fun?"

"She hasn't been in the basement. Brax and Beyer were both down there." Bart swung his gaze to land on Kara and growled at her tone. *Why was she even fucking here?* "We followed her scent to where his truck ISN'T parked. Basic math, Sweetheart." His lip curled with contempt. "When I get my hands on your mate..." He trailed off when her words about returning the key to the room started to sink in. He looked at her again, noticing that a few things had changed. Then his eyes dropped to her Panhead. One bike. Two people with windblown hair. Talk about your simple math. "Well, fuck."

"We found this," Beyer stepped around Bart, giving his brother an 'I told you so' look, pulled the dart from his shirt pocket and held it out to Brock. "I don't smell D on it, but you know how the hot head is. Once he sinks his teeth into something..." He rolled his eyes and flashed Kara a smile.

Brock wanted to growl at Bart, but he didn't. "I meant did you check the basement for Dane, dipshit." He looked at the dart a moment before he took and looked it over. "I smell demon or something other than shifter on it." He handed it to Kara. "What's your take on it, Cher?"

She ignored Bart and returned Beyer's smile before taking the dart and sniffing it. Her brows shrugged together. *What the hell?* What she was smelling didn't make sense. A drop of liquid formed at the beveled edge when she shook it. She caught the drop with the tip of her finger before it fell to the pavement and licked it off. "What?" The Bears were giving her a weird look and Beyer looked like he might blow chunks. "Three or more different kinds of demons. Not ones that usually get along. Maybe a poison or two that will make you trip your ass off." She turned her head and spit out the nasty tasting shit. "Other than that, I just get bear." She handed it back to Brock. "Not a hint of lion." She arched a brow at Bart.

"No, we didn't." Bart swept the hair back from his face and shook his head. "If Dane isn't responsible, we should check both, he could still be with her." He wasn't letting that go because something about the lion was making his radar ping like a son of a bitch and had been for a while. "Why would anyone mix that? What would it do?"

Brock wondered if he should tell his brothers about what happened, but it wasn't his place to say a word. "We need to do some looking and maybe call in Reese to help. The more eyes, the better."

Kara nodded her agreement and wiped her tongue on Brock's shoulder. The taste lingered. "I agree and how the

193

hell would I know what it does? Do I look like Yoda?" She gave Bart an annoyed look. "Cut him some slack, the lion was dead, and Bree helped to get him back, so him hurting her makes zero sense. Someone should call him and give him a heads up that shit is hitting the fan though. It can't be me." Her jaw tightened. "He wouldn't know who the hell I am, and no, I don't want to have a sharing and caring moment. Just trust that it's true."

Bart eyed her. She'd just licked his brother and Brock didn't get fidgety, the way he usually did when she was around. "Okay. Fine. Excuse the hell out of me for thinking you might have some insight with all of your," he waved his hands in a Jack Sparrow kind of way, "Powers."

Beyer had to turn his head away to hide his laugh. "Reese is watching the portal for me." He held up his hands. "Yeah. Yeah, I know."

"We need to go inside and not be out in the open. Just in case it comes back. The dart? I think we should give it to Asher or Ana let them do their thing with it. Like she said, Dane taking Bree wouldn't match up." Brock had never actually bothered to use his powers or any of that and right now he was regretting it. His brothers and sister on the other hand? Yeah, they ha that shit dialed in. He started for the back door. "Brax is where?"

Kara motioned for the others to follow Brock. If whatever it was, was still lurking, it was better if she brought up the rear. She could take more damage than they could. She turned, walking backward and sighing when her eyes fell on Dane's empty parking spot. She hoped that where ever he was, that he was okay. Pulling her head back into the problem at hand, she pulled the door closed behind her and followed the others into the bar.

Bart didn't like his ass being protected by a female, but he liked having his ass kicked by one even less, so he fell in line behind his brothers. "Brax is bringing a pair of newbs over to this side. He isn't back yet."

"Okay, so everyone is accounted for other than Bree," Brock said once he was inside. He wanted to ask if they'd spoken to the AP members that were working the doors last night, but questioning them at times was like pissing into the wind. "You checked her room, right? Did you notice if her phone was in there?" Brock asked remembering Brax bragging about activating an app that allowed him to track his littles sister by GPS when she began dating. At the time, Brock thought that it was over the top, but now his brother's paranoia was useful.

Kara pushed her hands into her pockets and watched Brock take control of the situation. She admired his level-headedness and that he was remaining calm while projecting the confidence that he had this. That was rare. How the hell had she never noticed it before? "I'm going to check if Jared or Ripper are around. I think I'll have some luck if they saw or heard anything." She stretched up and kissed Brock's cheek before wandering off into the crowd. "If you need me, you know what to do," she said over her shoulder, cutting through the crowd and moving towards the stage.

Beyer coughed and gave Brock a smirk when Kara left. "Bro." He shook his head and chuckled. "Maybe Caleb or the demon in the basement can shed some light on the dart thing."

Bart was about to answer the question and ignore whatever he'd just seen when Beyer opened his yap. "A fuckin what is where? Next to the portal? Are you fucking stupid?" Sometimes he could throttle the SOB, brother or not.

"What? He's in a cell. What is he going to do? Think about it really hard?" Beyer rolled his eyes and decided that now was a damn good time to disown Bart. "Anger Management Issues, over there, he checked her room."

Bart growled and wondered why their mother hadn't eaten the youngest of the Quint males at birth. "Her phone wasn't there, and she's not answering it."

Brock watched Kara wonder off as he listened. 'There's a demon in one of the cells down in the basement. Is there any way you can ninja your way down there? If it's locked up, it's for a reason. I don't think letting Heckle and Jekyll go down there right now, is smart,' he mindlinked Kara.

Brock put himself between his brothers. "I asked about the phone because it still has the GPS tracking on it. Do you think Alpha Pride would let a dangerous demon be close to the portal? Not if they want to keep their heads attached. Salvation wouldn't let Ozzy and the others do that. They've got rules, just like we do. Even if some of his team don't follow them, they've got them."

Kara's brow arched. 'You've got it, Babes." She ducked into the bathroom instead of going to the stage area and ghosted downstairs. She made a face at the caterwauling going on as the demon in the cell belted out Whitney Houston at the top of his lungs. When he missed the high notes, it was like a railroad spike being driven through your skull. She saw Reese, sitting in a chair with her ears covered and eyes scrunched shut. "The fuck is going on here?"

Kane fell silent and stepped off the bed to come as close to the bars as he dared. He'd touched them last night, and a jolt had knocked him against the wall. "Did you come to let me out, Goldilocks?" He wrinkled his nose when he picked up the scent of bear on her skin.

"Thank fuck!" Reese growled.

"That's above my pay grade." She glanced at Reese. "Everything under control?" She mindlinked Brock, 'I'm in, Babes. It's secure. Gonna send Reese your way.'

"Does it sound under control?" Reese raised her head, her eyes were miserable.

"Not really. I was being polite. I've got this for a few. The Bears need you upstairs." Kara turned to look at the demon again and tried not to laugh. "Don't suppose you can tell me anything about darts full of demon blood and a few roofies, can you?"

196

Kane eyed her and grinned. "I might be able to help with that. I'd need the dart and to get out of here." He glared at the bars. "It blocks my mojo."

"Pass that on to Brock?" She called up the stairs to the lioness who nodded and worked her jaw as if her ears were still ringing.

"Probably not," Bart admitted, rubbing the back of his neck and looking slightly ashamed of himself. "Still a demon being that close to the portal, ain't cool."

Beyer snorted. "Sure, when I say that, I'm full of it. It's the beard, isn't it? I've gotta grow mine out."

"Zip it," Bart growled at his smooth-faced brother before turning to Brock. "Okay, Einstein. Do you know how the GPS thing works?"

'Thank you, Cher.' Brock linked Kara back and sighed at his brothers. "No, but one of the techy people might. Like Reese, she might be able to get into it. Don't be a dick," he said to Bart. "It's a better idea than what you came up with."

Kara smiled when she heard Brock's voice in her head and eyed the demon. She didn't know what species he was, but while his wise ass breaker was flipped to on, she wasn't getting any aggression from him. Bone tired and annoyed, that he had in spades, but nothing about him said he was dangerous. "What did you do to get in here?" Kara asked and took a seat on the floor crossing her legs and leaning her elbows on her knees.

"From what I can tell? I was bleeding. Who knew that was a crime?" Kane shrugged and sat on his bed. *The Valkyrie didn't recognize him, and that was good.*

Kara's head turned to look over her shoulder when she heard footsteps behind her and Brax actually playing nice and explaining the program they had in place to help new shifters adapt to life on this side of the portal. She was shocked. Who knew he had that in him? She smiled and kept quiet when he gave her a confused glare and turned to take the newbs upstairs.

197

Bart growled and made a face, glancing up as Reese came toward them, looking like her head hurt. "I thought she was watching the portal?" He arched a brow at Beyer who shrugged.

"Kara says you need me for something." She rubbed her ear, still hearing Kane's awful rendition of "I'll Always Love You." If they got him on board and needed to torture someone, he had mad skill. "And if you get the dart to her, Kane might be able to tell us something about it? I have no clue what that is about, but she asked me to tell you." Reese didn't like being out of the loop. "So, what's up?"

"Can you help us hack into Bree's phone's GPS, to help track her down?" Brock asked hoping Reese could help. "You okay, Cher? You look like someone shit in your cereal." He could read the pain on her face.

"I think I'll make it." Reese shook her head and grumbled about loud ass demons that couldn't carry a tune in a bucket. "Yeah, if I can't, Ry can get in, but have you tried the Supernatural trick yet?" She grinned when all three bears looked confused. "You call the carrier, tell them about poor little diabetic Bree who went to a Justin Bieber concert and forgot her insulin?" She shook her head at them when they blinked silently. "I'll take that as a no. Same number that we have on file?"

Bart just stared at her. With all the intel and fancy equipment that even the CIA didn't have, she thought that they should just call and give Verizon a lame ass story? He didn't know what to say to that.

Brock laughed. "No, I was hoping for more techy stuff, but I'm willing to try it," he answered honestly. "If that doesn't work, will Ryker help us?"

Reese grinned. "We can skip the easy non-tech and head straight to Rycker if you'd prefer. All we need is the number and if Ry can't crack it? It can't be cracked." She held up her finger and pressed the button on her earpiece. "Ry. We need a location on a number. You got time?" She waited for him to answer and turned to the three bears.

198

Yeah, the irony of that was not lost on her. "I think we have the current number on file for Bree." She arched a questioning brow and waited for confirmation in the way of three identical nods. "And Ry? Make it priority, okay?" She dropped her hand and smiled. "Give him a few minutes. Anyone want to tell me what's going on?"

Bart saw Brax leading the newcomers through the bar and elbowed Beyer. "He's gonna have your ass for leaving your post. Who is taking watch?" When Reese told him, Kara, he burst out laughing. Yeah, Brax wasn't gonna like that, at all.

Brock waited for Brax to ask the million-dollar question. "Thank you, Reese. So, tell me about the demon in the basement. He a new pet of yours? Is he safe?"

Reese winced. "Honest answer?" She waited for Brock's nod. "I don't know yet, and that's why he's locked up. He was in rough shape when I found him. Starving, but when I offered my wrist he wouldn't take it, and he hasn't done anything, other than torture by bad singing, aggressive." She shrugged and kept the bite in the van to herself. That was reflex, not aggression. "I don't want to put him back out there until I know he's not going to be driven to kill someone because of starvation, but if I can convince him to join the team, that would be one hell of a help. Just what he knows about demons alone, could give us a leg up in the fight."

Bart shook his head. "And if it goes like the last time?" He snorted when Reese made a gun with her hand and mimed pulling the trigger. "That's harsh. I get it but, damn." He looked up when Brax joined them. "Before you go off, we're on it. Kara has the portal covered unless you don't trust her?" He arched a brow, waiting for a rant. She'd never let them down yet and had taken more than her share of injuries to save one of them or Alpha Pride. Maybe that would change, now that she was apparently not with D, but he didn't think so. Not after seeing how she was with Brock and good on his brother for going after what he wanted

199

after all this time. And he wasn't stupid. Having a Valkyrie fighting on your side, never hurt.

Brax wasn't sure what was going on. "Okay?" He said slow, waiting for someone to connect the dots. "Why is she watching it? I feel like I'm missing something."

Brock filled him in and watched his brother's face hurt red, then purple, with rage. It was incredible the colors Brax turned at times.

"I leave you all alone for a moment, and every time I do, something happens." He clenched his jaw and stared at them. He was sure if he slapped one of them Reese would put him down.

"We're working on it. Calm down, you'll give yourself a damn stroke," Brock said trying to keep the peace. Just once, he'd love to be the one having a fit. "And don't clench. Remember what Momma used to tell us."

Brax flipped him off.

"Okay don't cry when your jaw sticks and you can't chew anything for a week."

Brax glowered at his brother and crossed his arms over his chest.

Reese never got used to watching these four huge males bicker like kids, but it never failed to entertain her. Shaking her head, she heard Rycker tell her to check the printer behind the bar. "Roger that," she said, turning and leaving the Navarro brothers, wondering when the three stooges bitch slapping would start. Leaning her ass against the beer cooler, she pulled each page as it spit out, leaving her with three. "I fucking love you, Ry. Just saying," she said to herself grinning at the recon he was able to produce without breaking a sweat. She walked back and laid the pages out on an empty table near the bears. Waiting for them to stop the name calling long enough to get their attention. After a few minutes, she had a seat and cleared her throat loudly.

Bart was just about to tell Beyer that he was ugly and he dressed funny when he heard Reese make a noise and

200

looked around for her. Wow, he hadn't even realized that she'd walked away from them. "I blame you, whelp," he growled at Beyer and cuffed the kid on the back of the head before turning away and going toward the table the lioness waited at.

"Hey! I'm so Nairing his shampoo," Beyer growled low before following.

"I heard that!" Bart shot the youngest brother a dirty look.

Brock sighed and went to Reese. "I wish I was adopted," he groaned and took a seat, even though his bear wanted to pace. He waited for them to sit down. "So, what's the damage, Cher?"

Reese arched a brow at Brax until he uncrossed his arms and finally parked his ass in one of the chairs. One side of her mouth curled up at the victory. She clicked her mic of the earpiece on. "Okay, and Ry, correct me if I get it wrong. He was able to triangulate her position using the cell towers here, here and here." She flashed a sharpie into her hand and connected the dots. "That still leaves twenty or so square miles to search. Too much and would take too long and give them a chance to figure out what we're up to. So, he narrowed it down to two possibilities in the zone that could hold a bear that didn't want to be held and is demon friendly. Demon or not, they still don't want humans wandering in to muck shit up, and they still have to worry about security."

She made two x's within the triangle and tapped the first one with her finger. "This one we don't know much about, yet." She slid one of the pieces of paper closer to show them the aerial photo of the property and what was hidden behind the tall iron fence that surrounded it. "It's a possibility, but this one..." Reese pushed the last sheet of paper toward them. "We broke up an Einvigi fighting ring here last year. I know it doesn't look like much, small farm with a stone wall, but this doesn't show the labyrinth they

201

have underground. This would be my bet, but I say we hit both, to be sure."

Bart blinked and glanced at the bar clock. "Holy shit. He got all of that in fifteen minutes?" He rubbed his face, thinking that he really needed to upgrade his skills.

Brock listened to everything Reese said. "Okay. So, two teams of who? And how likely is it that this is a trap? I mean they left a dart behind, who does that on purpose?" He asked thinking that it was kind of stupid.

"Good point and it probably is, but we've never let that stop us before. The teams depend on what you all want. Do you want us to go in, or do you expect us to back you up? I think our best bet is to have my people, hit fast and hard from the outside and the center, meanwhile a smaller team searches for Bree. If you go, that's where you should be. You can sense her and know her scent better than anyone else. I'm down if you want to go, but I need my best right there beside you. Koen. Balden. Blade. Kara, if she'll agree to lend a hand. We're not fucking around, so if you don't feel it, be honest now because I'm trusting my guy's lives in your hands just as much as your trusting yours in ours. It has to be timed correctly, hit both at the same time and don't pull back until we have her, we're dead, or they are."

Beyer cursed softly beside Bart and looked a little pale. "Someone needs to stay behind on portal duty. It should be Beyer. Not busting your chops, bro, but you have the least experience, and I'm not gonna get Bree back and have our folks haunt her for us letting you get killed."

Some of the color returned to Beyer's face. "I want in."

Brock didn't want to argue with any of them. "Look, before we all start fighting, Reese has experience in this. We should let her make the teams. I'd feel better with someone that knew how to be tactful and not just go apeshit." He said looking at Brax and Bart. "Kara is willing to help us, so having her should make things a little safer. Bree trusts her. I'm not sure about the others. We need to do this right." He didn't know what to say other than that. He wanted to tell Kara to

202

light both places up. Well, first check for Bree and Dane, then blow it the hell up.

Reese nodded. "I'm not sending in anyone who is going to go cowboy on us. I'll let you work out your part, but if you go in, I can't let you go alone. If this is the size of what we faced last time..." She shook her head. "Let's just say, we need the count, but I'm not willing to send in anyone who isn't top notch. Bree knows Jared and Brian. They would be good choices as well."

She took this shit seriously, and the weight of having so many lives in her hands made her feel a little sick. There would be something wrong with her if it didn't. "No one, not any of you or any of mine are expendable. We can wait for a little bit, let Ry gather more intel and hope that Bree can shed some light. But we can't depend on it happening, and we can't wait too long. You all talk it over, talk to who you need to and get back to me." She smiled and hoped that she didn't sound like a royal bitch, but she was used to taking charge when no one wanted to. "I'm going to let Asher and Ana know, so they can be ready." She stood and pushed away from the table, talking to Rycker over her headset.

"Well, fuck." Bart breathed and looked at each of his brother's faces. "So much for the warm and fuzzies." He shook his head and pulled one of the pages closer to study it. "What do you think?" He looked to Brock out of habit. He was the level-headed one, and even though they would argue it until the end of time, Brock was the oldest, and when the shit hit the fan, Brock was in charge.

Brock nodded at Reese. "I want to go in with all the info we can gather. And the more faces she knows, the better. If she's lost in one of her shadow walk mode things... Sometimes she gets upset, and that part of her takes over. It's hard to get her to focus. And we don't know what she learned from her training on the mountain. I would hate for someone to die, because of our family. So, we wait until we've got something more reliable than a big ass map of maybe."

Reese bowed her head respectfully. "As you wish." She understood his concern and the weight of living with whatever happened because of their choices. "My people will be ready." She patted Brock's shoulder and walked away from the table, hoping that they didn't wait too long.

Bart let out a relieved breath. "We need to find Dane. If he's not with her, then his is another face that she'll trust." He sighed and grabbed a beer off the tray that was being carried by.

Beyer was staring at Brock. He wasn't sure that anyone had ever told Reese no before and lived.

"Thank you, Reese. We won't wait too long," Brock said over his shoulder to her. "Maybe one of us should go look for Dane before we go after Bree?"

Bart nodded. "It's you or me. Beyer, no, for the reasons I said, and we need Brax to keep the kitchen in line. I'm the most dispensable." Bart shrugged.

Brock nodded his agreement, even if the word dispensable chafed a bit. "Beyer and I will start asking for people to help us search for her and see if anyone saw or heard anything the night she went missing. Did anyone take the dart to the clinic?" Brock felt like his mind was overloading, and he didn't want to forget anything that could be important. Did Kara have the dart? At that moment, he couldn't remember. He growled at himself for being a moron.

Beyer fished it out of his pocket and held it up. "I still have it. I'll drop it off with the Docs."

Brax cursed. "No one tells me anything. She was darted? Like a common animal?" His growl rumbled low in his chest.

"I'm on it, then." Bart nodded and downed the beer. "When do we want to compare notes?"

Brock sighed at Brax. "I told you everything. Try listening when I speak." He looked at his other brothers. "Tomorrow night. We go, come hell or high water." Brock looked at Beyer. "Make sure you get it into the hands of one

204

of the doctors. Do not let one of the nurses or helpers get a hold of that. They might file thirteen it. The last thing we need is the only piece of evidence we've got, coming up missing."

"I won't let you down, Bro." Beyer slid it back into his pocket and pushed his chair back.

"Till then, Bitches," Bart grinned and pulled his phone from his pocket to work every contact of Dane's that he could think of and then start hitting the places he liked to hang.

Once his brothers left, Brock dropped his head into his hands. He couldn't shake the feeling that something big and bad was about to happen. He tightened his fingers in his hair. Why did she have to be so caring? Brock knew deep down that Bree went out there to see if she could get a feel on the stupid lion.

When Brax came down the stairs and waved her away, Kara wanted to blast his disrespectful ass, and she almost did, until she felt the worry that was coming off him in strong, steady pulses. Biting her tongue, she took the stairs two at a time and looked for Brock. She sighed and crossed the room when she saw him, leaning down to loop her arms around him from behind. "You okay, Big Guy?"

He relaxed a bit when she touched him. "No. Not one bit, but I can't tell anyone that. I'm not allowed to have a meltdown, though it has to be my turn soon." Brock's head was still in his hands, and he pulled on his hair a bit more.

Kara leaned down and whispered in his ear. "You can with me, Babes. I won't tell a soul." She hugged him tighter. "Anything you need, just say the word."

Brock let go of his hair with one hand and patted her arms around him. "I appreciate that Cher. I think the only thing I need right now is to eat. It'll take my mind off stuff, maybe."

"Then let's get you food. Do you want to go somewhere else and maybe breathe a little?" She kissed his cheek and stood up, a thought occurring to her. "My feelings won't be hurt if you want to be alone."

He shook his head. *Right and give her time to remember that he wasn't Dane? Nope.* Besides, if he was alone, he'd drive himself mad overthinking everything. "No. I'd like the company. We could go to the diner down the street. It has excellent wings. I feel like feeling bones crack and ripping flesh," he tried to joke.

Kara grinned and chuckled. "That sounds perfect." She held her hand out to him. "Is it close enough to walk?"

Brock took her hand and got to his feet. "Yes, it is. Another reason I like it. If I overdo it, I can waddle home pretty easily." He smirked, remembering the last time he and his brothers went there. They cleaned the place out of wings.

She laughed and leaned against him when he began walking toward the door. "No worries, Bear. I can roll you home if necessary. And if you need a distraction, I have ideas." Kara waggled her brows at him and grinned, hoping to lighten his mood, if only for a little while. She could feel the weight of his responsibilities crushing him.

He opened the door and let her go out first, blushing when Branden gave a wink of approval as Brock followed her out onto the street. "Ideas? I'm a bit scared." Brock smiled at her. "If you roll me home could you make sure to keep me out of the puddles, please?"

"Of course, I won't let you get wet. Well, unless I drool on you again," Kara teased. "You never need to be scared, I won't hurt you unless you ask me to." She stopped, turned and pulled his head down for a kiss. "That needed doing."

Brock smiled and lowered his forehead to rest against hers before he nodded. "Well, if I deserve it, Cher, I totally understand you kicking my ass." Holding her against his chest, he let her strengthen him and calm his mind. He couldn't explain it, but with her in his arms, he felt like he could tackle anything. Even the coming shit storm. If only he believed that it could last. Sighing, he took her hand and led her inside.

Booths lined the brick walls with red checkered tables dotting the worn commercial laminate floor. Cakes and slices of pie beckoned from a plastic display case on the short lunch counter, but it was the smell of the wings that made Brock's mouth water. "Booth or table?" He liked this place. It was homey. The prices were good, and the food was fantastic. Here, he was just a customer. Not a Quint. Not one of the Navarro Clan. Just a hungry patron, looking for a seat in the crowded diner. The only thing he disliked was their beer. Their drafts were always flat and watery, so he never got a beer when he came here.

Kara gave him an odd look for a second and then shrugged, looking around. "Booth? Maybe one in the back? Then we can fill each other in on what we found out, without worrying about someone overhearing?" She had no idea what had happened upstairs, but the demon was very chatty if she batted her baby blues and smiled. How much was true? Well, that was probably a different story.

Brock nodded and asked for one in the back. He slid into the cracked pleather booth and ordered a coke. "The beer here isn't that great," he whispered to her.

"Oh." Kara made a face. "Water with seeds, then" She shot Brock a grin. "With lemon," she clarified for the frazzled looking young man taking their order.

He chuckled and waited for the waiter to leave. "So, you want the long version or short version, Cher?" He asked, sliding the menu from the holder to her. He already knew what he wanted.

"Whichever version had you wanting to bang your head on the table." She pulled the menu closer, decided on the wings with a side of potato salad and looked up at him.

When the waiter came back with their drinks, he gave his order. "I want hot butter and garlic wings. No veggies with it. And I want the bucket." He waited on Kara to order.

207

Kara looked at the menu again and read off what she wanted, giving the young man a smile and dropping the menu back into its holder. "Thanks."

Once they were alone again, Brock sipped his coke. "I thought about using the GPS in Bree's phone to track her. Reese narrowed it down to where she was. A small farm or some other place. We decided it best to go in with AP's help. In two teams. We are going tomorrow evening. Till then, we're going to do some recon. Well, they are. Bart went to look for Dane. And Beyer took the dart to the clinic to see what the docs can get off it. It gives us time to find people willing to help with the search." he said in one breath.

"Wow." Her brow arched as it all spilled out. "Smart, thinking of the GPS." Kara sipped her water, wishing that she could wipe away the worry that clouded his sapphire eyes. "Probably a trap?" Because it always was. But still, her pulse pounded a little faster at the promise of a good fight. "Well, I'm in. What can I do to help?"

Brock nodded. "That's what I thought. I was hoping you'd be on one of the teams, so Bree has people she knows and trusts, in case she isn't totally herself. Though something Reese said is digging at me," Brock said, drinking his coke and wishing it would drown his thoughts. Maybe the sugar would do something to help him.

"Spill it, Bear." Kara hooked his pinky finger with hers.

"She said something about some nasty fighting ring or something like that. She said the last one they cleaned up was huge. What if they took Bree for something like that? I've heard stories about dog fighting. What if they are using my sister for bait or something even more messed up than that?"

"Then we'll kill them slow and bloody," Kara growled. She looked at him and sighed. "You said they had it narrowed down to two places? What if I check them out tonight and narrow it down a little more?" She squeezed his hand. "It's going to be okay, Brock. We're going to get her back. Have faith." She sipped her water. "Before the Docs do too much to the dart, we should let the demon in the cell look at it. He thinks he might be able to pick up on whose it is if he knows them, or has run across them before." She made a face. "If we trust a demon, that is."

Brock squeezed her hand back. "Well, Reese has the maps and all that. So, if you want to ask her for them, I won't say no to you taking a look before we waste time looking in a place she isn't." His brow went up at the mention of the demon's help. "Beyer took it to the clinic, but maybe we can get one of them to let him see it. Why would he help us though? Demons generally only care about themselves." He looked up as their food came and moved his glass out of the way so the waiter could put his bucket down on the table. "I need another bucket for the bones," he said, looking around the scarred table top. "And more napkins."

Kara shrugged and helped him move the clutter out of the way. "I think he has a little crush on Reese," she laughed and nodded, waiting for them to be alone again. "I was stuck with him, so we talked. He's one of seven of his species or was. In the last week, three have been taken out, he's scared, and he's been alone for a long time. I know how he feels with the lonely part." She bit into one of the wings. "I think he might jump at the chance to be part of something instead of waiting to be picked off." She bounced happily in her seat. "These are amazing." Kara shrugged again. "I could be wrong, though. But a lot of people would ask the same of me, why would I help you?"

He listened to her talk as he dug into the wings. A small growl came from him as he ate them. He hadn't realized how hungry he was. Garlic butter ran down his arm. Lifting it, Brock licked it off. "They should give a drop cloth with these." He joked. "Well if he wants to help, I'm okay with it. I can't speak for my brothers, though. Why you would help? Bree helped you, so you owe her one. Or maybe because you won't miss a chance to add a new skull to your collection of coffee mugs." He smirked at her. "I'm glad you're enjoying the wings."

Kara laughed. "Well, yeah, there's that, but you know what I mean. No one trusts anyone until they have a chance to earn it." She watched him lick the sauce off his arm and bit her lower lip. "Maybe they should, but you make making a mess look good, Babes." She teased, dropping a bone on her plate and picking up another wing. "Who else is going?"

He thought a moment. "We thought about asking Brian, Jared, and maybe Ripper. Oh, and Blade. I'm not sure who Reese wants from her team, but I trust her. I learned a long time ago she is one tough cookie. It's sad the guys still give her shit for helping Ozzy run the business," he said ripping into another wing. "I don't know about making this look good. When I get home, I'll have to watch my beard out, or I'll smell like this for a week." He laughed.

"Not the worst thing to smell like," she teased. "Good choices. Bree knows them." Kara wiped her fingers on a napkin before trying the potato salad, groaning happily and sticking with that. "I'd feel better if we could let her know we're coming. If she's even there." She sighed. "I wonder if we can get a message to her, I mean. One of the bloods in the dart was from the place we got Dane out of." She made a face remembering how the blood of the skitter that she'd ripped apart had splashed into her mouth. That was a taste she wouldn't forget anytime soon.

Nodding, Brock agreed with her. "Maybe we'll have some more info tomorrow, and we can do something like that. It would be nice not to scare the crap out of her. Or even have her be able to tell us what's what."

"Exactly." She nodded. "So, then the next question is, how do we keep you from obsessing about this all night and driving yourself nuts?"

Brock shrugged. He honestly didn't know, so he ate more of his wings and finally the waiter came back with the bucket and napkins. Brock dropped his bones into the empty container. "How's your potato salad?"

"Really good." Kara grinned and forked more into her mouth. "Almost as good as the wings. Almost." She grinned. "If we weren't doing a rescue mission, I'd just drop Fenrir in the middle and let the pup have a little fun." She laughed at the thought.

Brock smiled a moment before plowing through more of the wings, almost to the bottom of the bucket. "Is there bacon in it?" He asked looking at what she had left on her plate.

"And dill, I think." She scooped some onto her fork and held it out to him.

He leaned forward and took a bite. "Mmm. That is really good. Better than what I make."

"Really?" She looked at her fork and finished off the last that was on her plate. "But you're my cooking Yoda." Kara grinned and wiped her mouth on a napkin.

Brock laughed hard. "Well, I never said I was good at potato salad." He stuck his tongue out at her.

"I thought you were good at everything."

He roared with laughter. "Who told you that, Cher?" He shook his head.

She shrugged and grinned. "I thought it was implied and from my experience..."

He threw a bone at her. "Smartass!" Brock finished off his food. Taking a sip of his coke, he looked at her and grinned. "Like I'd have you make potato salad, you'd kill us all!"

Kara puffed out her lower lip into a pout. "I have one feeling left, and I think you hurt it."

He laughed hard. "Yes, Cher. I believe that shit."

She sighed. "Why do I always get that reaction? It could happen." Kara pushed away her plate.

"Sure. Maybe," Brock said, cleaning off his hands and face. "Are you full, Cher?"

"I'm never full. I eat like a linebacker." She wiped her fingers off and sipped her water.

"Well, then we should order their mountain sundae."

211

"Mountain and sundae in the same sentence? I'm in!" Kara grinned and scooted closer to him.

"It's huge. If we can eat it, our food is free, and we get our next two dinners, on the house." He grinned. "I haven't been able to finish it off. I blame the damn sprinkles."

Kara laughed. "I think we have a shot, Babes. Tonight, is your night."

"Sweet!" He laughed and ordered it when the waiter came back to clear the table. "I should warn you, it causes brain freeze." Brock tilted his head and thought for a moment. "Maybe that's just me."

"But worth it if we can conquer the mountain!" Kara grinned and bumped his shoulder playfully.

Brock laughed and took her hand in his. In his wildest dreams, he'd never dared to imagine that this time with her could be possible. "Maybe this time. If it takes me out, you can avenge me!" He joked

Kara nodded and stretched up to kiss his cheek. "The carnage will be epic. Stories will be told."

He laughed and bumped her shoulder as they carried the mountain of ice cream to the table. "See? I told you. Diabetes here we come!"

"I'm not sure if I should use a spoon or a shovel?" Kara blinked at it. Mountain was not an exaggeration.

"I know, right?" Brock handed her a spoon and took the cherries off the top. "Do you want them?" He asked eyeing them. "We can put them in your seed water."

Kara made a face and took the spoon. "That would be gross. I'll take one though." She opened her mouth.

He fed her one and ate the other before he dug into the ice cream. He was sure it was the sprinkles that always kicked his ass.

She chewed and grinned at him. "Meet you in the middle, Big Guy."

"Good plan." Brock shoveled in as much as he could, and then the ice cream headache started in. He ignored it, though he was sure his face showed that the ice cream was winning.

Kara ate like her life depended on it, laughing at the look of pain on Brock's face until a spike of ice was drilled into her forehead making her groan and push her hand against it.

"See? I told you." Brock moaned but kept eating, even though his head was one big ice cube.

"I thought you were joking. Food is not supposed to fight back once it's dead." Kara rubbed her head and scooped up more ice cream. "It's a rule. Or it should be."

Brock laughed hard. "You'd think that, but this stuff does. It's made by humans, so you do the math." He chuckled pushing ice cream onto her side of the bowl.

Her mouth fell open. "That's cheating!" She dipped her finger into a mound of whipped cream and dabbed it on his nose.

He crossed his eyes to see his nose and then licked it off. "Bear tongue." Brock laughed and put chocolate sauce on her forehead. "The blood of your enemy." He busted out laughing.

She arched a brow and felt her face flush a little watching him take care of the whipped cream on his nose. "Hey!" She laughed at the smudge on her forehead. "Keep it up, Buddy and we're going to fail when this spirals into a food fight." She ignored the spot on her head and stuck her tongue out at him. Ignoring the kid that was watching them over the back of his chair.

"Yes Ma'am!" He laughed and tried to eat, but he couldn't stop laughing at her.

Kara blinked at him and kept eating, glad that he was laughing and seemed to be enjoying himself, even if it was at her expense. Small price to pay to take his mind off what was coming.

Brock finished his half and leaned back. "Well Cher, can you do it or do we need to cheat?"

213

Still working on the smaller mound of ice cream, Kara thought that he might be right about the jimmies being the trouble causing bastards. She covered her mouth and chewed. "There was a cheating option, and you let me get brain freeze instead of telling me?"

He ghosted the bowl empty.

"Nah, put it back. I got this" She grinned and kissed his cheek.

"You sure Cher?" When she nodded, Brock put it back without the evil sprinkles.

Kara grinned, noticing what was missing. "Thank you." She hoovered her way through the mound of ice cream and finally put down her spoon. "Done, but I might explode."

Brock kissed her and groaned his contentment. "Now we sit here until one of us can move to roll the other home," he joked leaning back in the booth.

Kara laughed and leaned her head against his shoulder. "I hope they're open late," she joked back.

He smiled. "Twenty-four hours, Cher."

"We may need it."

He nodded and groaned. "Yes!" The waiter came back, and the look on his face said it all. "We would like the free meal coupons and maybe a barf bag," Brock said, leaning on her.

"Scratch the maybe and make that a definitely for the upchuck sacks." Kara laughed and groaned.

The waiter left them, laughing. "You know, I think I just gained ten pounds," he said patting his belly. "I look pregnant."

She rubbed his stomach, teasing, "I'm a fertile little Valkyrie."

Brock laughed hard, and that made his stomach hurt. "You're killing me, Cher."

"Awwww, poor Bjorn." Kara laughed at the look on his face.

"Yes. There goes my girlish figure."

"I like your figure, just the way it is." She wiggled her brows and bit his shoulder.

Brock smiled. "Thank you, Cher."

"No problem, it's true."

A few minutes passed, and the waiter returned with everything. "Okay Cher, on the count of three, I'm gonna get up. You ready?"

Kara eyed him skeptically but nodded. "I'll catch you if you don't make it, Big Guy."

Brock laughed and counted to three. On three, he got to his feet with a groan. "Sweet Jesus." he moaned, moving so she could get up.

"Oh, you wanted me to get up too?" She blinked at him and then sighed, following suit. She felt better once she was on her feet. "Not as bad as I thought." Kara grinned and slid an arm around his waist.

Brock left a generous tip on the table, and they started for the door. "I don't know if this was a smart victory," he said opening it for her.

She laughed. "We fought to the end, that's all that matters. Where we going, Babes?" She asked stepping outside onto the sidewalk.

"Where ever you want." He said following her out, still feeling overly full.

"I don't know. Depends on what you want. Do you want to be where you're just a knock away? A text away? Do you feel like alone time or company? You know, that kinda stuff."

"I honestly want to lay down and digest."

"Okay." She grinned and stretched up to kiss him. "I'll check in tomorrow."

"Please do. I want to make sure you don't die from the sugar." He teased, hiding his disappointment that she was leaving, not sure he believed that she would come back.

Kara laughed. "I'll walk it off and then go scouting. Have a good night, Babes."

Brock pulled her to him and kissed her passionately. It might be the last time he got the chance, and Brock wasn't going to squander it. Who knew what would happen when Dane came back? She could come to her senses and realize that he was just a bear and was beneath the Goddess that she was. His heart constricted painfully as he savored every second like it was his last. It might be.

Kara melted against him reaching up to curl her fingers in his long hair and took every bit of passion in that kiss and returned it, moaning softly. "You don't make it easy to remember to give you your space," she whispered against his lips and nipped his bearded chin.

"I'm sorry, Cher." He said grinning at her words and pressing his lips against hers again. "I'd ghost home if I were you."

"Okay. Why?" Kara tilted her head back, her arms still looped around his shoulders. All she could think about was getting him naked again, after that kiss. He was confusing the hell out of her.

"So, you don't waddle. I mean, I know I am."

She laughed and patted his chest. "Maybe you should ghost home then. I have a long night ahead of me. Be safe."

"I will. Please call or text me, if you need me. While you were sleeping, I put my number in your phone." Brock hoped that he didn't sound as desperate as he felt.

"I will. Same goes." She smiled softly and forced herself to pull back, even though she didn't want to, and began walking away. Pulling out her phone to ask Reese to send the coordinates of the two properties they thought that Bree might be held at, she looked back to smile at him over her shoulder.

Brock watched her go before stepping into a dark spot, off the sidewalk and ghosting himself home. Once there, he shifted into bear form and flopped on the floor on his side. He was so full he felt like he might puke.

Chapter 25

Brock lay on his side like a beached whale for a few hours, too uncomfortable to sleep. He'd hoped that the food would digest a bit faster. As he lay there, he thought about Kara and last night. A happy grin curled his muzzle and he chuffed. He worried that she'd get over whatever the fascination she had with him was, but the way she'd looked at him and the scent of her arousal when she'd walked into the darkness, gave him hope that it wouldn't be soon. He wished that he'd said that he wanted her to come home with him. He always thought of the right thing to say too late. He sighed.

His mind drifted to his brothers. The look on Bart's face said it all, his brother was not happy with Kara and him being chummy. Brock knew he needed to talk to Bart, but he didn't want to have a fight. His mind churned with too many thoughts. And his stomach growled a bit letting him know he needed to either fart or burp. "So full," he groaned to himself. Even though he felt like he might puke, he pushed himself to his feet. 'Brother, we need to talk,' Brock mindlinked Bart.

Bart was still going through his contacts when he heard Brock in his head. He thought about ignoring him. 'What?' He answered coldly.

Brock could tell by his tone that Bart was pissed off. 'Look, I know you're not happy about seeing Kara with me.' Brock's stomach made a disturbing noise.

Bart gave him a mental eye roll. 'Why would you say that? She has a mate. We don't even know where Dane is. Or Bree. And you're off skipping through tulips.' Bart really wanted to know what was so fucking special about this chick.

'I think you mean tiptoeing through the tulips,' Brock corrected him.

'Whatever. Not my point. Stop letting your dick lead you around. This is going to end badly for all of us,' Bart said through mindlink. He just knew something bad would come of all this. And he didn't want to see his brother be used as a rebound side piece.

Brock growled, 'I am not being led around by my dick. You don't know a damn thing about her.'

'No?' Bart snorted. 'Fill me in, dear brother. Tell me that fucking the mate, ex-mate, whatever the fuck you want to call her, of Alpha Pride's explosives operative is a good idea. How fucking a goddess who gets off on killing things is safe. What happens when her father finds out and comes looking for you? There are three of us that look exactly like you. Did you even think about that?'

Brock blinked. He hadn't thought about any of that, in all honesty. 'You're paranoid.'

"Am I? When you are putting a piece of ass ahead of your clan? What was I thinking?' Bart growled, sending out another text. 'Must be a gold-plated pussy or some shit, for you to have lost your fucking mind over it.'

Brock growled and curled his hand into a fist. If his brother were here, this would lead to a fist fight. 'That's not fair. Why is it so awful to want one thing for me? I'm not stupid. I know it probably won't last, but what's so wrong with me enjoying it while I can?'

'Maybe because we both know that you've been sniffing after her for a year. You seriously think you can just

218

walk away when she says, enough? Tell that lie to yourself, brother, because I ain't buying it.'

'What do you know about what I can and can't do?' Brock sneered and hated that his brother was right about that last part. When it happened, he was going to be broken in a way that not even time could heal, and he knew it.

'I know enough to know you've got a female on the brain and not the right one,' Bart said, cutting the mindlink.

Brock wanted to choke his brother. How dare he after everything Kara had been through? No, not even that. After what Brock had been through. Why was it so bad for him to be happy? If his brother didn't like it, too damn bad. Not that it would last long, but that was a worry for another moment.

Brock was suddenly exhausted. He lay back down on his side, on the floor. He closed his eyes and tried to think of something other than the worry that was creeping back into his mind.

Chapter 26

The first location was a bust. Not that it was unoccupied. In fact, it was overrun with humans swarming like wasps protecting a nest. Kara hovered overhead using the lack of light to mask her presence as she listened and tried to feel Bree inside. All she got was the chemical smell of meth being made. The place wasn't legit, but it wasn't their kind of problem, and the smell was threatening to squeeze the sundae she'd shared with Brock, back out.

She shook her head and ghosted to a stand of trees that crowded against the newly constructed stone wall of the second location. Her brow arched at the laser line of an alarm system that hit the grass between her feet.

Kara smiled. They had tricks, and that was promising. Closing her eyes, she scanned the compound or tried. Something was blocking her, and the idea of dropping Fenrir inside and letting him chow down on the ass hats hit her again. If he wouldn't tear through everyone... She sighed and carefully stepped over the red beam, checking that she wasn't stepping into another before crouching down to watch.

Kara scanned the wall for traces of an alarm or more of the laser trip wires. She needed to get closer and then find a way inside. Headlights cut through the darkness. She ducked lower and leaned her chest against the bark of a tree that allowed a clear line of site to the gate. The white cargo van inched toward the entrance, slowing to a crawl and then a stop when a man, he stunk of demon, stepped out of the shadows and motioned for the driver to roll down their window. Kara listened intently but could only make out a few words. "Master. Tiger. Bait." In any other context, they would have been meaningless, but after the update she'd gotten from Reese, it made scary sense.

The demon turned to the stone perimeter and waved his arms at something high on the wall. A whirring motor joined the drone of the van. Kara winced at the screech of metal on metal when the gate began to roll open. She should text someone, but she didn't have time. This might be her only chance, but she wasn't stupid. She sent out a mindlink to Brock and a select few AP members, "The farm is a bust. At the stone wall and going in."

The van began to roll forward again. Kara didn't wait for an answer and ghosted herself to lay sprawled on the roof of the van, wincing at the sound of the metal popping and groaning as it adjusted to her weight. If anyone heard her, the element of surprise would be lost along with the chance to find Bree and get her the hell out of here without bringing the entire compound down on them. A roar vibrated the thin skin of the van under her. Kara grinned. They weren't likely to hear much with that going on.

Bree stirred. Her body throbbed, and her mind was groggy. She blinked, waiting for her eyes to adjust to the dim light. Crap. She was in a cage. *'What the hell?'* Where was she? How long had she been where ever she was? Her large grizzly bear form took up most of the cage she was packed into like a sardine. She shifted her weight, and the metal bars creaked. She was too groggy to try busting out.

Her mind churned and seemed to want to focus on her family. Her brothers would be worried sick. Although for all Bree knew, she might have only been away for a few minutes, or it could have been days. She couldn't tell. She closed her eyes and tried to focus her mind, but she couldn't. Frustrated, she let out a growl.

221

"Quiet in there!" A deep, male voice yelled.

Bree growled louder.

"I SAID QUIET!" The voice repeated, louder and angrier this time.

Bree didn't quiet down. In fact, she got louder. She wanted to see who was doing the yelling. It was one of the first things that she'd learned during her training. Spirit or the living, always know your enemy.

"Goddamn it, I said quiet!" The owner of the voice cursed and stomped into the room. He was tall and lanky. Bree had to adjust her position to turn her head up to see the evil glint in his silver eyes. Jet black hair fell across his face, and his skin reflected tones of blue and green. The leathery wings folded behind him and dragged over the rough floor, reminding Bree of nails on a chalkboard. He turned slowly. Eyeballing the rows of empty cages, his pale lips curling up in a sneer when they landed on her.

Bree watched him, seeing the other cells for the first time when her eyes finally adjusted to the near darkness that surrounded her. She recoiled, pulling as far away from him as the bars that bit into her backside would allow. It wasn't far enough. She bared her teeth. A silent warning that she would remove any parts he dared try to touch her with.

Not impressed, the demon stalked closer to glare at her. "Don't you speak English or are you just a stupid fucking animal? When I say to shut the hell up," A spiked tail that she hadn't noticed slammed against the bars and echoed through the chamber. "I mean, shut the fuck up. What part of that is giving you trouble, Rug?" His tail banged against the bars again. He opened his mouth to continue the rant, exposing rows of jagged razor-sharp teeth, but stopped and tilted his head to the side, listening.

His chuckle made Bree's skin goose bump and crawl. There was no humor in it. Only cold, deadly delight. She watched the barbed tail cut through the air behind him, expecting it to be used as a weapon or torture device at any

222

second. The growl rolled up her throat as she readied herself for the attack. His laugh died, and Bree heard the skipping purr of an engine growing louder.

"If you make one more noise I'll slit your throat." He glared at her with those creepy silver eyes for a moment before he whirled around, striking the cage with his tail one last time and leaving the room.

Once he was gone, Bree closed her eyes and let out the breath she'd been holding. She was screwed. She tried to focus on an escape plan, but instead, her mind wandered and replayed the last few days. She felt sick inside about Kara and what had happened. Bree wished that she could do something for the Valkyrie. 'I'm so sorry Kara,' she said in her mind.

Tears stung her eyes, and she wasn't sure if it was from pain or sadness. The tears glittered green as they ran down her fur. Hitting the floor, they pooled under her chin. Her thoughts were as clear as pea soup as her body fought the poison from the dart, but she could feel something happening. Her magic was changing. The pool grew with each teardrop, seeping out through the bars. Bree blinked her eyes when she saw Kara's face reflected on the surface. Shaking her head at the mirage, Bree stared into it. 'Forgive me, Kara,' she said to the pool. Little did she know her thoughts were being sent right to the Valkyrielike a loud speaker from hell.

Kara gritted her teeth and held on for dear life when the van pulled through a minefield of potholes and watched the scenery crawl by. Demons. An ass load of them. Huddled around fires in big metal barrels warming their hands as they talked, laughed and in one case, punched another in the gut. Great. There were more shouts when the van stopped. Not of alarm, but instructions. Back up to the big double doors, leave it and get the fuck out so they could scan the van.

Scan it? What the hell did that mean? Kara's brows popped when a machine was rolled out beside the van that

223

looked like a monster version of the x-ray machine Asher had used when she broke her wrist last year. She glanced over her shoulder looking for somewhere to go before they discovered her. Pain blasted inside her head. Bree's voice filled it and expanded until Kara wondered if her skull was going to explode. Her vision dimmed. She blinked against it, feeling the trickle of blood roll over her lip.

'It's okay, Bree,' Kara linked back, trying to figure out how to adjust the volume. Before she got hit with another psychic sucker punch, Kara ghosted to the roof, staying low and wiping at the blood on her face with the back of her hand. 'Just tell me where you are and we can go get a drink and plot new ways to give your brothers gray fur.'

Bree's head cocked when she heard Kara's voice, not sure if it was real or a hallucination. 'Kara, is that you? I don't know where I am. I'm in a room with cages, and there's a demon guarding it. I think I heard an engine, but I don't know.' Tears were still rolling down her muzzle. 'My head feels like it's full of swamp water. The cage I'm in is too small. It's noisy.' She looked into the pool, still seeing Kara's face.

Kara had to steady herself with a hand on the rough tarred roof. Bree's volume dial was cranked up to eleven, and she didn't seem to know it. The trickle of blood coming from her nose became a stream. 'Yeah, it's me, Kid. I need you to dial it back a little. You're killing me, here.' She leaned forward to look over the edge as they scanned the van and bullshitted with the shifter versions of the human fishing story. Bigger than a whale. Fought for three days and nights. Blah. Blah. Blah. Only the fact that shifters were working for the demons caught her interest. 'Figure of speech, mostly. Just hold on, cub. We aren't going to let you stay here. You feel me?'

Kara pulled out her phone and shot a text to both Reese and Brock. [At the place with the stone wall. Bree's here. Alive. Not sure what I can do solo.] She tapped send and shoved it back in her pocket. 'Try to stay calm. The posse knows where we are. Hold on, okay?' She pinched her nose and rolled her head back, hoping to stop the flow of blood that if even one of those fuckers scented, would give away her location.

Hearing Kara, Bree didn't understand what she meant about dialing it back. She tried to whisper her reply. 'Okay. Hurry, please. The sounds coming from the other room don't sound good.' She wondered if Kara could hear them. Bree heard the clanging of chains and the whimpering of an animal, but she couldn't figure out what it was. The foul demon was talking to someone in the hall, but it wasn't clear who. What scared Bree most, was the sound of a buzz saw and the whimpering that grew to a howling scream and then stopped.

Brock laid on his side, snoring softly when his phone went off, roaring like a pissed off grizzly. He snorted awake and swiped his massive paw at the sound, knocking his phone onto his ass. The phone slid off his fur and under the bed. He growled and shifted to human form, before crawling under the bed and grabbing the phone. Unlocking the screen, he saw Kara's text.

"What!" He growled, jerking his head up. Pain slammed into him when his head connected with the bed frame. "Son of a..." He snarled and crawled out from under the bed. [I'll be right there. Hold tight. Thank you, Cher.] He texted once he was clear of the bed. Ghosting himself dressed, he went to find his brothers but had no luck. There wasn't time to dick around.

Rycker woke with a growl at the voice in his head, and he was already tapping the keys of the keyboard when Reese pounded on his door and burst in. "I'm on it," he mumbled without looking up or stopping. If they had a security system and internet, he could hack his way in, now that they had a definite target. He chuckled as he hit the fourth firewall. "Oh, you think you're good?"

He felt Reese hovering behind him. "Coffee. Black. This shouldn't take long." He heard her cuss behind him and

225

didn't care. He worked faster without the distraction of the Boss Lady hanging over his shoulder. Another five minutes and the wall of monitors lit up with scenes from inside the keep. "Gotcha." Rycker grinned and leaned back in his chair wondering where his coffee was.

Feeling the silent vibrating blip against her ass cheek, Kara pulled her phone out and read the text. [Stay calm. Get the others. She's ok, just scared.] She pressed send and then as an afterthought added. [No getting yourself killed. I'll take that personal.] She sent the text and sent a silent thank you to the sky when Bree's mindlink didn't take her head off this time.

'It's going to be okay, Bree," she linked. "I need you to stay calm, so this can go off smoothly. Okay? How many are with you or close by and do you know any of them?"

Bree tried to focus, but the wet sound of the saw was freaking her out. 'I think the other one is dead. I can hear a saw. Other than that, maybe two? Just a demon and someone else, I think. None smell or sound familiar to me.' She stopped for a moment as she heard a new voice come into the conversation. A scent that she remembered hit her. 'The thing that took me is here. I can smell it. It's powerful. Please be careful. It's evil, and it's angry,' Bree linked, trying to stand up in her cage. The metal creaked as she pushed against the bars. *Maybe if I can get out of this cage, I can break free,* she thought, giving the cell wall another push. She felt it starting to give a bit on the right side.

Brock's phone roared again as he was going down the hall to look for Reese. [Not sure where they are.] As he hit send he slammed into someone. A growl rolled from his chest.

Reese was coming back from the kitchen, trying to find the right speed that got her where she needed to be without splashing the coffee over the rim. She knew that Rycker had sent her away, just to get her out of his hair. She pulled out her phone to send the alert, typing furiously with

226

her thumb. [All hands. Suit up. Moving out in 15.] She hit send and hit a brick wall, spilling the coffee down her front.

"Fuck!" She growled and looked up, meeting Brock's wild blue eyes. "Good. You're up. Ry is hacking their security now." She ghosted another cup of joe into her hands and led the way to Ry's space. "Dayum..." She said on the exhale when she saw the wall of monitors already lit and showing them the inside of their target. She grimaced at the screen of the bear trapped in a cage. You didn't need to be a rocket scientist to figure out that it was Bree and the girl didn't have plans to stick around.

Rycker took the mug and smiled smugly before he took a long sip and purred. "Okay. The gate is here and runs on a remote link." He clicked the mouse on the screen that showed it from the inside. "Bree is here." Another click. "And as far as I can tell, Kara is almost directly above her on the roof. I can open the gates. There's another one in the back and a tunnel that comes out down by the swamp. If we hit all three at once, that should be enough for Kara to ghost in and grab her." He leaned back. "Or, you know, whatever you want to do." He shrugged and nodded a greeting to Brock. "S'up?"

Brock looked at the wall of monitors and growled when he stepped into the room. "Bree," he whispered, seeing his sister in a cage, two sizes too small for her large form. His eyes darted to the other monitors as he greeted Rycker with a nod. "Who the fuck are they?"

Reese shook her head and shot Rycker a droll glare. "No idea. Not the usual band of fuck-ups. Looks like a demon encampment. That's new." She glanced at Brock and then back to the monitors. She pointed to one of the screens that had something thin and wispy fluttering across it. "Does Kara know she's almost on camera?"

Rycker looked over at Brock and then to Reese. "I don't think she does. And there's another that will pick her up is she moves away from the ledge. The bigger concern is in eight. He clicked the frame. The shit they are doing to that

227

wolf, ain't right." He put down his mug and cracked his knuckles. "You give me the signal, and we'll open this thing up like a tin can, Boss Lady." He pointed out the locations of the sensors along the perimeter and clicked the keys of the keyboard, creating the bit of code that would take them all out with the push of a button.

'Okay, Bree. Try to calm down, Babes. I need you to keep your head. We have backup coming. As long as they aren't concentrating on you, we've got time. I need you to tell me if that changes. If they come for you, you've gotta let me know. I'm blind to what's going on down there.' Kara tried to keep her voice in the mindlink calm and steady as she felt Bree's panic grow again and caused more blood to spill over Kara's lip.

Bree listened to Kara and tried to take it easy. She concentrated on pushing on her cage. 'Okay, but if that thing comes in here, I'm not going to play nice,' she murmured and listened to the sounds coming from the next room.

Kara grinned at Bree's link and covered herself in her armor, glancing over the edge again when something roared. The tiger. They had three catch poles looped over its massive head and others tight around both rear ankles. She shook her head and fought the urge to release the poor beast, but as much as she wanted to, she had a mission to complete and that had to be priority. She wouldn't let Brock or the other Navarro brothers down. 'I don't expect you to go easy, Bree. But let me know if that happens because I'm not gonna let you face it alone. Feel me?'

Bree heard footsteps and froze as two demons came into the room.

"Put the new one over there," the latest demon said, coming into the room with the first demon. He turned to Bree. "And this one, I think we need to move her before her family comes for her."

Bree snarled at him.

228

Gore laughed. "What are you going to do in there?" He said, stepping closer. "Maybe we need to dart you again, bitch." He smiled at her coldly.

Bree wasn't going to let that happened. She roared at him.

He laughed at her and manifested a cattle prod in his hands. "First, I'm gonna have fun with you." He lunged at her with the prod.

'Demons!' Bree yelped through mindlink in a soft tone before she roared at the demon with the prod. As he came at her, she slammed her weight into the cage. The right side gave out and fell to the floor with a loud thud and rattle.

The other demon's eyes bugged, but Gore was unfazed when the bars that protected him from the giant pissed off female grizzly crashed against the floor, nearly taking him out.

Bree slid out of the cage and let her claws out. She roared at them in warning.

Kara ghosted to the hall outside the room that Bree was being held in, appearing behind a demon and turning his head on his shoulders like a cap on a broken bottle. The sound of crunching bones was drowned out by the tiger's roars as it was led inside and then Bree's as she squared off with an ugly SOB. Manifesting her weapons, Kara didn't hesitate, running the closest demon through with her sword and then using her foot to kick the still twitching body from the blade.

'I'm in. Can't wait.' Kara mindlinked Reese and Brock, planting her elbow in the teeth of a demon that grabbed a handful of her hair. She disappeared her sword and turned to shove her hand through his rib cage, curled her fingers around his heart and yanked it out of his chest to shove it into his face as he dropped. The slight tightening of her jaw was the only trace of pain caused by the broken ribs that dug long gouges in her wrist and hand.

Bree saw Kara appear behind the demon with the prod. She didn't give her away. Instead, she reared up on

229

her hide legs and started forward, claws bared. Gore tried to zap her. The prod touched her and gave a loud snap. Bree roared in pain, but it didn't slow her down. Her training had taught her to take the pain and fight through it. She swung her left paw out and caught the prod knocking it from his hands. Dropping onto all fours, she rushed him.

Gore cursed and blasted the Grizzly with a fireball.

Putting her head down, Bree took the fireball head on. As her body went up in flames, she started chanting in her head, a spell Salvation had made her learn for protection.

Brock watched Kara for a second then watched the demons go into the room with Bree. He couldn't hear Bree, but he could see her. His sister had freed herself, and she was out for blood.

Reese cursed as the events unfolded on the monitor and shoved her earpiece into her ear and pressed the mic button, as she tossed one to Brock. "We're up. Going in hot. Civies present. Check in and ghost out." She listened as her team answered roll call. Only a few were missing, and she'd deal with that later. "Come if you're coming," she winked at Brock and turned to Rycker. "Give us sixty and then tear it all down."

Rycker gave her a nod as she ghosted out and leaned over the keyboard, snapping his knuckles and watching the clock tick down.

Brock took the ear piece and shoved it into his ear. He ghosted out behind Reese. He hoped they got there in time. If anything happened to Bree, the family would never get over it.

Reese's legs were already pumping when her boots hit the dirt. Skirting the wall, she led her team toward the main gate. She glanced around to see who was with her and drew her Glock and dagger. Holding up her hand she counted down with her fingers in the air. Three. Two. One.

"Go." She growled over the headset as the gate began to roll open allowing her team to spill into the yard. Her face tightened when she heard two other commands and knew that the other two teams had breached their points of entry. She didn't have time to think. An arrow whistled by her ear and grazed her shoulder. Her head snapped up to see the archer on the wall. No bow. The fucker was shooting them out of his hands. Tossing her dagger so that she caught the blade by its tip, Reese threw it, catching the bastard between the eyes. His body fell, crushing a demon who was making a run for it.

Rycker's eyes bounced between the monitors, and his fingers flew over the keys as he opened locks and closed and secured doors and gates behind the team. "Mother fucker," he cursed, seeing Bree burst into flames. He activated the sprinklers, adjusting the water flow to soak everything in the room. He hoped that the Valkyrie wouldn't take it personally.

Kara's eyes widened when the flames appeared. "E-fucking-nuff," she grunted, jabbing her dagger up and into the chin of the demon who jumped into her path. Shaking the gurgling thing off, she laughed when it started to rain, the drops of water hissing and steaming as they hit Bree's burning coat. She was about to yell for the she-bear to ghost out, but Bree was chanting some next level shit that these fucks weren't ready for. Meeting the bear's eyes, Kara nodded and turned her attention on the ringleader. She hit him with a bolt of lightning that threw him back against the wall and held him there as she fought off the surge of demons that filled the room with her free hand.

Bree chanted and the pain faded. As the water poured over her fur, she relaxed a bit. A bolt of white light burst from her chest, breaking into spears that went through the demons that swarmed into the room. They turned to ash and bone in seconds. She snarled. She wanted to stay to help, but she knew Kara had come from her, so it was time to leave.

'Let's blow this popsicle stand,' she mindlinked the Valkyrie, ghosting out and to the rear parking lot of The Pit. Her body was still smoking from the fire, and the zap from

231

the prod finally did her in. She fell to the ground, breathing hard. *My hair is never gonna be the same*. Bree tried to ghost herself inside but was too weak. Instead, she started crawling slowly towards the door, hoping no humans saw her.

As all hell broke loose, Brock shifted into form. He charged the demons that had come for them when the first beast opened fire. He clawed a path through the bodies. He wasn't going to stop until Bree and Kara were safe.

"Well, dayum." Reese whistled, watching the bear cut a path through the stragglers that hadn't immediately abandoned ship or run for the shelter of the building. Nodding to Syn, they fell into formation, flanking Brock's sides. Their role was simple. Protect their kind and above that, protect the keepers of the portal. "Repeat." She barked when she heard Rycker's voice through her earpiece, but what he said was drowned out by the sounds of shouts, screams, roars, steel striking steel and gun shots.

Rycker growled and spun the volume wheel of the mic. "Bree is out. Kara's still inside." He sighed when Ozzy appeared at his side demanding an update. Rycker waved at the monitors and picked up the direct line to the bar below. "Keep a look out. Bree is out. Makes sense she'll come home. Send one of her brothers. No. Brock is with us. Get one of the others, damn it."

Growling his frustration, Ry hung up and eyed Ozzy, who was about to touch something that he shouldn't. "I work better alone if you don't mind." The old bastard could draw and quarter him later, right now he had shit to do. Hell, that look on the old man's face read that it was a certainty.

Brax felt his sister's presence and heard someone yelling that she was incoming at the same time. Not slowing as he neared the heavy security door he shoved it open, catching it on the rebound as it ricocheted off the brick exterior. His breath caught in his chest when he saw Bree dragging herself over the cracked pavement with smoke

232

wafting from her wet fur. "Damn it, Sis, what did you do?" He gently laid his hand on her and ghosted her to the clinic, hoping Asher or Ana were there.

Bree smiled at him weakly and nuzzled his hand.

Kara sighed her relief when Bree flashed out, but she could sense all of the others who were still here. She upped the amperage she was funneling into Gore and kept her eyes on the door as she dodged a spear that should have run her through. She wanted to take him alive and find out what he was up to, but killing him would be easier, and she was short on time. Kill it was.

Gore was sure he was about to be done in when one of his minions tried to take the Princess out. Not wasting time or the distraction, he vanished from sight.

Kara raised her arm to hit him with a twin bolt from her other hand when the demon disappeared. *What the fuck?* She ducked a blade, barely in time, and shoved the heel of her hand into another's face, feeling the satisfying crunch of bone breaking. "It's been fun, but..." She flipped them off and ghosted to where she felt Brock.

The rampaging bear was almost to the building when Gore appeared on the roof. That mother fucking Alpha Pride team that had been cock-blocking his plans were right beside him like a damn flock of migrating geese and cutting through his minions. Gore waved his hand, using his power to turn the weakest minds of the team members on themselves.

'The roof!' Brock yelled through mindlink when he spotted the silhouette and knew it wasn't Kara. They didn't need another one of those arrow shooting fucks raining death down on them from above.

Zar's head snapped toward Brock. Before Syn realized that there was a problem, his brother went after the Grizzly. "We shouldn't be here for your stupid sister!" The tall Wolverine sneered and opened fire on the bear.

Brock roared in pain as the bullets cut into him. He dove behind a van. 'Reese, what the fuck?'

233

Reese turned toward the sound of gunfire, shifted forms and jumped on the stupid bastard that thought he was giving orders and that his opinion mattered. A bullet blasted through her side and exploded out through her shoulder blade. She sunk her claws into the stupid fucking newbie before her right arm went numb and limp.

Moving quickly, she snapped her jaws closed on Zar's throat and yanked, closing her eyes against the spray of blood and not letting go until the geyser stopped and the body was limp. 'Anyone else want to break rank?' She growled through mindlink and spit out a chunk of skin, muscle, and windpipe. She wobbled, trying to lever herself up, even though her shoulder was ruined, glaring at her men and daring them to try her.

Rycker growled when Ozzy snatched the piece out of his ear. "Abort. NOW!!!" Rycker shook his head and eyeballed the older lion. Reese was gonna kick her Daddy's ass, and he wanted a front row seat.

Kara appeared just in time to hear Brock's mindlink and ghosted to the roof, grabbed the demon, wrapped herself around him and threw them both over the edge. Twisting, she forced electricity into his body as they fell. They landed in a heap and bounced. Pain sliced through her and the air was forced out of her lungs. Manifesting her dagger, she drove it into his gut and gave it a twist before she weakened from the lack of oxygen. 'Just stay the fuck down,' she growled through mindlink.

Gore was hoping to take out one of the bears, but the head bitch in charge, lioness had cock blocked him again. Stabbing his fingers into his dark hair, he yanked until his scalp burned. *Could not one fucking thing go right?* He was about to vanish again when the princess came out of nowhere and almost killed them both. Grunting at the impact of the hard earth, he headbutted her. Once she seemed dazed, he sunk his teeth into her neck and vanished, leaving nothing but his blood behind and wiping hers from his chin with the back of his hand.

234

"Fuck!" Kara yelled, hitting the hard-packed dirt with her fists and dropping back on the yard before forcing herself up to be ready for the demon to pull a repeat.

Brock hit the ground, bleeding and cursing as he heard Reese take charge. Then Ozzy's voice exploded in his head. He wanted to say, *too late*, but the bleeding from whatever fucking bullets he was full of, stopped him and made it hard to breathe.

Reese growled as her team began to disappear one by one after her father's order. Patricide was sounding like a damn fine plan, but he was the only one that outranked her. She didn't have to like it. She looked around at the bodies and the handful of her most loyal that remained. 'Get the wounded that can be helped back to the clinic and put down those that can't.' She took a wobbling step, and her muzzle hit the bloody dirt.

Growling again, Reese forced herself back to her feet and watched as her team did as she said, waiting until the last had gone before she tried to figure out how she was going to get back. Weaker then she let show, she couldn't ghost back to The Pit. Reese felt someone touch her back and turned, bearing her teeth, to find Blade. 'Help the bear.'

Blade shook his head no and nodded toward the Valkyrie headed toward Brock. Before Reese could say anything else, he ghosted her out.

Rycker rolled his chair back, out of the way as Ozzy continued to bark orders. "Clear the bar. We're closed for business. Prepare for wounded incoming. Some won't be able to hold form." Ozzy pushed a hand through his hair, growling. This was exactly why he didn't want his daughter to follow in his footsteps. *Why the fuck had the gods decided to give him weak sons?* He turned his glare on Rycker, who was watching him coolly. "Did you not hear me, Boy? All mother fucking hands on deck, in the bar!"

Kara still couldn't breathe when she dropped to her knees beside Brock. "Don't you dare die on me, Bjorn. Don't you fucking dare." She pushed her hand into his fur and

235

looked up in time to see that they were the last ones there. "Time to go." She ghosted him to the clinic and yelled for the doctors, and when they didn't answer immediately, she yelled for Jared.

Chapter 27

Jared was taking out the trash from the waiting room when the walls shuddered, and the floor shook under his feet. He dropped the Hefty bag in his left hand and braced himself on the wall. NOLA didn't have earthquakes, but that's what it felt like. That or a bomb had gone off somewhere inside the building. He heard Kara yell his name in a tone that he hadn't heard before. One that sent chills racing down his spine and spun into a ball of dread in his gut as his mind whispered, *Armageddon*. He dropped the other bags and ran toward the sound of her voice and the blast of barely contained power pulsing through the Clinic. The swinging door of operating room two, boomed against the wall as he shoved through it.

He skidded to a halt. Kara was drenched in blood, and her eyes were flared wide, bordering on madness. Jared swallowed hard, flexing his fingers, not sure what he was walking into. She slammed into him, hugging him tight and he saw the massive Grizzly Bear on the table over her shoulder.

"Thank God," Kara whispered against his neck. She'd never been so happy to see anyone as she was to see this panther, right now. "We need your help. Please?" She didn't care about the desperation in her voice.

Jared cursed and wrapped his arms around her to lift her and set her out of the way. The room was silent except for her ragged breathing and a steady dripping. The scent of blood made him gag, as he stared at the bear and realized that the leaky faucet sound was the bear's blood, dripping onto the tiled floor. Cautiously, he approached the mound of fur that was stained red and matted as the blood began to dry at the stiffening tips. His mandatory earpiece was in his pocket, and Jared was totally oblivious to anything other than his own thoughts about Serra and what she wasn't telling him.

"The fuck?" His eyes lifted to Kara's over the bleeding mess when she joined him. He wasn't sure if he was asking about the bear, that smelled like Brock, and his wounds, or if he meant the way she was leaning over the bear's face, begging him not to die and pressing her lips to its muzzle. Jared shook his head to clear it and instinctively pushed his hands against the grizzly's chest, covering the wounds and trying to slow the bleeding. He glanced at Kara, noting the worry and panic in her eyes. "What did I miss?" Before he could get anything out of her, Brax flashed in with another grizzly, yelling for Asher and Ana as he carefully lowered the bear to the other table.

"He's been shot. I don't know how many times, but he's fading fast, and I can't stop it." Brax appearing with Bree barely registered. Kara pushed the hair back from her face, pulling it tightly, using the sting of her scalp to focus her thoughts. "I..." She yanked again. "I yelled for the Double A's, but they haven't come, and I remembered that time that you healed me and..." She stopped, realizing that she was babbling. "He needs help."

She let her hands slide down over her neck, pulling her hand away confused that it was wet. Kara stared, transfixed by the maroon smear on her palm. *Did the fucking demon bastard bite me before he flashed out?* She shook her head, to get it back in the game. Honestly, she didn't know how much of the blood was hers, Brock's or the demon that she'd let the air out of. "You have him, while I go knock some doors down and get someone here to do their fucking job?" There weren't many people that Kara trusted in this situation. Jared was one of them.

Shit! Jared's mind raced. *Brock's not part of Alpha Pride. Not like that.* "I've got him. You go find the doctors or a doctor!" Jared looked down at Brock's large grizzly form. "Fuck man. A picnic basket ain't worth a fucking body full of lead," he joked, waiting for Brock so give him a mental *fuck off cat*, but nothing happened. He wished Brian was here tonight. He could use Baloo's help right now. He didn't want the wounded grizzly to eat him.

Brax snarled. "Get a fucking move on, Jared. Help him and then give me a hand with Bree."

Jared looked at the male and wondered what he'd missed. It had to be huge. Jared dipped his index and middle fingers into the bullet wounds he was covering, feeling for the projectiles. He used his magic to pull the slugs from the bear's body. Jared counted ten, but he knew there were more. A few didn't pop out, but it was a start. He hoped Brock could start healing or at least stop bleeding.

Asher woke to shouts and banging on his door. He hadn't meant to doze off. Hell, he wasn't even close to ready for the assault that Reese had planned for tomorrow night. Groaning at the stiffness in his back, he rolled up so that he was sitting on the couch in his office. He glared at the piece of furniture, almost sure that it was plotting to kill him. He scrubbed his face with his hands and blinked at the door that shook in its frame when the pounding started again.

"Keep your pants on. It's open!" Asher's brows almost hit his hairline when Kara threw open the door, looking more like Carrie in the prom scene than the Valkyrie. "They went early," he growled,

She nodded even though it wasn't a question.

"We're not ready for this shit. Why does no one kee..." His words trailed off when she grabbed him by the scruff of the neck and ghosted him into the room with the Bears and Jared.

Asher allowed himself a quick minute to visually assess the situation. Bree was severely burned, but Brock was in danger of bleeding out. "What the hell kind of war zone did you all find?" He growled, pulling on the purple nitrile gloves that he hated, but Ana insisted on ordering instead of the black ones he preferred, and gathering supplies.

"Less talking, more making sure the bear doesn't die, Doc. I don't wanna say that your life depends on it, but well... It does." His yapping was getting on Kara's nerves. This was her fault. If she hadn't gone poking around and sticking her nose in shit, Brock wouldn't be full of holes. She rubbed the bite again, the pain helping her keep her shit together. Looking at Bree, she realized that if she hadn't done what she had, then Bree might not be here, looking a bit charred, but breathing. Kara blew out her breath in a puff, "Sorry. It's been a shitty week. Put me to work and let me help before I lose my shit completely."

Jared tapped the sheet and the bullets he'd removed from Brock danced and clinked together. "I didn't get them all." He patted Kara's back, wincing when she jumped and seemed about to come out of her skin as the power around her began to build again. "Asher has this," he whispered softly, hoping to defuse the nuclear bomb that the Valkyrie was becoming. "I'm gonna help Bree."

Brax growled when Jared lowered his hands to Bree's singed fur and blistered skin. "Look, if you want me to help her, then get over me touching her. This ain't a dream date for me either."

Brax glared at the Panther, but dropped his hands to his sides, balling them into tight fists. He could lose two siblings if these idiots didn't get to work. Grudgingly, he nodded to Jared and clenched his jaw until his molars creaked.

Jared put his hands on Bree's flanks and closed his eyes, pouring his magic into her, attempting to heal her from the inside, out. Bree's organs and muscles were an almost perfect medium rare, but they were regenerating on

240

their own. She didn't need him for that, so he absorbed her pain, hoping that she could rest comfortably while her body did its thing. White hot, Bree's pain burned his palms as Jared siphoned it into his bloodstream. He growled, and his body began to smoke.

"You want to help? Suit up. You're going to assist. " Asher pointed at the sink, "Get as cleaned up as you can and get your ass over here." The Valkyrie was showing the textbook symptoms of someone slipping into shock, but he hoped that giving her something to focus on would hold her together until he had time to worry about it. None of this was ideal, but that was just too god damn bad. He arched a brow when Jared began to smoke but kept his voice calm. "Brax, if he goes flame on, the fire extinguisher is behind you." Asher turned back to Kara who was at the sink, scrubbing her hands and arms furiously under the water, scouring off skin and making her cuts bleed more. "That's enough. Leave some skin." He slid the Iso cone over Brock's muzzle and adjusted the dials. "How many more are we expecting?"

Kara shook her head rubbing her hands and arms dry on a towel and then pulled a clean gown on over her bloody clothes. "I came out at the end. I think Reese was hit. Other than that, I have no idea." She stood beside the bed, pulling on the gloves. "Don't be shy and don't worry about being nice, Doc. I think we both have the same goal." She rubbed the fur on Brock's head and mindlinked him. 'You're going to be alright. You have to be. I need you.' She twitched her nose and ignored the tightness of her throat. Concentrating and following instructions, she took over stitching when Asher realized that she had experience and skill in that department.

Jared took as much of Bree's pain as he could before his clothes started to go up in flames. He snarled and pulled his hands away. He growled and panted, looking down at his blistered palms. His body was literally crisping from the

241

inside out. "She'll start to heal," he said through clenched teeth.

Brax breathed out a sigh of relief and offered Jared a rare smile. "Thank you. I mean it Panther." He didn't wait for Jared to say anything before leaning over his sister and whispering softly into her ear.

Blade lowered Reese onto one of the beds, but that wasn't working for her as the team members drifted in and out of the room, while they waited. She couldn't relax and give into the pain. Not while her people were here and someone would use it as just one more opportunity to prove that she was weak and couldn't handle this shit. She pushed her legs back under her and levered herself up until her lion form was sitting up and seemingly alert, though her mind swam in pain. She was waiting. Waiting to hear how the Bears were. Waiting for the Doc. Waiting for her father to come and strip her of everything that gave her life meaning. She chuffed as the men joked about her taking it like a champ when she wanted to roll into a ball and pass the fuck out. Instead, she sat here taking field reports of who made it and who didn't and trying like hell to track it all.

Jared left the room and saw Reese and Blade. He shook off the pain he was feeling and went to her. "So, what can I do for you?" No way in hell was he going to put his hands on her without her say so. Sure, they were friends, but that didn't mean shit at times like this.

"Knock her out and fix her up," Blade said. "She's stubborn. If you let him do it, I'll get you a huge white girl coffee," he teased the growling lioness.

Reese eyed them both, curling up her lip and snarling. 'I'm all right,' she ground out through mindlink and eyed the other members of her team still in the room. She saw Balden peeling off his glove and hissed at him. 'You dose me with that shit, and I will rip you the fuck apart, Djinn.' She growled again when he laughed. 'Don't try me. You won't like how it ends, and you can shove your white girl coffee.'

242

She swung her head back to Blade when Balden pulled his glove back on.

Koen slapped his friend on the back. "Come on man, there are others that won't be so bitch... I mean picky, about who helps them." He smirked at Reese and herded the others out of the room. "We need to have an accurate list of who made it out and who didn't. You know she's gonna chew on our asses if it's not ready when she is." He chuckled and exchanged knowing glances with the Djinn.

Reese growled at them even though inside she was sending Koen a big ass thank you, for clearing the room. Well, mostly clearing the room. Her tail twitched back and forth as the Panthers stepped away from each other and came at her from different directions. She snapped her teeth at Blade when he reached for her, but she lost her balance and face planted on the bed.

Jared backed off for a moment, but when Reese ate mattress, he put his hands on her. He used what energy he had left to heal her. "You can pull your dick out and swing it around now," Jared teased as Ozzy burst into the room.

Reese growled at Jared, but it was half-hearted and became a groan when her father appeared. She didn't need this. Not now. Why hadn't she let them knock her out? Pushing herself back into a sitting position, she shifted and pulled a sheet around her. She felt naked anyway, might as well go with it. "I owe you," she murmured to Jared who looked like he'd been hit by a bus. She didn't have to see her father's face to know the rage she would find waiting for her. Reese turned her head and met his eyes. Yep. There it was, just as she knew it would be. "You don't have to say it, Dad. I fucked up. I got the memo. Call back the skywriters." She sighed and rotated the shoulder that minutes ago, had been in pieces. "We recovered the objective, so I'm still marking it in the win column." Reese sighed, suddenly feeling dead tired.

Jared moved away from her and slid into a chair. He mindlinked Kara, asking how it was going with the bears. He just needed a moment to rest, then he could get up and help more.

The last bullet clinked when Asher dropped it into the kidney-shaped metal basin on the cart, and he left Kara to finish the last of the stitches. She concentrated on what she was doing, focusing hard, so her hands wouldn't shake. When Jared's voice sounded in her head, she jumped a bit. 'Closing up Brock now. Bree is still out cold, and Brax is his usual charming self. How are you?' She linked him and tied off the cat gut, wiping the sweat from her forehead with the back of her gloved hand. Now that the adrenaline was gone, all that was left was worry and guilt. Leaning down, she pressed her face against Brock's. "Just tell me that you're still in there, Big Guy," she whispered, hating how much it mattered to her that he was alright. Sighing, she glanced up at Brax, who was looking at her funny. "How's Bree?"

"She's healing," he answered and kept giving her that look.

"What? Just spit it out." Kara braced herself for a verbal assault or to have something thrown at her head.

"Thank you." One side of his mouth curled up before Brax turned his back on her and sat down in the chair at Bree's bedside.

Of all the things that could have happened, that wasn't even on the list. *Fuck. Hell has frozen over.*

'I feel like a tank hit me,' Jared answered, glad that they seemed to have the bears under control. He waited for Ozzy to start screaming.

"Now, how about you let me take a look at you?" Asher pushed a chair under Kara, sighing when she shook her head no. "Okay, I'll check on the others, but you and I are going to have a sit down before dawn. Count on it."

Kara sank down into the chair and dropped her head on the bed beside Brock's as the Doc removed the cone from his muzzle and seemed satisfied with his vitals. "Don't hold your breath, Doc." She lifted her head to watch him leave and then dropped her head again, curling her fingers in Brock's fur. 'I think your mate needs you, Serra,' she mindlinked Jared's mate, closing her eyes as the ache of her body settled in.

Reese met Ozzy's eyes as he crossed the room and stood over her with his arms folded over his broad chest. "Go ahead. I can handle it." She braced herself for a rampage, not thinking for a second that Blade or Jared being here would soften her father's temper.

"What were you thinking, Reese?" He growled, and his jaw ticked.

She arched a brow and mirrored his stance as best she could while sitting down. "I was thinking about doing my job, Sir. Priority one, protect the Navarro's and get Bree back home to her brothers. Priority two, take out as many of the enemy and recover as much intel as possible. Priority three, get my men out alive, or as many as I can. Last, worry about my own ass. You have a problem with that? Fine. Spit it the fuck out to me, but you do NOT interfere with a mission. Ever. That was the first thing you taught me. We, you and me, come last. How fucking dare you take my command in front of my team? With all due respect, Sir, that was a bull shit, fucking move and you'd have my hide it I ever slipped like that." Reese's voice was soft but firm and deceptively calm when the rage churning inside her was considered.

Ozzy rubbed his mouth with his hand and arched a brow that reminded her of her place, but his daughter stood her ground. "You're right."

Reese almost let her mouth fall open but recovered quickly. When he tucked the stiff, blood caked hair behind her ear, she closed her eyes and leaned into his hand.

"She's going to be alright?" He looked to Jared and Blade. He should have asked her, but he didn't trust her to tell him if there was a problem.

Blade shrugged. "Define alright." He smirked at Reese's glare.

245

Jared waited for the biting and watched Reese take off her father's head. He hid the pleasure he got from seeing the old goat dressed down proper. Reese had balls of steel. He nodded when Ozzy's gray eyes fell on him. "I did what I could, and that's my queue to motor," Jared got up slowly. He hurt badly.

Leaving the Cubs with Daniel as soon as she heard Kara's mindlink, Serra ghosted to The Pit. It was a sea of bleeding bodies. Worry squeezed her chest as she searched for Jared in the crowd and then flashed to the clinic, sighing her relief when she saw him closing a door behind him and stepping into the hall. "Baby?" She went to him, reaching for him carefully. "Are you okay?"

Jared smiled weakly. "I'm tired, and I hurt. Can you take me home, please? I don't have the energy to ghost out." He took her hand and purred.

"You got it, Panther," she purred back and circled his waist with an arm lightly. "Let's go home and get you fed." She ghosted them home to their bed.

Chapter 28

Gore stumbled against the dresser as his knees dumped his ass on the floor. The clunky piece of wood and drawers wobbled, slamming against the wall. Something fell and broke. Shards of glass rained from above. Gore ducked his head, feeling their bite over his shoulders and arms. Fumbling and cutting his fingers on the slivers, he tried to push himself up, but only managed a bad imitation of man's best friend on all fours. Blood tickled his chin. He clamped his lips tighter. What was in his mouth was the only thing that might save him from Ty's wrath.

Dragging one knee to his chest, he forced the sole of his boot to the carpet, ignoring the crunch of glass. He lifted his head, eyeing the top of the bureau. It might as well be on the other side of the globe. Gore commanded his muscles to work and help him stand. The electricity the bitch had poured into him was fucking with his nervous system, short-circuiting the messages his brain sent, and his meat suit was giving out.

The scent of bowel, wafted past his nose, through the smoke that misted off his skin. Looking down he blinked at the loop of sausage casing that dangled from under his shirt. Cradling it in his hand, he covered the wound, remembering that the princess had tried to gut him before he could escape. He'd bleed later. Right now, he needed the thing on the top of the dresser. Silently he prayed that it hadn't broken with the mirror.

247

His body heaved upward, tilted to the side and dropped him against the wood. The dresser tilted over him dangerously, dumping everything on the surface to the floor. Gore hit it with his elbow and slammed it back against the wall. The movement cost him in pain and the lovely way the room turned to black and white for a moment. Blinking until everything returned to Technicolor, he dropped his head back on his shoulders and stared at the ceiling. Slithering against plaster and carpet grew louder, warning him that time was running out.

Gore let the hand that wasn't holding his intestines in, fall. A cold, smooth surface teased his fingertips. Tilting his head, he almost laughed or would have if it wouldn't have lost him his prize and lifted the glass vial to his lips to spit the Princess's blood inside, covering the end with his thumb as his eyes searched for the stopper. Grunting, he dragged his knees to his chest and pinched the vial between them as he strained and reached for the piece of rubber. His fingers brushed it, making it jump, catch in the carpet and rebound closer to him. Fumbling, with cold, numb fingers, Gore shoved it into the vial just as the tips of pale gray tentacles emerged into the room and the lights clicked off, dropping him and the room into darkness.

Bertha was coming, called by the scent of the blood that Gore was leaking. His heart hammered in his chest, making it pump out of him faster. Fear mixed with adrenaline. Gore held his breath, wiping the Princess's blood from his lips on the back of his hand. *Was this going to be the time when nature won over nurture?* He knew that Bertha loved him, but she was an animal, and even the best ones sometimes bit the hands that fed them.

His eyes adjusted to the dark, glued to the hall that led to Bertha's cavern under the home he'd built. He didn't worry about anyone stumbling upon it. Bertha's magic was strong and cloaked them completely. That also meant that if she turned on him, no help would be coming. He returned the high-pitched trill of her call, smiling despite the impending danger as she pulled her massive squid-like body into his bed chamber. The tips of her tentacle arms brushed his face and curled around him

Gore palmed the vial as his pet lifted him and carried him to the bed and lowered him to it gently. The bed sagged and creaked in the silence when she wrapped around him, her 'arms' touching and stroking him as though he were the pet. Hell, maybe she thought he was. Or maybe she was just tasting him before the meal began. Gore didn't know.

The door flew open, and Gore recoiled from the scream that burst from Bertha. Something hot and wet dripped from his ears and he knew it was blood. Heather filled the doorway, her blond hair falling over her shoulders and her golden eyes wide. Her lips were moving, but Gore couldn't hear a damn thing. Great. Now his eardrums were blown out too. He couldn't catch a fucking break. Bertha raised her head to bare her teeth at the female that she hated.

"Leave us!" Gore bellowed, even though he couldn't hear a damned thing over the loud buzzing and ringing. The door slammed, pushing Heather out with it and Bertha wrapped tighter around him. His bones groaned and creaked under the pressure of her affection. Gore blinked and fought the darkness that was closing in on him. A tentacle arm, slithered around his wrist, pulling his hand back from the belly wound. Fireworks exploded in his vision when something round and hot was shoved inside him through the ragged opening in his gut.

Gore struggled to get his arms free to pull it out, but Bertha wouldn't allow him to budge. Fire burned through the hole in his gut, leaching into his veins and racing through his body. A dull green light pulsed through his skin in time with his thundering heartbeat. *What was she doing to him?* Gore's lungs stuttered and collapsed. Something filled them and expanded, tickling their path up to his nose and mouth, filling them and bursting out of his body to wrap back around his face. Gore thrashed as he panicked. He was

249

dying. Bertha stroked his hair, and he could feel her purr vibrating into him.

Something popped, and he drew in a ragged breath. Then another. Whatever was on his face moved and settled into place. His eyelids sagged. The panic bled away with the pleasant buzz that simmered inside him as his strength began to grow. He didn't know what Bertha did to him, but it was helping. Gore surrendered to it and let the world fall away.

Chapter 29

Brock heard a slow and rhythmic beeping. It was beginning to annoy him. He slowly opened his eyes and saw something out of the corner of his vision. He turned his head and pain shot through his neck and burned through his whole body. His large grizzly form felt asleep and yet on fire at the same time. He saw the heart monitor machine thing. The beeping from hell was coming from it. He must be in the clinic.

Kara grimaced and wiggled, trying to stop the arm of the chair from digging into her back without falling on the floor. Groaning she dropped her face into her hand and pinched the bridge of her nose before rubbing the grit from the corners of her eyes. How many days had it been? One. Three? A week? She wasn't sure anymore. Nothing changed except for the faces that poked inside the room and looked at her like she had answers that she didn't have. Sighing, she glanced at the mound of fur on the bed and one corner of her mouth curled up. "Finally decided to join us, Big Guy?" She leaned forward and stroked the fur of his shoulder gently.

Brock felt someone's hand in his hair. He relaxed a bit, knowing that it was her. When she spoke, he couldn't really do much other than groan. 'I think so. How did I get here?' He tried to do a pain assessment in his mind, but everything hurt. Even his eyelashes. So, he couldn't tell what was wrong with him.

"You were shot. A lot. I brought you here, and Bree is back with us now. I'd ask how you're feeling, but," She sighed. "I know you hurt, Babes. I'm sorry. I didn't get there in time to stop it from happening."

He forced himself to move so that he could see her better to make sure she was okay. 'Shot. Like with bullets?' That was a new one for him. 'If it wasn't for you, Bree might be dead. So, I owe you.' Brock meant it. He'd give is life for his family. And for her.

Kara nodded and grinned. 'I know. Bullets. So .... human." She made a face. "No, you don't. I owed her. She and I are square now, mostly. But if you want to be all indebted to me, then heal faster so I can stop worrying."

'I'll get right on that, but if I was shot...' Brock's mind was slowly kicking into gear. He could smell and feel Jared close. 'Is Jared here?' He couldn't see the panther, but he knew he had something to do with him being here.

"He was. He helped get some of the bullets out and took the edge off your pain. I think he went home to recuperate, he helped quite a few, and I believe that it drained him."

Flashes of what happened came back to him. A big question boomed in his mind. Why hadn't AP... No, why hadn't Reese told them what had been going on? Why had she waited until one of them were almost killed to say a word?

His family had a contract with her, and in it, the rules were clearly stated. He knew that AP thought they ran this place and that gave them the right to do whatever they wanted. Bottom line? All caretakers of the portal could have just been murdered. Then what?

Brock wasn't the type to get angry quickly. He prided himself on being level headed and thinking before he spoke. Being a hot head was left to his brothers, but in this case, he was mad. No, he passed mad a few moments ago. He was livid with rage. His eyes and nostrils flared. The anger was making his blood boil and kicked his magic into overdrive. Brock started to heal faster. 'Reese, where is she?'

Kara's brow wrinkled when she felt his mood change from confused to bloodthirsty. She watched him, trying to figure out what was going on in his head until he asked for AP's CO. "Last I knew she was here in the clinic. She took a bullet, killing the one that shot you. Do you want me to get her, Big Guy?" She could feel the power and rage pulsing off him. She'd worry if she couldn't also see his vitals on the monitor growing stronger.

'Yes, please. If she isn't here, it's alright.' Brock hoped she was, though. He wanted answers. He deserved them.

She leaned closer and kissed his nose. "I'll find her, and I'll be right back." She didn't want to leave him, afraid that... Well, she didn't know what. "Stay put, okay?" She said over her shoulder as she left the room in search of the lioness. Kara walked through the halls, fighting the temptation to throw open the doors that were closed to her and just as she was about to give in to it, she spotted Balden and Koen leaning against the wall at the far end of the hall. They didn't go far from Reese these days. There was a story there, but Kara had no idea what it was, "Reese in there?" She waited for the tall blonde one to nod before she turned the knob and poked her head inside.

"Reese?" Kara's brows shot up. The female was fighting to pull the shirt over her head to hide the angry blue and brown bruises that covered her shoulder and rib cage of her left side. She heard that Jared had fixed the shattered bone. It must have been bad for that much damage to still be showing.

"For fuck sake! Who do I have to kill for a little damn privacy?" Reese growled, her head snapping toward the voice to lay a glare on the intruder. *Annnnd it did no good, at all.* "Kara." She sighed and forced herself to face and overcome the struggle to pull the shirt over her head and down over her torso. "You need something?" She arched a

253

brow when Kara shook her head no. "Then, want to tell me why you're here?"

Kara leaned her shoulder against the wall and eyed the female. She still didn't have her completely figured out, and that made her a little twitchy. "Brock wants to speak to you. Now." She kept her tone even, realizing that she didn't want the lioness anywhere near the bear. Not because Reese was attractive, but because she didn't trust her. Something was off, and Kara didn't like it. "You can follow me." She turned and left the room, not checking to see if she was being followed. Reese could tell herself that she ruled the roost all she wanted to, but if Kara had to deliver a reality slap about her will trumping the lioness's, it wouldn't be forgotten anytime soon.

Reese slid off the table with a hiss and reached back to grab her jacket, only to have to grab it with her other hand when her fingers refused to hold it tight enough. She jogged and fell into step behind the Valkyrie, knowing that Balden and Koen had fallen in behind her. It was like a freak parade making its way down the clinic hall, all they were missing were clowns and a guy on stilts.

Shaking her head to get rid of the image, Reese stepped into the room, arching a brow when Kara closed the door behind her and in her entourage's faces. Reese crossed her arms over her chest, still holding the jacket. The Valkyrie crossed the room to stand at the end of the bed, strategically placing herself to defend the bear if necessary. It wasn't, but Reese appreciated Kara's need to do it. "Good to see that you're getting better, Brock."

Brock wished he could shift forms, but the pain was too great to force it. He cursed his body for a moment. 'Thank you. I wanted to ask you a few questions.' He decided to fight through the pain and shifted anyway. As he did, he roared out. Once he was in human form, he pulled the paper on the table over his naked lower half. Looking down, he could see the bullet holes. Holy shit. He'd taken a

254

full clip to his chest. Or it looked that way. He swallowed his tears and pain and lifted his head, looking at Reese.

Kara kept the wince off her face when he roared his pain, but she stepped closer to him. She was going to be silent and not interfere. Unless one wrong move was made. Then she'd paint the room red.

"Sure," Reese smiled and draped her jacket over the sink, before pulling one of Asher's rolling stools closer to her with the toe of her boot and sinking down onto it without letting how much that hurt show on her face. "Always happy to help."

Brock got his pain under control before he spoke. "Why haven't we been kept in the loop on everything that has been going down around here? Before you tell me it's on a need to know basis or some A-Team crap, let me remind you that my family could have been wiped out. And if that had happened do you have a plan B?" He tried not to sound like an asshole.

Reese eyed him coolly. "What didn't I tell you? I said that the last time we went in there, it was a mess. I told you that we could take the lead, or play back up, but WERE going to go. You didn't complain about us taking the lead when we left, and we didn't take our toys and go home when you decided to cut a path through demons." She crossed her arms over her chest, regretting it immediately as the pain flooded her shoulder. "I have no say in you or your family choosing to put themselves in the line of fire. I gave you the best intel I had at the time. I do want to point out that we DID get you all out. I lost people. Good fucking people. There was no plan B. It was simple. Get your sister and get out. I didn't foresee a demon getting inside one of my men's heads and turning him on you. If I had, I would have made different choices."

Brock's mouth was dry as hell suddenly, listening to her talk about it like she had done them a favor. "I'm sorry some of your people died. I didn't know it was going to be this big of a thing. And I am talking about what you said that day we

255

were looking at the maps. That you'd seen stuff like it before. I've noticed a lot of secret things happening. And sure, why would having a demon in the basement, ten or so yards from the portal, not be a red flag? There is more to the story, and I just want to understand. It is our job to keep the portal safe. I know that most of you think I'm just the slow, quiet one, but I notice things. My brother has been trafficking a lot of bodies in and out of there lately. Having to fill positions a lot more than normal." He said fill positions in air quotes. And that made him groan in pain. "And your father has been on edge a lot more than usual."

"The demon is locked in a cell. He's secure. As for secret things?" Reese arched a brow and snorted. "It's nothing more than has always been done. Yes. The body count is climbing. That goes hand in hand with the threat growing stronger. Will it make you feel better to know that while I had seen shit like that compound before, the shit we see now is all new and scary as fuck? We are barely holding it at bay and away from nice shifters, like your family. One slip and it is going to landslide and roll over us. The fighting rings aren't new. You may not know that they've upped their game and are snatching unwilling shifters and throwing them in. They're cutting them into pieces and stitching them back together in a Frankenstein patchwork hybrid army. Does that make you feel better? Does it change how you do your job?"

Reese closed her eyes and let her head roll to hang loosely on her chest for a moment before lifting it to meet his gaze. "Simple fact. War is coming, and I'm not sure we can win. But I will fight with my last breath to try. If you don't like how I run things, then I suggest that you talk to Ozzy, and have another team brought in."

Brock didn't know what to say as he took in her words. All of this was happening, and his family was oblivious to it. "Actually, yes. It would have helped to know that the shit was going to hit the fan. We could have stepped to the side, so to speak. And after everything that happened with Kara

256

and Dane, things have gotten way creepy. You don't like going in blind, and I feel like that's what happened to us. We are supposed to work together to keep this place and the people in it safe. And we lend ourselves to you whenever you ask us to," Brock said as the monitors he was still hooked to started going off.

He felt his heart start racing and his chest was tightening. *Was he having a stroke?* He felt weak as hell at that moment. His world was being turned inside out. *How could she sit there and say all that and not understand that if his clan and himself had known that they would be safer, they would gladly fight beside her and the rest of the AP?*

Reese eyed the monitor and then dropped her gaze to him again. "If you want to be included in briefings, then I can add you to the list. I understand that you have a weight on your shoulders and that protecting the portal is a thankless job. I'm asking that you know that I am personally responsible for EVERY life under this roof and the rest of my team. I don't take that lightly. I've made the best decisions I could, with what I knew at the time. I'll move Kane to our home compound so you can sleep easier. I do think you should speak with Ozzy about a replacement CO, one you feel that you can work with. He'll be all over the idea like ants on honey. As for the shit with Dane and Kara? I don't know what happened. My operative is MIA, and all I can figure out is that you're knocking boots with his mate. So, who isn't out in the open with the caring is sharing?"

Brock wasn't going to ask for another CO. He was finally calming down when she made a comment about him sleeping with Kara. "As you just said, you know nothing." His voice was cold. "They aren't mates. It was all a horrifying joke that ended with them both being murdered," Brock growled, pulling the cords off his body, not caring that he was in pain and could stroke out. He got off the table. Kara stood between them. "But hey, as you said, MIA and shit." He walked around Kara and pulled a sheet off a table. The pain he felt didn't stop, but he had to get away from Reese

257

before he leveled her. He'd never hit a female, but there was a first time for everything. As he left, he threw one last comment over his shoulder. "Good job with that too. Letting a demon piggyback on a shifter under your roof while you watched, Boss Lady, Sir!"

Kara's jaw twitched as she watched the exchange between the two and when he decided it was time to go, she was right behind him. She wanted to offer her arm but knew that he needed to walk out strong and on his own terms. It wasn't until they were in the halls, away from the clinic, that she laid her hand on his shoulder, to remind him that he wasn't alone.

Once they were gone and the door slammed shut, Reese finally let her face drop into her hands as she blinked back exhausted and frustrated tears. Maybe Dad was right, and she couldn't do this. "Not now!" She snarled when she heard the door whisper open. She blew out her breath when it closed and shut whatever she was feeling away in a box. In her position, she couldn't afford to have feelings. She did her job. She was the job.

Brock felt Kara's hand on him as he tied the sheet around his waist. "I'm sorry, Cher. I should have just kept my mouth shut. And if I were you and could hit a woman, I'd have knocked her teeth out. How dare she? I'm not like the other males here. I don't shove my dick in anything that will let me. I thought Reese knew me better than that. Take me to your place, please, and if it's not a lot of trouble can I have some pants? This pink sheet is not really me," he said feeling sick all over. "Or maybe I should go throw up in her office."

Kara ghosted a pair of loose sweats onto Brock and stretched up to kiss him, hoping to stop his words and calm him down as she ghosted him to her apartment across town. "She knows. I know. Trust me, I don't want to be the voice of reason, but you're both exhausted and both in pain. A bad recipe for saying things that shouldn't be said." She led him to the bedroom and helped him get settled on the bed, ghosting in a tall glass of water and the canister of salve that she'd brought from home that would alleviate some of his pain. Pushing him back, she gently applied it to the stitched-up bullet holes. "Forget about her for a little while, Babes. She doesn't matter. How are you feeling?"

"Like a tank shot me and then mowed me down." Brock laid on the bed and let her apply whatever it was she had to his wounds. He yawned and knew that his brothers would have a cow when they saw he wasn't where he should be. "I think I just need more sleep."

"The bed is yours, Captain." Kara grinned and did a horrible impression of Scotty from the original Star Trek. "If you don't feel better when you wake up, I'm taking you to my hot spring. If that doesn't fix you, nothing will." She grinned and kissed his cheek.

Brock took her hand, the one not coated in stuff, and kissed it. "Thank you." Yawning, he closed his eyes, and a few minutes later he was out cold in bear form, snoring softly.

Kara wiped her hands and covered him with a blanket before settling into a much more comfortable chair in the corner. She flipped on the television and kept the volume low. Scanning through the on-demand options, she decided on a season of Ink Master. She texted Bart that Brock was with her and that he was okay. Pulling her chair closer to the bed, she settled in again and tried to make it past the first elimination, but she lost the battle and fell asleep.

Chapter 30

Dane pulled the truck into his space and eyed the phone on the seat beside him that was going off for the billionth time. He'd stopped checking the messages and texts because not a single one, made any damn sense. Everyone wanted to know if he was okay, why he was hiding out and laying low, and for him to know that they were there if he wanted to talk. Since when was going to his cousin's cabin in the next parish over a reason to think he needed to be put on suicide watch? For fuck sake. The world had lost its damn mind, and he couldn't keep up.

He eyed the back entrance of the bar. Maybe he should just go to his room and avoid the crazy. It was a solid plan, but he needed his check. This old beast ate up gasoline like a junkie left unattended in a pharmacy. He rolled the crank of the window and sighed at his grumbling stomach. Decision made. He grabbed the worn AC/DC t-shirt and opened the truck door, reaching behind the seat for his boots. Something about driving with his shoes on, made his skin itch, so he avoided it as much as possible. Leaning down, Dane stuffed his feet into his biker boots and crammed the laces inside before pulling the shirt over his head and snagging the keys from the ignition. He left his phone where it lay and stepped out to slam the door.

He headed for the door, pocketing his keys and wallet as he crossed the gravel covered asphalt. Dane rubbed the back of his neck. The weird vibe in the air was making the hair there stand on end. His head turned, his gaze crawling over the parking lot, trying to spot the cause. It felt like everything was spiraling into chaos but he had nothing to base it on, let alone answers to the five basics of the who, what, where, when, and why of it all.

He passed Syn by the dumpsters. Dane looked away quickly when he noticed the red-rimmed brown eyes and the wetness of the wolverine's face, but not before Syn gave him the stink eye. What the hell had he missed? Dane kept his feet moving and ducked inside, skirted the kitchen staff and then down the hall to Reese's office. He groaned at the smell of elk burgers and the way it made his stomach turn inside out to devour itself. The door was locked. Great. Sighing, he followed his nose to the bar.

That was it. The last straw. Heads were going to roll. Scribbling a quick note for Brock, Kara left it on the bed stand, along with plenty of water and a few snacks. She watched the rise and fall of his chest, chewing on her lower lip. Maybe she shouldn't leave him alone. The phone beeped again, and she had to swallow her growl. No. This shit had to stop, and three bears had to figure out how to wipe their own asses until Brock was up to playing babysitter again.

Fighting the urge to touch him, she ghosted to The Pit in search of the three pains in the ass. Smiling at Brandon, Kara passed the line and ducked inside. Searching the crowd, she didn't see any of the Navarro brothers. "Fine," she muttered to herself and began shouldering her way through the bodies. One of them would show up at the bar eventually, and whoever it was, was going to get a piece of her mind.

Dane beelined for the bar to place an order before the growling in his gut made the typical Saturday night clientele nervous. He jumped when a hand slid over his crotch, and a fetching brunette batted fake lashes over emerald eyes and licked her lips with hunger. If he weren't starving, he would

261

have chatted her up and had no doubt that he could have had her in his bed with little to no effort. He flashed a smile, shook his head and kept walking until he could lean his elbows on the bar. Pity. Maybe after he ate. Dane slid his ass onto a seat and tried to shake off the feeling that everyone was watching him. He pulled his wallet out and opened it to find two lonely one dollar bills inside. *Great*, he thought. *What the hell can I get with this?* He wanted to bang his head off the bar, and then he remembered that he had a tab and felt better.

Kara bumped into someone when she slid onto the only empty stool left. "Sorry," she muttered before she glanced up and her heart skidded to a halt in her chest. She closed her eyes and cursed loudly inside her head. Of all the people that she had to bump into, did it really have to be him? Pulling her shit together, she shot him a smile and tried to get Brian's attention. She needed a drink, and she needed it now.

Dane turned to see who had bumped into him, expecting to see the randy brunette. His dark brows popped with surprise. It was the blonde from the other night. The look on her face read, holy shit. When she smiled, Dane nodded at her, ignoring the way his lion stirred and purred. "No problem. I think I'll live." He looked her over curiously. She was pretty if you liked that drop dead gorgeous blonde type. He did, but he'd seen her with Brock, so he assumed that she was probably one of those bear chasers that were always trying to bag themselves one of the Navarro brothers. He could be a gent and let her know that she was barking up the wrong tree when it came to Brock, but it wasn't his business, and maybe the bear would lighten up if he finally got laid.

Either way, Brian was ignoring him, and Dane's stomach was beginning to hurt. His hunger was making him grouchy and Brian's slowness to fix it was annoying. "Yo!" He barked, trying to get the bear's attention.

262

Brian held up a 'just a minute' finger and went back to the drink he was mixing. His head snapped back to look at Dane, and his eyes bugged. He didn't mean to do the double take, but seeing those two, sitting side by side was the last thing he expected. Brian looked over the crowd, searching for Brock. The word was that he and Kara were a thing now, so her being here with Dane, mate or not, could be trouble.

Dane's brow quirked at Brian's holy shit look. What the hell was going on with everyone? Acid in the water or something? He shook his head. "Let's hope we get service this eon because I'm starving and I just might eat the bar."

Kara grinned and nodded. "Good, because that would have to be one hell of a bump, to knock you off." She pushed the bowl of what looked like Chex mix, closer to Dane, shaking her head when he yelled. Some things never changed, and that was both comforting and devastating at the same time. "I don't know, it's high in fiber," she teased, knocking a knuckle on the bar. "Could be good for your digestion. Just don't shift and get all growly like that time..." She snapped her mouth shut and cursed at herself. "So how have you been since I saw you the other day?" She snagged a pretzel and popped it into her mouth to chew before she said anything else idiotic.

He took a hand full of the stuff in the bowl and popped into his mouth. After he'd chewed it, Dane took another handful, trying not to think about how many hands had been in the bowl or if they were hand washers or not. "Well, that gives new meaning to shitting a log," he said, popping another handful into his mouth. Someone had fed the jukebox, and You Can Call Me Al by Paul Simon played. He swallowed the food in his mouth. "Okay, I guess. Been hiding out. People have been acting weird as hell. It's tripping me out."

The drummer in him never slept. Instinctively, his feet and hands started drumming to the beat of the song. Under his breath, he sang along. "A man walks down the street. He says why am I short of attention. Got a short little span of

263

attention. And wo my nights are so long. Where's my wife and family? What if I die here. Who'll be my role-model? Now that my role-model is Gone! Gone!" He stopped when he realized that she was looking at him like he was looney.

Kara smirked. "Don't stop on my account. I didn't expect dinner and a show, but I got no complaints." How was it possible that she could feel so completely at ease with him like nothing had changed, when her entire world had gone to shit? It wasn't fair. Like a dagger shoved between two ribs and wiggled just to watch her jump. "It'll get better. Just give it time." Kara wasn't sure if she was talking to him, or to herself.

He kept drumming along and finally Brian came over. "Christ dude, three people just dropped of starvation."

Brian gave him a bored look. "Don't get your bloomers in a bunch," Brian said, getting out his order pad and pen. "What can I get you two?" Brian wasn't sure about the status of Lion and Valkyrie, and he was smart enough not to ask.

Dane made a face. "First, take her order and second, fuck you. If anyone here wears bloomers it's you, Brianna," he said to the bear who was his band mate and couldn't resist giving him shit because Dane wasn't born and raised here in NOLA. He was British and though he did his best to Americanize himself, some days his accent and slang got the best of him. He gave him the proper Brit fuck you, two finger salute and then pulled the bowl of snack mix closer.

"I need a tall drink and a line on where I can find a Navarro bear to skin." Kara smiled sweetly and slid her card onto the bar. "Also, an order of whatever bears like, to go." Kara chuckled at Dane and the look on Brian's face. She ignored the arched and curious brow he directed at her and dropped her eyes to the bar top. "So back to bear skinning, not you. You I like. Where are they?"

Brian shrugged and gave her his usual smirk. "You might as well order Karabara, you know you'll just be stealing off his plate if you don't."

264

"Nah. I'm good." She smiled at Brian's yeah, right expression.

Dane waited for her to make her order. "Why is the office locked? I need my check. I want a double bacon elk burger with cheese and Cajun fries with it. And a Redbull to drink. I don't want one of those small cans you give to the humans. I want one of the large ones Ripper hides in the back of the cooler. I don't know if he drinks them, but I know he puts them there," Dane said, turning his head to the blonde again. Her name slipped his mind. "Forgive me, what's your name again? And why are you skinning a bear? Did they eat out of your trash, like so many of them do?" He said, loud enough for Brian to hear him as he left to fill their orders.

"Kara." She held out her hand out of habit. "And I'm skinning bears that won't stop texting their brother when he needs to be resting and healing, not telling them where the last box of Triscuits went or how to go to the grocery store to replace them." She blushed, realizing that she was ranting.

She smiled at Brian when he pushed the pint glass of tequila to her. "Thanks, Babes." She took a sip. "Sorry about that, but they need to grow up." She eyed Dane over the glass. "I heard that you bailed. I'm glad you're back, Dane."

He shook her hand and then took the big can of Redbull Brian put down on the bar. "Thanks," he said, opening it. "Maybe they're just having a lazy day," he offered, sipping his energy drink. Again, he had the feeling like they knew each other or she knew him. "And anyone who eats those bloody things needs a kick in the cunt." He made a face. Triscuits tasted like wicker baskets to him, or what he thought they would taste like. He realized his accent was creeping out. He cleared his throat and drank more of his drink.

"Maybe, but they need to stop before I have to stop them." She set her glass down, her lips quirking up when he went silent. Kara knew that look. *How many times had she seen it over the last year?* Shaking her head, she reached out and patted his hand. "Just be you, Babes. I've always found the accent charming, and I agree about the Triscuits." She let her stool spin slowly giving her a view of the room. "Hey! You!" She yelled. "Navarro! You and me gotta have words!" She growled as the bear, she didn't know which one, ducked and ran for safety. "Run now you little shit, I know where to find at least one of you twenty-four-seven." She muttered under her breath and turned back to the bar.

Dane held back a laugh when he saw Brax run for it, in the mirror behind the bar. "That was Brax. You can tell by the braided thing he wears on his wrist." Again, she was talking to him like she knew him. Normally he was good at hiding the accent, but it felt like he had forgotten how. He waited a moment and opened his mouth to ask her if there was a memo he missed about them, but Brian came back with his food and Dane's mind focused on the plate. "Can I get some ketchup and napkins?" He asked Brian, taking a fry and wondering where Kara's order was.

Out of habit, Kara stood and leaned over the bar to grab the good ketchup, not the watered-down crap that Brax insisted on ordering, and set it beside Dane's plate. "Oh, my God! Look at the size of that cat!" She pointed past him and stole a fry when his head turned, not remembering until it was too late, that she wasn't supposed to do shit like that anymore.

"What?" Dane asked, looking around. He saw no cat. He gave her a look and took the ketchup and squeezed most of the bottle on his fries and some of his burger. "So, tell me, Kara, why do I get the feeling you know something I don't?" He mashed his elk burger down before taking a bite of it. The moment his tongue hit the burger, he started to purr. It was so good. One thing about The Pit, you could get all kinds of good eats.

Kara laughed at the look, and for just a second, it felt like it had before. She pulled a napkin from the dispenser and finished chewing the fry as she wiped her hands. Her smile died when he spoke. "Probably, because I do." She drank half of the glass of tequila, hoping that people would buy that it was what made her eyes water. She made a face at the explosion of heat in her gut and had to turn her head away when he started to purr and a shit ton of memories, good memories, flashed through her head. It would have been so much easier if they hadn't been happy. Fate had taken care of that, though. Hadn't it? She took another drink and tried to find something else to focus on other than the dull ache in her chest and throat.

Dane held his burger over the plate and motioned between them with his right pinky. "We know each other? Like a friend of a friend, know each other, or one night in the bathroom, know each other? If it was the latter, I'm sorry I forgot. I'm not myself these days. My head is a bit dodgy lately."

Kara eyed him, not sure what to answer. She didn't want to lie to him, but she didn't want to crack a hole in the wall that held back the memories that had left him screaming. She looked around the bar. So many people knew the truth, at least about him and her. Someone was going to spill it eventually, and the idea of him being blindsided by it worried her even more, where that wall was concerned. "We were mated, for a year. Now we aren't. There was a..." She searched for a way to phrase it that he could accept. "An accident. Probably why you don't remember and why stuff feels a little off." She finished her glass and tapped the bar for Brian to hit her with a refill.

His jaw went slack, and his burger fell to the plate. Dane stared at her for a moment and then busted out laughing. "Mated. Right! I remember now. That was after my sex change, right?" He looked Brian. "Did you put her up to this, you Git?"

Brian winced and shook his head no.

"Am I being punked?" He asked staring at her.

She smiled sadly and nodded, downing the drink and sliding off her stool. Maybe it was better if that's what he

267

believed. "Yeah. Thought you could use a laugh." She looked up at Brian, hating the pity she saw in his eyes. "Tell the three little bears to lay off Brock for a bit? If they really have a problem, call me. Okay?" She smiled and patted Dane's shoulder as she turned to leave. "Glad you're back D."

"Have a good night Karabara." Brian watched her with more understanding than Kara was comfortable with, and made it hard for her to keep her shit together.

Dane was still trying to wrap his mind around what she'd said. Mated. He was, or they had been... Mated. "Wait," he called out to her. "Tell me what happened?" He could tell that her smile was as fake as that brunette's lashes had been and he didn't like how that made his lion groan. His instincts told him she wasn't bullshitting him, and that was some scary shit.

Kara stopped and closed her eyes. Any hopes of making it through all of this with her dignity intact went out the window. She should keep walking, get outside and remember how to breathe. Instead, she turned. "What do you want to know?" She hated the gravelly sound of her voice, but she couldn't help it.

He could see by the look on her face and the vibe she was giving off she'd rather be tar and feathered than to talk about it. "Did I fuck it up? Just a simple yes or no. And we don't have to speak about it again."

"No," She shook her head, hating the tears that were pooling in her eyes. "Fate screwed us both, Babes. No one's fault."

Dane nodded and thought for a moment before he spoke. "Well, I'm glad it wasn't me. You seem like good people. I'm sorry I don't remember. Maybe it's for the best, though. I've learned that some things are best forgotten and left unsaid. Leave well enough alone, but I hope we can be friends. Something tells me that having you as one, is a good idea. If your stones are big enough to want to skin a bear, then I would rather not be on the list of the animals you dislike."

268

Kara nodded and rubbed away the tear that leaked from the corner of her eye with her thumb. "You're probably right." She smiled. "And at least if you find something I left behind you won't drive yourself nuts trying to figure out how it got there, right?" She laughed. "I'm pretty sure I forgot to empty my underwear drawer, so, yeah. There you go." She leaned closer to kiss his cheek. "Friends. I'd like that."

He smiled and laughed. "I'll round up any bloomers and other things I find and make sure you get them back. Oh, you forgot your food," he said as Brian came over with the to go stuff in hand. He leaned over the bar and took the bags of food from Brian. "Here you go," he said wondering how in the world someone like her could end up mated to him. *The gods are a fucked up lot*, he thought to himself as he held out the bags.

"As long as we can do it publicly, and make as many bears as possible, horribly uncomfortable, I'm game for getting them back." Kara grinned. "Right. Food. Thanks." She took it and tucked it under her arm. "If you find yourself backed into a corner and you don't call for me, I'm going to be offended. We clear?" She arched a brow and smiled. "You're a good male Dane Lyons. Don't let anyone tell you different." She turned her head and raised her voice, "Unlike some good for nothing, soon to be my living room carpet, if they don't stop blowing up phones, Bjorns!"

Dane laughed and nodded. "You have my word." He shook his head. She was a firecracker, that one. He wished he could remember more about her. But as he said, better left unsaid.

"Good." She grinned and backed away before turning and pushing through the crowd to get back to Brock. Kara hoped that he was awake and feeling better, but if he wasn't then, she'd take watch until he was.

Dane finished his food and waited on Brian to bring his paycheck. He opened the envelope, looked at the amount and then back to Brian. "She was with me? No more bullshit."

Brian nodded and laughed. "We couldn't believe it either, man."

"Well, fuck," he folded the check, stuffed it in his wallet and signed the slip to tack the meal onto his tab. "The world has lost its damn mind." He shook his head and took the can of Redbull with him as he went back to his room, taking the long way, to avoid the brunette from earlier. If he'd forgotten Kara, what else had been wiped off the dry erase board of his memory?

Chapter 31

Ghosting home, Kara couldn't believe how much better she felt about where things were with Dane. She may have lost him as a mate, but she hadn't lost him completely. For the last year, he'd been her best friend and the idea of losing that was more painful than letting him go to find another that made him happy. Maybe Salvation was right, and they weren't true mates. If that was true, then it was better that she was out of the way. Dane deserved that.

Kara smiled as she unpacked the bag of takeout. Maybe she deserved it too. She snorted. That was probably a bit of a reach. Her kind was designed for two things. To reap the worthy dead and to serve Asgard. Love, family and all that other romance novel crap, was beyond their reach. They weren't supposed to want it.

She knew that she was being selfish, but until the Bear wanted to leave, she had no intention of letting him go. She needed him, even though that made her weaker. Kara liked the way that he looked at her as if she were a precious stone and he kept the nightmares at bay. Placing the food on a tray, she tiptoed into the bedroom, not wanting to wake Brock if he was still sleeping.

Brock pushed himself up against the pillow and looked down at his chest. Brushing his fingers over the puckered skin, he counted the holes. Would he still be here if he didn't know that dying would take his only chance to have

Kara, for however long she allowed it? He thought about what Reese had said. He probably should apologize to her, and Kara too. He tilted his wrist to read her note again. He hoped that she didn't come back with new furs to add to the pile already on her bed.

Kara poked her head into the room, smiling wide when she saw that he was awake. "I came back, and I brought food." She lowered it carefully to the bed and stepped back, sliding her hands into her back pockets. She wanted to crawl into the bed with him and feel his arms around her, but seeing him upright and his eyes open were a close second. "Feeling any better?"

"Food? Thank you, Cher." He dropped the note and patted the bed. "Yeah. I'm feeling better, physically. In other ways, not so much. I don't see any hides? Should I be worried my brothers are hog tied somewhere? If so, can I shave them bald first?!" He secretly hoped that she'd bearnapped his brothers and tortured them a bit.

She laughed and sank down on the bed beside him. "They're fine. All of them. The cowards hid from me, and I got distracted." Kara reached up and brushed the hair back from his face, looking for signs of pain that he was hiding. "How can I help you feel better in the other ways too, Big Guy?"

Brock wasn't sure how to answer that. "I want to apologize for last night. I said some things that were ignorant. I might need to apologize to Reese too."

She blinked at him, slightly confused. "You didn't say anything to me that warrants one, Babes. I mean thank you for saying it, but you and me, are good." She grinned and stole one of his fries. "Trust me, if we aren't, you'll be the first to know."

He smiled, pulled the tray over his legs and dug in. Brock had no doubt that that was true.

Kara crossed her legs and pulled her knees to her chest. "Dane is back."

Brock choked on a fry as she spoke. "He okay?" After a little more coughing he managed to dislodge the potato and get it down the right pipe.

She nodded and watched him until he stopped choking. "He seems to be. He's confused and feeling out of step with everything." She leaned over him to get the water and held it out. "We talked."

"How did that go?" Brock put the food aside, giving it a dirty look and took a long drink of the water. It figured. Survive getting shot and be taken out by a French fry. "I wanna hear all about it." He watched her nervously, waiting for the bad news. If it came, he'd still be there for her, but that didn't mean it wouldn't leave him a little raw. "Did he look okay?"

"He looked good." Kara smiled softly and dropped back, beside him. "It was weird. In some ways, it was like it always had been, well, it felt that way. But at the same time, it was just..." She blinked and rolled her eyes as they grew wet. "Sad." She reached out and laced her fingers with his. "I told him that we used to be mates. Once he stopped laughing, he took it pretty well."

Brock squeezed her hand and waited for the kiss-off to come. "That's good. How are you really feeling? I know he means a lot to you. If you need to vent, I'm here to listen. I'm glad he's okay and didn't flip out."

"I'm not going to lie. It hurts. A lot. It's not fair. None of it and I'm mad as hell. It's like he died, but he's still here to remind me of what we had. It was good." She dropped her chin to her knee. "But we left it in a good place. Friends. We always rocked that." She smiled softly. "I just have to learn to accept that he was a chapter in my life, not the whole novel." She looked up at him. "Do you worry about me going back?"

He listened to her, and he knew how their relationship looked from start to end. He wanted to say something to make the pain of it all go away, but nothing was that easy. "I worry about your happiness, Cher. You've been through a

273

lot and if it came down to it, bottom line, I want you to be happy. You're chained to me. Plus, I know the power you hold. I am not that stupid." He kept the rest to himself. If Kara chose to stay with him, it had to be because she wanted to, not because he laid a guilt trip on her.

One corner of her mouth curled up. "Chains? Didn't know you were into that," Kara teased before becoming serious again. "But do you know, when it was all said and done, what the most interesting part was?" She met his eyes.

He growled at himself for not saying it the way he meant. "I meant you aren't. Sorry I ain't all here. What was the interesting part?"

"Too bad. It had possibilities." Kara waggled her brows at him and grinned. "The interesting part was that when I left, the only thing that I wanted, was to come home to you. I wanted to know that you were alright. I wanted to crawl into bed beside you and feel your arms, furry or not, around me. I wanted to be surrounded by your scent and feel the peace that I only feel when I'm with you." She watched his face for a moment. "I wanted you, Brock. Just you."

Brock didn't know what to say. He'd been in love with her for a long time. And after what Reese had said, he wondered if others thought the same thing. The thought of people thinking anything other than respectful things about her wasn't okay with him. "I don't know what to say, other than it makes my heart smile to hear that. But why me? You could have anyone. What can I offer you? Other than a migraine?" *What was he doing? Was he really trying to talk her out of it? How stupid could he be?*

"Honestly?" Kara studied him for a moment as she thought about how to put it into words. "I don't know exactly what it is. I'm not sure that I'm supposed to. When I want to rip the world to shreds, your scent and touch sooth me. When I'm with you, I feel like I'm real and not dissolving into nothing. Wow, that sounds stupid." She sighed and ran her fingers through her hair. "You say I can have anyone,

274

Brock. Before Dane, I hadn't been with anyone in over two hundred years. I didn't need anyone. I didn't want anyone. I want you. What can you offer me? Everything! The chance, one more chance to have something worth fighting for. I've recently learned how short life can be, and I don't want to waste it."

Brock didn't say anything. He smiled, took her hands in his and kissed her palms. "It doesn't sound stupid. My mother always said, 'Sometimes things have to fall apart, to fall back together again." We go through hell, to appreciate heaven," he murmured.

Kara cupped his face in her hands. "So, stop selling yourself short and let me appreciate you, bear. Trust me, I'm getting the better part of this deal."

He barked a laugh and thought about a comment Jared had made about her, a long time ago. 'One of these days, man, she's just gonna drop a toaster in my tub. Zap, and that's it.' Jared's words had made him laugh then, and thinking about it now, made him laugh again. "Better end of the deal huh, Cher? I don't know about that. I'd rather be behind your shield than in front of it," he said still laughing, remembering Jared's face and his pretending to die from that toaster.

"Like I said, I'm making out better." She sighed. "I know there's no pay off for you. Like you asked. Why me? Because I don't get it. Hell, you should probably run now."

Brock roared with laughter thinking she probably had a long cord for that toaster if he ran. "Well I wasn't thinking about running and being full of holes now, I'm probably gonna be shitting lead for a month or two. So, running is out, but I can skip pretty fast." He grinned at her.

Kara felt like she was missing part of the conversation and wasn't sure if the one feeling that she had left was hurt, or not. She pulled her hand back and hugged her knees, not sure what to do. She'd put herself out there, and he was laughing. That math didn't add up to anything good.

275

Brock wrapped his arms around her and kissed her cheek. "I'm sorry, Cher. I was thinking about Jared. He told me once that he was worried that one of these days, you'd just off him. Toaster in the bath tub. Why? Because you have the power to! I can't help thinking that I've won the lottery here. Not every male can say that they got their dream woman to talk to them. Hell, if you even just called me, Hey, you with the hair, I'd be happy. I hope I can live up to everything you just said. I'm only a bear. I don't have a super powerful family like yours. All I've got to give you is my heart and my time. What you did for my sister and me is huge!" He nuzzled her neck slowly. "Taking care of me, as you are now? That is going beyond what you should be doing, and for it, I love you."

"Why does everyone think that I want to hurt them? That rat bastard of a panther is one of my favorite people." Kara growled. "I don't care about that other stuff, hell I don't want my family most of the time. I want you, the man, the bear and I want to give this a shot." She groaned and tangled her hands in his hair when his lips grazed her neck. "I can't promise that it will work, but I want to try if you'll have me?" She grinned and nipped his jaw. "And I kinda like taking care of you."

He kissed her and smiled. "It was a while ago that he said that. And I'll gladly have you. I am yours. Just remember to feed and water me. I can take my own walks," he teased.

Kara laughed and bit him harder. "I'm going to need a bigger watering can," she teased back. "I should warn you. I'm not going to hide this like a dirty little secret just so others can feel more comfortable. If I'm with you, I'm with you. I'm proud, not ashamed. That goes for my family too. Either all in or all out. I don't know how to be any other way. You think you can handle that?"

He nodded. "Of course. I'm proud to be with you and count myself lucky. I just ask one thing of you, Cher."

She pulled back to see his face, a little afraid of what if might be. "Shoot, Big Guy." She grimaced and then laughed. "Poor choice of words, but you know what I meant."

Brock laughed a bit. "Always be honest with me. No matter what."

Her heart melted a little. Of all the things that Brock could ask her for, that was what he chose. Kara reached up and cupped his face between her palms and pulled his lips to hers for a soft kiss. "No matter what. I promise."

"Thank you, Cher," he hoped that she meant it. If she changed her mind, he didn't want to be the last to know. "Are you hungry? I think the food you brought is cold. I'd ask you to nuke it, but I don't wanna die by French fry. It is a potato, after all." He teased her.

Kara gaped at him, slowly allowing it to become a smile and pushed his face away with her palm. "You will learn to love my cooking." Yeah, even she didn't believe that. "I can get you something else." She ran her hand over his chest, inspecting the healing holes that peppered it.

"How about pizza?" Brock looked down, his lips curling up as he watched her hand feather over him. "So much for my flawless skin."

"Pizza sounds good." Kara slid her hand over him again. "To my people, scars show strength and will. Not anything to be ashamed of. If you ever visit Asgard with me, you'll see mine." She smirked. "You might change your mind when you see my actual skin, but until then, just remember, chicks dig scars. What do you want on it, the pizza?"

He smiled. Kara mentioning the possibility of taking him to her homeland warmed him. Brock knew that she'd never taken Dane there because the lion bitched about it more than once. "Ladies choice. I'd love to go to Asgard with you, sometime."

Kara grinned and kissed him. "Really? Then I'll have to take you. I have a little cottage on the outskirts and away from everyone. I think you'd like it. I could even take you to see Dad's great hall for yourself, to drink mead and break

277

bread with some of the fiercest warriors to have lived." She eyed him, waiting for him to waiver. Most found being surrounded by brutal Vikings and Gods intimidating. She wouldn't blame him if he felt the same. "I'm feeling pepperoni, mushrooms, ham and maybe bacon. What do you think?"

"Sounds great, the cottage and the pizza. Do you like soda? I don't think I've ever seen you drink or order it?"

"I've never tried it." Kara ghosted the take-out menu for the pizza place on the corner, that was better than average, into her hand and passed it to him so he could peruse the options.

Brock was shocked. "Never?" He looked at the menu and saw that they had a large pizza and garlic breadstick combo. He tapped the paper. "How about that, with everything you listed off. And a two-liter of Coke. I want to see if you like it or not." He forgot that she wasn't from here so there might be a lot of things she'd never tried.

Kara picked up her phone and dialed the number to place the order and gave them her address almost forgetting the coke but remembering at the last second. "Should be here in thirty." She tossed her phone onto the bed. "So honestly, how are you feeling?" She couldn't seem to help but to worry about him.

"Parts of me are numb, and some parts are on fire, but healing, I think. Remind me to send the Panther a thank you card, or something. Maybe make Ozzy give him a raise. How are you? I know you must hurt, too."

"Or we could offer to babysit so he and Serra can have some alone time." She grinned and shrugged. "I'm okay, just a little bruised. I got bit. You know, the usual. My armor took most of the damage." She looked him over with concern. "Nothing, a soak in my hot spring or a little sunbathing, can't cure. I don't suppose the sun has that kind of effect on you?"

He shook his head. "No, but it's good to know that you're related to Superman." He teased and thought about the babysitting. "Watch Theo and JJ? I believe we can handle that."

"Superman's a wuss when it comes to a stupid rock." She snorted and rolled her eyes.

Brock chuckled. "Your snort is adorable."

She eyed him and laughed. "I can honestly say that no one has ever called anything about me, adorable. But thank you." She curled against him, tilted her head back and tugged on his beard until he leaned down to kiss her.

"Are you ready to try soda for the first time?"

Kara smiled against his lips and nodded. "If you think it's worth it, I can't wait."

"Well, it makes you poop funny shapes," Brock said with a straight face.

"Say what?" She blinked at him.

"It makes your poop funny shapes." The look on her face was priceless. He kept his poker face in place. "Is that why you haven't tried it yet? Scared of pooping out a Viking ship or something?"

Kara eyed him, ninety-nine percent sure that he was fucking with her. "Have you seen the size of a Drakkar?"

"No, are they big?" Brock struggled to remain stone-faced.

"You are a mean, mean bear."

He roared with laughter. "Why Cher, I don't know what you mean?"

"Mean," she growled and bit him, trying to untangle herself when someone knocked on the door.

Brock growled back and laughed harder as she jumped off the bed and walked away.

Kara opened the door, took the boxes that the guy pulled out of the red pouch and the plastic bag with the bottle of coke inside. She considered asking the kid if what Brock had said was true, but thought better of it and gave the kid a generous tip instead. She returned to the bedroom and lowered everything onto the bed, got two glasses from

279

the kitchen and returned to eye the red labeled beverage skeptically.

He held back his laughter at her expression. "Well Cher, you gonna try it?" Brock hoped she didn't punch him.

She looked at him and made a face.

"Well more for me then." Brock smiled and held his glass out to her. "May I have some please?"

Kara opened the bottle, sniffed it and rubbed her nose. "It tickles." Taking the glass, she filled it and looked at the dark liquid inside that churned like it was being attacked by the thousands of bubbles rising from the bottom and popping in a foam that reminded her of beer. Carefully, she sipped, gasping as foam filled her mouth and burned before she managed to swallow it, to continue the assault on her throat. The second sip wasn't as bad. "It's sweet." She handed the glass back to him and blinked her watering eyes.

"You okay, Cher?" Brock smiled, taking it back.

"I think so. You drink it on purpose?"

He nodded and took a sip of the coke. "Yes, Cher, I really like it. They have all kinds of different flavors."

She made a face and then grinned. "Maybe. God knows I didn't like tequila the first time I tried it, either."

He chuckled. "Thank you for trying it." Brock opened the pizza box and took a slice. "How many tries before you liked it?"

"Tequila? Just enough that my taste buds went numb," Kara grinned and leaned her head on his shoulder looking up at him. "Coke? Time will tell. You, though. You only took the one try, and I knew that I liked you."

He smirked. "Is that so?" He offered her a bite.

Nodding, she took a bite, grabbing a napkin when a little of the grease ran down her chin. "It is. You made my wings pop out, Babes. I didn't know that could happen." She laughed and wiped her face.

Brock laughed and looked at her. "I did?" He smirked. "That's not just a natural thing?"

280

"No. I usually have better control." Kara blushed and picked off a piece of pepperoni before pulling the slice from the others.

He grinned and ate his pizza, staring at her for a moment. "So, it's like a secret button or something?"

Kara choked on her pizza and laughed. "Something like that, but only you know where that button is, Big Guy." She bumped his shoulder playfully. She loved that being with him wiped away the crap of the day and she could just enjoy the time they shared.

He bumped her back. "I'll remember that. So, tell me about the last time you used them?" He reached for a napkin and set the coke on the night stand. "If you don't mind, that is, Cher."

"I never mind talking to you about anything. In all honesty, I don't use them often. Don't need to." Kara shrugged. "Sometimes, I mean, just for fun. It's a rush to throw yourself at the ground and miss." She grinned and picked at a stubborn crunchy piece of bacon, finally prying it loose and popping it into her mouth, licking off her finger and thumb while she tried to remember the last time she'd used them for fun and she couldn't. "When I was trying to figure out which place Bree was stuck in." She scrunched up her nose. "The first was a large-scale Meth lab, but the second paid off. How about you? How often do you let your bear out to play?"

Brock swallowed the last of the slice in his mouth and thought about it. "Lately, it only happens when I sleep. I don't shift that often, always busy. I try my best to blend in with the humans. If I had wings that would be awesome, I think. But people always say that about things they don't know anything about. I'm sure it's not as great as one would believe it is."

"It has its moments, and it hasn't sucked yet. Why do you want to blend with them? I mean, I get it. At the bar and stuff, but," Kara tried to figure out what she was saying. "I guess it's like you said, I don't know anything about it. That's got to be hard."

Brock thought about it. "It was something our parents use to say. I'm the odd one of the family. I haven't really gotten the chance to give in to my animal side, much. The last time I did, it didn't end well." He said with a sigh.

She dropped the crust in the box and pulled another slice closer to her. "How so? What happened?"

He chewed the inside of his mouth for a moment. "I almost got someone killed." Brock looked down at his lap.

Kara glanced up, surprised. "Oh. Wow." She rubbed his thigh. "You don't have to talk about it, Babes. Not unless you want to."

He shrugged. "I learned my lesson." Brock took another slice of pizza. He really didn't want to talk about it. It was utterly stupid and not the way he wanted Kara to see him.

She was curious, but if it bothered him, she wasn't going to pry. It was a shame, though. He should be proud of what he was, and Kara wondered if keeping his bear caged would backfire in the long run. "Yeah, lessons can knock you on your ass sometimes." She leaned against him.

He nodded, his mouth full of food. "I mean, I shift in my room, but like roaming free as one? Not in a long time."

"Don't you miss it?" She looked up at him. "I know when I go for too long not doing what I was born to do, I get twitchy as hell." Kara snorted. "Usually leads to some mess that I should have known better than to be part of."

Brock hadn't thought about it that way. "I do miss it. I guess because my focus is always on the portal and all that, I don't really get time to screw off. Or go hunting like I use to."

"The portal is important. I get that, I do." She put down the half-eaten slice, realizing that she was full. "But so is your mental and emotional health. You need to make time for you. It keeps you sharp when you need to be. Maybe I'm wrong. I don't know." She smiled softly. "But I have to ask, if

282

you don't have time for your bear, what makes you think you have time for me? I don't want to be a distraction that you come to resent or feel guilty about."

His brow quirked up at her. "That is an entirely different thing. Like I said, I let it out in my room where I know I'm safe."

Kara arched a brow and nodded. "Okay."

"Maybe you can teach me this thing I hear about, called time off and relaxing. Time for myself isn't necessary. Time for the people I love, is. Does that make sense?" Brock hoped that it did and that he hadn't upset her.

"Yeah." She watched him, getting a better idea of what made him tick. "Teaching you about that just moved way up on my priority list." She grinned and pressed her lips against his shoulder.

Brock smiled and leaned on her. "Great. So, you're eating the rest of this right? I gotta watch my girlish figure!"

Shaking her head, no, Kara laughed. "I'm stuffed. It's all on you, Bear."

"What, you wussing out on me?" He teased. "Well, damn."

"Yes. Yes, I am. You can make me pay for it when you're feeling up to it." She grinned and stretched up to nuzzle his neck.

Brock smiled, closed the pizza box and finished his coke. He let out a loud burp. "Jesus, I'm sorry, Cher. That was gross."

Her brow arched. "It had to come out, or you could explode."

He laughed. "Yes."

Kara pulled her knees to her chest and looked at her feet, not sure what to do or say now. She was trying not to let it bother her that he was cool with asking her questions about her people and her life, but not so much when it came to sharing about his own. "Then, there you go." She smiled stiffly and hugged her legs.

"So, anything else you wanna know? I'm sorry for not sharing much. It was kind of one of those stupid things. The last time I actually went all bear, I almost got my mate or whatever you want to call her, killed. She got caught in a bear trap, and hunters almost got us both. All because I was trying to be stupid and get a bee hive down for her. Not my proudest moment. I stepped in one also." Brock pulled up his pant leg showing her his right calf. "The scar looks so weird."

Kara reached out and traced it with the pad of her finger. "That's not stupid. It just didn't end as you planned, but you both made it. I'd think the lesson would be to watch for bear traps." She tucked her hair behind her ear. "If I decided to throw down my sword the first time I got hurt or almost got someone killed, I'd have been put down and been deemed useless a long time ago. Hell, this last thing, getting Bree. I almost got you killed. Doesn't mean I won't jump right back into the fight if I'm needed." She looked up, her finger still stroking the jagged scar.

Brock nodded. "Well no one ever said I was smart, but you're right. It's important to keep going, even if we're scared to. And I really can't thank you enough for what you've done for us. Even if Reese is pissed off at me."

She shook her head and gave him a look. "No picking on the bear, I'm kinda fond of him. It's just a different perspective." Kara pulled her hand back. "I wish that I could be comfortable with you thanking me and thinking that my reasons were noble. They weren't. I'm glad that you and Bree are okay, I really am, but I went because that's what I do. It's who I am." She watched his face, not wanting him to have a romanticized view of what she was. It would only leave him disappointed in the long run. She killed things that needed to be destroyed, and when the people that fought beside her died, she reaped them. "And I don't think that Reese is mad at either of us."

"Well, I might be an animal, but I have manners. If it bugs you, I'll stop. I'll just start bringing you dead animals, as gifts." he joked.

Kara laughed and nodded. "Nothing says love like a pile of dead things." She stretched up and kissed him. "What I want, is for you to be you. Man. Bear. You. I hope someday that you can trust me enough to know that I'm not going to judge any of it. You say that you're just a simple bear. I'm just a simple Valkyrie, no better than anyone else. If we can learn to trust each other at our best and our worst, then that is something that would be truly unstoppable and the kind of thing that songs are written about." She blushed a little. "Okay, yeah, see that sounded way better in my head."

He kissed her back and smiled. "I would like that, Cher, and I already do."

She looked into his eyes, and her pulse began to pound when the truth hit her. "So do I."

"If I seem like I don't, it's mainly my own stupidity."

She bit him. "It's not stupid. It takes time to let it sink in. It feels scary as hell, to be honest."

"Yes, it does, but it's a good thing." Brock smiled at her.

Kara nodded and leaned her face against his, smiling softly and biting her lower lip. "Thank you."

"For what, Cher?" He asked, confused a bit.

"For making me believe that, for once, I can have what I want." She smiled and pressed her lips to his neck. "And for showing me what that is." Closing her eyes, Kara spread her fingers over his chest, until her palm rested over his heart and whispered the words in old Norse that bound her to him. Not like she had when she thought he was in danger. This was deeper and more personal. Instead of claiming him, she was giving a piece of herself. It wasn't a sexual or physical thing. At that moment, with that vow, she sealed her fate.

He pulled her to him and kissed her slowly. "Ditto Cher," Brock growled softly.

Kara melted against him, sliding her hand up his chest to scrape her nails over the back of his neck as she lost herself in the feel of his lips against hers, smiling when he nipped her tongue gently. She shivered at the goosebumps that broke over her skin when he growled.

He rubbed her back gently. "You smell like the sun, Cher. I love it."

She grinned, content to stay where she was. "Like a fiery ball of gas?" She teased.

Brock laughed and nipped her jaw. "No, smartass."

"What?" Kara laughed and bit him back.

"You don't feel like farts. Maybe I should start calling you Sunshine."

"That's a relief." She sighed dramatically. "You can call me anything you want to Babes, just as long as you call." She grinned.

He smiled and raspberried her neck.

Kara squirmed and laughed, pushing against his chest carefully, not wanting to hurt his bullet wounds.

'Say Uncle,' he continued torturing her.

'Which one?" She squirmed, yelping and rolling in his grasp.

Brock started laughing and couldn't do it anymore. "You win." He shook his head. She was one of a kind.

"I did?" Grinning she tackled him, landing on top and tickling his face with her hair while he laughed, having no idea how she'd won, but not about to argue. "Is there a trophy involved? I do love me a good trophy." She nipped his earlobe.

"I can buy you one, Cher. What do you want it to say?"

"I have no idea." Kara shrugged, smiling wide.

"Well, bummer." Brock nuzzled her and sighed. Having her with him and this close was making him forget about his pain and being turned into swiss cheese.

"I'll just keep you for my trophy." She lowered herself down and held her chest hovering over his with her arms on the bed near his shoulders.

"Sounds like a solid plan, Cher." He grinned as a yawn slipped out. "Well damn, I'm not old. Where did that come from?" Brock frowned.

"Your body is working its way back from being broken, and I'm told that spending too much time with me is exhausting." Kara smiled and leaned down to kiss him before dropping to the side and tucking herself around him.

"Oh, ha ha, Cher." He yawned again and cuddled her to him.

"Dane said it more than once." She shrugged and pulled his arms around her. "I feel small when we're like this. I like it," she said against his chest.

"I'm a big guy. It's all this hair. I have fat hair."

Laughing, Kara brushed her lips over the underside of his beard. "Yay for fat hair," She yawned realizing that she hadn't slept since he'd been shot, well, before that really. The last time she'd woken up with him. "Have we made this sleeping together thing a habit yet? If not, can we?" She nuzzled him and let her fingers stroke his skin leisurely.

"I think we have." He yawned after her. "Yes, fat hair is a bitch, Cher."

She grinned and nodded, her eyelids growing too heavy to keep open. Kara opened her mouth to speak but yawned and tried to mumble through it. "Sleep n..." She fell asleep curled against him.

Brock smiled and held her for a while before he drifted off, thinking about how much he loved her.

Chapter 32

Brock's phone went off again, making him groan. "Cher, I think I need to come out of hiding. They won't leave me alone." He ghosted himself dressed. He felt better physically, but any other level? Not really. Everything that happened seemed to have him on permanent tilt. He pulled his hair back and put it up in, what some of the humans called, a man bun. Once the band was in place, he waited to see what Kara thought of him going back into the lion's den, as it were.

"Just say the word, and I can shut them up, permanently," she growled and continued towel drying her hair. Kara could tell by the look on his face that he wasn't going to let her do it. "Fine, I'll play nice-ish." She ghosted on clothes and tossed the damp towel into the hamper. "I'm not cool with making you deal with them alone, though, and I want to find out what the guy in the basement can tell us about the dart." She stuffed her phone into her back pocket and took one of the keys off her ring, placing it in his palm and curling his fingers around it. "So, you have a place to go to get away from them when you need to. You sure you're up to this, Big Guy?"

Brock wasn't confident that he was, but things had to keep moving. Life stopped for no one. "I'm ready and thank you, Cher. I appreciate it." He added her key to his ring, made sure he had everything he needed and took her hand before ghosting to The Pit.

Kara laced her fingers with his and gave a squeeze as the world went wavy for a second and then they were standing in one of the off limits to outsiders, halls of the bar. Glancing up at Brock, she grinned. "Remember, just one word, and I'll get them." She shook her hair back and stretched up to kiss him. "The 'safe' word is pineapple," she grinned against his lips hoping to make him smile. "I was thinking 'Kara No,' but who am I kidding? Someone is saying that twenty-four-seven."

She sighed at the sound of something breaking and an impressive string of curses coming from the bar. "We can bail if they make it unbearable." She cupped his face, kissed him again and patted her palm against his chest. "And if they don't like it, they can deal with me." Turning, she headed toward the loud voices yelling at each other.

Brock smiled as Kara kissed him and give her the okay to be his backup. He was about to answer her when all hell broke loose. "What is the issue?" He turned to see the stage in chaos. "Fuck," he muttered under his breath. He wanted to scream pineapple right then and there.

Kara watched Ripper, clawing, shoving and kicking at Koen. "You don't understand, the little fucker needs killing!" He snarled and rolled onto his back, grinding the hyena that was still holding on, into the floorboards.

Brock spotted Reese and her bodyguards. Well, today was a good day to have his ass kicked. *Let the kicking start,* he thought to himself as he headed for the stage after kissing Kara. "Okay, if I need you. I'll scream!"

"Never a dull moment. I'll be listening for you." Kara laughed and headed down another hall that led to the basement, glancing up at the lights that turned on when they sensed her. "Never get used to that shit," she said under her breath and took a right to go down the stairs.

"I was looking for you," Reese said, stopping beside Brock and watching the mini brawl.

"Oh?" Brock waved away some of the human bar staff. "Move it along, we've got this. Get back to work," he ordered, not wanting the humans in the middle of this tornado of shit. His eyes scanned the stage for anything out in the open that shouldn't be. A tiny land mine laid haphazardly, upside down and on its pin beside Brian's amp. "Holy shit!" He yelled, jumping for it. Grabbing the small package of big explosives, Brock winced as the pin dropped, sticking into the membrane between his forefinger and thumb. The thin piece of skin was the only thing keeping the pin from blowing the stage and the rest of them to kingdom come! He snarled in pain.

Kara groaned when she spotted Brax in a chair, leaned back on its two rear legs, against the wall and his feet in another, crossed at the ankle. She bobbed her head at his arched 'what do you want' brow and then her jaw hit the floor. The cell was empty. "Where the fuck is the demon?" Kara turned and stared at Brax, who just shrugged.

"Not here, that's all I care about." He went back to the game he was playing on his phone.

"But I needed to talk to him," she growled her frustration and pushed her hands through her hair.

"Well, then, it sucks to be you, Blondie."

Kara glared at him, her lips twitching from side to side as she considered kicking the chair out from under him, but knew it wouldn't do any good other than momentarily making her feel better. "Thanks for the help," she rolled her eyes and turned to bound back up the stairs. The AP crew circled Brock. The silence was deafening. The rising panic in the air could be cut with a knife. Kara pushed through them, following their eyes. They were all staring at Brock's hand. "Babes?"

Brock didn't take his eye of the landmine. "I seem to have a mine stuck in me." He tried to joke about it.

"Everyone out!" Reese yelled pushing her people toward the door. "Round up the Civies and get the fuck out, now! Koen! Get Ripper." She pushed a few more people to get them moving, ignoring the Valkyrie when she appeared. "Can you ghost it out?" She stepped closer. If the bear went bang, she'd be going with him.

"I don't know. If I do, where should I direct it?" Brock felt his skin ripping slowly, and blood was starting to ooze out. "What if I ghost out altogether?" He asked looking at both females. "If I explode, I don't want to take anyone with me. There are too many people in here, and if the human's media get ahold of it, Salvation will have my family's ass." Brock's mind was racing.

"No," Kara stated firmly. Brock dying was not an option. Dane had explained how these things worked when she'd found a bag of them in the closet and had tossed him one, turning him snow white. "Sorry, this is going to hurt." Kara reached out and pressed on the remaining skin of the webbing between his finger and thumb, holding the pin in place, but pushing it further into his skin. "I can get us somewhere safe, then let me take it. I'll probably live through it. You won't."

"Aren't these things supposed to be pin-less until needed? What genius would keep live ones in a populated place?"

"The god damn Lion, that's who," Reese growled and stepped back when Kara pushed her out of the way. She glanced around at the people watching instead of following orders. "What part of clear the mother fucking bar is hard to understand? Do it. NOW! Gawk on your own time, from OUTSIDE!"

Brock shook his head no. "No, Cher! What if I ghost into the ocean or something? Won't that work?" His hand was throbbing. "I mean, if we kill sea life, that would be better than blowing up the whole place with everything in it!"

"We're not going to blow up you or the bar." Kara could see in his eyes that he wasn't going to let her do it her way and so the decision was made. 'Incoming, Dad. If

291

anyone is near my cottage move them, now.' She stared into Brock's eyes until she had the all clear from Odin, ignoring his questions. "Trust me," she whispered and stretched up to kiss Brock ghosting them to her place in Asgard.

"Now it's just you and me. You're not sacrificing yourself, not today. You hear me? We can ghost it into the hot spring. Nothing lives there, and the humans can't hear or investigate it. When it goes off, hit the ground and I'm going to cover you." She flashed on her armor. "We're both going to be fine."

Brock was skeptical. "I trust you! Do what you need to, but if it musses my hair? I'll be pissed," he tried to lighten the mood, but his heart was hammering.

She grinned and rested her head against his chest for a second. "Note made. See that rock on the far side?" Kara waited for him to nod. "On the count of three. One. Two. Three!"

Brock listened to her count and then ghosted the landmine to the spot she was looking at. As it hit, the water exploded from the hot spring. For a moment, it looked like a black hole of water and rock. Things went into it and then shot back out, sending everything into the air a good thirty feet. Brock hit the ground.

Instead of Kara being the shield, Brock rolled and shifted, covering her with his body. Hot water and rock rained down on them. He grunted as the debris pelted him. His front right paw was bleeding from the mine. So was his back, or maybe it was just the water. Brock couldn't tell, but he knew it hurt. A rock smashed into his muzzle. If they had gone with Kara's plan, it would have hit her face and taken out an eye.

Kara growled and tried to roll him when he grabbed her and flattened himself over her. She pushed, but he wouldn't budge. Usually, she would push harder, but she didn't want to hurt him. The explosion made her ears ring and muffled the sound of debris hitting the ground around her. "We had a plan. A good plan. What the hell?" She growled into his fur. If he was dead, she was going to kill him.

Once he felt it was safe, Brock moved off her. 'Yes, we did, but I couldn't let you take any damage when it wasn't your fault,' he said through mindlink and flopped down on the ground licking his bleeding paw.

"It wasn't your fault either!" She glared at him and sat up. She was furious. "What if you'd died? Did you even think about that, Brock? Not everyone needs you to save them! It's not your responsibility!" She didn't know why she was so pissed, but instead of her rant lessening it, it was building.

'I didn't think about that. I thought about you and what would happen if you died because of me. Your father might end the world or something. I'm just a bear. Nothing too important.' She was beautiful when she was angry. Her eyes sparkled and her nose wrinkled. It was cute as hell. Brock grinned at her.

She stared at him. *Did he really believe that?* Kara blinked back frustrated tears. She didn't understand what was happening with her. Shaking her head, she pushed to her feet and started walking. "I can't do this."

Brock wondered if she was going to end him until she walked away and the words she muttered scared him more than anything she could do to his body. He shifted to human form, got to his feet and went after her. "I'm sorry. Please. I'm sorry. I won't ever do it again. I love you!" He meant the words with everything in him. "Cher, I can't thank you enough for the things you'd done for me. I don't know what I'm doing. Instinct kicked in. I'm sorry. I really am."

Kara found herself at the edge of the steaming water and waved her hand, putting everything back the way it should be. She wrapped her arms around herself and stared into the mist. All of it tackled her again. Being dead. Being stuck in hell. Coming back to lose everything that mattered. She'd been rolling with the punches or trying too, but this was too much. How could she let herself care about anyone, especially someone who was so quick to throw away his own life? How could she survive that again? She couldn't. She wouldn't, she decided, knowing that if she was having this argument in her head, it was already too late. A random thought made her brow arch. Can Valkyries get this PTSD thing she kept seeing on the news?

When she didn't respond, and seemed to be lost in her own head, Brock wasn't sure what to do. This was all new to him. He wanted so badly to know the right things to say and do, but all he could do was be himself. He hoped that she'd understand that his intent had been good, but sometimes he put his foot in his mouth.

"You're hurting. I can feel it. You should go into the spring. It will help." She rubbed her arm, willing herself back to numb. It wasn't hard.

"Only if you'll come with me. Show me how it works, Kara." He held his hand out to her, praying that she'd take it.

Kara pulled her eyes away from the nothing that she was locked on and slowly swung her gaze to his outstretched hand. She looked up into his blue eyes and swallowing became hard. Her nails dug into her arms, scoring the skin before she slowly felt her grip loosen and watched her hand slide into his. "It's easy. You just sit and relax. The rest takes care of itself." She felt like she was a spectator, not actually present.

He took her hand and pulled her to him. He kissed her softly before speaking. "I am sorry, Kara. Forgive me." Brock kissed her again, this time with passion. The pain his body felt was forgotten.

Her chest ached when he spoke. Kara was about to tell him that it wasn't him, it was her, when his lips and tongue made her forget everything but him and how her body fired back to life. If she didn't know better, she would think that he had cast a powerful spell that tangled around her and pulled her to him. But she knew that such trickery was beneath this Bjorn. She kissed him back, wishing that she could be the person that he deserved.

Brock lost himself in her lips and growled softly at her taste. He pulled away to go to the spring she'd pointed out. He ghosted himself into a pair of blue trunks and slipped into the water. He didn't pull her in with him. Instead, he held out his hand again. "Show me how it works," he murmured.

Kara stepped off the bank, not realizing, until the water filled her boots, that she was still clothed. She looked down at herself, a little confused to see her armor. What the hell was wrong with her? She ghosted away the armor and the clothes beneath, taking his hand and lacing her fingers with his. "Over here," her voice didn't sound like hers. She led him to her favorite spot where the bottom was made of a soft silt, and when she sat down, the water caressed her tired shoulders.

He let her lead and sank down beside her, moving closer until he was holding her. "Oh, wow. This is amazing." Brock groaned as he felt his body start to melt.

"I know, right?" She smiled softly and leaned against him, struggling to get out of her head.

"Yes. Does this help with your recharging?" He asked, not totally sure how everything worked with her.

She nodded. "The healing and recharging. If I can't get to it, the sun does too. If it's cloudy and I'm stuck, I just suck it up." She shrugged and grinned. "It should work for you, for the healing anyway." Until the next time that he decided to sacrifice himself and got hurt or died. Kara shivered.

He let himself sink further down into the water. And for some reason, Jaws came to mind. Still in the water, he mindlinked her with the theme music. He stayed under the water and let his hand come up like a shark fin.

One corner of her mouth curled up as the music filled her head, blocking out the other BS.

He moved around in the water a bit more and then popped up, trying to scare her. He took hold of her ankle, yanking her to him and raspberried her neck. 'Shark attack.'

She laughed and squirmed, pushing against his chest. "You're supposed to be healing." She wrapped her legs around his waist and nipped his shoulder playfully, throwing her body to the side and taking him with her in a splash.

"I am. I was turning into a fish. I have things on the computer about a shark-bear thing. I thought I was turning into one," he said, holding on to her. He growled then made a fish face at her.

"You are so not right." She shook her head and grinned at him.

"I'm proud of that, Cher," he said, laughing.

"Part of your charm and all of that?" She teased and held onto him tight.

He nodded. "Yes, but I feel incredible. This is amazing. And no fish smell."

She pulled back and eyed him, not sure what he meant. "I'm glad you're feeling better." Letting him go was going to suck.

"Rivers have fish. Most of the water I play in smells of it."

Okay, that made sense. "Nothing lives in this, it would cook." She grinned. "That's why I thought it was a good place to dispose of the mine. Nothing was supposed to get hurt."

He nodded and sunk into the water. He looked at the view around him. "This place is beautiful."

"I think so." Kara leaned back to wet her hair. "You're the first one I've brought to see it." She turned and pointed to the small cottage in the distance. "That's my home when I'm here. Not quite as grand as you probably expected." She did have mad skill at disappointing the expectations of others.

He looked at her, hid his surprise and smiled. "Wow. I'm honored. The cottage looks cute. If Viking things can be cute," Brock chuckled, pushing the hair out of his face.

She nodded. "It is cute. A little rough, but I like it." Kara reached out to brush a few strands of hair from his face that he'd missed. "Can I tell you something?" She suddenly felt fidgety, and her instincts screamed for her to keep her yap shut. Especially with him trying so hard to cheer her up. But she was at a crossroads, either do what she always had and just disappear or put it all out there and see what happened.

He nodded. "Of course, Cher. You can tell me anything!" He cocked his head, waiting.

Kara sighed and looked down at her hands, licking her lips, knowing that this was a mistake. "Okay. That stuff back there? You taking the hit? That scared the shit out of me. You could have been killed, Brock. I know this is going to sound selfish as hell, but then what do I do? How can I let myself..." she trailed off, having trouble finding the right words to explain what she was thinking. She made the mistake of looking up to his face and quickly dropped her eyes again. "I mean, I care about you. I do. But if you value your life so little, I can't put myself through losing someone again. I can't. I won't. I'd rather just stay up here and leave NOLA alone like I should have in the first place."

He frowned. "I'm sorry, Cher. I didn't mean it like that. I promise, next time, I won't go rogue on you. You have my word." Brock didn't really think of it the way she did. He was sorry for hurting or scaring her. "I promise." He took her hands in his, touched that she cared. "It won't happen again."

"You're not just a bear, you're my bear, damn it. Or I want you to be." She shook her head and closed her eyes. "I'm saying it all wrong."

"I want to be your bear. I have wanted it, for a long time." He squeezed her hands. "I've already said I love you, more than once. Maybe it didn't sink in. I don't know how to say it in Viking."

"It's the thick skull, makes me slow." She smiled weakly. "The truth? I think I love you too," she held her index finger about an inch from the pad of her thumb and scrunched up her nose as she teased him. "Just a little. That scares me, and I've got to admit, I feel guilty. I was mated, and now I love someone else. What the hell is wrong with me?"

"Nothing. Fate had a hand in it, Cher." Brock answered honestly. "Things happen for a reason, not all of it is meant to be understood."

"Okay," she wasn't sure she bought that. "Then I should just go with it?" She looked up at him and bit her lower lip, grinning sheepishly.

He kissed her. "You're amazing. Do you know that?"

Kara kissed him back, nipping his lower lip and shaking her head. "I'm really not, but it's sweet that you think so." She hoped that it lasted. "It's you, Brock Navarro, that is one of a kind."

"Nah, I'm a big pain in the butt." Brock's nose wrinkled when it started to itch.

She laughed and kissed the end of his scrunched-up nose. "I think we're going to have to agree to disagree, Bear." He was damn cute when he was trying to deflect a compliment and Kara felt her chest swell a little and realized the truth. She was doing things all over the damned place, things that she'd never done for another soul. She'd claimed him. Brought him here. Told him what she was feeling, instead of shutting that shit down and running for the hills. She'd already fallen for him.

"My hands are wet, and my nose itches." Brock wrinkled it again. "I hate that." He tried to will the itch away. "I think we will, Cher."

She tilted her head to the side, exposing her neck. "Rub away, Babes." Kara tightened her grip on his hands and pulled herself through the water to be a little closer. "Oh, and just so you know, I love you too. Thought I should say it without the jokes. So, no dying."

Brock nuzzled his nose against her neck. "Oh, thank God," he groaned once it stopped itching. When she said that she loved him, he stared at her a moment and then a smile set up shop on his face. "No dying, I promise."

Kara grinned and kissed him hard. "I'm gonna hold you to that."

"Of course!" He smiled and kissed her back. "No dying. Any other rules?" He teased.

She made a face at him and nuzzled his neck, sliding her arms around him. "Not that I can think of right now, if that changes, I'll let you know. What about you? Any rules that I need to know about?"

He shook his head no. His stomach growled loudly.

"We need to feed you, Babes. Do you want to go back or hit Dad's hall?"

"Odin's hall, for real?" Brock perked up.

Kara pulled back and looked at him, a little confused. "Yeah," she grinned at his expression. "I forget that it's something cool, I guess."

He chuckled a bit. "Yes, it's cool. To you it's normal. I'm a noob!"

She laughed and kissed him. "Then we should do it." Kara stood and held her hand out to him, "We need to dry off, and I assume you'd like to blend?" She backed toward the bank and shot her father a mindlink that she might bring a guest for lunch.

Brock nodded. "Yes, I would like to. And dry is good."

Kara led him out of the water and ghosted them both dry and into the soft brown leathers that the warriors wore here. Tilting her head, she added a dagger, because anyone who didn't come armed, wasn't taken seriously by her people. "Wow," she breathed, looking at him. "You definitely look the part, Babes." Her face flushed at the thoughts that filled her head. "You ready, or would you like to see yourself first?" She tightened the belt that held her sword on her hip and adjusted the torc around her arm.

"I'm ready." He tried to keep the excitement out of his voice and looked down at himself. That was a lot of leather. "I feel manly!" Brock laughed.

"You look hot, Babes. Think that guy in the Thor movie, but the dial cranked all the way up to ten." Kara grinned and

299

took his hand, flashing them into the stone corridor that led to the hall, encouraged by the quiet chatter, interrupted with loud laughs, not the usual roar of dinner time. That, was a little much for even her, to take. She could only imagine how insane it would seem to the bear. Calmer was definitely better.

Chapter 33

They strolled past the tapestries that hung from the ceiling and brushed the floors, the gold thread on the dark cotton, reflecting brightly in the torchlight. Kara let Brock set their pace, giving him the time to absorb it and tried to see it all fresh through his eyes. Finally, the hall ended, and they stepped inside Odin's chamber where food and drink were served around the clock. Fires danced in the hearths and stew bubbled in heavy cast iron pots, except for the one closest to where her father sat. There, a deer carcass turned slowly on a spit.

She laughed when a huge and bulging red headed male pulled her into a bear hug. "Good to see you, Ivan. Are you still telling that fishing story about the sea monster that took eight days and eight nights to pull on board?"

Ivan laughed and set Kara's feet back on the floor. "To anyone who will listen, Wee One. Looks like you've caught one of your own." He eyed Brock and chuckled.

"He'll have to tell you the tale. He landed me." She grinned. "Brock, meet Ivan. He's our resident storyteller, and he's Dad's wolf keeper."

Brock took it all in. He couldn't believe where he was, right now. Awestruck was an understatement. "Nice to meet you, Ivan," he said, a bit starry-eyed. "Are there any stories about Kara?"

Ivan's head fell back, and the roar of his laughter filled the room. "Oh, the Wee One was always into something. There was this one time when Fenrir was but a pup, and she stole her brother's hammer."

"We don't have to go into that, do we?" Kara groaned and scrubbed her face with her hands, blushing. "And he had it coming." She looked around the room for Thor, relieved that he wasn't there and dropped her voice, looking up at Brock. "I should warn you not to laugh when you meet him. You know how teenage boy's voices crack and squeak? Yeah, Thor never grew out of that."

Ivan shuddered. "Like nails on slate, it is. Now, back to the story," He put his arm around Brock's shoulders and led him to a table near one of the fires, leaving Kara to follow behind shaking her head.

Brock laughed and let Ivan lead him away. "This can't end well," he said, hoping she wasn't mad that he asked about her. He took a deep breath, reminding himself not to embarrass himself or Kara in front of her friends and family. *Please, no foot in mouth disease today.*

Kara laughed as she listened to Ivan tell Brock how she had used Fenrir to tree her brother with all of the embellishments that only Ivan could add, ending with his version of what ripping leather sounded like.

"And there the lad was, hanging from the tree by one leg, his bare arse flapping in the breeze and Fenrir running around with the seat of Thor's knickers dangling from his teeth. And this one, she took the boy's hammer and didn't give it back for two years. I swear the lad still pisses his pants when a dog growls." Ivan laughed hard.

Brock laughed at the picture Ivan painted for him with his story. He let his eyes drift back to Kara, trying to imagine her as the 'wee lass' that Ivan described. Sometimes, when she didn't understand something back home, he caught a brief flash of innocence. That must have been what she looked like back then.

"Keeping our guest entertained, Ivan?" Odin took a seat at the table. "Nice to see you home, Kara. It's been too long." He turned his single blue eye on the bear across the table curiously, as his raven's whispered in his ear. His head turned toward his right shoulder at one of the words, his brows rising before he turned his attention back to Brock. "She doesn't bring people home, Son. You must be special to her, especially if she is letting Ivan tell you his stories." He lifted his gaze to Kara. "Did you find what you were looking for the last time we met, Child?"

Kara glanced at Brock and thought about it for a moment. "I might have. Did you?" She smirked and pulled a horn of mead to her when the table was piled high with food and drink.

"I did." He chuckled and held his hand out to Brock. "Nice to meet a friend of Kara's, Son. I'm her fadir, Odin."

Brock looked up as Odin spoke and reminded himself not to gape. He was overly nervous suddenly. So many things could go wrong if he made the wrong impression. "Nice to meet you too, Sir." He wiped his hand on his leathers before shaking the Viking God's hand. "Brock Navarro." He added, forcing himself not to stare.

Feeling Brock's spike of anxiety, Kara rubbed his thigh under the table, arching a brow when a set of golden eyes glowed up at her, soon to be joined by another. "Geri and Freki, what are you doing under the table?" Kara leaned back to allow the wolves to shove their massive heads into her lap to be scratched and to sniff Brock curiously, tilting their heads and looking at her with confusion.

Odin shook Brock's hand and arched a brow at the warrior that had welcomed them. "Blame Ivan, he's been sneaking them scraps during meals again," he growled in a tired sigh.

"Aye," Ivan chuckled, not bothering to pretend to feel bad about it. "That I have. Only the choicest bits for my pups." He beamed proudly. "Pet them, Lad, they like a good scratch behind the ears." Ivan clapped Brock on the back.

303

Kara smiled. Ivan had already accepted Brock, and her father was playing nice, seeming more curious than menacing, and that was good.

"Did I hear an explosion earlier?" Odin glanced at her as he pulled one of his knives from its sheath to spear a piece of venison with its point and brought it to his mouth. "Dig in, Son. There's plenty for all."

"Yeah. Everything is okay, now." She waited for his nod before turning to Ivan. "You should see Brock's place in NOLA, Ivan. Plenty to drink and the best eats in the area. I think you'd like it." Kara grinned, knowing that having the huge Viking around would drive Reese nuts because there was no way he was going to find the 'wee kitten' intimidating, at all.

Brock relaxed when he felt her hand on him. He did as Ivan said, scratching their ears one at a time. "Yes, keeping bears fed is not an easy job. My family is very adamant about the place being stocked at all times with meat and all that. In the fall, we have the wild game added to the stockpile, but that is only for shifters. The humans don't know about it. Keeps things to a low roar." He smiled thinking about it. "I should add the wild game is brought in for us to hunt and we keep what we kill. If you don't kill anything, you get nothing. Well, that's the rule, but my sister ignores it and feeds others with it anyway." Brock chuckled and looked at the food in front of him. Leaning close to Kara, he asked her what some of her favorite things were.

Kara pointed to a few of the dishes and explained what they were. "The Rökt Fisk. I've tried smoked fish from all corners of the globe, and nothing is as good as what is made here. I'm also fond of the fresh fruit on warm bread, dripping with honeyed butter, but that's more of a desert." She eyed the table. "You may have to fight Dad for the Nettle soup," Kara gave her father a teasing grin. "I still say that Tyr didn't lose his hand to Fenrir, but to Dad, for reaching for the Nässelsoppa."

"You can prove nothing, daughter mine." Odin chuckled and pushed the soup closer to Brock. "One taste and you'll understand, Son."

Kara grinned. "Just don't reach for it when Dad has his stomach set on having it, or." She pulled her hand inside her sleeve and waved it around.

Ivan roared with laughter. "The ideas you have, Wee One! Aye, I never tire of hearing them." He leaned an elbow on the table, his muscular arm bulging around the gold torc that circled his bicep. "This hunt, is it only for shifters and how do you know who is an animal and who is shifter?"

Kara shook her head and whispered to Brock, "Ivan loves a good hunt, the more difficult, the better." She was pleasantly surprised at the ease that Brock was adapting to what had to be weird as hell for him.

Brock looked at everything Kara pointed out and laughed. "I like my paws. So, I'll leave it alone," he said, taking some meat and fruit instead. He thought about how to explain the hunt to them. "Salvation oversees it, along with a few elders. We have a spell we use to weed out the fakes and the ones not allowed to join in. Why Ivan? Do you want in on it? It's harder than it seems. We use it as a training exercise for the young ones and tool for..." His voice trailed off. Sometimes the hunt was used to kill off shifters too. Those who committed unforgivable crimes were added to the list of prey, as the elder's way of handling it. "A tool for thinning the herd." He picked up a turkey leg, quoting Sal's words.

"Aye, I do." Ivan nodded and ladled the chicken stew made with beer and honey glazed root vegetables into his bowl and reached for the barley flatbread that he dropped in, to both soften it and soak up some of the broth. "Would you allow an old wolf keeper to join?" He picked up a piece of the bread and popped it into his mouth. "Maybe even a rusty, one-eyed warrior who has been sitting on his arse for too long?" Ivan teased Odin, whose single eye was sparkling at the mention of a hunt.

305

"Don't let them pressure you into anything, Babes." Kara leaned closer to Brock and eyed the two males.

"Hush, Child. The bjorn has a mind and a voice of his own. And perhaps I should speak with this Salvation, and request to allow a select few of my warriors to join?" Odin grinned at the thought, his face softening. "As a show of respect, of course."

Brock considered the idea. "I think that would be interesting. Maybe we could learn another way to hunt, and teach the young some new skills as well. Talking to Salvation might be a good idea, respectful like you said. Of course, you don't have to be worry he'll liquefy your insides. That's happened a few times. He's a grouchy old man." Brock laughed as he said it, looking at Ivan and Odin, as he dug into the food on his plate.

Brock could see it now. Ivan kicking the crap out of his brothers and the wolf clan that thought that their shit didn't stink. Just because they always took down the most game. Not a surprise when the hunted in pack formation. Not one on one, like the rest of them did.

"I doubt that Sal will say no to you, Dad." Kara snickered and pulled the plate of smoked fish closer to her and Brock. "I swear, it melts in your mouth." She picked some up with her fingers and sniffed it. "Salmon," she moaned happily.

Ivan puffed out his chest proudly. "T'would be an honor to help with training the young. There are so few here now. Kara was one of the few students given to me. But don't hold that against me."

"Like we had a choice once Fenrir was left with you?" Odin scoffed and dropped a bone onto his plate. "The child was mean as an adder when she didn't get her way."

"I'm right here," Kara complained. "And my hearing works fine." She arched an annoyed brow. "I wasn't that bad, just because you two are old and couldn't handle the challenge."

306

Ivan chuckled. "Aye, she is a mean-spirited thing, for something so tiny."

"Some things do not change, no matter how much time passes." Odin teased, reaching up to stroke the beak of one of the Ravens.

Brock laughed as he ate, surprised that he felt at ease in the present company. The way they all teased one another and laughed helped. He almost felt like he was sitting at the family dinner table at home and not that of Gods. "Well, I think it would give some of the youngsters a leg up, to learn from someone other than their own clan members. And some of us could use some lessons on how to roll with things." Brock thought of Brax not wanting to follow any way, but his own. "Plus, the females may enjoy it. Fresh meat." He smirked and ripped off a chunk of the bread, or what he thought was bread, that Kara had dropped on his plate to try.

Ivan smiled wide. "Females, the most vicious beasts of all. Pray tell me that we don't have to treat them like delicate daisies."

"Like you'd know how?" Kara snorted. "You knocked me on my ass so many times that I started to think you were a giant, looking up at you from the ground, as often as I did."

"And you are better for it," Odin reminded her. "Never have you doubted that you could defend yourself or others, have you?"

"No," Kara shook her head. "I mean, what is anyone going to do to me that Ivan didn't already?" She grinned. "I think I like the idea of this cross training. It would be good for both of our kind, now and in the future. Don't you?" She glanced up at Brock.

He nodded. "No, they are no flowers. I think my sister may surprise you, Ivan. She is a lot like Kara in the, 'if you say no, that means yes and I'm going to ram it down your throat,' way."

Kara's jaw dropped open. "I do not do that."

Ivan and Odin burst out laughing.

"Well, I don't!"

Brock quirked a brow and continued eating. He waved his hand at the men laughing. "You sure Cher? Because you spike that kinda thing with a nice twist of fuck you, too."

She narrowed her eyes and sipped her mead.

"I like this Bjorn!" Ivan clapped Brock on the back. "You have met your match, Wee One."

Odin chuckled. "If you don't know, she gets quiet when she knows she's lost the fight." He sat back when the empty dishes were replaced with a new assortment of delights, sweeter than savory this time.

"Of course, she also gets quiet when she's about to open your throat with her dagger," Ivan joked.

"I'm not going to kill him," Kara made a face at the males. "I'm going to make him suffer and keep him. I know. The Horror!"

Brock laugh so hard that he snorted. "Yes, a quiet woman is a thinking woman, which means riot gear and death." He looked at the cup on the table in front of him. "What's in this?" He asked, not sure if it was mead.

"It's mead, from Dad's private stock, like what you had with me." She let the corner of her mouth curl up a little. Brock fit into her world almost as smoothly as if he'd been born to it. "There's beer or wine, if you prefer." She nodded to the ones walking along the rows of tables and stopping to pour as they were summoned.

"If my daughter says that she's keeping you, and she has brought you here, then I must respect that. Although, I will have you know that it is not a hardship. You are welcome in my hall anytime, Brock." Odin raised his drinking horn in salute and then drank deeply from it. "Perhaps a new age is dawning, in which my kind will not be seen as nearly obsolete."

"Aye. I will drink to that." Ivan held his horn out to the server as she passed. "To old friends and new, loyalties forged in steel and new alliances born of laughter and wisdom."

308

Brock took the mug and raised it. He repeated what Ivan said and took a drink. "I'm honored to be here. I really am. I do have a question, though?" He looked at Odin.

Odin lowered the horn to rest in one of the holes that had been burned through the table, wiping the drops of mead that clung to the hair over his lip on the back of his hand. Leaning forward, he rested his elbows on the table and met the bear's gaze. "Speak freely, young Bjorn."

"I heard a rumor that Viking ships sails are made from the skin of your enemies. Is that true and if so, do you oil them to keep them from ripping?" Brock asked with a serious expression.

Odin's brow arched and he blinked. Kara turned her face away to hide her smile. Ivan, on the other hand, burst into a hearty and loud peel of laughter that seemed to make the walls shake.

Odin turned his eye on his daughter. "Is this more confusion caused by that damn television show?"

Kara shrugged. She wouldn't know, she didn't watch it.

Brock lost it laughing. "No," he said between snorts. "I was kidding. I do wonder what you do with all of the dead bodies? Fire or what?" He asked still laughing.

Odin smiled warmly. "Trust me, Son. Only the dead know." He winced when his eyes fell on Kara. It was only a flicker, quickly hidden, but Kara noticed and stiffened slightly. "Fenrir has a hearty appetite as do my two boys here." He nodded toward where the wolves, Geri and Freki snoozed, appearing harmless though they had been known to choke down entire villages.

Brock nodded and finished his food and drink. "I should have worn my fat pants." He said patting his stomach. "I think I'm pregnant, Cher."

Kara choked on her drink. "Already? Well, fuck, I'm fertile," she teased rubbing his stomach affectionately.

Ivan roared with laughter again, and Odin arched a brow as the fact that his daughter had indeed lain with the Bjorn, was confirmed. The Ravens murmured low into his

309

ears before stepping away and perching on the edges of his wide shoulders. The Bjorn would bring change, and not all of it would be easy or go well, but it would happen.

"Should I get you home before your ankles start to swell, Big Guy?" Kara teased.

"I think it's too late. I have cankles and tank ass, I fear. And my breasts hurt." Brock joked as he watched Odin, he got the feeling it wasn't good news the birds were telling him. "Something wrong?"

Odin watched them, amused until the bear turned to him. "No, son. The winds of change can't be stopped. I hope that you are ready for it. I hope that we all are." He smiled at Kara's wrinkled brow. "Worry not, Little One. The future is bright." He tried to be reassuring, "If you want to stay, you are welcome. Kara's room is always kept ready, should she choose to return to us."

Brock nodded and hoped that he was right. "I'm sure whatever happens, I'll handle it as best I can. I'm not always the brightest crayon in the box, but I try." He watched Odin's birds a moment and wonder what they would taste like. Probably stringy as hell.

Kara laced her fingers with his and grinned. "If you can handle all of this, you'll be okay. I know it."

He squeezed her hand and smiled. "If not, I'm sure you'll put a boot in my ass the whole way." Brock looked at her. "You're not eating?"

She grinned and wrinkled her nose. "Maybe. Probably." She looked down at her plate and shrugged. "I ate some."

Brock frowned. "I know you've been through a lot, but you need to eat. You're home and with your family. I won't tell you how to feel, but if I could spend any time with my parents, even for a moment, it would make me feel better. If it's because of me, I'm sorry." He squeezed her hand again. "I'll feed it to you if I gotta," he joked.

Kara looked at him, and none of the things that popped into her head were appropriate, and very few were kind, but she bit her tongue. "It has nothing to do with you. I was eating for pleasure, not because I was hungry." She pushed the plate away and held her horn out for a refill.

He cocked his head and said nothing more about the food thing. Brock drank his mead, taking in the hall.

Once topped off, Kara drank about half of it, lowering her eyes to follow the grain of the wooden table top, not able to look at her father for the moment. Ten years. Ten fucking years that he'd left her there to rot. She shook her head and pushed the hair back from her face. She was trying to get over it. She was, but it gutted her when she thought about it.

"Fortunate for us that Freya finds eating with us beneath her." Ivan chuckled, not sure of what was going on. "No one can clear a room like that female."

"For good reason," Odin rolled his one blue eye and shuddered. "Although watching Kara take a bite out of her mother's pride is always entertaining," he teased.

Brock arched his brow. He didn't know much about Freya. "Oh? Do tell," he said, looking at some weird yellow Jell-O mold thing. "What is that?" He poked it with his fork.

"Ambrosia. Mother imports it from the Greeks, I think?" Kara looked questioningly at her father, who nodded and made a face. Neither of them cared for it. "I should warn you, it boosts your powers and is like mainlining really strong coffee." Kara made a face. "I have no idea why she insists that they put the mini marshmallows in there, though."

Ivan jiggled the plate making the gel wobble, chuckling. "It tastes like honey and potatoes. It's an acquired taste, like Freya herself. Although she would like you." Ivan smirked at Kara's sound of disgust. "She likes to collect males that she finds pleasing to her eye." He shuddered. "I could not stand the mental scarring of thinking long on what she might do with them."

"Over my dead body," Kara growled.

"No more dying for you, daughter mine. I will not allow it." Odin patted her hand affectionately. "Marriages and

311

matings are not always based on love or affection. Not even for the gods. Freya lives her life in her home on the far side of the village, and the rest of us live over here, or further out like Kara has chosen to do."

Brock eyed the thing as it wobbled. "I don't know about letting her collect me. I'm not interested in someone that likes Grandma Jell-O type things. She sounds a bit like a woman that would love to keep a man's parts in a jar on the mantle. I'll pass. I'm happy with the one ornery female I've got. Ivan, any advice on how to handle her?"

"Shin guards and armor," Ivan nodded. "Aye, thick, strong armor. Never compare her to her mother and when she is too angry to talk, let her walk away because blood will flow if you try to stop her." He pulled up his tunic showing a nasty scar in the middle of his hard abdomen. "I tried. Once. Wee One ran me through for the trouble."

"I told you, I had it," Kara smirked. "I can't believe that you're still complaining about that little scratch."

Ivan scoffed. "Ran me through, you did. I was leaking every drink of mead I took, for a week!"

"You got in my way!"

"You were surrounded and the only one coming to your aid is skewered by your blade, and you want to blame me! She is your child, Odin. If there was ever doubt, I know the truth of it now."

Kara rolled her eyes and flapped her fingers against her thumb. "And you're still yapping and sniveling about it, how many hundreds of years later? For fuck sake, Ivan, I was twelve."

Odin chuckled. "We must seem strange to you, Brock. Hell, sometimes we seem weird to us. Our kind, fight with everything we have, and we love just as fiercely. If you can capture her heart, you'll never have a need to handle her because she will move the sun and the stars for you."

Brock nodded at Odin's words. "I get the feeling that is entirely true. And if she wants to run me through, then I'm sure I deserve it. I never argue with a female. It always ends badly in some way, shape or form."

"Wise man," Odin chuckled. "I may be speaking out of turn, but if she brought you here and let me meet you, then you are special to her." Odin smiled as his eye drifted over his daughter. He had so many regrets, he hoped that what Huginn and Munnin whispered about him being her Ingolf were true, but that the path would be easier than the Ravens warned. "But when she lets you see her true skin, the one that shows the scars and tells the tales of the battles she's won..." He took a sip from his horn and sucked the dampness off the hair over his lip. "Then you will know that you own her heart. Tend it carefully."

"Well, I can only hope she finds me worthy of all that. I've been in love with her a long time. To her, it seems only a few days maybe a week. A small blip on the radar, but to me, she's been a beacon for a long time. I don't know how to explain it. She's questioned me more than once. Words can't really do it justice. I tried and came off like an ass." Brock shook his head remembering the look on her face.

"No, you didn't." Kara leaned against him. "You did just fine."

"Ingolf!" Muninn screeched from Odin's left shoulder.

Odin watched Kara's head rock back, and her eyes flare at the raven's statement. Heads turned, and murmurs grew louder at the tables. "That's what the Ravens tell me, Little One." He turned his eye to Brock. "Ingolf is the old Norse word for two souls that are two sides of the same coin. They can, and do, exist on their own, but once united, they cannot be separated, even by death.

Ivan's laugh echoed through the hall. "It seems you be stuck, My Friend."

Brock pushed the hair from his face as his head cocked to the side listening to the bird's screech. "Come again?" He wasn't totally sure he heard all of that. "Like reincarnation or something?"

313

Odin thought about it. "For you, perhaps, but Kara has only had the one very long life, with a brief interruption. It is rare when two, who never should have met, are tied to one another this way. It can be a gift, and it can be a curse. I think the people of your time come closest to explaining it as a soulmate."

"I see. I hope it's true. And if not, I may have to eat your bird," Brock said being totally honest.

"Can we eat it either way?" Kara asked hopefully as the raven squawked and stepped closer to Odin's head, hiding his head in the Alfather's hair.

"Hush, Kara." You know he believes you," Odin scolded.

"The bird is smart. Wee One has been plotting to serve up the flying rats, as she calls them, for some time." Ivan laughed.

Kara grinned and looked up at Brock. "Be careful what you wish for Babes. I'm not easy to live with."

Brock chuckled. "Well, as I'm pregnant, I guess we'll see."

She laughed and tugged his beard to pull his face down and kissed him. "I guess we will."

Odin watched them and smiled softly. He'd expected her to react badly to hearing that she may have found her ingolf. He reached out with his magic and touched her aura. His brow arched at the way she became calm and centered when she touched the Bjorn. Perhaps the raven was right. He arched an eyebrow at Ivan who just shrugged.

Brock kissed her back. "I warn you, what I do in my sleep is not my fault."

Kara smirked. "Ditto, Big Guy. I get handsy, as you know."

He turned red and then laughed. "Yes. I recall. That was interesting, to say the least. I guess I should be glad that you don't make balloon animals in your sleep, Cher."

Kara burst out laughing, pulling more looks from the other tables. "I'll try to remember that."

314

He laughed harder at her comment. "Do I need to sleep with armor on?"

"Please don't. Your fur keeps me warm," Kara teased.

Ivan looked at them oddly. "Fur?"

"Don't ask unless you want them to enlighten you, Ivan," Odin shook his head and made a face. "Do you have armor, Brock? We can't have my daughter's ingolf going into battle without the armor to protect his life."

Brock laughed at Ivan and shook his head no. "No Sir, I don't have armor. And when I sleep I turn into a grizzly bear. Literally!"

Kara laughed when Ivan's brows popped, and for the first time in history, he was speechless.

Odin chuckled and mindlinked his armorer. "We will see to it. The armor. I have no urge to watch you sleep."

"I hope not. Though, I've learned that Kara is a bed hog."

"I am not!" She gasped. "I just migrate from one side to the other, and I like the way your fur tickles my skin."

Ivan made a face. "is it true that bears have a bone...." He shook his head. "Nay, I don't want to know."

Brock roared with laughter and nodded. "Yes, that's why balloon animals are out!"

Odin closed his eye and couldn't help the laugh that rolled over his tongue.

Ivan joined Brock in the roaring. "Aye, you will want to keep that a secret from Freya or she will indeed be trying to add you to her collection."

Kara blinked. "What did I miss?"

Brock made a face. "A world of hell no." He shook his head.

Kara looked confused.

Brock leaned close to her and whispered into her ear. "If there is a real bone in there."

"Oh," her lips made an o, and her face flushed, making the males laugh harder.

"You asked, Cher." He laughed and rubbed her back.

315

"I did, and I demand a demonstration to prove it's true. Later, not here," she teased.

"I was about to say, Cher, that is not happening."

"About to?" She grinned and bit her lower lip.

He laughed and shook his head. "Your father might cut off my bits."

"Don't pull me into this, Bjorn." Odin held up his hand. "I gave up trying to tell Kara who she could and could not bed on her millennial day of birth. And she has always been pickier than most."

"So? Put your money where your mouth is. And yes, I did think of taking the dirty route with that, but I thought it would sound wrong." Kara smiled sweetly

He roared with laughter and shook his head. Brock couldn't speak, he was laughing so hard.

Kara just watched the three men laugh around her. Damn, it was good to be where people got her humor, again

Brock started to choke a bit, laughing so hard. He reached for his cup, but it was empty. He laughed and coughed harder.

She passed him her drinking horn and patted his back hoping that he wasn't choking on a bone. *Okay, wrong choice of words, or thoughts, whatever*. Kara chuckled.

He took it and drank from it. It took a moment to stop choking. "Damn bones."

Kara busted out laughing so hard that tears streamed down her face.

His stomach hurt from laughing so hard. "Cher..."

Kara wiped at her face and looked up at him, "Yes, Babes?"

"You are too much," Brock said trying to calm himself.

"I was serious." She grinned, glancing that the Ravens who were mimicking the laughter.

Brock eyed the birds. "That's some creepy crap right there."

"I know, right? And they rat you out about every little thing. They're worse than that annoying little yellow bird in the Loonytunes cartoon."

"Tweety is his name," Brock said still looking at the birds. "What if I just pop off a wing?"

"Yeah, not a good idea. Dad is fond of the flying rats."

"How about some rice and water?" He grinned.

"Rice and water?"

"You don't know about that Cher?" He asked.

She shook her head no. "I mean, I know what they are."

"Rice gets bigger when you add water. Birds eat it, then drink water, and they blow up!" He said laughing.

She shook her head. "You were doing so well with Dad...."

Odin arched a brow as he listened.

Brock laughed. "I would never do it, but Brax used to feed the birds and charge people to watch them blow up!" He chuckled. "Ten bucks a pop!" He lost it laughing at his own pun.

Kara shook her head again.

"I'm sorry, Cher. The things young males do when they are bored."

"Wouldn't work with these two anyway," she eyed the Ravens. "They only eat meat, maybe a little fruit."

"Well, what a bummer." Brock eyed them.

Odin arched a brow and turned his gaze on Kara and Ivan excused himself. Clapping Brock on the back, Odin followed the man, talking about the new trainees.

Once Odin left Brock looked at some of the things hanging in the hall. "Are there reasons for some of these?" He asked pointing upward.

Kara looked at the assortment of carvings and tapestries. "They tell our history. Dad doesn't trust one person to hold it all, he prefers that it be out in the open for all to see. It's harder to change the details that way. That one," She pointed to a weathered carving that spanned an

317

eight-foot section of the stone wall. "It tells the story of Dad and my uncles slaying Ymir, the frost giant and with his remains, they built the nine realms. Beside it, that tapestry depicts the same motley crew finding their way into a realm unknown to us, the battle that ensued and him bringing the lovely Gaia home to Asgard. The carved dragon heads, the Drakkar, are from longships that did not make it back and took with them to the bottom, countless worthy warriors whose souls were wasted. It's all we can do to honor them."

He looked at it all as she spoke. "That makes sense. Having knowledge be something everyone can know and learn from." He looked at the carvings. He'd started some of his own but hadn't told Kara about that part of him and his family heritage.

"Yes, and it's harder for some to twist for their own gain if everyone has the same facts. And they're beautiful." She broke off a piece of bread and popped it into her mouth. "Tell me more about your kind, I feel like I know next to nothing, other than the stuff with Gaia and Dad."

Brock wasn't sure what to say. "Shifters or Bears?" He picked up some more meat that looked like it was jerky.

"The bears, or at least your family. I honestly don't care about the rest. I know that sounds bad." Kara shrugged. "But it's true."

He chewed the jerky like stuff and laughed. "Anything you want to know specifically? We can start there," he joked.

"Everything," she grinned. "I want to know what makes you tick. What you like, what you despise. What were the best times of your life? What your family is really like, not just what you all let us see. Everything."

Brock wasn't used to people asking him about himself. "Umm. The best times in my life were when my family was complete. My family is close, or was. When my parents were taken, things changed for us. I know Bree takes it the hardest. She was away when it happened." Brock took another drink of the mead. "Things I despise? I don't like lima beans, the circus, elephants, and women with long nails," he said, trying to lighten his own mood after talking about losing his parents.

Kara checked her nails and smiled, taking his hand and lacing her fingers with his. "I'm sorry about your folks. I wouldn't know what that's like. If we're not killing each other, that's as good as it gets in my family." She tilted her head. "You're not used to having people ask about you, are you?"

He looked at their hands laced together and shook his head no. "No. I'm the quiet one in the family. I do have a unique talent I have never told anyone. Want to see it, Cher?"

Kara smiled wide, surprised that he wanted to share something personal with her when she felt like she had to pull every tiny bit of info out of him. "I'd love to."

He pulled his hair out of the way. "I can wiggle my ears." Brock wiggled them for her.

"Impressive," She grinned. "I can only do my nostrils." She wiggled them and blushed. She remembered trying so hard to learn to do it when she was a kid and now it was just a stupid human trick.

"Let's see. I like the color green, and I don't really much care for the summer. I can't dance, and elephants scare me."

"Why are you scared of elephants? And you told me that you do dance, in your room alone and I'm still holding on to seeing that."

"I like to dance, but can't do it well. I don't let it stop me. I'm stubborn," Brock said, laughing. "An elephant almost trampled me when I was a cub. I don't get near them. Also, why I hate the circus. Humans tried to put me in one, but that's a story for another time."

She stretched up and kissed him. "Let them try it now, and I'll light them up but good." She grinned. "I like when you talk about you. It makes me feel closer to you. I don't want to be with you and one day realize that I don't know you at all. Been there, done that, have the t-shirt and shit."

Brock laughed. "I wonder what they would taste like? Well, ask me anything I'm an open book," he said honestly.

"Extra crispy KFC, I think," she laughed. "See, there is just so much that it's hard to pick specific things. I know that you want the best for your family, that's obvious. But what do you want, for you? If you could paint your life exactly as you want it, what would it look like? Now, in the future. You know what I mean?"

He thought about it for a moment. "I would love to have a family of my own. That's all I really want. To be a father so I can pass on our family traditions and all that. At heart, I'm a simple guy." He shook his head. "I know that sounds stupid, but a family is all I want and a house with some land so I can shift and all of that without fear. A place to teach my cubs and my brothers and sister's Cubs things."

"That doesn't sound stupid, I don't need to shift, but there's a reason why my cottage is away from everyone else. It's good to have a place to just be you and leave the BS behind." Kara winced a little, knowing that if he chose to be with her, he couldn't have what he wanted. Not with the way shifter breeding worked, and it wasn't likely that she would get a second bite at the apple when it came to being given a mate. One was all you got, and she'd fucked it up. "You sure I'm the person you want, Brock? There are others that could give you that. I'm not sure that I can."

Brock nodded. "Yes. I'm sure. I left out that I want a dog. I never had one, but I really want to see what it's like to have a pet." He kissed her cheek. "There are ways around the cub thing. Nothing is set in stone. If we decide we want them, I'll go to Salvation. He has the power to make it happen or not to happen at all. He turned one of the jackals that use to work for us into a eunuch. Another he blessed so that he and his mate could have children. It all depends, but it's not an easy thing to ask." He thought about Jared. "We can always adopt."

320

"You sound pretty sure of yourself, and that's one hell of a list of obstacles. And you don't even know if I can. Hell, I'm not sure if I can. None of my sisters have." Kara sighed. "I don't want you giving up on what you want and then hating me for it later." She thought about the dog idea. "I can definitely get on board with the fur baby, though."

He smiled. "Well, we will see what happens. A fur baby would be a good start. Is there a breed you like more than others?"

"My only experience is with Fenrir, and I doubt that Hel will give him up." She laughed. "I guess I'm pretty open. We'll have to decide who gets custody, which nights." she teased.

He laughed. "I don't like small dogs. They are bear bait." The humans always said that and it made him laugh.

"Any dog that fits in a purse is not a dog," Kara made a face. "I would want something that we could play with, without worrying that we'll break it."

He nodded in agreement. "Are you a cat person?"

"Other than Jared, Serra, and Ripper, not so much. You?" She rubbed his hand between hers and looked up at him. "Maybe we should decide if we want to live in one place and if so where that is, first?"

"I like them too, and Daniel isn't too bad. The kid is mouthy, but his heart is in the right place. And I'll let you pick where we live. I just have to be able to get back to The Pit if I need to defend it."

"Yeah, the kid is okay, I guess." She grinned. "Is my place alright? It puts a little bit of a buffer between you and your brothers and between Dane and me. Dealing with all of that is still a work in progress, at least for me. But you can ghost back if you're needed or Rycker could install a bat, I mean bear signal or something."

Brock chuckled. "Great idea. A bear signal. I'd pay to see that."

Kara laughed. "So would I. Thank you for making this so easy on me. If you change your mind and need us to be at

321

The Pit, I'm open to that too. So how do we go about getting a dog? Because once we have one, we're parents and you're stuck with me forever," she teased.

He laughed. "Oh, the horror!" He said shaking his head. "There are pet stores and adoption places. We can look online and in the paper."

"What about that place that has the parolees? I saw it on TV once. I mean if anyone can handle difficult animals, I think we can." She shrugged. "How hard can it be? Ya'll managed to housebreak Brax."

Brock laughed hard. "I would love to go to that place and check out their dogs."

"Even if they won't let us have one, we should leave a donation. They seem like good people, for humans."

He nodded. "Yes. I'd like that. They appear to need all the help they can get with housing and feeding the dogs. And the vet bills, I'm sure, are insane."

Not caring who was watching or what might be said, Kara cupped his face and kissed him long and slow. "I love how you think, Bear."

Brock growled softly and melted into her kiss. He forgot where he was until he heard someone cough.

She grinned against his lips and nuzzled him before pulling back and looking for whoever thought that a cough was necessary. "That's right. I'm with the Bjorn. Anyone wants to make an issue about it then we can discuss it in the yard? No? Then get a fucking lozenge for your throat and zip it."

Brock lost it laughing. "Oh, geez," he said, smiling.

"What?" She blinked at him innocently and drank her mead. "They expect me to be a crazy bitch, I can't disappoint them."

He just shook his head, laughing still.

"Okay, I could have been nicer," she admitted, her brow wrinkling when she spotted Loki in a corner and not with his patented mischievous grin. "I wonder what's up with him?" Kara murmured, not meaning to give the thought a voice.

Brock looked at him a moment. "I get the feeling it's no good."

"I think you're right, but with Loki, you have to weigh just how badly he can leave you screwed over by helping him and if it's worth it. I love him, but my brother always has ulterior motives that only benefit him." She glanced up at Brock. "Like I said, our families are different."

"Most people do, Cher. It's just how life is," he said honestly.

"I guess you're right. What would you like to do next? I'm thinking selfies in Dad's throne," she grinned.

"We can do that? I wanna touch Ivan's beard. I'm jealous."

"Yeah, we can, I'm thinking Christmas card. The beard envy, you gotta talk to Ivan about that." Kara snickered.

"Okay, he won't stab me, will he?" Brock asked wondering if he would or not.

"Probably not, he seems to like you."

He chuckled. "Could be interesting."

"Maybe you should just say, 'Nice beard, Bro' and not take the chance?"

Brock roared with laughter.

Kara grinned. "I wonder if they think we're dead, back home?"

Brock tilted his head and shook it. "I bet they do. I really don't care, Cher."

She laughed and leaned against him. "Well, if a case of the conscience does start to hit, just remember that time passes differently here. The ten years I was gone was just a few days for you. So, to them, we've barely been gone. I have to admit, I'm enjoying showing you my world."

"I like being here. Thank you for sharing. Is there anything else you wanna show me?" He kissed her forehead.

Smiling Kara nestled tighter against him. "I don't know. None of it is that interesting to me, anymore. If you want to let your bear out to stretch, it doesn't get much safer than my cottage, but if you'd like to explore or see the throne room or the stables, we can do that. Or we can just nap naked in the sun. I'm easy."

"That might be fun. Naked? Wait. What?"

"Just throwing that out there," She grinned.

"You are a trip, Cher. You know that?"

"Is that good or bad?" She tilted her head back to see his face.

"Good." Brock smiled.

"Yay me!" Kara smiled wide and nipped his bearded jaw. "So, what's next, because my butt is falling asleep."

"Let's go see if Ivan will be a good sport." Brock stood. His ass was asleep too, along with the back of his legs. "I think we need to invest in padded benches, Cher."

She laughed and grabbed his arm when the pins and needles sensation attacked her ass cheeks. "I think you might be right, Big Guy. Ivan will be in the stables or the training yard, kicking the crap out of some poor fool." Kara took a step and hissed. "Okay, a slow stroll through the halls it is," she chuckled.

Brock nodded and moved slowly with her as his legs tingled and felt rubbery like they might give out on him. "If he's training, I don't wanna be in the way." Brock hit his leg, hoping it would help.

"You won't be." She patted his arm reassuringly. "He might toss you a sword and a shield and make you play too, but you won't be in the way."

Brock hoped that Kara was right. Of course, Ivan would probably put him on his ass, quick as shit. He laughed "Well, thank god my ass is already numb."

Chapter 34

Kara led Brock through the maze of halls until they finally came to a heavy door that towered over them. Waving her hand, Kara grinned as it swung open slowly. In the yard, people bustled around and chickens ran underfoot. Hanging a right at the outside kitchen, she followed the short wall until they found themselves at the back of the stable. She stopped to rub Sleipnir's muzzle and to feed him the apple that she'd slipped into her pocket. She missed having her own mount, but couldn't bring herself to pick another. She laughed as the horse sneezed at Brock. Kara slipped the bear an apple to avoid his getting an annoyed bite from Odin's horse. "Just keep your hand flat," She demonstrated, holding her palm out and her fingers straight. "It hurts like a bitch when he gets your fingers." Her smile grew as Brock made friends with her father's freak of a horse and heard steel striking wood, with Ivan bellowing at someone.

"It t'aint a tine of a fork for picken' yur teeth. Aye, it can be if you want to die, Lass. It's steel, and the steel is thirsty. Now git off yur arse and swing it like a man, not a pretty little pansy."

Kara rolled her eyes and chuckled. She remembered hearing those same words, more than once.

Brock held the apple in his palm and flattened his hand as the horse ate it. He heard Ivan kicking the snot out of someone. He looked at Kara, thinking that he'd rather annoy the eight-legged horse than having Ivan kick his furry ass all over Asgard.

"Awwww, he likes you." She ruffled the white mane as Sleipnir rubbed his face against Brock's chest. "I think whoever Ivan is yelling at, might enjoy the interruption." She snickered. Although in truth, what that tough old bastard had taught her had saved her more than once, and she owed him everything.

Brock petted the horse and sighed. "Alright. Let's get the ass kicking over." He motioned for her to lead the way.

Kara shook her head. "He'd be the first to tell you that if you think you'll lose, you will indeed lose." She took his hand and led the way, past the stalls, ignoring the heads that poked out to see who was here. She began humming TAPS as they neared the gate that led to the training yard. Instead of going through, she leaned against the rough beams that made a crude fence and watched. "He has tells. He leads with his shoulder. If he's going to swing high, he pivots slightly on his left foot just before he strikes. If it's low, he sticks his tongue out, just a little. You can tell if it's coming from the left or the right, by watching his hips. Do you see what I mean?" She spoke softly so that only Brock would hear and glanced up at his face.

"Yes," he whispered back and watched the warrior intently. His eyes narrowed as he tried to follow Kara's example of sizing up his opponent. He was surprised that the more he broke down how Ivan worked, the less anxiety he felt. A smile played on his lips that wouldn't have been possible before. Brock hopped over the fence and leaned his ass against the rail. "Is this an ass beating for one, or can anyone join in the game?"

Ivan threw back his head and laughed. "Aye, all are welcome. Gunner, get weapons and a shield for our friend." He eyed Kara and grinned. "I thought you liked him, Wee One."

"I do." She dropped a bag of gold coins in the dirt. "I'll put that on the Bjorn." She arched a brow and enjoyed the shadow of 'oh shit' that crossed Ivan's face before he covered it.

"Darlin', if you want to give me your money, I am happy to take it." Ivan lifted the string on the bag with the tip of his sword and tossed it to the girl he'd been yelling at moments ago. "Aesir rules. There are three shields and three bouts. Each round ends when the shield is broken. And then I take Wee One's money." Ivan chuckled.

"Put your money where your mouth is, Ivan. Match my bet. I have confidence in the Bjorn." The gathering crowd began to chatter around them.

"It is done, Aye." Ivan laughed and tossed his own bag of coins to the girl. "You backed the wrong steed, Wee One."

"We'll see, Ivan. We will see." Kara grinned back.

Brock wasn't sure about taking on Ivan. His fighting skills were honed using claws and teeth, not sword and shield. He was given his choice of an ax, a sword, and a shield. He tied his hair back from his face, eyeing the weapons skeptically. After a few minutes of consideration, he lifted the ax and picked up his shield, not sure if one was better than another. Brock said a little prayer to himself before raising his eyes to Ivan's. "I'm ready," he said, knowing that it was a lie.

"We begin as thus." Ivan banged his sword against his shield twice and waited for Brock to do the same. "And so, it begins," he chuckled and swung the massive sword at Brock's shield, just to see what he was made of.

Kara winced, knowing how the sword striking the wood vibrated up your arm. 'Remember what I told you and no matter how much you want to, DO NOT drop the shield.' she mindlinked Brock.

Brock's blue eyes flared when the sword struck his shield and felt the impact reverberate up his arm until his teeth rattled. So much for the slim hope that Ivan would take it easy on him. He lunged, shoving his weight into the shield and pushing the sword upward and away. Brock spun from Ivan, rolling the ax handle through his fingers and testing his grip. The ax felt more natural to him than a sword would have, because of the large-scale woodworking that he did. The trees he used, didn't cut themselves.

Eyeing Ivan and trying to remember everything Kara had told him, Brock wondered what Ivan was. Was he a man who had earned his place here, or was Brock raising his ax to a God? How much did Ivan know about the human style of fighting? Brock was about to find out. Gripping the ax handle tightly in his hand, he swung. Brock's eyes mapped every detail of the shield that Ivan raised. The grayed weathered surface and rusty stains that bled into it from the iron bolts, dent's, the bites taken by previous hits and more importantly, the grain of the wood and how it flowed. The wood shield has seen better days and had not been cared for properly.

Brock studied everything, the reach of Ivan's blade, the Viking's style and the way he moved. He'd always relied on his ability to out think an opponent, and Brock fell back to his comfort zone now, even though there was nothing comfortable about this situation. Still, brains before brawn had served him well. Anyone could beat the hell out of another person, but if you could out think them, it shattered their confidence, and they made stupid hotheaded mistakes. Well, that was his plan, as he hammered against Ivan's shield. His blows seemed to be nothing to the Viking who showed no discomfort. In fact, he was laughing and his green eyes twinkled with good humor. But the rules were about breaking the shield, not the man, Brock reminded himself.

Kara kept her poker face in place when Ivan swung on Brock. Even though she was flinching inside, no one would know that she had anything but complete confidence in her Bjorn. Her eyes sparkled as he found his rhythm and comfort zone, changing the fight to what he knew and refusing to let Ivan play his own game.

Ivan laughed and met each strike of the ax with his raised shield. Finally, a real opponent. He swung the sword, landing a blow before Brock forced him to duck back behind his shield, but the light was beginning to peek through the wood. The loud crack of breaking timber and metal snapping rang out and ended the first bout. Laughing, he slapped Brock's back affectionately. "I'll stop taking it light on you now, Lad." He chuckled and waited for Gunner to bring him another shield, leaning close to Brock he spoke low. "I would have you at my side in a battle any day, Bjorn. Aye, any damn day."

Brock grinned and nodded, trying not to let the compliment go to his head. "I'd be honored." His eyes sought out Kara in the crowd. She looked relaxed and confident, and he allowed that to bolster his confidence. He could do this. Tossing the Viking a smile and slapping his shoulder, Brock moved out of Ivan's reach giving himself time to readjust his shield in his hand. He watched Ivan's body language and braced for the next rain of attacks.

Ivan grinned good-naturedly and slid his arm into the leather straps of the shield, gripping the second strap with his hand and giving it a bounce to get a feel for its balance before banging his sword against the wood and waiting for Brock to do the same. Then he swung at the bear's legs, trying to use the Bjorn's height against him.

Kara pulled her phone from her pocket and snapped pictures of the fight. Brock had earned bragging rights, just for stepping into the ring with Ivan and if he chose to do so, he was sure as hell going to have proof for the naysayers back home.

As Ivan swung at his feet, Brock did a cartwheel with the hand that held his shield and gripped the ax. Most misjudged how quickly he could move, expecting his large, six foot eight frame to slow him down or make him top heavy. That was their mistake. Brock could thank his sister for it. When they were cubs, Bree went through a phase of wanting to be an Olympic gymnast and Brock had been the only one who would join in her cartwheeling and tumbling. Over the years, the skills learned from their play had helped him more than once.

Brock landed on his feet, pulling the shield in to cover his midsection. His ax blocked and protected his throat. He banged the handle of his ax on the shield letting Ivan know he was ready and grinned at him.

Ivan roared his approval and circled, looking for his opening before lunging to strike the spot that he had previously weakened with his blows. The bear was not an easy one to read, and he was enjoying the hell out of finally having a little sport. Letting out a yell, he charged and began trying to bash the shield to pieces, ducking a chunk of wood that blew back toward his face.

Brock changed his approach as his shield started to vanish from Ivan's blows. Screw defense, offense was the way to go. He raised his ax to connect with Ivan's sword. The sword's blade slid into the groove between the blade and the handle. Brock twisted his wrist as the sword blade dug into the wood of the handle, becoming snared. Brock smiled and yanked his arm downward, pulling Ivan to him. Brock used that momentum to hit the warrior in the face playfully with his shield and seemed to take the Viking by surprise. Ivan's grip on his sword loosened. Feeling the resistance against his weapon lessen, Brock pulled back with the ax. The sword came free, clattering to the packed dirt. Instinct screamed for Brock to step on the sword and prevent Ivan from picking it up. But this was for sport, not blood, he reminded himself, and stepped back, leaving it open and available for the Viking.

The crowd leaned forward in a collective gasp. Most had never seen Ivan disarmed and in the field, this could have been a fatal mistake. The chatter kicked up a notch as bets were placed as to the bear's honor, did he have it? Cheers and groans rang out depending on which side the spectator had laid their money when Brock stepped back and let his elder collect his weapon.

"Good show, Lad." Ivan beamed, wiping his stinging nose with the back of his hand.

Kara smiled proudly from where she leaned on the rail. 'Nicely done, Babes,' she mindlinked. She could tell he was having fun and was feeling less out of his element.

'Thank you, Cher.' He linked back. "My pleasure, Sir." Pride bloomed in his chest when Brock realized that he wasn't as bad at this as he'd thought he would be. "I take it, that doesn't happen a lot?"

"Nay," Ivan laughed and shook his head. "It does not." Seating the pummel in his hand, Ivan arched a questioning brow. "Ready?"

"Yes." Brock grinned and adjusted his stance, waiting for Ivan's next attack. His shield was on its last legs, but he didn't care if he won, as long as he didn't make a fool of himself. There was no shame in losing to an ancient Viking warrior in Asgard. He blinked. He'd never dreamed that he would be able to say that.

Ivan eyed Brock's shield and growled his displeasure at its condition. It was going to come down to a winner take all bout. Both would save face, and that was good. He attacked the shield, pulling back when it fell in two halves to hang on Brock's arm. "One more to go, Lad." He chuckled.

"Yes," Brock said waiting for his new shield. He and Ivan circled each other. "A fight to the death," he joked.

Ivan laughed, "All or nothing, Bjorn. Either way, tis been a pleasure." He waited while Brock slipped on the new shield and adjusted it for comfort before he banged his sword against it and waited for the bear to make the first move.

Brock decided to make it fun. He ran full force at the Viking, shield up and ready. It reminded him of a Red Rover death match.

Throwing his head back in a roar of laughter, Ivan did the same.

Kara held her breath, worried that this would knock them both unconscious.

They collided in a crash of metal and wood. Splinters exploded and rained down on them and the surrounding crowd causing the spectators to duck and turn their heads. Both men landed on their backs hard, grunting at the impact. Silence fell over the yard until Brock met Ivan's twinkling emerald eyes and they both broke into a peal of laughter.

"I dare say, it was a draw," Ivan laughed, lifting his head to look at the bear.

"Yes, Sir. I would say so," Brock said sitting up. "Thank you for letting me play. And not shaming me in front of Kara," he said low enough for only Ivan to hear.

Ivan clapped him on the back, "Aye and to you for not doing the same before my students." He grunted and pushed himself to his feet, holding out his hand to Brock. "And for letting an old man enjoy a worthy opponent."

Kara slipped through the rails of the fence and walked over to the two males, who were still dusting themselves off and laughing. Taking one of each of their arms, she held them up, and the crowd cheered their approval. When she dropped them, she grinned at Brock, "I knew you could do it."

Brock smiled. "Oh, he was just kind to me. Next time, I'll end up a rug. Won't I, Ivan?" He said laughing. "I'm just glad I have all my parts still."

Ivan shook his head. "Nay, the Lad put up a hell of a fight. You chose well, Wee One." He ruffled Kara's hair, laughing at her scowl.

"Modesty isn't a familiar character trait with my people," she swatted Ivan's big hand away. "A draw is almost better than a win and very rare. You're allowed to be proud, Babes. I know I am."

"Well, we'll have a rematch soon." He grinned at Ivan. "And I am proud. Mostly to be yours."

Ivan gave him a thumbs up behind Kara's back and began barking orders at his students to make ready for more training.

"See? It's when you say stuff like that, that you melt my heart just a little bit more." She grinned and stretched up to kiss him.

Chapter 35

"You do realize that they're going to be telling stories about this for months? You'll be a legend around here." Kara beamed, not so much because of the notoriety he'd have, but because no one was likely to try to screw with him. Not many walked away with their dignity when they went up against Ivan. This had shown them all that Brock wasn't hiding behind the Valkyrie, but walked beside her.

"I don't know about that," Brock said taking her hand as they walked. "I would love to do it again, to see what he could teach me. I'm sure a lot."

"Trust me. It's a pain, I know, but it comes with respect, and that's good." Kara squeezed his hand and grinned. "I think you should. Maybe invite him to Nola to do something that you enjoy. Ivan is a good guy, and he's been wanting to check out the 'world of man,' as he calls it. This would be a good excuse." She swung their hands happily as they walked.

Brock arched a surprised brow, looked down at the top of her head and grinned. He couldn't remember seeing any of the people that he'd met, here in Nola. It meant a lot that Kara wanted to mix her two worlds and make him part of it. "I didn't realize that Ivan could leave here. I'd think I'd like to have him visit." He shook his head, imagining the looks on his brother's faces when his new Viking friend popped in.

"So, what can I reward you with, for fighting so well?" Kara nodded her approval and glanced up at him. Her kind was becoming fat and lazy. It would be good for them to play a more active role in the worlds they were connected to.

"As a prize? Do you have a TV here?" Brock smiled and thought about cuddling and watching something on the tube.

"In my cottage, yes. Gotta love those satellite dish, things." Kara grinned. "Is it bad that I just want to be with you and maybe rub any sore spots you might have?" She watched his face, loving the way that he seemed to take everything in and process it without it being too much. "I never brought anyone here, because I knew that few were able to roll with our brand of weirdness. I'm glad I brought you. OH!" She pulled out her phone and pulled up the photos. "And I got pics!" She grinned and showed him.

"Oh, geez," he groaned as she scrolled through the photos. "What? No video?"

"I forgot I could do that." She cursed at herself for it. "You two look very vicious and manly."

"Good, how was my hair?" He chuckled.

Kara shook her head and slid the phone back in her pocket. "I'm not going to tell you."

Brock laughed at her tone. "You're so mean."

"Not me. Sweetness and light, here."

He nodded and tried not to bust out laughing. "Light only because you need the sun to charge, Cher," he teased.

Kara shrugged and stuffed her free hand into her pocket. "Sure, if you want to be all technical and shit. Fine. I'm mean, awful and a bitch. I was trying to be nice."

Brock growled, picked her up and tossed her over his shoulder. "Yes, so utterly awful. So, tell me, Cher, since you got photos of Ivan and me. What kind of blackmail do you have in mind? Whips and chains? Feathers or the whole chicken?" He began down the dirt road that led back to her cabin.

335

Pushing her hands against his lower back, Kara tried to lever herself up and twist to see over his shoulder. "Ooh, whips and chains, who's getting chained up?" She grinned. "I wasn't thinking blackmail. You earned bragging rights, just for doing it."

"I don't know, Cher. I never tried it. Do you know how all that works? I'd love to learn." Brock wasn't sure what kind of things she liked in that department. 'The damn TV show,' as her father said, painted a picture of a full world of kinky things. His brow quirked, thinking about it.

"Never chained anyone for fun, but it has possibilities. Please, tell me we're getting close. I drank too much mead to be spending this much time upside down with jostling, and it's kinda weird talking to your ass."

Brock moved her to carry her in his arms. "Is this better? I never tried anything like that. Are you saying your drunk, Cher?"

"Much better." Kara circled her arms around his neck and nuzzled him, groaning at the way his scent filled her and made her feel real. "Not drunk, just too much liquid in there to be upside down. I can't help it, I've gotta ask, do you want to try something like that?" She looked up at him, pinning her lower lip between her teeth. "Honest answer and I won't judge."

He laughed hard and made his way into the cabin. "Honestly? I don't know. It kinda scares me. Chains and all that."

"Fine take the fear out of it, not that you couldn't snap them if you wanted to anyway, and you're not the one wearing them. Still scared?"

Brock thought a moment. "If you want to, we can try it. Do I have to call you Master?" His brow arched.

"I prefer Kara, but you know, if that gets you off..." She grinned. "And I'm not sure that I want to, I just wanted to know if you did. Believe it or not, the last thing I want to do is hurt you."

He set her down. "I'm not really into that. I believe it, Cher. And I'm glad you're not into it either. A little too far out there, for me."

Kara looked around the small space, still leaning against Brock because she liked feeling him there. "See? Now we know and no awkward forgetting of safe words and all of that." She laughed. "What do you think?" She stepped back and gestured to the minimalistic cottage. Everything was simple but functional. Where many of her family went for the over the top, her tastes were more concerned with comfort. Except for the television, an enormous flat screen that ate up an entire wall.

Brock looked around at her things. "Would you like some wall to go with your TV, Cher?" He said, gaping at it. "That is a thing of beauty. I like your place, it's not super girly, but you can tell a woman lives here. Of course, the chain mail bra might also help with that idea."

She laughed. "It comes in handy too, but it's torture on a cold day." Kara impulsively stretched up and kissed him. "If we spend much time here, maybe you can help me butch it up a little," she teased and nipped his lip.

He kissed her back. "Butch it up, huh? Well, my taste is pretty much tools and things to trip over. I'm not that graceful. As you know. Falling out of my own bed. Super smooth."

"But you looked good doing it," Kara smirked. "And if I hadn't hogged the bed and groped you after you were sweet enough to humor me, it might have gone differently." She shrugged. "I don't know, I like the idea of your stuff being underfoot. It means you're here with me." She made a face. "God, that sounded almost pathetically girly. What are you doing to me bear?"

Brock laughed. "Well, we both can't be men. I can try and be feminine for a while. If you promise to braid my hair for me," he teased. "I don't have much stuff, honestly. I could buy new stuff to leave all over the place, if you like."

"No, that's okay." She tugged his beard and stepped back to look for the remote.

"Oh, come on!" He begged. The look she gave him was priceless.

"I'll braid your hair anytime, Babes. I don't want you to go out of your way. Not for me."

"Would you braid it now?" Brock asked, thinking about what she had said. "Okay, I'll bring some of my things here, if you like."

"Sure," She left him to get her brush and a hair tie from the bathroom and returned looking around for a place that would make it easy for her to reach. She wasn't used to feeling short, but damn if Brock didn't make her feel petite. She was going to have to improvise. She took his hand and led him to the sofa and pointed at the floor with the brush. "Park it, Big Guy, and I'll make you pretty," she teased.

Laughing, he took a seat. "No pigtails," Brock said leaning his head back, looking up at her.

Kara eyed him before dropping onto the sofa and hugging his shoulders with her knees. "It would be hella cute, though," she grinned, tilted his head back and leaned over him to drop a kiss on his lips. "Okay, so a manly braid like my kind wear into battle, or fancy? Are you trying to make a fashion statement?" She asked pulling the brush through his hair, loving the softness of it against her skin.

"Surprise me!" He said laughing.

Kissing him again, Kara leaned back and pushed his head forward, adjusting her position when something poked her ass cheek. Reaching down she came back with the remote and held it out to him over his shoulder. "Find us something, Big Guy." She closed her eyes and inhaled deeply as brushing his hair seemed to fill the room with his scent, and she wanted to wrap herself in it. Forcing herself back to the task, Kara began sectioning his hair carefully before weaving it into the preferred plated pattern of warriors.

"Thank you." Brock studied the remote and finally located the power button before pointing it at the wall of television and clicking the button. He opened the guide option and started looking for something to watch. "Oh! There's an old MMA fight on that I haven't seen. Is that okay with you? I love MMA!" He said not moving his head as she braided his hair, being far gentler than he'd expected.

"Violence and half naked men, what's not to love?" She teased and wove a rogue strand of his hair that was fighting her into the pattern, working her way down the tail.

Brock selected the fight and set the remote down. "If you ever wanna wrestle, let me know," he joked.

"If I ever want to?" Kara laughed. "You have an open invitation to throw down with me anytime." She wrapped the tie around the tail of the braid and leaned forward to slide her arms around him and rested her chin on his shoulder.

"Am I purdy now?" He asked smiling. "I don't know, you'd probably kick my ass."

"Drop dead gorgeous, Babes," she smiled back and wasn't lying. "If you're afraid... I understand." She teased. "Besides, my kind almost sees it as foreplay, so yeah, I understand the fear."

Brock laughed. "Thank you, and I'm scared you'll muss my hair."

Kara laughed and nipped his shoulder.

Watching the fight, Brock made a face. "Damn, did you see that? His teeth just flew out. Damn."

"Yeah, no more solid food for him." Kara winced, wondering if the guy's jaw was broken.

"Shit, man! Protect your middle," Brock barked at the screen, starting to get into it.

"When blood bubbles come out of your mouth like that, tap the fuck out," Kara growled at the television. She didn't understand why the human didn't. He wasn't fighting for his life, but he could still lose it. "Do shifters ever do this?" She glanced at Brock and then her eyes were sucked back to the screen. "I mean, humans would be easy pickings, and they'd hardly have to break a sweat." Of course, she did know the fighting elite of the shifters, so maybe she was off the mark.

Brock watched the two men still kicking the snot out of each other. "Do what? Be this stupid? No, Cher, we know when to say when, unless it comes to someone we love."

"I meant, compete in these things." She arched a brow. "Yeah, I've seen what it takes to take you down when your family is in danger."

He chuckled. "Actually, I know a few shifters who do this for money when they need it," he said watching the fight end. "About time. Dude had nothing left. Brutal."

"Really?" She slid onto the floor beside him. "Anyone I know?"

Brock thought for a moment. "I don't believe you've met her yet," Brock said trying to think if Kara had met her. "No Cher, I don't believe that you have."

"Her?" This was more interesting of a topic than she'd thought. "Tell me more, please?" Kara blinked at him, trying to be cute and irresistible.

He laughed at her expression. "Yes, her. Not too many people know about it. Her name is Abigail O'Conner. She's a rabbit," Brock said, trying to remember what else he knew about her.

Kara blinked. "A bunny shifter? You're screwing with me."

"Nope. I'm totally serious. A few males have the balls to call her a Bunny, not thinking much of it, and she punches their lights out. My father used to call her Jabby Abby." Brock laughed.

"Good for her. I watch how females are treated differently at The Pit, hell in NOLA in general. I don't get it." She shook her head and let her confusion show. "You've known her for a long time, then?"

"Yes, it's disgusting. I was raised better than that. My brothers too, but you wouldn't know it sometimes." Brock thought about when Abby came to The Pit. "I was a cub when she came through the portal. She comes and goes. I guess you could say, I've known her for a long time. I haven't seen her in years, though. Last I knew, she was put on some mission by Salvation. That was a few years ago."

Kara tilted her head. "Salvation sends you on missions? Like what?" She didn't really understand her brother's role or why he was always so damned cranky about it.

"There are places he can't go without being known, I guess. I've only been on two, myself. Are you thirsty?" Brock tried to change the subject, getting up off the floor.

"Yes. What did he have you do?" She watched him stand and craned her neck back. "Or is it some super, secret decoder ring required, kinda stuff?" She grinned, sobering when she wondered who Sal had sent to take out her and Dane.

He got himself a glass of ice water and sat down on the couch with her. "Sometimes it seems like you need one. He had me scout out places for safe houses," Brock said taking a drink. "For females and children. I'm not sure if it had to do with them having not having mates or if their clans kicked them out, but my job was to check out the area for him and report back about it. The other was guarding a family of leopards against demons, while he took care of the problem. Nothing too exciting." He downplayed it, drinking more of his water.

Kara nodded and ghosted off her boots, tucking her legs under her and leaning her elbow on the back of the sofa. "It sounds interesting, though, to an outsider, like me." She smiled softly.

"Really?" He asked, surprised as he watched her get comfy. He offered his water to her.

"Yes," she took the glass, sipped it and handed it back. "It's weird. I've been watching from the outside, almost like through a window. I can see what is happening, but I miss the whys of it. On occasion, when I can be useful, ya'll let me in to help take care of a problem. As soon as it's done, I'm back out in the cold." She shrugged and watched his sapphire eyes. "I died for something, I'd like to understand

341

what it was, you know? It makes it hard to trust much of anything that has to do with that world. And when I do, I usually regret it."

He took the glass and nodded. "Honestly, I get the need to know basis. I don't always get the whole story. I get the part that's tied to me. After that, I don't know. I wasn't allowed to ask about the family I helped or the safe houses. I don't know why Sal won't tell me, but I can understand your feelings, Cher."

"I appreciate that, Babes." She rubbed his arm and smiled softly. "I think that's part of why I suck at being subtle or mysterious. I prefer full transparency, not secrets and tricks. I try not to let you feel like that, with my world. If we are going to do this, I want you to be comfortable wherever we are. I didn't do that with Dane, in my defense, he never showed any interest in it." She made a face and shook her head the red flags that were popping up in hindsight. She couldn't help but wonder what she did not see, where Brock was concerned, that would come back and bite her in the ass. She felt herself take a step back from him, emotionally and that just made her feel a little sad. "I'm trying to learn from my mistakes."

He smiled. "Well, you're totally right. Won't work with half the picture or information. And what happened with you and Dane, is between you and him. That's not us. I don't even let that come to my mind." He lied. Seriously, how could he not worry about her ex popping back into the picture, and saying that one thing that she needed to hear, to fall back into the lion's arms?

Kara nodded and leaned her head on his shoulder. "I try not to."

He reached up and stroked her cheek, forgetting that hand had the water glass in it last. His hand was a little wet and cold. "Sorry," He said, feeling bad for using her cheek as a napkin.

She gave him a confused look and pulled away.

"My hand was wet. I'm sorry for that. Ignore the derpy bear," Brock shook his head. "Tell me more about your place. Any rules or limitations?"

She laughed. "I thought you meant that you were sorry for touching me. I'm not sure what you mean. In Asgard or in NOLA?"

"Goof." He laughed. "Yes, here. I know my sister and my mother had things that were not for us guys to touch. Momma had a large coffee mug that was a special gift she got, and if anyone drank from it, she has a fit. Bree doesn't like anyone touching her stuff in the bathroom."

Kara thought about it for a moment and shook her head, "No one ever comes here, but no, I don't believe. I mean I would prefer that you not try to wear my underpants. You'd stretch them out, and they'd never fit right again," she teased. "I'm an open book, Babes and I'm not overly sentimental about stuff."

"Well damn it, that was the first thing I was going to do." Brock pouted.

"I had a feeling," she nodded trying to look serious.

"How about as a head warmer?"

She twisted her lips back and forth as she thought about it. "Depends on the situation, but as an eye patch? Aye, Matey."

He lost it. "Cher! Oh, my God," Brock said, laughing so hard that he held his sides.

Kara blinked at him innocently. It warmed her to see him smile.

"A Viking pirate..." The thought made him roar with laughter.

"You'll never look at Dad the same way again," she grinned and leaned against him, looking up into his face.

Brock shook his head, laughing. "No, I will not."

"What is it they say? If you get nervous just imagine everyone in their underwear. This is like that!' She smiled wide.

343

"Oh, my gods!" He was laughing so hard that he was crying. "Jesus, Cher."

Kara curled against him and sighed happily. "Just remember, you started it."

Brock snorted. "I'll do that," he said, wrapping his arm around her.

"I like you. You get my humor." She grinned and patted his chest, stretching up to kiss the underside of his jaw. "And I like how you smell and that you make me calm and excited at the same time. I guess I gotta keep you."

"My smell? Well, I love everything about you. Even that bloodthirsty part!"

Kara nodded. "You smell like the woods after a soft spring rain, with a twist of sweet grass. And when you hold me like this, you feel like home, not a place, but where I belong." She scrunched up her nose and hid her face against his chest. "That made no sense and was the opposite of bloodthirsty. My ancestors will be ashamed." She chuckled.

Brock grinned. "Well, I'm glad you like my stink. I get what you mean about feeling at peace," he agreed, honestly.

"Good." She tilted her head back and crooked her finger at him. "Kiss me, Bear. Please?"

He growled softly and did as she asked. Brock felt like she really saw him and who he was, deep inside. Maybe she even saw things that he didn't. That last part worried him a little, but he'd never had that with anyone else, not even his family and he liked it. He'd miss it if she came to her senses. He'd miss her. Was it wrong to pray that she never did?

Kara smiled against his lips, shuddering slightly as his growl vibrated through her. She tangled her fingers in his hair as much as the braid would allow, never wanting to let this sweet and gentle bear go. He wasn't weak, his bout with Ivan had shown that, as did how he handled his family. It was an unprecedented combination that made him truly priceless. And he was hers. Her chest swelled aching painfully at the amount of emotion it was being forced to hold within. She placed her hand on her chest, wondering if he could feel how hard and fast he made her heart pound. "My heart is yours, Brock Navarro."

He could feel her heart beat faster as they kissed. When she spoke, Brock smiled. "Mine has belonged to you for a long time, Cher. Even before we met." He hugged her close.

She clung to him, pressing her face into the crook of his neck and smiling as his hair tickled her cheek. "Now that I know, I'll be careful with it, and if anyone tries to hurt it, I will kill them, dead." Kara grinned at the redundancy but didn't care. She'd lost once, and it had been gut-wrenching, but in the end, she couldn't regret it. The time with Dane had taught her that she wanted what she had with Brock. It was different than anything she'd experienced before. She KNEW him, even though she knew very little about him. Something deep in her soul recognized his and returned the call that it heard. Perhaps Odin's ravens had been right. Perhaps he was her ingolf. She smiled even as something deep down inside shivered at the power that gave the Bjorn over her.

"Ditto, Cher. Let's watch one of the weirdo movies you like. Teach me the ways of B-movie trash," he joked.

"It's not an old B movie, but it reminds me of one..." She took the remote and found what she was looking for in the list of films. "If you don't laugh once, you have no soul." Grinning Kara snuggled into him and pressed play before Tucker and Dale vs. Evil filled the screen.

"Okay. Let's see if it's any good." Brock got comfortable and stroked her hair while they watched the movie.

Kara kept looking up at him to see what he thought and let the movie give her a break from the cluster fuck going on inside her head.

He watched and laughed. "It's not too bad." He shook his head laughing. "Is it sad I know some guys like that?"

She laughed. "I know, right? I think that this could so happen to The Pit crew."

He nodded. "Gods, you're right." He thought for a moment. "I think I've heard of this movie before. There's a wood chipper in it?"

She laughed hard and nodded.

"Okay then I've wanted to watch it, just couldn't remember the name." Brock took her hand in his.

She ghosted in snacks and drinks and smiled as his palm slid under hers. "Lucky for you that I like my, what did you call them? Oh yeah, weirdo movies." She arched a brow and teased, tilting her head back to see his face.

Brock laughed and thought about the last time he sat down and watched anything on television that wasn't at The Pit or something Bree made them watch. He watched Vikings, yes, but that was because Bree thought Travis Fimmel was hot. In all honesty, he felt the character of Ragnar Lothbrok was a little odd, like he was trying too hard. He did like Floki and Rollo, and when he saw Lagertha, he thought of Kara. Her courage and the set of balls they both had, was incredible.

Still snickering, Kara settled back against his side and put her feet up.

"I love his dog," Brock reached for some chips.

"Me too. His face is a little floppy in the muzzle, but he's cute."

Eating some chips, he nodded. "I wanna mush his little face," Brock remembered their talk about getting a dog. "So, when are we going to have our first fur baby? I know the magic of my fur wears off."

"I like your fur and how it feels against my skin." She grinned. "You tell me when, Babes. We just need to find it."

Brock smiled at her. "We can look online first. I've heard that's one way that people pick them out. I don't have a computer. Bart smashed mine. Don't ask. Temper trauma over some game or porn site. I didn't get the full story. I just know he killed my laptop."

"Trauma on a porn site?"" Her brows edged toward her hairline. "I don't think I want to know what could have caused that."

"Like I said, I didn't get details. He saw something, and the laptop ended up paying the price. Maybe it was his girlfriend!" Brock laughed.

"I thought..." her brow wrinkled. "Never mind. I must be thinking of someone else." She shook her head and added that to her list of things to consider later. "I have one at my place. He touches it, and I will zap his ass." Kara smiled sweetly.

"He owes me a new one. I'm thinking about breaking the TV in his room. See how he likes it."

She shook her head and laughed. "Brothers, gotta love them. I just take Thor's hammer when he acts up. With Loki, there's no point, it just ups the ante. Before you know it, someone has a weird rash that can't be cured."

Brock's eyes widened, and he made a face. "Rash? Where?" He put his hands up. "Never mind I don't wanna know." He didn't want to think about her having a rash on her butt or something.

"All I'm going to say is, if Loki gets one over on you, laugh and let it go. He is NOT one to prank war with." Kara smiled remembering the itching that had covered her from head to toe until Dad had threatened her brother's life if he didn't remove it.

"Okay I'll make a note of it, but you could always Roshambo him for whatever it is he wants. " Brock laughed hard. It was something Jared had taught Bree. Brax had learned the hard way not to play that game with her.

"I have no idea what that is. He's tricky enough when he's nice, not gonna chance it again. We have a deal. When he deserves it, or when he pushes me to the point that I scare him, he doesn't reciprocate. It works for us."

"That's where, most of the time, two guys kick each other in the balls over whatever they want. Whoever is left standing, gets it. My brothers had no idea what it was,

347

either. Brax played along with her until the first strike."
Brock laughed thinking about Brax's face and the noise he made hitting the ground. Leave it to a Panther to come up with something like that.

Kara winced. "Ouch. Not saying I wouldn't or haven't, but by the time I get to that point, it's to add insult to injury after the broken bones."

Brock winced. "I'm glad you two have a thing worked out. But I would be okay covering you in that pink stuff from head to toe. I bet Asher has some stuff for a rash." Brock joked

She perked up a little. "We can always pretend."

Brock laughed. "Just tell me where the evil man made you itch, Cher," he said, trying to be serious.

She scratched at her side and grinned. "Under here."

"You may have to take that off, so I can see it better."

"If you think it will help." Kara pulled away, her legs still folded under her, and pulled her shirt over her head, looking down at her side and glamoured the skin reddish.

"You poor thing," Brock cooed, looking at the redness. He ghosted in calamine lotion and cotton balls and prepared to dab it onto her skin.

"Yes," she pouted, stretching her arm up to show him, biting her lower lip and giving him sad, puppy dog eyes. "What do we do if it spreads?"

"I guess you'll have to stay naked. The air getting to it will help a lot." Brock couldn't help but chuckle at the look on her face. "Cher, you are too much," he said wiping some of the lotion on her side.

"Naked. You think that will help?" Kara grinned and jumped at the coolness of the cream. "Maybe, but I've got my shirt off and your hands on me, so I don't see a downside."

Brock pretended to think that over for a moment. "I don't see one either. Other than maybe you getting cold." He wiped some of the lotion on the tip of her nose.

She crossed her eyes to see the dot of pink. "How can I get cold with you here to keep me warm?" She leaned closer and wiped the lotion from the tip of her nose to his neck. "Just in case it's contagious." She grinned and nuzzled him.

He growled softly. "We wouldn't want both of us to be itchy, now would we?" He said nipping her lips.

"That would be a shame, but I'd lotion you if it happened." Kara tangled her fingers in his hair, or tried, messing up the braid and kissed him. Goosebumps broke over her skin in response to his growl.

"Well, as long as you'll lotion me, I think we'll make it." Brock felt the goose bumps surface on her skin. "Cold, Cher?" He asked, taking in her scent, even if she did smell like that weird pink stuff.

"No," she shook her head. "Feeling really warm. I blame you."

"How warm?" He whispered into her ear, his hands slowly running over her sides.

Kara groaned softly and rubbed her face against his bearded jaw, tasting the skin of his neck with her lips and tongue. "Burning up. I need help."

"My poor, Cher," he said, kissing her softly, at first.

"Yes, it's torture," she whispered against his lips, and moved on to his lap, wanting to be closer to him as her blood began to boil.

"Tell me what I can do to make it better?" Brock ghosted away the lotion from her skin and brushed the long hair from her face.

Kara tugged at his shirt, pulling it up so that she could slip her hands underneath and stroke his skin. "I'm not sure, we'll have to experiment." She turned her head to brush her lips over his palm.

Brock pulled his shirt off and shivered as the braid in his hair tickled his back. "I guess it is best, to keep the problem contained. Do some troubleshooting on it."

"It's our duty to prevent an epidemic." Kara nodded gravely, turning so that his legs were nestled between her

349

thighs and her chest leaned against his. She gasped softly at the electrical charge that danced between them, making her skin hum when they touched. It felt the same as her fingertips did when she created lightning, except this was burrowing into her to swirl in her stomach and made her core spasm. "Whatever it takes."

"Oh, yes," Brock growled low. "Whatever it takes." He cupped her breast and lifted his gaze up to stare into her azure eyes. "Does it itch there?" He squeezed the mound in his hand gently and wet his lips.

Kara bit her lower lip and nodded, her eyes locked with his, groaning at the swipe of his tongue under his mustache. The warm pressure of his hand caused her skin to tighten under his touch. She had to concentrate to stay in character, feathering her nails over the rippling muscled that covered his ribs kept her grounded.

Brock let his thumb glide over her nipple, barely brushing the hardening nub. "What about here? We can't have you itching. That would be horrible." He moved his thumb back and forth, teasing it and watching her face.

Her body jumped and tensed at the light whispering touch of the pad of his thumb. Her universe shrunk to his sapphire eyes and the way he touched her, stoking the flames licking up her spine and wetting her panties. Moaning, Kara rested her forehead against his and nodded. "There too."

Slowly, his hands inched around her sides. His bear stirred at the softness of her skin and the fire burning in her eyes. Spreading his fingers to feel more of her Brock tilted her back, letting his eyes crawl over her, savoring the gentle rise that bloomed into full breasts with dusky rose nipples in the center. The tips were peaked and hard. She was perfect. His mouth watered and when he could no longer resist, he dipped his head, dropping kisses and licking, moving painfully slow closer to her nipple. Ignoring the demands of his bear, Brock brushed his tongue across it lightly and breathed over the damp skin.

Kara shivered at the heat of his mouth and the soft scratching of his beard, as he leaned her back. Trusting him to hold her, she dropped her eyes to his bent head and felt her core clench and the wetness spread. Cupping his head, she slid her arms around to lightly scratch the nape of his neck under the braid. She wished his hair was free so she could tangle her fingers in it and pull him closer. A whimper rolled up her throat as he teased her. Her head fell back at the explosion of sensation under his tongue and the ache that slammed into her core. "I think that's helping," she whispered huskily.

Brock smiled and moved to the other nipple, teasing it too. 'Are you sure, Cher?' He was addicted to the taste of her skin, and her whimper sent a bolt of heat to his length making it kick and grow. The ungiving leather began to feel more like a vice than pants. He shifted his weight to ease the pressure so that he could stand it and ignored his own need. He wanted to hear her whimper again. It was a sound that he'd only heard her make with him and it let him believe that she was truly his.

"Yes," she sighed softly, coming to her senses enough to pull her head up to see what he was doing and that just cranked up her internal thermostat. "I mean, more tests may be needed," she teased in a breathy whisper, feeling the walls that she's spent centuries building to keep everyone out begin to crumble when it came to her Bear. It took all of her strength not to beg him to take her. Here. Now.

He smiled and glanced up at her face. Role playing had never been his thing, but with Kara, he didn't feel weird or clumsy about it. He wanted to play along, just to see what she'd come up with next and he knew that it would end with him buried deep inside her, with his name on her lips. Pulling his mouth away from her body grudgingly, he growled at her nails on his neck and tried to look thoughtful. "We should take this to a more secure environment. To the lab!" He slid his hands down her back and under her ass. He cradled her to his chest as he stood and carried her to what he hoped was the bedroom.

Kara tightened her legs around his waist, locking her ankles. "Yes, we need a lab." She grinned, using her thighs to move her core over the hardness in his leathers. "God," she groaned. It made her need for him so much worse, and it was beginning to hurt. She needed to touch him. Taste him. Growling, she nipped, licked and kissed his neck, holding onto his shoulders loosely, trusting him not to drop her.

Once in her room, Brock kicked the door closed with his foot and made for the giant bed in the center of the room between two large windows with a view of the hot spring. Her lips and teeth on his neck were making him forget his own damn name. His bear demanded that he push her into the bed and get inside her, now! Brock ground his teeth against the urge. Instead, he leaned over the bed, grinning when she let go of his shoulders so that he could lay her down and pull back. He narrowed his eyes as he studied her. "You know these tests are required to be conducted without interference." He gestured at her still half-clothed body. "I can't do my job properly with that in the way. We want the best results. Don't we, Cher?" He asked with a small smirk.

"Oh!" Kara covered herself shyly and forced her cheeks to flush, her eyes sparkling as they met his. She loved that he was playing with her like this. "Are you positive?" She waited for his nod. "In the name of science, you have my full cooperation." She slid her hands over her stomach, to the button, popped it open and then moved on to pull down the zipper. Lifting her hips and wiggling, she pushed the soft leather down her thighs, towards him.

"Now. Cher. You didn't follow instructions." Brock shook his head and frowned to show his disapproval, pulling her britches off over her feet and dropping them to the floor. He made a tisk tisk noise. "This is important. If you can't take this seriously, then things may have to change." He dropped his eyes to stare at her panties and arched a brow at her still wearing them. "You said, for science." He leaned over her on the bed and steadied himself on his right arm. With his left, he slid his hand down over her body, remembering every curve as if he saw it for the first time until he reached her thigh. He slipped his hand between her legs, dragging his fingers further into the crevice of her legs until his fingertips hit the bed. His hand was sandwiched between her thighs. He watched the lust bloom in her eyes as he turned his hand, using his pinky finger and thumb to move her legs apart.

Brock smiled looking down at her and had to swallow a growl as he tried to be serious. "So many tests, Cher. I hope you're ready for them. But first things first. No interference. And this?" He sighed and hooked his forefinger into the soft lace of her panties. His brow arched. They were damp already. He grinned as he pulled them away from her core. "Commitment, Cher. This is serious business. What if it infects the world and only you and I can save it? Did you think about that?" Fighting the urge to rip through the delicate lace, he pulled them down her long legs and tossed them after her pants.

Kara shivered as the cool air hit her and she moaned at the heat of his hand so close that she wanted to scream for him to touch her. Hell, she might beg. It balanced on the tip of her tongue when he began to scold her. She shook her head and did her best to look ashamed. "I was selfish. Please forgive me," she apologized. "You're right, of course. We must keep the world safe." She stretched out in the center of the bed and looked up at him innocently. "I think I'm ready." She could already feel her skin become damp at the heat of anticipation and briefly wondered if she could burst into flames from this overwhelming, burning need for him.

"That's better, Cher." Brock ghosted himself naked. He didn't think he could tear himself away from her long enough to undress and he didn't want to try. Still leaning on his right arm, he let it take most of his weight and what was left fell over her and the bed. Bringing his hand back to rest

353

between her thighs, he cupped his hand over her core. She was hot, wet and ready for him. Knowing that made a growl rumble in the back of his throat, but he didn't let it past his lips. "Where else do you have problems, Cher?" He asked, sinking his forefinger into her slowly.

Kara's eyes fluttered shut, and her hips lifted off the bed when she felt his hand cover her finally touching her but not enough! She opened her mouth to beg but instead moaned his name when she felt his finger slide into her. She whimpered as her core tightened around it and she had to bite her lower lip to stop from crying out. Kara reached for him, her fingertips skimming over the red dimples of the still healing bullet wounds. Opening her eyes, she remembered the game that they were playing. Fighting through the lust that was clouding her mind, she reached down to cover his hand at her core, rocking her hips against him as she pressed his hand harder against her "Here." She arched up to nip his lip. "And here." She flicked her tongue over his lip. "And how about you, Brock. Are you feeling any symptoms? I think I noticed a swelling." She arched a brow and looked down at his cock, standing tall and proud, begging to be touched. Kara tried to breathe normally, even though her lungs wanted to pant.

Brock growled softly as her core tightened around his finger. "We need to fix that then." He said kissing her after she nipped him. "Me? I have some swelling, yes. I've got an idea of how to fix it, but I think that there's an itch that needs to be scratched first," he said as she moaned louder. He let his finger plunge in and pulled it back out. He added another keeping his hand turned so that his knuckles didn't rub or ram into her. He didn't have to worry that he was doing something wrong or that she didn't like it as she raised her hips to meet his hand and the sounds she made... That alone might make him come if they kept this up.

"It seems I have a strange dryness in my throat." Brock pretended to clear it. "I think it's getting worse." With his left hand still exploring her core slowly, he pushed off the

354

bed and rocked back into a crouch at the edge of the bed. He used his magic to lift her legs for him and slide between her thighs, pulling her to him and dropping her legs gently over his shoulders. "I need to test a theory." Brock let his tongue join his finger for a second before taking it out and running up and over her clit. The sounds coming from her were driving the bear in him crazy. He wanted to take her roughly, but he wouldn't let the grizzly take over. This wasn't about him. She had been through a lot, and she needed to be shown love, not just used for a good time.

Kara growled her protest when he pulled away, and she was lifted and set down again. It was hard to track what was happening. Her body tightened, feeling like the skin was shrinking and left her teetering on the edge of exploding when his fingers moved and sounds that she'd never heard before filled her ears. It was her. Raising her head, she watched him taste her, and her frame rocked as his tongue flicked over her clit. She fought to keep her eyes open and used the hand that had slipped back to cover his wrist holding open her folds to give him clear access to her. Her other hand balled into a fist in the furs. She whimpered and moaned.

"Is it helping?" Her voice was rough, and she blew apart when his blue eyes flipped up to hers. "God Brock!" The tension and pleasure were already building again, wiping what she'd planned to say from her mind. Her brow arched as she lost control over her form and the scars that covered her began to appear faintly. She wanted to hide them, for the first time feeling self-conscious of them, afraid that it would change how he saw her.

He couldn't believe how good she tasted and the fact that she was coming apart made it even better. Or so he thought until he looked up at her as she came and then for the first time, he saw her for who she really was. He moved his fingers more, hooking them up to brush against that slightly rough patch of flesh and locked eyes with her. "You're beautiful. Cher," he said honestly, smiling as she cried out again. "I think the rash is healing, but this swelling isn't getting better. I'm worried, Cher!"

One side of her mouth curled up and Kara unballed her fist to stroke his face. That single statement, a single act of kindness on his part shattered any reservations she still had, and she knew that she was done hiding anything from him. "You said that you had an idea of how to bring the swelling down. It seems only fair that I do anything I can, after you've helped me so selflessly."

Brock grinned and nodded. "I do appreciate your cooperation, Cher. You don't have to do anything but lay there for this experiment." He pulled his fingers from her and lowered her legs to the bed, crawling between them. "All I need for you to do is get into a comfortable position," he said, putting his fingers in this mouth to taste them. He sat on the edge of the bed on his knees waiting for her to get comfortable.

Kara licked her lips and groaned softly as he tasted his. Nodding, she wiggled further up the bed to be sure there was room for his long legs and then grinned up at him before locking down her expression into a serious one. "I'm ready. Don't hesitate to tell me if there is more that I can do to help with your 'condition.'" She had to clench her hands into fists not to reach for him.

"I'll do that, I promise, Cher. Since it's for science and all." He moved closer and settled himself between her legs. Brock leaned over her, dropping his weight onto his elbows before he lowered his body to cover hers and groaned at how perfect she felt under him. His tip brushed against her core, pulling a moan from them both. Tangling his hands in her silky hair, he captured her lips possessively and rocked his hips, feeling her core slide over him slowly. He growled at the slick heat and the tight satin feel of her. It was almost too much. Even his bear groaned at the pleasure of it.

Kara moaned when he slowly filled her, rolling her hips into him to take him deeper, kissing him deeply and trying to push all that he made her feel for him into it, hoping he'd feel it. Relief came with the slight sting of her stretching around his girth, but it was short lived as his stroking her inner walls only caused her need for him to grow stronger. Kara smiled when the conversation from earlier ran through her head. "I'm sorry. I moved, was that alright?" She blinked at him innocently, softly scraping her nails down his back.

"Just can't follow directions. Can you, Cher? The data might be skewed. We may have to start all over again," he said in a husky tone. Thinking and making words were the last things on his mind right now. He was fighting his grizzly for control. A growl rumbled from his chest. What was it about her that made him loose control and common sense? His form wavered, but Brock managed it.

"I've always been bad at that. We can run the experiment again later to see it the results differ." She grinned and cupped his face. She could feel the duality of him, and his holding form seemed to get difficult. Kara shook her head and kissed him again. "You don't have to hide who and what you are from me, Babes. I'm not going to run." She looked into his eyes and then nuzzled his ear, pulling back her hips and rolling over him again, moaning, "Oops, I think I did it again." She grinned.

Brock growled, and his form wavered again. "Kara," he groaned a warning, his mind was swimming.

She tightened around him as she shuddered at the growl and she grew wetter. She had no idea why his growl alone could have her on the verge of coming. It only happened with him. "I love you," she whispered. "Both sides of you." She hoped that his bear would hear and realized that he didn't have to fight the man for control. They were one. Brock was in there, no matter the form he wore. Wasn't he? And while the packaging was oh so pleasing to the eye, it was his soul that called out to her. She moved again, whimpering as a wave of bliss flooded through her.

He couldn't hold it anymore. He roared as he came hard. He shifted forms and growled his body vibrated, still coming harder than he thought was safe or healthy.

Her head jacked back as his release hitting her walls knocked her over the edge again. His name ripped itself from her throat. She clung to him, curling her fingers in his fur, shaking and gasping for breath.

When he stopped filling her with his seed, he shifted back to human form, but his body was still vibrating. Panting hard, he closed his eyes trying to calm himself. "I love you too," he whispered, his eyes still closed. He held her and rolled, so they were laying on their sides cuddled together. "In the name of science. Holy fuck!" He chuckled, panting hard.

She nodded and chuckled. "Can't wait to read the research notes," she teased, snuggling tighter against him.

"Me either, Cher." His heart was pounding hard. "You know, we may have to start all over. I had something in my hair. Does that count against it?"

"Yes," She tilted her head back to see him and grinned at his expression. "Yes, it does. We need fresh data!" She reached up and stroked his cheek. "You know that you're not going to hurt me, right? I'm rocking that whole immortal thing."

Brock nodded and smiled. "I know, but if I told you what I really thought of you, you'd sock me in the gut." He grinned bigger. "Screw it. Hit me if you want. I don't see you as some unbreakable thing. To me, you're a delicate flower."

She arched a brow and stared at him before she burst out laughing. Finally, after Kara got herself under control, she kissed him softly. "You can think of me however you want to, Babes, as long as I get to curl up with you at night. Serious question, though. Do you think your bear wants to hurt me?"

Brock didn't need to think to answer that. "No. Why?" He asked confused.

"Curious, mostly." She shrugged and rubbed the bridge of her nose on his chin. "Just trying to figure stuff out. Nothing bad. I promise."

"Well, it's not you, it's me and my own weirdness," he said scratching his chin. "Oh, god I itch. It didn't work. I'm doomed... Doomed, I tell you," he said, laughing.

Kara laughed. "Back to the drawing board, I'll get the lotion." She didn't move but looked up at him, smiling end enjoying having him relaxed. She kept her thoughts to herself not wanting to spoil the mood.

He roared with laughter. "It puts the lotion on its skin, or it gets the hose again." He hugged her tight and kissed her face all over.

"You trying to get me all hot and bothered again, bear?" She joked and laughed, closing her eyes when he started raining kisses.

"Maybe," he said, still kissing her face.

Kara cracked one eye and laughed harder.

He sighed happily.

"How did I get so lucky?" She opened her other eye and stroked his face, beeping his nose. "To find you, I mean."

"I think it's that ingrown or in clone thing. Whatever Odin said."

Kara's brow wrinkled as she tried to work out what he meant and grinned. "Ingolf? Maybe. I always thought it was a myth. Not so sure now."

"Yeah, that." He chuckled. "Well, I think it's true, whatever it's called. You won't tell me differently, Cher!"

"I'm not going to try, Babes." She nuzzled him. "But you have to admit, it's some pretty iffy stuff. What if we'd never met? I mean we only did by chance, really. And that was after we were supposed to be mated to others. That is fucked up and kinda pisses me off."

"Maybe this has nothing to do with my bloodline, perhaps we need to see this from a Viking point of view."

"Okay," She thought about it and braced her head up on her arm. "I'm listening, whatcha got?"

He tried, but couldn't put it into words. "I wonder if I could show you, instead of telling you."

"Can we try?" Kara smiled hopefully, wanting to know what he thought.

Brock took her hands in his, even though they were laying a bit weird. He closed his eyes and tried to let his magic flow through him and into her, so she could feel what he did. He didn't move, hoping it worked and not wanting to take the chance of messing up the connection if he did get it right.

Kara took his hands and watched his face as he concentrated, not closing her own eyes until she felt the heat build between their palms and a tingling move up her arms. She waited for it to get to her head, but it stopped and swirled in her chest. Part of her broke at the ferocity and strength of it. It was pure and unwavering. Tears welled in her eyes. How could she doubt that it was true? "God, Babes. I am not worthy," she whispered when her voice failed her.

Brock opened his eyes to see her. "Yes, you are, Cher." He smiled. "Do you understand? Did it work? Words aren't my friends, sometimes," he said honestly.

She nodded and opened her eyes. "I felt it all." Kara let his hands go to cup his face and kiss him softly. Pulling back, she met his eyes. "I'm not, trust me, not with the things I've done. But I will be, no matter what I have to do to get there because I am not letting you go. Not now and not ever. Not until you want me to."

"Ditto, Cher," he agreed, grinning.

Kara smiled and hugged him tightly. "Then it looks like we're stuck with each other."

"Yay!" He said in a goofy voice. "I'm going to pet you, and love you, and named you George!"

She laughed and then pouted. "But I don't wanna be a George!"

"Who do you wanna be?"

"I like being me because I get you." She nuzzled him. "Damn, that was sweet as hell!" Kara laughed.

Brock shook his head, grinning. "Okay you can be you, but I'm calling you George the next time we do things for science."

"Fine, then I'm calling you Dr. Navarro," Kara wiggled her brows.

He chuckled. "Isn't there a movie named that or something?" Brock scratched his chin again thinking.

"I have no idea, but I'm going to do it." She laughed.

"You're the boss!" He said smiling. "Maybe we need google to help us."

Kara crawled to the edge of her bed, flopped down and pulled her pants over by the leg. Once she had them, she fished her phone out of her pocket, crawled back to Brock, and placed the phone on his chest before falling onto her back and looking at him expectantly. "Get to googling." She grinned.

Brock laughed. "I hear it's a handy tool. Like a sword or claws." He looked down at his chest trying to see the screen.

"Off subject, but can you shift parts of you or is it an all or nothing kinda thing?"

His brow quirked. "I can change parts of me if I want to, or have the control. Why do you ask?"

She shrugged. "You said claws as tools, I thought, that would be fantastic if my back itched and then the question." She grinned. "Yeah, my thought patterns are a weird combination of a squirrel and a hit and run."

He roared with laughter. "Oh, my God, Cher."

"Or if you can change only parts back to human when you're bear, you could have the best man in a bear suit costume, EVER!"

Brock lost it, laughing so hard that he started to tear up. Never, in a million years had he expected this playful and goofy side of the Valkyrie and he was thoroughly enjoying it.

Her brows popped up as she watched him and she grumbled under her breath. "Well, it would be."

He couldn't breathe he was laughing so hard.

Kara shook her head.

He held his aching sides. "Oh, Lord. I haven't laughed like this in a long time."

She grinned. "Why not?"

"Have you met my family?"

"I laugh at them all the time." She grinned and then made an O with her mouth. "But they aren't texting me to tell them how to pick up a fork and important stuff like that twenty-four-seven. Point made. We can run away from home and just stay here."

"We can? I hadn't thought about that. Wait. A fork? Are you serious? Did you get a hold of my phone?" Brock had wondered why the last time he checked it, all his texts were cleared. It was the same for the call log.

"Yes, we can and yes, I did," Kara answered honestly. When you were shot and needed to heal, I manned your phone, thinking that if something important came up, I could help and try to handle it. But your brothers are sniveling, useless, annoying SOBs. That's how I ran into Dane the other day. I went to tell them to back the fuck off, or I was going to kill them, but they all hid from me like cowards!" She growled. "Sorry if that was the wrong thing to do and sorry about the rant." She smiled sheepishly.

"No, Cher. I appreciate it." Brock smiled at her protectiveness. Everything about being here, with her, was surreal.

"Yeah?" Kara grinned and touched the red spots that marked where he'd been hit with the bullets. "I'm glad because I'd do it again. They're so busy worrying about who's gonna take care of them, they forget that sometimes you need to be taken care of."

Brock nodded. "It happens with a large, pain in the ass family. Not that I don't love them to death, but as the oldest, it's my job."

"But it's not your job, and they should appreciate that you've chosen to take it on. I would love to have a brother that looked out for me. I know, it's none of my business. I'll

362

shut up." She pulled a pillow down and stuffed it under her head, for the first time noticing the furs that covered her bed. "And I should probably invest in blankets. Wow, how fricken insensitive am I?"

He laughed. "I don't mind, but I can't help wonder how many of these are bear? I don't like the room of death that you have going on here."

She made a face, not wanting to answer. "Two. I didn't think. Most are reindeer. Yeah, I don't blame you. I don't mind changing it. I'd rather have you in my bed, than them." Kara grinned. "And I've learned that I prefer the fur on the living bear. It's much cozier."

Brock chuckled. "It's okay. I love the fact it's not me on the bed, dead. Well, not yet."

"You're not allowed to die." She rubbed her chest as it tightened and tried to breathe through it as his joke hit her hard. It brought back the possibility that he could die like she had. Like Dane had, and this time, she would be utterly lost.

"I know," Brock said, thinking about the furs. "What else is on the bed?"

"There are sheets, under it all."

He laughed. "Other animals."

She looked at him confused. "I was always better at hunting than sewing. But I bought the sheets and brought them here."

"Well, I can sew, so I'll make a good wife someday." He smiled.

Kara felt like she'd let him down somehow.

"That was a joke. Our mother made us learn that kind of thing. So that we could share in household duties. The female shouldn't do it all."

She nodded. "She sounds like a wise woman."

"She was." Brock smiled. "I have photos of her on my phone. Do you wanna see them?"

"I really do," Kara nodded. She could feel the pain it caused him and understood too well what it was like to have your world turned upside down by death.

Brock found his phone, opened his photos and handed it to her. "There you go, Cher. The goofy cub with a brown bow on its butt is me. Don't ask why."

"She was beautiful, and you were adorable, bow and all." Kara grinned, scrolling through the pics and moving closer to him on the bed, holding it so he could see too, if he wanted to. "I'm sorry, Brock." She rubbed his arm, deciding that she didn't like it when things hurt him. "You look like your Dad, and I can see your mom in Bree."

He kissed her temple. "You think so?" He asked looking at the photos.

She grinned and nodded. "I do. Why is Brax scowling in this one?" Kara looked up at him, she'd recognize that expression and body language anywhere.

"Zoom in. You'll see why," Brock said, laughing.

Kara placed her finger and thumb on the screen and pulled them apart, making the image bigger. "Oh. Is that a…" she laughed seeing the black lines and the mushroomed shape of something drawn on his forehead under the hair that he'd obviously tried to pull down to cover it. "Sharpie?"

"Yes," Brock said, laughing so hard he was in tears again.

"Who did it? I gotta shake their hand." Kara lost it.

"I did," he said proudly.

"You?" She laughed harder. "You are my new personal hero, Babes!"

Brock grinned. "Yes. The butt beating was worth it, for this photo."

"How hard did they have to try not to laugh while they did it?" She grinned and cuddled against him.

"Mom lost it. She had to leave." Brock shook his head.

"It's got to be tough when your kids do stuff that cracks you up, but you have to punish them anyway. I don't think I would be good at it."

"Right?" He laughed thinking about it.

She passed his phone back to him. "Thank you for sharing that with me."

"You're welcome." He put the phone on the nightstand. "My pleasure."

Closing her eyes, Kara rolled, pushed her back to his chest and pulled his arm around her, kissing his knuckles and smiling. "You wore me out, Babes. Can we stay long enough for a little nap? I promise, back home, they'll barely miss us."

Brock didn't have any doubt about her knowledge of the time difference. "I'm on board with a nap." He let her get comfortable before yawning, as his eyelids grew heavy. It didn't take long before they were both fast asleep, Brock in bear form and Kara next to him snuggled against his fur.

Chapter 36

Loki watched as the warriors gathered around the table that Kara and Brock sat at, laughing and regaling the Bjorn with their stories of valor, pillaging, plundering, and conquests. The bear was well liked, with his strange combination of humble and strength that charmed even the harshest critics. Kara had chosen well, and the bear's feelings for her showed clearly when he looked at her. She cared about the one they called Brock, too. Not that she flaunted it. To do that would paint a target on the Bjorn that Loki wouldn't wish on anyone. His sister had never been good about holding her tongue or throwing a fight to spare another's pride. She had enemies. Ones that would revel in her destruction and not understand that when it came, they were all doomed.

He had yet to say hello to his sister on this longer than usual visit to Asgard. Not because he didn't want to, but because she had always been able to read him like a book. He had no doubt that she would see his plans in his eyes. He also had no doubt that she would support him, but only after it was done. Loki pushed back from the table unnoticed, and kept to the shadows, as he left his father's hall and ghosted to his daughter's realm.

Obsidian walls surrounded him. The torch flames danced and scattered the shadows but never actually illuminated the space, giving it a gloomy and eerie feel.

Stuffing his hands into his pockets, he walked with his head down, taking the same route he had countless times before, until he found himself before the thick slab of wood that served as the door to his son's cell. The familiar fury over the unjustness of Fenrir's imprisonment churned in his gut, disturbing the light supper that he'd eaten. To lock a being in the darkness for most of its life because of a stupid prophecy was cruel. To do it after the wolf had run and played in the sun and learned to love and be loved, was torture.

Loki waved his hand, willing the door to soundlessly swing open exposing a pit of darkness. His heart ached at the growl that greeted him. "Forgive me, son," he whispered, bowing his head and stepping inside. If his child tore him to shreds, Loki would understand and in many ways, it would be a relief. Heavy chains rattled and scraped against the stone, moving closer to him.

'Fadir?' Fenrir mindlinked his father. The wolf strained to see in the darkness, but it smelled like his father.

"Yes son, I've come to make things right. It's long overdue." He held out his hand, not sure if he would be allowed to keep it, but smiling when the massive head slid under his palm and butted against his chest.

'I don't understand.' The giant wolf turned his head so that the scratching fingers found that sweet spot behind his ear. Fenrir groaned his pleasure.

"I know Kara visits you, son. Has she told you about where she spends her time?" A smile quirked up at the sounds the wolf was making. It was too rare that it happened.

'Where men and animals live in peace in the same body, and they walk among the humans unnoticed?' Fenrir sank back on his haunches and tilted his head trying to figure out why his father was asking.

"Yes. Would you like to see it?" Loki's chest constricted as though a ton of boulders were piled upon it when Fenrir's tail began to wag.

'Aye. But why do you torture me, Fadir?'

Loki winced at the hurt in his son's voice. "No more torture, Fen. It's time for you to be free and to live." He took the wolf's face in his hands and dropped his forehead against Fenrir's. Whispering his plan, Loki knew that he could be locked away for doing this and he didn't care. "You won't know who you are, but you can have a life." He finished and pulled back to see his son's glowing eyes.

'Will I see Kara?' Fenrir nuzzled his father. Hope beat in time with his heartbeat for the first time in eons.

"I don't know. You will be where she is. I promise you that." Loki smoothed the fur between the wolf's ears. "You can say no, Son. This is up to you. I wish I could have offered you a better life, but this is all I can do."

'Will I see you again?'

"I will never be far, Fenrir. I never have been." Loki smiled sadly. "What say you?"

'Yes. For as long as it lasts, I want to walk in the sun again.'

"Then it is so," Loki embraced his son and sent him back through time and space to a place that he prayed would be safe and give his son a chance to be part of a world with a life worth living. "Be safe, my son," he whispered, ignoring the shuddering of the rock around him as dread rippled through him. With another wave of his hand, he created the vision of the giant wolf, asleep on his pallet in the corner. It could be decades before anyone noticed that the boy was gone. He hoped that it was longer.

Chapter 37

Bree sat in what they'd grown up calling, 'Indian style' and rested the backs of her hands on her bent knees with her palms facing the ceiling, trying to ignore the hard floor under her. To get past the discomfort was always a struggle. Closing her eyes, Bree tried to shut out the world and the growing worry that swirled in her stomach. No one had heard from Brock since he'd flashed out holding a live landmine in his hand. Blowing out her breath, she forced her mind to empty and concentrated on her breathing as she tried to focus her energy like she had been taught by their clan's shaman.

Instead of her mind floating and gaining insight from the spirit realm that she walked in, it turned to the past. *Heat licked at her skin as sweat trickled to places it shouldn't be. Steam hung heavy in the air, tasting like smoke as it filled her lungs. Drums beat rhythmically in the distance, or maybe that was her heartbeat. Bree knew that if she opened her eyes, she would find herself in Gray Claw's dark hut, sitting in the center with a pile of stones over glowing embers and his colorless eyes staring back at her.*

"Do not let the bear rule you or let yourself be led by your magic. They are one in the same. Always remember that. To control your magic, you have to control who you are," the shaman said as he ladled more water over the embers and another hiss of steam filled the hut.

Bree didn't know what it was called, the sacred pile of stones or the magic that it induced. All she knew was that she was melting. Even though she was not in form, she felt like she was wrapped in the thick fur coat of her bear. As sweat poured down her face, Bree kept her eyes closed.

"Release your spirit into the world. Let your bear roam free!" Gray Claw's voice droned soothingly.

Bree had no clue what he meant until she heard a sound. It was a bear roaring so loud that her pulse quickened and her body tensed, ready to run.

"That's it, Bree. You're doing it." The shaman smiled as Bree's bear appear in spirit form.

Bree opened her eyes to see a shimmering bear in front of her. The female grizzly was roaring as it shimmered in all colors of the rainbow.

"This is just the start of what you can do. This is called spirit release. We use this to do many things. If you can control it, it can save your life and the lives of others."

Bree wiped sweat from her eyes. "I don't understand." She looked up through the bear to see Gray Claw's face.

He smiled and closed his eyes. "You will." Gray Claw lifted his face to the small hole in the roof of the hut where the steam escaped. The moonlight cast shadows over his sharp features as he stood still as stone for a few moments. A blue shimmer came from him, churned and took the form of a grizzly. The bear grew so large it seemed to swallow them both.

Bree felt the power of it hum over her skin. The shaman spoke three words in a language Bree didn't know. The bear outline started to spin as if someone had pressed a hidden fast forward button. The shaman's chanting grew louder, and Bree could feel Gray Claw's power as scenes of the times he'd freed this magic in the battles to save their people flashed in the air between them. It was why he was the shaman of the Navarro clan.

Gray Claw clapped his hands together over his head and turned his palms to the sky. The bear became a blue

370

beam of light and exploded through the hole in the top of the hut.

Bree's heart pounded so hard she could hear it as she stared after the blue bear in awe.

"With meditation and focus, this is one of many things you can do Bree." He lowered his chin to meet her eyes as his hands fell back to his sides. "If you are willing to try."

From that night on, Bree meditated every night, when The Pit finally grew quiet and most slept. She wanted to make her clan proud. As her consciousness drifted, she could feel her brothers and their emotions. They thought she was a fragile cub, but that was not really the truth.

Brock lay with Kara curled against his side. His fingers feathered over her bare hip as he stared at the ceiling and worried about Bree. He hadn't seen his sister since before he'd been shot. The feeling that something was wrong nagged at him, and he felt like a jackass for not having spoken to her since. Sighing, he reached out to her with the magic that he rarely used, hoping that his bond with his sister was strong enough for this to work. 'Bree, can you hear me?'

Bree's lips curled into a soft smile. This wasn't the first time that she'd thought of Brock and he'd answered. Her brother had no idea of the power he held or how tightly linked he was to her. 'Yes, are you okay?'

Brock's brows popped in surprise at how clear her voice was in his head. It must be the power of Asgard, or maybe it was the water of the hot spring's magic. 'I'm safe. I'm with Kara. How are you? I feel like there are things you haven't told me.'

Bree wasn't going to tell him the whole truth. Not what she saw with Dane and what had happened with Reese. There was time for him to be bogged down with the bad news when he came home. If anyone deserved a short reprieve, it was Brock. 'Brother, I'm fine. Maybe a little tired, but as father used to say, 'We all have our own path to follow, and only we can travel it.' I promise you, I am fine.'

371

Brock hated when she did that. 'I know Bree, but as the only female of our clan, you are precious to us. You know you can talk to me about anything.'

'I know, and you can do the same. Like, what is going on with you and Kara? The Valkyrie hides a lot about her, and she doesn't share well. I know how much you love her. I don't want you to get hurt, Brock.' Bree liked Kara, but there was something dark and dangerous that came from her, something had happened, and she wasn't ready to let anyone know. Bree worried that whatever it was, it would rock their clan's world.

'I'm not a big sharer either. I haven't told her what happened to our parents and I know she wonders about me. About why you all use your magic and embrace your bear, but I don't. She asks me questions at times that I don't know how to answer. I'm scared that if she knew the truth, she wouldn't love me. I've hurt so many people.'

Bree's heart ached for her brother. He was only a cub when the incident happened. His actions shouldn't have been counted as marks against their clan. Every time she saw Salvation, she wanted to pull him aside and ask him what the hell his problem was. How he could have done what he did to her family? But Bree knew that would be like pissing into the wind. 'We've all hurt someone, in some way. That's life,' she said through their link. 'You'll be home soon, right?'

'Yes. Until then, please be safe and try to keep everyone in line.' Kara rolled and elbowed him in the side, making him grunt. Brock sighed as the link between them was lost.

Bree felt her brother's magic leave. She opened her eyes and felt tears running down her cheeks. Brock bottled up his emotions so tight that sometimes it scared her. She worried what would happen if anyone hurt their family. What he'd do. The humans were so lucky they'd lived through Kara dying. Her brother could have uncorked his fury and taken out the whole city.

Chapter 38

Ivan ghosted to the edge of Kara's hot spring and eyed the cottage grimly. Maybe she wasn't home. Aye, that would be better. His leather armor creaked as he flicked the long auburn braid over his shoulder. Ivan didn't want to be here and more than that, he didn't want to be the one to share what he'd overheard with her. Wee One was likely to kill the messenger. Groaning, he decided to get this over with and began walking toward the small stone cottage.

Kara stepped into the doorway, her corn silk hair fluttering around her face in the gentle wind. Ivan groaned, and raised his hand in greeting when Brock appeared behind her, wrapping his arms around Kara's waist from behind and nuzzling her neck. Ivan paused, not sure that his timing was right. "Nay," he sighed and shook his head. "Ere is no good time for this." He resumed his walk toward them, playing out his own bloody death in a hundred different ways.

Mayhaps having the Bjorn here would temper Kara's reaction to the news Ivan brought, but he doubted it. Shedding blood was the only way to soothe the beast that lurked within that Valkyrie. Ivan himself had considered taking up his sword when he heard the news, but it was Kara's place to right the wrong done to her, and this time her brother had gone too far. He smiled as he neared them, his brows wrinkling at the pale circles that peppered the center of Brock's bare chest. "Ye made fun of her cooking.

Didn't ye?" Ivan shook his head and tried not to stare at the injuries that undoubtedly should have proven fatal. *Pray tell me that Wee One hasn't taken to cheating death*, he thought. The repercussions of such would be deadly.

Brock laughed and clasped the older Viking's wrist, pulling him in to bump shoulders. "Only Kara can turn a potato into an explosive."

Kara elbowed Brock lightly. "He'll believe you."

Brock's brows popped. "Well, you did. Don't blame me for the bomb de terre, Cher. Next time you'll take out someone's eye!"

Ivan chuckled as Kara dropped her head and pinched the bridge of her nose. Watching the Bjorn tease her, and that Kara allowed it, spoke volumes.

Kara shook her head and looked up at Ivan. "I thought the hot spring might help the healing, but I'm rethinking that now." She narrowed her eyes and pretended to glare at Brock over her shoulder, her menacing look switching to a smile when he circled his arms around her waist and pulled her back against him again.

Leaning down to rest his chin on her shoulder, Brock caught a whiff of anxiety in Ivan's scent. "It's good to see you again, Ivan. What brings you by?"

Kara's smile faded, and her brows shrugged together at the sudden tenseness of Ivan's face and the way he didn't seem to know what to do with his hands. This wasn't a friendly social call. "Just spit it out. What's on your mind?"

Ivan scratched the back of his neck. Mayhaps he should do this privately. Nay, when Brock had a hold on her was probably better. "We found out who was behind where you went when you died, Wee One, and you're not going to like it."

Kara felt her blood turn to ice in her veins. Her fury was calm, cold and deliberate, it just needed a target. "Who?"

"Aryan. Thor's..." Ivan met Kara's eyes as he tried to choose the proper word. "Mistress."

Brock tightened his arms around her when he felt that blast of cold that filled the air. His brow arched when he realized that it was coming from Kara, who had gone stiff in his arms. "Cher? What am I missing?" His voice was soft, and something told him not to let go of her.

Kara's jaw ticked, her attention laser focused on the burly redheaded Viking in front of her. "He knew? You know this to be true?"

"Aye." Ivan nodded gravely.

"Cher?"

Kara forced her body to soften in Brock's hold and leaned back, turning her head so she could see him. "What it means is that I'm going to kill my brother."

Brock blinked. He could not have heard that right. "Isn't he immortal?"

Kara's smile was cold. "I guess we're going to find out." She turned back to Ivan. "Meet me in Dad's throne room in an hour?"

"Aye." Ivan watched the emotions flow over Brock's face. Was the Bjorn prepared for what happened when these siblings quarreled? He didn't think so. "And what of him?" He nodded toward Brock. Ivan liked the Bjorn, but if Kara wanted him removed to a safe distance, Ivan wouldn't hesitate to make her wishes reality.

"I'm right here," Brock reminded them. "And what do you mean? If Kara is going to fight anyone, I'm going to be there, with her," he growled, his bear growing irritated with the situation. He wasn't a cub, and he would not hide when she might be hurt or need him. He'd lost her once, and there was no way in hell that he'd be left behind to wonder what had happened to her. Not again.

Kara let her eyes close as she struggled not to allow her anger to lash out at the wrong people. "I'm just going to go get him and take him to Dad, Babes." She leaned her head against his before she turned in his arms to face him. "Why don't you splash some water from the hot springs on your

375

chest and meet me there? I'll be okay. I promise. I just need maybe an hour." She stretched up to kiss him softly.

Brock eyed her skeptically. He had a feeling that there was a lot more to this than either were telling him. He shook his head no but knew that he couldn't stop her if she decided to go. "Promise?" He sighed when she nodded. "One hour, Cher. Then I turn this place inside out, looking for you."

Kara smiled and kissed him again. "Understood," she whispered against his lips. "Don't worry. You can't get rid of me that easy."

He squeezed her tighter and searched her eyes before he pressed his lips to her forehead. "You had better mean that, Kara." Brock rubbed his hands up and down her arms before he forced himself to let her go.

"I do." She reached up to cup his face and ran her thumb over his lower lip. When his hands dropped, she stepped back and willed her armor to wrap around her and her weapons to fill her hands. "If he has questions, answer them, Ivan. He and I have no secrets."

"Aye, Wee One." Ivan grinned and then turned his gaze to Brock when Kara ghosted out.

Brock met Ivan's jade eyes and then began towards the hot spring, needing something to do while he waited. He hated this. "This all has to do with when Kara was dead, doesn't it?" He asked without looking up as he knelt at the edge of the spring. He flexed his shoulders and growled. They were stiff, and although the skin had closed, his chest throbbed in time with his heartbeat. Every time he thought of Kara getting hurt, it beat faster.

"It does." Ivan sat on the bank beside him.

"Tell me about it." Brock looked at Ivan before he dipped his hands in the water, splashed it onto his chest and rubbed his wet hands over his shoulders.

Ivan looked out over the shimmering surface of the hot spring as he spoke. "She didn't die in battle. Usually, when that happens, the soul would have gone to Helheim, the realm of the unworthy dead."

"It's like Hell, right?" Brock splashed more water on himself, amazed that the throbbing was already becoming little more than a dull ache. These waters were a miracle cure.

Ivan looked at him, trying to make sense of his words. "In a sense, aye. However, Kara has always loved Hel, so time in Helheim would not be so bad. Sometimes, when a bloodline is pure or protected, they cannot enter Helheim, even if they die as a frail old man. Where Kara went was worse. Much worse." Ivan sighed, his sense of honor screamed at the injustice of it.

"Worse than Hell? How?" Brock let the water drip down his torso as he tried to wrap his head around it.

Ivan waved his hand over the water beneath Brock. "Watch," he murmured and let his magic weave the spell that showed Kara, day after endless day, waking, and taking the battlefield to kill or be slain by the ones she loved most. "Like I said, it was worse."

Brock watched the scenes unfold, over, and over again. He gasped, surprised to see his own face and her allowing the hundreds of him to run her through. He splashed his face, pushed at the wet hair and sank back on his heels. "Her brother made that happen? Thor?" He couldn't help it, to Brock, her brother wore the face of the actor that played the god of thunder in the Marvel movies.

"Let it happen. The cowardly whelp knew, and did nothing." Ivan's nostrils flared with outrage.

"Then he deserves what he gets." Brock braced his hands on his thighs and nodded. "I want to go with you, Ivan. When she brings Thor to her father, I want to be there for her."

Ivan shook his head. "Are you sure? This isn't like it is in your world. She isn't the same. The rules of combat are different here."

377

"Fine," Brock touched the scars on his chest, surprised that they didn't hurt at all, now. "How are the rules different?"

"There are none," Ivan answered quietly.

Brock stared at him for a moment as a cold chill raced down his spine. "I'm going with you," he stated firmly. For better or worse, he wasn't letting her face this on her own. That female was his Valkyrie, just as surely as he was her Bear. He would be there for her.

"Aye," Ivan sighed and skipped a flat rock across the water's surface.

Chapter 39

Kara appeared in the gaping archway of Odin's hall, the hard soles of her boots slapping against the stone floor as she trudged down the hallway. Lightning flashed around her, the statically charged air crackled and caused the torches to flare as if gasoline splashed over the flame. The dull expanse of gray stone walls was broken with intricately woven tapestries, rich in color and threaded with precious metals. Kara saw none of it. Her armor moved with her like a second skin, and her weapons were sheathed, but not for long. Her jaw ticking was the only outward sign that someone was about to fucking die. Well, that and the big blocky hammer in her hand and the larger meat sack of struggling god that she dragged behind her by his braided red hair.

Odin and Loki glanced up. Kara may not be able to read minds, but their twin expressions of 'Oh fuck' as their eyes widened and brows headed toward the hall's high ceiling wasn't hard to decipher. Odin's Ravens ducked against his neck, hiding in the Alfather's hair, falling silent for the first time that Kara could remember. Loki chuckled and leaned his arm against their father's throne, trying to appear relaxed as he offered her a curt salute. His hand sliding down to rest on the hilt of his sword told a different story.

Odin stood, his one eye questioning as it bounced from Kara's blood splatted face to Thor's beaten and slightly carved up body that kicked and whimpered at his daughter's feet. "Kara?" His voice, deep and strong, echoed off the walls.

Brock felt her presence before Odin spoke and turned away from the window where he'd been watching for her. They were early, and he'd hoped to see her coming and in one piece before she arrived. It didn't happen that way. He started for her, wanting to see for himself that the blood on her wasn't hers. Ivan's hand on his shoulder stopped him, reminding him that he was a guest here. He could observe, but not interfere. Unless they tried to hurt her and then all bets were off. His bear was ready to claw its way through some Gods to keep her safe.

Kara didn't answer. She just kept putting one foot in front of the other, grinding her molars to dust until she stood at the bottom of the stone slabs that built the stairs to her father's throne. Swinging the heavy male, like he weighed nothing, Kara tossed her brother to skid across the basalt platform at her father's feet. "Tell him," she ground out with all the warmth of a glacier.

Loki chuckled, shaking his blonde hair back from his face before glancing down at a thoroughly worked over Thor, now missing most of the bushy beard that he was so proud of, his left ear dangled by a stubborn sliver of flesh and this nose and teeth were shattered. Rolling his amused eyes to Kara, the only sign of his trepidation was the flatness of his usually laughing sapphire eyes. "About time you figured shit out, Little Sister."

Kara's eyes swung to Loki. Her blonde brow arched as lightning struck the floor between his boots, daring him to flinch. "You knew." It wasn't a question, but a cold, chilling statement of fact that sounded like a death sentence. She flew up the steps, two-handing the heavy hammer and swinging it up to crack her brother under the chin in an uppercut.

Loki flew back through the air to collide with the wall, breaking stone and leaving a cartoon impression of his body when he crumbled to the floor and shards of granite rained down over him. Loki landed on one knee, his palm spread on the debris-covered floor and snapped his broken jaw into proper alignment before he looked up to meet her cold gaze. "For fuck sake, Kara. I didn't know until you were out."

Brock's jaw hung open. The condition of Thor and what Kara had just done to Loki, shocked him. He'd seen her fight before, but not like this. This was brutal, bloodthirsty and terrifying. He shared his bed with her, but never would he have thought her capable of this. This was what her wrath looked like, and he realized that he had grossly underestimated the power and strength that she held. He loved the Kara that he knew, but this version, he didn't know and was afraid of. So were the others. Their scents stunk of it.

Odin turned his head from watching Loki take a shot that would have splattered the skull of a human like a melon, looked down at his other more broken son at his feet and then back to his daughter. Kara lifted her chin with defiance. One of the Ravens whispered into his ear, its voice like gravel over stone and what it said chilled Odin to the bone. War. Death. Ragnarok. Extinction of the Norse pantheon at his daughter's hands. It fell silent when Kara turned her eyes on the black bird, her brow a threatening arch that left the raven quivering. Crossing his arms over his chest, he eyed his daughter as his mind raced to find a way to defuse the ticking time bomb that would be the end of them all. "What happened Kara?"

She snorted at Loki, not buying his claim of innocence and not caring. She snorted again at her father's question. "You, who knows everything, are going to pretend ignorance, fadir? Really? Is that how you want to play this?" Kara glowered at the male, her lip curling up in disgust. "Fine," she growled, her nostrils flaring and the lightning in the room building in its intensity, making her father flinch slightly. Turning her wrath on Thor, who had finally managed to pry his face off the floor and was balancing on his hands and knees, Kara kicked him in the gut, flipping him onto his back to groan pitifully in that god damned squeaky voice of his. "His whore, fucked her way through half of Valhalla to send me to the lower levels. I demand her blood and he..." She kicked Thor again. "Is hiding the bitch."

Odin's brow shot up. Well, that explained why his little girl was going terminator on her brothers. He eyed Thor and the mix of snot and blood bubbles that came from his broken nose and mouth. "And how was it that I didn't know of this?" He demanded of his son as his Ravens whispered the truth of Kara's words. Thor's answer was a wet gurgle. "You will hand Aryan over, now."

Thor shook his head no, his hands wrapped around his middle as he coughed and wheezed.

Odin's face went dark, and the temperature in the room plummeted until their breath turned to plumes of smoke in the frigid air. "Oh, I beg to differ, boy." He turned his one blue eye back to his daughter. "You will have vengeance, Little One. I vow it."

"And Baulstrad. The whore's whore." Kara sneered. "I'll give you twenty-four hours to produce them both. If I don't have them then?" She kicked Thor soundly between the legs, knocking him back a full yard and smiling coldly as he assumed the fetal position. "I will cut my way through the nine worlds until I find them. Don't test me, fadir. I spent ten years being forced to cut down the ones I love most, not many here mean shit to me anymore." She spat on the sobbing and huddled Thor and shot Loki a look that promised a toe tag. "Oh," she tilted her head and lifted Thor's hammer. "And this is mine now."

Only giving her father the time to nod once in agreement, Kara turned to Brock and let her face relax and the rage to be replaced by worry when she saw the shade of horrified white that he'd become. She stopped in front of him and held out her hand. "Do you want to come with me or should I send you back home, Babes?" She had to remind herself to breathe while she waited for his answer. "The choice is yours. I swore to protect you, I can't do you harm."

Brock stared at her, not sure what to say. He should run as far as he could get from her. The shit he'd just watched her do to her own family... He swallowed hard, finding that his tongue had gone dry and opened his mouth, but nothing came out.

Kara's blue eyes closed and she nodded. "I understand. It's okay." It was the truth, but the hole that he would leave in her was so much larger than the one she'd thought she'd felt for Dane. Her hand fell back to her side before opening her eyes and giving him a soft smile.

His hand cupped her face, and his thumb wiped away a smear of blood before Brock pulled her to him. He'd almost let her send him back to NOLA, but then he'd seen the pain in her sapphire eyes and Brock knew that he couldn't let her go. "I go with you, Kara." He whispered against her hair. "I'll always go with you." He felt her nod, and the throne room blurred, disappeared and was replaced with her cottage.

Chapter 40

Freya let her eyes sweep over her things and nodded. She was ready. Ghosting to Odin's hall with her twenty most favored warriors behind her, she strode into the room and paused as she watched her daughter punt Thor, throw down a threat and disappear with a very attractive male that Freya would love to add to her collection. In fact, the idea of postponing her plans until she could convince the giant blonde male to leave her daughter for a much better offer, gained legitimacy when she caught his eyes over Kara's head. But then he was gone, and Freya remembered the things that she'd seen and would come to be. Staying here to die with the rest, was not an option. Not for her.

Swallowing her disappointment, Freya strode forward, clasping her hands at her hips as her men straightened her gown and made sure that not a single hair was out of place. "I'm leaving." She said to everyone and no one.

Odin cringed at that all too familiar voice that he despised, turning his head to look over his shoulder from where he squatted beside his bleeding son. "This is not the time for your bullshit, Freya," he growled and turned away to fuse Thor's ear back where it belonged, ignoring his screams. "You brought it on yourself. Stop whining and try to act like a man, for fuck sake."

Loki gave Odin a 'did you hear what you just said' look before he broke into a fit of laughter when Thor whimpered again. "Why start now?" He laughed harder.

Odin glared at Loki, rolled his eyes and sighed when he heard the rustling of skirts still behind him. "Fine." He stood, crossed his arms over his chest and turned to glower at his wife. "When are you leaving, and can I help you pack?"

Freya narrowed her eyes and hit him with a droll glare. She had planned to warn him of what the future would bring if he continued down the current path, but now? She mentally shrugged. Let him learn for himself. She smiled tightly. "No need. I have everything I need. I only told you as a courtesy." She slapped away the hand of the male who had been honored to be allowed to touch her hair. Usually, it brought her pleasure, but it annoyed her now. "I shan't bother you further."

Odin groaned silently. "Where are you going?"

"Home."

"For how long?" He eyed her pinched features and knew that she was pissed. Too bad, really. She was breathtaking when she wanted to be. The depictions of angels couldn't compare to Freya's beauty. It was one of the only things that Kara had inherited from her mother that was useful. If only Freya weren't such a vile cold bitch. Odin sighed again. "So, we can have everything ready for your return."

"I haven't decided." Freya shook the silvery blonde hair back from her flawless porcelain skin. "I may not come back at all."

Odin rubbed his beard thoughtfully, more to hide an accidental smile than because there was a lot to think about. He nodded. "You will be missed, but as you wish." He kept his expression grave and a little hurt because he knew that she'd like that. In his head, he was dancing with joy and singing, *'Don't let the door hit you in the ass on your way out.'*

385

Freya stepped forward, lifting her skirts to step over the bleeding Thor and making a face that showed her disgust. She didn't want his blood on her dress, not even the hem. She turned her face and waited.

Odin swallowed the bile in his throat and pressed his lips to her smooth cheek. "Be safe, my wife." He murmured when he pulled back and suppressed the urge to spit, not trusting her not to have splashed poison on her own face to bring him discomfort. He had no doubt that they hated one another. Nor did she.

Freya's head gave a curt nod as she stepped back. "I will be taking my men with me," she said as she turned and descended the stone steps.

"Of course you will," Odin ground out between clenched teeth and watched her float out of the throne room and down the hall into darkness. She was up to something, but he didn't have time to worry about it now. Odin turned back to the torn to shreds redheaded male at his feet and shook his head. "Ivan?"

"Aye," Ivan answered from near the large windows.

"Keep an eye on her until she leaves the realm?"

Ivan bowed his head and left to do just that.

"Now, son." He knelt beside Thor. "You're going to tell me where your pet is, or I'm going to finish what your sister started."

.

Chapter 41

Kara was in Brock's arms when they appeared in her cottage. She didn't want to know that he'd seen too much, but she had to. A ghost of a sad smile crossed her face before she looked up at him. He still looked a little pale. Dropping his hand, she stepped back and wiped at the blood splattered on her face. She must look like something out of a horror flick. "You can change your mind. If you want to go, I'll understand." She glanced up and dropped her eyes. Why the fuck had Ivan brought him there to see all of that?

Brock was still processing everything. He knew Vikings did things differently and Kara was no different. Scratch that, she was different. She wasn't just another Viking. She was truly the daughter of Odin. And that meant that she was no normal Valkyrie, but one of the oldest and fiercest in creation. Brock didn't fully understand what happened to her when she died. He had been too busy being thankful she was alive to really consider everything that she went through and how she felt about it. Now, he knew. She was pissed! He'd always been a little afraid of her because she was immortal. He was just a bear, nothing special. If she wanted to, she could turn him inside out with a blink of an eye. Even though he'd gone toe to toe with Ivan and didn't end up dead, didn't mean he wouldn't with her. His mind was swirling with so many thoughts.

"Go? Go where?" He asked still staring at her. Brock cocked his head, a little confused.

She tucked her hair behind her ear and shook her head. "I don't know. Anywhere. Away from me. Ivan shouldn't have brought you there. You weren't supposed to see..." Kara's voice died as she realized how it must have looked to an outsider. Hell, it had been brutal as fuck for her kind. She hadn't missed the matching looks of shock and fear on her father's and Loki's faces. But seeing it on Brock's had hit home. Even then, it didn't quell her need to make Thor pay for what he'd done, and she wasn't done yet. Carefully, she lowered Thor's hammer to the countertop and leaned against it, looking up at Brock. "I don't want you to see me as someone to be afraid of, and I'm worried that you do."

Brock's mind flashed to the female fox he'd killed as a cub and the things that happened after that. No one was perfect, and he was no one to judge another for their actions when it came to pain or fear. He knew from the moment Kara appeared in NOLA that she was a force of nature. Making people pay on the daily was her job. He couldn't fault her for what she had done. Not when he'd done some ugly things of his own. Hell, he'd almost killed that little snot nose kid when he'd seen him with her jacket. If the others hadn't been there to stop him, the kid would be pushing up daisies. So, no, he couldn't judge or turn tail on her. She deserved better than that.

"Cher I'm not going anywhere. Yes, that was brutal, but I have no idea what was going on in your head when everything went down. I only have part of the story, but I know you'd never hurt anyone that didn't deserve it. I know that one hundred percent, deep down. You've taken a lot of crap from others that you could squash like a bug, and did nothing."

Kara sagged a little with the relief his words brought. "Thank you for saying that, and I hope that you're not just afraid not to say something else." She willed away her armor, the blood splatter and ghosted on a clean tank and shorts. "I'm not joking when I tell you that I am not capable of hurting you. It's one of the catches of claiming you. You're safe and in control until you decide differently. Even then, if you released me, I am bound from harming you." She had no idea why, but she couldn't stand the thought that he could fear her.

He nodded. "I forget that stuff. I'm just glad you like me." Brock chuckled. "I didn't say it because I was scared that you'd pop my head like a grape, or something. I said it because I meant it. When it comes to you, I've almost killed a few innocent people. So, you doing what you did, was for a reason. You don't fly off the handle." That made him laugh, she could fly for real. He lost it, laughing and shaking his head.

She watched him laugh, not sure why, but she was learning to get used to him doing that every now and again. "I'm glad. Wait. You almost killed innocent people because of me?" Kara tilted her head to the side, her fingers playing with the soft leather wrapped around the Hammer's handle. "Who?" She grinned because that was sweet as hell.

"Two little fox punks. I don't remember their names. They were the ones who found your body. If there had not been others there, I probably would have put one's head through the bar, literally, and ripped the other one to pieces."

Kara smiled softly and nodded. Yep, hearing that made her heart melt a little more. "I bet your brothers shit themselves," she chuckled. "The stuff with Thor was different. He has this ignorant little human twit that thought, for some ridiculous reason, that if I was gone, then she could improve her standing in Dad's Hall, just because Thor keeps her in his bed. It wasn't going to work. She's human, for one, and I don't have a spot in the hierarchy of Dad's hall, so lots of faulty logic there, but that didn't stop her. She traded sex to anyone that, when the opportunity presented itself, could help her fantasy happen and she did. Thor's hiding her. That's the short version."

Brock listened and decided that she was too merciful. "Well then, she got what she deserved. So, what will you do with Thor's hammer?" Brock wanted to touch it but didn't. "As for my brothers, they just didn't wanna have to hose off the ceilings and walls."

She nodded, "She hasn't yet, but it's coming. I can hear Brax complaining about it now." She lowered her voice to a low growling imitation of his brother. "I didn't make the mess, I ain't cleaning it." Kara laughed. She saw his eyes fall to the hammer and grinned, "You can play with it if you want. It's ours now. If Thor wants it, he can fight me for it."

"I.. I can? I don't know how it works." Brock forgot things were not like the movies he'd seen. "Your impression was spot on." He grinned, looking at the hammer.

"You just pick it up. The lightning thing was a practical joke that one of my sisters played on him. The idiot thinks he makes the lightning happen and gets mopey and afraid that he's fallen out of favor with the hammer when it doesn't." Kara rolled her eyes. "Now they take turns, following him around, so he doesn't sulk." She picked it up and held it out to him. "It's heavy as fuck though."

He frowned. "No lightning! Well, that bites." Brock wondered if it was like the sword in the stone kind of thing. "Has anyone other than your bloodline tried to use it?"

Kara thought about it and shook her head. "I don't know. I'm not sure that many would try."

"Well, let's test this out. If this thing kills me, tell my family I died in some cool way," Brock eyed the hammer. Slowly, he reached out for it, taking hold of the leather, or what looked like leather, wrapped around the handle. "Is this skin?" He asked as he felt it. His brows raised a bit.

"Of something. I'm not sure what. It's dwarf-made. I don't think it's human, maybe frost giant."

"There are dwarfs here?" Brock got a good grip on the handle. As he did, he felt a jolt of power go through him. It wasn't normal electricity. It was something else. He waited for it to make him shift, but it didn't. He lifted the hammer off the counter and realized that she wasn't joking about how heavy it was. As the power surged through him, he felt different, like his body was vibrating. Flashes of battles and what he figured might be warriors who had used this before him, filled his head. "I can see now why Thor likes this and why he cried like a girl when you took it from him."

Kara eyed him and could tell that something was happening, but wasn't sure what. "Do not tell me that it's fricken testosterone activated." She narrowed her eyes to a glare and stared at the hammer. "Un-fuckin-believable," She growled and shook the hair back from her face. "When I held it, it did nothing. What's it doing for you, Babes?"

"I feel like a power surge is pumping through me. Like lightning, but not. And the things I'm seeing are amazing. Battles and warriors that I assume held this before me. My body feels like it's vibrating. Have you ever used hair clippers?" He asked. That was the closest thing to what he was feeling to explain it to her. When you use hair clippers too long, and the vibration made your hand and arm feel weird. His whole body felt like that.

She shook her head no and reached out to lay her hand on his arm. "I can feel it through you, though. Weird." Kara looked down at the hammer. "If it's showing you all of that, maybe it likes you." She grinned and kissed his cheek, scowling at the static shock that snapped as her lips touched his bearded skin.

Brock smiled as she touched and kissed him. "Oh, sorry," he said when it shocked her. "I wonder if it's because I'm not a Viking." He rotated his wrist a moment. "I'd be honored if it did. Is it bad that I'm kinda giddy?" He asked honestly. "So, what happens when you touch it?"

Kara grinned. "No, it's not bad. Some things are destined to be. Who is to say that this was not intended all along and maybe Thor being an ass, me taking it from him and it finding its way to you was its plan all along. I know that no one else can touch Dad's spear. Many have tried, and all we find is a pile of clothes and ash." Kara laid her hand on the blocky hammer. "All I feel is cold iron." She shook her head and dropped her hand. "I don't think it has anything to do with you not being Viking, but more with you being you." She looked at him with a bit of awe.

He looked at her and then at the hammer. "Well, I was scared it would shock me and make me shift or kill me." The idea that he was meant to have something this cool made Brock's brow arch again. "Have you touched the spear? I'd like to see it. I bet it would be good to roast the crows on!" He joked as he changed hands with the hammer. "You don't get fuzzy feelings when you hold it? What about seeing the history of it?"

Kara shook her head no. "I dared Loki to once, and he was thrown into another dimension for fifty or so years. I don't have that kind of time to waste." She eyed the hammer and then turned her eyes back to him. A smile had taken over his lips, and his eyes sparkled as pride and disbelief seemed to do battle. "I get nothing. Just cool metal under my hand. That you do, means something, Babes."

"Well, maybe you should give the spear to Thor, somehow? Has anyone thought of wearing gloves or anything when touching it?" Brock put the hammer down on the counter. As he did, his body felt a little weird. "What could it mean? That I felt something. It could be because I've been in your hot springs, maybe?" He rubbed his hands on his pants. The belief that he was chosen was too alien for him to wrap his mind around. He was nothing special. There had to be another reason.

"I think Dad would have a problem with me giving away his things." Kara grimaced and figured that that was a pretty quick way to finding death for real. She listened to him try to find ways that he was not chosen and that this was a cosmic coincidence that could happen to anyone. "Maybe, but I've been in the hot spring too. Don't worry, Babes, you don't have to do anything with it. I'll just shove it in the back of the closet. All I know is that Thor ain't getting it back."

"Hell no! I want to keep it. Maybe take it home with us to scare the shit out of my brothers with," Brock said smiling. "No, I wouldn't want Odin angry. I've seen you mad, and you're only a small part of him. I'd rather live."

"You and me both." She laughed when he claimed the hammer. "Then it is yours, Babes. Do with it what you will. I have to finish what I started tomorrow. Do you want to stay here or go back home?"

"I want to stay with you. Unless you don't want me here. My place is beside you." He said, knowing this was hard for her in more ways than one.

Kara laced her fingers with his. "I always want you with me, but I'm afraid that I'm going to scare you off. I'm not going to lie. I'm going to kill people tomorrow, and I'm going to enjoy it. Not because there's any honor in it, but because if I don't, then more will try to screw with me and what is mine. That's you, and I can't allow anyone to think that shit will fly for even a second. Not even my father or brothers."

Brock squeezed her hand. "My mother once told me something that I've always held close. *'When you love someone, you have to love them on their bad days too. If you cannot, then you do not deserve their good days. And when you love someone, you must love all of them. If you cannot, then let them go, so someone else may.'*" He pulled her hand to his mouth and kissed her knuckles.

Kara smiled softly as his lips brushed the back of her hand. "Then, I have to ask, can you, Brock?" She met his eyes and prepared herself for the worst, but hoped that he could.

He nodded. "That I can, Cher. I'm worried you may not be able to do so with me. My family is not like Dane's was, or lack thereof. And I come with some unusual baggage." He never spoke of the lion, because he was afraid she'd go running back to him or try to rekindle what they had. He would never tell her this, but he feared it. They had been

393

mated. The powers that be saw it fit for them to be together. Though it was broken by death, it still meant something. He'd secretly prayed that when he and Kara slept together, he would wake with her mark. He hadn't, and it crushed Brock, cutting him deeply. Yet another thing he wouldn't tell her. What good would it do if he spoke of it? None, because they didn't have the power to make that happen. Without the mark, he was still hers.

Her brow wrinkled with confusion. Kara hadn't thought about Dane since she'd talked to Brock about him. This bear had that kind of power. He kept her grounded in the present and breathed life into her when she'd been little more than a husk. Kara cupped his face with her free hand, stroking his jaw with her thumb. "I love you, and I can accept anything that comes with that. But anyone stupid enough to try to do you harm will face my wrath, no matter who they are. If they're your family, I'll try extra hard not to kill them." She smirked and tried to joke. "Unless you tell me to let you go, I'm holding on tight, Babes."

Brock growled softly as she said she loved him. "I love you too, Cher. I hope no one is that stupid, but some people do like to poke the bear, so to speak." He smiled in her hands. "I appreciate you trying not to off my family. It's even hard for me, at times."

Kara shuddered at his growl, wondering if the tingling that raced through her was what he felt when he held the hammer. The corners of her mouth curled up at his words. Rolling up on her toes, she kissed him softly. "I think you'll see that I understand your family pain, as you meet more of mine."

Smiling against her lips, he thought that she was probably right. Brock cupped her face and just looked at her. "Gods, you're beautiful," he whispered, staring into her eyes.

She smiled and blushed. Groaning and shaking her head slightly, Kara brushed her lips over his. "As long as you think so, Brock."

Brock kissed her again, harder this time, wanting to stamp her as his possession. "I do, Cher. I very much do."

"Gods, you are perfect, bear," Kara sighed against his lips.

He nuzzled her and rubbed her back, gently pulling her against him. "No, I'm just me." His lips brushed her neck.

Kara growled softly and bit his jaw. "For me, that is perfect." She grinned and tugged at his lower lip with her teeth. "When did it get so damned hot in here?" *Whenever he is in the room,* her mind mocked her, but Kara ignored it.

Brock groaned as her teeth grazed his skin. "I don't know, but it is warm in here."

"Do you have anything that you need to get back for?" Leaning back, Kara bit her lip and watched his face as her hands slid under his shirt to roam over his skin.

"No." He growled at her touch, lifting and setting her on the countertop. "Why Cher?"

Grinning, Kara pushed his shirt up with her wrists as her fingers and nails feathered up over his sides. Rolling her eyes up to his, she smirked. "I wanted to know if I should plan on a cold shower." She leaned closer to kiss him and growled against his lips. "You make my blood boil, bear."

"Ditto Cher." Brock wanted her badly. He let his hands roam the dips and curves of her as his blood pressure spiked.

Kara bit her lip against a groan at the feel of his hands and the goose pumps they caused. Sliding her thighs open to fall to the outside of his she hooked his legs with her heels and pulled him closer. Leaning into him, she whispered into his ear. "Take me to bed and show me." She nipped his lobe and nuzzled him.

Flashing them to the bed with Kara on top of him, Brock disappeared their clothes. His mouth watered at the sight of her. Pulling her down to him, needing the taste of her on his tongue, he licked her flesh, growling, "So beautiful."

395

Kara shuddered as the growl vibrated through her, straight to her core that spasmed and grew wetter. "Gods Bjorn, I love when you do that." Her hands roamed over his chest, taking one of his hands and sliding it down between her thighs. "Makes that happen every time." She nipped at his chin and lifted her hips. Releasing her hold on his hand, she dipped hers lower between them to tease his hard length with her fingers.

Moaning, Brock let his fingers find out just how wet she was. The moment his fingertips felt it, his cock jerk hard. "Every time, Cher?" He teased moving his fingers deeper inside, wanting to hear her scream his name.

Her breath hitched in her throat, her core tightening around his fingers as hers tightened around him, stroking slowly. "God, Brock." Kara moaned. She was so hot that she expected to burst into flame. Nodding, she dropped her head to lick and nip at his nipple. "Every time."

Brock smiled and groaned, moving his fingers faster until she felt close and then slowing to tease her. She whimpered and moaned on top of him as her hand danced on his length, making him groan his pleasure. "Gods."

She bit his neck when he teased her, taking her to the brink and then backing off, leaving her panting and wanting to scream her frustration. "Mean bear," she growled against his neck and returned the favor. Kara loosened her fingers until her hand only feathered over the hardness in her palm, her thumb whispering a slow circle over the head. God, this was killing her. She wanted him so damned badly that her body ached and rioted against the game they were playing.

His tip started to leak as she teased it. Growling again Brock moved his thumb over her nub in circles. "I love you," he whispered.

"Brock," she whimpered, sweat breaking over her skin, pleasure building and feeling his tip weep under her thumb made her mouth water to taste him. The growl was too much, it was all too much. Kara screamed his name so hard that her throat hurt a little as she broke and came hard. She dropped one hand to the bed to stop herself from falling as her body shattered into a million pieces leaving her panting. "Love. You. Brock."

Grinning, he pulled his hand from her and brought it to his lips to clean it. Her scent and taste made the bear he truly was, roar inside. Gods, he wanted to take her hard. Sucking and licking his fingers, he stared at her.

Growling and arching a playful brow as he licked his fingers, Kara saw the glow to his eyes and felt his energy change. His bear was waking. She could feel it. Biting her lip, she stroked him again, smiling as he leaked a little more. She pulled her hand to her lips, shuddering at how addictive the taste of him could become.

"I want you, Kara," Brock growled. He grabbed her and rolled them on the bed, putting her under him and sliding himself between her silken thighs. With a growling thrust, he entered her. The feel of her folds made him shiver and his length jerk so hard he almost lost it. Moving his hips, he thrust into her deep and slow.

"God, yes, Brock!" Her head jacked back when he entered her, the air leaving her lungs in a moan and her very bone marrow quivered at how perfect it felt to have him inside her and when he jerked she careened into another orgasm that left her breathless. Forcing her eyes open as she panted and rolled her hips to take him deeper, Kara lifted her head up, her eyes crawling over him, meeting his eyes before dropping lower to watch as he slid into her. Gods she loved watching him move. "Fuck." She whimpered, a sound she'd only ever made for him.

"We are, unless you want something else, Cher," Brock teased and moved his hips faster. He was so very close, and her moving didn't help. He moaned her name, fighting to hold on. He didn't want her to think he was bad in bed. "Jesus."

Kara shook her head no. Her body coiled tight when he moved faster. Her hands reached for him pulling him down for a hot and demanding kiss that pushed her over the edge again, arching her back and meeting him thrust for thrust, his scent washed over her and wreaked havoc on her senses. He drove her to the point of insanity until she wasn't sure where she ended, and he began, only that every inch of her was exploding, pulsing, tightening around him and panting his name.

As she kissed him, Brock's body tumbled over the edge, and his seed filled her hard. He didn't slow as she came. He smiled as they clung to each other. Brock slipped one of her legs over his shoulder and the other into a more comfortable spot. Groaning again as she moved on him. The walls of her core were pure heaven. "Kara," he moaned.

"Gods." Her cry sounded more like a strangled sigh. Kara bit her lip and slid her hands over him, her nails leaving soft red welts on his skin when he changed their position. Raising one arm over her head against the headboard, she grinned at him, her other hand sliding between them, spreading her fingers to feel the push and pull of where they were joined. The brush of her palm over her sensitive nub made her body jump against him, and she gasped his name.

Growling, Brock thrust faster. The headboard banged against the wall. "Oh, gods." He kissed her leg and nipped it. "That's it, Cher. Let go." He urged her on, wanting to please her.

Panting and shivering at a cool breeze that flowed over her sweat slick skin she arched into him, meeting his tempo. The friction of him so snug against the walls of her core and her palm brushing over her nub was too much to stand. Kara broke hard and fast. "Gods, Bjorn!" She screamed, slipping into a mix of English and her native tongue. Her core seized around him and pulsed so hard that her heartbeat fell into its rhythm.

Enjoying her in a roar, Brock exploded, and sweat covered his body. He looked down at her, loving the way her lips parted and her face flushed. "Sated or do you want more?"

398

A smile curled up one corner of her mouth as she looked up at him. It took longer than it should have to get her breath under enough control to talk. Pulling her hand back from between them, shivering a little as cool air hit hot skin, Kara licked her fingers moaning as the mixed taste of them burst on her tongue. "Both?" She teased with a grin.

Laughing, he looked at her and felt his canines burn to be as deeply in her skin as his cock was. The need was overpowering and scared him a little. Cursing in French, he leaned over her and rolled onto his back, taking her with him. He didn't want to leave her body. Not yet.

Kara felt the turmoil of his emotions and reached down to touch his face. "What's wrong?"

Brock shook his head, not wanting to tell her because it was stupid. It was something that a bonded male would do, not a boyfriend.

"Tell me," she whispered against his lips, nipping them and tightening her core around him as she moved. Her eyes closed as she slid over his hot, hard, pulsing cock. "God, I can never get enough of how you feel inside me." She moved again and whimpered when his hips surged off the bed to fill her completely.

"Cher," his voice was barely more than a growl. He could feel his canines lengthening against the inside of his lips.

"Please, tell me." Kara gasped as he seemed to grow inside her, locking their bodies together. She tried to move on him, but he was so thick that she couldn't. Another gasp became a whimper when his cock began to pulse, stretching her wider and touching her deeper. "Brock?" She panted, her eyes searching his as fear began to grow. Every pulse of his length sent a toe curling shock wave of pleasure that forced orgasm after orgasm. She had no control over her body, and that scared her, but only made her come harder.

Brock didn't know what was happening with them. They had locked. He'd heard of it happening, but only with true mates and in stories passed down from the elders. His

399

brows wrinkled as he tried to remember, but all he could think about was the need to taste her blood on his tongue. He needed it so bad that he was afraid that he would hurt her, or worse, but he couldn't help himself. He let his lips part to show his elongated canine teeth.

Kara's eyes flared when she saw what he'd been hiding. Her mind screamed no, but her body just broke harder, instinctively knowing that if he didn't, they could be trapped here, like this, for days and she would go insane from the constant building pleasure or burn up in the process. Holding herself up with one hand on the bed beside his head, she nodded and swept the hair away from her neck. "Please," she begged, not sure what it meant, but knowing that this was bigger than both of them. "Mark me. Please." She lowered her head and licked one of his fangs.

Brock cupped her face and stared into her eyes. He couldn't do it. He wouldn't. Then the pleading tone of her voice asking him to mark her snapped his control. Primal instinct roared inside him, turning him feral. He reared his head and struck, moaning at the sweet tang of her blood on his tongue. His arms wrapped around her, holding her still and tight. He could feel what was coming and didn't want to tear her skin when it happened.

She cried out when he broke her skin with his teeth. The sharp sting was a shock, but the slow draws on her neck woke her body, bringing every sensation into focus and smothering her. She could feel every hair on his body that brushed her skin, his scent grew filling her pours, his heat burning inside her and God she was coming so hard that she thought that she would turn inside out with the pleasure. She tried to move, but couldn't. Somewhere deep in her groggy mind, she knew it was part of his claiming her. Instead of fighting, she held his head to her and whispered, "More. Take more."

He growled his answer and gave over his control to whatever was happening between them. His hips surged, pounding into her body as her blood filled his mouth, his body tingled with it as though it were waking and the feelings that she had for him rocked him to his core. The more he drank and the harder his cock took her, the more of her he got, the more of her he knew. It was addictive, and he never wanted it to stop, but her heart was beginning to slow when it should be racing. He pulled his teeth from her skin, hooking and tearing the tender flesh to ensure that his mark would show, as he sunk his length into her slick hot core one last time. He came so violently that his back arched off the bed and he was sitting with her in his lap and her legs wrapped around his waist. Her name was torn from his lips, and he swore he felt the room shake around them as his release exploded deep inside her so forcefully that her body jerked in his arms.

"Brock!" She screamed as the hot jets of his release scoured the deepest parts of her and moved organs that she couldn't identify with its punch. It hurt and at the same time was the greatest burst of pleasure Kara had ever known. Panting, her hands still holding his head, she pulled back and kissed him. "Holy. Hell."

"Yeah," Brock agreed, resting his forehead against hers as the air sawed in and out of his lungs. His mind and body were floating as the word, *mine*, echoed in a loop inside his head. Her heart beat to the same rhythm as his. He could feel it against his chest. He didn't know what had just happened, but it was something powerful and fear churned in his stomach as a voice whispered inside his head, *"If she chooses to reject you, you will never have her. Offer her the oil of the nettle if you dare know the truth, for until she decides, she will never truly be yours."*

Kara nodded and stroked the back of his neck with her nails, trying to get her breathing under control. Nettle oil. She needed nettle oil, but she didn't know why. She opened her eyes and found his staring back with worry. "What?" She asked, pulling back a little to make him less blurry.

401

"Do you know anything about oil of the nettle?" He felt foolish for asking such a strange question and waited for her to laugh in his face, or at least pull away.

Kara shook her head no. "Only that I need some," she whispered back, brushing her nose against his.

Brock's heart leaped in his chest, and a tiny bottle of the oil ghosted itself into his hand. He raised his hand and uncurled his fingers to see the bottle. "I think I have some here, Cher." He pulled his arm from around her to show her what he had. Some next level shit was going on, and he didn't know what to do other than to go with it and if she laughed in his face then so be it. All he knew was that the next few minutes could decide the rest of his life, though how he knew it or how it would change, he had no clue.

She stared at the small bottle, her brow arching. Something weird was going on here, but instinctively, she knew what to do and that she had to do it while their bodies were still joined. Her arm shook, feeling a bit like Jell-O when she reached for it and popped the cork with her thumb. She tilted her head back and poured the oil over the bleeding wound on her neck, dropping the bottle on the bed and rubbing the oil into her torn skin even though it burned like a bitch.

Brock watched her, holding his breath and his eyes bugged when his bite healed before his eyes but left a crisp black scar where the skin had been torn. "Cher, what have we done?" He blinked at her, touching the mark lightly with her fingers and meeting her eyes.

Kara chewed at her lower lip and stared back. "I think you just claimed me and I agreed to be it." She wasn't sure how to feel about it, only that she wasn't sorry.

"So, you're mine?" He arched a brow skeptically.

She nodded. "In the eyes of Asgard, yes. I belong to you."

"And in your eyes, Kara?"

"I already did." She smiled and touched his face.

402

Brock smiled his relief. "Good." He kissed her softly and wrapped his arms around her, holding her to him tightly.

She held him just as tight as his bloodline imprinted itself on her bones. An Ingolf binding was unheard of, but every fiber of her being told her that it had just occurred and it felt right.

Mine, Brock thought.

"Yes," Kara agreed with a smile.

Both were so caught up in the moment that neither realized that he hadn't spoken or mindlinked her, but she'd heard it anyway.

Chapter 42

As the time drew closer, Kara's muscles coiled tighter. Between her mood and the fact that she was dressed in her armor with her weapons visible and ready for use, spared her from the chit chat. Not Brock though. Ivan and other warriors were gathered around the bear, laughing and welcoming him to their ranks as he told them about the world of man. She shook her head and stabbed a chunk of venison on her plate with her dagger, forcing herself to chew and swallow. Her eyes were pulled to her father's empty seat, again. Kara pushed the plate away and waited for a break in the guffaws, questions, and bragging. "Brock, it's time. I've got to go."

He turned and took her hand. His eyes were still smiling, but worry and trepidation flowed through him. The males surrounding him eyed her warily. "I'm ready when you are, Cher."

Ivan slapped Brock's back. "Hurry back, Sven was just about to tell yer 'bout the time he slew a Drakkar with 'is bare hands and wit." The massive redhead chuckled and rolled his eyes.

The men erupted in laughter and Sven's dark brows slid down over his eyes, not enjoying being the butt of Ivan's joke. "At least if your Valkyrie dies, you need not worry about her mother adding you to her brothel."

Brock growled. "That was never going to happen."

404

"Aye," Ivan chuckled again. "Not now that she's left Asgard."

Brock raised his hand to rub his nose with his middle finger, causing another peal of laughter.

"Do we know where she went?" Kara broke into the conversation, and the laughter stopped. She'd overheard the rumors but didn't put much stock in them until it came from Ivan's lips. She swung a leg over the bench and eyed the group, waiting for an answer.

"Aye," Ivan nodded. "She took everything and returned to Vanaheim. She took EVERYTHING. Don't think she'll be back."

Kara nodded. "Good. Hope she stays there." She doubted that Freya went without an ulterior motive. The goddess was cold, calculating and did nothing unless there was a benefit for her. She forced a smile. "I'll have him back before you know it."

Brock arched a curious brow but then was descended upon by each man gripping his forearm and slapping his back in a show of respect. He fit in here, more than he did back home, and he was both baffled and awed by it. He looked around the dining hall and shook his head. He could live out the rest of his life here, with Kara and be happy. But that was not his fate, and he knew it. Sighing heavily, he swung his legs over the bench and stood, tugging Kara to her feet to stand beside him. *Please don't let what happens today change everything*, he thought to himself as he followed Kara through the full to the gills hall.

Kara didn't see the walls or the tapestries as she walked with her Bjorn. Something was up and the way her luck ran lately, it wasn't going to be in her favor. Fine with her, but she worried about Brock getting out of here safe until she spied Ivan slip into the throne room and lean against the wall with his arms folded over his barrel chest and his hand resting on his sword. She arched a questioning brow, swinging her eyes to Brock and then back to Ivan. The

405

Viking nodded, and Kara felt some of the tension drain from her shoulders.

"You don't have to..." Her words died at the bear's expression. It read, I ain't leaving. Tucking some loose hair behind her ear, a ghost of a smile slid across her face. She wasn't worthy of him. "If it goes wrong, promise me that you'll let Ivan get you out of here."

Brock blinked at her and snorted. He nodded even though he had no intention of doing any such thing. He had her back whether she liked it or not.

"Liar," she smirked and bounced up the slab steps and dropped into the throne.

Brock chuckled and followed, his hands itching to touch the incredible carvings that scrawled over the seat, fit for a god.

Kara tilted her head back and smiled. "Go ahead. Dad likes it when people appreciate his stuff." She sighed her relief when he stood behind the throne and busied himself with studying the craftsmanship. Today was going to be bloody and brutal. It would be better if Brock didn't see any of it, but she wasn't going to lie about who and what she was. If he couldn't handle it, then it was better if they both knew it now.

She wiggled around until she was comfortable and threw her legs over one of the arms. Kara knew that just finding her here would irk some, and the utter disrespect she was showing, would turn irked to pissed. A bitter smile shone in her eyes as she manifested a sharpening stone to drag along the edge of her sword. They were late. Go ahead, make her wait, because that always ended well.

The steady scrape of pumice against steel was soothing and annoying at the same time. Every minute that ticked by, the darker Kara's mood grew. Sure, she could go looking for them, but this was the heart of Asgard, and everyone ended up here eventually. Tilting her head to the side, catching her reflection in the aged blade, she mentally listed all that would die today. All those in Valhalla that had betrayed her.

There were those who swore up and down that killing a god would catapult the world below into darkness and death. Maybe today was the day to test that theory. Just as she was about to give in to her baser urges and begin the massacre, if one person cutting through a few hundred qualified, her father strolled into the hall, followed by Thor and Loki.

Brock straightened when he heard footsteps, resting his hands on the high back of the chair and leaning forward a bit. If they tried to hurt one hair on her head, his bear was going to find out what God meat tasted like.

Kara's brow quirked upward. She didn't move and barely breathed. So be it, if this was the answer to her demand. She sighed and did her best to sound bored even as her blood began to boil. No one could disappoint you the way that family could. "So, I take it the answer is no?"

Odin turned his head to glare at Thor with his one crystal blue eye. "He will produce the female, but there is a complication, Little One." Shaking his head, he looked up at his throne and the way she was sprawled across it, his jaw ticking. Kara wasn't sure if it was because of her or her brother but was guessing it was a little of both.

Sliding the whetstone along her blade, Kara lifted the sword to check her work by running her thumb over its edge, smiling as a paper-thin line of blood appeared on her skin. "Your complications, as you call them, are not my problem, Fadir." She turned her gaze to his, her smile tightening as an arctic blast rolled and churned in her gut. That Thor had not been allowed to heal was a sweet gesture, his smashed face and now very crooked nose telling one and all whose side of this fight Odin came down on. "Might as well spill it, so I can get this shit over with."

Odin raised one muscular arm and flicked his fingers, glowering at Thor one more time and making his son flinch. "Bring her in."

Kara watched with interest as the nothing special human was dragged in by two armored warriors. Aryan kicked, she screamed, and she begged. Kara felt nothing but contempt and that didn't change with the next words to fall from her father's lips.

"She is with child."

Kara's brows shot toward her hairline as she turned in the throne to place both boots firmly on the floor. "And I care why?" She flashed away the whetstone and eyed the female who had the nerve to sneer at her. Suddenly the pieces of the puzzle fell into place. It was so fucking stupid that she laughed. "You, pathetic little idiot." Kara shook her head and leaned her elbows on her knees, giving the woman a good view of the weapons that were going to end her life. "You honestly think a whelp of yours has a place here? My place? God, you're as stupid as my brother." She raked her disgusted gaze over Thor, who apparently had fallen for her faulty logic, before turning to Loki. "I don't understand how you play into this, Brother."

Loki laughed, strolling forward like he didn't have a care in the world. Slowly, his eyes never leaving Kara's, he took each step until he was standing at her side and nodded a silent greeting to Brock who didn't budge.

Brock growled a warning. He didn't like Loki being so close to Kara, not when he could feel the tension crackling in the air. Nor did he appreciate the man's sense of humor about the situation.

Leaning down to rest his elbow on the arm of the throne, Loki spared a glance at the Bjorn, standing over his sister like a watchdog. He lowered his voice so that only she and the bear could hear. "Who do you think loosened the lips of the guilty so you would learn the truth, dear sister?" He smirked as her jaw tightened and Brock's head tilted to the side barely enough to be noticed. "There's more to be known if you just listen."

"I fucking hate when you talk in riddles," Kara growled her annoyance. Loki loved to do that shit, thinking it made him sound wise instead of just the annoying ass he really was. Experience had taught her to strip his words down to their most basic meaning, so she listened. Squinting her eyes as her ears identified each sound in the cavernous room, a smile curled up her lips before she barked a cold laugh. "I get your meaning." Kara shook her head and pushed off the throne, descended the stairs and stopped toe to toe with her father. "If there is young in her vile womb, why does it not have a heartbeat?"

Loki, held out his arm to block Brock when he tried to follow, shaking his head.

Brock growled and curled his lip, showing the longer than usual canines. "Move."

"Not your fight, Bjorn," Loki smirked.

Odin's one eye flared as did his nostrils. His head turning to pin the female with a glare that turned the air cold enough to frostbite the flesh. He did not flinch when Kara slid her dagger into the swollen front of the female. Thor gasped making a strangled gurgle in his throat as the blade slid in and then a string of ancient curses when stuffing and sawdust spilled onto the floor. Kara arched a blond brow at her father. "She's not worth the time it will take to wipe her blood off my shoes. Her whore is here as well?"

Odin pulled a repeat of the calling forward of the prisoner. This time a weeping and snotty nosed male who didn't even bother to struggle, shuffled forward. How the hell did such a coward ever end up here? His very existence was an insult to her people, and she would not give him the honor of a warrior's death. An idea formed out of nowhere, the perfectness of it causing a slight shiver of delight. "When was the last time Fenrir fed?"

Odin's head fell back on his shoulders, and his deep rumbling laugh echoed through the chamber. Thor turned paper white and began to sputter. Kara silenced his babbling with an elbow to the face. The blood gushed, and his nose sat more to the left than running a vertical line down the center of his face. Loki snickered behind her, still leaning against the throne. "Since before his last escape, Little One."

Odin chuckled and reached to cup Kara's face in his palm, his blue eye sparkling with life. "I'm sure his appetite is ravenous by now."

"Then I say we ring the dinner bell and watch the show." Kara smiled coldly at Thor. "And he will watch, or be part of the meal." Just when she thought that Thor couldn't turn paler, he proved her wrong. "Those are my terms, or we're back to the original plan." She arched a brow and let the ravens whisper into her father's ears.

"Your terms are accepted." The room swirled and changed around them until they all stood in the bowels of Helheim. Water dripped over the chipped cavern walls, landing in puddles that couldn't be found by the naked eye. The female began alternating empty threats with pleas for mercy from Thor.

Brock hadn't fully recovered from thinking that Kara was going to open a womb and spill an innocent life onto the woman's shoes when the throne beneath his hands disappeared, and he had to recover before he fell on his face. He wasn't sure what was going on, but he knew it wasn't good.

Loki laughed at Brock's expression and whispered, "How are you at wolf growls and throwing your voice?"

Brock blinked at Loki, confused and opened his mouth to speak, closing it again when Kara's voice cut through the air and echoed, but he was focused on the god beside him. Something was off. Loki was moving his hands and chanting in a language Brock didn't know. The feel of strong magic raising the hair on his arms told him enough. Loki was up to something.

Kara snorted at the woman. "Get with the program twit. He has no say or power here, and if he begs to differ, he will join you." Humans never got the way their kind worked. Life was brutal and bloodthirsty. Those born of Asgard were no different. They were not soft, and if they chose to be, it was a gift for a special few. Even then, they were what they were. Not good. Not evil. They just were, and as a race, they were colder than most.

A wave of Odin's hand opened the heavy stone and steel of the cell door. Furious red eyes glared at them from the darkness, a low growl vibrated across the floor and caused the hair on the back of Kara's neck to prickle as they stood at attention. Jaws snapped in explosions of bone hitting bone, leaking the fetid odor of rotten meat caught between teeth to decay. Chains rattled a dragged over the stone floor as the giant beast inched closer, the air crackling with the tension as they all waited for Fenrir's lunge. The ancient wolf wasn't stupid, he knew every inch that his bindings would allow him and denied them all that moment of heart hammering adrenaline rush.

"The whore's whore goes first," Kara said in a calm and even tone, turning her head to her father. "And she will give him the push so the pup can reach him." Her jaw ticked, waiting for someone to speak against her. She got nothing, which was both a disappointment and relief. Odin nodded and directed her orders to be followed.

The human female shoved her lover into the cell, turned and ran directly into Odin, who spun her around and held her to face the brutal ripping of flesh from bone. "Keep those eyes open, Little Liar, or I will remove your lids." His whisper barely registered over the screams and tearing flesh or the disgusting chewing and swallowing of hunks of meat. The male's head was torn from his shoulders, silencing the not entirely human sounds he was making and rolled across the rough stone, still spinning at Odin's foot before he drew it back and punted the cranium back into the darkness. The female broke into a series of frantic blood-curdling screams that quickly chewed at their nerves.

Brock paled and took a step back. He knew that wolf and its name wasn't Fenrir. What the hell was going on? Was this how they settled disputes here? What the fuck had he gotten himself into?

411

"Gods!" Kara growled. "Thor, give her to him and shut her the fuck up." She arched a brow when he shook his head no. "Fine, then I will send you with her, brother mine." She smiled coldly and stepped back to move behind him. Ratcheting Thor's arm up behind his back, she smiled at Loki. "Count of three?"

Odin shook his head when Thor turned his pleading eyes to his father. "You made your bed boy, now you must lie in it. If what's between her thighs is worth dying for, who am I to deny you your wish?"

Loki nodded his head, counting down for a synchronized tossing, his blue eyes sparkling as he silently chanted to keep the spell in place. If they knew what he'd done, it would be his head rolling today. He was aware that it would, in time, but not today.

"Wait! I will do it." Thor dropped to his knees sobbing and screamed when Kara's grip on his arm popped it from the socket. Still, she did not let go. She yanked him back to his feet and shoved him at Loki.

"Do it." Odin's voice rumbled and echoed back at them like gunfire. "Or join her. Do it now, before your sister grows bored." Thor shuffled forward, still sniveling and acting utterly broken.

Kara wanted to feel sorry for him, he was her blood after all... Wait. No, she didn't. She wouldn't shed a tear for the stupid son of a bitch. Not now. Not ever. A cold smile curled at her lips, her arms crossed over her chest, and she ignored the heavy arm of her father as it fell over her shoulders. After what felt like way too fucking long, Thor shoved the human forward so hard that her feet left the floor and she caught a little air. Nodding her satisfaction, Kara savored the new pain filled screams, and sounds of a feral animal devouring its kill assaulted her ears.

"It is done?" Odin slid the monstrous door back into place with a wave of his fingertips.

Loki sighed his relief and shot Brock a grin. He knew that the bear noticed his slight of hand, but would he give him away?

Brock arched a brow at the blonde god, not sure what he should do and still in shock at seeing the humans torn apart by the same wolf that he'd pup sat when he was barely old enough to watch after himself. Venom, next in line to lead the Canis pack had been MIA for almost three years. How the hell had he ended up here? Brock shook his head and looked away from Loki.

"Yes." Kara agreed, sheathing her weapons. "As soon as you agree to one stipulation." She rolled her head back to meet her father's single eye. He inclined his head and raised a brow. "All of you stay away from what is mine. What he calls my…" Her lip curled up with distaste as she eyed Loki. "Pets. If I even hear a whisper of one of ours sniffing around one of mine, I will be back, and I will not stop. Am I clear?" Kara tilted her head and rolled her eyes as Odin stopped to listen to the damned black winged rats on his shoulder. Odin's nod was her answer. Kara turned to Loki.

He too inclined his head in agreement. "If they don't screw with me, then I won't screw with them." Loki looked at Brock and arched a brow.

"Good." Roughly, Kara embraced her father. She didn't miss the look Loki hit Brock with, and she didn't like it. She would slaughter them all if they reneged, and she would start with Thor. She stopped in front of Brock and sighed at the disbelief she saw etched into his face. "Let's go home, Babes." She held out her hand, not sure that he would take it.

Brock searched her eyes, looking for the funny and easy going female that had stolen his heart, but the regret he saw there was enough. He slid his hand into hers and pulled her closer, kissing her forehead. "Yes." He smiled and looked past her to the three Gods watching him with interest. Why did he have a feeling that he'd made at least one enemy today?

413

Brock thought Kara needed to know about the wolf in the cell, but he couldn't tell her here. Not with them staring at him. Loki's eyes seem to be boring into Brock, and he locked eyes with the God.

Loki smiled at him. 'I wouldn't say a word, Bjorn. Not to her or to anyone, about what you saw. My sister may have a thing for you now, but you are nothing of importance to her or any of us. You are a pet, like a thing in a cage. She keeps you, and that is all. I wouldn't make an enemy of me.' Loki's voice filled Brock's head. His tone was cold and deadly.

"Lead the way, Cher," Brock answered Kara, wanting to get as far away from here as he could right now. He wouldn't leave Venom, not if he could help it. For now, he'd have to, and it made him sick. 'Cher, what is going to happen to the wolf in the cell? He just eats people, right?' Brock linked her.

Kara's brow wrinkled at the way Loki was staring at the Bjorn, not sure what was going on but she wasn't going to ask. Not here. Flipping the sobbing Thor off one last time, she ghosted them back to Brock's place at The Pit. "Mostly he gets left alone, in the dark." She made a face, hating what Fenrir's life had become. "Why do you ask?"

Brock rubbed the back of his neck. "How sure are you that Fenrir is the one in that cell? Let's just say for a moment, that he wasn't. What would happen?" Brock hoped that she'd tell him he was full of shit and that there was no way on god's green earth that it could be anyone but Fenrir. But it wasn't god's green earth. It was Asgard, and there, things were different.

She blinked at him and arched a brow. "It would be the beginning of the end of everything. How could it not be Fenrir, only Loki..." Her voice trailed off as Kara replayed what had just happened. She'd been so wrapped up in making Thor pay that she hadn't noticed the little details. Fenrir hadn't uttered his usual chuff in greeting. She'd dismissed it because Odin was there, but it had never caused him to ignore her before. The light had been bad. She hadn't seen the wolf clearly. What if? "Why?"

Brock's face went white for a moment. "I... I don't think that's Fenrir in there. He smells like someone I know. Loki knows that I know, or he senses it. I don't want to make trouble, Cher, but I honestly don't think that is Fenrir in that cell." He said hoping he was wrong, but his gut told him otherwise.

She felt the color leave her face. "You think, or you know?" Kara's tone was deadly serious. Her mind reeled with possible outcomes. "Wait. Did he threaten you? I mean..." Kara pushed the hair back from her face and cursed at the ceiling. "Fuck."

"I know it's not Fenrir," Brock said seriously. "As for Loki, not in the I'll slit your throat kind of way, but yes, he did threaten me. I don't care about myself I care about what this all means to the big picture. Why would Fenrir not be there?" Brock didn't know a lot about her world. He had heard stories about the wolf, but every time he thought he knew things about it, it was always ass backward. He was learning to assume he knew nothing for certain.

"Because Loki is shady as fuck. No one knows why Loki does anything!" She growled and dropped her hands. That wasn't true. She knew why Loki would release Fenrir and it wasn't necessarily to fuck with everything. She sighed. "Fenrir is Loki's son, and he's been locked down there for eons because of a prophecy. It's not fair, but it's how it is." Kara began to pace, battling between being happy for the wolf and waiting for the world to burst into a ball of flame. "If you're right," she rested her hand on Brock's shoulder. "I believe you if you say you know the wolf in the cell. We need to get him out and figure out how to fix this before it goes bad."

Brock held her a moment before he spoke. "I'm sorry, Cher. The last thing I wanted to do was pile on more to your horrific day. So, how would we get Venom out of there?"

Kara dropped her head against his shoulder. "I don't know. I have to figure out how to defuse Loki. You might not care if anything happens to you, but I do." Going to Odin was out. He'd demand both the wolf and her brother's heads. Hel might be a better choice. "First, can we make sure that Venom, that's his name, right?" She looked up for his nod. "Once we know for sure that he's MIA, I'll visit the cell. If he tries to rip me apart, then it ain't Fen."

Brock didn't like that idea. "Do I have to like this plan? And I am coming with you. Venom might not try anything if he remembers me." He wondered how dead he was going to be when Loki learned that he ratted him out.

She thought about it and shook her head no. "It will be easier to sell that I just went to visit the pup and figured it out myself if you're not with me." She smiled. "And no, you don't have to like the plan. I don't."

Brock growled. "I am not letting you go alone. What if something happens? Who is going to protect you?" He knew she didn't really need it, but damn it, she was the love of his life. He made himself a promise to keep her, even if it killed him.

Kara arched a brow. "Okay, hold up there, Buddy Bear. Who is going to what? If I'm splitting my attention between keeping your mortal hide intact, chances are higher that I'm going to make a stupid mistake. And, so what if I get hurt? I'll heal. You won't. Dead is dead. You can't come back from that, Brock. Me? I might look like a Picasso for a while, but it will get better. So, shelve the testosterone."

She was right, and Brock hated it. The bear in him snorted. "Fine," he grumbled. "I'm still calling Bullshit."

"Call it anything you want to." She shrugged. "Besides, there is going to be plenty to do here if what I think is going to happen, does."

He didn't think of that. Brock's facial expression became an oh shit one quickly. "Cher, how bad could it be? Would there be signs?" He probably sounded like a moron to her, but he wasn't used to the end of the world in large doses. He was used to small ones that AP or his clan could manage.

"If you see something and you think it's not possible, kill it. Quick. It can be anything from weird weather or natural disasters to things that have been locked down and under control that aren't anymore." She sighed. "Imagine the worst-case scenario and multiply it by a hundred."

Brock's eyes bugged out for a moment at what all this could mean for not just him and his family, but the world. "Holy shit." His mind started to race. "I guess we divide and conquer. Should I warn Salvation? Or wait until you know for sure?" *Gods, what does an aneurysm feel like*, Brock thought to himself.

"Warn everyone. Salvation. Reese. Do you all have a 911 system, because this is the time to use it." Kara rubbed her hands up and down his sides. "If we're wrong they can all cuss us out later. But if we're right..."

Brock closed his eyes for a moment. "Okay, def-con one it is. It's better to overreact than underreact, right? Shit, Cher, this is some next level stuff."

"Yes, it is," she agreed. "You watch your ass and keep it safe, or else," Kara growled and hugged him tightly.

"I promise, Cher, and you do the same," he growled, hugging her. He couldn't lose her again, he'd just found her.

"I have to, I have something to come back in one piece for." She grinned and stretched up to kiss him.

"Mead. I know," he teased and kissed her back.

Kara laughed. "Yeah, and you, Smart Ass." She nipped his jaw. "I'll be back as soon as I can, Babes. I love you."

"I love you too, Cher." Brock hugged her tightly one last time and let her go. He couldn't let his own fear get in the way of things that had to be done.

Stepping back, even though she didn't want to, Kara flashed him a smile and ghosted to Fenrir's cell in Helheim.

Chapter 43

Ty sat in his throne room, staring at nothing and absently stroking a groove in the arm of the chair under his hand. Reddish-brown hair fell against his ears, annoying him. Raking his fingers through it, he pulled it back. Where were they? His minions weren't answering when he called. They always answered, not doing so was a death sentence. So, either they were suddenly stupider than normal, or they were vanishing. He shifted his weight in the chair. It creaked, sounding like tortured souls but brought him no pleasure. His minions joked that his massive copper throne was built with the bones of children. Bones? Yes. Children? Maybe. Ty really didn't remember anymore.

His left hand fell over the side and dipped into one of the pouches tethered to the frame of his macabre piece of furniture. The material had been dyed to match the copper tone of his throne precisely, to blend in at first, second and third glance. Only when his hand found its way inside, was it visible. The tanned flesh of his sister's first love was buttery soft under his fingertips. Ty didn't remember the poor fool's name, only the reason that he'd slaughtered the son of a bitch and that was a secret that he guarded carefully. Dipping lower, the things inside clicked and chattered as his fingers swept through them, stirring them and assuring Ty that they were still there. He smiled to himself and stroked the disks that appeared to be nothing more than those cheap plastic poker chips the humans used. Ty knew the truth. Fingering the disks and feeling the essence within each one, he was interrupted when he sensed his head Shadz Warrior and most trusted minion close by.

Gore ghosted into the arched doorway of the throne room, in human form. His short, dark hair was gelled into a faux hawk and a few days of scruff shadowed his jaw. He didn't know what Bertha had done to him, but when he woke today, he felt like his old self. Well, except for the feeling of something occasionally stroking the inside of his meat suit, and the unease that burned through his veins. He hoped that Ty wasn't in the mood to tear apart his freshly healed hide. Something was happening. Gore could feel it, and it wasn't their usual brand of bad.

He remained still, groaning inwardly at the sight of Ty lost in thought with his hand in one of the pockets. One did not interrupt the Master when he was thinking. Not if he wanted to keep his insides where they belonged and not splashed over his boots. Silently, he clasped his hands behind his back, his fingers curling tightly around the vial in his palm and watched. Gore's head tilted at the sound of soft clattering. He never understood what the hell was up with those poker chips. As far as he knew, Ty didn't even play the game. *Weird*, Gore thought, shaking his head. He cleared his throat. If that didn't get Ty's attention, he'd come back later. Bad juju or not, he wasn't ready to die today.

Ty blinked when he heard someone clear their throat and raised his eyes to find Gore standing there. Motioning him forward with his free hand, Ty pulled the other from the pouch, dropping the flap to hide the treasures inside. "It's about time. Did you bring me the princess?"

Gore shook his head and stopped at the foot of the throne.

"How hard is it to find and capture one fucking Valkyrie?" Ty growled angrily.

419

Gore opened his mouth to explain but snapped his jaw together when Ty leveled that look of impending pain on him.

"I don't want to hear any more of your bullshit. I want Kara, and I want her, yesterday. Leave me and don't return until you have her," Ty sneered and waved Gore away.

"I'm trying my best, but it's not that easy. That's not why I'm here. Something bad is coming. I can sense it. We need to be ready."

Ty gave him a look of contempt. "What the hell are you yapping about? If something was coming, don't you think I'd know about it? Who the hell do I look like to you? Just another demon king of dipshits? Why must you always test me, Gore? I should reach down your throat, grab you by the balls and turn you inside out. You're lucky to be alive. You know that, right?" Ty growled coldly, leaning forward on his throne.

Gore was about to ignore the warning and tell him about the vial in his hand when the air in the room began to vibrate, softly at first and then growing more violent.

Ty's eyes rolled up to look at the ceiling and the creatures that shifted restlessly as their sleep was disturbed. Arching a brow at Gore, he bolted from his throne as the floor quaked beneath them. "What in the hell?" Ty demanded, but the deafening groan of shifting stone drowned out his voice. It was loud, reminding him of the time he put his running shoes in one of those industrial dryers the humans built buildings around.

Gore tried to move, his eyes darting back to the safety of the doorway. He couldn't. He was locked in place. Surges of power prickled his skin. His eyes grew wide. The pit beneath them. Ty kept everything evil, dark, and deadly there. Had it been breached? Gore met Ty's eyes. He could see the Master's lips moving, but Gore couldn't hear what was said.

The dark marble walls shuddered. Cracks bloomed in the smooth stone and grew into fishers, racing toward the

420

floor, exploding in clouds of rock shards and dust. Both men gaped as everything fell silent. Another rumble filled the chamber as stone ground against itself. The pressure was building, and something was coming. Blood sprayed from the cracks in the floor like lava erupting from a volcano.

Something cold closed around Ty's heart, squeezing painfully as ice filled his veins. Was this what fear felt like? He didn't like it. He stared at the jets of blood spurting through the floor and tried to move when it began to rain down over them. He couldn't.

The spray sizzled as it hit their skin. Gore snarled in pain. "What the fuck?" He growled, turning his eyes to Ty, waiting for him to protect them. At least himself. His brows popped when nothing shielded the Master. They were both trapped in place as the room became a bad acid trip around them. It only lasted a few minutes, but to them, it seemed eons.

As quickly as it came, it drew back. The spewing fountains dwindled to a bubbling gurgle, then to still pools. Panting, the males stared at each other, both wondering if they could move and if they did, would it start again? Blood dripping from their soaked clothes was the only sound other than their ragged breathing. The smell of cooking flesh filled the room as smoke rolled from their skin.

Ty ground his teeth against the bloody acid as it chewed through his skin and the sleeve of his shirt slithered wetly down his arm, taking a layer of his flesh with it. He blinked, not believing his eyes. Everything looked as it did before. The gaping fishers in the walls and floor were gone, leaving flawlessly smooth stone. Flexing his fingers, his face tightened at the pain that danced over exposed muscle. His eyes swept over the room, waiting for the blood geyser to erupt again. If this had happened in the pit... Ty's heart pounded as he tried to move, but got only a sluggish response for his trouble and the pain that wrapped around him was perfect agony. "Gore."

Gore's eyes were wide, showing a thick band of white around his dark iris. He wanted to wipe the blood from his face, to rub his eyes, to remove what he was seeing. His arms were too heavy. Even breathing could be considered an Olympic sport right now, the lingering effects of whatever had just happened was a vice, squeezing the life from him.

Ty stared back, annoyed at the shock and horror on his Shadz face. "What the hell are you looking at?" Ty snapped. *How dare he look at Ty as if he were grotesque and not the perfect specimen that he was?*

"Your face. It's..." Gore didn't know how to explain it. Ty's face was a twisted, mangled mess of flesh and other horrors. It shifted from one nightmare to the next, too fast for Gore to find the words. At that moment, Gore saw a part of Ty he'd never seen before. One he never wanted to see again. The Master was truly terrifying.

"What about my face?" Ty fought gravity to reach up to touch it. His fingertips sizzled in the sticky blood that covered it. "Forget my face. We have bigger problems," he snapped at Gore. "The pit. I want you and the others there now. Make sure nothing escaped. And for the love of god, do not tell anyone what happened here."

Gore, still held captive by the terrifying twisting and changing of Ty's features, nodded. He hadn't thought that anything could really scare him, but he was wrong. They didn't call Ty the god of monsters and everything evil, for no reason. Some said that he was once filled with love and happiness. That it changed when he and his sister were separated. Whatever had happened that day, turned Ty's light to darkness. Love became hate, and his emotions had twisted, like his face was doing now. He was powerful before, but his fury took form and created the first monster and through the beast, Ty gave humans their first taste of evil. Because of his pain and sorrow, the world was changed forever.

Gore sagged when whatever held him rooted in place, released its grip. He slid the vial into his back pocket and concentrated on the new mission. The Viking bitch's blood was powerful, and Ty wanted it. If the shit hit the fan anymore, Gore might very well need a bargaining chip to save his hide. Snapping his hanging jaw shut, he nodded and flashed to the gate, praying that the barriers held.

Chapter 44

Still reeling from everything and what it could mean, Brock left his room and headed to the portal to summoned Salvation. He knew the ghuardian wouldn't be happy he was called like this, but Brock didn't care.

Salvation sat on the floor of his hut, deep in meditation when he felt himself being pulled away. One of the Navarro clan was calling him. He opened his eyes, sighed and ghosted himself to the barrier between the sanctuary of The Mountain and the New Orleans stronghold. He didn't have time for this. Reports of strange and unusual happenings were coming from every corner of the globe, and he'd hoped that maybe just one clan would have their shit together and be able to handle something without him holding their hands. No such luck. His mood was already dark when he stepped through. Seeing Brock was a surprise. The bear was pale, almost white with fear. Whatever the problem was, it couldn't be good because this bear never did anything like this. His brothers, yes, but not Brock. "What is it?" The ghuardian asked.

Brock tried to control the panic and fear, eating away at him. *Shit had not hit the fan yet*. He kept telling himself that. As Sal appeared, his bravery drained. The Ghuardian's face read, this better be fucking important. "We have a problem. A huge problem. We should talk in private."

Salvation's brow arched as he watched the bear. The cub was a ball of anxiety and fear, but he was trying to fight through it. Sal sighed and scratched the stubble that peppered his jaw. "In private? You're starting to freak me out a bit, Bear." Salvation ghosted them to Brock's room and leaned his ass against the arm of a chair, crossing his arms over his chest and eyeing Brock. "Don't worry. I've locked your room down. Now tell me, what is going on? There's always a problem of some kind. You'd better not be wasting my time with bullshit."

Brock wasn't sure how to go about this. So, he just blurted it out. "I don't know if it's one hundred percent, but we think that Loki has uncaged Fenrir. According to Kara, the repercussions of this are going to be world ending. I am not trying to be Chicken Little here or the bear who cried wolf. I was there, by Fenrir's cage, and I saw the wolf inside. It smelled like Venom. Kara has gone to Asgard to confirm it."

Sal took in everything the bear said. He didn't know his father or that world well, but he did know his sister. Even if they'd had their fall outs, and she could play crazy bitch better than anyone he'd met, he was aware that she wasn't the type to get worked up over nothing. If she was worried, then there was a good reason. The same with Brock, the bear didn't usually get riled up, though his brothers did. He was the calm and cool one of the clan. "Venom?" The wolf had been MIA for a while, and even Sal couldn't find him. If the wolf were in Asgard, that would explain why Salvation couldn't find or sense him anymore. He cursed under his breath. "Have you told anyone else?"

"Yes, Venom. I'm sure of it. His scent is unmistakable." Brock watched Salvation process everything. He shook his head no when he was asked if he'd told anyone else. "No. I came straight to you. My next stop is Reese. I think she needs to know what might be coming."

Salvation sighed. Reese was going through a shit storm, as it was. This may just be what she needed to refocus her thoughts. "Okay," He nodded and stroked the hair over his lip as he thought. "Please, do that. She needs to know. I'll handle the rest." For once, he wasn't battling his uncle. He was shocked that Ty wasn't behind this, but he knew that the bastard would take advantage of it. "I'll send you someone to help watch over the portal," he said. "I'll be in touch. When you learn more, I'm your first stop on the info dump. We clear?" He eyed the bear and once satisfied, ghosted out.

Before Brock could ask who he was sending, Salvation vanished. His brothers would be insulted that Sal didn't have confidence in them. Though, this time it wasn't about that. It was about the sheer magnitude of the shit storm coming for them all. Brock pulled his phone from his pocket and texted Reese. [911. Find me ASAP and keep it quiet please.] He added his name, because the last time he'd texted her, she didn't recognize the number. Something about a slime demon oozing all over her phone and she'd decided, fuck it, no phone was worth the trouble. Brock hit send and pushed a hand through his hair. Now that he had a second to breathe, he was worried about Kara.

Reese sighed when her phone chirped and vibrated in her jeans pocket against the floorboards. Crawling over the bed and pushing Blade's leg out of the way, she pulled the pile of denim closer and fished out her phone, groaning at the text. "Looks like it's time to get back to work," she sighed and ghosted on clothes, ducking the pillow Blade threw at her head, laughing. [I'm at The Pit. Where do you want to meet?]

Brock's phone went off as he sat down and scrubbed his face with his hand before reading the text. He assumed that once Salvation left, the wards in place to keep his place private had disappeared with the Ghuardian. [I'm in my room if you're cool with meeting me there.] Brock hit send. He knew that only minutes had passed here, but he was worried that Kara wasn't back yet. "Please, be okay, Babes," he said to himself.

426

She read the text and leaned down to kiss Blade, purring against his lips. "I'll be back, and I'll yell if I need backup." Reese grinned and ghosted outside Brock's room, looking up and down the hall before she knocked. A shiver raced down her spine, causing her brow to arch. *What the hell*, she thought to herself.

Brock got up and open the door. "Come on in." He stepped back and then closed the door behind her. "You'd better sit down for what I'm about to say." As he spoke to her the look in her eyes was different. "Are you okay?"

"Yeah, I think someone just walked over my grave or something. Glad to see that you're still breathing. I wasn't so sure." Reese rubbed her arms to warm away the goosebumps, as she crossed the room to sink into the sofa. Her nose twitched. Kara's scent was everywhere. "So, what is worthy of a 911, Bear?"

"Thanks. It worked out, and there were no casualties." Brock smiled. It felt like the stuff with the landmine had happened weeks ago. For him, it had. Brock eyed her for a moment before speaking. "How much do you know about where Kara comes from, and the god, Loki?" He asked, wanting to know if he could cliff notes it or not, to get the lioness up to speed.

"Not a lot about where she comes from, but I know Loki cheats at cards, has a love of Irish whiskey and likes those nasty ass cigars in Ozzy's desk drawer. Why?" Reese tilted her head and shook the blonde hair from her face. Something had the bear worked up. The question was, was it a little problem or something that was in her wheelhouse?

Brock sighed, realizing that Reese didn't know much and he was going to have to do his best to get her up to speed. "Kara, like Loki, is from Asgard. She took me there, and I kind of foiled one of Loki's plans. Or at least, I think I did. Short version. Venom is in the cage there, and the wolf who was supposed to be in said cage is Loki's son, Fenrir. We think he's missing and because of that, shit may be about to hit the fan. They have a prophecy about him ending

427

the world. I already told Salvation about it. You're the next stop on the end of the world tour." Brock tried to make a joke, but inside he was trying not to freak out. "And before you ask me why this should matter to you, or whatever, it does. Trust me. Forgive me for sounding like a dick, but Sal thinks it's bad enough that he's sending someone to help with it. I don't know if it's just for the portal or what. Before I could get more info, he vanished."

Reese listened silently as the story spilled from Brock, like air from a full balloon, dropped to fly around the room. She tugged up the sleeves of her shirt and leaned her elbows on her knees, tilting her head up to look at the bear. "Okay," she paused as she digested it all. "Mind sitting down? Watching you pace is making my neck ache." She smiled and looked down at her hands hanging between her knees. "If Sal wants us on it, then we're on it. Any idea what we're looking at?"

Brock lowered himself into the chair across from her. "From what Kara said, it could be anything from weird weather to anything out of the ordinary. 'If you see anything off, kill it quick,' she said. But I had a horrifying thought myself. If this is as powerful as she says, I'm worried about the portal and our ability to keep it locked up tight. It was only verified when Sal said he was sending someone to help with it. I don't want to send anyone into a panic, but we need all hands on deck," he said, pushing his hair out of his face. "Kara left to go check everything out, and I'm hoping she'll be back PDQ. I don't think I left anything out. I'm not used to being the one to give the briefing."

"Lovely," Reese sighed and glanced at the clock over Brock's shoulder. "Bart should be starting his shift on portal duty. I'll send someone down to back him if shit gets weird. We're going to keep this in the need to know loop. The last thing we need is a bunch of civies panicking. Portal keepers and AP. Is Sal going to let the keepers of the other portals know, or is that on us?" She watched Brock for a few moments and gave him a reassuring smile when he

428

shrugged. "You did fine. Take a breath. We'll handle it as it comes. Okay?" Yeah, she was shitting bricks on the inside, but the bear didn't need to know that right now.

Chapter 45

Kara stood outside the heavy door and closed her eyes. If her brother had done what she thought he had, they were all screwed. Sighing heavily, she waved her hand, wincing as the scream of old hinges that didn't move much, pierced her eardrums and echoed inside her head. Chains rattled within, and the low growl rolled over her and vibrated in her chest. Kara's head tilted to the side. "Pup?" She called out, keeping her voice calm. "I brought some Tums, in case those nasty humans gave you a stomach ache." She forced herself to smile and step inside. If Loki was watching, then she had to play this like she was clueless.

The wolf lunged, dust was kicked up from the floor and made Kara's eyes water from the grit. 'I know, Venom. I'm here to help,' she mindlinked the wolf that most definitely was not Fenrir. *Loki, what have you done?*

Venom snarled and gnashed his teeth, warning her that if she came closer, she would regret it.

"Calm down, Big Guy," Kara crooned, closing her eyes as she reached out her arm. This was going to fucking hurt, but it was the only way Loki would believe that she hadn't found out about this from Brock.

Venom tilted his head, watching the crazy woman and waiting. She was going to hurt him too. He knew it. They all wanted to hurt him, they had for years. First in the fighting rings. Then as bait when he was wounded. Then the blonde

430

God had won him in a game of cards. A game of fucking cards! Venom had dared to hope that his new enslavement would be better, but the bastard had locked him in here. It was dark, cold and damp. No matter how much bedding he piled in the corner, he couldn't get warm. He couldn't even use his voice, other than to howl because the asshole had slapped on these chains that blocked him from shifting. Howls just brought that woman. The one with the beautiful face, who talked sweet but was a half rotting corpse. Venom shivered. And then they were throwing people at him. He'd gone from Creep Show, straight into The Twilight Zone.

He sniffed at the air. She was one of the ones that had come, and from her words, he knew that she was a cold and evil bitch. His muzzle pulled back, baring more teeth as she moved closer. Her words were a lie, just like the others who wanted to trick him into submitting to something degrading for their entertainment. Jumping forward he snapped his jaws on her arm and glared at her. 'If you want it back, get me the fuck out of here now. I swear to God, I'll rip it off.'

"God damn!" Kara barked, gritting her teeth against the pain that raced up her arm. Breathing through it, she opened her eyes and met the glowing golden orbs that were all in. He had nothing left to lose, and he knew it. There was no fiercer opponent than that. She nodded. 'That's the plan, Big Guy. Brock asked me to take you back home.' She was going to fucking kill Loki if she lived through this.

'Liar!' Venom roared. The Navarro clan would never lower themselves to associate with the vile trash that stood before him.

'Fine. Don't believe me, but if I'm lying, why would I do this?' Kara snapped her fingers and the chains that bound the wolf clattered to the floor. 'We can argue some more, you can rip me apart, or we can leave. It's your call. You're the one with a mouthful of me. You're calling the shots. Look at me, I brought no weapons.'

'Tricks," Venom hissed through mindlink, his eyes narrowing when the chains fell away, and he felt his magic return. He tried to ghost out, but couldn't. He was going to need her help if he wanted to go back home, but he wasn't sure that she wouldn't take him somewhere worse. 'Why would one of you, help me?'

"You're not Fenrir. You should not be here," Kara said out loud and reached up to stroke his muzzle, ignoring the tightening of his jaw and the growl. 'Because it matters to a bear that I care about. Don't judge us all by one bad example.'

'I heard you before when you pushed those people in here to die. He's not the only bad example.'

Kara smiled. The wolf had a point. 'True. But it's, either trust me just a little, or stay here. You don't have to let go. Keep the upper hand, if you want. I'll ghost us to a cell at The Pit.'

Venom snorted. Just when he was starting to think she might help him. 'Another cell,' his tone was flat.

'Just until I know you're not going to eat a mess of folks that I don't hate. Yes, a cell. If you glass half full it, you can call for the others once we're there. If I'm not what I say I am, they will let you out and leave me in. Tell me I'm wrong?' The pain lancing through her arm was getting harder to ignore.

He listened, and he wasn't buying most of it, but she was right about the people back home. Alpha Pride wouldn't care what kind of a Goddess she was. If she was dangerous, they'd take her out or die trying. And he was out of options. 'Fine, but I'm not letting go of you until I'm free. One twitch that I don't like and we'll see how immortal you really are. Understood?'

Kara bit her tongue against the smart-ass remarks that balanced on the tip. 'Understood. Ready?' She waited for the wolf's nod, which hurt like a bitch and yanked her to slam her knees against the stone floor with a cracking sound. Kara growled and shot the wolf a dirty look. He was lucky that he meant something to Brock or she'd just fry his furry ass.

432

The cell wavered around them like the air over hot asphalt and was replaced by a better lit and homier cell in the basement of The Pit. Venom scented the air to decide if it was another trick. He smelled bear, coyote, lion, panther, wolverine and booze. It smelled right. Still, he concentrated to be sure. He wasn't falling for any bullshit this time or letting his hostage go.

"Either let go or call in the cavalry because one more clench of those chompers of yours and I'm losing an arm." Kara's hand was cold and numb, and the blood that was trailing down Venom's chin was spurting in time with her heartbeat.

Venom loosened his jaws and was about to do just that when he spotted Bart coming down the stairs. 'Gimme a hand, Bear.' His legs almost sagged in relief. He was home.

Bart's head turned as he tried to locate who was mindlinking him. He spotted Kara on her knees and a giant wolf staring at him over her shoulder. "Venom?" That's what the scents told him. Though they didn't do shit to explain why he and Kara were in a cell and why he could smell blood and pain. "Why you in a cage, Wolf?"

Venom chuckled and dropped Kara's arm, shifting to his human form and ghosting on jeans and a t-shirt. "Long story, Bear." He wiped the blood from his mouth with the back of his hand and moved closer to the bars. "But good God damn, it's good to be home."

"Let me get the keys." Bart jogged down the hall toward the portal and sprung the hidden wall safe, disguised as just another brick in the wall and fished out the keys, returning to open the door for Venom. "Go get something to drink and I'll be up in a second." Bart stepped back and let Venom pass before he stepped inside and closed the door again, looking down at Kara, who was still on her knees. "After I have a word with the Valkyrie.

Venom arched a brow but didn't ask what had a bee in the bear's bonnet. "See you up there. Jager, right?"

433

"You know it," Bart nodded, not looking away from Kara. "You and me. We've got to talk."

Kara rolled her head back to look up at the bear that looked like Brock but wasn't and cradled her arm to her chest. "Can we make it quick, before I bleed out?" She could feel herself weakening, and that was the only reason she wasn't forcing herself to her feet to meet him eye to eye.

"Fine. Short version. If you're playing with my brother and he gets hurt, I will take you out." Bart crossed his arms over his chest. "Or you could just cut the shit, since you seem to like to play the flavor of the month game, and leave him the fuck alone now."

Kara blinked at him. She wanted to laugh, but she had a feeling that would just draw this out, and she needed to go stitch herself up. "I'll take option one." She splayed her good hand on the floor and used it to push herself to her feet. Her left kneecap crunched, making her hop and shift her weight to her right leg. "We done here?"

"No. I'm serious. I don't care what it takes. I won't let you do to Brock what you did to Dane."

Kara blinked at him. *What she'd done to Dane? What the fuck was this bear on?* "I heard you, now get out of my way," Kara said tightly and began limping for the door. She stopped when Bart held his ground. "Look, I don't know what your problem is, and I don't care. Brock is a grown ass bear, and as long as he wants me around, I'm not leaving. So, put your dick away, I'm not impressed." She gave him a second to move and sighed, tossing him aside with the flick of her good wrist. "Nice talk. Later."

Bart landed on the cot, wondering how close he'd come to being a bloodstain on the wall as he watched her limp out of the cell and disappear.

Chapter 46

Kara was trying to remember that Bart was Brock's brother and that it was wrong to kill him, but as she appeared in the bar's bathroom and her knee locked up with that first step, it wasn't easy. She limped to the vanity, glad that Bree was back and seemed to be making sure the restrooms were being cleaned. She banged the paper towel holder until she had a long tail of them hanging from the machine and ripped them off. She tucked them under her arm before waving the bitten arm around the faucet. She growled as the motion sensor seemed determined to ignore her and when it did work, the water ran until she put her arm under it and then cut off.

"Bloody fucking hell," Kara growled, giving up and wrapping the paper towels around her bitten arm and pulling her sleeve down to cover it. She wasn't sure where Brock was. He could be with Salvation, Reese or anyone really. No matter what, her first priority was to make sure that he was okay and let him know that they were right. Then she could worry about getting her med kit from under the sink in his room.

Brock sighed and was about to leave his room when his brother's voice filled his head.

'Your woman has an attitude problem.' Bart mindlinked his brother as he left the cell.

435

Brock perked up, that must mean Kara was back. 'What did you do to her? Right now, is not the best time to piss her off.' Brock linked back.

'Oh, sure. I did something.'

'Brother, I know you.' Brock replied as he started to pace again. Why hadn't she come back to the room? 'Is she okay?' He asked Bart.

'She was bleeding and holding her arm,' Bart mindlinked, going back to his post.

Stepping out of the bathroom, Kara grunted when she had to jump back to get out of the way of a waitress with a tray loaded with drinks. "Not my fucking day," she grumbled under her breath and limped to the bar.

Ripper looked her up and down, arched a brow and pulled a bottle of Patron off the shelf to shove into her hand. "You need a hand, or you got this Karbear?"

"Thanks," she said holding up the heavy square bottle. "Seen Brock?" She ignored his question and leaned her hip against a stool.

He shook his head no. "Not for a while. Maybe an hour ago he went downstairs. Brax isn't in the kitchen if you need a place to ghost." He eyed the growing maroon stain on her shirt and then looked back to her face.

"Thanks again," she smiled softly. She missed the talks that she and the leopard used to have. Grimacing as she got fully upright again, she hobbled toward the kitchen, only to feel Ripper's arm around her waist as he helped her through the saloon style doors.

"We need to make time to catch up, soon. Okay?" He stepped back, ready to jump forward if she wobbled.

"You're right. We do." She grinned. "But I'm gonna go deal with this first."

"Solid plan. Who knew you could come up with one of those?" Ripper teased with a grin.

Kara made a face at him and ghosted outside Brock's door. If he was dealing with shit, she didn't want to just barge in, so she tapped the bottle against the door instead.

436

Brock bolted to the door and pulled it open to see her standing there. "Cher, what the hell happened?" He asked letting her inside. He took the bottle of Patron from her. "Sit down, and I'll get the kit," he said once she was inside and the door was shut behind her.

She watched the Patron go away and sighed as she hopped inside and dropped into a chair. "The good news is that Venom is back. The bad news is that he's a bitey little bastard and I might have tossed your brother across the room a little." Kara peeled up her sleeve and began unwrapping the scratchy brown paper towels from her arm, wadding them up and looking for a place to set them down. Not seeing anything that she wanted to have to clean later, she ghosted them into the trash, although she'd considered putting them in Bart's private cookie jar. "Other than that, everything went smooth."

Brock put the bottle on the coffee table and got her first aid kit from under the sink in the bathroom. "I wouldn't call that smoothly." He said when he was returning. He knelt in front of her with the kit and opened it. "I spoke with Salvation and Reese," he said pulling out antiseptic and bandages.

"How did that go?" She watched him calmly unpacking the kit and reached out to tuck the hair in his face behind his ear to just enjoy looking at him for a moment. *Yeah, Bart had another thing coming if he thought he could chase her away from her bear.*

He spoke as he worked to patch her up. "Salvation is sending someone to help with the portal he said he would handle the rest himself. And I let Reese know what was going on. We are keeping the loop small on this. Only AP and portal keepers. If anything goes sideways, we are supposed to tell Salvation." He sat back on his heels once she was patched up and looked up at her. "So far everything has been normal other than Reese got a bit weird when she came into the room. She said something about it felt like someone walked on her grave."

437

Kara let the sound of his voice sooth her as she tried her best to ignore the iodine chewing a hole through her arm. "Small is good. No need to have the masses doing something stupid." Her brow arched at what Reese had said. "Yeah, that's weird. I wonder if she's feeling the energies shift. I hope not, but this hasn't happened before, so who knows what will come of it?" She ground her teeth together and fought the urge to shake the foul brownish stuff from her skin. The bandage seemed to help a little, but it still felt like battery acid in the punctures.

Brock put the kit down and opened the Patron for her. He knew how she liked it. After all the times he'd made it for her, it was easy. He made her a drink and kissed her forehead as he handed her the glass. "I didn't ask any more about it. She said it as she was coming in. Did you feel anything out in the hall?" He asked cleaning up the mess and getting up to put it away.

She shook her head no, smiling at his lips on her face and then took a long drink. "I wasn't there very long."

As he went into the bathroom, the air in there seemed to shudder. The sink, flush and shower had shimmered before it disappeared completely. Brock stopped short. The face of some creature blurred into focus and popped out of the air like some weird fun house trick. It screeched at him. The scream was so loud, and the force of it knocked him back onto his ass. "The hell?" He growled, staring into the bathroom from the floor. Brock blinked. The face was gone. He wasn't sure if Kara heard it or if it was just him. Maybe his imagination was fucking with him.

A weird surge blasted through the air, causing Kara's hand to spasm and drop her glass to break on the floor. Instinct had her on her feet and her sword in her good hand. Turning at the screech, she leaped forward, but her knee wasn't playing fair when it locked, forcing her to bite back a string of curses that would make the guys at the bar blush. She pushed forward, her only thought was keeping Brock safe. Kara tripped over him when he landed at her feet but

438

regained her balance and planted her boots with his thighs between them in time to see the thing disappear with a tiny popping noise. "I guess it's starting," she sighed and waved her hand through the doorway, to be sure it was gone.

Brock looked up at her, standing over him, ready for battle. "Yes, I would say so. I have no idea what the hell that was." He got to his feet and looked at her drink on the floor. "Let's try this again." He cleaned up the mess and put the kit away still leery that the thing might pop out at him. He got her another drink and held it out to her. She was still holding the sword in her hand. "Cher?" He said shaking the glass at her. The ice made a clinking sound.

It was a hard choice. Her sword or that yummy glass of pain be gone. "You don't play fair." Kara narrowed her eyes and slowly lowered the sword to the coffee table where she could grab it if needed. Eyeing it, she also ghosted in the Hammer that seemed to have a fondness for her bear. Only then did she reach out for the glass and leaned against him. She wondered if she could wrap him in armor twenty-four-seven because the idea of him getting hurt filled her stomach with ice. "I'd feel better if you kept that nearby," she nodded toward Thor's hammer.

Brock glanced at the hammer. "If that's what you want Cher, then I'll do it." He took a seat on the sofa. "So, what's next? Other than the end of the world."

"I don't know." Kara plopped down beside him, holding out her drink so that it didn't spill. "I'm gonna have to call out Loki on his shit, but I'm gonna wait until I can stand and look menacing." She grinned and sipped the tequila, groaning happily at the slow burn as it made its way to her stomach. "Have you told your family?" She eyed him over the glass. "Oh, and Bart gave me the 'if you hurt my brother, I'll take you out' talk." She rolled her eyes although it kind of warmed her that Brock's brother was looking out for him. That must be nice. Hers either managed to get her trapped in Hell or destroyed the world.

439

"I was about to tell them when you came back. That explains why he said you have an attitude problem. I asked what he did to you." Brock chuckled and rubbed her thigh. "Let's use the element of surprise with Loki. I would really like to ram my fist through his face."

"I have an attitude problem? Me?" She scoffed and then shrugged. "Could be true and I'm on board with taking his head off." Kara leaned her head on his shoulder. "Don't let me being back, stop you, Babes. All that has changed is that we know it's true."

He smiled. "No, not you." Brock thought about going to tell his family. "Would you want to come with me? So you can answer questions they might have. If not, that's okay, I get it. My siblings, as you already know, are a bit gruff."

Kara grinned up at him. "They don't scare me. Bring on the big bad bears." She stretched up and kissed his cheek.

"My brothers are not the ones to watch out for. Bree is the one that'll sneak up on you, and you'll be on your ass before you know it. My sister has ninja skills. Or maybe we're just old and slow." Brock smiled and then laughed when he remembered something from their training as cubs, about knowing your opponent. As their sister, Bree knew them well.

"Makes you easier to catch though." She grinned up at him. "Just tell me when, Babes, and help me up. Then, I'm ready when you are."

Brock helped her up. "Let's get this over with because we don't need anyone fighting blind." He sighed, taking her hand.

"You are very wise." Kara grinned and laced her fingers with his, not putting down her glass.

He ghosted them into the store room that was closed to everyone but the staff. It held empty boxes and other things. Once they appeared, he opened the door for her. "Ladies first." Brock waited for her to hobble through, before closing the door and taking her hand again as he mindlinked his siblings to meet them at the portal. "We're meeting them there, Cher." He hoped they didn't freak out.

Gritting her teeth, Kara forced herself not to limp and waited for him to join her, not letting his hand go. Touching him, no matter how slight, made her feel better. "Makes sense, if Sal thinks it's an issue, we don't want to leave it unguarded for even a second."

Kara growled when they arrived at the stairs that led to the basement. Her knee and stairs weren't going to be fun. Grudgingly, she downed the rest of her drink and ghosted away the glass. Kara smiled softly as Brock slowed his pace to allow her to use the rail and his arm to make her way down the steps.

Brock wanted to carry her but knew that she was stubborn and wanted to face his brothers on her own two feet. It took longer than normal to reach the old stone floor, but a little more time to think wasn't a bad thing. Looking her over to be sure that she was okay, he led Kara past the cells and down the long maze of halls. It was strange to have someone by his side when things were bad. Stranger that he knew that she had his back. A smile curled at his lips. It was something that he could get used to.

To most people, it looked like any other hallway. Bart leaned against the wall at the end. Above him, there was a sign that read, VIP SECTION. If anyone made it past Bart, one of two things would happen. Humans would find a dead end with a small door that opened to another set of stairs that led to the side alley. It was warded, so a human's memory would be wiped clean of stepping foot in the basement. Any supernatural being would be ghosted into a secret room with doors on every wall. Only the Navarros knew which ones went where. Choosing the wrong one almost always led to death, the type and how painful was dictated by the being's worst fears. The portal to the mountain wasn't something to play with.

Kara eyed Bart and stifled the growl that rolled in the back of her throat. This was not the time or the place for

441

petty bullshit. She leaned on Brock to take some of the weight from her knee and waited. She chose to ignore Bart's snort and eye roll and turned her head when she heard Brax's bitching coming closer.

Brax and Beyer didn't understand why they needed to meet at the portal when they were about to leave for a trip to the swamp camp for a few days. "This is some bullshit. It better not take long," Brax muttered, coming around the corner.

Bree trailed behind her brothers. As she followed them down the hall and around the corner, she saw shimmers of colors and felt sparks of cold. She slowed. Her brothers didn't seem to notice anything out of the norm as Brax continued to complain. When Bree jogged to catch up, something cold shot through her. She looked down her legs, and her eyes flared. She could see through her feet. They were still there but only as a pale shadow. Staring, she walked into Brax.

"Excuse you, Miss. Pushy. Jesus!" Brax growled when his sister slammed into him.

Kara shivered. The air seemed to bounce between frigid and scorching. Sweat broke across her forehead, and she swore she could feel ice crystals form before they melted again to run down her face. She dropped Brock's hand and ghosted in her sword.

Bart's eyes bugged out. "What? You wanted everyone here to see you kill me? I stand by what I said," he snarled at her.

Beyer saw the sword. "Whoa! Now come on, kill the loud mouthed one. Leave the rest of us alone." He stared, wide-eyed at Kara and the sword.

Brock sighed. "She isn't going to hurt anyone. Something is coming, and we all need to be ready."

Bree followed Brax as he moved around Beyer. "Yes. Coming down the hall, something odd happened," Bree said.

"Something happened that has messed with the balance of things. Salvation is sending someone to help us protect the portal." Brock didn't wanna blurt everything out, in case one of Loki's spies was lurking. 'Loki set his son free and had Venom locked away in Asgard. Kara released him, and he attacked her, that's why she's hurt. I have no idea what this will do to things here. Some weird stuff has already happened. Reese is fully aware.' He mindlinked his siblings and Kara.

Bart snorted again. "And here I thought she was trying to pick him up and it got rough when she wouldn't take no for an answer," the sarcasm was heavy in his voice.

Kara glanced up at Brock. "I don't have to save him, do I?"

"Don't do me any favors, Sweetheart," Bart smiled.

"Maybe my coming with you to explain this, was a mistake." Kara sighed and hopped back to lean against the wall. "Pretend I'm not here."

Brock growled at his brother. "Knock it off, asshole. This is serious. We're all in danger. Not just us, but the whole world if we don't figure out how to fix it." Brock's voice grew deeper, and his nostrils flared.

Bree knew what that meant. She put herself in between her brothers. "Kara, please explain what this means from your standpoint. Ignore Bart. Please, for me. How can I help?" She asked in a soft tone trying to help defuse the situation.

Kara sighed. "Okay. A quick history of the fucked up that's my family. I'm sure you've all heard of Fenrir. The wolf son of Loki, blah, blah, blah. What the books and the movies don't tell you is that Fen wasn't always a prisoner. He grew up with me, we played, and he is one of the sweetest people I know. Little did we know that he is the one who will bring about Ragnarok, the end of everything, by killing my father. I don't think Loki did it to end anything other than Fen being trapped in a cold dark cell. I think he just wanted his son to see the sun again and have a life, but it's not that simple." She looked around and then dropped her eyes to the floor. "I don't know exactly WHAT he did yet, but my guess is that he knocked the scale off balance or caused a crack in multiple realities. I'm not sure what's coming, but it's all bad. The old ones talked about the barriers between worlds thinning or breaking and the things that were locked away finding freedom like Fenrir has." She shrugged. "That's all I know, and it's a whole lot of nothing."

Bree listened to what Kara said, and her jaw went slack. "My vision was right. Holy shit," she whispered.

Brax and Beyer turned to her. "What?" They asked their sister in unison.

Bree's face turned red. "I had a dream or vision about a wolf in a cage. The spirits in my dream told me it would be free, and hell would walk the earth."

Brock looked from Kara to Bree.

Bart glowered at Kara. "What's next, a rain of toads?" He felt like this was a test to see if he went ape shit.

"I could arrange it, just for you, Bear." Kara smiled back tightly before dismissing him and turning back to Bree. "Did they say how, Bree? If we can be ready for it, maybe we won't lose as many." Without a doubt, they would lose some, but Kara's goal was to keep the body count low. She shivered as the temperature went schizophrenic again.

Bree tried to remember her vision or whatever it was. "There was a large pit. It was old, and it opened up to vomit out souls and darkness." The memories made her shiver inside. "The smell was like death itself. The spirits in my dream kept saying something about a sceadugenga or something I couldn't make it out entirely." Bree remembered the flashes of it. It was giant and ugly.

Kara made a face. Yeah, that sounded like a carnival ride she'd rather miss, and she was clueless to what that word might be or mean. "I'm going to kill my brother," she muttered under her breath.

"Well, isn't that just grand," Beyer groaned.

"I think we need to start keeping ourselves armed," Brax said.

Brock put his hands up. "Now, wait a moment. We can't just start acting all crazy before we know all the facts. We do not want a mass panic. This needs to stay with us and AP. We have humans to think about."

Bart growled. "All the more reason to be armed."

"Course you'd side with him," Brock said in a growl.

"Big picture, brother mine," Bart answered through clenched teeth.

Kara twitched her lips back and forth, hating what she was about to say. "They're right Brock. I'm not saying that everyone should carry something big and obvious, but they need to be able to defend themselves. Knives. Tasers. Weapons. Most of AP is packing something, so it won't seem out of place if you are too." She winced as he turned his eyes on her and Bart laughed. "You know damn well, that you're going to feel responsible if they need one and don't have it." She shrugged. "Just my opinion. Not my monkey. Not my circus."

Brax looked at her for a long moment. "But it is your monkey and your circus, Viking. If your brother hadn't done this, there wouldn't be a problem. I'll arm myself, and no one will tell me not too. Now, if this little meeting is over, Beyer and I have shit to do." Brax turned to leave. He didn't give them time to stop him. He was sick to death of other people fucking up his life.

Beyer followed his brother as he left. Leaving Bree, Bart, Kara and Brock there.

Bart saw a group humans coming down the hall. "Sorry, this place is off limits." He pointed to the sign above their heads. The people glared at him. "Move it along, nothing to see here," Bart waved them away.

"I'm not saving him, either," Kara growled and crossed her arms over her chest. "This has been fun, but I think I'm over it for today." She started down the hall, her limp slightly better and glared at the humans. "Don't make me show you the way. I'm not in the mood to play nice." One opened his mouth to say something, smart ass. Kara could

445

feel it coming off the kid in waves. He didn't get the chance. She shoved the heel of her hand into his nose, breaking it. "Don't say I didn't warn you. Now go. Bleed somewhere else."

Brock watched her leave, wincing at the shot the human took and the blood that erupted from his nose. "Bree, talk to your brother," he sighed before chasing after Kara.

Bree slapped Bart in the head. "Mom should have eaten you," she said before leaving.

"Cher, wait up!" Brock called after Kara. He caught up and scooped her into his arms. "Let me help you," he said, carrying her. "I'm sorry about my brothers. You don't have to save them. We could feed them to the gators if you'd like."

"Brax is right, and that pisses me off, but he's still gator food." She sighed and leaned her head against Brock's shoulder and whispered, "I was going for an epic exit, but this is good too."

"You stormed off like a pro, but like the love-sick puppy, I am, I don't wanna be left behind. This way, I've got you with me." He kissed her cheek. "Wanna leave a horse head in his bed?" He teased.

Kara grinned and circled his neck with her arms. "You read my mind."

Chapter 47

Sipping from the to-go cup she'd bought at one of the many cafes in the French Quarter, Kara walked through the crowded sidewalks, weaving between the people while the excited chatter of tourists bombarded her from every direction. Shaking her head, she chuckled, doubting that they would be so cheerful if they knew all of the beings that walked among them and that most saw humans as an annoyance or a meal. Sliding her free hand into the front pocket of her jeans, she stepped aside to let a stroller pass, smiling softly at the gurgling babe inside, wrapped in nothing but baby blue.

The heels of her boots clicked on the pavement once mother and child had passed and her mind wandered so far that she didn't notice the man who fell into step beside her until he touched her arm. Swinging her head and giving a fuck off look that made the attractive, well-groomed man take a step back, she slid her thumb through her belt loop instead of striking his nose with the heel of her hand. That was her usual 'How do you do' when folks she didn't know laid hands on her. "Can I help you with something?" *Like a broken limb?* She arched a brow and stared him down.

The male stammered, raking a nervous hand through his dark curls and his ice blue eyes crinkled at the corners with his smile. He was pretty if you looked past the stink of human that clung to him. And no matter how pretty he was, he left Kara cold. He had nothing on Brock. She almost smiled when he closed his eyes, muttered an old curse in Norwegian and shook his head before meeting her gaze again. "Please forgive my intrusion, but you're Kara. Aren't you?"

Kara's eyes narrowed and any amusement that may have been peeking through vanished. "Who's asking?" Her tone was bored as she sipped her coffee and considered if this human needed to die or was just a patron from the bar.

"Ulrich." He held out his hand, then slowly lowered it when all she did was stare at it and arch an annoyed brow. "I have a problem and a mutual friend, said that you might be able to help me."

"I think you have the wrong person." Kara shook her head and started walking again, groaning her annoyance when he fell in beside her like a well-trained dog. Rolling her eyes, she glanced sideways at him and angled her shoulders to slide between two clusters of people on the sidewalk. "Look. I don't have many friends, and I don't help the living. Die heroically, and then you're my problem. Until then? I'm not your girl. Go away."

"I'm and Omega Delta scholar," Ulrich said in a low voice, his eyes darting around to the people milling around them. "With a demon on my ass."

Kara laughed. "As I said kid, not my gig." She paused to check the display window of a shoe store when a pair of boots destined to be hers caught her eye. "I thought you had people for this kind of thing."

"We do, but they are busy with some big whatever that I'm not important enough to know about." He growled and rolled his eyes at the display. "Ripper, from The Pit, said you might be able to help."

She shrugged and started walking again. "Funny. He didn't mention you." Gently, Kara used her boot to push away a small pug that had taken an interest in how her leg smelled. Living at The Pit, she was a walking smorgasbord of scents, and this happened more than she'd like to admit.

Sighing heavily, she turned her head and tried not to gag at the hopeful expression on Ulrich's face. Kara was going to kill Ripper when she saw him. "Who did you piss off and what kind of demon are we talking?"

"I defended myself." Ulrich raked his hand through his hair again. He turned his pleading eyes on her before they darted to the small oasis of green, littered with benches, across the street, his tan skin going pale. "Who knew that its mother was a Gorgon and would take it personally?"

Kara snorted. "Funny how that shit happens, eh?" She followed his gaze across the street. Kara flexed her hand grimacing at the twinges in her mostly healed wrist. "If looks could kill, and with a Gorgon they can, you're gonna be in need of a body bag." Stopping, she leaned against the brick façade of the bakery and inhaled the delicious scents that hung heavy in the air. She should get something and take it back home with her. "If she's still at her post, I don't get why you're bothering me with this."

"That's the problem. I think she's following me, just waiting for me to slip up and turn me to stone." He followed Kara inside when she shook her head, deciding that he was out of his mind. "You are really ordering pastries when a Gorgon is loose in NOLA?" Ulrich gaped, reminding her of a goldfish in a bowl.

Shrugging, Kara read the menu board and gave her order to the friendly bear on the other side of the glass case full of deliciousness that made her mouth water. "The Ursus Major Special. Two, please. To go." Kara ignored the annoying human, pulled the cash out of her pocket and dropped the bills pushed back at her into the tip jar beside the register. "Thank you." Kara smiled at the pretty blond bear and tucked the boxes under her arm, almost running into the human that was in her way. "You're paranoid. Why are you still here?" She pushed him away with the hand that held her coffee, splashing some of it onto the front of his crisp white button up. "Get away from me, kid. You bother me." She left the shop, looking for a place to ghost out.

"You're really not going to help me?" Ulrich shadowed her before stepping directly into her path and trying to make her stop.

"You're delusional. Look around. Green and scaly doesn't exactly blend in, even here." She rolled her eyes and tried to resist the urge to bolt his stupid ass. "Now get out of my way before I demonstrate the difference between what I am and what you are." Kara shook her head and started walking again when he dropped his gaze to the sidewalk and stepped back out of her way. "About fucking time. Be sure to tell your doyen about this. I'm sure they could use the laugh," Kara threw back over her shoulder and turned down an alley. She stopped and listened to be sure that the pesky human had given up.

A hiss from deeper in the shadows drew her attention to the row of dented and scarred construction dumpsters. Arching a brow, Kara downed the rest of her coffee and ghosted the cup into the steel rectangle, watching and listening carefully as the wax coated paper bounced over the trash inside. Glancing behind her to be sure she was alone, Kara walked slowly forward. The hair on the back of her neck stood. Something was hiding back there. Normally, she would enjoy a little sparring match, but she had pastries, and she was hungry. It was not the time to play.

Passing the first dumpster, Kara saw nothing. Passing the second, the shadows grew darker, and the hissing became louder. Oh yeah, there was definitely something hiding back there. Edging forward cautiously, Kara's eyes flared at the glowing red eyes that met hers. Okay, and the green scaly skin wasn't what she'd been expecting either. "The fucking OD recruit wasn't full of shit, after all." She laughed, but it was short lived when the Gorgon bore its teeth and lunged at her. Shaking her head, Kara sent a bolt into its chest. "I don't have time for this," she growled at the reptilian female that flew back and slid down the wall twitching on the broken pavement in a puddle of something nasty that dripped from the dumpster.

Kara growled. She couldn't leave the damned thing here to be discovered or turn some poor unsuspecting male to stone. Shaking her head, she manifested her sword and stepped closer, avoiding the puddle of rankness and swung the blade. "Like a hot knife through butter." She grinned as the Gorgon's head slid off its severed neck and fell into its lap. Kara watched for a few moments, hoping it would turn into dust or something. She had a genuine appreciation for the self-cleaning demons at times like this. "Figures," she grumbled and ghosted the body back to the gates that separated and protected the Shadowlands from the pit of Niflheim where it belonged, so it could be attended to by loved ones if it had any.

Looking around once more for prying eyes, Kara ghosted home to deliver the goodies and the bad news. Omega Delta was noticing the weird happenings that were popping up everywhere and soon, the humans would too.

Chapter 48

Dane tossed and turned, churning his neatly made bed into a pile of twisted blankets and sheets. He was forgetting something. Something important. He was exhausted. His mind wouldn't quit, chattering in a nonstop loop, and what it was trying to tell him was like smoke through his fingers. He could touch it, but holding on, was impossible.

Growling, he threw off the blankets and navigated his apartment from memory, finding himself in the bathroom, leaning his hands on the basin with his head hanging over his chest. *What was it? Did shifters get Alzheimer's? Dementia? Maybe it was just insanity, finally needling into his gray matter and twisting everything.* Dane turned on the faucet and splashed water on his face. "Fuck," he growled as the iciness hit his skin. One more thing that he'd forgotten. It took a few minutes for the water here to warm up. *'That was never a problem at her place.'* His head tilted.

He could see it in his head. The labradorite counter that held the stone bowl of a sink. The warm sage walls and soft plush towels the color of slate hung over the brushed nickel bars. The feel of the softness, wicking the moisture from his skin felt like velvet. The warm hand on his chest as nails lightly scraped the nape of his neck. Goosebumps springing up at the touch as heat rolled through his body, stirring his lion and making them both purr. Laughing blue eyes, the color of the sky, marred only by the trace of hazel, his hazel, around the pupils. Soft lips that smiled and dropped kisses on his skin. Hair the color of corn silk that tickled his flesh and felt like heaven when he curled it around his fingers.

Bits and pieces. What he wouldn't give for the full picture of this female that haunted him. She was his. He was hers. He felt it all the way to the marrow of his bones, but he had no clue who she was or why she was torturing him. A laugh echoed inside his head, pulling a purr from his chest. It was soft, delicate and it made Dane buzz with anticipation as his lion chuffed with contentment. It was the sound of being... "Home." Dane jumped at the sound of his own voice.

Growling again, he flipped on the light, dragging him back to his tiny, lonely, bare bones bathroom. He wiped his dripping face on a towel that he yanked off the hook on the back of the door, wincing at the scratchiness of the cheap terry cloth. Shaking his head, he balled up the towel and dropped it into the basin. Leaning close to the mirror to eyeball his reflection. His jaw was sprinkled with a few days of not shaving, and his eyes were the same mix of gold and gray that they had always been, though they did look a little sunken and bruised. '*Not always*,' a voice whispered in the back of his mind.

They had been different. He'd been different, and it was all because of the ghost woman who haunted him. Dane's head turned at the sound of a door closing in the hall. '*Go. Now,*' the lion inside him growled. Dane hesitated, but not for long. He grabbed his jeans off the floor, yanked them up his thighs and shoved himself inside, realizing that his dick was hard and fastening them with a grunt. They pinched, but he didn't have time to think about it. He grabbed a shirt and stepped out into the hall.

His eyes closed at the scent that filled the corridor, purring as it rolled over the organ in the back of his throat that allowed him to taste it. It was almost perfect. Like pure sunshine after a summer rain. His lion growled. It did not

453

like the woodiness of bear that tainted its purity. Dane followed his nose, not because he had to, but because he could not get enough of that scent. His feet already knew where they were going. To the roof, where the female would be sitting on the ledge and looking out over the city like a guardian angel in the dark.

At the top of the stairs, he pushed the door open, and there she sat, right where he knew she would be, although he had no idea how he knew. Dane froze. *What was he supposed to say? "Sorry that I've been stalking you, but I can't control my lion?" Yeah, that didn't sound pathetic or crazy.* His eyes closed and the hand that he wanted to face plant into, ran through his hair.

"The city is beautiful at night. Isn't it?"

Her voice broke through his mental rant and muscles that he hadn't realized were coiled tight, relaxed. Stepping onto the roof, he let the door whisper shut behind him and shrugged on the shirt in his hand. Dane walked closer to the edge slowly, closer to her, taking it all in. "It really is."

Kara smiled and glanced up at him. A wave of sadness washed over her, but she tried to ignore it. "Trouble sleeping?" She pulled her knees to her chest and turned to see him better.

"Yes," Dane lowered his ass to the raised ledge. "For days." His eyes swept over her face, putting together the flashes of memory into perfection. It was her. "How about you?"

She shrugged. "Nightmares are kicking my ass tonight." Kara shook her hair back and looked down at her bare feet. "It all takes some getting used to, doesn't it?"

Dane nodded, swinging one leg over the edge and using his hands to hitch himself closer to her. He was trying not to purr and keep his lion in check. It wanted to rub on her and cover the bear's scent with his own. "I think I'm losing my shit."

"Do you want to talk about it, Big Guy?" She snorted and shook her head. "You used to. I know you don't remember."

He watched her, and the scent of her sadness and the salty air of threatening tears made him feel better. Even if it also confused him. The word was that she was with Brock now. Hell, she'd come from the bear's room and wore his scent like a perfume. Still, knowing that losing him hurt her, was a soothing balm. "We spent a lot of time together?"

"We were mates for almost a year." She nodded and hugged her knees to her chest, resting her chin on them as she looked up at him. "It's hard to just forget what you're used to. I'm here to listen, Dane. I always will be."

"You loved me?" He brushed back the hair that fell over her face, his brow wrinkling at how familiar it felt.

"Yes." Her voice was rough before she cleared her throat. "Tell me what's got you worried."

He sat back as he watched her and then put his hands on the ledge between his thighs and leaned his weight on them. "I wish I remembered. I get flashes and that déjà vu shit. Mostly I can feel it all there, but just out of reach. I'm losing track of what's real, what isn't and what happened, but I can't remember. Add in not sleeping, and I'm close to snapping like a cheap plastic toy."

Kara listened and chewed her bottom lip. This was her fault. "It sounds like it's all coming back to you." She gave him a weak smile and rubbed her arms, suddenly feeling cold. "What if knowing would drive you mad?"

"Not knowing's not really fostering good mental health." He arched a brow, trying to concentrate over the purr of his lion. "What do you know, Kara?"

She let go of her legs and pushed both hands through her hair. *Should she tell him?* Her chest ached as she met his worried hazel eyes. She'd never seen fear in Dane and seeing it now, crushed her. Sighing, she closed her eyes. "I don't know everything."

455

Dane hitched closer and reached out to pull one of her hands from her hair, noticing the tan line where a ring had been. His thumb rubbed the pale strip of skin. "Please. I got left with nothing. I need this."

Kara groaned and stared at her hand in his. Tears bit at the backs of her eyes and white-hot fury at what had been taken from them flooded her veins. "It's not fair." She wiped at her eyes with the back of her free hand.

"No," Dane agreed. "But it's the hand we were dealt, Sweetness."

She smiled softly and nodded. "Yeah. It all started when we died." She snorted as his brows jumped. "Our brilliant plan that combining our life forces would keep you alive had a major flaw. If they got you, it took us both out." She shook her head and smiled. "Maybe making decisions after half a keg of mead wasn't the best way to go."

Getting over the shock that she hadn't only been his mate, but had allowed them to bond, he laughed. Her humor was entertaining, and he began to understand how they could have worked. He chuckled. "Why mess with a tried and true method?"

Kara laughed. "That's what you said then, too." It hurt, being here with him. "Unfortunately, we both went to different versions of hell. After Dad finally got around to breaking me free from mine, I began searching for you. We found you in the Shadowlands." She watched his face.

Dane whistle low. The Shadowlands, ripe with awful soul sucking beings, was a story that parents told their cubs to keep them in line. It was second only to the stories of Damion Mangus. Aka, the Panther Bogyman. "It's real?" He had to concentrate to quiet his mind. "You got me out?"

Kara shook her head no. "I tried. I agreed to stay if he would let you go, but then I got sucked out of there and dumped back here."

A smile crept over his face. *She'd been willing to trade herself for me?* His lion chuffed, wanting to rub on her. "You really did that?" He couldn't keep the awe from his voice. "You cared that much?"

"Yes. You're…" Her voice trailed off, and pain flashed in her blue eyes. "You were my mate. I couldn't leave you there."

"But you can leave me now and take up with the bear?" He winced at the harsh words. He didn't know where they were coming from. "I'm sorry." And he was. He hated seeing the pain that flickered through her features and made her pull her hand away as her spine straightened.

"That's not fair, Dane. You have no idea the shit storm I was dealing with, and he was there for me." She held up her index finger and began ticking her points off by adding another finger. "I went to a hell where I had to kill you, every fucking day, for ten long ass years. I come back, wake up in the morgue, yes with a toe tag, and I can't feel you at all. We both know what that means. I somehow get you back, and you beg me, BEG ME to take the memories that leave you unable to do anything but fucking scream. The cherry on top? Only the memories that involved me were infected and hurting you. So, I got to choose. Watch you shatter mentally or erase me and everything we had. And then, because, yeah, this had been a cake walk, I get to come back here and learn how to let you go without caving to the need to reduce this stupid fucking rock of a planet to ash. News flash, it tore me apart. You got to forget, but I had to remember. So, fuck you and your judgment. I've only made it through because Brock saw a glimmer of something worth saving. Without him? There would be nothing left but rubble."

She was stunning when she was pissed. Fire flashed in her clear blue eyes as her perfect features hardened and her nostrils flared slightly, giving her a wild and feral aura. Dane glanced at the lightning that began to flash and fork through the clear night sky. That was her too, but he didn't know how he knew that. Blood surged to his cock, making it kick as it hardened to be strangled by the denim of his jeans.

457

Pain exploded through his head. His eyes slammed shut, and he had to grab the ledge to hold himself upright as his body tried to curl into the fetal position. "Fuck," he growled through clenched teeth. Images flashed through his head, flooding through his consciousness and ripping at his sanity.

The hand on his arm strengthened him and kept him rooted on the roof top with the Valkyrie even as his mind churned, doing its level best to drag him into the darkness of madness. "Don't let go," he whispered, his knuckles turning white with the death grip he had on the concrete that he felt beginning to give under his hands.

"Never."

Her voice calmed the raging storm taking place between his ears, and he thought he felt her wrapping her arms around him and holding him tight against her. True or not, Dane clung to it, to her, as the scenes of his life with her unfolded and tore his heart to shreds. *Why would she take this from him? Why would she throw him away?* Silk slid over his wet face, sticking and tickling his nose. And then shit got dark.

He remembered the thing forcing its way into his body, twisting his mind and the blood on his hands. Dane choked on the bile that bubbled in his throat as every vile thing the demon had made him do, came back in hi-def clarity. So many screams, begging for mercy and the mangled bodies...

He'd almost been grateful when Salvation's words forced their way through the veil the demon had wrapped and trapped Dane behind. His lion had roared its consent as Salvation explained the risks of separating the beast against its will. It refused to let him go, and he remembered the regret and sorrow in Salvation's voice when he was forced to admit defeat. 'Do it,' Dane had whispered, battling to the surface for a split second and then everything had faded to black.

Dark laughter and the clicking of razor sharp, pointed legs echoed through his head. Dane cried out when his

458

claws punched through the tips of his fingers and sunk into something soft. The smell of blood filled the air, its only competition was her scent, and that was what he clung to as he remembered the Shadowlands. His body that had been little more than a wispy fog. The skitters. Ty's cold eyes and promises. Kara coming for him just before he was cast away. Pain. God, the pain.

Dane opened his eyes and could see nothing. Adrenaline kicked his heart to jackhammer against his sternum as the fear and certainty that he was still trapped there suffocated him. A hand cupped the back of his head sliding through his hair, and soothing murmuring slowly broke through his silent screams. He tightened his arms around the warm body that held him, rocking him gently and forced himself to pull it together. It felt like an old zipper that was missing teeth finally pulling itself closed. "God, Kara," he whispered, realizing that the silk that his face was buried in, was her hair.

"It's going to be okay, Babes." She didn't pull away or stop rocking him.

She was holding him together when his mind was trying to rip him apart. His lion purred, and Dane gave into the impulse to nuzzle her that felt as natural as breathing. His claws retracted, but still, he clung to her. "I'm sorry," Dane whispered into her hair. "I never wanted to hurt you." He wasn't sure if he meant the claws or everything else he had done.

"I know," her broken whisper found his ear.

Dane wasn't sure how long they stayed like that, holding each other. His heart ached at knowing that when he finally let go, it would be the last time that he felt her against him. His lion growled and spit its disagreement and the word '*mine*,' echoed through Dane's head. But she wasn't. Not anymore. She'd given him up to save him. Anger churned in his gut. "It's not fair. You should have left me there."

Kara stiffened and pulled away. "How can you say that?" She didn't understand.

"Because," Dane wiped at his face with his hands and then pushed them through his hair as he sat back. "This is worse."

Her head snapped back as though she'd been slapped and pain filled her eyes, turning them a stormy gray. "Then, I am sorry, Dane. I truly am." Kara slid off the ledge and walked toward the door that would take her back to her bear, wrapping her arms around her middle and letting her shoulders and head sag from the weight of the ache that filled her. "No good deed goes unpunished, right?" She shook her hair back and turned away.

"Yeah," Dane said gruffly to her back. "Something like that." There was an empty pit in his chest that ached to be filled with what had been there before. It ached for her. Without thinking, he ghosted into her path and pulled her into his arms, mashing his lips against hers.

Kara gasped, shocked for a moment and then pushed him away. "What the hell are you doing?"

"I don't know." He reached out and closed his fingers around her wrist, closing his eyes at the warmth of her skin. "Stay with me, Kara. We were good together. We can be again." He tugged her closer, flashing the smile that she'd never been able to resist.

Kara shook her head and cupped his face in her palm. "No. We can't." She slid her thumb over his lips, a smile flickering across hers when he pursed them to kiss it. "You've got to let me go, Dane."

"I can't." He slid his other hand into her hair, tangling the silken strands around his fingers.

"You can. You have to." Her head bowed, and her hand lifted to his chest, to push more space between them. "I'm sorry."

Dane stared at her in disbelief. How could she walk away from him and what they'd had? His lion surged under his skin, tightening his hold on her and walking into her until

460

her back was against the door. Growling low in his chest, he lowered his head to kiss her again.

"Dane, no." Kara sighed, hating that she was hurting him.

"Just one, Karbear." He brushed his lips over hers, and a jolt of lust kicked through him, pulling him to her and pressing her against the steel door. He grunted when he was tossed backward and lost his balance, landing on his ass.

"I said no." Her tone was even and her eyes cold. "I'll let you get away with that one, it won't happen again." Kara turned and yanked open the door. "Goodbye, Dane." She slammed the door behind her and began down the stairs. *This shit had to get easier and stop hurting, didn't it?*

Dane stared at the door as it banged shut and braced his elbows on his bent knees, bowing his head.

Brock watched from the shadows. He'd only meant to check on Kara, not to intrude. Which was why he'd stayed hidden, knowing that he should leave, but he couldn't. He watched, fully expecting to see his life circle the bowl. Even when the lion had kissed her, he'd stayed put. She had to decide, and she had. She chose him. Brock Navarro. No one could kick the grin off his face, not until the lion had manhandled his female. When the door slammed, he stepped out into the dim light and crossed his arms over his chest.

"And the hits just keep on coming," Dane growled. Rolling his eyes up to see the bear.

"You need to leave her alone," Brock stated calmly even though his jaw was ticking.

"Why? Because you say so?" Dane snorted.

"No," Brock shook his head. "Because she does." He was trying to be patient, but the lion was pushing it.

"Why do you care? She was my mate! I love her."

"So do I, and I won't let you hurt her any more than you already have."

461

"Let me?" Dane laughed. "You finally growing a set, Navarro? How about you back off MY MATE and let us get back to how life should be?"

Brock shook his head and took a few steps, squatting down so that he was at eye level, but still looming over the lion. "Don't mistake my easy-going nature for weakness. Not where Kara is concerned. She chose me. Respect that. I know you've heard the whispers about what I can do. Don't make me show you. Let it go. Let her go."

"Could you?" Dane arched a brow at the out of character threat. He'd heard the rumors, and after seeing what Brock's siblings could do, he wouldn't be surprised if they were true. Brock's scent reeked of sincerity and the need to protect.

"I did once," Brock growled. "I won't do it again."

Dane answered his growl. "We'll see, Bear."

"Yes," Brock stood. "We will." He turned and went to find Kara, hoping that she'd be waiting for him in their rooms.

Dane dropped his head into his hands, wishing that he'd never remembered her and their life together.

Chapter 49

When Kara woke, the bed beside her was empty and the sheets cool. Brock must have slipped out without her noticing. Her eyes crawled over the ceiling, replaying what had happened with Dane last night. There was so much going on, they didn't need that too. She sighed. Well, if nothing else, he remembered the missions that he'd gone on while they'd been mated and that was necessary experience for the shit storm crashing down around their ears.

Yawning she dragged her legs over the edge of the bed and rolled herself up, scrubbing her eyes with the heels of her hands and blinking away the blur. She felt like she hadn't slept in days, probably because the nightmares were back. Groaning she ghosted a strong cup of coffee into her hand, grimacing at the bitterness. So much had happened in the last twenty-four hours. Dealing with Thor's PITA. Fenrir was who knew where. Dane. Weird shit popping up everywhere. That kid from Omega Delta.

She wondered if Alpha Pride knew about them. They must. Ozzy was on top of everything. Kara shrugged and downed the wake-up juice. Time to hit the shower and go find Brock. She didn't like him being anywhere without her by his side to make sure he kept breathing.

Brock pumped his legs to the rhythm of the old school Disturbed that leaked from his earbuds. He still couldn't believe it. Kara had chosen him. A smile stretched across his face as he pushed the jog into a sprint. His muscles burned, and it felt good. He felt good, as his mind wandered. When she'd first come back, he knew that she would have gone back to her life with Dane in a heartbeat. He would have missed so much. He needed to do something for her, just for them. It may be selfish, with everything that was going on, but that didn't change the plans that were forming in his mind.

He slowed to a jog and then a walk and then stopped to bend and lean his hands on his knees while he caught his breath. Lifting his head, he looked out over the levy. The water was crystal blue, and the sun reflected off the waves in bright starbursts of light. *Like her eyes.* He smiled again and turned around to retrace his steps, turning up the volume on his iPod, for the first time not running away from anything, but running toward the future that he wanted with Kara. It was his, and he was going to take it. Anyone who got in his way would rue the day.

Kara looked at the clock as she pulled on her boots. After noon. No wonder Brock hadn't been here when she woke up. She slid a knife into the sheath inside her boot and pulled her jeans down over the feminine biker style of footwear and went to find Brock. He wasn't inside. Stepping out into the bright sunlight, she found him crouched against the wall, breathing hard and sweaty. A smile curled her lips as she appreciated the acreage of bare skin not covered by his sweats and running shoes. In a perfect world, he would be shirtless all the time. Scratch that. Naked would be perfect.

She copped a squat beside him, leaning her back against the rough wall and ghosted in a large bottle of water for him and another cup of coffee for herself. She sipped from the travel mug and tilted her face back, sighing as her skin absorbed the sun's warmth.

Brock opened his eyes when her scent seemed to surround him. His body leaned toward hers just a bit as he turned his head to see her. His bear chuffed its affection and Brock couldn't agree more. "Is that for me?" He lifted his wrist to point at the Icelandic Glacial bottle.

She nodded and held it out, her eyes still closed.

"Thank you." Brock unsealed the bottle and took a swig, groaning at how good it was. Rubbing his palm on her leg, he wiped the sweat from his face on the back of his arm and chugged the water. It was the little things like this that made him love her.

"Anytime, Big Guy." Kara opened her eyes and brushed her lips over his shoulder, sighing happily.

"How do you feel about us getting a pet together?" Brock sucked the moisture from the hair over his lip as his eyes caressed her face.

Her brows shrugged together as she rolled her head against the brick to look at him curiously. "A pet? What are you thinking?"

"Like a dog. Maybe a fish?" He grinned. "A cat?"

One side of her mouth curved up and Kara shielded her eyes so she could see him better. "I don't get the fish as a pet, thing. They just look at you. Dogs or cats make more sense." She shrugged and sipped her coffee. "Are we allowed to have pets here?"

"Like you care," Brock laughed. "The place is full of animals. What's another one?"

"Good point," she grinned and dropped her ass to the asphalt, stretching her legs out and crossing them at the ankle. "Do bears prefer dogs to cats?"

"I like dogs, myself."

"Me too. Not tiny little ones that you carry in a purse though." Kara shook her head. "Might as well get a pet rat as one of those things."

"My thoughts as well."

"Puppy parents, eh?" Kara sipped her coffee and thought about it. Turning her head, she pressed her lips to his shoulder and grinned. "I think we should do it."

Brock smiled and draped an arm around her shoulders. "How about today? What breed?"

"Today is perfect. I don't know enough about breeds." Kara settled against him and tilted her head back to see him. "Help me out, Big Guy."

"I've always wanted a pit or lab." Brock shrugged. "But I want you to be ok with it."

Lifting her hand, Kara laced her fingers with the one that dangled over her shoulder. "We'll know it's the one for us when we meet them." She smiled, having no idea if that was true or not. "I'm okay with whatever we agree on."

He kissed her forehead. "Would you like to go now or later?"

Kara shrugged. "Now is good. I've got no plans but if you do..." Her words trailed off when he flashed himself clean and dressed. "I'll take that as a no, to the plans."

He brushed himself off and got up, holding his hand out to her. "Nope, just time with you."

Reaching up, Kara took his hand and let him pull her to her feet. How quickly he got ready, never ceased to amaze her. She finished her coffee and flashed the mug into the dishwasher. Keeping his hand in hers, she leaned her shoulder into him. "Any idea where to start the search?"

"I'm not sure. Google maybe?"

Kara laughed and sandwiched his bigger hand between hers. "Google does know everything."

"Other than that, I don't know. We just go pick one out."

"I'm ready for the pick out and cuddle with, part." She grinned up at him.

"I'll see if I can borrow Brian's truck." He pulled her closer and kissed her, growling softly before letting her go.

"Okay, Babes." Kara tucked the hair behind her ear, pulling out her phone to google the supplies they would need and trying not to be distracted by the view of Brock walking away.

Brock left her to speak with Brian and came back a few minutes later. "Got the keys. We just need to put gas in it and lay stuff in the back seat, so it doesn't get anything on them." He said, rolling his eyes.

She laughed at the eye roll and ghosted the blanket from the back of the sofa into her arms. "Kinda makes me WANT to make a mess, but I'll play nice." She smirked and kissed his neck before climbing into the truck. The ride was short, or maybe it just felt that way because she spent the entire time fiddling with the radio and chasing down music that she liked.

"We're here," Brock killed the engine and the constantly changing tunes blasting through the speakers. "You ready, Cher?"

Kara grinned and bounced excitedly, opening the door and hopping out to wait for him to join her by the hood of Brian's restored classic truck. "I am," she nodded her head and eyed the brick and mortar building they were parked near. She could hear dogs barking inside, pulling her in. Struggling not to run, she made her feet behave and stepped inside when Brock held the commercial glass door open for her. Her nose twitched at the faint smell of urine under the stronger disinfectant scent.

Brock chuckled. Kara couldn't hide her excitement. It was leaking from her pores and made his skin pebble. This was one of his better ideas. Reading the signs, he smiled at the staff and placed his hand on the small of her back to guide her to where the kennels were.

Her brows popped toward her hairline at the rows of cells filled with canine inmates. Kara shook her head. Humans were weird as hell. Slowly she walked down the painted concrete between the kennels, wincing at the echoing barks and her head tilting as she met the hopeful eyes of each dog. "God, this is sad. Can we take them all?" She glanced over her shoulder to Brock.

"If I had my own home, yes," he answered sadly, looking over the dogs.

467

Stepping back, she took his hand and leaned against him. It didn't seem fair that they had to pick one and leave the rest behind. Kara glanced up at the sign that promised that they were a 'no kill' shelter. A wave of pissed off flowed through her when she realized that some must kill their residents if this one felt the need to say THAT. Scooching down she held her open palm against the chain link, smiling as a Shepard licked at her skin. "Are any talking to you?" Kara meant that quite literally, though the humans around them had no clue.

Brock looked around trying to see if any of them spoke to him. "Not yet."

Nodding, she reached out to the pit in the next enclosure, noting the board between the chain link walls and her brow arched a little. Chocolate brown eyes under twitching pale brows met hers. Her lips curled up as she scratched his muzzle through the diamond shaped holes.

Brock watched her, smiling when Kara stopped to make a new friend. "Hey there." He scratched its left ear.

She smiled up at Brock, watching how gently he touched the canine and the open, calm energy that he surrounded himself with. No wonder she loved him. He was truly one of a kind, and he didn't have a clue. "This is one of the breeds you mentioned earlier, right?" Kara tilted her face toward the dog and laughed as the end of her nose was licked.

"Yes, this is a pit bull. They get a bad rep for being dangerous and vicious."

Kara eyed the dog and turned back to Brock. "He doesn't strike me as very dangerous or vicious." Kara closed her eye as its tongue almost licked her peeper.

"Animals are only like that when pushed or trained to be, Cher." He eyed the dog and saw one of the workers coming toward them.

Kara nodded. That made sense. 'People' were the same way, back anyone into a corner and you got what you got.

She followed Brock's gaze that fell on the khaki-uniformed employee strolling their way.

"Did you find one you want?" The man asked, looking at the pit with a hopeful smile curling his lips that fell when his eyes fell on Kara. He sighed, doubting that the Daddy's Little Princess type would be up for the challenge. "He's a lot to handle. We have some puppies in the next room if you'd like to see them."

She met Brock's eyes and then looked back at the dog in the kennel that was trying to push his body through the two-inch holes in the chain link to get closer to them. 'Would you rather start with a puppy?' Kara mindlinked the bear and slid her hand further inside to scratch the dog who was pinning her, and then Brock, with those pleading dark eyes.

'No. I want one that's already housebroken and all that.' Brock mindlinked back and decided to let Kara handle this because the human may end up in a cage if he did.

Smiling, she leaned closer and kissed the 'hard to control' dog on the nose, turning her head to eye the scraggly looking human who was sucking on a toothpick while giving THEM the speech. She crossed her arms over her chest and squared her shoulders, glancing up at Brock. "This is the one we want." She arched a questioning brow at Brock, hoping she was right because she'd already fallen in love with the pit bull.

"Yes, we'll take this one."

The man arched his brow and motioned for them to follow him. "Okay, we have paperwork to fill out, and there are fees for the dog."

Smiling wide and hugging Brock tight, Kara linked the dog that they would be right back when he started to whine at their retreating backs. The link seemed to get through. He plopped back onto his butt, his tail thumped against the floor, and his tongue lolled between his teeth. Annoyed by the formality, they filled out the papers, paid the fee and gave the bribe that the human called a 'donation.' "Our dog please?" She arched an inpatient brow.

The man went to get the dog and brought it back collared and leashed. "I should tell you he has a problem with chewing. His last family couldn't break him of wrecking the house and pissing all over everything."

Kara grimaced and tried not to smile, since being house broken was on Brock's list of must haves. 'You can change your mind, Babes. I won't be mad.' She linked him.

"Thank you for letting us know." Brock took the leash and paperwork before heading outside with the dog. "What are we gonna call him?"

She smiled and kissed his cheek. Eying the dog, Kara tilted her head to the side. "He doesn't look like a Steve," she teased.

Brock laughed and looked the pit over. "He looks like a Bob, to me."

Kara nodded and bent over to ruffle the short hair on the top of the pit's head. "Bob works for me. We're going to need a bigger bed."

Smiling, Brock petted Bob's head. "He's not sleeping with us."

Bob barked as if to say, oh yes I am.

Brock shook his head. "So, what's next? Dog stuff?"

Kara pulled out her phone and held it up so that Brock could read the list. "I will break my no shopping rule for you two, or we can just ghost it in."

"I vote ghosting, so we can get him home. I was thinking beer and pizza, later." Bob jumped on Brock. "You like that idea too?" Grinning Brock scratched his big head. "You'll fit right in."

Laughing, Kara nodded her agreement. "Sounds perfect, right down to the beer and pizza."

The drive back to The Pit didn't take long, and this time Kara was too distracted by their new pet to mess with the radio. *Thank god*, Brock thought as he parked the truck and double checked that the leash was still attached, before getting out. "Welcome home, Bob." He grinned as the canine jumped out and began sniffing the ground.

"Can we teach him to do things to Brax's shoes?" Kara grinned up at Brock before reaching back into the truck, taking out the blanket and checking that there was no mess left behind.

"If you want," he laughed. "I wonder how we'll get him past Brandon?" Brock looked down at Bob. "The back door by the dumpster may be best."

Kara eyed him, wondering how aboveboard all of this was and was about to ask when it struck her how much funnier it would be if shoes were chewed, but no one knew there was a dog in the house. Kara crept up to the back door and held her hand up as she peeked in the window. Finally, when the coast was clear, she flagged Brock and Bob in, trying not to laugh.

Breaking into a run with Bob in tow, Brock bolted through the back door and then up the stairs. Seeing Brax coming down the hall, he ghosted himself and Bob to their room.

Kara skidded to a halt when she saw Brock ghost out and acted like there was nothing to see here. "Hey Brax, how 'bout them Sox?" She arched a brow as he grumbled at her and looked confused. "Yeah, baseball. Never mind." Kara sighed and bounced up the stairs, shutting herself inside Brock's rooms and sliding down the door to sit on the floor laughing and being licked by Bob.

"Mission accomplished," Brock grinned. While Bob licked her face, he ghosted in all the things that they needed and stared at the pile. He whistled. "This is a lot of stuff."

Kara sputtered, pushed away Bob's head and herself to her feet, looking at it all. "Wow. You sure we didn't go overboard?"

"I got what was on the list. This is all you." He laughed and picked up the purple collar. "That's a little girly."

She grinned and took the purple collar, hiding it behind her back, blushing. "Okay, maybe I went overboard."

471

"You can put that on him if you want. I was hoping for something less purple." Brock laughed at how cute she was.

"I can go with less purple, but only because I love you, Bear." Kara grinned and ghosted it away.

Shaking his head, Brock picked up a black collar with a Viking ship on it and knelt to put it around Bob's neck, removing the shelter collar.

"Perfect!" Kara stretched up and kissed his face, her hand rubbing his back as she looked down at Bob. "I've never had a pet before that couldn't talk. What do we do with him now?"

"Let him hang out while we order food." Bob barked. "I think he's hungry."

Kara eyed the monster-sized bag of what was labeled dog food. That was a lot of kibble. She made a face when she opened the bag, and the smell hit her. She hoped that Bob liked it. Reaching in, she scooped some out with her hand to fill a bowl.

Brock laughed at the look on her face and filled another bowl with water. "We need to get him a self-waterer and feeder."

"I forgot something? Well Damn!"

He nodded and watched Bob dig in, satisfied that the basics were covered before ordering their food. After hanging up, he went through the pile of stuff and got Bob's bed ready and stocked with toys. Maybe with this much to chew on, their things wouldn't be as appealing. Brock hoped it worked like that.

Kara googled a self-waterer and feeder on her phone and ghosted them in, waiting until Bob is done to set them up in an out of the way corner so that they wouldn't trip over the containers. She wrapped her arms around Brock from behind and sighed happily, watching as Bob circled before laying down and rearranging the toys. "I'm happy we did this, Babes. Damn, we make cute kids," she joked.

Brock chuckled, holding her to him and kissing the top of her head. "I am too. I call not being the pooper scooper."

472

"Fine," Kara shrugged and bit him softly. "I'll take one for the team, for now. If we ever do the kid thing for real? That's all yours." She grinned and gave an evil laugh.

"I'm great at diapers."

She nodded and smiled up at him, dropping her head against his chest. "You will be an amazing Dad someday, Brock."

He kissed her and quirked a brow. "If Salvation lets me."

She shook her head, genuinely annoyed that her moody brother got a say. She kissed him back and called the fates a collection of not so nice names and expletives, in her head.

"I love you, Cher. So much."

She tightened her arms around him. "I love you too, bear. More than is good for either of us."

Bob jumped up and ran to the door, barking and wagging his tail so hard that his hind feet slid back and forth on the hardwoods.

"Food must be here."

Kara smiled and pulled Bob back by the collar so Brock could get the door. "I have cash in my jacket if it's my turn, Babes." She scratched the top of their dog's head between his ears, cooing to him softly.

"I've got it." Brock fished his money out of his jeans and opened the door to get the food and pay for it. Thanking the delivery guy, Brock kicked the door closed with food in hand.

She groaned at the smell of tomato sauce, melted mozzarella, veggies and meats that filled the air and made her stomach growl and Bob drooled a little bit, making her grin. After washing her hands, Kara pulled down plates and got cold beer from the fridge. "Smells amazing!"

Nodding, he eyed the whining Dog beside his leg. Brock shook his head as he dished out the pizza onto the plates. "No people food, Bob."

Bob whined louder.

Kara laughed at him and waited to see whose will was stronger, Brock or Bob. Brock had the arched brow and stubborn chin working for him, but Bob was rocking the pitiful eyes. She already knew that she was a pushover for either of them, so she was staying out of this one and popped the tops off two bottles of beer, pushing one towards Brock.

Taking his beer, Brock sat with Kara as Bob tried to cute some pizza out of her. "No, Bob!"

She groaned and tried not to look directly into the big brown eyes *of I've never eaten before in my entire life*, sadness, and sipped her beer. "Gods, he knows how to do that naturally? No wonder I never win an argument with you, Bear. You have an unfair advantage!"

"Just remember dog vomit and the other gross things that come from sick dogs."

Kara sighed heavily. "Okay, you win with that." She made a face and bit into her slice trying not to groan her contentment too loudly.

Brock ate, watching Bob huff at them and lay down. It oddly reminded him of Bart when he gave up after a fight with Bree.

Kara grinned when Bob curled up on his new bed, pushing the toys off with the end of his nose. Yeah, she couldn't help it, she already had a soft spot for the canine. She tore off a couple paper towels and handed one to Brock before wiping her mouth and then fingers. "So, do you want cubs someday?" She looked up at him before grabbing up another slice and laughing when Bob sighed heavily.

His mouth full of pizza, Brock looked at her, not sure where that had come from. He finished what was in his mouth. "Well, I am not certain how that works, with you being you and me being me. I don't know about children. I want some most days and others, no, not at all, because the way the world is and seeing the hell my own family has been through. If my mate wants them, then I'll give them to her, or try to."

474

She nodded and chewed as she listened, wincing at the reminder that he had a mate out there somewhere, waiting for him to find her. "Yeah, I never thought about it much, until it was a possibility and now it's not again, I guess." She shrugged and sighed. "I try not to think about it most days." Kara grinned and bumped his shoulder with hers. "I don't know how it works for us either. We are not in the handbook."

"Damn the manual anyways. It would probably be something we'd have to talk to Sal about. I'm not sure if anyone else would know how that works. Would we get Bears with wings?"

Kara laughed. "Maybe, tough little bears with wings that can bolt people." She shook her head and sighed. "Doubt that Salvation is looking to do me any favors. He doesn't seem to like me much, with the killing me and all." She left out the part about the feeling being more than mutual. "I could ask Dad, he might know. Hell, I probably should, but he's gonna be grumpy the next time I see him." She rolled her eyes.

"Let's see how it works out with Bob before we get ourselves killed over Cubs. Or vubs, as it would be." Brock laughed and drank his beer

She snickered and agreed with a vigorous nod of her head. "I'm not saying we should, just wanted to know what you wanted, Big Guy." She grinned up at him and stole a mushroom off his slice. "Vubs." She fell back laughing.

"Balkyrie?" He said thinking about it. "No, Vears?" He got himself another slice of pizza and wondered what their species would be called.

"I think we might get to name them if it happens." She snickered and sipped her beer. "Never heard of it happening before, but then again until recently, I never spent a lot of time with shifters." She shrugged.

"And now you're stalking us, all over," Brock teased.

Kara made a face at him and stuck out her tongue. "You're the only shifter I'm stalking, and I'm pretty obvious about it." She shook her head and took another bite. "Might be a bjornkyrie. Bjorn is our word for bear," she said thoughtfully and shrugged because it probably didn't matter, her eyes rolled to Bob. "How often do we walk him?"

Brock liked her idea. "Sounds cool." He looked at Bob. "I'd say every few hours until we get into a routine with him."

She pressed her lips to his shoulder and grinned. "We can do that. He seems to be rolling with being surrounded by bears and what have yous." Kara smiled at the dog affectionately. She liked having something that she shared with Brock. It made their situation feel more long term, and that was comforting. "Are we gonna catch crap for having him here?"

"I have no idea, and if we do, I'll handle it. As I said, it can't be no pets allowed, when we let all kinds of creatures live here. I don't see how one dog could hurt anything. Brandon lives here." Brock laughed. "And once we got Koen to stop humping legs and peeing on everything it worked out well. So, if they have a problem, oh well."

Laughing as she imagined Koen being that nasty, she kissed him and nodded. "Yeah, Bob is way better behaved than that, already."

"Yes, and he smells better." Brock laughed, hoping no one had an issue with it.

Kara looked up at him and grinned. "You are something special, Brock Navarro, just in case no one has told you that today."

"I think the cuteness of Bob has gone to your brain, Cher." Brock smiled and got up to take his plate to the kitchen. Bob placed himself in his path with a rope toy in his mouth.

Kara rolled her eyes and disagreed wholeheartedly. Anyone that could put up with the hot mess that was her and made her feel like that was okay, was extraordinary. That he never saw it was what had hooked her but good.

She pulled her feet up onto the sofa and finished her pizza, her head tilting to the side as Bob insisted that Brock play. A smile curled up the corners of her mouth, *okay that was just damn adorable*.

Grabbing the rope with one hand and pulling Bob along to the kitchen, Brock set the plate down. Bob growled and shook his head trying to make Brock move. Brock let his arm be swung back and forth before getting on the floor with the pit and wrestling with him. In the end, Bob ended up standing on Brock's back with the rope in his mouth like he'd won a game of King of The Mountain.

Laughing hard, Kara took her plate to the kitchen and patted Bob, who seemed very proud of himself. "Good boy, you teach him who's boss." She put both plates into the dishwasher and leaned her elbows on the counter waiting to see how the bear was going to get himself out of this.

Brock pulled himself across the floor with just his arms until he was close to Bob's toys. He grabbed a squeaky bone and squeezed it a couple times. As it made noise, Bob cocked his head, and Brock threw it. Bob jumped off him and took off after it.

"Nicely done, Babes." Kara snickered and offered him her hand to pull him up.

Taking it, Brock pulled her down to him and kissed her deeply, growling at the taste of her.

Her hands tangled in his hair as she kissed him back, pressing against him when he growled. "God, I love you, Brock." She growled against his lips, laughing as Bob tackled them and licked them feverishly. "You're right. He definitely doesn't sleep in our bed." She laughed, pushing the canine back.

"I love you too," Brock said as his mouth was invaded by Bob's tongue. He made a face and wiped his mouth. "Bob, not cool, man. Not cool."

Hiding her head in Brock's neck, Kara laughed hard and added mouthwash to her mental grocery list.

"Thank god, he didn't just lick his ass." Brock got up and went to the fridge to wash his mouth out with beer. "So gross."

Kara rolled up and hugged Bob, laughing and watching Brock try to get the taste of dog out of his mouth. "I don't think he liked that, pup." She grinned and patted the pit's shoulder, eying the dog sideways. "Don't get any bright ideas though. I'm good. I promise."

Bob licked her face and stuck his tongue up her left nostril. Then got her mouth. Brock turned in time to see it all. Laughing, with a mouth full of beer, he choked and spit it everywhere.

Kara groaned and wiped her tongue on the tail of her shirt. "That is just nasty!" She pushed herself to her feet and took Brock's beer, poured some into her mouth, swished it around and spit it out in the sink. Wiping her mouth with the back of her hand, she shot the bear a look. "It's not THAT funny." She growled and took another sip, this time swallowing. "We've gotta teach him not to do that." She shook her head and laughed. "You okay?"

Nodding, Brock choked a bit more and laughed as Bob watched them and then ran to the door. "He may need out." The word *out* sent Bob's tail wagging.

Scraping her tongue with her teeth and still making a face, Kara nodded and grabbed some of the waste bags that Google told her she needed. Thank the Gods, there was a dumpster to drop it into outside. "So, are we going for stealthy until we're caught, or do we just want to walk him through?" She glanced up at Brock and clicked the leash onto the toggle of Bob's collar.

Brock shrugged and ghosted them to the park.

"Stealthy it is, then." Kara wiggled her brows and let Bob smell his way to a cluster of shrubs.

Chapter 50

Kara lowered her spoon back to the bowl of Honey Nut Cheerios, her head tilting to the side. The hair on the back of her neck stood, as a cold chill crawled down her spine vertebrate by vertebrate. Something wasn't right, and she didn't mean her choice of a snack. Someone... No, scratch that. Something that shouldn't be inside the building was, and it was setting off all kinds of internal alarms. Did this have something to do with the text she'd gotten from Ripper earlier about some demon asking about her?

Brock had gone to restock their dwindling grocery situation, not trusting her to not come home with bags of things that could be nuked. According to him, that wasn't really food. Kara had shrugged and not argued because Brock's cooking rivaled Brax's and she was learning a thing or two. No potatoes had turned into shrapnel since he'd been here.

If Brock came back while whatever it was, was out there, he was a sitting duck, and that wasn't something she could allow. While it was nice to spend a few days with Brock and Bob at her place, they didn't have the added security of Alpha Pride being just downstairs and running interference.

She moved her feet from where they rested on the chair and pushed it back as quietly as she could before ghosting into the hall outside her door. Her bare feet made

479

no sound as Kara carefully avoided the strategically placed floorboards that creaked and worked her way silently, down and through the building, searching for the intruders.

Gore had asked around for an hour before he got answers and found the address. He stopped a good two feet from the steps. He wondered about the best way to make the Princess come out. She'd probably been tipped off that someone was asking about her and that made things more difficult. Then it hit him. Smirking coldly, he called for Heather and waited for her to appear. When she walked from the shadows between two buildings, Gore waved his hand giving her the face and body of Bree Navarro. He chuckled at her pout. "Don't worry, Kitten. This is temporary, I'm too fond of your body to let it go for long."

Heather beamed at him and looked down at herself holding out the loose flowing tunic top before rolling her eyes back to his. "I don't know, Baby. This could be fun for playing with as long as you promise to make it hurt." She grinned and bit her lower lip, thinking of the many ways he could torture this body and the things she could do to him in return. Her face flushed with the heat that raced through her.

Gore groaned as he imagined making the innocent face and body before him bleed as it screamed his name. He reached into his pants and adjusted the part of him that grew hard as stone at the images flashing through his mind. "Such a tease. Why do you torture me so?" He jerked her to him roughly and pulled the fabric off her shoulder to sink his teeth into the ivory skin, moaning at the taste of blood on his tongue.

Heather's head fell back, her hand slapped against his neck and held him in place as her nails sunk into his skin and yanked him away from her. Her smile was cold. "Because I can." Nails still in his neck, she pulled him closer to lick her blood from his lips. "What do you need me to do?"

Gore growled and sliced her tongue with one of his fangs, returning the cold smile. Her words were like a splash

480

of ice water, enough to get him back on point, but doing nothing to extinguish the flames caused by the idea of tearing the new body apart while he fucked her how he wanted to. "Knock on the door and tell her that The Pit is under attack, or whatever you have to say to get her out here."

Heather bit his lip hard, the pain from the ragged and torn skin caused by his teeth, making her throb. There were advantages to being what she was now, and Gore knew how to push every one of them to the breaking point. "Not until you promise that later, you will rip this poor," she bit his lip hard. "Innocent." Another bite. "Little Bree, to shreds."

Gore growled, barely able to resist the urge to do it here and now. "Do a good job, Kitten and I'll make you pay for it later."

Her lips curled into an evil and knowing grin before she pushed him away roughly and pulled the tunic top back over the skin he'd ripped open. "You'd better, or else." Heather turned and followed the path to climb the steps to the stoop and knocked.

Kara had been through the building and made it to the first floor but still hadn't found fuck all. She growled her frustration and paced through the halls one more time, searching for what had tripped her Spidey sense. She came back to the main entrance and arched a brow when she noticed the human-shaped shadow that fell across the bubbled glass in the door. Manifesting her dagger, she held her hand behind her back and threw open the door to find Bree standing there, looking bored. "Hey?" Kara leaned against the frame and eyed the blonde female that didn't seem right. The smell was off, for one thing, and so was the bear's energy. "Can I help you?"

"Yes, The Pit is under attack by demons, and I was told to get you. Please, come quick, before more die!" Heather made her eyes wide and let her voice rise in a panic.

Kara eyed her, knowing it was crap, but curious as to where this was going. She pressed her hand to her throat

481

and blinked with wide eyes. "Oh no! We'd better save them!" She battled with herself not to let her eyes roll. *Why the hell would demons attack The Pit when they should be partying it up with all the weird otherworldly shit that was happening?* If it didn't make sense, then it wasn't true, as a rule. Sighing, Kara stepped outside, already growing bored. "Okay. Let's just lay our cards on the table. I know it's bullshit and you ain't Bree. Just tell me what the hell you want and stop insulting my intelligence."

Heather frowned for a moment before attacking Kara. Grabbing the Valkyrie by the throat, she whipped her into the yard. Gore watched from the shrubs that lined the walkway and covered the Princess in a heavy metal suit head to toe. It would weigh her down, but he knew it wouldn't hold her for long. Gore gnashed his teeth at Heather and vanished to the Shadowlands to dump the Princess at Ty's feet.

"Well, well, looky here. It's a scary Viking." Ty smirked and gave her a droll stare.

Kara ghosted out of the metal suit, dusting off her jeans with her hands and shaking her head. "Well, that was dramatic and shit." She glanced up at Ty and snickered. "You have idiots working for you. You know that, right? If they'd simply said, 'Hi Kara. Ty would like a word,' odds are I would have come on my own or at least agreed to meet with you." She rolled her eyes and cursed in ancient Norse. "So now that you've gone through all this unnecessary trouble for little ole me, what do you want?"

Ty narrowed his eyes at her. "You took something of mine." As he looked her over, he could tell her soul was broken. She may play a good game of I'm all right, but deep down, he knew the truth of how she felt. She was one step away from surrendering to the darkness inside her. Things that had been done to her. Things others didn't know. Things he could use to control her. He grinned and crossed his arms over his chest.

Kara shoved her hands into her back pockets and kicked out one foot, checking the rounded toe of her boot before shrugging and looking up at him. *A throne? Really? What was it with everyone needing a damned throne to feel important?* "Sorry. Not sorry?" One corner of her mouth curled up. "Not sure what you're talking about. You need to be a little more specific," she lied, not liking the smugness of his grin or the way he sat there like he knew something that she didn't.

"The lion was mine."

Kara snorted. "He was mine first. How can one little lion matter to you?

"That isn't your business. I had plans for him. Time was spent, setting up the dominos so I could watch them fall. Your interference may have cost me a lot." Ty leaned forward, turning the ring on his finger. "And you may have just killed everyone you care for. Well, at least in this realm. Not that Viking hell hole you call home. Tell me something, Kara. When you had Salvation rip the lion from my realm, did you think about the consequences?"

"In the Shadowlands?" Kara laughed and looked around. "There's no one here I give two shits about." Her brow furrowed, his tone telling her that his question went deeper than Dane. She examined the copper and fused bones on the arm of his throne. He couldn't know what she'd done while trapped in the bowels of Valhalla. Only two, maybe three, knew about that. She shook it off and went with the obvious, not willing to admit shit that she didn't have to. "Honestly? No. I never gave it a lot of thought. He was mine, so I took him back." She shrugged and met his dark eyes. "What should I have been thinking?"

Ty sighed at her stupidity. "I meant realm, as in earth, all levels, all things not Valhalla. Does it really matter now, since you may have set in motion a war to end the world? What is important is what happens next. You need to be punished for what you did, but I know you won't see the old laws the same way I do. So, I'm going to make this easy for

483

you." His lips curled up in a smile but showed no warmth. "I know the truth of everything you've done. I'm sure there are a lot of people who would be interested in this knowledge. Many will turn on you if I make it public. The price for my silence is small. You will work for me until I see fit to void your services. If you try to weasel your way out of it, I'll kill your precious lion, but not your bear. For him, it will be watching each of his family die horribly and knowing that it's because of you. It will leave him broken and ruined. Then, after that, I'll go down the sadly short list of the few you care for. Now, before you try to tell me Salvation will have a fit, I'm already aware, and I don't give a damn about the Buffalo, or whatever he's pretending to be now."

Ty leaned back and crossed his leg in front of him, letting his right foot bounce while he waited for her to make her decision. She may be too far gone to care anymore. It was ironic that he had Salvation and her family to thank for it. Stupid fuck that Salvation was, he didn't understand that Norse laws of life and death are different than his. The sentence he gave Kara had changed everything for her. Ty wasn't sure if she knew that, or not. In time, she'd learn the truth.

Her brow arched and Kara looked down at the black marble floor, following a vein of quartz with her eyes while she ground her molars to dust. Yeah, it would suck if what she'd done became common knowledge, but in all honesty, she didn't care what most thought of her and trusted them just as much with or without the knowledge. She snorted at the idea that Salvation would even flinch at anything that had to do with her. Ty only had one card to play, and he'd thrown it in her face. Dane and dear gods, Brock. The bear didn't know, and she doubted that he could look past it. Ty didn't need to threaten his life to reign her in, but the fact that he had, pissed her off. She shook her head and closed her eyes for a moment before reopening them and looking up at the God of Monsters, her lip curling up with the disgust she felt for him and the fact that she had no choice.

"Fine. What do I have to do?" She spat out the words that left a bad taste in her mouth.

Ty ran his hands through his hair and cocked his head to the side before taking her by the hand and performing the ritual that would make her one of his. When it was done, there would be no place that she could hide from him. Not even in her precious Asgard.

Kara watched as he did whatever the hell it was he was doing, biting her tongue against the vile words that wanted to flow over it and probably seal the fate of the few she loved. She yanked her hand back when he was finished and glared, stepping away from him.

After they had finished, Ty hoped she would be smarter than most on her first mission and concentrate on the job, not a way to get out of it. "Now that is done, and out of the way, your first mission is to find out where my Gatekeepers have been going off to. Other than the one you already killed, that is. And if you don't know what the gate is, I'll give you the short version of it."

Giving a curt nod. Kara flexed her hand, not liking the lingering stiffness of her fingers from what he'd done. "Cliff Notes version," she growled out, not missing his disapproval of her tone. She shook her head and raked her hair back from her face, setting aside her pride that was screaming bloody murder about all of this. "If you would, please."

Ty ghosted them to the middle Gate and let her see the hell and horror of it. A heavy corroded steel grid covered a ragged hole torn through the ground and was shored by the still-twitching bodies of the fallen as far up and down as the eye could see. He smiled and began to walk around the crooked ellipse. "This is all that divides the real evil and myself, and I am the only thing that keeps them here and out of the world of man. These barriers hold the horrors of the universe in check with the service of the Gatekeepers and others like you. Or my Shadz, as I like to call them. Souls of demons and creatures that have eaten their own worlds but are still hungry come here to get free. It's always a

485

bloodbath. One slip up and it all becomes," he used the Norse word for the end of the world, "Ragnarok."

Kara held the back of her hand over her nose, but it did nothing to block the stench of burnt flesh and death. "Hate to break it to you, Big Guy, but Ragnarok has already begun. You can thank Loki."

"And knowing that changes nothing. The humans aren't ready for true evil to take over. The gate must remain secure. The gorgon that you killed was a Gatekeeper, her spot was a hard one to fill, in the middle, fighting what is above and what comes from below. Maybe I should let you have a crack at it." He eyed her, wondering if she could handle it.

Kara studied him intently before glancing over the edge and tried not to think blah, blah, blah as he recited his problems and told her about the barriers that were supposed to hold back the tide of evil. She shook her head, not believing that was possible. Evil hid in the most unexpected places and jumped forward at even the slightest chance of gaining ground. She doubted that he was ignorant of that fact either. "So, do you want me to spy on your minions or take a place at the gate? Because, while I am good, I doubt I can do both at the same time." She crossed her arms over her chest and looked up at him arching a brow.

Ty glared at her, not appreciating her mouth and that decided her fate. "You will take her place, and if you let anything get past you, I'll make your hell realms look like Disney-fucking-land. Down here you have none to save you or to stop me. None of your Viking horse shit will work here. It doesn't matter if Odin himself came to get you, he'd be powerless here," Ty said calmly as he watched something fly by them, screeching. He shielded himself as it went for her.

Well, fuck. Playing spy sounded way more fun. Kara sighed and looked down at the scars that covered her bare arms. At least she was back in her real skin. It wasn't much, but it was something. "If anything gets past me, it's because

I'm dead," she muttered. Glancing up at the screech, she covered herself in her armor, and her weapons appeared in her hands. Did he really think Odin would come for her? They may be a treacherous lot, but honor and keeping one's bargains still meant more to her kind than it did to most. Ghosting onto the cross between a pterodactyl and giant canary's back, she grabbed a fistful of leathery feathers and sunk her sword into its back, angling between the ribs and piercing its heart. Gods, the stench of its blood was fowl, like a bloated corpse left in the sun, for days. Kara gagged as it dropped, jumping free and rolling to her feet as whatever it was, skidded across the stone and twitched for a few moments. "You're going to have to make it clear what I can kill and what I can't because you know what my first instinct is." She wiped the black tarry blood off her sword using the wing of the dead thing.

Ty watched Kara kill the Trivium, he spoke. "You bare my mark," he paused before speaking again. "My Shadz and Gatekeepers will know not to attack you. If anything comes at you here, it's meant to die and if you kill something other than what is intended to be dead?" He shrugged. "You'll find out quickly what that means for you." He turned and began walking away from her. "I'll give you twenty-four hours to take care of your shit, topside. Once on the surface, you can hide as you always have, but my Shadz will see the true you, now. If you don't come back within the time frame I gave you, I won't need to come for you. I can just end your life, no muss no fuss." Ty snapped his fingers.

"You're all heart," Kara muttered and sheathed her sword. "When I come back, are there hours or am I just here for good?" Kara turned, tracking his movement as he walked away.

He shrugged and started to vanish, leaving her. Ty hoped that she was as strong as she thought she was because, in all honesty, he figured the gate would kill her. If she died, so be it she owed him a warrior and either way he was going to get it. If she lived, she might be his ticket to

Asgard. He smiled to himself as he appeared back in his throne room.

"Thanks for the clarity dick wad," Kara growled under her breath and flashed back home to hit the shower and wash the stench of the blood off. Yeah, this was going to be a fun night. Ghosting her clothes away, she stepped under the hot spray of the water and tried to wrap her mind around the death sentence she'd just agreed to and blinked back the tears at the thought of having to leave Brock after everything that had just happened. Thank God, she didn't share a mated mark with him. When she died, or he got tired of waiting for her to come back, he was free. Like Ty had said, 'No muss, no fuss.'

Brock pushed the cart up and down the aisles of the local Rouses Supermarket, dropping in anything that caught his eye. The cupboards at home were bare, and he was looking forward to making new things for Kara to try. He'd never seen a woman eat like she did. The Valkyrie could put it away. He liked that about her. She wasn't afraid of food. Though cooking it, was another story. He chuckled and smiled at the small boy that glanced up at him, holding a box of Captain Crunch.

As he strolled through the store, putting things in the cart, Brock grew uneasy. He felt like something was off. He tried to ignore it, but the bear in him wasn't letting it go. Brock glanced through the store's giant windows near the checkout. The sky looked fine. Just another beautiful day in NOLA. But the weather here was always changing. One moment it was sunny and perfect, the next it could be pouring cats and dogs.

Brock shook his head. It wasn't the weather or the chance of a sudden downpour that made his bear restless. It was something else. The ether around him seemed off. Not able to shake it, he quickly finished up and headed back. He wanted to talk to Kara about the feeling that something was wrong or looming on the horizon.

488

Chapter 51

Kara stepped out of the shower, scrubbing her hair dry with a towel and found the soggy bowl of cereal still on the table. Maybe she hadn't been gone as long as she'd thought. Shrugging, she drained the milk into the sink, scraped the mush into the trash, rinsed and stacked the bowl inside the dishwasher. Now what? Padding across the cool hardwoods, she went to the bedroom and pulled a pair of slate gray yoga pants from the drawer, shook them out and pulled them on, snagging a loose tank top, she did the same. She might as well be comfortable while she could, because life on Thorn's wall was likely to be anything but comfy.

She glanced up at the clock, her brows popping toward her hairline. Kara didn't have as much of her twenty-four hours left as she would like. She decided that if Brock wasn't back by the 2-hour mark, she'd text him that they needed to talk. Leaving a note just didn't sit right with her. She would if she had to, but as much as she didn't want to tell him that she had totally fucked her life, she felt she owed it to him to put in the face time. Sighing, she dropped onto the sofa and stared at the wall, trying to figure out how she had gone from being hopeful for the future to not having one at all.

It had been a rough day. After his trip to the grocery store and finding Kara gone, his brothers and sisters had gathered at the place where his parents used to take them when they were young and honored their mother on

Mother's Day. Brock dreaded this day, every year. Father's Day was more of the same. Wiping his eyes, he collected Bob from his room, took him for a short walk and appeared at Kara's. After the run in with Dane, they'd been spending more time at her place. He liked it here, it was so much quieter than The Pit.

Kara rolled her head against the arm of the sofa toward him when Brock appeared. His scent had the tinge of sadness to it that always reminded her of the woods after a hard rain. She scrubbed her face with her hands. And here she was, about to make it worse. God, she should have gone into stasis, and not pulled him into the cluster fuck of her life. Maybe she deserved to be in that damned pit of death, just to repent for being a selfish bitch. She sighed and offered him a weak smile. "Hey. How did it go?"

"Fine, I guess." Brock sniffled a bit. "How are you, Cher?" He sat down beside her, rubbing his face.

She groaned inwardly and rolled up to hug him tight. "I'm sorry, Babes," she whispered against his neck, wishing all of this was coming at a better time but not sure that it existed. Kara shook her head and closed her eyes. "Not so good, but I'm more worried about you right now, Big Guy."

Brock shook his head. "I'm ok. You have that, we need to talk, face. So, what's going on, Cher?"

Kara sighed and winced a little when she pulled back to look up at him. How the hell did she explain this? 'Um..." Kara chewed at her lower lip searching for the right words. "I pissed off the god of monsters, between killing a demon that he liked and Dane escaping the Shadowlands. Now I'm in trouble."

Brock stared at her and then laughed. When she didn't smile, his jaw tightened. "Cher, how could you do something like that?"

Her brow arched and her own jaw tensed as Kara returned his stare. "It's not like the SOBs are marked. I didn't wake up and think to myself, 'Oh gee... How can I piss off the evilest guy I know, today? How can I totally fuck

490

anything good in my life? Yeah, let's do that!'" She sat back crossing her arms over her chest and pulled her knees up in front of her. "Trust me, if I'd known this would happen, I wouldn't have." Kara shook her head and looked out the window.

"I mean killing demons in general, that's heavy shit." Brock tried to wrap his mind around this and sighed, hugging her to him. "So, what now?"

Kara was confused. Why would she not kill demons? "Babes, it's kind of what I do to work off frustration, it keeps me level from the real heavy shit, as you call it." She hugged him back, hating this. "He's making me work for him as a guard or something. I don't remember what he calls them..." She sighed and growled. "He's putting me on this gate that he has. Don't know for how long. The dick bag wouldn't say."

"The Shadz," Brock said as rage gripped him. "And you can't get out of it? When do you start?"

She shook her head no. "He was pretty clear about that." She blew out her breath, not able to meet his eyes to see the disappointment there. Glancing at the clock, she sighed, ignoring the tightness of her throat and chest. "I'm supposed to go back in eight-ish hours. I am so sorry, Brock." She blamed Salvation for all of it.

Brock sighed and nuzzled her. "It's okay, Cher. We'll get through this." He kissed her. "Together. You hear me, Kara? Together, because I love you."

"I love you." Kara sighed and leaned her face against his chest, inhaling deeply hoping his scent would calm her and convince her that the rest that she needed to tell him would be better off left unsaid. It didn't. "You don't know me, Babes. When I died, I did some nasty shit, stuff that makes even me, sick to my stomach. I came back wrong." She chewed her lip and shook her head. "Somehow, I'm not quite so fucked up when I'm with you. I don't want to ruin your life. I love you too much, and I'm afraid that this is going to kill me. For good this time."

491

"Don't say that, Cher." Brock played with her hair and nuzzled her neck. "Be positive."

Kara snorted and smiled a little. *Yeah, telling him that she was positive she was going to die, probably wasn't what he was going for.* Instead, she nodded and nuzzled him back.

"I already know what happened while you were gone. Ivan showed me. " He kissed her again and held her. "When do you leave?"

Holding onto him tight, not wanting to let go, ever, Kara had to clear her throat before she could speak again. She looked back at the clock. "Supposed to report back a little after nine. I think. I don't want to be late. Apparently, he kills you for that." She sighed.

Brock made a face and shook his head. "Should you get ready? You know, weapons and all of that?"

She shrugged. "I kinda just flash them in as I need them. If you have stuff you need to do though, I understand. I didn't want to disappear on you after I promised I wouldn't."

"No. I was gonna lay down and rest. Rough day, and now, it's even worse."

Cupping his face, she kissed him softly, closing her eyes against the stinging. "Don't blame you." Kara tried to smile and nodded. "I am sorry."

He hushed her, "I know you are, Cher." He nuzzled and kissed her while his mind rejected that any of this was happening.

Nodding she dropped her forehead against his. "I will come back," she said with more confidence than she felt. None of this was fair to him, and she hated it. The last thing Brock needed was one more person piling shit on his plate.

"You'd better, or I will come for you," Brock growled softly.

Kara laughed. How that happened when she felt like there was a knife in her chest, she had no idea. It was all part of the miracle that was Brock. How had the fates gotten it so wrong? They seriously deserved to have their bitchy

492

little asses fired. "That, I don't doubt." She grinned and kissed him again. "And I pity the idiot who tries to get in your way."

"They will be sorry." He felt sick at the thought of her not being here, in the land of the living, anymore.

Kara nodded and nuzzled him. Standing up, she held out her hand and tugged him up from the sofa when he took it. "Come lay down with me, Babes? I want to hold onto you until I need to go." Rolling up on her toes to kiss him, she smiled when he scooped her up and carried her. "Gods, I love you, bear," She whispered against his neck.

He lowered her to the bed, memorizing everything about her. It was cruel to let him have her and then snatch her away. "I know," he said as he laid beside her. He hated that he was exhausted. He wanted to savor every second that they had, but his body was shutting down. "Promise that you will come back to me."

She stared at him and tried to speak, but her throat had closed off. "I vow it," Kara whispered, stroking his face with her fingers. She didn't stop, even after his eyes fluttered shut and skin was replaced with fur. She should rest but she couldn't. If she did, she was afraid that she would oversleep and get them both killed. Not that the thoughts tumbling through her head would have allowed it, anyway.

Kara sighed and snuggled against the warmth of her bear, not taking a single thing for granted. Not his scent. Not the mix of soft and coarse hairs that tickled her skin. Not the rise and fall of his barrel chest. Not the heat that bled from him and warmed her even though her blood was running colder by the second. Most importantly, not the way she had no doubt that she would fight with everything she had, to get back to him. Brock was her reason to make it through whatever was coming.

Picking up her phone, she shot an email to her lawyer to make sure her will was in order and that the recent changes were all in play. Leaning over to open the drawer in

493

the bedside table, she pulled out the pad of paper and a pen and wrote a note that could never say what she felt. She hoped Brock knew, because if he didn't, then it wouldn't matter anyway. Gods, this was killing her. Leaving and not being here to have his back if the shit hit the fan, was chewing at her gut like a diseased rat.

Kara flashed the vials she'd prepared after her shower, into her hand. Dropping them to clink together onto the bed beside her, she eyed them and didn't give two shits who her giving them to Brock, pissed off. Sighing deep, she began writing:

Babes,

I know it's gross, but these are vials of my blood and water from the hot spring. If you get hurt, or backed into a corner and need a boost, it should help. Use it for yourself or someone who needs it. Be careful and be safe. I need you to be here for me to come back to. I love you, Brock.

~Kara

Yeah, that was lame as hell, but there wasn't much she could do about it. She flashed the note and the vials to the table on his side of the bed, hoping he would find it. Kara rolled to face him. Sliding her fingers through the thick fur of his chest, she blinked against the tears that wanted to flow and had to remind herself that this wasn't goodbye because she would fight through hell to get back to him, literally. Finally, her fingers brushed against his warm skin beneath the sleeping bear's hair. Closing her eyes, she whispered a pledge. If he were in trouble, she would know, and she would find a way to help him.

Pulling back slightly, she looked at his sleeping face and hoped that if this went badly, he would find someone who deserved him more than she did. Her phone blared and vibrated, reminding her that her time was up. Sighing, Kara reached behind her and silenced it. When she looked back to him, his eyes met hers and her heart shattered. Taking a

494

stuttering breath, she kissed the tip of his black, leathery nose and tried to smile. "I gotta go, baby. I love you." Rolling out of bed she grabbed her bag. "I'll be back" she promised him, and herself before she ghosted to her post in the Shadowlands.

Brock stared at the place Kara had been and wished that he'd told her that he loved her once more before she'd gone. He turned his head when he heard the sound of Bob's nails against the floor, coming closer. Sighing, he shifted into human form and ghosted shorts on himself. He sat up, rubbing his eyes. "Okay, boy. I know. Give me a moment to get all my marbles rolling."

Bob barked at him as if to say, hurry up. Brock stood and looked around the room. His brow arched when he spotted the paper and vials of what looked like blood on the table next to him. "What the hell is this?" He picked up the note and read it.

He didn't like this at all, not one damn bit, but what could he do? Brock left the vials where they were while he found his shoes. He knew Kara meant well, but he couldn't use her power like that. Bob barked again, reminding him that they were about to have an issue.

Brock opened the small safe hidden in the false bottom of one of his dresser drawers and put the vials in there with the note. He closed the drawer and ghosted himself and Bob outside so the pit bull could do his thing. He knew as he stood out there, waiting on the pit, that Kara doing that was serious. They didn't give their blood, or anything like that, haphazardly. That she thought she should, meant that she thought it was more than possible that she wouldn't make it through this.

He pushed the hair from his face, thinking about it all. "Cher, you'd better come back, and you'd better be in one piece," Brock whispered, mostly to himself.

Chapter 52

Kara's low heels scraped over the gravel strewn stone blocks, mortared and fused together, building the ledge that she walked on. Leaning over the side, she stared down into the dark abyss. God, it was a long way down. Far below her she could see the occasional winking of flames and wondered who the poor fools were that had to take this shit on at the ground level. Up here was bad enough and all she had to deal with was the shit that could fly or climb. She sighed at the screams and screeches that never seemed to stop, but at least they were in the distance, for now. That never lasted for long. She didn't know how long she'd been here. Minutes, days, years? In the perpetual darkness, there was no way to tell. The amount of time didn't matter, she'd learned the rules of this realm fast. Kill or be killed.

The hair on the back of her neck prickled and a chill slid down through her spine, leaving gooseflesh in its wake. Kara's hand tightened on the hilt of her sword, her fingers falling into the grooves worn in the soft leather from centuries of use. Tilting her head right then left to work out the kinks, she squared her shoulders and turned slowly, her blue eyes scanning for anything out of place. Kara ignored the green scaled Gorgon in the distance at his post on the ledge, he was not the cause. The air over the opposite edge of the wall began to shimmer, like heat rising off hot pavement. Her eyes narrowed, and her free hand fell to her side. Energy began to swirl and warmed her palm. Lightning crackled in the sky above.

A smoky black mist crept over the crumbling stone edge, drifting closer, sniffing the air and looking for fresh blood. It was what everything here wanted. Back in NOLA, the currency had been money, here it was blood, and these creatures didn't care whose if it was fresh and warm. Rolling her eyes heavenward, Kara raked the sky for more incoming. She had no idea what half of the things she'd fought here were, but was getting one hell of a crash course. The first lesson she'd learned was that they never attacked alone. Everything went silent, leaving only the soft whisper of her breath and the calm and steady beat of her pulse. Silence was always dangerous, the held breath before all hell broke loose.

Kara's brow arched as the scarred skin on her sword arm began to bubble, blister, char and then crack open as the black mist licked it. One corner of her mouth quirked up as she welcomed home her oldest friend. Pain had never let her down. It never offered to be anything other than it was. It grounded her and kept her mind clear. It reminded her that she was alive and not back in the hell of the lower levels of Valhalla. She was finding it harder to remember that with each passing hour as she fell into the old rhythm of fight or die. She was mechanical about her kills, taking no pleasure in any of it, and not fearing death. She was numb to it all, like she had been before. She knew she had a reason to survive this, but it faded in her memory as the bodies fell and stacked up against the base of the wall so far below. Kara was growing tired of it all.

She flexed her fingers, sending a bolt of energy into the swirling dark mass. The only sign that it's high pitched scream made her eardrums cringe as the sound sliced through her skull, was a slight tenseness at the corners of her eyes. The blackness pulled back in a rush, slithering back over the edge of the ledge but it did not flee. Kara could feel it lurking, waiting until she dropped her guard and it could

497

claim another drink. Again, it was silent. She felt the air being vacuumed away from her. Rolling her eyes skyward again she scanned the horizon, turning in a slow circle. Here, there was no safe way to protect your back, and if you forgot that simple fact, you paid for it.

A single flap, like a sail catching a gust of wind, shattered the silence. Then another. Growing closer and louder each time. It was coming from everywhere and nowhere, making it hard to pinpoint. Kara turned, knowing that whatever it was, it would try to attack from behind. That was lesson number two. Slow, the same way a gator broke the surface in the swamp, Volkswagen-sized glowing red eyes drifted above the lip of the wall, only to sink again before reappearing. Kara stared back, not caring enough to flinch as she widened her stance and sunk down, lowering her center of gravity and creating a smaller target.

Unblinking red eyes bored into her azure blues. Each was sizing up the other, and the big, whatever-the-fuck-it-was had the size advantage. They both knew it. Neither moved for what felt like years and then it opened its beak to roar, showing uncountable rows of sharp and nasty teeth. All were angled back toward its cavernous throat to keep anything swallowed alive from climbing back out. The fetid air blew back her hair, loosening the tight braid and forcing her to lean into the gust so that it didn't knock her on her ass. The stench left the taste of sour milk and copper on her tongue.

A dark scale plated claw crept over the edge, long talons sinking into the stone, shattering it and sending the shrapnel exploding outward, both at Kara and to tumble into the darkness below. She didn't flinch as shards of sharp stone penetrated and cut her skin. Her only reaction was the tightening of her fingers holding her sword. The smell was far worse than the discomfort. Kara's eyes danced over the creature that appeared to be a mix of bird, dragon, and bull, searching for a weakness that she could exploit.

The claws dragged over the stone, making the sound of nails on a chalkboard sound like a lullaby and setting Kara's teeth on edge. Tilting her head to the side, she watched as it poked at the burnt flesh on her arm, using one talon to scrape off the top layer of cooked flesh before pulling it back for a taste, licking the claw with a long slimy forked green tongue. Only then did its eyes close and she swore the damn thing purred. Kara's jaw ticked at the obvious pleasure the thing was getting from it. It wouldn't last.

Another clawed foot pushed over the lip of the wall, the creature slithering closer, its beak gaping as it sniffed her. Kara's brow lifted, and a smirk played at her lips. Rolling her eyes skyward, she waited until the beast too glanced up and then she called down the lightning that had been crackling and building above them. The thing screamed, rolling along the surface of the wall as it tried to dodge the bolts.

Kara's head jerked back on her shoulders when she noticed it had no hind legs. Its tail flicked, snapping across her middle and slicing her open as she flew backward and tumbled over the rough stones. Levering herself up with her elbows, she sighed her relief that her sword was still gripped tight in her fist and pushed to her knees. Something warm and wet ran over her abdomen, soaking her pants through to her skin. Glancing down, Kara realized that it was blood. Hers, but she didn't have time to bleed as she jumped to the left to avoid a crushing stomp of the creature's palm that tried to squash her like a bug. Rolling out of the way as the other hand came down, she grunted when she was pinned with sharp talons framing her head and the heel of its hand pressed against her hips like a five-point harness. The only thing she could move were her arms.

She went limp when it lowered its head to sniff her, blowing a puff of air into her face. It eyed her, tilting its head and turning it to see her better with one of the glowing red eyes, the lid spreading slowly from the corner to cover the surface and leave Kara in sudden darkness. When the eyelid

499

began to slide open again, Kara tensed and shoved her sword into its eye with a war cry, twisting the blade and turning her head as its blood poured over her face, smothering her.

Kara grunted, gritting her teeth as the talons sliced into her shoulders. She had to end this now, or she was going to die. Calling down the lightning, she hit it with bolt after bolt, not stopping until its massive body finally fell limp. Panting, Kara winced and tried to pry its clawed hand off her, but it was a no go. She laughed and wished she could wipe the blood from her face, but she was stuck and too drained to do a damned thing about it. Survive to die. Fucking figured.

Chapter 53

Ty appeared in the shadows, watching the Valkyrie.

Feeling eyes on her, Kara turned her head, searching the shadows for the next thing with teeth that wanted to take a bite out of her. Sighing, she gripped her sword tighter and waited.

"How goes it?" He asked showing himself to her. He magicked a shield around the two of them. Ty didn't want anything interfering with their little chat. She was still alive, and that was a pleasant surprise. Maybe she was a better asset than he'd first thought.

Kara's brow arched, and she tried to brush the hair back from her face, but the dried blood made it stiff and uncooperative. "Hey." She eyed Ty skeptically. "I'm still breathing." She turned to look over her shoulder expecting something to be ready to attack. "What brings you out here?" She turned her eyes back to his.

Ty looked her over and smiled. "I've come to relieve you of your post."

Her eyes narrowed a little, not really believing him and waiting for the punch line. "Okay." Kara glanced over her shoulder again, because being on the gates made you paranoid as shit. "What's next, Boss?" Her voice lacked it usual sarcasm. She was too damned tired and relieved to be leaving here.

"You'll be reassigned to a new post."

Sighing, she nodded. She knew it was too good to be true. Kara didn't let the disappointment show on her face and straightened her back a little more while she waited and ignored the aches and pains that made her body throb.

They vanished and reappeared in Brock's room at The Pit. Ty left her there, without a word. He like keeping her off balance.

"What the fuck?" Kara growled and looked around. Ty must have something against letting his people know what the hell was going on, because this was the second time he'd left without any damned answers. It was starting to piss her off.

Shaking her head, completely baffled by the lack of clarity Ty seemed to thrive on, she checked the rooms and found them empty, except for Bob. Kara patted his raised head before she closed herself in the bathroom and leaned her sword in the corner, not trusting that she would be staying here. Glancing up, she caught her reflection in the mirror and grimaced. Dried blood covered her and her armor, cracking and flaking off in places. Her blonde hair was stiff and stained red. The skin under her eyes was puffy and showed how little sleep she'd gotten while she was gone. Kara had learned quickly that it was better to be sleep deprived than wake up to a reaper sinking its claws into you.

Suddenly she felt the exhaustion tackle her, weighing down her arms as she reached to begin unstrapping, unlacing and peeling off her armor piece by piece. Too tired to flash them where they belonged, she piled them beside her sword. Every movement pulled at tired, achy muscles and reopened cuts wept, leaking blood and a strange pus that she'd never experienced before. Usually, her body healed quickly, but either something in the air or the beasts in the Shadowlands had something in their claws and saliva that made everything fester with infection and slowed healing to a snail's crawl. More of her skin was an angry purple color than the usual healthy tanned tone. Closing her

502

eyes, she let her head roll forward and ran a hand over the gash across her stomach.

Turning mechanically, she stepped into the shower and turned on the water not reacting to the ice-cold blast that hit before the water warmed. Kara groaned softly at the feel of the water rolling over her skin. Gods, it felt good. Curling her fingers around the soap, she lifted it to her nose and inhaled, savoring the delicate scent. After too long smelling nothing but sulfur and the foul stench of blood, it was heaven. Kara sighed and rolled it into a lather, slowly covering her body with suds and scrubbing her skin until anything not bruised, was pink and clean. Pulling the tie from the end of her braid, she leaned her head back under the spray, letting the now hot water dissolve and break up the blood before she reached for Brock's shampoo and squeezed some into her hand to repeat what she had done to her skin.

Finally, when she thought she was as clean as she could hope to be right now, she wrapped herself in a towel, barely able to muster the energy to rub her hair to less than dripping. Avoiding looking at herself in the mirror, she zombie walked to Brock's bedroom and collapsed on the bed. Reaching for the pillow that smelled like him, she pulled it to her and hugged it tightly. It was a piss poor substitute for the male that she missed horribly but would have to do for now. Barely conscious as her body began to shut down, Kara linked Brock that she was in his room and going to pass out. She would have texted but had no idea where her phone was. That was a problem for another time.

Brock stood behind the bar, pouring a draft when he heard Kara's mindlink. A smile instantly took over his face, and he breathed deeply for the first time since she'd gone. 'Are you ok?' He linked back. His eyes swept over the crowd. He wanted to sprint to his room, but they were swamped.

Kara hugged the pillow tighter and smiled when she heard Brock's voice in her head. 'Yeah. I'm okay. Missed you.'

When Daniel stepped behind the bar to check on his paycheck, Brock grabbed the young panther. "Cover for me? I have to go." He tried to keep the pleading out of his tone as the kid arched a questioning brow.

"I don't know, man. I had plans." The bear was all but coming out of his skin to get out of here. What was up with that? Brock was never like this.

"I'll match your pay for the shift. That's double time." Brock spread his hands, palm up and waited. "Double. Time," he repeated with a drug dealer's grin.

Daniel laughed. "Yeah, okay. But only because you've covered my ass so many times."

"Thank you." Brock smiled wide and tossed Daniel his bar towel. "The drinks in the well are for table seven." Backing away as he talked, he bumped into Ripper. Turning, he slapped a hand on the leopard's shoulder. "She's back," he grinned and dove into the crowd to fight his way through to the kitchen.

Ripper arched a brow at Daniel who shrugged and began putting the drinks on a tray. "Apparently, she's back. Whatever the hell that means." Shaking his head and laughing, Ripper slid a draft to a regular at the end of the bar.

Brock bounded up the stairs and threw open the door, petting Bob's head as the pit lifted it to look around with a yawn. "Cher?"

Kara winced and lifted her head to look over her shoulder, pushing up on one elbow so she could see. Her body sagged when he appeared in the doorway, and she knew that she was really home. "I'm in here." She pulled the towel tighter and sat up, thinking she probably should have stolen one of his t-shirts or something.

He wanted to scoop her up in his arms and never let her go again, but the bruises and cuts that covered her bare arms and legs forced him to control himself. Instead, he sat on the bed and stroked the back of her hand with his thumb. "I'm happy you're back. Are you hungry? I can get you something to eat." He wanted to do anything that would make her more comfortable and didn't care if he was babbling.

"Me too." Holding her towel, she crawled into his lap and wrapped her arms around him tightly. "Starving, but I need this first," she whispered against his neck, letting his scent soothe her.

He held her, reminding himself to be gentle, and stroked her hair. Seeing that she was struggling with the towel, he ghosted it away and replaced it with baggy sweats and a tank top, but not before he saw how badly she'd been abused. He swallowed his growl, wanting a piece of the son of a bitch that would do this to her. "What do you want to eat?"

Kara smiled as the shirt covered her. "Thanks. Anything I don't have to kill first and can identify." She shuddered slightly as she remembered the lack of options at the gate.

"How about spaghetti and meatballs? I made some for lunch. I went overboard with it. I also have some wine if you want that too."

She kissed his jaw and nodded. "Sounds amazing." It really did, but she couldn't bring herself to move just yet. "Sorry to pop back in with no warning, Babes."

"Hush. You're back, and that's all that matters." Brock gave her the remote from the nightstand and kissed her neck as he lowered her back to the bed and tore himself away from where he wanted to be, to make her dinner. After a long ass ten minutes, he returned with the tray of food and wine, half expecting her to have been a figment of his imagination.

Rubbing her face as she flipped through the channels, Kara listened to him making noise in the kitchen and let the sounds of home sooth her. She pushed her back against the pillows and leaned on the headboard, needing to know nothing was creeping up behind her and felt guilty. She should be helping, not sitting here doing nothing. She groaned when he appeared with the tray of pasta, moaning

505

at how good it smelled. Not as good as he did, but it still made her stomach rumble. "If no one has told you how amazing you are yet today, Brock, let me be the first." She grinned up at him.

Laughing, he sat down with her. "Need anything else? Cheese? Salt and pepper?"

Shaking her head no, she leaned over and brushed her lips over his shoulder. "It's perfect." She blinked at the pile of food, enjoying the anticipation of how it was going to taste until she couldn't torture herself any longer. Picking up a fork, Kara twirled the pasta and blew on it before sliding it into her mouth, moaning happily as the garlicky tomato sauce danced on her tongue. "So good," she sighed before taking a sip of her wine.

Brock's grin grew as she dug into the food with enthusiasm. He couldn't stop touching her to assure himself that she was truly home.

After inhaling about half of the plate, Kara sat back and rubbed her stomach, feeling too full. Wiping her face with the napkin, she glanced up at him and blushed. "Sorry, my table manners are usually better than that. God, I missed you!" She cupped his face sliding her thumb along his bearded jaw, loving how it felt against her skin. "How long was I gone?"

"Not long, a few days." He grinned and licked her fingers. "Drink your wine." He hoped she liked it.

Groaning, she bit her bottom lip and watched him lick her fingers, feeling the room suddenly become way too warm. "Felt longer." She had no idea what she'd said, every bit of her attention trained on his mouth.

"No, only a few days, Cher." He licked her fingers again. The mix of her and the tomato sauce on her skin was delicious.

She didn't want to wrap her head around that, not when he was here beside her. She cleared her suddenly dry throat and reached for the wine, closing her eyes and savoring the rich oak flavor. "Did I miss anything important?" Other than him, because even the most everyday and mundane things took on new importance to her if this bear was involved.

Shaking his head no, he removed the tray from her lap.

"Good," she smiled and watched him move the tray. "Thank you." She eyed him and wanted to crawl back in his lap and hold onto him, but that sounded clingy as hell, even to her. Instead, she slid her palm under his and lifted his knuckles to brush her lips over them.

Smiling, because he couldn't seem to stop, he kissed her hand and pulled her close. "Are you tired?"

Kara sighed happily and slid her arms around him. "Yeah, I hate to admit it, but I am a little." Flat out lie, that. She was exhausted, but she didn't want him to go. Yeah, it was selfish, but she could live with it.

"Good, because I could use a nap, myself." Brock snuggled up with her.

Gods, he was perfect or humoring her, but she was sticking with perfect. Grinning, Kara wiggled closer, until all she could smell was him and moaned softly. Pulling back to kiss him, she met his eyes and smiled. "I love you, Brock."

"I love you too, Kara." He kissed her again as a yawn slipped from her.

"Sorry." Kara shook her head, a little embarrassed by the yawn and snuggled against him again. Closing her eyes, she felt safe for the first time in days, and it had more to do with him being here than where she was.

He held her and felt his body relax. He'd been coiled tight, worried that she wouldn't come back. Relief made his eyelids heavy and, although he tried to fight it, he drifted off.

Kara smiled softly, feeling the softness of his fur appear against her face. Spreading her fingers, she pushed them into his warm coat and then she was out.

Chapter 54

Brock woke and groaned, stretching out his massive grizzly bear body. He chuffed his contentment at the lump he felt burrowed partially under him. Kara was home. He'd been worried that she wouldn't come back, not alive and if she was, not to him. He still couldn't believe that she was his. Well, for now. She could leave and shatter his heart at any moment. But for now, he had her, and he wasn't going to ruin it with what could happen. He had the female that he loved beside him, and that was as good as it got.

He breathed in her scent, his brow arching. She smelled different. The tinge of pain was expected, but that wasn't it. Was that because of the time she'd spent in the Shadowlands? He shifted off her so that he could look her over. He glared at the bruises and cuts that covered most of her exposed skin. Rage simmered in his chest. She didn't deserve this. Yes, he knew that her way of life was brutal, but this was too much.

Kara's hand crept over the sheet until it tangled in the fur that covered his chest. Brock sighed at the sense of calm it brought him. It had to mean something, that she sought him out even in her sleep. Didn't it? At first, Brock had thought it was a fluke, until one night he'd experimented with moving out of her reach repeatedly and each time, was rewarded with her migrating over the bed to him. In his weaker moments, he allowed himself to think that maybe, just maybe, she needed him as much as he needed her.

As if reading his mind, she rolled over until her back was against his chest. Brock circled her waist with his paw, lifting his head from the pillow when she hissed, and pain overtook her scent. Shifting human, he tugged at the hem of her tank top, arching a brow when it stuck to her stomach. Dropping the white cotton, he stroked a bare patch of skin on her hip and pushed up on his elbow to take a look. A maroon and yellow stain slashed across the white fabric that covered her abdomen. When he touched it, the fabric was stiff and crusty. "My poor, Cher," he whispered laying down again and holding her against him.

Kara's face rolled toward him, but her eyes didn't open. Her skin was glossy and her blond hair stuck to the dampness there. Brock brushed his lips against her forehead and pulled back to look at her with concern. She was burning up. He didn't know much about Valkyries and if they could get fevers, but she wasn't usually this warm or sweaty. He swept the hair back from her face, surprised at how wet it was. Something was wrong.

Brock considered ghosting her to the clinic to have the Docs look her over or try to summon Odin to take her to her hot spring. His eyes swept over her face in the dim light, and he used his magic to open the heavy curtains to let the morning sunlight spill over her. Kara sighed, and her lips curled when the rays touched her skin. Maybe it was wishful thinking, but he thought that her color improved a little. Brock's brow arched as he watched the dark purple spots fade to a russet brown before his eyes. It made sense. She'd told him that sunlight recharged her and helped her heal, but seeing it firsthand made him believe it and calmed the worry that was chewing at his gut.

A knock on the door turned his head. Pressing his lips to Kara's damp hair, he carefully untangled his body from hers and rolled out of bed. Stretching, he ghosted on a pair of sweats and smiled when Bob fell in beside him. Brock was surprised when the dog didn't bark at the knock, but grateful. Kara needed to rest. Maybe Bob knew that too. He opened the door a crack and peered out.

"Morning, Bubba." Bree smiled at him, holding out a cup of coffee.

Brock smiled, let the door swing open and took the mug as he gave his sister a one-armed hug. "What do you need Bree?" He asked and stepped back so she could come into the small kitchen and closed the door behind her.

"That's why I keep smelling dog," Bree grinned and knelt to pet Bob, whose tail wagged furiously as he licked her face. "What's his name?"

"Bob." Brock watched his sister with his pet, pleased at her reaction as he sipped the coffee.

"You can visit me anytime, Bob." Bree kissed his nose and stood up. "They sent me to tell you that it's your shift for the portal." Her eyes turned to the open bedroom door. "Is she okay?"

Brock groaned and scratched his bearded jaw. He'd forgotten about them doubling up the shifts on the portal, and he didn't want to leave Kara. "I think so. She's pretty banged up, but breathing."

"I'm glad she's back." Bree kept her concerns to herself. The spirits had told her what had happened in the Shadowlands and how close Kara had come to forgetting everything, even Brock. He wouldn't listen to her anyway. Her brother had blinders on when it came to the Valkyrie.

"Me too." Brock smiled and hugged his sister. "I'm not as dumb as you think I am, Bree," he said, resting his chin on top of her head. "I know it might not last, but that doesn't mean I can't be happy for now, does it?"

She looked up at him, surprised that he knew what she was thinking. "No. It doesn't."

"Good." He released her and grinned. "I'll be down after I take Bob out and hit the shower."

"I'll tell them that you're on your way." Bree left quietly, relieved that Brock was still thinking with his upper head and not just the downstairs one and his heart.

Chapter 55

She didn't feel right. Kara wiped at the sweat beading on her brow. She pushed off the sofa and fell back down with a thump. The muscles in her legs quivered and her joints throbbed. Breathing heavier than she should, she dropped her head back on the cushions and eyed the ceiling. Crap. This should be getting better by now, not worse. Scrubbing her face, she tried to remember the last time she'd felt what humans would call *sick.* Other than deliberate poisonings, she was coming up empty. She shivered and pulled a blanket over her as a cold chill raced over her skin.

Kara tried to flash herself to the roof to recharge and speed the healing with the sun's help but got nowhere. When she woke, she'd had to shower to loosen the scab that had pasted the tank top to her wound. Afraid that it was happening again, she rolled down the blanket and pulled up her fresh shirt to look at the oozing wound that refused to heal. Wincing, she slid the pads of her fingers over the ragged edge, sitting bolt upright when they brushed over a raised dot of black. Her entire body clenched at the pain that shot deep into her abdomen before her nervous system picked up the scream and ricocheted it through the rest of her body. Biting her lip to muffle the groan, Kara pinched the black thing between her broken nails and tugged.

Her head jacked back when the thing moved. The black tip had pulled out about a quarter of an inch but was still firmly rooted in her flesh. Kara's eyes rolled back in her head, and the room dimmed. Blinking her eyes rapidly, she breathed through the burning lightning bolts of pain. Slowly raising her head and looking down, she grabbed the hair-thin spike again and yanked. Blood flooded her mouth as her teeth sunk into her lip. Her vision reduced to a single pinpoint of light. The air exploded from her lungs, and her body went limp. Raising her heavy hand, she held the thing in front of her eyes and attempted to focus. It was four inches long, sharp for easy entrance, but barbed for not so easy extraction. Nice. Blood dripped from the barb, ruining the new white tank top. Her head dropped back, and she blinked at the ceiling.

Panting, Kara wiped at her forehead, preventing the sweat from rolling into her eyes. She sighed. Ty should have warned her about this shit. Then again, he wasn't big on explaining anything, other than how much she sucked. Taking a deep breath, she glanced down again and groaned at the neat line of black dots embedded in the swollen red, with tinges of green, gash. She couldn't do all of this by herself and asking Brock to help... Yeah, she knew he would, but it was just too damned gross. If they all felt like the last one when they came out, she didn't trust herself not to hurt him.

Another chill made her teeth chatter. Heat bled from her skin, causing the air to shimmer around her. Sighing heavily, Kara wrapped the blanket around her and forced her shaky legs to stand and hold her weight. Her body screamed its protest, but her will was stronger. Progress was slow. One foot dragged and shuffled in front of the other. More than once, she had to stop and lean her shoulder against the wall. 'It's okay, Bob,' she linked the pit who whined and tried to push his muzzle through the crack under the door.

Pushing off the wall, she began moving again. Her fingers brushed the wall, ready to catch her if she faltered. Kara didn't see anything as she focused on her destination. Just when she doubted that she'd make it, she found herself propped up against the frame of the door to Asher's office. Wiping the sweat from her forehead with the back of a quivering hand, Kara cleared her throat.

The combination of the nasty smell and the sound got Asher's attention. His jaw fell open when he saw the Valkyrie. She looked like hell. Her blonde hair was wet and plastered to her face. Her blue eyes held none of their usual light. She trembled, and her teeth clicked together. He could feel the fever that burned inside her from across the room. Flipping the patient file that he'd been reading closed, he rolled back his chair. His sharp chocolate colored eyes swept over her with concern. "You okay, Kara?"

Kara shook her head, locking her knees when her legs began to sag. "No. I don't think so. I need your help." She held out the barb to him with a wobbly arm. "I have a bunch of those in me, and I can't pull them all out myself."

Crossing the room to her, Asher's dark head tilted as he took what she held out to him. He turned it in his hand, studying it. Sniffing it, his nose wrinkled. Poison and infection, the barb reeked of both. If she were a shifter, she'd already be dead. His brow arched before his gaze rolled back to meet her eyes. "You did the right thing, coming here. No bolting the nice doctor. Deal?" One side of his mouth curled up in a grin as he helped her into an exam room and onto the table. "Show and tell time."

Kara's smile was as shallow as her breathing when she settled on the exam table, not caring that she was crinkling the hell out of the paper liner. "No worries. Seems my powers are on the fritz." Blowing out her breath in a huff, Kara opened the blanket and lifted her shirt for him to see. Watching his face for a clue as to what he was thinking. The Doc had one hell of a poker face.

"Do I want to know how this happened?" Asher's voice was soothing as his hand palpated the area. He held his breath when Kara's hands dropped to grip the exam table, and the metal frame beneath the padding groaned.

Kara gasped and gritted her teeth together when he touched her. It felt like she was being gutted with a dull knife. Not able to open her mouth or make her voice work, she shook her head no.

Asher chuckled and got a pillow from the closet, fluffing it before he placed it on the table and helped her turn and lay back on the bed. "Anything I need to know about your kind before we do this?"

Kara grimaced and tried to get comfortable, which was damned hard to do when being in the fetal position sounded like the best course of action. "If you could ghost me to the roof when you're done, I'd appreciate it. I need the sun." She eyed the doctor wearily. Trusting did not come easy and was alien to her, but she was out of options.

"Good to know." Asher moved around the room collecting supplies and snapped on a pair of nitrile gloves before offering a reassuring smile. "You ready?"

"Yeah." She shook her head no, making him laugh. Her hands death gripped the exam table as he got to work. Kara tried not to flinch, flop or do anything to make his job harder. Grinding her molars and jacking her head back on the pillow, her body was taut. Kara made it through the first barb being pulled loose and heard it clink into a stainless-steel basin. She felt the pull of the second as it chewed its way out through skin and muscle but passed out before she could hear it join its friend.

Chapter 56

Kara smiled when she rolled over, and a furry clawed paw hooked around her hips and dragged her back against the soft fur of the bear behind her. Groaning softly, she wiggled back against Brock tighter, tilting her head at the leathery nose that brushed her neck. Kara covered his arm with hers and slowly opened her eyes, blinking the sleep from them and nodding her head deeper into the pillow and closing them again.

Yesterday, she'd barely been able to move, and today, she was just a little sore. What a difference a day made. She didn't remember coming back inside after Asher had left her on the roof, with plenty of water and Bob to keep watch over her. It seemed their secret was common knowledge to the shifters living in the rooms over The Pit. That was a little disappointing, but she was glad to have the company. Brock must have come for her. She ran her fingers through his fur, smiling.

She'd never expected any of this when she'd stumbled into The Pit in nothing but a lab coat, shell-shocked by what she'd just escaped. The one thing Kara had been able to count on since she returned was Brock. She didn't deserve him. "Did you bring me inside?" She asked, her voice soft and a little groggy.

Brock's muzzle nuzzled her neck, licking it as he groaned at her scent that was almost back to normal this morning. 'Don't you know, Cher? I'll always come for you,' he linked her, holding her tighter. He had no intention of letting her know that Asher had come to him after leaving Kara on the roof. The Doc was worried, more so with all the weird creatures popping out of the shadow as of late. Asher had shown Brock the four dozen spines that he'd removed from Kara and explained the poison and what it would do to shifters. Stone cold death. Quick and painful. Kara had only survived because of what she was, but still, Asher was worried and had told him to keep an eye on her. Who knew what the after effects of such a lethal dose could do?

Kara's smile grew, and her hand reached up to stroke his face, laughing when his long tongue wrapped around her fingers. "I do. Now."

'Good,' he growled against her ear. 'I think someone wants to say good morning.' Brock watched Bob's eyes slowly rise above the edge of the bed to peer at them.

Brown eyes watched them from the side of the bed. Pale gray brows worked as the canine looked from Kara's face to the bear behind her. Reaching out, Kara rubbed Bob's head and yawned so wide that her jaw made a cracking noise. He probably needed to go out. Sighing, she wiggled out from under Brock's arm, mumbling something about taking the dog outside, at least that's what she meant to say but wasn't sure she was even close to making those words come out of her mouth.

Kara was rewarded with the sound of Bob's tail thumping on the floor. Rubbing her face with her hands, she pulled her hair back in a messy ponytail and ghosted on a pair of shorts and a t-shirt before she crawled out of bed. Yawning again, she zombie shuffled into the living room and blinked, trying to focus long enough to find Bob's leash. Okay. It wasn't going to work without coffee. Bob whined and looked at the door, telling her it would have to wait. Crap.

Kara caught herself on the counter top in the kitchen when her feet tangled in the leash, and she almost faceplanted on the floor. Arching a brow as she bent over to pick up the nylon lead, she snapped the toggles onto the ring of Bob's collar and was about to ghost out when she remembered the little plastic bags. Shuffling back to the living room, she shoved a couple of them into her pocket and looked down at the pit. "You ready, Big Guy?" He chuffed what she assumed was a yes, so Kara ghosted them to the parking lot behind the bar.

Rubbing her face again as she walked and let Bob wander and take in all the smells that came with The Pit, she remembered that she could ghost herself some coffee. Yeah. Her gears were not really turning yet. Kara snorted at herself and made a paper cup with a lid appear in her hand, grimacing as the hot creamy beverage burned the roof of her mouth. Better. She smiled and watched Bob. He was adapting well. He was already used to ghosting places, and the plethora of scents inside didn't seem to faze him at all. Sure, she could walk him down the stairs, but it had been kind of fun to keep him as her and Brock's secret until the jig was up.

Glancing up, Kara watched as the sun finally rose above the buildings around her. She sipped her coffee again and decided that she would take Bob for a run after he did his business. Stretching their muscles would be good for them both. It would be even better if Brock decided to join them.

Chapter 57

After walking Bob, Brock slipped in through the back entrance and into the kitchen. His plan was simple. Sneak in. Steal a couple of steaks. Go unnoticed by Brax.

Crap. Kara had lost track of time and forgotten that someone depended on her for some of life's most basic needs. 'Hold on Bob, I'm coming,' she mindlinked the canine, having no idea if it worked because he had never linked back. She jogged through the people and poked her head in through the saloon doors of the kitchen, ready to duck if necessary. She spotted Brock, grinned and pushed inside to lean against the counter saying nothing as he rifled in the monster of a refrigerator.

With his head in the Frigidaire, Brock didn't look up when Kara came in. Her scent told him who it was. Bob poked his head around the island in the middle of the kitchen. His tongue was hanging out, and he was ready for whatever got dropped for him.

Kara snickered at Bob, who had already learned to keep a watchful eye out for Brax. "You are a brave bear to do that without a look out in place," she teased and grabbed an apple from a crate that hadn't been dealt with yet.

Giving her a thumbs up, he pulled out four steaks, two whole chickens, and one ham steak. Kicking the door closed Brock set the meat on the island.

Both of her brows popped up as Kara eyed the pile of food. "Hungry Babes?" She used the tail of her shirt to shine the apple before she looked up at him again and took a bite. The crunch sounded louder than she expected. Her neck lowered into her shoulders as she looked around for an armed and angry bear.

"It's for Bob." He laughed and started making dinner for them all. Bob pawed at him. "Okay, water. Right. Can you please get him a bowl of water?"

Kara froze in mid-chew and stared at him until he laughed. "You've got it." She snickered at the image of Bob looking like he'd swallowed a bowling ball. Kara rubbed her hand across Brock's wide shoulders on her way across the kitchen to the sink. Holding the apple between her teeth, she pulled down a bowl and filled it with water.

Brock smiled and seasoned the steaks after he cut away the excess fat. He dropped meat for Bob here and there. "Hungry?"

She nodded her head yes, and set the bowl down for the pit, before taking the apple out of her mouth. "You know me. I'm always hungry. Just not sure I'm THAT hungry." She pointed at the pile of food and laughed.

"Sure, I've seen you eat before," Brock teased her.

Kara rolled her eyes up to his, arched one brow and calmly leaned up to bite his shoulder. Grinning against his shirt, she laughed. "You know a nothing but salad kinda girl would drive you nuts, Big Guy." She patted her hand where she'd bitten him and kissed his bearded cheek.

He growled and then so did Bob. Brock laughed. He deboned a piece of the chicken, pulled it off the plate and let it hit the floor for Bob. "Salad is not food. It means food is coming. Nothing more."

She laughed and eyed Bob, who seemed to be siding with the bear. Kara wasn't sure she liked that turn of events but forgot about it as soon as she saw Brock's smile. "Agreed. So, what are we making?" She took another bite of her apple and watched what he was doing, hoping some of it would sink in somehow.

"Making steak and fries. The ham is for Bob. The other chicken I'm gonna soak overnight, and tomorrow we're going to the park for a picnic." Bob perked up at the word park.

"We are?" Kara smiled and threw the apple core into the trash can, snickering as Bob tracked it like a pro. "I don't think I've ever done that for fun."

Brock smiled at her. "It's simple. We play with Bob, eat like pigs and maybe even get drunk. All depends." He dropped the fries in the fryer when Brax busted in.

"What the hell are you doing?" Brock's younger copy demanded, his Cajun accent thick with rage.

Kara had to admit, that sounded nice. She was just about to ask what the getting drunk depended on when Grumpy Bear burst into the kitchen. She looked from the food to the fryer and then up at Brock. "He doesn't really want us to answer that, does he?" She watched Brax seethe and wondered just how they could look so much alike on the surface and beyond that, not have a single similarity.

"You're just in time brother, for dinner," Brock said as Bob bolted up from the floor and snarled at Brax.

"A dog! You let a dog into my kitchen?" Brax exploded.

"Why not? Sirus and Drew come in here all the time." Brock smirked, pulling the fries. He plated the steaks. "Calm down before you give yourself hemorrhoids from trying to shit out that stick you've got in your ass. What's the matter Brax? Another girl laugh when you tried to give her your number?"

Brax ignored the dog ready to attack him and backhanded his brother, hard. "We can't all fuck lion leftovers," he snapped and started away.

Brock licked at his lip, tasting blood. "Yes, she might be leftovers. But that's better than being overlooked and unwanted because I'm a twat," Brock said in French.

Brax spun around and launched himself at his older brother. Taking Brock down, they slammed to the floor. Bob barked and snarled as he jumped on them both and sank his teeth into Brax's left calf.

"Momma should have aborted you." Brax raged.

"No. She should have stopped after me. Let the humans have you, you fucking cunt." They battled and insulted each other in French.

"Um, standing right here..." Kara watched as they both ignored her and continued to hurl insults at one another. Lion leftovers, original true, but not exactly complimentary. Her brow arched and her head snapped around when Brax and Brock hit the floor and Bob jumped into the fray, drawing more blood. "Fuck my life" she muttered, not that anyone could have heard her over the blue streak of cursing in French going on. Why didn't Kara think she could live here full time? Exhibit A was slugging it out on the kitchen floor.

First, she grabbed Bob and learned exactly why so many were afraid of pits. Either his jaws her locked as he shook the hell out of Brax's leg or he had a stubborn streak that rivaled the gods. "Let go, Bob," Kara growled and was again ignored. "Remember, you made me do this." She sent a weak bolt into his mouth until he spit out the bear. Grabbing the dog by the collar, she held him back and considered sending a much stronger bolt into Brax. Yeah, that made her smile. "E-fucking-nuff, you two!"

Brax punched Brock in the face one last time as Brock shoved him off. Growling, both brothers huffed as blood poured from their mouths, noses and foreheads.

Brax spit blood out and stood. His leg throbbed in pain and he couldn't feel much else from it. "That dog needs to be put down, or I will fucking eat him!" Brax snarled.

Bob barked and snarled back.

"He was protecting his owner." Brock's tone implied that he was talking to an idiot.

Brax shoved Kara out of the way and grabbed the dog by the muzzle. Bob whimpered in pain.

"That's it," Kara growled as she bounced off one of the stainless steel, work tables and bolted the bear, and only at the last minute remembered to hold back enough not to turn him into a pile of ash. Brax let go of Bob, before the electricity reached the canine, and dropped to the floor switching forms as his body twitched. Kara kicked him in the ribs. "If you want to fuck with me, come at me. Touch my fucking dog, and I will kill you. Last." She kicked him again. "Warning." She turned around looking for Brock and Bob, pulling the hair back from her face and trying to calm the hell down before she did something terrible. "Are you two okay?"

Bob ran to Brock. "I think so." Brock stood up. "I'm sorry, Cher." He looked down at the floor ashamed of himself and his brother.

Kara snorted and cupped his face, looked at the damage and reconsidered that pile of ash idea. "Why are you sorry? I just bolted your brother. I should be apologizing. And I am sorry if you get shit about it, but not at all sorry I did it." She stretched up and kissed him carefully before glancing down at Bob who was peeking out from behind Brock's thigh. Holding out her hand, she grinned when he slid his head under her palm. "So where were we, before we got interrupted?"

"Dinner!" Brock ghosted them and the food back to their room, mindlinking Asher about Brax.

She laughed as they appeared back in Brock's room and Bob trotted around like he was staking his claim on his territory. "And we were talking about being drunk in the park?" She snickered and dropped her head against Brock's chest, sliding her arms around him and tilted her head up to look at him.

He groaned a bit and nodded "Sounds like an excellent plan."

She nodded her agreement. "It really does. We should get you cleaned up before you eat, Babes." Kara winced at the blood on his face. One of these days, either he was going to snap, or she was, and all that would be left was a pile of dead bears. Sighing, she leaned into him and inhaled his scent, groaning softly before stepping back to go and get the bag of first aid supplies she kept under the bathroom sink.

Running a soft washcloth under the tap, Kara wrung it out and grabbed the bag, hoping that the cuts weren't too deep, before returning to find Brock sitting in a chair and possibly mind melding with Bob. She opened the bag, taking out what she needed and placing the supplies on the table before stepping between his spread thighs and tilting his chin up so she could see his face. God, she loved looking at him. Not only was he drop dead, fucking gorgeous but there was a softness in his face and a mischievous glint in his eyes that made her melt. And the male underneath the mask? She was in awe of him. She dabbed at the cuts, doing her best not to hurt him.

"What?" He asked seeing her staring at his eyes. Brock was glad she was gentle. "I hope you know, I don't see you like Brax said."

She shook her head no and smiled softly. "Brax is Brax. No one sees things the way he does." Well, she hoped that was true because that was one miserable bear. There were only a handful whose opinions mattered, where she was concerned, and one was sitting in front of her. She refolded the cloth to expose a clean surface to continue to clean his face. "I was just thinking that meeting you was the best thing that ever happened to me, Bear. I love you like crazy." She grinned and kissed the end of his nose, reaching for the A&D ointment.

"Ditto, Cher," Brock said as she finished patching him up.

"Good!" She grinned, biting her lip and gathering up the unused supplies to stuff into the bag before she turned and knelt to check Bob. "Did that big mean bear make you bite him?" She cooed and scratched behind his ears. "I think he's okay." She looked back over her shoulder at Brock. "How about you, Babes?" He took too much crap over having her here, and it wasn't fair. She knew that her past with Dame didn't help, but she loved Brock and wasn't leaving, so they could all fuck off.

"I'll heal. I'm just a little sore." He wondered if the Doc had found Brax yet. "Are you ok?" He knew Brax had knocked her into shit pretty hard.

Standing up she put stuff away and looked over at him, wishing that she'd been blessed with the power to heal instead of kill, but she was what she was. Kara pushed the hair back from her face and did a quick inventory of her body. Other than a tender hip, she was good to go. "I'm fine. Your brother hits like a girl." She grinned. "Just saying."

Brock laughed, even though it hurt his face. "Pushing a female, that's a new one for him." Though he had manhandled others before. He was a psycho.

Kara snickered. Most didn't think of her as a female once they knew what she was, and that was all right with her. Doing it in a fight would just get their ass kicked quicker. "Yeah, well he has issues, I guess. Maybe he should visit one of those head shrinkers that I keep hearing about or maybe Asher can remove whatever 'blockage' he has." She had a feeling that things were not going to end well for Brax if he didn't get his head right. The only reason she cared was that it would hurt Brock. Her stomach growled. "Is dinner ruined?"

"No, let me warm it in the oven for a few minutes."

"Thanks." She kicked one of Bob's balls with her toe, sending him chasing after it. She stepped back between Brock's thighs and pushed her hands into his hair, pulling it back away from his face. Leaning down with a grin, Kara ran her tongue over his lower lip and kissed him carefully. "Sorry. That needed doing."

He took her into his arms and nuzzled her.

She smiled and held him to her. "Love you, bear."

"I love you too."

Nuzzling him back, she laughed when Bob pushed his way between them and tried to find a hand to drop the ball into.

Brock laughed "Okay, Bob." He took the ball and threw it.

She grinned. "I think he likes it here."

"I hope so."

"Me too." She kissed him again and winced at the cuts on his face. "They've got to stop thinking it's okay to hit you, Babes."

He shrugged. "Used to it."

Kara growled softly and grumbled under her breath. "You might be, but I'm not." She tried to shake it off and offered him a soft smile. She knew it wore on him, but it was his way to put up with it and say nothing. That was part of what she loved about him, but it also drove her nuts and scared her a little. What if she crossed a line? Would he ever tell her or just keep on keeping on even if it hurt him? Kara sighed and shoved her hands into her back pockets.

Brock warmed their dinner in the oven. As he stood in the kitchen the scene with his brother played in his mind again. He knew why his brother... No, all his brothers, were like this. One stupid mistake had totally fucked their family, once upon a time. Brock had learned his lesson, and he'd kept to himself, to avoid repeating it, for decades. But there was something about the Valkyrie that told him deep inside that this time was different. What he had with Kara was kismet.

Nothing and no one would change his mind about that. Even if it meant taking an ass whooping from his siblings for it. It was something he'd gladly do. You can't undo the past, but you can learn from it. Though Bart, Brax, Bree, and Beyer may not think he'd learned, he had. Brock had learned that one, and how meaningless life could feel when you lived in seclusion and had nothing to wake up for in the morning. Fortunately, his siblings had never had that experience. Brock hoped they never did.

Chapter 58

Brock paced, his hand going to his pocket to feel that the box was still there. Everything Brax had said about Kara in the kitchen replayed through his head. He growled. His family might be cool with how things had gone for him up until now, but Brock wasn't. He finally had the chance at something real, and he'd be damned if he wouldn't grab onto it with both hands. He was tired of not knowing and worrying that Kara could change her mind and he'd be left broken, with nothing but memories. If it was going to happen, he'd rather it be done now before... Before what? He was already screwed if he lost her. His heart couldn't rebound from that.

He wiped his palms on his thighs and prayed that he was doing the right thing. *Please don't let her laugh in my face.* Brock pushed the hair from his face and ghosted himself next to a small but lovely waterfall he'd discovered near the spot where the forest met the swamps. Before he lost his nerve, he mindlinked Kara. "Cher, I need to talk to you as soon as possible. Can you come? Alone, please?" He swallowed hard and waited for her to appear.

The smoke had finally cleared from Kara's attempt to cook, and Bob had stopped hanging his head out the window gasping for fresh air. It wasn't that bad, and she was almost positive that the canine was trying to make her feel sorry for forgetting Brock's most important rule, Kara does

527

not cook without supervision. She was just about to explain to the pooch that it wasn't nice to guilt trip the bringer of the kibble when she heard Brock's voice in her head. As soon as possible was never good. Sighing, she pointed her finger at Bob's nose, "This isn't over, Buddy Boy." Kara grinned when he licked her finger. She patted him on the head and ghosted to the bear.

Brock smelled the smoke mixed with Kara's scent and closed his eyes to gather his thoughts. Turning, he looked her over, concerned at the smoke that clung to her clothes. "Is everything okay?" He asked, staring at her, expecting to hear that the 'nice firemen,' as she called them, had paid another visit to their home. She didn't look hurt, but that didn't mean she wasn't. Brock's heart started to race a bit, and he had to stuff his hands into his pockets to stop them from reaching for her. His fingers closed around the small box, reminding him why he was here and his heart pounded faster.

Kara blushed lightly and smiled. "Yeah, I made burgers. All buildings are still standing." Her brow arched slowly as she watched him, his body language was anxious as hell. "Babes, what's wrong?" She stepped closer and hugged him, rubbing her hand in slow circles over his back as her eyes took in their surroundings. Damn, what a beautiful spot.

He tried to relax, but he couldn't. "I'm glad. Wait. You tried to cook? Is Bob okay?" Brock tried to keep his voice stern, but when she hugged him, his mind began to race like a hamster on a wheel. Brock stepped back, out of her reach and bit his lip as he stared at her. What he was about to do could ruin everything. "I need to say something to you, and I want you to close your eyes while I do it. It'll be easier that way for me." His mouth went dry. Damn it all to hell.

"Of course, Bob is fine, a bit of a drama queen, but fine." Kara's brows shrugged together when he pulled away and stepped back. Since when was, 'I need to tell you something, but don't look at me,' a good thing? Groaning silently, she dropped her eyes and tried not to think the worst, but damn, it was hard. It would explain the anxiety, he was probably afraid she'd bolt his ass when... She shook her head and smiled tightly. "Yeah, sure. Hit me with it." She closed her eyes and waited.

"You know I love you and that I've never met anyone like you. I don't think I could love anyone more than I do you, but I can't do this anymore. Not like this. Something has to change." Sighing loudly, he pulled the small box from his pocket and sunk down on one knee. "Open your eyes, Kara." As she did what he asked, he opened the hinged box to show her the ring inside. He watched her eyes and his voice was barely more than a whisper when he asked, "Will you marry me, Cher?" Brock's heart pounded in his chest so hard that he hoped he didn't have a heart attack.

Kara ran the scenarios of what she was expecting through her head, and this wasn't on the list. She blinked at him with her jaw hanging open. Her eyes bounced between the ring and his face. Her legs failed, and she dropped to her knees, searching his eyes as she cupped his face between her palms. "Don't ever scare me like that again," she growled, trying to look angry before she kissed him softly and rested her forehead against his. When she could breathe again, she nodded and flipped her eyes to his. "I would love to marry you, Brock."

"I am sorry, Cher." He chuckled as the weight that had been crushing him slipped away, and he kissed her hard. Remembering that there was unfinished business, he forced himself to break away from her lips and held his hand out for hers. "I want to make it official before you change your mind," he teased with a grin.

She blinked back the tears that had flooded her eyes and gave a shaky laugh as she slid her hand into his and watched as he slid the ring onto her finger. The sun reflected and sparkled off the blue stone recessed in the gold setting. "It's beautiful," she whispered.

"It's the color of your eyes, Cher. I know it's not huge, but I wanted something that wouldn't get in the way when you fight." Brock rubbed his thumb over the band as pride bloomed in his chest. She was wearing his ring. He still had trouble believing it, even though he saw it with his own two eyes.

Kara shook her head, staring at it and then flipped her eyes to his. "You thought of everything. It's perfect."

Brock smiled, pleased that she liked it. "Thank you for saying yes. You've made me the happiest male on the planet." He kissed her again and pulled her into his arms to hold her close.

She laughed and kissed him back, melting against him. The smile that was frozen on her face couldn't be pried off with a crowbar. Holding him tight she closed her eyes and inhaled his scent, moaning in the back of her throat. "Gods, I love you, Brock." She kissed him again.

He nuzzled her after she kissed him and grinned. "I promise to always love you and be there for you. No matter what, Cher."

Biting her lip, Kara watched his face. "I promise the same." She bounced excitedly. "I can't believe that I REALLY get to keep you. I can't imagine life without you anymore."

"Yup, now you have two pets." He joked. "I know we'll be happy together. If not, you can always make me into a beautiful rug."

She jabbed him lightly in the ribs and laughed. "And you've got a full-time pain in the ass." She winced. "Let me apologize in advance for the crap that comes with my life." He'd seen her at her best and worst, mostly her worst, and he still wanted her. She wiped at the drop of wetness that trailed over her cheek.

"I'll put that in my back pocket, my love." He smoothed the tear away with his thumb and growled softly. She was amazing. Everything about her made him feel special. He fell more and more in love with her every day. Grinning, he playfully nommed her neck and chuckled.

Laughing, she squirmed and nipped his lower lip when he growled, making her body shudder slightly. God, there was no one like him, and she never took a single moment with him for granted. "You might need bigger pockets," she teased and kissed him, licking and sucking at his lips.

He cuddled her to him and ghosted them home to bed. Bob pounced on him as soon as they appeared licking Brock's face and wagging his tail. "Did Momma try to cook you?" He asked as Bob looked at Kara then sat on Brock's legs.

Kara gave an offended gasp. "I would never..." She crossed her arms over her chest and looked back and forth between them. "I see how ya'll are." She growled and tackled Brock, laughing as Bob jumped on her and stuffed his cold, wet nose in her ear."

"Get her, Bob. Don't let her hurt Daddy!"

Bob sneezed in her ear then licked her face, before trying to wedge himself between them. He barked when he couldn't do it.

"EWWW! Dog snot!" Kara laughed and tried to push Bob's head back so she could wipe her ear on Brock's shirt. Ghosting one of his toys into her hand, she shook it and threw it. "Ha! I win." She stretched up and nuzzled Brock.

"Get off me with that snotty ear!" He growled trying to move away, but she was laying on his hair and couldn't. "Damn, my gorgeous hair!"

"You're my prisoner." Kara laughed and nuzzled him some more, making sure to rub her ear against him, knowing that he could easily move her, if he wanted to.

"GIRL GERMS AND DOG SNOT!" Brock pretended to freak out. "THE HORROR! You devil woman, you!"

Laughing hard, Kara collapsed on him and laughed until she snorted which made her laugh harder. "Get used to it bear, you're stuck with us both," she wheezed out.

Brock hugged her tight and raspberried her neck, grinning as she screamed and wiggled.

531

Chapter 59

Kara watched the wolf across the dusty parking lot. She'd found him. She'd been minding her own business, sitting at a little café, enjoying a light meal and thinking that she needed to get back home and check on Bob. Maybe she would take him to the park to play in the small pond that had no alligators thanks to her bolting it three times a day, for the last week. Yeah, she was probably breaking a dozen fish and game laws by doing it, but they couldn't prove shit. Just as she was finding a dark alley to ghost home in, her body hummed at the beacon of power that sliced through the ether. Fenrir. Kara's eyes narrowed as she appeared where she felt him, but at a distance, and watched his body all but blowing apart with what was shoved inside it. He didn't know. She could tell by the fear and confusion that drifted off him in a dark smoke. Just as suddenly as it had appeared, the energy signature faded down to almost nothing. "The fuck did you do, Loki?" She muttered.

Fenrir's head turned, his brown eyes locking with hers in a silent challenge. Kara was just about to step forward and accept when Ty's summons rang through her head. Shaking it with regret, she ghosted home to get her armor and gear up for Gods knew what. Walking past Branden and into the bar, her eyes searched for Brock, finding him fighting with the printer, again.

Stepping behind the bar, she slid her hand over his shoulders and pushed her phone that wouldn't work where she was going, into his back pocket. "I've been called back," Kara explained when he turned to look at her with questions in his blue eyes.

"Asgard?" He asked hopefully.

Kara shook her head no. "I don't know how long I'll be gone."

"Fuck," Brock cursed and pulled her to him, hugging her tightly. The last time she'd gone, she'd been hurt. According to Asher, she should have died. Thank the gods that she was a Valkyrie and the poison had only made her weak and sick. "I don't want you to go."

"Neither do I," she whispered into his chest. "But I don't have a choice."

"I know," he growled and kissed her, not caring how many people stopped to watch them. "Be careful and kill anything that gets in your way, Cher. We have a wedding to plan."

Smiling, she cupped his face and ran her thumb over his lips. "I promise, Big Guy. Nothing is stopping me from coming back. Nothing." She pressed her lips to his and hoped that she wasn't lying. "So, you'd better be here, and in one piece, when I do."

Brock nodded, and bear hugged her, not wanting to let go. "Yes, ma'am."

"Good." She tried to pull away, but his arms were steel bands around her. "You have to let me go, Babes," she whispered.

"Never," he growled back. Brock knew she was right, but his arms were still in denial. Finally, he forced his grip to loosen, and she slipped free. Lunging forward, he held her face in his hands and captured her mouth, pouring every drop of his feelings into it. "Remember that I love you, Cher."

Kara's breath was ragged when he tore his lips from hers. "Always." She smiled slowly and forced herself not to

533

hold onto him. "And don't you forget that the feeling is more than mutual."

"Never," He promised and watched her walk away. 'Mine,' his bear growled.

Kara jogged into the kitchen and ghosted to The Shadowlands, wrapping herself in her armor and weapons as her molecules became solid. Sighing, she glanced up at Ty on his throne and inclined her head respectfully. Hate it or not, she had a duty to do, and she would do it with honor. "You called, Boss?"

Ty sat back, his gaze amused but not exactly warm, as his eyes swept over her. In all honesty, he hadn't expected much out of this one. She had a mouth and an attitude to rival most of her Viking brethren which warned of nothing but trouble. In truth, she hadn't offered much, seemed to fall in line and had yet to complain about her new job. Even at the gate, she had fought through the pain, exhaustion, and hunger. She might not have been happy about it, but she hadn't wasted his time with whining as most new recruits did. And what surprised him most was that she hadn't complained to anyone else to get her out of it either. He wasn't sure if that was a Viking thing, or simply Kara.

"Yes." He leaned forward and turned the ring on his finger. "More of my guards are missing. I want you to find out where they've gone. I don't want them dead. Find them and bring them back, if they still breathe."

Clasping her hands behind her back, Kara tried to hide the way her body vibrated as it was given permission to do what it was bred for, to dole out violence and death. She'd tied her own hands, so to speak, on that front, not wanting to make her sentence any worse than it was. Without the outlet that fighting for her life gave her, she was getting dangerously twitchy and soon, the fake veil of calm she was selling to those around her, was going to shatter. This was better.

"You want your guards alive if I find them that way." Kara met his eyes and repeated his orders back to him,

534

simply for clarification. "And if I encounter hostiles that are not your guards?" She arched a brow, her eyes following a dark shadow slithering along the arched stone ceiling, one corner of her mouth curling up as she watched its progress. "Do you know if they have fled The Shadowlands? I only ask because I intend to do this as efficiently as possible. I have no need to waste your time, or mine, with needless crap."

He shook his head no. "The reports I've received point to them being here. And if they are not mine, I don't care if they live." Ty watched her, annoyed by her worry about wasting her time and waiting for her to balk about this job. He glanced up at what she was looking at and reached inside her mind to view her memory of dealing with the mist that burned and charred her skin until it split to feed on blood. His eyes narrowed, looking for any signs of fear or anxiety and got nothing back but vague amusement and excitement. "Has the Princess missed the killing?"

"Yes, I have." Her eyes left the blackness, now creeping down a wall and swung back to Ty. Her lips curled up at his laugh. Tilting her head to the side, she reached out for the energy signatures of those who had shared her post on the stronghold. Three were still where they belonged, the rest were all new. Arching a brow, she expanded the search. "Why did you wait so long?" She watched him curiously.

"Who says you're the first I've asked? I hope for your sake that you do a better job than the last Shadz to give it a try." Ty leaned back and crossed an ankle over his knee, his foot bouncing as he measured the Valkyrie before him. "Not that I care, as long as your debt is paid in the end."

Kara grinned and bowed her head. "Point taken. Shall I start now?" Her eyes darted to the black mist that she could feel sniffing toward her. A growl rolled up the back of her throat as she rubbed her fingers against her thumb, sparking and offering to shock it. Kara felt, more than heard, its angry groan as it changed direction, slithering down a hallway instead to search for its meal.

535

Ty stroked his jaw, watching her stare down the mist and win. He wondered if she realized how at home she was here and how far she had fallen into the darkness that lived inside her. He chuckled as her sapphire eyes rolled back to him with calm determination. Many thought they were badasses, but a stint on the wall knocked that out of them if they lived. This one was going to be harder to break. She would though, they always did. "No time like the present."

She smiled and nodded before turning and following her instincts. It was strange, not being able to use scent to track by, but everything here smelled acrid and burned. Even topside it had taken her almost a week to make the smell go away. Now, if Kara were tracking one of Ty's in her world, she knew what smell to chase. Her low square heels scraped over the stone tiles of the floor as she was faced with three hallway options that looked more like tunnels. Reaching out with her senses, she picked the third and dampest, groaning silently when whatever the glowing green liquid was, found a way inside her boots to squish between her toes. On the bright side, the same slime illuminated the space until it ran dry, a few hundred yards in.

Slowly the area grew darker, her boots glowing for a while but soon they went dark too. Skimming her palm and fingers over the cold stone, Kara inched through the inky darkness, her head turning toward the things she couldn't see that scurried past and reached out to touch her. They seemed particularly entranced by her hair, and that was creepy as hell. Sure, she could illuminate the cavern, but warning a possible enemy that she was closing in wasn't part of the program, and she could feel the life signatures of some of the ones she sought up ahead. Unfortunately, that did not tell her how many were already dead.

Closing her fingers around the worn leather hilt of her sword, she pulled it from her sheath without making a sound and ignored the plethora of hands that reached out to touch her as she passed. Breath on the back of her neck sent a shiver dancing down her spine, and her feet moved a little faster. Light bled around a corner up ahead. She crouched lower and winced as one of the things touching her, became more insistent and grabbed her ankle, tripping her up a bit. She refused to look down or to slow. If they could have hurt her, they would have by now. One thing about The Shadowlands, nothing was shy about drawing blood, if they were able.

Carefully stepping across the hall as soon as there was enough light to see the opposite wall, Kara leaned her back against the rough stone, inching toward the brightness and finally coming to the turn. She heard a dull thump, one she knew too well. It was a body hitting stone. Blinking her eyes and waiting until they adjusted to the brightness, she peered around the corner. "Fuck." Her lips moved but made no sound as she ducked back into the shadows. This was so many kinds of wrong that she didn't know where to start the list. Waiting or turning back wasn't an option. She didn't know who the demon that was slicing the throats of Ty's guards and holding the bodies so that the blood sprayed under a closed door was, but she guessed they weren't on her side.

The scrape of metal against metal made her arch a brow and look around the rough stone of the corner again. The demon cursed, trying to turn a large key with both hands and failing before kicking the door. It stomped to the next of Ty's bound and gagged guards, dragged him across the floor and repeated the cutting of the throat ritual. Kara didn't know what was behind that door, but if it took an ocean of a particular kind of blood to open it, wasn't anything good. Taking a deep breath and rolling her eyes toward the ceiling, she sent a silent prayer that the ones she cared for would be taken care of because she was about to do something really fucking stupid.

Stepping into the open, she strolled down the hall, glancing at the walls and looking over the row of Ty's guards kneeling and waiting to be slaughtered. "Is this a private party? Or can anyone join?" Kara grinned and tapped the flat of her sword against her palm nonchalantly.

The demon screamed and threw itself at the door, trying to turn the key. Leaping forward, Kara sliced off its hand, just above the wrist, leaving it twitching and trying to grasp something on the stone floor. Any feeling of triumph was short lived when the slime demon surged toward the door again, its head back as it yelled a word she didn't understand, at the top of its lungs. Swinging the blade of her sword upward, the scream was silenced, and the head slid off the neck to clunk against the floor and roll toward the pile of bodies, staring vacantly at nothing.

The click of a lock mechanism tumbling, turned Kara's head. The floor beneath her feet began to rumble. Dust and chunks of rock fell from the mortared ceiling. "Son. Of. A. Bitch," she growled as she watched the key turn in the headless body's hand as it crumpled to the floor. A low roar filled the air, building in intensity. The wood and iron of the door bent and splintered. Running to the bound guards, she sliced through their bindings and pointed them in the direction of their Master. "Tell Ty what's going on," Kara growled as the last of the six were freed. She reached out and grabbed his green scaled shoulder drawing a growl. "What is it?"

The Gorgon laughed at her and shoved her hand off him. "Titan. Good luck, Viking." Still laughing, the demon turned his red eyes away from her and bolted down the tunnel to safety.

Throwing her weight against the door as something inside boomed against it, Kara tried to hold it closed. The walls shook with the impact. "What the fuck is a Titan?" She growled, not wanting to find out. Another bang against the door, blew it open, the wood exploding in splinters and throwing Kara against the stone wall, bouncing to the floor and missing the soft pile of bodies by inches. Blood filled her mouth. She wedged her hands under her chest and levered her body up to her hands and knees before rolling back on her heals and bolting the moving shadow still cloaked in darkness.

It retreated. At first. Then it returned fire. Kara dove out of the way, rolling to her feet and raising her hands to zap the hell out of the fucker. A loud cracking noise sounded above and made her curse. Throwing bolts with both hands, Kara had to dive out of the way of the return fire again when the ceiling collapsed with a crash.

Kara was forced to the floor by the huge chunks of stone that rained down on her, filling the air with dust and turning everything dark. Her bones cracked and splintered. Kara pushed at the huge blocks of stone, trying to find the light. She coughed at the dust that filled her lungs and felt the wet coppery splatter of blood on her lips. Panting through the pain, she tried to shove herself free again. The rocks settled and were compressed, squashing the air out of her lungs and snapping a few more bones. The fucker had stepped on her, and it was huge.

Waiting until the crushing stopped and she could convince her lungs that they really were meant for breathing, she ghosted herself into the shadowed tunnel that she had come through. She couldn't manage much more than that until she healed. Panting through the pain, she dropped her head back against the stone and waited. She wasn't sure if it was for help to arrive, for the Titan to return and finish her off, or for Ty to reward her failure with an easy death. All options sucked and still, Kara was stuck here waiting.

Chapter 60

Ghosting in to The Pit, Kara leaned against the railing and looked over the bar below. The buzz of anxiety and confusion filled the air, wafting off every shifter and non-human in the place. Her eyes scanned the bobbing heads, searching for Brock and not finding him. She growled her frustration. She did not have time, and she needed to know that he was alright. She looked for any of the quints, but again, nothing.

"Where the hell is everyone?" She growled as she turned toward the stairs, stopping short when she caught her reflection in a mirror. Strolling into the bar in bloody leather armor with weapons strapped everywhere probably wasn't going to make anyone feel calmer. Still, she considered it. Scaring the nonessential out of the bar might make it a smaller target for the nastiness that was loose in NOLA.

No need to cause panic until it was necessary. Flashing on a clean pair of jeans and the top that she'd bought last week, she hoped that if she was still leaking anywhere, it wouldn't show. Moving stiffly down the stairs, she felt every step rattle her broken bones, but she didn't have time to hurt right now. Plenty of time for that, if they failed.

She sighed her relief when she reached the main floor to weave through the patrons on the way to the bar and clapped a hand on Brian's back. "Seen Brock?"

Brian glanced up from mixing drinks, and his hands froze. Pain tensed the corners of Kara's sunken eyes, and the scent of blood surrounded her in a fog. Her cheek was bruised and swollen, and multiple patches of red were growing larger before his eyes. All of that told him that something had gone wrong. But it was the feral and bloodthirsty look in her eyes that cemented the knowledge that the shit had hit the fan. "What happened, Karabara?"

"Just tell me that the last time you saw him, he was okay."

Brian nodded and absently put the drink on the waiting tray. "Yeah. About twenty minutes ago. He took Bob for a run, I think." He eyed her, wanting to ask more, but he had a feeling that she wasn't going to tell him. Not yet.

"Reese around?"

"I don't know." He caught her shoulder as she started to list to the side. "Maybe you should sit down?"

"No time, but thanks," She tried to smile, but her face hurt too much to pull it off. "Be careful, Bear. Shit is about to get real." Before he could ask anything else, Kara slid back into the crowd and ducked down the hall. As soon as she knew that she was alone, she let her mask fall for a few seconds and sagged against the wall before she rapped a knuckle against the office door. "Reese? We have a situation that needs dealing with ASAP," she talked to the closed door.

Kara eyed the wood of the door, appreciating the craftsmanship of the carved panels, but got no answer. Sighing and shaking her head, she stepped back and walked slowly down the hall and to a door that led outside.

She had every intention of briefing the necessary people about what was headed their way if it wasn't already here, but she needed a few minutes to just sit in the sun and recharge. She pushed out through the door at the end of the hall and dragged her shoulder against the exterior wall of the bar until she found the sunny side of the building and let gravity do its thing of pulling her to the ground. Kara winced as bones pushed together wrong and let herself steep in the pain that was swallowing her whole. She wanted to drop her head into her hands, but lifting her arms was too much trouble. Instead, her head rolled forward on her neck.

Power pulsed, close to qualifying as a sonic boom and her head shot up. *Fenrir. How could she forget?* "Loki, get you trouble causing ass down here, now," Kara growled at the heavens. "If I have to come looking for you, what I did to Thor will look like a scraped knee compared to what I do to you." She was in no condition to back up that promise at the moment, but she was willing to give it one hell of a try.

Loki stood inside Fenrir's cell, gaping at the chains coiled into puddles of links. *That god damn bear!* He growled. He was going to kill him. He'd gone through a lot of trouble to find a wolf that could pass as Fenrir to those who didn't know him. Sure, he'd been surprised when Kara fell for it, but the heat of the moment and all that shit. Now Kraven was sniffing around, asking questions and about to ruin everything. Loki's ass was going to pay for what he'd done, and he was fond of his ass so he would do anything that he could to save it.

Kraven. Loki scrubbed his face with his hand. A bored Valkyrie turned bounty hunter for the gods. She was as quick witted and deadly as she was beautiful and he was screwed. If it wasn't for the chaos of the walls between the nine realms crumbling and Odin being distracted by having his precious Gaia back, Loki knew that his ass would already be toast. He needed to come up with plan B, and he needed to do it fast.

He kicked the pile of empty chains and cried out at the pain that shot through his foot. Limping, he paced, growing more irritated as he moved. He froze and tilted his head, listening. It was faint, but he knew that voice laced with threats. Glaring at the chains, he left the cell and locked it before ghosting to New Orleans to answer his sister and maybe kill her Bjorn.

Kara felt her brother's presence. "I know you're there, so stop your bullshit. We need to talk."

"Yes, we do, Little Sister." Loki allowed himself to become solid and stood over her. His damn foot was throbbing. "I assume you are the one who took my wolf?" He crossed his arms over his chest and glared at her, his eyes narrowing as he breathed the air heavy with her pain. Good. He liked it better when her threats were idle.

She nodded and leaned her head against the building. "I went to visit Fen and found Venom, so I returned him to his family," Kara lied and met her brother's angry eyes. "I get it, Loki. I do. I've almost done it, too many times to count. But now we have a problem."

Loki's shoulders relaxed, and he sighed. He should have known that if anyone was his ally when it came to making things better for Fenrir, it was Kara. "What's the problem?" He ghosted in a large oak tree stump and sat, leaning his elbows on his knees. How much did she know?

Where to start? Kara's mind churned. "First, I saw him."

"Where?" Loki's heart pounded. "Is he alright?"

Kara shook her head. "He's stuffed into a shifter body, and it's barely holding his power. It won't work for much longer." Hissing, she pushed her ass closer to the wall when she began to slump. "Fuck," she growled. "His being free has consequences, Brother mine.

"But he was okay? Happy?" Loki couldn't keep the hope from his voice.

"Yes," Kara smiled softly. "For now, he seems to be." She let her brother enjoy the moment before she gave him the rest of the news. Not able to take the pain marinade that she was soaking in, Kara ghosted in a random bottle of booze from the stock room. She growled when she couldn't grip the bottle tightly enough to get it open.

Loki leaned forward, took the bottle and broke the seal before passing it back to her. "So, what happened to you?"

543

"Thanks." Kara took the bottle and tipped it back. When half of the bottle had made it down her throat and made her stomach glow with its heat, she made a face and looked at the label. "Amaretto? Really?" She wiped her tongue on her arm and shuddered. Ignoring Loki's chuckle, she lowered the bottle to the ground and closed her eyes. "I got stepped on." Her voice was flat. "By something called a Titan. Like a frost giant, but no ice and bigger." Sighing, she opened her eyes to glare at his bark of laughter. "It's not funny."

"Beg to differ," Loki managed to get out as he laughed harder. "Was it like the drawn television shows? Were you a pancake?" He laughed harder.

If looks could kill, Loki would be wearing a toe tag. "No. Don't you get it? Ragnarok has begun."

Loki's laughter died. "This keeps getting better." He reached down and took the bottle finishing it and shuddering. "You drink this shit? On purpose?"

"Not on purpose," Kara grimaced, the taste of it still coated her mouth. "What do you mean?"

"Someone called in Kraven."

"Fuck," Kara cursed. "Dad?"

Loki shook his head. "I think it was my daughter. No one else seems to realize that he's missing, but Hel is a smart cookie."

Kara rubbed her face, opening the jagged cut on her cheek. "Great. Just great." One problem at a time. Was it too much to ask?

"Exactly." He reached forward and touched his sister's face, pushing his power into her through the tips of his fingers. It wasn't enough to heal everything, but it knit her bones back together. "Sorry, freeing Fen took a lot out of me."

"Thank you." Kara wiped the blood that dripped down her face with her fingertips. "So, what do we do, Loki? How do we stop this?"

544

He shook his blonde head. "I don't know, Little Sister. I wish I did."

Kara sighed as her mind worked the problem. "We need to find a way to shut down the holes that are opening. So far, stuff has only been able to stick its head through before the tear closed, but that won't last. Then, we need to stop Kraven." She glanced up at the pained look on her brother's face. "And we need to do it all, without sacrificing Fenrir. We on the same page?"

Loki's eyes closed for a second as relief washed through him. "We are."

"Good." Kara sighed and pulled her knees to her chest. "Maybe the dwarves have something..." She trailed off and shook her head.

He nodded, picking up her line of thought. "I'll check with them. We have Fenrir's chains. If they could hold him and block his powers, then maybe they can do the same to this Titan thing."

Kara grinned. "Maybe they can. I like how you think, Brother Mine."

Loki chuckled. "It's not much of a plan, but it's a start."

Kara nodded her agreement. "Let's get to it, then." She grunted as she pushed herself to her feet, watching Loki do the same. "And Brother?"

He looked up from dusting the dirt from his leather britches.

"I love you."

Loki flashed her a smile. "You're going soft, Little Sister," he teased before disappearing.

Kara eyed the stump he left behind and sighed. Well, Bob had a new thing to water. Now, to find Reese and Brock.

Chapter 61

Brock growled and tightened his hand around his phone, squashing the urge to throw it. Kara wasn't answering, and shit was spiraling out of control fast. The regularly scheduled programming on the flat screen over the bar was being interrupted every ten minutes with 'breaking news' concerning some new shit storm. There was no hope of hiding this from the humans. Not when a damned Dragon had just dive bombed the French Quarter. Bob was going nuts. Barking and growling at one door and then running to repeat at the next. Brock tried to mindlink Kara, but again got nothing but radio silence.

"Screw this," he growled and ghosted outside. Using the doors wasn't an option. They were all locked and the glass boarded over to keep the onslaught of strange and frightening beasts outside. Brock ducked his head as something streaked past him and into the shadows. Arching a brow, he followed it, slow, expecting the worst. He edged around the corner of The Pit and froze at the deep, grumbling growl followed by a wet saliva filled snarl behind him.

His hair tickled his face and chills raced down his spine as his heart jackhammered in his chest. Another gust of hot air blew more hair over his shoulders. Turning slowly, Brock stared death in the face. A mouth full of sharp serrated teeth with spit dripping from the sabretooth fangs, over its muzzle to pool on the ground. Glowing red eyes, narrowed in the scarred black skin peppered with tufts of raven hair. Claws on the front paws dug into the pavement, leaving cracks in the asphalt.

Bob going nuts and barking inside the bar, barely registered as Brock's mind tried to work out what he was seeing. He'd heard about these from his parents, was told bedtime stories about the hellhounds that would come and take away little bears who didn't listen to their parents, who only wanted to keep them safe. A hellhound. Holy shit. Pivoting, Brock backed away slow, staring at it in disbelief. "Nice doggy. Good doggy," he murmured.

Kara circled back toward the bar, retracing the same steps she'd taken earlier. She didn't like how the buffer of space between The Pit and the war zone was shrinking a little more each day. She dodged the dumpster that a sudden gust of wind overturned beside her and dropped into a crouch. Another huff of wind, picked up dirt and debris, sandblasting her skin. Kara looked up and sneered at the demon hovering above and eying her while it licked its lips. Black skin, split in places and seemed to glow red underneath reminded her of cooling lava. Topaz yellow eyes gleamed, and it smiled or snarled, showing her a nasty set of teeth that, given half a chance, she would be happy to knock down its throat. Leathery onyx wings stretched to fill the alley, the barbs at the tips cut grooves in the brick buildings on either side of her.

Kara turned to face it, manifested her sword and arched a brow, hating that she was less than a block from home. It was too damned close. "Come and get it," she growled. Smirking and gesturing like she was ringing the dinner bell, Kara planted her feet as it swooped down at her.

Brock tried to hush Bob through mindlink, but Bob wasn't listening. The hellhound turned and started towards the bar. "Bob, go upstairs!" He yelled. Shifting forms, not

547

caring if anyone saw, Brock reared, threw back his head and roared.

The canine nightmare barely spared the massive grizzly a glance. It smelled the blood inside the building. So much food was inside, and it was hungry. Ignoring the threat behind it, the hellhound loped toward his next meal.

Dropping his front paws to the cracked pavement, Brock charged after the vile mutt. Gods, it smelled like something that Branden had rolled in that time. His lip curled in disgust and curled back exposing his teeth. Brock leaped, hoping he could crush the thing under his weight. Stabbing into its back, he shivved the beast with his claws. It's scream, made up of the souls it had consumed, echoed off the buildings around them and made his ears bleed.

The damned thing didn't even slow down, dragging the bear toward The Pit. Brock's skin and fur were grated off on the rough asphalt, leaving a bloody matted trail behind them. He wasn't letting go. He couldn't. Too many lives depended on it.

'MOVE,' Brock bellowed through mindlink when Ripper appeared before the main entrance swinging a piece of chain and holding a damned rocket launcher. *What the hell was he going to do with that? This was how he was going to die? Blown to bits by a crazy ass leopard. Fuck.*

The world switched to slow motion. Ripper's brown eyes flared. His arm raised. A sneer curled up his lips as he let loose a primal yell. He ran at them. They collided. The force of the impact exploded through him. Brock struggled to hold on, sinking his claws deeper into the rolling muscles of his runaway mount. Ripper was mowed down, and the thing wasn't slowing. The hellhound wasn't going to stop. It was going to try to break through the barricaded door ahead. Brock closed his eyes, tucked his head and braced for impact

Rolling on the pavement and breaking a glass bottle with her shoulder, Kara dodged a wing barb. She didn't move fast enough and hissed as the black talon sliced through her shirt and the small of her back. The ground under her shook as the barb slammed into the earth, splitting it apart and throwing chunks of tar into the air. Kara growled at the acidic burn of her torn flesh and rolled to her feet. Her lips curled into a smirk. The demon had stabbed the ground so hard that it was stuck. Smiling coldly, she moved closer, ducking wing number two as it tried to separate her head from her shoulders. This was going to be fun.

Kara heard the yell, recognized the voice and then the words sunk in. Brock and Bob! Her heart pounded in her chest, and she had to fight not to look over her shoulder at the bar. The demon shot forward in a blur. She threw her arms up to defend herself. The distraction cost her when he sunk his claws into her side. Kara grunted in pain and swung her sword, chopping off its hand at the wrist. Pivoting and ignoring the thing still stuck in her side, she shoved the pummel into its face. Kara laughed, not allowing herself to wince at its high-pitched scream of fury.

"I don't have time for this shit," she snarled and grabbed the demon by the throat, ignoring the talons of its other hand digging into her forearm as she shot a bolt into it. She didn't let up or let go until black smoke rolled off its skin creating a fog around them. Kara pushed the body away from her as it went limp, crumpled and burst into flames. It smelled like a mix of burning tires and vomit.

Jumping over the burning trash, Kara made a face as she forced her body to remain calm and ghosted to the bar. Her jaw fell open when she appeared in time to see the hellhound mow down Ripper and crash through the front door in an explosion of glass and wood. Her heart stopped. Brock was all over the mangy SOB. "Fuck!"

Brock bit into the hellhound's shoulder, but the damn thing didn't even flinch. If anything, it picked up speed after it had breached the entrance. He tried again, locking his jaws on its neck and straining to snap it. This wasn't working.

549

The terrified faces of his loved ones burned into his brain. Bree stood on the bar, her blonde hair blown around her face by an invisible wind as she chanted, holding her hands out to her sides and raising them toward the ceiling. Brax threw open the kitchen doors and had a meat cleaver in each hand. Bart leaned over the bar at Bree's feet, pointing their Pappa's shotgun at the intruder. Beyer was frozen, blocking the path to his sister with a snapped off bar stool in his hands. Alpha Pride, closed in around them with an array of weapons drawn.

"Don't hurt the bear," Reese barked as she blocked the beast's escape.

Growling loudly as they thundered towards his family, Brock threw his weight to the side. Nothing happened. He did it again. Harder. The hound's feet faltered, slipping on the worn hardwood floors. It tilted off balance and fell. The force of Brock's yank pulled them into a roll. They fell. Brock took most of the impact with his back as they spun and crashed through a booth. Trying to breathe through the feeling of his lungs collapsing, Brock caught a glimpse of Kara in the broken doorway. The sun shined behind her making her look like an angel. Brock fought not to lose his grip on the beast.

Kara vaulted over Ripper, who was dragging himself back to his feet and ran inside. Bob snarled and barked, his body tight and rigid before he jumped forward and bit the hellhound's paw. Kara ghosted Bob into the kitchen and linked Brax that if he touched her pet, she would wear the bear as an ugly fur coat. She wasn't joking and meant every word. Her mind churned with the best way to kill this thing without killing Brock. Growling, she realized that the easiest option of bolting the damned thing was a no go. If Brock let go now, he'd be torn apart. The Bjorn was pinned under it, holding tight with his back against the broken half wall of the booth.

She did the only thing she could think of. Yanking free the demon's hand that was somehow still dangling from her side, she whistled and tossed it. It was a canine. Maybe it would fetch. Dropping her weight down into her thighs, she raised her sword and held her dagger flat against her arm, ready to leap even if he didn't chase the 'toy.'

The hellhound howled and struggled to break free of the bear's hold.

Brock growled. He couldn't see shit with his head wedged under the booth's seat. He kicked his rear legs, hoping the hellhound would move enough for him to find some kind of leverage and gain the upper hand.

Kara growled as she watched Brock try to get the monstrous mutt off him and got nowhere. This was going to hurt like a bitch. Dropping her weapons, she jumped forward and grabbed the beast by the scruff of the neck and the tail. Teeth snapped loudly, less than an inch from her nose, and a gust of putrid breath turned her stomach. Yanking and throwing her weight backward, she tried to peel the beast off her ... Kara's brow arched as she almost thought *mate*, and had to rephrase to *future husband*. "Quiet, Bob!" She yelled, hearing him barking and alternating between throwing himself against the door and chewing on it. If she could just get this son of a bitch off the bear...

Brock shifted to human form and started punching his way through the chest of the hellhound. Blood splattered on his face and burned his eyes. He turned his head to stop it from pouring into his mouth, through his sneer of gritted teeth. His fist snapped bone and pushed out through the animal's side, and dead weight pinned him tighter against the floor. He couldn't breathe and thought he might be passing out until he felt the weight shift. Blinking his eyes to clear the black spots, he saw Kara and Koen dragging the corpse off him.

Heads began popping up from behind overturned tables and the bar. "So that's what one of those looks like." Kara raised a brow and shook her head, stepping around the

551

hellhound to offer Brock a hand up. "You okay?" Her concerned eyes scanned him looking for blood that was his.

Brock nodded and called for Balden. "What's going on? Demons and now these things!"

"These are just the small stuff, trust me." Kara sighed her relief and scrubbed her face with her hand. "We need to get everyone out of here. It's not safe anymore." She dropped her hand and looked at him, her lips curling up on one side. "Nice punch you have there, bear."

"Thanks." Brock grinned, still holding her hand and using it to pull her closer. He dropped his forehead to rest on the top of her head. "You need to answer your phone, Wee One," he teased, growing serious. "I was worried about you, Kara. Don't do that shit to me, again."

Kara closed her eyes, and a smile played at her lips. "I had a demon trying to shish kabob me." She tilted her head back to see him better and kissed him softly. "I won't. I promise." Someone cleared their throat behind her causing her to turn her head.

Koen shifted uncomfortably, rubbing the back of his neck and glancing over his shoulder. "I think a dog has Brax cornered in the kitchen. When did we get a dog?"

Kara grinned, and Brock chuckled. "Guess what? We got a dog."

Balden left the last people, pulling on his black leather gloves and stood over the hellhound, looking down at it. His hands rested on his hips as he studied the creature and shook his head. "The fuck," he muttered, glancing over his shoulder when Reese slid the doors shut behind the last of the civies, closing them inside the billiards room to trip their asses off. Snorting, he poked the mangy furred body with the toe of his boot. "Anyone else want to forget this shit?"

Beyer raised his hand and leaned back against a bar stool, before helping Bree down off the bar.

"Too bad, cub. No Djinn juice for you." Reese snorted, standing beside Balden and staring at the dead animal and the shattered entrance. "Okay, we need to get that door secured ASAP," she barked at her men.

Grumbles filled the air as supplies were ghosted in and soon the sound of hammers hitting nails filled the room.

Kara could still hear Bob barking in the kitchen, punctuated with a bear's growl and threats. Sighing and sliding her hands over Brock's arms, she pulled away from him and crossed the room to open the kitchen door. Brax was perched on one of the stainless-steel prep stations, holding a cleaver between him and Bob waving a heavy rolling pin, ready to swing.

"Get the fucking mutt away from me, or we're having dog stew for dinner," Brax growled.

Kara arched a brow at the threat and tried not to laugh. She pulled her phone from her back pocket and snapped a photo before laying a calming hand on Bob's back. "It's okay, Bob. I won't let the big bad bear hurt you."

"Hurt him? Who cornered who?" Brax raised the rolling pin again when Bob gave him one last growl and trotted off, wagging his tail.

Koen's sawing laugh sounded behind her. "You gotta send me a copy of that."

Kara grinned and nodded while Brax cursed, jumped down and stormed up the stairs to the living quarters. "Christmas card," she whispered, her brow arching at the yelling coming from the other room. "What now?" She sighed.

"Nothing good," Koen growled and pushed through the saloon doors, holding them open for Kara. His brow arched at Bob trotting through the room with a clawed humanoid hand in his mouth. *Fuck, his life was weird as shit.*

"I told you this would happen, that she would bring a shit storm down on our family. I fucking told you!" Bart yelled, nose to nose with Brock and his hands balled into fists.

Kara arched an annoyed brow and crossed her arms, watching the confrontation. What had she ever done to the

553

bear to make him hate her so damned much? Brax she understood, but not Bart.

Brock growled and bumped his brother a step back, with his chest. "Not the time. We have bigger shit than your petty BS. She's not going anywhere. Live with it." His eyes bored into his brother's, daring him to keep kicking this up a notch. Brock didn't enjoy pounding the snot out of his little brother, but he was damn close to making an exception.

"Stop. Both of you." Bree pushed herself in between them and tried to use her arms to gain more space.

"I fucking told you," Bart snarled, ignoring his sister and shoving Brock's shoulder. "She ruined Dane's life, and now she's gunning for you. No piece of ass is that good. Grow the fuck up before she gets us all killed."

Brock opened his mouth to tell his brother to shut the fuck up about shit he knew nothing about but stopped when he heard a cough near the doors to the kitchen. He wiped at the sweat that beaded on his forehead and turned his head.

Koen stood beside Kara and tilted his head to the side toward her before stuffing his hands in his front pockets and shaking his head.

Brock's eyes closed. The look on her face said it all. His family was too much of a pain in the ass to tolerate for her to be with him. His already speeding pulse pounded harder, making him cold and light headed. "Kara…" his voice trailed off, not sure what to say.

"Enough," Bree growled at Bart and pushed him back further.

"Fuck this and fuck you, Brother," Bart snarled and stalked off.

Brock let his head roll toward his chest and sighed. Leave it to his family to screw up his one chance at happiness. He rubbed his face with his hands, not sure why he was sweating so damn much. When he opened his eyes and lifted his head again, Kara was standing in front of him.

"He's not wrong." Kara's voice was soft as her eyes searched his face.

"He is wrong," Brock growled back.

Kara nodded and touched his face. It was a talk for another time, to be had privately. "Okay, Bjorn." She smiled and caressed his lower lip with her thumb. "Is everyone alright?" She asked, turning to look at the crowd in the bar and then falling on the hellhound. Waving a hand, she ghosted the body out into the delta, where the fishermen rarely went, because no one needed to be dragging that shit up in their nets. "Ripper. You seeing in triplicate? You got bulldozed hard."

"I'm cool. Can't hurt this thick skull." Ripper knocked on it and grinned, picking up Kara's weapons from the floor and handing them back to her. "You're bleeding though, and he's," He pointed at her side and then looked at Brock. "Looking like Carrie, at the prom."

Kara looked down at her side and then at Brock. She didn't like the film of sweat that was coating his face. "You sure you're okay, Babes?"

"You don't look good, Bear," Ripper agreed. "Might want to have the Doc's check you out. I'm going to go calm Bart down and check on Brax." There was a thump. Ripper turned his head to see Bob, sprawled on the floor with his brown eyes rolled up into his head and his body quivering. "That can't be good."

Brock took a step toward their pet, his legs each weighed a metric ton. The room tilted and the voices around him echoed. "Is hellhound blood..." His voice died, and his legs gave out dropping him to his knees and making his teeth clack together. The floor was coming closer, and then everything was dark.

Kara lunged when Brock began to fall, but only got dragged down with him. She rolled her body to cushion his fall. Her mind raced, trying to remember everything that Ivan had told her about the hellhounds that he'd raised, but none of it was coming back. Holding Brock to her, she reached out to lay her hand on Bob's quivering flank and ghosted them to the clinic and pulled herself out from under

555

Brock. He was still in human form and unconscious. He couldn't do that! "Bear down!" She yelled at the top of her lungs making the windows shake and lightning flash outside.

Phelon caught her as she struggled to hold both the bear and the canine. "Through here," he took the dog and eyed the bear with worry. His form concerned the RN. Only a few things could cause that, and they were all deadly. He lowered the dog onto one of the two beds in the room. "What's all over them?" Phelon took the severed hand from the dog's mouth, curled his lip in disgust and tossed it into the red biohazard bin by the sink.

"Hellhound," Kara grunted as she settled Brock on the bed and swiped the hair back from his face. "He killed it and then they just dropped." Her eyes moved over him, checking the rise and fall of his chest. He couldn't die. He couldn't. She stroked his hair while the nurse put a stupid cuff on his arm that wasn't going to fix a damn thing and pumped it tight. Inside her head, she screamed for anyone she could think of that could help. Ty. Salvation. Ozzy. Her father. Even Kraven, who hated her.

What the hell was a hellhound? Phelon yelled for Asher and waited.

Asher stripped off the bloody scrubs, hit the shower in record time and was pulling on a fresh pair of pants when he heard Phelon yell. Grabbing a pair of gloves, he raced down the hall trying not to think about the patient that had just flat lined on the table for the last time. He bumped open the door and the fact that he was shocked only showed as a slight hiccup in his step. He listened intently as Phelon filled him in on the bear's vitals and a short synopsis of what had happened.

He glanced up at Kara seeing a disturbing mix of fear and fury in her eyes that sent a shiver down his spine. "Hellhound blood." He repeated back. Great, because they weren't bad enough when they were tearing his people apart. He turned the bear's neck, taking the cloth from Phelon who was trying to clean away the blood gently when

556

fast was what they needed. Wiping skin clean, he gasped at the purple lines that told him they were racing the clock against a toxin that had leached through the bear's skin. "We've got to get this off him, now!"

"Can you ghost in a hose? We can hook it to the sink and hose him down?" Phelon suggested, adjusting his gloves.

Kara watched and as soon as Asher said to get it off him, she ghosted away Brock's clothes and made a garden hose appear, waiting for the nurse to hook it to the faucet impatiently. "Let me do it. If I go down, it doesn't matter. We need you two." She didn't wait for permission or put on gloves. Kara already had the blood on her and in open wounds. If she was going to be affected by it, she was already a goner. Once Brock was wet but clean, she ghosted a blanket over him for modesty's sake and looked at the doctor. "Now what?"

Asher watched Kara work and didn't argue, but did he noticed that she was wearing a good deal of splatter, never mind her own blood and she was still standing strong. "Are you immune?" He watched the bear's veins turning a dark royal purple and branching out over Brock's skin.

She shook her head. "I don't know. I haven't dealt with one before, but others of my kind have, and this never happened. Why?"

"Because if this doesn't let up, we are going to fight fire with fire. Or in this case, your blood. You up for that?" Asher smiled when she didn't hesitate to nod.

Phelon cleaned up the bloody clothes with a broom and dustpan, careful not to touch any of it. Seeing what it did to the bear, it was best not to let any of it touch his skin.

Kara stroked Brock's shoulder, hating that he was going through this and more scared than she would admit to anyone but Brock. "Drain me dry, if you need to." She looked down at him and felt her throat tighten. The world needed him in it. "Is whatever it is, stopping him from

557

shifting? He should be in form. This isn't right." And that scared her as much as everything else did.

Asher blinked at her and waited for Phelon to hook Brock up to the monitors, his vitals were holding steady for the moment. "It must be." He didn't admit that he was worn so thin and too caught up in the moment to notice that he should be working on a bear, literally. "Get cleaned up and be ready if we need you."

"No. Do it now. Him and Bob."

Asher arched a brow when she shook her head at his demand. "Get cleaned up first. We don't want others dropping because they touch some of that stuff on you."

Kara eyed Brock, not wanting to leave him, even for a second, but knowing that the Doc was right. Gods knew the shit was hitting the fan enough without that happening too. She ghosted into the shower, sent her clothes to the dumpster and came back out wearing clean scrubs and still dripping wet. Her hand stroked Brock's hair as she checked the machines again. "We do it now." The lilt of her voice sounded like a question, but it wasn't. She didn't like the hesitation she saw in the doctor's eyes. She would trade everything she was to be able to heal them, but her powers were bringing death, and the buzz growing at the base of her neck told her that time was short.

She couldn't lose them both. Kara felt her world crumbling to ruin. The anger and fury that she'd felt when she returned from her hell of death, bubbled in her chest and chewed its way through her veins like acid. She closed her eyes, trying to find her center, something to ground her when she heard the machine that beeped out Brock's heartbeat begin to slow.

Asher groaned, his tired head rolling forward on his shoulders. The hits, they just kept on coming. Pushing his hair back from his face as he lifted his head, he nodded at her, wincing at the lightning that flashed nonstop outside the windows. He knew it was Kara's doing. He'd seen it before when she was upset, and the last thing they needed was a power outage. "We do it now. Phelon, we're going to need two transfusion lines. Hook up Bob to another monitor. We start with the bear."

He met Kara's eyes, watching as a whole lot of bad shit flashed in the azure depths. "Can you handle both?" A cold shiver ran its icy fingers down Asher's spine. The scent wafting off her reminded him of when she'd come back, and again when shit had gone bad between her and Dane. Nothing good could come of that. His heart sunk when Brock took a turn for the worse. "We need to do this now." *Gods, let this work,* he prayed silently because his senses told him that if this failed, Kara would destroy everything.

Asher slid a chair behind her and pushed her down into it with a gentle hand on her shoulder as Phelon slapped a transfusion line into his hand and got busy shaving spots of hair and hooking Bob up to his own monitor. "I've got the bear. You can do yours?" Asher didn't wait for and answer, knowing that she had experience in field transfusions. He turned and pierced an easy to find, dark purple vein in Brock's arm.

Kara nodded and tore the sleeve of her shirt open, jabbing the beveled point of the needle where it needed to be and working the valve until her blood dripped from the end of the soft tubing. Her eyes searched the room. Kara felt a familiar presence, and if she was right, then it might already be too late. Grinding her molars to dust, she whispered that everything was going to be okay through mind link to Brock, hoping that it was true. 'You are not going to die today, bear, so don't even think about it.' The base of her neck prickled again as she was called to collect a soul, but her mind hit the decline button. Let one of her sisters do it.

Her sigh of relief left her lungs on a hard puff when Asher stood back, and her blood was flowing through the tubing and into Brock. Her eyes were glued to the monitor, willing the numbers to climb back to where they needed to be, bouncing to the rise and fall of Brock's chest and then darting around the room of shiny stainless steel furnishings. She felt Phelon preparing her other arm for Bob but didn't pay it any attention. If she felt what she thought she was, they were running out of time. "Mist, if you're here show yourself and get the fuck out. You can't take him." She growled.

Asher's brows raised and he glanced around the room when Kara spoke. What was she talking about? His heart kicked when a brunette female appeared, her features almost identical to Kara and she was armed to the teeth. One break. That's all he needed, but he wasn't going to get it. He cringed at the power swirling in the room as the females stared each other down. "And the worst timing fucking possible award goes to..." He shook his head and muttered sarcastically. "Phelon. I think you might want to get to safer ground." Nodding, the nurse slid his hand over Bob's flank and took the long way around whatever was about to go down and bolted out through the door.

"You should go too, Doc," Kara said without looking at him. Her eyes were right where they needed to be, on her sister who wanted to reap the soul of the bear Kara loved. "This is going to get messy." She smiled tightly.

"You know the rules, Kara." Mist crossed her arms over her chest, not wanting to take on her older and stronger sister. "They don't change, even for us. You have to let him go."

A feral growl rolled up Kara's throat and filled the room making the windows shake, and her sister took a step back. "Over my dead body. That's what it's going to take." Kara opened and closed her fingers, making the blood flow out of her faster.

Mist's eyes flared wide as she keyed on the movement and spotted the transfusion tubes. "What you are doing is forbidden!" She gasped. Mist drifted closer, her eyes locked on the blood flowing from her sister and into the canine and the male. "If death is what you want, sister, you are going to find it." Mist reached out her hand toward Brock.

"Don't." Kara's tone was soft and deadly. If Mist laid her hand on the bear, he would shudder his last breath and be gone. Kara was not going to let that happen. Her eyes shot to the monitor and saw that the peaks of his heartbeat were growing smaller. "Don't touch him. Don't force me to do something that YOU will regret."

Mist's hand froze in midair, her amber eyes rolling up to meet her sister's. "You won't." She eyed Kara, and she wasn't so sure about that. Kara had always been a bit of a loose cannon, and since she'd returned from her decade of hell, slicing through bodies wearing the faces of those she loved most or dying at their hands, she'd been off the rails. Thor was still limping from his last encounter with Kara and Loki claimed his jaw still ached when it rained. Did she want to push her sister? No, but she didn't want to face their mother's wrath either. Mist was in a no-win situation.

"Try me." Kara arched a brow and waited. She didn't flinch at the loud crack of lightning hitting pavement outside. She shook her head and sighed when Mist's hand twitched closer and barely missed brushing Brock's toe that stuck out from under the blanket. "You always were stupid, Mist. Probably why you're Mother's favorite." Without thinking twice, Kara swung her head, and using her powers, threw the Valkyrie out through the window. Glass shattered, and the wind gusted through the window before Kara closed her eyes and replaced it.

Asher watched the exchange, not sure exactly what was happening. He wanted to take Kara's advice, but he worried that she wouldn't be able to defend herself with both arms tethered. He feared that she would let herself be killed before she so much as twitched either arm and disturbed the flow of blood. Then that worry went out the window, with the brunette. Just damn. He hadn't seen that coming. His jaw hung open as he wondered just how powerful the usually cheerful and bouncy blonde was?

Alarms on the machines sounded, and Kara's heart froze as Asher began yelling medical jargon and then there

561

was only the steady drone of an even tone. The blipping line that showed the beat of Brock's heart was flat. "No!" she growled, tears rushing to her eyes as she stared and felt her sanity cracking apart.

"We're losing him!" Asher's voice boomed and echoed as Kara's vision changed, bathing everything in red tones. She backhanded someone who tried to yank the tubing from her arm, barely noticing them hitting the wall and crumbling to the floor.

"Clear!"

The electricity shot through the bear, arching his body off the table, and into her arm through the needle in Kara's vein. She didn't care about the jolt that froze her heart. She could feel Brock's spirit struggling to remain inside his body and losing. The lightning outside the windows grew in intensity, striking the buildings around them. Shrapnel of walls rained over the streets and fires blazed. So what if her heart stopped? Without Brock, she didn't need one.

"Epi! Now! If we lose him, she's going to kill us all!" The building began to shake and the tiled walls cracked.

The Doc was right. Kara couldn't hear anything as she watched them fight to bring back the bear as her control crumbled and she unleashed her fury on the city outside. The only thing protecting The Pit was Brock's soul remaining inside his body. When that changed, Kara was done, and she didn't care how many she took with her.

About the Authors...

Misty and BJ began writing together in a small role player group centered on one of their favorite book series in 2015. It didn't take long before they realized that this partnership was something special.

Pulling away from writing the story lines for another author's characters, they began developing their own characters, world and applied the nail-biting plot twists to their own work. The Creation Inc Series was born, and readers were begging for more!

Black On Black: THE MATING was released in 2016 and the second in the series, KISMET, was released in June of 2017. Also coming in 2017 will be a novelette that continues the story of Jared and Serra, the first characters that came to life for them. Book 3, ALPHA PRIDE is also expected for 2017.

The Creation Inc world is growing rapidly and expanding, and nothing can stop it...

It's all about you....

If you liked what you read, please leave us a review where you bought it. If it was a gift, then Amazon is always a great place to let us know what you thought. Reviews help our books raise in the ranks and receive better visibility. We plan to bring you more from the Creation Inc world for years to come, please help us do that.
Amazon: https://www.amazon.com/dp/B0718WGGFS/

Want to be kept in the loop? Join our newsletter...

Receive updates of upcoming releases, contests, giveaways and newsletter member only freebies just by clicking the link below and signing up. If you decide it's not for you, you can always unsubscribe.
http://eepurl.com/cMmPWb

Printed in Poland
by Amazon Fulfillment
Poland Sp. z o.o., Wrocław